W9-BLV-895

WAKE OF THE RED WITCH

.25

WAKE OF THE RED WITCH

by Garland Roark

LITTLE, BROWN AND COMPANY · BOSTON

1946

ABIGAIL E. WEEKS MEMORIAL LIBRARY
UNION COLLEGE
BARBOURVILLE, KENTUCKY

8/3.5
R628w

COPYRIGHT 1946, BY GARLAND ROARK

ALL RIGHTS RESERVED, INCLUDING THE RIGHT
TO REPRODUCE THIS BOOK OR PORTIONS
THEREOF IN ANY FORM

PRINTED IN THE UNITED STATES OF AMERICA

TO
LEOLA

CONTENTS

PRELUDE

I, SAM ROSEN, *have a tale to spin; and the reader is hereby warned: —*

I have followed the fruits of the pen, I have devoured many stories dealing with the eruption of human passions, and in my travels I have heard things which stand one's moral tufts eternally on end. But they remain windows in a house of fancy still to be built.

From Mayrant Sidneye I learned what half the world has scarcely imagined; from Ralls I learned what Mijnheer Sidneye forgot in his erratic and activated imagery; from a feminine creature, as mysterious as any lagoon under tropic skies, I learned what I had never mentally conceived. Combining my accretions, and I stand in the flesh among them — in the wake of three ships — I soon made a discovery.

I could build a house around those windows.

PRINCIPAL CHARACTERS

SAM ROSEN — Part owner of the tramp schooner, *Quean of Melbourne*, who tells the story of Books One and Four.

RALLS — Rosen's strange, implacable partner, former captain of the *Red Witch*.

TILDEN KING CARTER — A handsome, carefree, and sick man. Friend of Rosen and a member of the crew of the *Quean*.

VAN DER RUYSDAAL (an alias) — Wealthy Dutch owner of the island of Little Soembawa.

HARMENSZOON VAN SCHREEVEN — Ruysdaal's half-brother.

TELEIA VAN SCHREEVEN — Daughter of van Schreeven.

MAYRANT RUYSDAAL SIDNEYE — Ruler of Batjak, Ltd., famous Dutch East Indies maritime empire.

BATJOEK OF AMBOINA — A Moluccan, one of Sidneye's top lieutenants.

DOKTER VAN ARKEN — A scientist in experimental medicine, and a power in Sidneye's firm.

ANGÉLIQUE DESAIX — Niece of French *commissaire* in Polynesia.

MR. LORING — First mate aboard the *Red Witch*.

MRS. LORING — His wife.

MR. BULLIT — Captain of van Schreeven's yacht.

RITTER DU BUYS — A seaman on the *Quatrefoil*.

PIET DE TURFFS — Host to the crew of the *Quatrefoil* in Bali.

xi

MR. RODRIGUEZ — First mate of the *Golden Hind* under Ralls.

RIPPER ARREZO — Seaman for Ralls and Rosen.

JAN HOOCH — Teleia's suitor, youthful member of Batjak.

MR. VERY — Prosecutor in the *Red Witch* case.

MR. SUGGS — Defense lawyer in the *Red Witch* case.

MAYRANT VON STREICHER — German diplomat in the Netherlands.

ZULINDE SCHOUTEN — Sidneye's aunt.

STEFAN MEER — Captain of the great ship *Quatrefoil*, later Sidneye's partner.

VEE VOSSLER — First mate of the *Quatrefoil*.

NAND VOSSLER — his wife.

RAAS VOSSLER — their son.

CHRISTIAAN VOSSLER — their son.

WILDE YOUNGUER — One of the fiercest of Batjak's captains.

LIDJ VAN DER GLOTZ — Able seaman on the *Quatrefoil*.

HERR KLINGG — German employed by Sidneye.

FATHER VAN SKIKE — Priest in Bali.

VAN CORDTLAANT — One of Batjak's successful sea captains, who rose to be captain of the famed *Golden Hind*.

TEER NOORD — First mate of the *Golden Hind*.

JACQUES DESAIX — French *commissaire* of Polynesia.

LONYTA — a beautiful Balinese girl.

UA NUKA HAVU, UTI MOPO, KUIRINUA — Polynesians.

MR. SHERATON — Australian Mandate official.

BOOK ONE

Little Soembawa, 1939

CHAPTER I

1

ABOARD our aging schooner, the *Quean of Melbourne*, we lazily inched out of a becalmed stretch in the Bismarck Sea, our yellow, weather-shredded sails hanging onto every pitiful breath in an exhausted sky; our one Diesel was minus the necessary fuel to drive us into a livelier clime. With course set north by east we checked position twice that morning, peering between times at the desolate horizon for a break in the eternal line; the lower Admiralty Isles were overdue on our starboard bow. All was quiet on deck, and above; we coasted along without purling the water, it seemed. And when nature finds inclement mood, seamen tag along in her wake, leaning on the rail in listless manner, lifting an eye occasionally when a sail rustles or throws a shadowy hint at bellying — but only one eye; the other is too busy moving ahead or in retrospect. I eyed the sheeted sea with both the future and the past seeking a meeting place in that desolate present. I frowned out of it, seeing nothing but a cargo of hemp, gewgaws, and hodgepodge, all a mask to our inordinate desires.

Far off, topping the roll of the earth, a brown-masked green came into view. Soon its opaqueness danced out of the heat waves and away, pulling the *Quean* up for a glimpse at a palm-fringed atoll lying flat and long in the middle of the sea. The faintest breath of wind put a hand in our sail and hove to for a long quarter hour. By that time we stood close enough to view a gap in the coral that bespoke an inlet. We moved up and circled to the south.

Ralls raised his thumb and pointed leeward, and the bow swung slowly around to draw a finger on a palm-fringed lagoon, the likes of which one might dream about. Ralls, senior owner and partner of our floating home that bore a bawd's title — *Quean* meaning a wench — gazed at the stretching atoll through parched slits, his strong, hairy arms akimbo, and his swarthy face screwed up by the sun under a once white sea cap. He wore it in jaunty fashion, but he was the word itself, and more.

3

He was cool as a clam in thirty fathoms and menacing as the vortex of a hurricane when his anger upped, and a human hell when his brand of anger closed in. Ralls was a rakehell who looked the part, one in whom no man ever failed to see a swashbuckling eye, a roaming, inculcated wisdom heightened by greed. His expression reminded me of a rattler's warning, and I had long since catalogued it, like its metaphor, a gift to humanity in general — for by his very face he had turned angered men from him, from marked avenues to their own graves; he had left men quivering in their own reluctance to answer his fluid curses. But a hasty picture of Ralls is only a weak portrayal. It is better that one should meet him slowly.

The skipper was not an unhandsome man. His eyes — they expressed the pains and joys of life, the close-pressing past and future in waxwork of cunning, of callousness, of heroic certainty; black and ever slitted, they had a way of blandly covering a hole card and digging out the detailed marks of another's hand. For a nose he drew a perfect thin, aristocratic shape, neither sensitive nor numb. His mouth, a thin slit that seemed ever ready to smile, was chiseled by one whose parsimony with marble had not affected his aim for perfection. No lines showed on his face, no extraordinary shape was given his pointed chin or hand-me-down jaw. His features, excluding his heavy brow, were regular, and only by their co-ordination did the dreaded depths of his eye lend satanic qualities to nose and lips.

I have never seen Ralls ruffled. Under pressure he seemed to glorify calmness until his moment arrived, a moment in which he seized the initiative and pressed his ends without fear or compassion. He respected neither the halls of justice nor their antipodes. A woman was a creature designed to assuage a man, and his sexual desires were interlaced with brutish whims. Ralls was inexorably bound to Ralls, a man of odd passions and prodigious thoughts.

He had two definite sides, and one of them he voiced when the cream-white beach inside the coral barricade met our eyes in the distance. "I hope there's a woman in this forsaken place."

I motioned to the helmsman to bring her starboard beam about easy in order to flank the right edge of a coral head for a sea eye into the channel. The ship's stern coasted to side and slow sail in a slow breeze eased her across the fifty-yard gap of a mouth. I eyed the bottom, threw a lead over, and verified my sounding. The outer sand hump wasn't heavy enough to bar the *Quean*, which meant the inside hump was probably safe. Then I saw the middle channel, deep at six fathoms and running blue straight into the lagoon; it was like a man-made

4

passage, I thought, but then it was not unusual for a lagoon to empty through more than one opening, thus decreasing the sand deposit of each. But the perfect running gash along the middle evoked a frown of perplexity. I walked to portside and heaved a line: it struck bottom and rolled down the shelf of sand that seemed almost precipitous.

Back at the starboard beam I peered at the mouth intently. The light on the water ricocheted a lesser glare from our position, and I saw a shaft of iron, then another, and another, each about twenty feet long and staggered from left to right across the deepest part; they seemed less a dumped cargo by their orderliness. I spoke to Ralls about them and he eyed them without comment. It was then I noticed a maze of heavy cables running from them and disappearing in the coral wastes.

"Probably some fool plantation owner's idea of holding a low delta," I said, dismissing the subject in words, while raising the bars in my imagination: up they rose, by compressed air, to block any ship that sat the water. Then I laughed and turned to Ralls with: "What say, Skipper, shall we venture inside?"

"Seems navigable," he said. "We'll see."

Soon the *Quean* pointed out to sea for a circle back, and I gave the order for easy sail and all hands to stand by the ropes. The schooner then caught hold of a sickly breath of wind and we glided slowly toward the gap we'd flanked some minutes before; soon the bow edged sluggishly into the opening between the coral heads. Again I peered at the lonely iron bars, and my eye followed them past the beam and the stern.

Ahead I saw the emerald of shallows and the blue-green of navigable depths, and the twisting run of the colors called for an alert eye. Then the wind left the sail and we poked along almost at a standstill.

"More sail," I said, and with it we stepped up the *Quean's* pulse. She entered the channel in a lazy step that gave ample time to swing her helm over and into the path of safety. To Ralls I said, "We'll probably find some lonesome old man and a few blacks."

"Yeah," he returned, not moving his eyes from the palm grove a furlong ahead. "Where there's a black man there also is a black woman."

I paid him no attention; my blood, too, was red, but too red for a blend with the primeval; though I've heard there's no equaling the exquisite abandon of savagery. I squinted at the alabaster beach, beyond which rose every shade of green. I gazed into the lucid bosom of the lagoon. There coral in a nightmare of shapes blossomed into a heaven of color; fish-white blended with shell-pink, violet, and tan.

5

Castellated shapes moved into view, under, and on back of us, disappearing like a magic slide portraying a color chart of fancy, daring me with its very beauty, with its mystery, speaking loudly of iridescent pearls, and of even stranger mysteries. I continued to stare and dream until a sudden jerk of the ship returned my lookout eye.

The jibs bellied, and the forestaysail and foresail flapped, sending the ship like a hand pushing a toy boat. The water, suddenly choppy, purled about the bow, and we had, we knew, that breeze we'd hoped for during the last thirty hours.

"Hey, Ripper, are you chancing a run in?" I yelled back at the Dago helmsman.

"Hella no," he said. "She'sa no got fiva fathom, no!" We drew enough water to keep the lead sounding, though we were safe enough except for jagged teeth and shoals that made a lie, sometimes, out of surface colors.

"Well, there's pink jackknives rising to meet the ship," I thundered. "Hard-a-port!" The *Quean* responded nicely before idling by a thick serrated finger that almost dried in the sun. It was hard over wheel for the next hundred yards, with quick hands to furl all but the weakest bellies of our sail. Tewelliger, our fourth man, other than our Malays and useless Carter, busied himself with the sail — he seldom opened his mouth, though he could eye one with eloquent disesteem.

I glanced at our top hamper — the *Quean* was a fore-and-aft-rigged lady, a two-master, her mainmast stepped nearly amidships, and carrying two upper triangles and a sweeping mainsail; her shorter foremast carried her jibs, forestaysail, and fore gaff-topsail; but from her deck up she seemed aureoled in pawnshop gloom: the dirty, shredded sails, sallow gray shrouds, and flaked paint all shouted of lean pickings; something must be done to her canvas or the next good blow would rip off the mainsail and more, leaving her to the one Diesel with a toy screw, and no fuel.

I sighed and turned away before Ralls barked a gentle order: "Get Carter up. One slug of gin, and no more. And slap him around a bit if he starts that damned jabbering again."

I eyed him and then the water. There were no currents to throw an idler about, so I sauntered off toward the hatch, not wondering why I always swore to leave the schooner at the next port, but curious as to why I gave resolve the lie. There is nothing so irksome to a man of spirit as lengthened bondage, be it in the shape of a ship, a strip of land, or a woman's face; one can hate each with a passion and at the same time give of love. I shook my head forlornly and renewed my oath to the schooner's ears.

6

Carter was a vagabond romancer, a bard, and a fallen professor rolled into one; but a sense of humor, and guts, he had, along with a strange malady that paraded its symptoms upon face and body. With the knowledge of his plight pressing against his poetic soul he continued to display a physical courage that seemed to buoy him up and above the Stygian clouds of hypochondria. Ralls said we'd ditch him next time we berthed. This was it, this forlorn atoll. Perhaps I was glad, for he was, it seemed, getting worse.

I gave thought to Carter's aversion, on that night weeks before in the Rabaul pub, to the fellow who walked to the bar and gave off a tale in guttural Dutch about a remote lagoon. It was full of pearls, he said, big black pearls, and hundred-grain drop-shaped pearls. Sure — we'd know the spot by the map he'd sell us for enough to throw a good drunk: a pound note! And why didn't he go after them, himself? "Mijnheer," he said, growling at Carter, "the seat of the Australian mandate is here, and I am known, and I should be followed. That is why. *Verdomd!*" And Carter had laughed at Ralls the sucker, swearing under his breath that the Dutchman was a fake. But here was the island, and we sat on the lagoon above pearls as big as birds' eggs. Apocryphal, or true? We would soon know.

I ambled on to Carter's bunk, wondering how we'd rid the ship of what he would leave behind. I was little worried, however, since I reasoned that the Lord, if there was such an entity, meant us to escape or be damned. Either way, none of us would sit up nights with long faces. It was not that I was callous, rather it was the tropics.

I came upon him hunched over his guitar, banging out an island tune. At my entry he lifted his eyes without any change of expression.

"Get your rags together, son," I ordered. "You're making final port."

His eyes mocked me at length before he said, "So we are in Frisco, eh?"

Contrary to Ralls's opinion he was sane as a missionary returning to the States. Without grimacing unduly at what met my nose, I uncorked a gin bottle and tilted it to my mouth. I peered at him as I wiped my mouth with the hair of my wrist and saw him purse his lips. They were like a woman's, and so was his hair that held to ringlets. I cursed him *sotto voce* for being a wastrel instead of a smiling hero of the films. He grinned and sang: —

> The gin we drink is mighty sweet
> On this son-of-a—— of a Diesel,
> But hand me the bottle, Sam —
> Pop — goes the weasel!

"You'll drink from a cup," I said. But no sooner had I turned a wondering eye to the companionway when the *Quean* veered sharply, than he made a lightning stab for the bottle. I saw him too late, but I turned and slapped the quart from his mouth, leaving a streak of weak red on his grinning lips.

"Scared, eh?" he said. "And so you and the admiral think you can ditch me in the coconut groves. Fruit rats and hermit crabs for playmates and nothing to drink but water." Then he laughed. It had a lonely ring.

I felt useless and mean. Carter had been my fraternity brother in the long ages past when we were gentlemen at a Midwestern university; there I'd busied myself getting him out of various and perpetual scrapes. We had been that close during our first four years in the tropic seas. It was none other than Sam Hart Rosen who had coaxed him from an assistant professorship in journalism to take a tramp steamer out of Frisco to Singapore.

The laughter died and he said: "Pour me a drink then, Sam."

"I wouldn't touch that bottle with a ten-foot pole," I replied. "It's yours now."

"Thanks, pal," he said. It was the strange inflection he lent to the word that brought my eye around. "I'll do you a favor some day," he added with a meaning. "You and Ralls both."

I went on deck, mad as hell, wishing the wop, or Tewelliger, or a Malay would give me an excuse to cram my fist into a mouth. Ralls still leaned against the starboard rail, and in his direction I walked. Tewelliger, sounding with a deep-sea lead, reported four fathoms, then five.

"Sam," said Ralls, "there's a ship in the lagoon — just around that hook."

I peered, and saw only the dirty white of small sails, much smaller than our own. "So there is," I flung back at him. He said nothing more, instead he slowly lit a cigarette. Ralls possessed that gift I have seen in but few: a silence that turns a half-minute into an hour. At last he played out the line, saying: —

"Sam, there are pearls here, all right."

"Yeah, wise guy. So there are. There were pearls on that toadstool isle east of New Hanover. They're still there." I glanced at the water and drew in safe wide fathoms.

"They're here, all right," he said. "They're easy to get in this water. Big sisters, I hope, and black as a Solomon Islander's teats."

Carter arrived on deck. He flung a greeting at the wop, asked Tewelliger if his blood called for a native, and then headed our way.

8

"Well," he remarked in his nice, icy tone, "if it isn't the admiral, the Chieftain of Blup Blup, planning to mulct the natives."

"Easy, Carter," I said. "Ralls hasn't the patience I have."

"Patience!" He laughed. "If either of you has anything in your veins but dry ice, it's refrigerated gin. See any pearls, Admiral?"

Ralls turned about and ordered Ripper to pull up near the boat and cast the mudhook over. Then, and only then, did he let his eyes fall on the curly head above the dirty white dungarees, and that ubiquitous guitar.

Both the wop and Tewelliger stiffened and forgot their work as they eyed first Ralls, then Carter; Ripper craned his neck from the stern as if a seventh sense coupled with long experience would suffice to haul the ship by any reef; and silent Tewelliger's arm dangled over the rail with the lead. I felt a scrape but paid no attention to anything except eyes locked in fierce challenge. Tewelliger reported six fathoms.

Carter grinned while Ralls maintained a rising blank. He was, of course, afraid of Ralls way down inside him, as scared as he was of anything that had life, which was a matter of rigid conjecture in itself. Perhaps it wasn't fear; instead it could be a thorough awareness of that which made up Ralls.

And Carter, the fool, invited the worst. He grinned with those talkative feminine eyes, and even Ripper, out of range, could see he expatiated upon a long and hideous suffering for Ralls. His over-all expression, a sane calm, shouted of stark insanity.

Without batting an eye, Ralls lifted the pistol from his belly holster and pointed it at Carter. It was not a move of defense, but a cool, deliberate act. One shot would remove the scourge of Carter — forever — and Ralls would not lose a puff of his cigarette after it was done; it was like stepping on a wounded bird. And the man had a way of lending magnificence to brutality, a way about him that released him from the black onus of crime.

"Watch your course, Ripper," Ralls said calmly, as the gun sight leveled on Carter's head.

I spoke up, why I don't know. "Ralls, lay off. Can't you see that's what he wants?"

"Perhaps you're right, Sam," he returned, slowly lowering the gun. I sighed as the crux joined the past.

"You and your notions!" Carter flung at me. "The bastard hasn't the guts to do it."

But Ralls placed his elbow on the rail, his back to Carter, leaving himself open to the whims of an insane man. Carter, however, ambled

9

off, cursing before pausing to gaze at the island, before turning the gin bottle to the sky.

Ripper and Tewelliger relaxed.

2

The sound of the surf breaking against the coral outside the lagoon and the wind in the coconut palms ahead broke the quiet of the deck as we edged in. Tewelliger droned out six fathoms, then five, then four.

"Hard-a-starboard!" I said, and Ripper brought her up nicely, with no more than two feet to spare between the thick, jagged coral strands. Below a deepening blue-green went all the way to anchorage. A large sting ray lay flat, underneath us now, waving its tail and holding its deadly spines erect.

"Strange, isn't it, no natives running out with pigs and coconuts to trade?" I said.

Ralls said nothing as he eyed the other boat. I surveyed the depth, evoked five fathoms from Tewelliger, and chose a place where we could pull in almost to the beach. A neglected bamboo wharf lay ahead and I shouted to Ripper to bring her in there, bow and stern. Tewelliger gave the cable a rattle and we moored her in line with the beach, casting warps to the trees to hold her fast.

The craft within a stone's throw of us was a beautiful yacht of at least ninety-five feet. She posed graceful and white with eighty-five feet on the water; her beam ran out seventeen feet, her draft eight or nine. She was equipped with permanent aft canopy, and her name in gold, in a jet-black plate across the white, round stern, announced her the *Flores Tandjoeng* of Soerabaja. I noticed that her wheelhouse was well forward of the beam, meeting the ketch-rigged foresheet, almost, though there were ample deck, white ventilators and roomy hatchway in the enclosure of brass rail to the bow. A flat white canopy with rounded sides crossed her at the beam, roofing deck cabins and alleyways. Cabin doors opened to flank the round visored house with wheel, indicator, and other appurtenances. Two lifeboats aft paralleled the sail boom. She could easily accommodate a dozen guests in manner grand, in addition to her complement in uniform.

The red, white, and blue bars of the Netherlands flew from her stern; and that answer to a seafarer's dream stood there gleaming from trucks to water line, throwing down a resplendent shadow into the silence of the lagoon. Her design seemed odd, and I attributed the passing thought to the steel-sheeted bridge standing atop the wheel-house. Were she mine, I said, I'd elevate the wheel.

But strangely, she seemed deserted.

Rubbing my chin, I turned about to peer at the island for some sign of life through the vegetation and palms. Large elephant ears told the same old story — taro and poi; dried coconut meat in long over-cupping strings spelled the anonymity of copra. Blooming hibiscus fringed the rise over which we knew there was life. Farther to the right, where the thick growth was best described as dense, where the cove lost its depth and circled to a gentle beach, the fronds of banana trees met the sun in emerald green with ribs of flaming yellow.

We were on one of those sanded coral juts that Ralls dubbed "half a fly speck." It was that, and not exaggerated on an enlarged map of the Archipelago. But due south of Manus Island we were, between Papialou and Alim. Ideal for a passionate tryst, I thought satirically, and the climate lived up to its blood allegations: in the tropics one seldom defies nature, one merely succumbs more to her moods, giving lazily, ecstatically — and eternally. But I was used to the rot of the islands like this one.

Instead I saw the tropics for what they were: four months of rain and eight more of torrents, or vice versa. It's all the same. We were almost upon the equator. The lovelier islands begin at a half-thousand miles above and below.

A noise caused me to snap my eyes forward. There coming toward us was as strange a procession as I've ever witnessed in our off-chart landings. Three natives with pierced nasal septa, their foreheads smeared with yellow ochre, led two stubborn goats. Behind them, a wizened Amboinesi, his hair and mustache white, his face a million wrinkles, carried a bright green parrot. He wore knee pants of dungaree supported by a heavy leather belt. The sight was reminiscent of my days in the Moluccas. Had he possessed a bamboo flute, the picture would have been perfect. But that was not all I saw.

A wheel chair came over the ridge, a young Moluccan behind it, another flanking it on the left with a frond to sweep the flies and mos-quitoes from its startling occupant; and on the right a native gun bearer, a general naked between his navel and his flowery headdress, strode importantly. In the chair was a two-hundred-pound man, as bald as he was short and fat. A set smile lingered on his face as he peered at Ralls, then at me, and then on to the sails of the two-masted *Quean of Melbourne*. As he drew near I could see the blue welts on his legs; sickly veins standing out like Braille declared their varicosity. He was pale and drug-colored — his ears giving off the purplish glow born of sedatives; there was evidence of a skin ailment that looked to me like frambesia, a grasping cousin of syphilis. He wore immaculate white knee-length trousers, pressed as neatly as the open collar of his sleeveless blouse, and a large black pearl in a lead-colored mounting was a conspicuous addition to his groomed hands.

I was shaken by surprise when he said: "Welcome to Soembawa the lesser, Mijnheer Ralls. I named the place that when I traded for it three years ago come the rains." He gazed at Ralls with narrowed eyes that bore little real welcome. Thin lips hovered in a fixed smile over bright large teeth. Definitely Dutch, said his speech, and definitely a man of force and decision, the ring of it added.

Turning his eyes upon me without losing their fixity he said: "I am Mijnheer van der Ruysdaal. You would be Sam Rosen? And your crew, the Dago Ripper, and Americans Tewelliger and Carter, and the Malays, where are they? Ah, here comes Carter." It was Carter, all right.

Ralls drew my astonished eyes with: "So you follow me closely, Mister?"

"Indeed," came the steeped-in-ice reply.

"That wasn't your name when I last heard of you," Ralls said easily.

"True. True. But van der Ruysdaal will do. It seems the name you knew had something to do with ships, and pearls, and trade in general. Is that correct?"

"I seldom gossip," returned Ralls.

"A commendable trait, Mijnheer Ralls. But that is only one of your ennobling qualities. But tell me what brings you to this edge of the world? My copra has its contracted market, and there is little else."

"Fuel," said Ralls.

"And why should this spot suggest a supply? You saw no signs of life from outside the lagoon."

Carter, standing apart from the strange group, moved forward and spoke. "Look at me, sir. Peer closely. I think one answer to your question is me."

The Dutchman slowly turned his massive head and lifted his eyes from Carter's feet to his face. There he was met with the challenging grin and insolent eyes that seemed to be Carter's last will and testament to a world down under. Mijnheer van der Ruysdaal said nothing, nor did his expression change. He continued to dissect our unwanted cargo with growing interest. At last he extended his hand, a gesture that opened wide my eyes. Carter, reluctant to take the stranger's

12

hand in his, was put at ease by the light in the Dutchman's eyes. Their hands locked in firm clasp.

"Tilden King Carter, sir, or Mijnheer," said Carter. "I'm delighted to meet you."

"I return the compliment, young man. It is good to meet a stranger who is a friend. Too often youth has little patience with age and it is so the other way around. But age has the advantage, since it can peer closer than youth — and truer. After all, my friend, a man's eyes remain the only organ he cannot hide." He turned to his Moluccan wheelman and spoke in a rapid mixture of Dutch and native jargon. Again he spoke to Carter.

"A man's eyes are the reflection of his inner self."

I wondered what went on between the two. Was he finding Carter clean? If not, then why did he calmly touch the polluted hand?

"So the two wish to be rid of you."

"Yes," said Carter. "They're frightened." He laughed, and the Dutchman laughed, and together their contagion increased until both shook. The wizened Moluccan joined in, and the servants, their apish eyes darting about, thought it wise to fall into congruous spasms.

"Ah me," the Dutchman sighed. "It is good to laugh, is it not?"

"Indeed it is," returned Carter. "Particularly when one gazes at such comedy." His finger jerked toward Ralls and me.

"Well, you're welcome here, Mijnheer Carter. Come. I shall see that you meet my house as becomes a guest to Little Soembawa." At his signal the coterie turned about-face.

"Wait," said Ralls, and the man raised a hand to stay his servants. "Whose craft is this, Mijnheer?"

"It belongs to Mijnheer van Schreeven. He pays call from Soerabaja."

"A hell of a poor sailmaker," reflected Ralls.

"And a great man," returned our cold host, "as you well know."

"Could I purchase fuel from either of you?"

"Had I a supply, my dear Ralls, I should give it to you and sigh with relief at your parting. But, alas."

"Then I'm afraid we must impose upon your hospitality until we can trim sail," said Ralls.

"That decision," said the Dutchman with cool authority, "remains the prerogative of a Ruysdaal. A village of armed natives lies beyond my mansion. But how long will your sails detain you?"

"A week perhaps. With help, half the time."

"Then remain," came the order. "But on the *Quean*. I shall set guard.

Water and sago flour will be sent you. And," he paused to emit a devilish chuckle, "you may amuse yourselves by diving for pearls. There is fabulous wealth in this lagoon." His gaze said more — to Ralls.

Again he gave the signal to move. He laughed again, louder than before, and as we watched the whole party joined in. Slowly they moved up to the ridge and the sounds of their mirth rose and fell even as they grew smaller against the leaning palm trunks and showy vegetation.

3

      I gazed up at the palms bending toward the sea, and somehow I felt that their trim tropical silence also mocked us. A gentle breeze moved the arched fronds, causing a subdued rustling in the endless ceiling. From somewhere a cockatoo broke the heavy quiet, and again faint peals of laughter were wafted to our ears.

I gazed at the *Quean*. Tewelliger and Ripper leaned on the rail staring at us. The lagoon rippled, or I thought I detected a racing lap of the water. Below her hull the purple stillness presented four pairs of rapacious eyes: sharks enjoying the shade. Far beneath them the tan of a four-foot moray eel slithered into an unseen door of a magenta and rose castle. Ralls, hands in jeans, was walking toward the *Flores Tandjoeng* with a contemplative eye on the craft. He stopped short when a sound from the trees invaded the oppressive silence. I, too, turned about and saw Carter. He had not gone with the party, but sat with his feet in the shaded sand.

He stood and stretched lazily as we watched him. Then, peering intently, he said: —

"Ripper, Tewelliger, good luck." A moment of quiet punctuated his next words.

"Sam, Ralls," he said, bowing low. "So long, you bastards!"

With that he turned his back on us and walked slowly toward the ridge. He was soon swallowed by a wall of ferns and creepers.

"Ralls," I said, "who the devil is this van der Ruysdaal?"

Chuckling, he replied, "Just an old trader, Sam."

CHAPTER II

1

THAT was the beginning, or rather it was a prelude to the past, as well as the strange future; the past was van der Ruysdaal's long story, out of which the mystery surrounding Ralls was cleared like fog before a lusty wind. None of us knew the long story of Ralls's past; all we knew was that which we had picked up here and there and pieced together in a somewhat distorted patch-quilt of knowledge. Such is the danger of gullibility to gossip: a lamb becomes a jackal and a lion is falsely tamed. Ralls's pattern entered my mind, adhering more to the tiger shark; thus, one must realize I was somewhat surprised to learn that I viewed him falsely.

I could, perhaps, conjure up a wordy paragraph picture of Ralls the man and leave it there — I have done so — but the lifeblood of the definition remains strangely missing. It is there, but without the throb, without the pulsating life of environment that studs each mind with his unforgettable portrait.

And of portraits! If van der Ruysdaal created a picture of dissipation and its boomerang, why shouldn't Ralls? Simply because every man revolves about an entirely different core. Call it inherent, or whatever you like, but always return to that fact. Every man finds his own axis.

Ralls ever viewed the forbidden with patience — gracefully, I might add. His week's leave to trim sail, under orders to confine himself to the *Quean* and lagoon, failed to stem his thoughts. His first words at sighting the island, "I hope there's a woman in this forsaken place," remained uppermost in his mind. His second thought was pearls, and his third, fuel. A woman to Ralls was the prettiest feminine form available on a given spot, be she white, brown, yellow, or black; and his methods of obtaining satisfaction were most curious, that much I'd learned from far-reaching sounds over the distance he put between people and his individual acts. But it required the substance of Mijnheer van der Ruysdaal's words to execute a true portrait of Ralls.

We spent the night aboard our craft, and Ralls again paced the beach beyond the *Flores Tandjoeng* until far into the night. I knew why,

15

for as I joined him that afternoon in a close-up of the craft I, too, saw through a cabin window a wisp of pink silk with borders of ecru lace; it lay innocently still atop the mahogany sill. Van Schreeven had brought civilization with him in its most perplexing state: a white woman.

Van der Ruysdaal presented an atoll of beauty, a mysterious pearl floor in the palm of Soembawa, plus steeped hatred of an uninvited guest. The *Quean of Melbourne* gave to the union Ralls. All were known quantities; each one had its values, its plane, its wide dissimilarity. And with such a setting the stage could only yield promises.

And out of the visible stage a tropic moon shot up from the horizon out over the surf; first gold, then yellow, then white. The nearer the equator the larger the old man; he almost winked at us from the receding end of the mast. Ralls, pacing out there, was a moving pattern that propelled an inky shadow back and forth. Lazily I gazed beyond him. The island itself was a patchwork of swaying tufts against a garish sky, a synchronized mirror of tropical silhouettes below. A breeze, warm though almost comfortable, swept from the inland, bringing with it the perfume of a million blossoms.

Seeking sleep I turned over and over, then raised my head to peer through the rail; I scarcely blamed Ralls. I was getting that way myself as I continued to view that mahogany sill in the moon. I cursed and got to my feet.

"Damn!" I said it again. "All white women are in the moon as far as we're concerned."

"Sa no good," said Ripper. I turned, not aware of his proximity. Then Tewelliger laughed.

"Well!" I flung at them.

"Stilla say sa no good."

"What's no good?" I asked of the wop.

"Dreamsa no good. Me, Giusep' Arrezo longa time ago forgetta biga curves of Vittoria Goldonio. Take leetle the curve, so where? She makesa no diff-erence. All same." He crossed himself, laughing.

"How about your say, Tewelliger?" I said lighting a damp cigarette.

"I never opened my mouth," he said, not moving his head on the hairy arms he used for a deck pillow.

"You seldom open it," I said. "Sometimes I wonder what goes on in your head."

He shrugged without removing his eyes from the moon. I turned to the cask of water our host had so graciously sent; there I raised a dipper to give the tepid stuff a run from my head down into my blouse.

16

"Sometimes I find myself picturing the jail you escaped from, Tewelliger," I said. "I know it's back in the States, but whether San Quentin or Sing Sing, I'm not in the know." I took a mouthful of the liquid and then spat it out, deciding in favor of gin: since one must sweat out whatever goes inside, I might as well enjoy myself, I soliloquized.

"However, I can see you were sent up for refusing to comment on your crime. A word or two," I raved on, giving my imagination free rein on a subject I wasn't even thinking about, "might have saved you from the jury that wanted a few facts. But noncommittal you decided to chance silence."

Said Ripper: "Non-a-committal she mean he no do it, eh?"

"Yeah," I said, after running my tongue around my uppers. "It means he hired somebody else to do it."

"*Ges-ù-Cristo*!" exclaimed Ripper. "Anda he tell, eh, Tewelliger?"

"*Mister* Tewelliger," suggested the American.

I tilted the bottle again and slowly set it down. The beach met my eye and I felt something missing. It was Ralls. Quickly, smiling out of sheer relief for a break in the eternal sameness, I glanced at the *Flores Tandjoeng*. I saw nothing except her glossy lines, a mass of silver and ink, but somehow I knew Ralls was aboard her.

Of course, I gave thought then to van der Ruysdaal's words about setting a guard. Perhaps Ralls had reconnoitered to his satisfaction. For a good hour I stared at the beach, the *Flores*, and back at the beach. Perhaps Ralls was aware of my vigil; it had always been that way, the other sensing the watch without a word of warning.

"Ripper," I said quietly, "fetch me the bottle."

He obeyed, pausing only to verify my expression as that of "schooner alert." Tewelliger roused himself, carefully adjusting belt and holster. More than once, with our back to the wall, with outriggers belching savages on deck, we had turned the tide by the sheer nerve of a rush.

2

The moon reached for the western horizon, and I was getting drowsy. It was after I drank from the bottle that I again looked toward the beach.

There, as if they had popped up out of nowhere, sat a half-dozen armed natives. Calm as the weather and patient as the silvered lagoon, they only peered at the *Quean* in statuesque solidarity. I neither moved nor showed surprise as I met their gaze for a full quarter hour, but I

17

was aware of their menacing, too quiet presence; I was not in ignorance of that strategy which presented a few and concealed a multitude. I'd been moving about in Melanesia too long. The first military law of the native is calmness, the second ambush, the third ferocity. If there's a fourth, the *Quean of Melbourne* has yet to find it.

I wasn't at all surprised to see Ralls strolling down the beach a half hour later, unperturbed by the presence of visitors. Nor did I give it a second thought when he stepped up to a fierce squatting warrior and scratched a match on his kinky head before offering the brute a cigarette. The sounds of chop jargon reached my ears. What was said I did not know; all I caught was the evaporation of sound.

"Rosen," Ralls said, raising his voice a trifle.

"Aye, Skipper."

"Rations to the boys," he said.

"Ripper," I said slowly, "it's on the way." He understood. "One jigger of special for our guards. No more. Maybe two for the one Ralls puts a finger on." Our special meant grain alcohol with sweetened water: under such dynamite they talked more and forgot quicker — and came back faster when we wanted them.

Soon a score of them appeared, clamoring, glub-glubbing, and laughing excitedly. Whoops of pleasure sounded from the few Ralls singled out. I did not take the weight off my elbows, and at the stern quarter Tewelliger eyed the scene with his own brand of tranquillity. Before long two glistening guards, their thin bodies oiled except for loincloths and stilted headdresses, came near the boat with Ralls. Pointing, one of them jabber-jabbered and pantomimed. His subject was, of course, the pearl bed, and he gave an ostentatious account of its wonders.

Dipping his hands into the sand and jackknifing his knees, he grunted and straightened out in a simulated return from the watery floor. Panting, he presented the huge shells to Ralls, retrieving one and placing an imaginary knife in an imaginary lip. And lo and behold! The pearl that wasn't there was bigger than an American half dollar. I could not refrain a chuckle — the black was shooting the full force of a *Quean* special to his imaginative organs. He dived again, lying on his belly in the sand, performing with arms and legs; his head bobbed in search of shells. He slowly got to his feet, jerked convulsively, tore at his arms and neck to rid himself of the monster. This went on for several minutes before he fell limp on the sand, a victim of the sea beast.

Ralls asked the location of the bed; his greedy mind asked for more.

18

Ripper was sent ashore with more tonic. And under its influence the giddy boys bragged. Out of the bedlam Ralls secured three who would bring the bottom of the lagoon to the surface. Black heroes for the moment, I said, corpses in the next.

Ripper leaned on the ratline, grinning. "Nota so long Skipper calla for boat overside." He was right, the order came in a hurry. Tewelliger and Ripper put the boat over while I hooked the searchlight to battery and lowered it. Ralls ordered me to stay aboard ship and let Ripper take the oars. That suited me. I eyed the mute Malays, asleep near the stern.

"Watch out for Santa Claus, Skipper," I said as the boat pulled away.

He gave no answer but grabbed an oar and lent his weight to it. With an occasional eye to the beach, to see that our inebriated chums behaved themselves, I followed the boat until it rounded the jutting beach and was out of sight. I was glad when they shoved back into view and ceased rowing. They were no more than a hundred yards from the *Quean* when Ralls hooked the clamps onto the battery and submerged the light a foot under: and I could hear the bottom panel of the boat slide back as he uncovered the sea glass.

The last time I had lain on my belly peering down at the bottom from that boat, Carter had been the diver. Standing erect, in his healthier days, he had dropped straight into a school of sharks, waving his arms and heading straight for the hungry but bewildered creatures. The old native trick had worked again, though I have seen it fail. When a shark's hunger exceeds fear there's a lightning dart, and blood — and blood brings the pack — and there's nothing left of the diver but a short, foolish memory.

Evidently they were not over the thick bed, for I saw the moon-beams high-light the outstretched arm of one of the blacks before Ripper set the oars in motion. They pulled closer in and to the right, slowly, pausing occasionally for Ralls to get up and let a black peer through the plate. A faint jabbering reached my ears against the wind, telling of the heightened excitement of guards turned helpers.

This went on for some time, and I could sense Ralls's growing impatience. Whether the big bed existed or not, Ralls, I knew, would send the boys down for scattered shells. At last I heard an excited flow of yammer and saw a black shrink from Ralls's pointed finger. Something down there was a counteracting agent to alcohol. Ralls's gun was in his hand and his arm was stiffened in the direction of the water. Then the butt was descending and the thud reached my ears, a somber echo of Ralls. Such medicine was not necessary for the next fellow. I saw him break the water almost without a sound; the lagoon closed over him, and there was a long interval of silence. He was up, alongside the boat and holding two large shells. Each looked to be almost a foot in diameter, and I guessed their combined weight at ten pounds.

To Tewelliger I said, "A hundred to one they didn't get pay." Had I said one thousand to one the limits of safety would still be with me.

But Tewelliger possessed a mania for odds and he weighted a greasy note under an anchor cable without any comment whatever.

Again the black went under, and I waited long minutes for his appearance. My eyes sharpened: I could not credit any set of lungs with that endurance, but I continued to wait until a long five minutes passed. There was a moaning sound from the boat, and I saw Ripper give her the oars in rapid strokes that lessened the distance between us. Somehow, I felt that the episode spelled finish to further trial diving that night. I saw Ralls jerk his light, and the scrape of the panel going back into place reached my ears.

"Like a coffin lid, Tewelliger," I grunted, casting a surreptitious eye his way. He had seen, and already his hands opened and closed convulsively.

The black was down under there, though his presence did not change the beauty of the night. Five or six fathoms above him the moon fell upon his watery ceiling, garnishing it with wave after wave of evanescent diamonds that rolled on in toward the beach. A flying fish joined another; and a night bird struck a note, disdainfully pronouncing the only eulogy the grave would ever know. I yawned, cursed the mosquitoes, and said I was ready for sleep.

I was mistaken about that, however, for no sooner had Ralls and Ripper put the boat within arm's length of the *Quean* than I perked my ears and tuned them to the beach. The commotion took me in long strides across the deck, my gun in hand, my mind ready to signal its use. All I could imagine was the reaction of the horde to the death of a comrade, since I was positive those on shore had witnessed his fate. I expected them to charge in screaming force, hacking, yelling, and shooting as they came. There was nothing novel about such an experience except that one's mind ever finds the same running thrill first experienced. The idea is to kill without getting killed, and to date we had shown ourselves skilled reflections of success in the mirror of that idea.

Trouble of a different sort caused me to lower my gun. Tewelliger, at my side, was ordered to advise Ralls of what was going on, and soon the skipper leaned nonchalantly on the rail by my side. Together we stared.

The first howl emitted by our guards came when the slow wheel chair, the same of the afternoon before, moved speedily toward them. Mijnheer van der Ruysdaal had, as was evident, schooled his Moluccan in the art of maneuvering the vehicle, for he came down the slope in a swooping charge that was fleet and sure; a descending wraith. Belying his sluggishness, the Dutchman brandished a long flowing whip that was many-tailed. Its bark was resounding, sharp as a pistol crack, and indicative of lightning. Charging upon his erring flock, the Dutchman emitted a fiendish yell, high-pitched and sounding all the world like "Hy-eeah," though that wasn't the word at all; it seemed out of another world. And strangely, the body of servants did not break and run. They cringed and fell to their knees, arms forward and backs in position for the lash. And come it did, once for each of them. The crack came and following each sound, without deviation, a black jerked and fell to his belly in writhing pain. The wheel pusher seemed to be responsible for timing and distance — he performed with the speed and éclat of a genius.

Three of the blacks ran, and it was after these that the chair sped. We saw from our front-row seats what happened to one of them as the other two disappeared among the shadowy trunks. One flash of the whip caught the black as he fled, striking him on a buttock's cheek and pulling a fearful scream from deep inside him. He fell, we saw, tearing away his loincloth and clawing at the flesh that popped open like a hacked melon. Ruysdaal drew close and ordered the culprit to stand. Quivering and babbling, he obeyed, aware of that entree of pain to follow the cocktail.

"Ten to one he gets it where it hurts," I said.

Before any answer could be made, the whip came from the side and around; it was jerked back by a wrist movement that set the tails deftly, and with rebounding, excoriating force, into the flesh. The black fell, writhing.

"A gentle lesson in birth control," Ralls said.

Some time later the flying Dutchman's fury was spent and his panting pushman resumed the pace of the afternoon. Our host then toured the field, ordering his servants to their feet and away. Ruysdaal turned his chair in our direction. Quietly, menacingly, he approached us, and on the beach not more than twenty feet from the *Quean's* stern he waved a halt. We stared down, and he up, and no word escaped any lip there for long, long moments.

It was the Dutchman who broke the silence. "Mijnheer Ralls, I'll thank you to produce my three servants," he said in the manner of one asking for a match. If there was malice, and there was, it was concealed in manner grand.

Ralls was ever unpredictable. He did not move a muscle except to grin as nicely as Ruysdaal had spoken. Then he ordered Ripper to row the boat to portside.

"Have a cigarette, Mijnheer?" said Ralls, tossing the pack to the beach. The Dutchman accepted, and gave it a light just as Ripper turned the bow.

"There is one missing, Ralls," said Ruysdaal.

"Yes, one missing, Mijnheer," the skipper replied slowly.

"That is regrettable." It came in the tone of a question.

"But unavoidable," returned Ralls. "I accepted your generous offer to do a bit of pearling, Mijnheer."

"Yes, I know."

"And it was kind of you to furnish me with night divers. Next time, however, send me experts. Your clumsy man stepped into one of your sea pits, a two-foot clam."

Puffing his cigarette with casual indifference, the Dutchman kept his eyes on the skipper. And the skipper yawned before relaying the macabre scene to all of us.

"I held my light on him. I left him a few minutes later, picked clean. There's a monument to you, Mijnheer, dangling out there."

I slept well through the three hours before that steaming sunrise. Perhaps I was tired. At any rate, I was in a good mood when I heard Carter's voice upon awakening. I was glad he was near, very glad — somehow I missed him and his guitar-sweetened poetry.

CHAPTER III

1

FROM the west a rain cloud dipped low and bent its head in our direction, its heavy bosom bursting in pearl-gray sheets. Slanting down in rainbow hues from a peeping sun it raced across Little Soembawa, drenching every foot of her until almost upon the *Quean;* then it veered sharply and sent tons of rain to the beach, and

22

atop the *Flores*. On it traveled, hugging the surface of the lagoon; and about a mile away, out over the plumes of the breakers, a mist was all that was left of it. Five minutes later there was no sign of our heavenly visitor, only the rain smell of steaming verdure. All was quiet, tropically peaceful, serene.

Why Carter strolled alongside the *Quean* that morning was put into question from the moment I saw him.

"One of my bad habits, Sam," he said. The *Quean* was in his blood, all right.

A newly pressed suit was on his back, and his hair glistened, giving him a well-groomed look that one seldom sees in remote spots. A powdery film almost hid the nodules from view: too bad, I thought, that such a hell-raising and debonair lad should find the scourge of the tropics settling in him. Tilden King Carter was a goner, I knew full well. He knew it, too, though he covered beautifully.

My words reached his ears but not my thoughts. "Mijnheer Carter," I scoffed, "has turned Hollywood on us." I was thinking that he came nearer than anyone I'd ever known to symbolizing adventure in the raw. He took his fun in big gulps without looking back, and he put his everything into it. I had never known him to shun a dare, and out here they are hair-raising and frequent. He was the type that could retch and grin at the same time.

"Thanks," he said. "Where's the admiral?"

"About," I said. "Looking for him?"

"Yes. I came to offer my respects, and invite him to make himself at home on our island."

"How nice of you. May we pluck a coconut or two for lunch?"

"Just don't overdo it, my man," he said. "And keep yourselves on this side of the rise. Oh, hello, Ripper," he said as the wop cocked his head at the shiny bad penny. "How's pearling?" He laughed.

"Tewelliger, the boys have a skeleton out there for you." He laughed heartily at the blanched face of Tewelliger. "By the way, Sam, better tell the admiral to keep off the *Flores*. Miss van Schreeven doesn't like having him aboard."

"Miss van Schreeven, eh? Pretty?"

"She's white, which is in itself beauty," he said. "But she's really a prize — nitrate of glycerol — T.N.T., Sam. And that's not all that's over there. So, Sam, since rape would be justified, I warn you in all seriousness to keep the admiral away. You know him."

"So you don't want any interference," I said, trying to bridge any thoughts of Ralls on the loose.

"Have it your own way, bo," he returned. "Say, pass over a drink,

Sam. Honest-to-goodness eggs and American hotcakes with Frisco coffee have sort of upset my belly."

So Ralls had investigated that bit of silk, I kept saying over and over in my mind. Aloud I laughed and said, "You'll be getting the gout, Carter."

"Yeah. I thought you boys were to trim sail."

"No hurry."

"Well if you knew what I know, Sam, you'd exercise your right to half ownership and get the hell out of here."

"And just what does the little man know?"

He shrugged, caught the bottle I flung at him, and said, "Well, here's to the girls in Moresby, to the females of Celebes; may they all have ninety children — planted in twos and threes."

Ripper laughed. I had heard that one before.

"Ah." Carter glanced up at us and again put the bottle to his lips. "Good old gin," he said, grinning. "Well, well! Look, boys, coming toward us. None other than the admiral."

"Meet the dandy, Ralls," I said. "Pretty, isn't he?"

Ralls, I noticed, had blossomed forth under a new cap. His open shirt was also a clean white, and his trousers were the ones he had salted down back in Kieta. He walked almost to Carter and stared at him from head to foot, grinning easily and saying much in silence.

"Look!" Carter cried. "The admiral took a bath."

I laughed. "Skipper, you going soft on us too?"

"Soft?" Carter jeered. "Did you say soft? Why, he has on Miss van Schreeven's panties right now. How does lace feel, Admiral?"

Ralls stared from a face of wax, at last saying, "Are you here, Carter, to bring any message from over there?"

"Yes," said Carter, still smiling and casting a surreptitious glance at Ralls's midriff. "How was the *Flores*, Admiral? Didn't know you liked silk in delicate shades," he paused to wink at me, "any more than Dutch like thieves in the night."

Ralls said, "If you weren't scheduled for torture, Carter, I'd enjoy killing you."

"Ten to one, Admiral, I'll outlive you. Yours is catching up with you faster than mine, and don't think it isn't. And as for torture, I'll not linger like a weakling, not this lad. When things get worse I'll spit in your face, make myself bleed a bit, and start swimming in the lagoon. So don't think you can frighten me."

The morning passed without further interruption. Ralls held one of his rare conferences with me in his cabin, and after I relayed the message from Carter — "If you knew what I know, Sam, you'd get the hell out of here" — he asked for my opinion. Despite his singularity he harbored a certain respect for my opinion, realizing that I held a counterweight at the other end of my running line. I was catalogued as a tough one due to the company I kept, though I was less dreaded, simply because I failed to emit such deadly force as the skipper, and, too, I was a known governor to his domineering qualities. Although Ralls was the accepted head of our various enterprises I was often consulted before him.

"Really want to know?" I put slowly.

He played solitaire when engrossed in thought. A red jack fell atop a black queen as he answered, "Yes, regardless."

"The black four will play there, Skipper," I said. "Personally, I think we're in for trouble around here. And for what? Let's just suppose pearls are the number one attraction — which is an error — they're less valuable than our good health. Yeah. I suggest we really trim sail and take to the first breeze."

"And — with pearls the number two attraction, what about the first?" He did not glance up at me.

"Well, find out for yourself in a hurry, and if there's no go, let's move. You know the Dutch boy, so you'll know how far it is from taw to naw. I haven't seen the girl, have you? And just who is this Ruysdaal?"

He raised his eyes, but not his head; he peered at me, half grinning. I caught his question and answered it. "I'm with you all the way, Ralls, as long as you don't throw my neck in a noose." The deuce of spades was lifted to the ace and a three of diamonds found the four of lowly clubs. "But there's one thing I want you to do, Skipper, and I mean it. Lay off Carter. Get it?"

"He makes my trigger finger nervous," he said.

"Yeah, and if you shot him, he'd still laugh at you. What the hell, Skipper, are you nursing a weak spot?"

"Okeh, Sam." He poured two stiff whiskies and set one before me. "Here's to a try."

"Yeah," I returned. "A *safe* try. And I hope you mean pearls."

I went on deck and told the boys to really trim sail, that we would pull with tomorrow's wind for Lorengau. They eyed me with a mixture of admiration and surprise, but they said nothing. I, for want of something better to do, went down the ladder into the boat and shoved off for a look at the lagoon. Out of sheer curiosity I worked out to where the trial moon diving took place and slid the sea eye. After some time I peered through and saw it.

25

ABIGAIL E. WEEKS MEMORIAL LIBRARY
UNION COLLEGE
BARBOURVILLE, KENTUCKY

There lying on the floor was the one-legged skeleton. The clam had opened up and I could distinguish it by the high brilliance of its color. It was every bit of two feet and I knew its lip was no plaything. The skeleton's foot was caught in a coral cleft, and there it would remain unmolested.

"This isn't the bed," I said aloud. "If it is, pearls will never hold us here."

I rowed farther out, peering through the glass window after each two or three strokes, letting the boat glide slowly under its own power. The floor took on depth, I noticed, and the coral formed larger rooms in this courtyard of Neptune. I put in a good hour of this, crossing and crisscrossing, and edging farther out as I did so. Then, after what seemed a lifetime of viewing wild colors and shapes, I came upon what I sought.

I am not given to the appreciation of beauty for beauty's sake, yet every now and then I find myself deeply entranced. My mother did oils and my father struck a musical note on almost any instrument, so I credited the mood to them — a fellow must find a little of the classic good in a dish with raw opposites. As I peered down into four fathoms that mood closed in on Sam Rosen. There on all sides of a circular room, some thirty feet in diameter and nosing into a long tail nearest the island, was coral and more coral. If color caught my eye, shapes held me. Lacy clusters and rich sawtooth edges met against the shafts of mirrored sky blue. In the shadowy caverns light beams danced about. Where they came from I did not know; the porous growth simply reached up for the sun.

Even a poor imagination could make a world out of this.

"A beautiful graveyard," I said reverently.

I threw off the spell and turned to more practical things. They were there — on the floor of this amphitheater and on up the narrow trough — pearl oysters, big, almost as large as the pair Ralls brought in early that morning. As I stared at them and sought to pick them from the film of growth, I reckoned that at least one pearl was down there. And one could be a fortune, depending, of course, on its color, shape, and size.

At that moment, as I lay on my belly in the drifting boat, the bug that bit Ralls nibbled on me. Not the girl I had not seen, but the second — wealth you could hold in your hand, spherical and iridescent — layered nacre from a bosom that could not eject a grain long years before. Pearls spelled wealth if genuine, despite the fact the Japanese had torn the market asunder with cultured pearls. I sat up in the boat and jerked viciously at the panel. Ralls would laugh at me if he knew what was in my mind. Thus I debated, wisdom against desire, greed against rationalism: pearls versus what I felt to be our only sane move. I thought of the odds against us, the eventual locking of wits and perhaps open combat with the Dutchman, but so strong was the serum now in my blood I glanced at the shore grimly and then chuckled contemptuously.

Pearls! I would have them. But I did not know the future. The pearling ended with the death of the native.

My departure from the *Quean of Melbourne* had been that of a man in possession of his faculties; my return was without them — I left them on the liquid floor of a coral paradise.

The next move was mine and I felt the weight of it as I got on deck. Snatching a bottle from Ripper I moved to the port rail and guzzled a good two inches. Ralls was nowhere in sight, a fact that was a pleasure in itself. Ralls possessed the faculty of reading a man's every secret. However, there was little cause for worry on that score; events were about to take a turn. My decision would remain a secret.

2

I had never laid eyes on van Schreeven until that moment, though I, as well as Ralls, was aware that he must sooner or later come into view. I saw him then, a tall, athletic figure with wide shoulders and a firm body. His hair was sandy against a pleasing bronzed face, out of which blue eyes peered in friendly manner. In his face was written strength of purpose, unrelenting decision, and complete assurance of self; all that plus polish. He approached his yacht in military fashion, sending curtains of smoke from a long cheroot. Why he chose to pass the *Quean* I did not know, and I cared less, but he was staring up at me in another moment.

"Ahoy, there, *Quean*," he said.

"Greetings," I returned. "You're van Schreeven?"

"Right, and you'd be Rosen, eh?"

"Right you are. Care for an afternoon finger?"

"A pleasure," he said. "But be my guest aboard the *Flores*. Whisky and soda with ice."

"Coming right down, Skipper," I said. Ice was a luxury we lost a day out of Rabaul, and it tempted me more than pearls at the moment.

On van der Ruysdaal's island I shook hands with the fellow. I judged him to be in his fifties until I felt his grip, and then I dropped my estimate a good ten years; he was, I later learned, much older. But a man either grows old young or retains a deceptive youth in the tropics — the alternative is to die young.

Sitting under his fan in a cushioned chair with a cold sweating glass of Scotch in my hand I found the sweet lethargy of contentment. I observed every detail of his cabin, even to the coat of arms on the fancy, but weak, cigarettes he proffered: mahogany throughout, with a thick coat of wax to save it from the ravages of a damp clime; fluffy curtains on the ports, gilded frames screwed to the enameled bulkheads, and thick carpets of rich crimson on the floor.

I answered his question with, "No, I don't mind telling you. Light cargo of hemp. But of course, we handle a bit of all cargo. A silver bell, for example, from an eccentric old fool in Kieta to a church in Lorengau. Then there's a chest of dental tools we're holding for a drunken doctor in Port Moresby — he missed the boat to Madang. Oh yes, he'll pay," I laughed, "or we'll use the tools on him before selling the stuff to the Chinks."

He laughed. He sat sprawled in a carved chair in the manner of a man accustomed to riches and having his own way. My drink went the way of all good things and the excellent host lost no time in extending me another.

"And, if I may inquire, what's your occupation, sir?" I asked. "Your name is familiar, though I can't seem to —"

"I am not exactly following any definite occupation, Mr. Rosen," he said. "You see I have a hobby. I can afford one. I indulge in, shall we say, nursing a fondness for anthropology."

"Well, sir, you should feel like the fisherman who threw his net in a hatchery," I said, grinning at him. "The anthropoids abound in these seas."

The conversation was leading up to a point, I thought. The ease of van Schreeven's talk and posture suggested as much. Again I found his English too perfect, and without faulty accent; to strike a true picture, I was sure his Dutch would be affectedly English. So, for all the man's veneer, I felt myself a match for him.

"Just what on earth prompted you to choose this island for a port?" He asked it blandly enough, and I countered as nicely with a tale of calm winds, poor sails, and exhausted fuel.

"Which prompts me," I said, "to put a question that may sound impertinent, though I assure you it springs from curiosity pure and simple." His expression bade me proceed. "Why does such a beautiful yacht display rotten sails?"

He laughed. "Yes, to a seaman they do stir up disrespect. Frankly, they were thrown up from sheer necessity by Mijnheers Bullit and Trago, my captain and chief mate, out of what was available. You see, we sprung our screw on a reef one night in Jomard Entrance, out of the Coral Sea." That was strange, I thought. But he cleared it by telling me they had pulled out of a cove in a hurry and were forced to pull astern. "Bullit and I had to mount the machine gun, while Trago handled the *Flores.* A hard gust ripped our sails before we could reef them."

Making a mental note of the armament, I said, "So anthropology has its wars, too."

"Yes." He frowned into his glass and then began biting into the meat of his objective. "Mr. Rosen, I presume you are aware of my host's antipathy to your — er — schooner's visit here. Of course, since you witnessed the meeting of Ruysdaal and Ralls; you were also present at their little tête-à-tête before sunup." I nodded and he continued: —

"Bad blood exists between them. I am sorry to say that every day, or hour, that the *Quean of Melbourne* lingers in these waters, the nearer sound the drums — I mean, frankly, open strife. There is more than lost love between those two. Ralls is known for a thousand miles in any direction as a — let us say a very, very strange character, rather smooth, though implacable. You are none the less publicized, but your role is seemingly that of satellite and regulator. In other words, Mr. Rosen, you indicate, by reputation, a man with whom one may do business. If I am —"

I interposed with, "Sir, if you're waxing into a trading mood, I must again indulge in your hospitality." I lifted my glass with a grin. "Of course," I added lightly, "I think you are making a mountain of a molehill. Ralls is a very mild sort." I lied glibly. Ignoring my remark, he said: —

"Mijnheer Ruysdaal is a sick man. He even exceeds that. If I may have your confidence I shall enlighten you with certain facts pertaining to his condition. He does not accept his physical condition as an event incidental to his years. It maddens him. He is at times moronic, at other times he is vitriolic, and again he falls from the plane of man. He becomes a slave to his moods, and he is not content with imagery."

My eyes opened at this remark.

"He's an old man with fevered, drug-clogged visions. He lives to humor his body — he lives to eliminate his troubles — and his enemies."

I was beginning to understand. Van Schreeven's lack of emphasis behind his words coated the stinger with slow drops of poison. He was bidding desperately for our pulling anchor. Why? What was all this to him? I turned my eye on him and he met my gaze for some time before striking back with more of the balm of persuasion.

"He is engrossed with the idea that he is endowed with supernatural powers. He is on this island solely to experiment with cures. His coterie assumes the role of just so many guinea pigs."

"You mean, sir, these natives are living test tubes for his —"

"Those who live," he returned easily. "Of course, he is not a scientist in the accepted manner. He does not employ the laboratory conception altogether."

"Then," I asked, "what does he use?"

"A radical form of psychogenesis is about the nearest definition I can give. He uses mental influence, dealing in origination, development, and evolution. He is aided, of course, by the eminent Dokter van Arken."

"Then how does he use the natives?"

"As opposites. They are labeled antipodes."

The whole thing was over my head. I was getting bored with explanations I knew nothing about and, too, the more I drank the nearer I approached sobriety: Scotch was a gentleman's drink that touched one off to surfaces, and niceties, and not pay talk. I wished for our potent mixtures aboard the *Quean:* van Schreeven would have painted me lucid pictures under its steam.

"Why did the old boy take such a liking to Carter at first glance?" I put squarely.

"He," explained my composed host, "was an enemy of Ralls, of yourself. He is afflicted. Therefore, he's an opposite. Ruysdaal will take good care of him. Carter is like rubber against a live wire."

"How do you mean that?" I asked, leaning forward.

"Literally," he said.

"Well, what do you want me to do?" I fired the question to shorten his words.

"To weigh anchor," came the blunt answer, softly spoken.

I got to my feet slowly, smiled at him, and thanked him for a pleasant visit. That was my way of asking what he had to offer. He stopped me with the seriousness of his tone and the unnecessary words: —

"I'm very serious."

"Well, Mijnheer van Schreeven, your craft is as seaworthy as the *Quean.*"

"But, Rosen. I suppose I must tell you. Ruysdaal is — my brother."

So! I pursed my lips and stared at him. "Just who is this Ruysdaal?"

"What is your price?" he said.

I was about to name it when the boat gave off vibrations of someone

30

walking about. It was a light step with a quality foreign to a masculine tread. It drew closer and I could hear the measured fall of feet. My eye was upon the door as it opened —

And I stared at something that sent opaque shadows over the coral castles I'd seen that afternoon; forgotten were the pearl bed, the menace of Little Soembawa, Ralls, and every other thing in the world of the present and the past. A girl, the girl, claimed my eye.

I had scarcely acknowledged the introduction when another presence made itself known on the *Flores*. I saw the shadow travel ahead in casual jerks and, at last, end abruptly as its owner stood in the door, leaning calmly against the brass stripping.

It was Ralls.

And so it came about that I was freed from any admission of the pearl bug's bite — I saw in his eyes a clear-cut beam of determination that said we would disregard van Schreeven's supplication as well as our own inner sanity; we would remain on Little Soembawa.

CHAPTER IV

I

THE sun goes down in a hurry in the tropics. One does not see a lingering twilight of the temperate zones, but one broad jump that takes your breath away. Just before the sun dropped the Moluccan made his way to the *Quean*. I was, as usual, leaning on the rail lost in thought. Ralls was in the cabin getting drunk, which meant he stirred the first winds of the whirl. Ripper had just come on deck with my supper and his expression was a mental shrug. He knew what always came with Ralls's sprees.

The Moluccan came closer and held forth his knotty cane. On it was a scrap of paper. I reached for it and opened the sheet while he stood there. Inscribed in flowing hand was: —

My dear Mr. Rosen:
Mijnheer van der Ruysdaal joins me in inviting you to dine with us one hour after sunset. Please write your answer on this sheet and return it via messenger.
Cordially,
Harmenszoon van Schreeven

Lord, how I wanted to accept that invitation. The thought of good food and drink, my enlarged curiosity concerning the Dutchman's island over the rise — and another sight of the girl I had met — almost caused me to throw caution overboard and accept. Instead I cursed Ralls under my breath and scribbled out a reply: "Regret I cannot come. Too busy. How about a rain check?"

A half hour later the messenger brought an answer: "Tomorrow evening then."

"Harmenszoon," I reflected. "What a monicker. And just how much will you pay, Harmenszoon?"

I gave thought to the advantages of waiting until the morrow for another talk with Ralls. By morning he would welcome sane discourse, and together we could converge our opinions into definite shapes. I remembered that I hadn't informed him of the meat in van Schreeven's talk that afternoon. Brother to van der Ruysdaal, or liar supreme, called for our veriest scales; we never undervalued an expectant enemy, or friend for that matter. I classified Harmenszoon as a smooth customer who knew a whole lot more than he divulged. His talk of his brother's black magic was surface chatter, defining his reserve as either deadly or treacherous, or both. He scarcely fitted my idea of a naïve Dutchman, notwithstanding the fact that there were a few in existence. But one learns to respect the Dutch in these parts.

The stars came out with the drop of the sun to hug given spots in a luminous ceiling just beyond the *Quean's* masts; in pearl white against a growing velvet, they seemed to radiate a strange heat. As I glanced again to the coral atoll the glint of their fire struck the silent coconut sentinels overleaning the lagoon and ricocheted from one silhouette to another, penciling the long lashes of sweeping fronds in radium against tropical indigo.

Called out of their torpor a million night insects fell into their season with raucous savagery. Their fierceness was the raw tropics and they did not know the decorum of constraint; they were bent on pillage. Shrilly, dully, they chorused the oncoming hours of night.

"Well, Sam Rosen," I said aloud, "the night is young, and Ralls is drunk, and yonder comes the advance guard of the moon."

Thereupon I turned about and walked down to Ralls's cabin, and hammered on the door. There was no answer so I barged on in.

Ralls sat under the light, his cap hugging the back of his head, his elbows on the table, chin in one hand, a pencil in the other. He did not raise his eyes as I entered, but continued to trace sharp lines about an object on an old sheet of parchment. Beside him was a clear bottle of gin with penciled lines on the label. Each line meant one degree nearer the sought-for — drunkenness; he ordinarily drew twelve marks, four on one bottle, eight on another. Then when the last line was behind him he invariably stood, three feet from the fine print of Genesis I, and read aloud before strolling on deck. His next procedure was to perch himself on the rail of the *Quean* where the ropes were thinnest and start walking. With premeditated purpose, always the same — to find out if he could walk it. Sober, he could not, drunk he could. If he fell on deck or into the water he was, therefore, sober. I have seen him fall in either direction, I have also seen him scare the wits out of a gray nurse, the worst shark in any ocean, with his splash. But he had other reasons, and why he stood the rail shall be duly explained.

At my entrance I took sights on the bottle and saw three marks. Desiring a finger myself, I walked to the shelf and took a bottle down; to have poured a drop from his liquid scoreboard would have invited trouble. Without a word, I poured a drink and downed it, then another, not evincing in the slightest the fact I was not alone.

At length he said: "Sam, it's no use. I can't get my mind on this thing." He penetrated the sheet with a vicious jab of his pencil.

"You meant to say that you couldn't get your mind off other things?" I grinned playfully and met his mirthless smile evenly.

"What other things?" he said. He eyed me for a moment before turning to the bottle. He gurgled deep and at last set it down, empty. Only eight drinks to go before Ralls would emulate a hurricane.

"Never did I expect such glamorous handiwork in this edge of the world," I said, as if talking to myself. "Like the gossamer threads of evening — riding in on a South Seas moon — and the perfumed essence of beauty — from a Balinese festoon —

"With a ray of imprisoned passion — in the eyes of a golden typhoon — and the sapphire of the tropics — in her winy, whirling rune. The girl, Ralls."

"Enough," he said quietly. "You remind me of Carter."

"His verse," I returned. "He's good at it, that boy is."

"Sam, ordinarily I don't seek company when I set out to drink."

"Okeh, Skipper," I said. "Just paying call." I arose and tossed off another drink.

"Sit down, Sam. I might as well tell you now that I've changed my mind."

"That's quite all right by me, Ralls." I returned, again finding my chair. "She almost upset me, too. But, of course, not quite."

"Why the 'of course'?"

"I just thought I'd save you the words, Skipper."

"You can tell Ripper and T'welliger they can hang from the sails as far as I'm concerned. I've got other plans."

"Other plans, huh? Well, Skipper, that's just lovely. I was saving my news for tomorrow, even turned down an invite for dinner at Ruysdaal's — in order to put you in the know. The *Flores*, Skipper, packs a Gatling gun."

Thereupon I gave him the story in detail. So careful was I not to miss any word or inflected meaning, I almost burped a Scotch taste onto my tongue. He downed drink number five when I finished, enough to brush off any bloke in the sea, but then he could drink level with Lucifer himself.

"Well, that should change things up a bit," he said.

"Yes," I answered satirically.

"But it doesn't," he fired in slow motion.

I sat up straight and eyed him. "Just a second, Skipper. Since when has either of us decided to set up any dictatorship on this tub?"

"You don't get me, Sam," he said, frowning into my eyes. I didn't give ground as he said, "I don't see any use in us squabbling over any decision. We're both after dough, and there's plenty lying around this island."

"Come again, Skipper," I said, not lowering my gaze. "I might as well come clean, since you won't. You'd trade the *Quean*, my part along with yours, and see us all floating out to sea as shark food for a smile from that girl. Now wait — I'm not through.

"You rode into this place in a mood, Skipper. Well, up pops an orchid instead of buffalo grass. And you build to the fact instead of against it. Now wait, Skipper. I'm human, too, but not to the point of courting positive suicide."

"Are you through, Sam?"

"Not quite," I said nicely.

"Then wind up — and get out."

"No, Ralls." I smiled at him and removed my cap. "This thing isn't that easily settled. If you're set on your aims, then remember one thing — we have never fought odds alone. We usually figure out ways and means and then stand together. Right?"

"Right, Sam," he said, mollifying somewhat his strident tone.

"But," I added the thorn, "only where there's profit for both of us."

His eyes danced, and he got to his feet. He calmly marked off number six and said: "Sam, you win — temporarily. I'll wait until your conference is over before I do anything."

34

"Well, you forget, Ralls, there's price to name. That's not my sole joy, or duty, as it were." I got to my feet and walked to the door; there I turned about and said: —

"Think it over, and decide on a price they'll pay. Not one we can't divide — or spend."

He grinned; he seemed to pity me.

2

When I went on deck the ship was bathed in moonlight, a matchless patchwork of light and shade. Slow shadows quickened into flowing silver, and shapes found enchantment that was massive, lucid, and grotesquely beautiful. Towering above the fluid roll of the beach line, and leaning almost over the stern of the *Quean*, a gaunt palm spread an umbrella that was as eerily menacing as the calm before a storm. It simply hung up there, not stirring a particle in the oppressive atmosphere.

I mopped the sweat from my face and neck and ordered Tewelliger on watch. I might add that the reason for a bodyguard during Ralls's orgies was merely to gratify a whim. Ralls was a lordly man in his morbid and hellish moods, and it cost nothing to humor him.

"He'll be out within the hour," I said. "Ripper, keep an eye about, will you? I'm taking a walk."

The beach glared up at me as I trod the cushion of sand. A score of land crabs scurried away as I approached. I paid little heed to these creatures as my mind swung around to Carter. Since morning he had been noticeably absent from the fold, and the noisy memory of him seemed to cast a pall on the home he no longer claimed. I hoped he was enjoying himself.

I walked aimlessly, having only one purpose in mind, seeing new ground and water and losing sight of our schooner for once. I came to the jutting tip where the beach continued to hold a fifty-foot margin from a dense garden jungle. The odor of heady perfume clung to the stifling surface air and I threw a glance at the bushes. For one moment, an incalculable eternity, I stared into the face of a white man who froze in his attempt to duck out of sight.

I played a long shot and said, "It's rather close in there, isn't it, Mr. Bullit?"

It was two bucks on the nose that paid off, for the man, a strapping fellow with a broad face built around a broken nose and a sidewise smile, trained his beady eyes on me in silent apology before lumbering

35

forward. I appraised him as one does a prospective antagonist. His wide shoulders and ham hands were connected by giant muscles that sweated oil to a harem of tattooed beauties. As he approached I saw that his smile was guided by a bucktooth his thick lips had learned to clear.

"Me apologies, sir," he blurted from a bullfrog throat. "I was eyeing the flying fishes when you popped up. For jimminy crickets, I says, if it isn't one o' the blokes from the *Quean.*"

He stood before me offering his hand. I merely stared at him from head to foot holding my arms akimbo. "A likely tale, Mr. Bullit," I returned. "You may advise Mijnheer van Schreeven or his host, or both, that I don't enjoy being shadowed."

"Aw, haw, haw, haw, haw," he bellowed. "Can't you take a joke, sir?"

I thought fast, at last deciding to take a chance on fathoming him with words. "Not from guys who know that I know about the concealed wealth on this wet clod."

"Wealth?" His surprise was genuine.

"Yeah," I said, giving him a contemptuous grin. "You miss a lot in life, Mr. Bullit. All blind men do. I don't know whether to take you in to the skipper, cut you in, or cut your throat."

He spread his feet apart and slowly raised his hands to his hips before saying, "Well, sir?"

"There's little profit in knocking hell out of a guy like you, Mr. Bullit," I said nicely, "though it would give me great pleasure."

"Haw, haw, haw! That's funny, since there's nothing holding you."

"And if I win?" I said.

"Ye can take me before Mr. Ralls, though I'd as soon meet the devil himself."

"And if I lose?" I said.

"You can cut me in on your treasure."

"But you wouldn't change sides," I thrust at him. "You get your pay from the *Flores.*"

He laughed. "Not so anyone would know but us."

There was something about the fellow that belied the brutish lout who confronted me. I did not doubt his greed, his ready arm, or his rugged agility in giving them combined use, but there was this fact to alter his outward show: the *Flores Tandjoeng* did not travel in the same style as our schooner, and had the fellow actually slipped into the man he pretended, he would be elsewhere now. Van Schreeven would first of all plant his skipper's sights in a man not only fearless and clever, but loyal to the nth degree. My mention of treasure would reach

36

the two brothers who would see in us, Ralls and me, men lingering here with an inspired, conspired purpose. That was exactly the way I wanted it; they would fall to the defensive and not put the offensive power they held into play — then too, they would not suspect the true aim of the skipper of the *Quean*. It was beside the point whether or not there was treasure here: if so they would reveal the fact; if not, the same — but our cover lay in first play.

"Well, I'll tell you what. If things shape up as I think they will, you'll find me at this very spot at sunrise day after tomorrow. Until then, keep mum."

"Aye, aye, sir," he said. "But about a little fist work, are you still in the mood?"

"No," I said. "I scarcely see any need for it now." I turned to leave him, saying, "There won't be any need for your spying now, Mr. Bullit."

"Aye, aye, sir," he grunted. I saw him disappear under the giant leaves of a banana tree.

I walked farther on, skirting the trunk of a coconut palm. I sensed the island was like a huge tooth, its concave roots encircling the lagoon, the promontory I trod merely an inner root. To my left the palm trunks rose from fern, bush, elephant ears, and thick jungles of vine life, while on my right a long sloping beach dipped into the shallows of the lagoon only to rear its head again in a sandy toy island some fifty yards away; and straight ahead the shoal ran into its large molar root that curved back around the lagoon.

My ears caught the notes of a blaring phonograph that gave off screechy Dutch or English, I scarcely knew which. It was heady and dank here. Soon I stumbled upon a rise that lifted me a good ten feet above the surf. It was a honeycomb of porous rock. Imagine my surprise when I saw a running stream of swift water at least two feet deep and easily that wide. I tasted the stuff, and it was cool and sweet. In another jiffy I was out of my clothes and sitting in the middle of it. I doused my head and felt the cool stuff part my hair. Before long I noticed a presence in the water, faint signs of civilization's cleansing agent — soap. That was my first thought about the spring's headwater.

Hastily I dried myself with my shirt and donned my remaining garments. I cautiously followed the stream on up to its head. As I approached I heard a gentle splashing, and a voice. Warily, on all fours, I crept to the pool, hiding behind a thick trunk that was flanked by blooming hibiscus bushes. I rose to my knees and parted the foliage, frowning as I did so.

3

I saw a pool bathed in moonlight, water gushing from a fountainhead in the rock directly across from me; I saw a setting of tropical lilies and water plants beneath graceful fronds, thick, quiet, and fierce. That was the background, an incidental stage soaking into my lesser sight while I viewed the work of art that was the actress: Teleia van Schreeven.

The same girl I had met aboard the *Flores* stood naked in the pool, a lively tonic to my eyes, even as she had been that afternoon in rose blouse and mannish blue dungarees. Out of the encounter I drew a picture, one that nestled sanely in a mind's eye, the opposite of beauty unveiled in the moonlight: she was Dutch and Balinese, and minus the harshness of face one meets down Java way; she retained all the animation of the gay Balinese. Her face, proud, creamy-bronze, and outfitted with deep, intelligent eyes and smile-drawn lips made to order from Sam Rosen's pattern of beauty, was but a parade ground for radiance. Her hair, a rich brown setting for her face, neck, and shoulders, seemed designed to guide an eye to the supporting carriage. Of medium height and weight, and slim of waist, she was proportioned, it seemed, to glorify her plain attire. In complimentary manner, in amazement, I had lifted the Rosen brows; and the woman, eternal since Eve, seemed to flash understanding. Another quality leaped from her eyes; it was that brand of assurance that goes with poise and knowledge — a positive air of superiority minus any trace of arrogance.

That is how she met my eyes; that was how she met Ralls's, only his stare had been more penetrating. Perhaps he saw that afternoon what I saw in the pool. Teleia van Schreeven minus rose blouse and blue dungarees.

She stood before me in water up to her calves, a statue of toned bronze. She faced the bank of the pool, bending once, twice, to cup water to her shoulders. She seemed a nymph at play, toying, sighing, and dreaming before slowly turning to face the moon, and me. Swift was that eternity in which I stared.

But Sam Rosen was no artist — instead he was a human being who gave his red blood up to a fast run through redder veins — he was at the moment the lost trader, who had, during that one day, given himself first to pearl lust, and then to the creature for whom Ralls staked everything. He was a caldron of desire. Thus artist, trader, and adventurer met the man.

As she turned her longing eyes upon the moon and raised her deep-throated voice in a Balinese song of love, I met the Sam Rosen who rubbed his sweaty hands together. I took a quick inventory of the stage. Inside me I seemed to be ripping the turquoise depths and bubbling surfaces of a Balinese lagoon with a dorsal fin, and from the welter of blood and foam I sought that mad beauty of the eternal in a moment's grasp. The smoky Sam said: Beat Ralls at his own game while no one is about.

I got to my feet slowly and stalked into full view of her. For a moment she stared at me in frozen surprise. Then in a most unfrightened manner she stepped to the bank and drew a robe about her.

Facing me, she said: "Good evening, Mr. Rosen. We missed you at dinner."

There was quality in her cool defiance, and I could not hold back an admiring smile. I said as calmly as the moment allowed, "You are beautiful. Beautiful!"

I stepped nearer, having crossed the narrow outlet that wound its way into the lagoon. Then I was within arm's reach of her, and she peered up at me while wrapping a towel about her head in nonchalant manner.

"Miss van Schreeven," I said, lending my voice authority, "I warn you not to ever make the mistake of coming here alone. You aren't exactly safe here, especially in the nude. Do I make myself clear?"

She stared at me for a moment, the moonbeams playing about her lush lips and narrowed eyes. She said, openly defiant, "Sir, I take orders only from my father."

"Then," I said, and I caught her wrist and yanked her to me, "he's indeed a negligent father. You'll do as I say about this! Do you understand?" My hand tightened, and she winced.

Her eyes opened wide but not in trepidation. She only stammered, "Y — yes." Then she asked me why, what danger confronted her. She asked a question like that! When a jerky vice held her, when eyes turned a hellish red burned into her not a foot away, she asked a question like that! I laughed, I could not help it.

In another moment I almost threw her away from me and headed for the beach in long rapid strides, and all the way back I gave myself up to mounting rage; I cursed Sam Rosen for every kind of fool, for the damn fool he was. Her stupid wonder had provoked the laugh, and that sudden expression of another thought had broken the spell like a pin in a bubble. And I knew then I would be haunted forever by the ineffable quality of that upturned face. There was more there to stir a man down to his innermost black pits than could ever spring from a detailed memory of her unclothed body glistening in the pool. Something walked into her eyes in that moment. In that vast eternity, comparable to a whole century moving slowly by in the snap of a finger, I had stood there, and read those eyes. She had inherently called for a lover in her song; and I read of disappointment.

As my head spun like a senseless hurricane, I stalked on toward the curve and the *Quean*, upbraiding myself in one rash outburst, and decrying her wantonness and beauty in another. I had won a victory only to retreat. I had owned her soul; and from her no voice but that of supine acceptance. I had let her slip my grasp to wait for another man less noble.

"No!" I said aloud. "No! It was her innocence." The blood rushed from my head, and in saner mood I gave emphasis to that definition. It was not until I rounded the promontory and met the *Quean's* eye far down the beach that I quelled the awful disturbance inside me. Stooping to cup the salty brine to my forehead, I heard a noise in the bushes. Quickly I raised my head and again met the bulk of Mr. Bullit.

4

He stood twenty feet from me, chuckling, his hands hanging from thumbs in an ornate Chinese belt. I arose, walked slowly in his direction, and said something about our meeting again. He chuckled all the more and adjusted the pistol slung under his arm. I thought he was putting on a queer act for a man who succumbed to my apocryphal bait less than an hour before and, as he rocked to and fro in sarcastic glee, I was certain he had learned something in the interim. What it was, I soon learned.

"Mr. Rosen," he said. "Sir," he added after a brief pause. "See this gun? I see you do, sir. Well, you are a very, very smart man."

"Yeah?" I queried, walking closer.

"Yeah," he said gruffly. "Numbers ain't often put on steel jackets, and seldomer initials, but I'm telling you, I cut yours on the one coming up around the cylinder. Aye, aye, sir, I did that.

"I still say, you're a smart man." Then he laughed.

I, slow of mind in this cheap surprise, finally caught on. Said I: "Have you been spying on me, Mr. Bullit?"

"Why, Mr. Rosen," he said with mock hurt.

"Come, Mr. Bullit, let's open up and cease the mystery. Just what are you talking about?"

"Oh, swimming pools and fairies, maybe." He added in a mirthful baritone, "You're a man of brains."

"You mean —"

"Yeah, Mr. Rosen. I mean I had the bead set on your bonnet and my finger itched. There is some treasure we didn't discuss. She, by the way, is it."

So. Mr. Bullit was a man of many moods, of few masters. I, in all seriousness, eyed him as a mortal enemy, one who must be put in his place once and for all. I was not viewing the stock of Rosen at par and that thought angered me as much as did his interference. Twice that day I'd slipped from a state of sanity upon which I prided myself. There was pearl lust, there was a woman's figure and face. It was no wonder then that I invited any opportunity to set my stock soaring again.

I'd seen his type in action, and the thought was reminiscent of slow torture that comes with ribs cracking in a grizzly hug, of ponderous weight behind a thumb gouging at an eye, or even worse. My redeeming self had already said he must be beaten, and my calculating mind was racing forth with a plan of attack. My weight, one eighty raw, was not hanging flesh, but there before me was over two hundred in steel.

I was about to yell out to Ralls, who wasn't there, over Bullit's shoulder and wade in, when he, facing the open lagoon, pointed past me with "Look, Rosen!" With the speed of a mongoose I leaped backward to await a bull's rush. But he was not fooling. "Hey, Rosen, I mean it. Look out there — a man almost done for!"

Out of the corner of my eye I peered. Sure enough, there was a man out there floundering with his last ounce of strength. He splashed aimlessly, about a hundred feet away, while circling him with water purling white in the moonlight I saw the dorsal fin of a shark. I dove before Mr. Bullit could co-ordinate his beef and unwrinkled cerebrum. My eye followed the shark as it drew near the helpless man, and as I cut the distance down, I heard Mr. Bullit's shout: —

"Get the man, Rosen, I'll take the shark!" Proving his words, he fired. The aim was true but only the fin felt the impact. Enraged, the beast cut toward the victim, leaping to the surface in a foamy whip. That, evidently, was Bullit's idea, for he placed two fatal shots in that split-second interval. The man I pulled out of the lagoon had a face beaten to a pulp. Blood oozed from lips, nose, forehead and hair, while red flesh marked one ear. His body was a mass of red weals that bespoke the whip.

In my maddened state I gazed at my friend Carter, the victim. I thought of Mijnheer van der Ruysdaal.

"So!" I said. "Mr. Bullit, you'll get the scrap you've invited." Nor did I await his answer. In a swift exchange of blows, Bullit failed to cover his jaw. For a moment he stared up at me in foolish manner, his elbows and back in the sand. Then he arose and lumbered toward me, grinning.

Sam Rosen was watching his stock climb, but over a grave mistake; he had erred in his snap judgment and accused wrongly.

CHAPTER V

1

WITH Ripper and Tewelliger rising from their watch to stare at me for the insane man I was, I heaved Carter on deck and proceeded to douse his open wounds with raw whisky. I growled incessantly, and when Ripper ambled over with words about my making a great mistake in bringing him to the *Quean*, I flung a bottle at him. It struck the wheel, almost dislodging a spoke. Next I raised Carter's sore head and poured down enough of the remedy to raise the dead. For my efforts, a choking, fighting Carter rose up in protest.

"Now," I said, panting. "Ripper. Tewelliger. You two watch out after him. Don't let anyone touch him. I'm making a call. Do you hear?" I stared at them and then at Carter, inwardly ablaze. For answer both men flung their guns to the deck and faced me in open defiance.

"What in the name of hell goes on here?" I barked.

Ripper, of course, answered: "I meana no for to buck ya, sor. But — he walka the rail."

"Well, so what? What did you expect him to do, fall off?"

"Sa no good, sor, sa no good. He'sa wild."

"Who's wild?"

Tewelliger said, "The skipper, sir. He's the one who done it."

I was fast losing that last bit of control I retained. "Tell me," I thundered, "who the hell ever walks a rail but Ralls?"

"Sa nota that, sor. Mother Maria, nota that! He'sa one who threw him over." He pointed to Carter. "The Creeper, sor, the Creeper."

"You mean to tell me Ralls took the Creeper to Carter?"

Both men nodded.

"You mean to tell me he used his fists on him?"

"No," said Tewelliger. "The butt end of the whip."

"And then slung him into the lagoon?" Again both men nodded.

I spread my feet apart, and showly reached out to grasp the gin bottle Ripper extended. Aloud, ringing clearly in the night air, I heard my voice as it gave off with: —

"The dirty son-of-a-bitch!"

2

Perhaps I should explain why Ralls walked the rail. I could tell you in three words — he contemplated action — but such brevity does not suffice. One must, like me, view the underlying props to such inadequate explanation; not the actual and widely separated reasons for action, but the primal drops to the unique display. There is little need for wasted words that proclaim Ralls the possessor of savage traits. That has been gleaned. But of his idiosyncrasy, there was something too calm and violent, too placid and deadly. He moved with the heart of a hurricane in its first stages, slowly forming winds and thoughts, holding them centered and in tow until more winds and thoughts were gathered; the whirl continued under the superb disguise of lackadaisical calm. Then quietly, ominously, the wind increased in velocity, the thoughts whirled faster and faster, until a mighty roar lent itself to the whole environ. A hurricane is wholesale destruction, but there's never a more becalmed spot than its vortex, its dead center: that was Ralls directing, thrusting out a vicious hand, holding out one more bit of hell like that he had given Carter. Then his hand was drawn back to the vortex and he traveled on.

Call it madness if you like, but strike the superlative.

My first taste of his standing the rail came after I was forced to sign up and mulct advance pay from some willing soul in order to pay for Carter's appendectomy. That was in Sydney. And we met in a strange manner: I was the verbal target of two burly Chileans who'd just made port, and everything else they could, before singling me out for a bit of lewd ribbing. I said little but kept right on drinking until one of the greasy tramps asked me if I was by any chance part native. I swung three blows, two at that one and one at his chum. It ended in a hurry. Ralls, unknown to me by sight, had witnessed the whole mess, and when the police persuaded me to accompany them, he suavely disarmed them with a word and an eye; it was after several drinks at the bar he invited me to join up. He advanced me the money I needed upon my promise to board the *Red Witch* next morning.

43

I boarded her at sunup and we hoisted sail into a robust trade wind within the hour. The boat seemed less of a banker's proposition — she was chartered by a bank on this trip — and more of a mystery ship with a free roaming master. Short of an Australian windjammer, her sails bellied from three masts. She was minus skysail, leaving her five high, topped with royals. Ralls was merely captain and he ordinarily followed the routes via the Caledonias, Fijis, and on up to the Ellice group, catching the lesser Hebrides and Chesterfields on the home swing. Carter was left on his own, which suited him fine, and I, happy at a chance to serve even the devil if necessary, fell into my place along with the motley crew.

I noticed that undercurrent of respect the crew as a whole accorded Ralls, and it was a source of amusement. I had heard plenty, but minus that trait known as gullibility, I sold rumor short. The second morning out, however, running before a strong southeast trade, and strangely north, two seamen took to fists on deck. The scrap was a halfhearted affair until Ralls came on deck. Eyeing them, he said: —

"I don't allow fighting, so you can take your punishment in a continuation of that forbidden pleasure."

He made them slug one another until each was fighting mad. Then he watched them lose energy, sweat, and blood until each was thoroughly exhausted. They stood panting and wiping little rivulets of gore from nose, mouth, and ear, afraid to continue, afraid to stop. The sight was pitiful.

"Don't stop, lads," Ralls ordered. He leaned against the mizzen fife rail with arms folded, grinning steadily. In another lapse of minutes neither was able to raise an arm, but Ralls ordered us to douse them with water. Lying on the deck in blood and brine they lolled their eyes at Ralls for mercy and, not finding it, crawled toward one another. Again unconsciousness, and more water. Ralls kept them at it. I remember the one called Camille was sporting a pair of lips that were red raw and three times their former size. The other could not see through the purple puffs that continued to swell.

The crew grumbled, but held its sullen distance. Only I had my say.

"Isn't that carrying the show to the extreme, Captain?" I said quietly. I wasn't heroic and I was never accused of voicing impertinence, but somehow the punishment versus the crime simply failed to strike any harmony in my mind.

"Did I ask your opinion?" he said without turning his eye my way.

"No, sir," I replied, "but you're getting it just the same. Now what's my punishment?" I was mad as hell by that time.

44

Then he slowly turned an eye on me. For some time he stared and then turned to scan the horizon, his brows arched and his tongue making a tent pole for his starboard cheek.

"Follow me, Rosen," he said.

I did. If he sought to shove Mrs. Rosen's boy around, well and good, but he would not do so and remain in the pink. He walked slowly toward his cabin, and once inside he locked the door. A bottle was atop the table and he reached for it, asking me politely if I'd reach for the glasses behind me. I backed toward them, and he laughed.

"Cautious, eh?" he said. My "Yes, sir" was without the proper ring of maritime courtesy.

"Have a drink, Rosen."

"Thanks — sir."

The tension seemed to stir up silence; in his favor, of course, since he alone knew the next move. But I was satisfied, and I faced him without any show of expression. That was fine.

"Rosen, what would you say if I told you I plan to use the whip on you?"

"Well, sir, the law, while against you, is ever on your side. If I objected — mutiny. But Captain Ralls, you're staring at a man who doesn't give a tinker's damn about laws that don't work both ways, so I'd say you'd be making a slight mistake."

He grinned pleasantly and said, "I've had an eye on you, Rosen. You've got guts. Here, have another."

"Thanks, sir," I replied.

"I'm considering an idea, Rosen, that means money. Would you like to be cut in?"

"Aye, sir. Nothing like an honest dollar," I said tentatively.

"A dollar's a dollar," he returned brusquely, "but this idea might lead us to a court of inquiry."

He mentioned courts, which meant murder or scuttling, or both, and giving me credit for understanding he watched me closely for any signs of moral repugnance. It was not forthcoming as I stared straight into his eyes.

"Very well then, Rosen. Our log calls for a meeting with an American steamer at Davao in the Philippines. Our course calls for the Carolines and then due west. Somewhere near one forty-nine at three degrees south I shall probably need a new chief mate — Mr. Loring is religiously inclined. Your papers aren't the best, but they'll do."

He arose, walked around the table, and offered me his hand. I took it. Then, smiling, he took a swing at me, almost breaking my nose.

45

He tapped a fountain of blood that turned my white blouse a rich crimson.

"That," he said easily, "is for the benefit of the crew."

The *Red Witch* made Nouméa in Caledonia, Kira Kira on San Cristobal, Tulagi in the Solomons, taking in her slow swing to the northwest more than her share of fair weather and smiling winds.

Too long I had been Americanized, which meant, in the South Seas, mechanized slavery to eventual nothing. I gave thought to "Isn't it so?" On a ship or an island one can have everything without the constant motivity, relative, of course, to one's idea of the word. Laziness they call it in Omaha, Columbus, and Dallas; heaven they call it from Honolulu, Tahiti, to Singapore. I chose the heavenly, and so would a Wall Street clerk or a Chicago merchant — once they tasted the fruit. The *Red Witch* took me through the core.

And such a ship needs another word. Her name was, it seemed, purposely conceived before the ship; she was carefully designed to carry the stirring title. *Red Witch!* Batjak, a Dutch firm of Java, owned her; it was rumored the big man of the firm had named her. And she fell beautifully into title, for she gracefully towered into the wind hand and swept through the water like a fleet swan done in Chinese lacquer. She split the luminous troughs with a passion, and I felt her artisans deserved a page in history. Her decks were long and scrubbed white, her hull glistened of red, and her bulwarks were white, and her masts and spars gleamed in the sun against white sails with fast bellies. Many were the hours I spent under her sighing uppers watching her bowsprit nose on into the blue-green seas, listening to her ropes creaking and her canvas volleying as she picked up the wind; and I've stood her deck while she scudded, ever praising those men who gave her stern a feather; I've seen the trimmers run her ratlines and rigging while the water cascaded from her deck, while Ralls bellowed. Aye, I've heard her talk. I've almost heard her rebuke a helmsman for "pinching her" too close to the wind.

She was one of those ocean queens favored by Neptune, it seemed — until the devil took the helm. Her bow carried a figurehead, a gilded lady, seldom seen on the too few remaining ships under sail, her head facing the water, her breasts cooling in the shade and running spray. Watching the lady from wharf or boat, I've heard men wager on the size of her golden nipples: some squinted and said apples, others plums: but all of them said she was a painted witch. I never took the trouble to cup a hand over her nipples. Her name stood out in carved and gilded letters on her stern, *Red Witch*, and her trim lines augmented the ornate words from fore to spanker.

46

On that trip she traveled light. In her hold was wheat, though scarcely enough for good ballast. But she sailed proudly, her eye bent leeward. The crew was in fine spirits, having tasted of wine and shore-cooked food. Some had renewed their acquaintance with human flesh, caring less for its color or virtue and more for its sprightliness. Mr. Loring, lean, and chaste in appearance, despaired of their souls in profound terms, and sought prayer among them; but with all their respect for his office, the men mocked him openly. He grew diffident, then morose, then cantankerous.

All that time the captain of the *Witch* was collecting wind for his hurricane. In Nouméa I felt the brush of it, in Kira Kira it was a whirlwind of noticeable size, and out of Kieta it sent a dive into the barometer. I was a daily companion in his cabin, and over our drinks we thinned the air, after a fashion. I learned we carried gold, bars of it from Kalgoorlie's "Golden Mile" marked for Frisco. Its true worth I left alone, awaiting Ralls's spilling the news, if and when it suited him. But the very disclosure of our cargo painted all sorts of possibilities, almost lending verity to my already seething imagination. With gold aboard we could do any number of things, though the still vague shape of any procedure must be tied to his words concerning the "court of inquiry." At any rate he drank more and walked the deck with his mind in the royals, and, I thought, his feet implanted in hell.

Mr. Loring came out of his cabin many times during that leg of the wind with his brows knitted and a huge paw rubbing at his chin. Plagued with the mystery in the air and the skipper's reticence and penetrating stare, he evinced bewilderment at its highest pitch.

The second mate was a quiet and easy man selected for obedience first, and that same quality second — he would have fought a shark with his hands tied had Ralls ordered him to do so.

His name was, in short, Ripper. The selfsame Ripper of the *Quean of Melbourne*. His orders were relayed through Mr. Loring, to whom he paid little heed; Ralls always countermanded them and took Mr. Loring to task for not getting them straight in the first place. And at the chief mate's whiny expostulations Ralls always replied in slow placating tone: "Mr. Loring, get more sleep. Your mind needs rest from worry." It was small wonder then that the poor man was almost insane before we reached the Bismarck Sea. On the morning of that day in which Ralls stood the rail I was informed that Mr. Loring had been put aboard as second in command for one reason, namely: his pronounced uprightness; by the charterers, of course, who felt safer with a man of probity riding herd over their gold.

47

"Poor Mr. Loring," said Ralls. "He's losing his mind. Out of Tulagi he told Ripper I said point due west, and to my face he declared that I told him exactly that." I could not suppress a grin, nor could Ripper. Ralls ignored us and talked on, calmly, easily. After several shots of gin, he ordered Ripper to fetch the "parson." He arrived moments later, his long frame bent, his huge eyes hollow, his bulbous nose flared, his mouth twitching, his "Aye, sir" creaking from a quaver to a high note; and when he wasn't asked to sit with the underlings who shared the welcome mat of his superior, he gave off a grimace one might expect from an officer who is a stickler for discipline.

"Mr. Loring," said Ralls, "point the ship due north, for an hour, then west by south for St. George's Channel."

"Aye — but, sir, that is off our course."

"Is it, Mr. Loring? Don't you know our destination?"

"Why, sir, Davao."

"Then which route would you follow, the southern or the Caroline skirt?" Ralls queried gently.

"Our course was mapped north from Kieta." He sweated and stared. At last, he mumbled respectfully and departed. Ten minutes later Ralls again asked Ripper to fetch Mr. Loring.

"Mr. Loring, what's your course?" Ralls said. The gaunt mate gave it. Ralls eyed him for a full minute before saying, "Mr. Loring, I distinctly told you to point her two points west from north, didn't I?"

"But, sir, you — I'm sorry to contradict, sir. You said due north, and — I, sir, distinctly —"

"Mr. Arrezo," said Ralls. "What did I say?"

"West, sor."

"Mr. Rosen, did I say north or west?"

"West, sir."

Loring stared, popeyed, then fell to a chair, wiping sweat from his face.

"Mr. Loring, I did not ask you to seat yourself."

"Sorry, sir," he said, arising. "May I inquire, Captain, if I'm being shunted around, or have I — I actually been hearing things? I'm beginning to suspect something is wrong with me, or —"

"Or what, Mr. Loring?"

"Or that I'm traveling aboard a hell ship," he said weakly. "The men up there will think I'm crazy changing orders about."

"Are you, Mr. Loring?" Ralls asked, leaning forward with simulated concern. "Of course you're not. You're merely a sick man who needs attention. Look at me, then turn your head to the left." When the mate

48

complied, Ralls arose as if startled. "Put him to bed at once, Mr. Arrezo. And exert every precaution," and in undertone he said so Mr. Loring could hear the forbidden, "to protect the crew."

"*Ges-ù-Cristo*!" exclaimed Ripper. "Sa no wonder the rats she leava the boat."

"No!" said Loring. "No!" His voice grew higher. Whether he feared for himself or for a ratless boat wasn't made clear. Perhaps he connected the two and feebly fought joint disaster. That was, however, beside the point; the import was his thorough cracking-up. He had ever taken life too seriously, he had elevated his temperate zone mind into the clouds in defiance of the tropics, childishly unaware that the expanse under the hot southern arch takes its toll in one way or another, and without fail. But the company he kept on the *Red Witch* helped the laws of the tropics in speeding his collapse.

3

From Mr. Loring's molded degradation I inherited the office of chief mate, and Ripper, proud of second mate's place, a lofty perch exceeding his aptitude, addressed me with a pleasant, "Aye, sor." Thus, with amusement ruling the sympathetic emotions of my new and short-lived rank, I trod the deck of the graceful ship that day with a wary eye cast toward Mr. Ralls's office. It was not until the black night dropped over us that he sent for me.

On his round table sat two bottles. In one hand was a cigarette and in the other a stub of a pencil. His cap fell to the back of his head, and his eyes shone glassy and calm; he invited me to drink with him. To my surprise he did not pour from the bottles before him, instead he reached for another at his feet. After pouring he gave a glass a bartender's on-the-line coast. We bent elbows as he drank from his bottle and I drank from mine. After his every lengthened quaff, he used the pencil on his container, drawing a mark.

"Mr. Rosen, can you imagine a more interesting cargo than bullion?" I couldn't, nor did I waste any thought over his chatter. I awaited only the meat of his words. When he said a storm was coming up I still awaited his jump from metaphors to sensibilities. I was aware of a storm brewing on board ship, and I was equally positive that none was hanging in the heavens near our position. So I downed another drink and awaited his pleasure. "Mr. Rosen, I want you to remember every detail of this day; and tomorrow. The courts will connect the stories we give, mine, yours, and Ripper's." He bade me drink up, marking up the

49

second on his strange scoreboard. "One other thing. Tomorrow, see that our position reaches the ears of the crew — this position." He handed me scribbled figures on a sheet almost as yellow as the falsehood I was to drool. While I engraved them into my memory, he pulled the string on the mariner's chart, and said, pointing: —

"By flying under short sail we should be about here by sunset tomorrow. Right? You and Ripper take over the watch." He eyed me for any surprise the chart might pull from my eyes. "And see that the last two hours of the day finds our bow in the sun's eye."

"Aye, sir."

"You're a cool customer, Rosen. Why in the hell don't you ask a few questions?"

I raised my head and met him squarely. "I scarcely see any need for them." I omitted the "sir" purposely. "I'm merely following orders."

"Are you wondering about your share?"

"No, nor worrying about it," I said truthfully.

"Mr. Rosen, I might be planning to cheat you of treasure — and life, for all you know."

"You might," I said evenly. He continued to level stabbing eyes at my face, holding them in place for many long minutes, without lowering them as he poured again from the dusty white bottle. In a gesture that underscored my own initiative I reached for his pencil and drew the third line.

"But I won't," he said, and I knew he meant it. There was some attraction in our personalities and, inexpressible though it was, we both felt ourselves engaged in a warm mental handclasp. The devil and a mortal.

I walked the deck of the *Witch* as she ate up knots during the earlier part of the starless night, watching the sea and the riding lights up in the rigging; and only a savage squall drove me off deck. Before midnight a running wind plucked at the sails, clearing the sky wringer and lifting the red girl to greater speed. I came on deck and watched Ripper and the imbeciles shorten sail, saw him lead the lads up the ratlines. The stars were out, hanging low and still dripping, and I was occupied by their pulsations when I thought I heard a stilted moan. The wind was against me but the dismal sound came again.

Soon I knocked at Ralls's door; no answer was forthcoming so I barged in, saying as I came upon him: "Just trying to locate a moan, sir."

"Well, you've found it, *Mister* Rosen," he said in a voice of steel, pointing to the floor behind him. "Just what do you do after such a find?"

I stared at what met my eye: Mr. Loring, almost nude, lay on the floor; on his shoulders and back large red hunks of flesh stood out in puffed lines a good inch high. They oozed blood. Panting, he threw a foot and arm up in telltale spasmodic motion; he had taken almost too much.

The velocity of the hurricane increased; the wind inside Ralls's skull was working; his eyes were glassy pins of placidity, the vortex of the storm that had yet to rear itself into the pinnacle of fury before quieting down for the backlash. But hurricanes present miracles, too, for some things remain untouched in the very splendor of ruin.

"Well?" he said. "Do you want a taste of what Mr. Loring got?"

I said nothing, as I slowly counted the marks on the bottles. Twelve in all. I was amazed at the quantity of gin he was able to consume and still sit there without thickened tongue or mind. I saw he was sober as a judge as he sat there drunk as an owl.

"Well, Mr. Rosen, can't you speak?"

"Yeah," I said recklessly. "He'll look good to that court you spoke of, or is he planning to be absent?"

"You're farsighted, too, aren't you?" he said.

"No special talent in that direction, sir. But when Sam Rosen straddles a tight wire with a companion, he dislikes seeing the other fellow inclined to cut that wire." I held my tongue until he faced me again soberly.

"And as for a taste of the whip, what do you think?" I inquired, smiling.

"Mr. Loring, Rosen, will be in court. His dementia will clear us." His hurdle of my question did not surprise me at all. To myself I said he might decide to answer it that night or five years hence. "Mr. Loring imagines he was beaten tonight," he added.

"Well, sir, his imagination wears a visible coat, now and for some time," I said. "Enough to sway a jury. Just what is the idea of beating him, sir?"

"Since you scarcely know me, Rosen, we'll just call it a periodic whim." He made no mention of the effect that pulpy back might have on the censuring eye of any jury. Instead he went on deck, walking under his own power with the nonchalance and pomposity of a prime minister.

4

He ordered Ripper to doctor Mr. Loring's wounds in the manner of one brushing a fly off his face, before proceeding to cast a weather eye at the sails and beyond. Around the deck he strode, eyeing every man there with strange lingering glances that I couldn't fathom; and each poor fellow who felt the stare grew nervous. The impelling force of that hurricane was mounting.

The next thing I knew he stood on the rail — as easily as I met the deck under me. He slowly walked a rope-free stretch, glancing neither at his feet nor at the ship, but up into the tail of the sky. That he would walk off the stern and land in the water I was sure; but then I wondered if he would not just keep on walking through the thin air. Upon my word of honor, he turned about-face, still glancing off, and slowly retraced his steps. At the quarter he stood for perhaps a minute before continuing his eerie, unwarranted tread.

I could bluff facts into a picture of Sam Rosen not in the least concerned, but such insouciance was far from claiming me. The quantity of drink inside him could not condone such sureness, I said to myself, unless his very drunkenness shut out fear and thereby gave him the supernatural power to walk a narrow rail as though it were the deck; by that reasoning he could walk the ropes. I viewed concentrated, calculated inebriation that sharpened every faculty of the man's being into precision timing and pointed, sensitive control. No, that could not be. The laws of nature, while elastic to an incalculable degree, are seldom reversed to match what I viewed. But there he was on the tiptoe of the atmosphere.

Back and forth, back and forth, he kept on, his pace increasing, his tempered monotony speeding into a climax that was long overdue; but it did not come. A sandy-haired youth near me murmured "My God!" in a voice that shouted of disbelief. I watched his eyes and saw them almost popping from their sockets — someone had told him of ghosts and hellish apparitions in his childhood, and he was seeing them at twenty. A Manila American, working his way back to the Philippines, spread his mouth like a dying fish and said something about the dance of the skeletons.

The sails dripped their last of the shower and flapped feebly in the trade, while the gilded lady on the bowsprit remained quiet and unconcerned. The splash of the warm sea tapped again and again at the sides, rolling streaks of phosphorescence into the wake with equal composure. Ripper kept his weather eye cocked like the accomplished seaman he was, never giving Ralls more than a passing glance. He had seen the act before.

There is no suspense equal to that which is without reason, to that which departs from the human sphere and lingers eternally before sane eyes. Such exorcism is reminiscent of one's conception of the world of lost souls, wherein the wailing wall is crowded with séances, with shapes that are not shapes, but shadows of evil earthly forms — they howl in long tremulant, rising sobs without the physical voice from which to emit sound. And the captain, himself of flesh, and bone, and blood, standing a rail of tangible wood on a ship we all felt underneath us and saw over us, was somehow in tune with the spirits of that nether world.

The sandy-haired lad shook from head to foot. I saw him clutch at his throat once; and then, as Ralls held to the rail like an eternal ghost, his imprudence got the better of him.

"Stop it!" he cried. "For God's sake, stop it!" Then he sat down on the deck, weak and unnerved.

Ralls, his spell broken, halted, stared down at the interloper and, after an eternity, stepped to the deck. Without a word he walked to the lad and stood over him.

"Up, Harrison, up!" he said.

The lad obeyed, backing away, his eyes fixed on Ralls in widened horror, his one hand at his mouth, the other thrown forward convulsively, as if for defense.

"The Creeper, Ripper," Ralls said, slowly stalking the lad. And Ripper, relinquishing the wheel to the quartermaster, moved off without a word. Men cleared a path for Ralls and some banded together. Quietly I eased into their midst and raised a warning palm.

"But 'e'll kill 'im!" a cockney whined. "'E's a devil, 'e is. Gawd!"

"And I," I said, "will do the same to any man of you who interferes. No mutiny on this ship, lads." That stayed them until Ripper delivered the Creeper, a seven-foot plaited rawhide affair that had long since taken on an oxblood depth of color from its leaded butt to the farthermost tips of the five uneven tin-tipped strands — the latter were designed to flick where they fell.

"So ye're in cahoots?" a burly one grated into my ear.

"Gentlemen," I said with mixed authority and persuasion, "he is the captain. Unless you wish to be logged, hold your heads." I faced them, and as others came up to protest, I added: "You fellows are getting worked up over something that doesn't concern you." I was calm and my voice attested to the fact. They realized, I think, that I would have used the heavy pistol that went with my office, not in defense of Ralls or his dehumanized passions, but as insurance against mutiny on the high seas.

In the excitement I noticed the *Witch* had slipped past the Duke of York Isle.

5

The early morn passed and the day broke clear and red-eyed. I opened my eyes at the sound of Ralls's voice: "Mr. Rosen, you're needed on deck — the compass needs a reading." I understood. I peered at him and saw him sober, although he had, I knew, bolstered his twelve-marker momentum with the same howling fluid that brought the winds.

We were through St. George's Channel, about four under at one fifty-one and a half.

"Ripper," he added, "is getting everything shipshape." I could imagine more than he implied.

After a hasty breakfast of fresh flatfish and potent coffee I trod deck fresh as a daisy. The *Red Witch* remained under faked canvas, and although the trade was solid and unpocketed, she rose slowly and leaned to the rocking swells with timed rhythm, giving no signs of the prevalent hush she had experienced during the night — she seemed ignorant of all imprecations as her trim sails flapped and bellied and hung bulged in her many attempts at a gallant charge. Such a thoroughbred should, I said to myself, be given full rein, but not so. The bit was drawn tight in her teeth.

I gave our false position in casual manner, not bothered in the least by my conscience; I said more — "We'll ride her into Davao soon." Some frowned, others held their thoughts under blank eyes, while one lad said, "She hugs the wind, that she does, sir." He was minus the mutinous swelling of last evening. The general opinion: we had driven north during the night.

The sun was thirstily seeking the water line when we swung the crimson lady slowly into its eye. The maneuver was so timed as to attract little attention; a slight pull to leeward gave the deck an easy slope, but it passed unnoticed. Heavy clouds followed the sunset and wrapped themselves beautifully into overlapping patterns for the gold lacework they inherited. They dimmed in luster and accepted purplish bellies with a bronzed sheen before their final red and crimson coverlets, and as the minutes passed, and our eyes, Ralls's and mine, awaited the hole card, the whole western shoulder was incarnadined. The *Red Witch* was meeting her color. The final dip was but a matter of minutes as the sun broke clear and flooded the sea with its hue. The sails took on a bloody glint, and drove the proud lady westward. Then slowly the bit was freed in the sails; slowly, and the *Red Witch* ate up the sea.

Ralls stood apart from the bow rail, smoking, his heavy lids closed to shield the bright pin points from the red glare that fought vision in its wake. I stepped to his side and took my position on elbows at the rail, shielding my eyes with one hand and peering straight ahead. The sun was a half ball winking at us when I felt the girl scrape. It was gentle and only rocked the craft in the manner of a changing trough, but it was a harbinger that sent my flesh tingling.

"Suppose," I said, chuckling, "she picks her way through with a blind eye." As I said it, the leadsman, Red Galt, heaved a line overboard and jumped back when it limped at nine fathoms. He uttered an exclamation, "We're riding a shoal!" Ralls eyed me, and I laughed aloud. "You'd better take a drink, Galt," I said. I watched him amble off, scratching his coppery skull as he sought an explanation to what he had seen.

Then the sun swung under, bringing the swift night upon us. The ship's lights blinked on in a jiffy. I saw Ralls saunter toward the boats, peer into them a moment, and then quietly fall into the role of leadsman. Satisfied, he came over to where I stood and said, "No bottom." If she struck, and there were enough jutting crags there, I knew, she should be down deep enough to defy anything but a native's eye from an outrigger; and we were far enough out to lessen that gamble to infinitesimal odds — unless she ran head over and perched herself on a submerged reef.

But for some unknown reason the ship was alive with questioning eyes; intuition, I thought. Ripper calmly manned the helm and gave his raucous voice to an Italian lullaby, aware that he awaited the sharp, strong antics of a furious wheel. From the galley came the matching discord from the throat of our Filipino cook: before long the call to chow would sound. Mutton and rice, I said, with slim chances for a surprise. Raw tea without enough ice to cut the brackish taste. I sought the eye of the giant from Singapore as he walked close, and in it I saw anxiety as he peered over the side. I laughed when he said, "I been sailin' long enough to feel it, sir. We're not meetin' with a push down there."

6

A long hour passed, giving us two rough scrapings on the starboard beam. An old sea dog mumbled something about "damn fools sailing full in the dark," and another voice sounded in my ear, asking why we held her to top canvas in the reefs. I was met with still another question: "Why the reefs — aren't we to the north o' 'em?"

"Unless the compass is screwy," I said, "we are."

To Ralls, I bellowed, "What do you make of it, sir?"

His answer was what I expected: "I can't account for it. The chart shows no reefs or uncertain circles with E.D. [Existence Doubtful] or P.D. [Position Doubtful]."

"Shall I shorten sail, sir?"

"After I check further," he said.

As if the devil lorded over the obedient elements, a stiff puff of wind caught the sails before Ralls could move. By its feel I could tell we would keep company for some time. I followed the skipper to his cabin and sat down in silence to drink with him. He was wrapping the doctored log in oil silk. Twice I drank, and the third was lifted to my mouth when it came: a jarring scrape and the tearing of merciless teeth into her hull. It threw us almost across the room, sending bottles and other odds and ends across the floor and against the bulkheads. Judging from the sound and the inertia, I reckoned, and rightly so, that she had struck to starboard and almost at the beam. She creaked and leaned, moaning as her wounds gathered in brine to swirl with her bilge.

On deck there was wild uproar. Ralls calmly brushed off three or four heavy slugs and followed me. Ripper bellowed orders and sent men scurrying below; he had the boats well stocked in short time. Ralls shouted for someone to get Mr. Loring safely into a boat.

I chuckled.

Under full sail and tearing ahead like a wounded fawn, and crying out her pain in strange voices, the *Red Witch* seemed unaware of her mortal wound. She jumped forward only to emit another groan from her innards as she listed heavily. She was free of the ragged rocks and moving slowly, floundering in the direction she had last seen the sun. I saw the wheel spinning wildly and I knew Ripper would have lashed it before leaving had he not been in the know. Ralls had gone below but he was soon up again, yelling for us to abandon ship. In his arms was a burlap sack, and after he placed it in the boat I saw him pant from exertion. Three times he went below for samples of virgin gold. The ship's masts leaned perilously, and her every stanchion met the angle. The starboard deck was soon under water. Before long her sails would flop over into the inky sea. In the dim light of the lamps the scene was ghostly.

From the boat I saw her go down a half hour later, her lights aglow, her sails flattened to the water line, her hull sucking a fill of the Bismarck Sea. With a sob she slid under, carrying herself proudly, I thought, a lady to the end.

56

Ralls stared until the waters closed in over her: a hellish smile covered his face. The hurricane's fury was spent; its backlash disappeared with the *Red Witch*.

Ralls was happy; he had not stood the rail in vain — for the beautiful girl lay at rest in many fathoms off Albert Reef.

*　　*　.　*

Though the sinking of the *Witch* was of the past, it would always live in my memory as a first impression of Ralls when he drank himself into his hurricanes. And so it was, as I stared at Carter on deck of the *Quean*, I felt the proximity of that same fury that had buried gallant sails under lonely waves. Yes, for Ralls had also used the Creeper on Carter.

CHAPTER VI

I

So Ralls had used the Creeper on Carter! The black diamond of his eye possessed many facets. I owed apologies to Mr. Bullit, to Mijnheer Ruysdaal, and I said they could all wait, if needs be, until the day Gabriel blew; I had forgotten in the madness of those moments the spell of Teleia van Schreeven, for which I was joyously thankful — I was not in possession of my faculties under so high a tide of passion, and I admitted uneasily that on that night I had already set new records in the doings of fools. And Ralls had stood the rail, which was, as the past bore out, the forerunner of things to come. I had warned him to leave Carter unmolested. I had no choice in the matter.

Such reasoning led on and on, its saner side advising that our own differences must greatly aid the enemy. But I cared little for anything but personal revenge. So, it was good fortune that held from Ralls's ears my outburst of profanity — for surely I would not have retracted it, and equally positive, his resentment would have been shown by his various signs. One of us, Sam Rosen or the hurricane, could only have met defeat in a battle to the death. And I could remember the old saying: —

The odds are ever with the devil and the elements.

Carter's voice brought me out of the truculent mood, on the safe side. I was aware then that I could wait with the patience of Ralls, himself, to even the score. A showdown was due, overdue, I realized, and when it came we should see who employed the greater cunning. Smoldering anger and sweet determination flooded me with an emotion akin to joy. I grinned and turned to the fraternity brother of ages past, saying: —

"How about taking a peep at yourself in a mirror and getting off this ship? You aren't exactly welcome here, now as in the short past."

"Thy will be done," he returned. "It seems I got a hell of a good trouncing from some quarter. I'm beginning to get it now. Ralls — and then I thought I was swimming."

"You were, Carter. And how you got as far as you did without the sharks making off with you is a wonder. You were rescued off the point yonder."

"By whom — my dear friend?"

"Does it make any difference?"

"I could have guessed it was you, Sam."

"Save yourself from mental endeavor," I said gruffly. "Get yourself off the *Quean!*"

He stared at me, wincing from the pain that claimed him, and grinned as if to say he'd taken a whole lot but he could take more.

"What's the admiral up to this time, Sam?" he fired at me. "Gold or women — or should I have said woman?" His words were effervescent.

"Why didn't you inquire when you two were playing?"

"I did," he said ironically. "He seemed to relish no discourse on the subject."

"One of these days, Carter, Ralls will get fed up, and when he does you may be sure your damned aggravating laugh will haunt us no more. There is plenty I could tell you but you would, of course, scoff. It seems to me your observing eye could acquire a memory — mine would, with your sorry marks and damned foolish scars rising up as gentle reminders. Oh well," I said with a shrug, "some people never learn."

"Bravo, Sam!" he said. "That's the longest lecture you ever gave. But you forgot to say, 'Carter, you go around in an epic mood too much.' Want to try again?"

"No, Carter. I'm all washed up with you. You can go straight to hell." I turned away from him for his own safety — he had a way of provoking one into nastiness.

"Wait, Sam," he said seriously. "I kept up a run of chatter to keep alive. I really want to talk to you."

58

"Well?" I turned about savagely. That's what I wanted him to say.

"Let's get off this damned tub and find a place where I can see an ear for a hundred yards. What's on my mind? Plenty."

I glanced at him again, closely, and decided he wasn't pranking. I sent a second glance at the deck and sails — schooled precaution. Ripper and Tewelliger lay stretched out on the opposite deck forward and only occasional stabs at mosquitoes evinced their alertness. The Malays snored. Peering over the side I saw the land rested in absolute stillness under the bright moon. I saw no shadows of guards, no movements whatever, though I felt sure Ralls was out there somewhere. So I decided to see what Carter had on his mind.

We strode past the *Flores Tandjoeng* and on around the bend. I had never seen this side of the island. There the outer sea met a wider beach. Carter led the way; it was his party, to which all I had agreed to furnish were refreshments, and ears. He was shirtless and the welts on has back stood out under the brilliant moon like long dried fillets of buffalo meat on tan cloth. He was followed by swarms of flies and mosquitoes which he ridded by an occasional bathing of the sore parts with a gin-saturated cheesecloth. What a fool he was, I said.

At the widest strip of beach Carter walked to an excavated sago trunk and there we sat down, Carter with the cloth flung over his back, and I with elbows in the sand. Without further ado he raised his bottle.

"Sam," he said, "you know how I love Ralls." His pause, in which he soberly eyed me, brought mirth to my lips. "Yeah, I really love the admiral. So much that there's nothing I wouldn't do for him. I'd gladly cover him with syrup and stake him in an ant bed, though I'd fight off the little fellows who got in a hurry. Well, let that stand for the time being. Of course, I know how well you two get along. You're the governor to an erratic engine. Without you he'd shake the works to pieces in a hurry.

"Sam, you're pushing twenty-nine, aren't you? I thought so. Well, for many years now you've been tied up with him, and for what? Your despicable obsession, gold. Have you got much of it? I doubt it. Traveling around with a few strands of worthless hemp, and a lousy mess of gilded pewter and gimcracks for the natives — delivering a damned bell across a half thousand miles! Sure, I know he's always conjuring up ways of getting gold. And suppose he does find it, what's the picture? In one word it's — trouble. As I said, without you he'd simply disintegrate.

"Now about you. What does he give you? Yeah, what, Sam?" He leaned toward me in all seriousness, demanding an answer. I had none, so I drank from my quart, and he lifted his own. "So you admit he gives nothing to you: I mean it in a sense of mental and moral marrow for your being. He gives you not a goddam thing: but — he takes away from you! He drains you of your very best, like a vampire bat.

"I have no motive in saying this to you, except — I want you to think about it, turn it over in your mind every day and every night — and then when you see the truth of my words — begin to hate him; as I do. Without a brain to his hellish soul, he'll be lost. You, Sam, are that brain. All you need do is draw apart from him in spirit. Let him make all decisions for a while, and then when the crux arrives, bow yourself out. Easy, isn't it?"

"Carter," I said contemptuously, "is that all you got me out here for?"

"Sam," he returned, "every story has some sort of prelude. You scoff at my words, turn them about like a boomerang. But down inside you, you don't. No, Sam Rosen, you don't. You make a pretext of my words, thinking outwardly that I'm bidding for your favor, that I want you to crush Ralls for me because I'm too weak for the job. But you must know that I don't ask one goddam thing of you for myself. You know that. But as for finishing the admiral, I'd simper to the blackest savage on bended knee. So let's be square with each other, Sam."

"Yeah," I said absently. "Let's be square." I was already turning over in my mind those words, "He takes something from you — gives nothing." I applied detail, added and subtracted a thousand events, their shaping, their doing, their end; I multiplied fancifully and subtracted with practicality. Ralls burrowed in and out of my plagued mind. At last I made a violent effort to free myself of the enfeebling grip — silently I cursed Carter, less for his facts, and more for what they did to my mind.

2

Carter viewed his libation to hate with satisfaction. "Many are the laws," he said, "that could trip him, but — they deal out only bigoted justice. Mercy is too good for fungus." I listened, merely to lessen the damage of his first thrust, though in the silence, his pause for effect, I found my inner self voicing full agreement to everything he had said.

"What the hell?" I snapped. "Carter, your brand of insanity is worse than violence. Why don't you get a hold on yourself and —"

"One moment, *Mister* Rosen. Can't you take it? I'd be proud, in your case, of the fact I still had a mind that could be fashioned into a second trough — for the truth!"

He raised his bottle, not relinquishing my eye for a moment. "Why don't you practice your speech about being square — why not start with yourself?"

I, pinned down tighter than ever before in my whole life, refused to voice the truth. "On with your story, professor," I said, twisting my lips into a cynical smile.

"The mind and the tongue differ with abiding harshness — yours," he countered. "Why don't you give your aggrieved tongue the blessing of a confession every now and then? It's a delicious morsel, Sam. You leave me the criminal in thought and deed while you sit there in bloated stubbornness. You are, advertently, a damn moron."

"Thanks," I returned. "And you're a damn fool. I'm sure Ralls would quake in his boots if he knew of your captious plotting, my little man. I venture his ears are burning now, burning from laughter." I sighed, and made as if to rise. "Well, if that's your story, that's it. Sorry I can't encourage you. If I were you I'd put the proposition up to your friends, the Dutch."

"Oh, they're ahead of me," he said seriously. "But I did want your skirts clear. You see, Sam, those Dutch boys aren't fools. They're letting Ralls — and you — hang yourselves. First it will be Ralls, unless he makes you the scapegoat. Then you won't have a chance to come around for they'd think you were merely trying to save your own hide."

"Just what," I said evenly, "are you talking about?" I gathered he knew something I did not.

"Isn't Ruysdaal playing out the rope to you two? Isn't Schreeven's man Bullit on his toes trying to find some reason for killing one or both of you?"

"Are they?" I inquired innocently.

"Sam, you bore hell out of me. If you were free of mind, you'd be walking in the big time. But jeer on, jinni of Aladdin Ralls." He eyed me again, searching for a hole in my armor.

"One question, Sam. Remember the landing here? Was it not queer that Ruysdaal called you and me by name, that he named our crew?" To that shot I answered in the affirmative. "You never heard of a Mijnheer van der Ruysdaal before, and neither had I. But he *had* heard of us. Why? Why was he following our movements? What interest had he in our tramp schooner, in her whereabouts, in her pulling in here?

"Sam, we've both seen Ruysdaal's face in a newspaper; but he's changed, he's years older now. So I can't hold that against you. But back to the name, you'll remember that soon. Ruysdaal — place it yet?"

I could not, nor could I remember ever having seen his face in print.

"Well, Sam, let that stand for the moment. Remember the Dutchman who sold us a map of a pearl lagoon back in Rabaul? Why did he pick on us? He'd been waiting for us!

"Do you think for one minute that Ruysdaal is anything but a huge, sleepy spider with beady eyes? He spread his net and awaited the fly — the one fly."

"If he is all that," I put lightly, "why did he want us to up anchor and pull out?"

"To create a desire for our most peaceful and kind admiral to remain. That's why." That sounded reasonable enough; Ralls was like that, all right, and then there was that opposite thinking of the Dutchman. "Sam, do you pluck plums or enigmas?"

I covered my heightened curiosity with: "Carter, after the beating you took you should be in bed." I actually marveled at his staying power.

"I can't sleep on my back, can I?" he returned. "And I could never relax on my belly." He gave my interest the silence it deserved — dismissal — before going on with his revelations. "And there's one surprise over there that I wasn't supposed to view. The rambling mansion — and it is just that, a gorgeously appointed place fit for a city home, here in the jungle — houses a number of guests. This morning Ruysdaal rolled out in his chair, followed by one of them. They moved to the veranda. Sam, this will interest you as well as prove me not the damn fool you enjoy calling me. It has a strange connection with things I've said, or rather I should say that it alone sort of connects things one can't quite grasp. Listen closely, Sam, and see if you can name the picture I am about to give the Dutchman's guest."

"Carter, I just thought of something that hardly coincides with your talk. Why did van Schreeven ask my price for influencing Ralls to quit this island?"

"Did you strike an agreement? No. Well, let me say this much — why don't you set a price and see what happens? The other four months of my life against one drink of gin you don't collect."

"Why?" I asked.

"Sam, you poor fool!" he said, laughing. "Can't you see that is more bait?"

"Hell," I snorted, "we weren't invited to this place!"

"No," he returned, "but you — we have haunted this sea for the past four years. Why? Sooner or later we were due here. The drunk in the Rabaul pub was, I'd swear, an agent of Ruysdaal."

I gave thought to our reason for always heading back up here during every slack in the routine of earning a living. For three years we had consulted the old worn parchment chart in Ralls's cabin drawer; we had put every penny we could rake and scrape into equipment that had to do with sea helmets, lines, pumps, and amphibian experts; we had peered into the depths of the wash, never far from this Eden or hell, until our eyes could distinguish the fish as Johns and Henrys and Sams. But how did Ruysdaal know about us and what business was it of his? I asked aloud.

"The spider and the fly," said Carter. He poured gin on his cheese-cloth and swung it again over his shoulders. I said Carter needed a doctor for his wounds. "Don't worry about me, Sam. Ruysdaal will doctor me, and he'll be the angel nurse when I tell him how I came by these loving marks."

"I'm not worrying about you in the least," I said. "I'm only wondering how the devil you stand it."

"Oh," he said. "Well, Mr. Rosen, I am highly impassive, a stoic, as it were." He raised the once handsome corner of a swollen lip and gave one brow an arch in taunting manner.

"But as I was saying — the man who walked out after Ruysdaal was a man I'd seen before, one you've seen, one the admiral has seen. Listen closely, Sam.

"He was tall, gaunt, and hollow-eyed. His hair was salt-and-peppered, and it gave his big eyes a godly glow, only his big mushroom nose took it away. Speaking of stoics, he *is* one. Standing there peering down at the corpulent Dutchman, he seemed missing only one thing — a Bible. Do you place him?"

"I'm afraid not," I said. "I've seen several people answering that description. Any other clues in the guessing game?" I added sarcastically.

"Yeah," said Carter, enjoying the suspense. "In his hand was a cap, the likes of which one sees in a witness chair in a Sydney courtroom — or on a fellow with a share of authority on a ship — a ship that went down. Now —"

"Wait a minute, Carter!" I exclaimed. "You don't mean Loring!"

"Hurrah," he cried. "Simple Sam goes to the head of the class."

"You mean — Loring, from the *Red Witch?*" I could not grasp the

63

fact; it was too foreign for my blood. I raced into a dozen ideas that ended with blocked walls of hard stone.

"Yeah. I saw him last as you did — on the witness stand telling the court — telling the court — and you and Ripper and Ralls playing fast and loose with your lies after the poor devil, ever scheming to put him in the insane ward. I'm sorry I missed that trip on the *Red Witch*, Sam. Even then I'd have sworn against Ralls in any court on any charge. Queer, my dislike of him sprouting before I even knew him, isn't it? You remember Loring on the stand. Remember the prosecutor asking him about the course on that last day; remember how the prosecutor wrapped the barratry charge around Ralls, and how the defense responded; remember what Loring did, what he did to the verdict?"

I remembered well; I could never forget that trial. I saw Mr. Loring on the stand; I heard the question as the court scene once more paraded into my mind.

3

Loring took his time in answering. Drilled by the damning element, a foreground of legal minds against a background of obdurate, and wise, ensurers of both ship and cargo, he fought frightful nervousness with a too stiff mask of calmness. From the first I told Carter he would eventually crack and thereby give all his fine testimony certain refutation. Our defense, a paunchy and bald, fierce-eyed, and truculent veteran of the Sydney courts, Robertson Velame Suggs, of Suggs and Trallerque, Barristers under the Crown and commonwealth, a highly successful firm in cases having to do with graduated crime, was advised of the former chief mate's skin-deep weakness; as a result he smiled through the testimony in which the ensurers' chief witness bared his shoulders and revealed the scars from Ralls's Creeper. Mrs. Loring, Etta Rose — I remember her name and face — swore vehemently against the perpetrator of the crime, and gave the court to know her husband had never a mark on him until that fateful voyage. She tore her emotions from hate to tears of pity for her churchgoing man's plight, saying, and causing Mr. Suggs glee and the cocky prosecutor a wince, "Mr. Loring hasn't been the same man since."

"And, Mr. Loring," the legal mind of the underwriters said, "tell us why you could not prevent the disastrous course of the *Red Witch*."

"I was, sir, on the night before the crime" — Mr. Suggs protested, and not in vain — "before the — er — disaster, called into the captain's cabin and asked why I chose to sail north instead of north by

64

west. I answered truthfully, advising him that he had ordered that course for an hour, then west by south, to be exact, after one hour due north. We were sailing with the trade at our back at the time. Then he proved me a lie by Mr. Rosen and Arrezo before hinting at my insanity. I protested, never having met with such from a superior officer before — and I've sailed the oceans from Capetown to Buenos Aires with never a mark against me. My next surprise came when he struck me with a pronged leather whip. He enjoyed his crime, I could see. Such people I have heard of, but never before had I met one of them. I did not cry out for two reasons, the first being that I was a man; and when the pain made me less of a man, I could not — I could only moan. My senses left me and I knew nothing else until the next day. I awoke to find myself in bed with my door guarded."

The next question again brought me into the scene by its answer: "Yes," said Mr. Loring, "Mr. Rosen and Mr. Arrezo conspired with him, I'm sure. You see, at that time Mr. Rosen was only a member of the crew. A few hours later he became acting chief mate, giving the *Red Witch* two such officers.

"For a while the *Witch* was a ship with two chief mates, and then, there were two chief mates without a ship." Irrelevant, said the defense, and a waste of the court's time. Then Mr. Very, the suave exponent of justice, asked for a detailed account of the crash and events following the sinking.

"I remember the men throwing me headfirst into the boat. There I waited and viewed with a sad heart the efforts of the noble ship. She tried to sail on. When she listed more —"

"Was she under full sail?"

"She was, sir. And sail wasn't lowered when she scraped several times. There's men of the crew to bear out my words."

"Did you see the captain after being thrown into the boat?"

"I did, sir. In his arms was a burlap sack, and the contents were heavy. He placed it in the boat opposite and ordered — no, he ordered abandon ship before depositing his bundle — no, sir, I did not know what was in the sack. Yes, he carried the whip over an arm and the coil about his neck. . . .

"No, sir, it was too small for a case of liquor."

"Continue your story, Mr. Loring."

"Well, sir, the hold was filling fast and her starboard side was so heavy my boat was soon in the water and the sails towering over me, and dipping lower and lower. We were some yards from the reef by that time, the pull of the full canvas yanking us loose and forward until

65

the leaning sails were full before the wind. Every man was off her and safely in the boats — Captain Ralls drove everyone off except Mr. Rosen and the second, Mr. Arrezo. They jumped some five minutes before he did."

"Why did Captain Ralls remain on board?"

"He stood the portside as best I could see in the dim lights that lit the deck; and he busied himself tying a float to the rail. I saw the deep reel line holding onto it."

"What kind of a float did he use?"

"A spar buoy, sir," Loring replied.

"Did the captain beat anyone during the voyage?"

"Yes, sir."

"Why?"

"For various small breaches of discipline — for example, fighting. He made two of the crew, Camille and Sharnwort, fight past their physical endurance, and then he had water thrown on them to revive them."

"No one interfered?"

"No, sir, except Mr. Rosen, at that time only a sail hand. I, sir, applied my rigid code of nautical subservience to a superior and held my tongue — and then, sir, my religion forbids personal strife."

Again the ensurer's solicitor winced; he quietly ordered Mr. Loring to hold his answers to terse facts. Mr. Suggs, I saw, smiled in a greasy manner.

"Did you witness Mr. Ralls's sensational walk of the ship's rail?"

"No, sir." Then, asked to tell of events following the sinking, he slowly fell into the narrative: "We pulled oar all night, sir, taking turns of one hour, and keeping on the tail of the boat carrying the officers and the rest of the crew. We moved before a strong southeast trade until morning, under makeshift sail; and when the sun rose, we shifted our course to due north. A mistake, I thought." Here Mr. Suggs protested; it held. "Toward midafternoon of the second day, after hours in heavy squalls and blistering sun, we sighted a small island. We pulled toward it, every man thanking his God for shade from the merciless sun.

"We pulled onto the beach and a scouting party returned a half hour later to report the place uninhabited — except for land crabs and two goats. The latter tasted mighty good that evening. Our provisions were very low, and there being no fresh water except in stagnant rock holes, we were rationed until the sheets were spread for a rain. For a week we remained there, the officers drinking heavily and the men roaming the place at will. We left the island on this day three months ago, sir, under improvised sail and outriggers attached to our boats.

66

"We were at sea for two days and one night, and at sundown on the second day out we sighted a Japanese ketch plying the islands with a cargo of gewgaws and silks.

"Mr. Ralls boarded her and spent more than an hour with the grinning heathens before ordering Mr. Rosen and Arrezo to tie on and then come aboard. It was dark, and a fierce squall kept all of us bailing the boats until midnight. Then we were given a mess of cold, tasteless rice. And thus we traveled for two days, prisoners in two small boats. Fights broke out. Two of our men were lost when knocked overboard — sharks. It was planned murder." He gazed at Ralls.

"On the third day we reached Lorengau."

I thought it strange that Loring said nothing about the direction the Jap ketch took to Lorengau; I thought it even more strange that Mr. Very passed up that point.

4

The long trial wore on. Mr. Foggart of Singapore, the giant who remarked, "We're not meetin' with a push down there," was called to the stand. He said in brief: "We was crawlin' on our ship's belly, sir, with the sacks full of wind. We scraped aplenty, but the cap'n wasn't concerned: he just acted like he'd a loony compass on her. But the bottom wasn't under her at times, and that alone was enough to warn a seaman o' his rank that heavy sail was suicide."

A question was put: "Regarding Mr. Loring's tale of the agonies at sea attached to the Japanese ketch, can you corroborate his statement in full?" The giant blinked and asked for the question in the King's English, and when it was extended he answered it in the affirmative, voicing regret at having knocked one man into a shark's mouth, adding: "Every bloomin' man of 'em knowed I couldn't stand bein' goosed. I almost jumped o'er the sides meself."

Mr. Timothy (Red) Galt said: "Aye, sir, only Mister Loring didn't tell the tale as it should a been. 'Is words uz true, but they weren't enough o' 'em. There was cholera in the boats, and the cramps o' it, and the er — a —"

"Purging," said Mr. Very, helpfully.

"Aye, sir, 'twas done at both ends. They's them 'at's got it yet."

"Did, in your opinion, Captain Ralls do everything possible to prevent the sinking of the *Red Witch?*"

"'At, sir, 'e didn't. A blimey macaw ud of knowed to douse the rags with no bottom under 'er — I, sir, seen a line in me own 'ands go limp at nine fathoms! When? Why at afore sundown, about a round and some before she struck."

Mr. Harrison was called forth to tell in his own words every detail of Ralls's standing the rail. He botched it somewhat, not in words so much as in feeling. I followed him through his timid loquacity without having seen Ralls conjuring up the devil for expressions of brotherly love. Then Mr. Very popped the question of fathoms and sails, to which Harrison replied: "I'm scarcely enough of a sailor to know, sir, but — it seems logical that our speed should have been lessened. The captain made soundings. I, myself, saw Mr. Galt's line limp at nine, sir."

"At what time did you see Mr. Galt's line at nine fathoms?"

"I remember it was just after sunset."

The stocky fellow representing the charterer of the *Witch*, a placid Dutchman — I later learned his name was Michiel Tulp — held his poker face at the amassed evidence pointing to crime. The stakes were high. A ship worth a bank's ransom, and a cargo of bullion rumored to reach almost a million dollars, a combined loss that was enough to waver and topple fortunes by their vibratory mention, or by the rattle of the gilded paper that bound their fate, let alone a court's decision. Both ship and virgin ingots lay at the bottom of the ocean, marked by false positions, and a spar buoy that was purposely tied in a loose knot to the rail of the wind girl; it was probably floating toward Guinea, the Carolines, Gilberts, or New Britain; and the only true position of the *Witch* was a matter of hours and compass, in co-ordinate reckoning, from an uninhabited island. Once there, by such calculated means, the treasure might be miles away in any direction. I say this with authority.

Mr. Camille followed Mr. Sharnwort to the stand; their tales were anything but conflicting. Following them were lesser lights, but always the weight of numbers followed each man's word to the stand. I happened to follow Ripper, who, by his very terseness and assumed stupidity — rehearsed to Mr. Suggs's forensic liking — gave Mr. Loring positive dementia in word and neat emphasis by making the sign of the cross over his heart. When pertinently questioned about fathoms and sails, he swore to seventy, admitting full sail. Mr. Very's "Why full sail in such shallow water?" was answered with "Sa known to be done all over whena sail by chart — no? The ocean she no cana be so light alla the time whena the marks saya no."

"But when you scraped, Mr. Arrezo?"

"We scrape," he said with a shrug.

"But why did you hold to full sail after that?"

"Mother Maria, sor! We was on our way to Davao, and the wind she

68

good. Yes? So. A littla scrape she no meana we sink. So why, I aska you, so what'sa wronga witha that? Crime?" Questioned further, about Ralls's idiosyncrasies, he declared that Mr. Ralls, the quietest, most thoughtful and considerate skipper in the seas, was a victim of fear and imagination from a damn poor crew who jumped at a chance to rebel.

In the long half hour before Mr. Very's finger, he beamed, sneered, scoffed, and crossed himself, and it was Mr. Very who sweated in the end.

I was on the stand for one hour. Mr. Very sought to turn my answers, though I never failed to pronounce the insanity of Mr. Loring. Not once did I say the word, but by subtlety I inferred it until the court eyed him with misgiving. As to our trip I paralleled the story Ralls gave after me, to the minutest detail, claiming, and with some truth, mutiny.

5

Ralls came to the stand, with the composure of a Queen Victoria in marble, adorning any square in His Majesty's far domains; and he gave Mr. Very a mild taste of the slits of his eyes. Casual enough, decorous to perfection, unworried, and lazy in his movements, he seemed scarcely the demon or criminal he was alleged. His dress was new and of the sea, his hair was combed slick and it glinted of blue; debonair, he was, every inch of his six feet.

Said Mr. Very: "Your name, sir?"

"Ralls," came the answer.

"The full name, Mr. Ralls," crisply.

"Ralls," evenly, glancing beyond the interrogator.

"Am I to understand —"

"Exactly what I tell you," said Ralls. "No more. No less. I should deem it unwise of a man in my position to falsify on so trivial a question." He chuckled. "The consequences hardly warrant my doing so."

Mr. Very asked if he had once captained another ship of the Batjak line of Soerabaja. Ralls had.

"Is it true you beat your men, and if so, why?" Mr. Very fired.

"True. They disobeyed orders, and were inciting mutiny."

"You realized you were violating maritime law, of course. But why such an unnecessary beating?"

"I was the sole judge of necessities on board the *Red Witch*. I'll thank you to reword your question." Mr. Very did so, at a marked loss of repose.

"Why did you not limit your strokes to what ordinarily constitutes a good flogging?"

69

¨Men who sail under me find me very strict. I do not tolerate homosexuality aboard ship.” Mr. Very skipped that in a hurry.

“Were you drinking when you stood the rail?”

“I was.” Then Mr. Very said, “Drunk?” and received: “Taking the word at its face value, does it sound reasonable for a drunk man to perform such a feat?”

“You’ll answer me yes or no, Mr. Ralls!” thundered the barrister, to which Ralls replied, “Only when you extend sensible questions.” I noticed he omitted the “sir,” and I kept my ears on tiptoe for the sound of it.

“Why did you relieve Mr. Loring of his office?”

“Because he was a sick man. Here.” He touched his forehead. “He was unable to set course as ordered.”

“Is that all?”

“No. Mr. Loring was a religious maniac who provoked open disrespect from the men. They jeered him for holding prayer among them. Such a man is hardly one for a command. I feel that he is responsible for the mutiny that broke out.”

“Is that why you beat him?”

“I regret that I did not beat Mr. Loring,” said Ralls, chuckling. “I had a legal right.” Mr. Very asked if he meant the answer as denial or actual regret. Ralls said, “Both.” When asked how Loring came by the marks if not from Ralls, he was met with, “Another of your foolish questions — which I shall answer. I’m sure I don’t know how he acquired them. No one on the ship saw me beat him, no one heard him crying out — and when I beat a man it is before all — to quell mutiny. I held no personal dislike for the poor fellow; and when Mr. Tulp, representing the charterer, asked that he be given the position of chief mate, I was not only pleased, I commented, as Mr. Tulp will confirm, ‘I hear he’s a good man and a veteran seaman.’ I met Mr. Loring in maritime respect, and unaware of his deplorable mental state, invested in him the full responsibility of his office. I first suspected him of possessing a childish mind when I came upon him one night while he was prying with the compass. Mr. Arrezo, at the helm, saw this, heard me say in kindly manner, ‘Mr. Loring, let us confine our mechanical attentions to less important objects.’ He shed tears and departed.”

“So you deny beating Mr. Loring?”

“Emphatically,” answered Ralls.

“Then how is it that Mr. Galt, on the day before, saw no stripes on his back when he stood before him with a change of clothing? How is it that he produced a blood-covered shirt at the Mandate’s office in

Lorengau? How is it that Mr. Creed and Mr. Voorhees pulled a bloody sheet off his bedclothing on the morning of the *Witch's* last day? Answer me, Mr. Ralls."

"I know the three gentlemen you mention to be reliable until — that is until they can profit by enacting the opposite. In Auckland — and Mr. Suggs has proof — Mr. Creed served time for perjury. Mr. Voorhees is easily led, and as for Mr. Galt, I think any physician will say his mind is slightly enfeebled. He is given to self-pollution. You will notice in the log my statement declining an opinion on the particulars. I request the court to investigate these charges before pledging their evidence to the records of this trial. Only Mr. Voorhees puzzles me. I have known him for many years. He is a good man and a good sailor."
I glanced at Voorhees, saw him pale, and then smile at Ralls. Suggs later swung his testimony to our side.

It seemed that Mr. Loring's stripes were charged with more than their share of weight, causing me to wonder if they were being trumped up to represent the whole. From that moment I gazed at the figure of Mr. Very for what he symbolized, and my respect for him grew somewhat. He was a relentless creature, never dying, but digging ever deeper into the core. Why, I asked; for what reason did he linger there?

"And how do you account for what we are about to show the court?" said Mr. Very in caustic tone. He then proceeded to order Mr. Loring and young Harrison to bare their backs. They obeyed, facing the bench while medical men examined the scars on their ugly backs. It seemed Mr. Very had won a fine point.

He turned to the court: "I think we have shown that there is ample proof of criminal maltreatment. I beg of the court to vindicate properly all woundings and beatings. If mutiny is the excuse, there has been no proof shown of its existence. Thus, with the court's permission, I shall now attempt to show that the sinking of the *Red Witch* was barratry premeditated. I shall attempt to show that it (the court) cannot sustain the defense in a plea that barratry was not planned; I shall also show that negligence was not the remote cause. Thus, maritime law says that where policy covers the risk of barratry, as in this case, it will exculpate the underwriters from obligation and charge to the owners and charterers of a vessel. The clause, 'and fire be the proximate cause,' shall be shown to rest, as in example cases we shall name, as attending verboseness used for emphasis."

The maltreatment of the crew was none of his concern, nor that of the underwriters, but proving it meant that the master of the *Witch* was guilty not only of perjury and false entries in the official log — which

71

a mate must also sign — but of a deeper prevalent dishonesty. Mr. Tulp showed no fear or pleasure. He remained cool and outwardly indifferent to a decision. But, of course, he was on our side as an idle bystander who could not insert word or weight into the hearing. But — should the verdict go against Ralls, Tulp, representing the vast financial structure, would, like the ship's owner listed in the customhouse as the famed Batjak, Ltd., of Sydney, Melbourne, and Soerabaja, turn upon us with bared teeth. No longer would the inquiry be a scramble for huge sums of money. It was said the head of Batjak, Mayrant Sidneye, followed the case with heightened interest.

The Naval Court had the power to cancel or suspend the certificate of any master or mate, to prosecute offenders for tyranny, high crime, and/or highest crimes. But the fight was for insurance first, owner and charterer versus underwriters. The charterer, a rich banker, took the stand only once. The owners of the *Witch* made no appearance in court.

6

Again the thorough Mr. Very stood before Ralls. The charge was past the preliminary lead questions opening the chapter on the master's fraudulence and well into the core. The court's ears and eyes were welded to the compass and the close bottom of the *Red Witch*. Said the solicitor: —

"Mr. Ralls, you had ample time to check the compass after the first brush of hull and reef. You were enough of a seaman to realize a slowing of her speed was necessary. If your compass had gone wild you knew the constellations well enough to right her course. You claim she went down at a certain position. The charts show a safe depth at that position. You struck a reef, we admit. Therefore you sailed into it with criminal intent, covering your cunning with brutality. But — most important to this court — insurance is nullified because the ship deviated from her voyage."

He turned to the Naval Court with a simple shrug. "Gentlemen, the facts in the case establish themselves. Never in the history of maritime iniquity has such solid purpose been brought to the attention of His Majesty's Court. The *Red Witch* was a doomed ship before leaving Sydney. Doomed to die in the seas where her master could again find her, where the charterer and shipowner could not find her — due to false positions. I recommend the suspension of the certificates of the master, the chief mate and second mate, as well as their trial for perjury, brutality, and barratry. I recommend that the Board of Trade exercise

72

its right to purchase this wreck and make it unlawful for this trio ever again to approach the waters of the Bismarck Archipelago."

Then Mr. Suggs took over. His steam was ample, though throttled to the tempo of a beginning. The gleam of his eyes and his pink hairless head were one, and the folds of flesh, sagging from his cheeks into sacks supported by cheek gristle, swung loosely, like his rotund belly, as he gathered momentum. His small mouth, tight and firm, belied the great bellows that took over the bass throat. His record was an enviable one and he did not choose to find its interception here. Success for the charterer and owner meant not only another triumph for Suggs and Trallerque but a further fattening of its coffers; their services came high, and even higher for the personal appearance of the wily veteran and senior partner, Robertson Velame Suggs.

One by one he called up the crew, never hesitant, never tiring in his trenchant pace, never at a loss to direct his questions at the level of the witness's mentality; he had catalogued each man according to a standard. Thus when he broke off niceties with hammering and potent questions that had to do with uprising on board the *Witch*, Mr. Foggart, the giant from Singapore, was taken completely by surprise. The question, "Did you, Mr. Foggart, have a gun pointed at you by Mr. Rosen, chief mate? If so, why?" brought forth an answer that sprung the trap. "The master was a beatin' Harrison, and we was aimin' to stop him. Mr. Rosen held us back wi' a Luger."

"So you admit mutiny?"

"Now, I ain't said I was in no mutiny."

"But you were going after Mr. Ralls, eh?"

"Yes, sir, all o' us was. The law says a master can't do that to a man." Suggs scored fast. He was a man worthy of admiration. His first thrust proved the existence of mutiny.

The second night watch was called and these members were positive only of Mr. Loring's shunting the ship about in the afternoon and evening of the day preceding the crash.

"So," said Suggs to the last of them, "you sailed north by east as far as you know, only for Mr. Loring's change about? You did? And you could not censure the master for full sail under the circumstances? You could not? And can you believe — answer yes or no — that the *Red Witch* was deliberately sunk?"

"Er — no."

"Mr. Galt, please," said Suggs. The cockney ambled forward and swore to the truth. "Mr. Galt, can you swear that the ship was off her course before, or at the time of, the accident?"

73

"That, sir — no."

"Then how do you account for only nine fathoms on your line?"

"I, sir, and I've racked me 'ead, can't."

"Could some fresh reef have happened along due to — say Mr. Loring's toying with the ship's compass? I said, is such possible? You're a good seaman, Mr. Galt, and you should know."

"Could 'ave, sir. Aye."

"Give me your opinion of Mr. Loring up to that time, Mr. Galt."

"'E uz a man who fell to preachin' 'cause we took to women in port. I never cared much fer 'im. 'E seemed weary, sir, and 'is changin' orders around wasn't natural. The whole crew said 'e uz a bit balmy, sir."

7

The case wore on. The evidence was hashed and rehashed and still I had not been called by the defense. Nor had Ralls. The case was on every tongue along the waterfront, and I heard it was a choice morsel in those circles frequented by bankers; and certainly it was no hushed affair among shipowners and underwriters. It was in a Sydney bar one evening that I chanced upon a heated discussion of the affair. Two men sat at the table nearest the bar and blew foam from glasses and smacked their lips with a gusto foreign to palatable enjoyment. Each seemed unwilling to allow the other a full voicing of his opinion. One was a Britisher of middle age, a shipper's clerk, I thought; the other seemed a man who had chosen the sea, his face being ruddy and leathery and his huge biceps decorated with a blue and red anchor and a misshapen September Morn.

The latter said: "Jest you wyte till tomorry. Mr. Loring comes up, I 'ear, and the blimey Suggs'll 'ave 'is stinkin' 'ands full. 'E'll show there was intent to —"

"Come, come, Turner," the other broke in. "Hasn't the honorable Suggs almost shattered everything the crew said? Hasn't Voorhees swung over with a story that he wasn't sure the bloody sheet came from the mate's cabin? And since when —"

"Rot!" scoffed the seaman. "I spose ye'll be syin' nex', Mr. 'Awkins, 'at Mr. Creed uz wrote off cause 'e owned up to perjury at Auckland? S'pose 'e was. Ayn't Loring, sir, the 'ole kyse? Ayn't 'e, I sye, ayn't 'e?" He leaned forward, enjoying in full the flavor of his insolence and deduction.

Mr. Hawkins laughed. "Turner, your ignorance is indeed amazing.

Righto. You know jolly well Mr. Suggs has purposely held him back until the court is weary. Only one pipsqueak from the ex-mate and Suggs'll sew the case tight."

"Wyte and see. Jest you wyte. I 'ear things to the contrary. I 'ears Mr. Loring'll be syvin' 'is 'ole card, 'at 'e'll damn the devil Ralls and 'is myte, the Jewish-lookin' bloke, Rosen, tomorry. I ayn't in the know, I ayn't, but the news is from good 'ands."

"Mr. Turner, you're gullible. Rumor is one thing, fact another. I'll wager you a pound note against five schooners of suds that you're wrong."

"Ye're on," said the seaman. "And I'll arsk this gen'lman 'ere to bear witness." To me, he said, "'Ere, me good man, could ye lend a ear to a 'onest lyin' o' odds?"

"Gladly," I said. "Mr. Turner, I hope you lose to Mr. Hawkins, for you see I'm Rosen, late of the *Red Witch*." I grinned at the pair, the most surprised men in all of Sydney. They seemed to strangle on their ale. The seaman, empurpled with embarrassment, eyed me curiously from beneath a solid black brow for some time. At last he said: —

"Well, I 'opes I win, Mr. Rosen, for lessen I do, the likes o' me'll 'ave a 'ard time livin' down the suspicion cast us by all shippers. No 'ard feelin's, sir, but I 'opes they 'ang Mr. Ralls from a yardarm."

True to rumor, Mr. Loring was called forth before noon. He had lost weight during the hearing and his eyes glowed dully from purple caverns. He eyed Mr. Suggs inanely; his lips, calm before Mr. Very, now twitched at a sagging right corner; his brow had lost its serenity and his hands were folded and unfolded many times before Mr. Suggs leveled a question — and the paunchy barrister chose to let the ace of the opposing force sweat; once he held a pointed finger in Loring's face, only to turn about and address the court in lengthy review; again he put a forthcoming question on his pointed finger and allowed the witness a thorough wringing of his hands before saying to the court: —

"I am pleased to approach this witness, the last bastion of my opposing team, with the issue no longer in doubt. The evidence of each member of the crew upon cross-examination has deliberately cleared the accused of any change in the course of his doomed ship. You have heard the men before Mr. Loring admit they could not swear to any supposedly settled charge by the opposing side. You have heard Mr. Loring state, under Mr. Very's questioning, the ship's position. Therefore, with the position given by all in accord, with the absence of proof of the course being changed, the court can only assume that nothing contrary to diligent and honorable seamanship was employed by the ship's master. This, therefore, up to this moment, exonerates Captain Ralls of the charges my opponent thrusts upon him. So, regardless of the statements of the present witness, remember the weight of numbers has already cleared Mr. Ralls.

"I do not expect this man," he pointed at the apprehensive witness, "to readily submit to the truth of the situation. He is clearly bordering on *non compos mentis* and should, to my compassionate mind, be saved from the ordeal which my office, in legal decorum, must vigorously prosecute. It is clear to all that the personal injuries, corporeal or otherwise, that Mr. Loring chooses to magnify are primarily designed to distort facts into pure and simple avenues leading to revenge. Revenge, arbitrariness, malice, and all other issues of a personal bearing must be, as this court realizes, held as irrelevant to the major premise. This court is not interested in the color of the sunset or the number of men in a boat tied to a Japanese ketch — after the *Red Witch* went the way of all ships. Nay. The sole purpose of this court is to determine the cause. It was either premeditated or it was not. So far, and the court must accept the evidence as the sole evidence obtainable, there has *not been the slightest proof of barratry*."

At his mention of the Japanese ketch I wondered why the captain of that craft had not been brought before the court.

Mr. Loring wet his lips, sweated, and exercised his hands as Mr. Suggs talked on. "There remain two important facts — Captain Ralls's whip, which he unfortunately lost in Lorengau, and which, I am sure, could lift the stigma of brutality from his wronged shoulders if it could be found; and the other — the disposition of the heavy burlap sack which Mr. Ralls placed in the boat in a race against a sinking ship. The latter will be duly explained, and to the full satisfaction of the court, as well as to any doubters of Captain Ralls's integrity. But, to further impress this honorable court, these issues are trivial — the main issue is the charge. Therefore, may I request this court to adhere to facts and only facts pertaining to that serious charge." He turned to face Mr. Loring after a pause of some seconds.

"Mr. Loring, were you not once a missionary?" A weak answer in the affirmative caused everyone to lean to the stand. "And why did you give up that work, Mr. Loring? Remember you are on the stand and under oath."

Loring squirmed, turned a horrified eye toward his wife, and said the question was unfair, that it had no bearing on the case. Mr. Very objected but Mr. Suggs was calmly adamant. In the end the court allowed the question to stand. The ex-mate hedged. The bald solicitor put the words into question form and tied them to an answer.

"Did you not meet a native girl of rare beauty and physical charm?" The witness nodded sadly.

"Had you not for some time eyed the ripeness of her uncovered breasts, entertaining a growing desire to drink from her savage lips the wine of wild fruit? Yes or no?"

After an age, Mr. Loring whispered, "Yes."

"Did you not marry her?" The answer was the same. "Did she bear you child? If so, how many?"

"Three," the broken man said, daring not raise his eyes to the awed wife, who turned from the red of embarrassment to the purple of anger. Only Mr. Very influenced her silence.

"And what became of them? Did you leave them?"

"I left them. I do not know —"

"And you continue to worry about them, don't you? And you lost your mind for a period of one year, did you not? You were in a home for cure, in the outskirts of Melbourne, were you not?"

Loring broke. He shook in his grief and his sorry cheeks glistened with tears. Mr. Suggs moved away, wiping at his eyes and blowing his nose as if the ordeal tore at his heart. Aloud he kept saying, "Poor man. Poor man." Then he addressed the court: —

"Gentlemen, I regret that I am forced to press certain facts to a greater degree. I assure you I do not enjoy this cruel pursuit of realities — but since I have no alternative —" He turned upon Mr. Loring.

"You, therefore, my poor man, had no right under existing laws to marry Etta Rose Dehring, did you?"

"No."

"Therefore," said Suggs, his belly shaking as he thrust a finger at the weakling, "she is not your wife. You are therefore, Mr. Loring, a bigamist, are you not?"

Etta Rose "Dehring" swooned. The swift severance of the marital tie was too much for her, that and her husband's perfidy of former years. She must have seen her spouse with his eyes on a brown girl, or perhaps she saw an inky shape; she no doubt saw him embracing a dusky shadow; she must have seen a devil and a black wench. How fitting, I thought, her refuge in a fainting spell. Once out of it she could face the future, present, and past without further surprise, and thus with the complete fury of her sex.

Though not a beautiful woman she was pleasing to the eye. Many years younger than Loring, she was yet carrying invitation beneath her heavy lids, and her haunches rippled provokingly; only her upper arms were stout and hinting of flabby flesh, though her face would bloat not many years hence. Nothing in her expression denied that she sought to humor her senses, though one could derive without undue exertion her fidelity to the old man in the witness box. And he, shocked into a craze, eyed her calmly, as he eyed Suggs, and Ralls. He was now a madman hating even the sight of the woman he loved, the woman who had, at last, sought out his sin and viewed it in joint public shame with him.

Out of her comatose state she slowly eyed everyone within her range, at last leveling her eyes upon her man. The intensity of her stare grew, and her face was drained of color, and as her eyes remained glued on him, a wild light formed in them: it was hate, deeper than the word, and her lips curled under the killing weight of it. The court sent a man to stand beside her lest she rise up and seek a pardonable revenge then and there. Mr. Suggs, aware of all possible repercussions, swiftly sought a flushing of the tense atmosphere. He turned to the hardened face of Loring, saying: —

"You are the last to represent trumped-up charges, my good man. Have I your leave to continue? Then," he said, when a murmur of assent followed, "can you give proof of the *Red Witch*'s change in course?"

"No, sir" — meekly. "I was in bed."

"Can you then say the course was changed?"

"I — I don't know. I — don't know anything any more, sir. Nothing! Nothing except —"

"Come, come, Mr. Loring," said Suggs in the tone of address that went with "you blithering fool" instead of the formal court "Mister."

"Except that — I know, I know as sure as there's a God in heaven that the *Red Witch* was deliberately scuttled." There was something in his tone, in his rigid calmness, that carried more weight than any statement that had yet come out of the affair. It was felt all over the room, I knew, for I saw men lean forward, and, too, I saw and heard Mr. Suggs's quick attempt to block the blow. His voice quivered with uneasiness as he said: —

"Mr. Loring, you're a broken man. Why not confess that your testimony was but a figment of the imagination? Would you not feel better?"

"Yes, I'm a broken man, Mister, thanks to you — no, just Captain Ralls. I have nothing to live for, nothing to die for but the sins of my years. May God have mercy on my soul when I swear that I shall live only to return what has been given me. As to your question," he said wearily, "I cannot confess to that lie, for you see, unless we had been off our course we could not have reached the uninhabited island below Rambutyo by rowing due north. Fifty hours due north of the sworn course would have taken us, with twelve hours north by west, almost to the Hermit Islands. The island, as you can see on the Admiralty Chart, is west by north from the sworn position of 3.2 degrees south by 145.7 east. It is strange that directions or sound reckoning have played no part in this trial."

How clearly he sounded the truth. That was Mr. Very's ace. But in holding it back he had ruined his chief witness.

A breathless silence fell over the court. I stared, not at the man who had spoken his piece, nor at the famous barrister whose finger froze in midair; nor did I gaze at Mr. Very — instead I turned my eyes upon the court, upon the five men, three officers of His Majesty's Navy, one shipowner, and one merchant. Two leaned forward, their hands stilled, their faces tense and rigid as marble; the remaining three frowned, exchanged significant glances and leaned into a whispered huddle. It was then my eyes left them and came to rest on Ralls, then Very, and last, on Mr. Suggs. Ralls held his statuesque calm, Mr. Very smiled, and the paunchy interrogator, Suggs, dabbed a handkerchief about his dew-covered baldpate.

The woman Loring had illegally married was no longer in the room, and the sole remaining woman, attached to the court because of her unerring accuracy at shorthand, forgot to write. She was not alone in her display of surprise. Every sailor there, most of them from the *Red Witch*, struck various and bemused poses in assuming outward stupidity; jaws dropped, frog eyes bulged, and faces craned forward on their necks in the manner of a flock of inquisitive fowls.

Into Loring's last sentences the great Suggs strode triumphant — out of them he wobbled in defeat. It was that quick. Only one short minute before the lull the ruthless lawyer had almost counted ten over his crushed witness, a slow excruciating count that broke tissues into sagging flesh with the "eight — nine —" And then came the answer of all answers from that hulk that asked for God's mercy in his hate. Robertson Velame Suggs, of Suggs and Trallerque, had evinced the power of the blow before the court by his failure to parry or return the thrust. And in allowing that momentous pause an echo, the future fees for the great firm slid from lofty heights to within the reach of the masses, who, ever prone to mimic the moneyed class, avoided the firm as it would a plague.

8

The case did not pause at that point for a verdict — instead it wore past its natural ending into a long anticlimax that taxed the reserve of both sides, that made wearier the weary; even the patient public, loquaciously drawing conclusions a week before, now settled back with sighs of boredom and watched the affair out of the corners of its eye.

The proceedings fell into a feeble state of pointless squabbling, in which the prosecution built up, with numbers, Mr. Loring's log of the lifeboats against a poorly launched counteroffensive by Mr. Suggs; Mr. Very merely kept the stagnated routine alive for a very special purpose: the court had ordered a seaplane to chart the direction and distance from the *Red Witch's* sworn position to the island named, the latter to be authenticated by the crew of the plane who had orders to fetch evidence, photographic and material, that would satisfy the court. Aerial distances, plus generous miles for a floundering boat, would be applied to the speed of men pulling at oars in directions sworn by the majority; which of course would clarify the debated position. And, too, the captain and crew of the Japanese ketch would be questioned.

Such proved to end the case, as I had known from the moment Loring cooked up contagious doubt. Ralls, Suggs, and Mr. Tulp held many long-faced conferences, which I attended with marked silence. But their efforts to pluck a plum from the ashes were futile. The charge of barratry was justified, said the court. Thus our former colleague, Mr. Tulp, became our enemy, and joining him in criminal prosecution of the ship's officers, Messrs. Ralls, Rosen, and Arrezo, was the firm of Batjak, Ltd., the owner of the *Red Witch*. Batjak's loss was a ship. The charterer, said rumor, lost a cool million in bullion.

Then came the unexpected, a surprise I could not fathom: the charges were dismissed before the date set for our trial. We were free to go our way, though our certificates were canceled. Ralls, grinning, advised that P.O.B., the Power of Batjak, was responsible. The Dutch tycoon, Mayrant Sidneye, had assumed the role of Santa Claus. Completely bewildered, I asked why; and Ralls only grinned, shrugged, and said, "I thought he'd come through. He always has." But in the bars and along the quays I heard: "Sidneye says legal justice is too mild for Ralls."

Ralls only grinned and said nothing.

But poor we were, except for the one bar of gold Ralls had failed to declare; two lay in the possession of the charterer, having gone from the naval hearing in the very same sack in which Ralls had placed them while on board the sinking *Witch;* the remaining bar was legally hot, and to turn it into negotiable form we were forced to book slow passage on a Chinese floating department store, one of the many boats given to island trade by the crafty Orientals, from Port Moresby. In Bangkok, after meetings with high-caste Chinese and a blunt German, we realized a tidy sum. But we were still without papers to sail a craft under the Union Jack, and minus the necessary money or credit to purchase any seagoing tub under any flag. But our fame, a glaring notoriety, had spread and we sat tight with our eyes and ears open; and before long we were engaged in unsavory, but highly profitable, business.

Out of it came the *Quean of Melbourne,* an aged but healthy craft which we planned to use, when the stink died down, to tear the bullion from Neptune's bosom. And on board her we sailed the seas from Singapore to the Fijis, and north and south of our home port; sometimes under the French colors, but when we got a break we adopted the Stars and Stripes. Lax as hell they were in Manila, in many, many respects. And there were days when I was ashamed to raise my eyes to the beautiful flag whipping in glory before a roaring trade wind.

But on we sailed, biding our time, pulling along the palm-swept shores of the Celebes; floating into the harbors of Batjan and Amboina, where the spice winds meet lazy sails with strange invitation; coasting before an afternoon breeze to a distant landfall, to anchorage beneath a volcanic peak nestling in lonely southern clouds; putting our sail into the teeth of the under trades and viewing the swampy shores of Dutch New Guinea; past the Schouten Isles and ever down past the southeast hind of the Admiralty group. There, somewhere in the coral bosom of the quiet waters, was a magnet that tugged at our helm — the molded yellow that caused insanity and suicides, that built pillars of hate in the souls of temperate men, that shifted fortunes never to be repaired, and drove bankers into cancerous ruin — the gold of the *Red Witch.*

That was the past. Before me, on the sand, sat the last victim of Ralls's whip, who had just said, "Remember what Loring did to the verdict?"

CHAPTER VII

1

THE curly-haired exile from the *Quean* arose and walked back and forth for some time, then sat down again in the shadow of the sago trunk. The moon beat down on the sea facing New Guinea, and only the singing surf added to the sounds of the heavy tropical night. Towering palms kept their distance from the waves; those wise old sentinels eyed the sea like watchful, bearded sailors in the rigging.

I sighed heavily and sought to free my mind of the maze of questions Carter's words evoked. But in vain; one thought piled atop another, each a layered stone in a pyramid of riddles. Why did Ralls stand the rail this time; why should Ruysdaal court our destruction; what was between the Dutchman and the skipper; where did van Schreeven enter; was Carter being fattened for the kill; why was Loring there; what proposition awaited me at dinner next evening; what about Bullit; and — what about the girl whose beauty stirred my blood with inordinate warmth?

Were all events, big and little, tied together by a thin unraveling thread, one end at Soembawa, the other in the grave of the *Red Witch?* I cursed aloud in profound disgust, causing Carter to laugh knowingly and raise his bottle as if in a toast to utter confusion.

"You met the girl, didn't you?" he said. I nodded. "She's rather chipper, don't you think? Balinese. There's a certain buoyancy in their faces that lifts them above their Oriental kin, a love of life resigned to joy, a piquant flavor of suppressed mischief and passion.

"Yes, sir, she's some doll," he added with a sigh.

Grinning savagely — a mixture of fire and regret — he ran his hand through the short locks and gazed up at the moon. Carter symbolized the rhythmic beauty of mind even in the scum of environment; perhaps the green mold of circumstances, a setting for his jeweled mind, amplified the beauty of his words; contrasting elements did that, I admitted.

I was again thinking of the girl, of her strange haunting eyes with that ray of imprisoned passion. Wilder than the sea, the tropics! Again

I saw her parted lips, moist, and faintly quivering. I gritted my teeth and said: —

"What part does she play in all this?"

"I'm afraid she's the flower in a parching wind. She is, my chum Sam, the stronger lure. That's my version, at least. The lure for sinners like Ralls — and yourself."

"Me!" I flared.

"And why not?" He answered with the wisdom of Solomon. "Since when are you immune to the charms of femininity?"

"There are things a hell of a lot more important," I said.

"Now, Sam," he said facetiously. "Why not spruce up a bit and go out after her yourself? Why? Because I think there would be less hell with you in the picture."

"How about you taking my place?" I asked without interest.

"No," he said painfully. "I'm above that."

"Since when have you turned lily-white?"

"Oh, I've learned to appreciate flowers — the botanist in me, Sam. I couldn't offer her a permanent glory, and damned if I play her temporarily. She's an orchid I'd sooner not crush."

"Which one died, Carter, the doctor or Mr. Hyde? You were better company when you lived the split personality."

"Yeah," he grunted, "wasn't I? But, Sam, you could sparkle a bit more and woo her. You know it isn't a man's dress that appeals to a woman so much as his attention to dress. Reflect the bearing of boldness, of immaculateness, and the battle is half won."

"Go to hell!" I said. It was a mistake. Carter could not have seen me better had I spilled my soul with a wordy confession. His eyes quickly locked with mine and a new light played in them. I wanted to rise up then and there and extinguish that glint of discovery; but I merely raised my bottle and made the best of a good draught before turning the subject to Mr. Loring.

"What earthly reason could Ruysdaal have for keeping Loring here?"

"Oh," he said. "Loring?" Suppressing a grin he added: "He's the man I saw, wasn't he? The abrupt change, Sam, floored me momentarily. So, forgetting the girl, I'll say that Mr. Loring is here for a purpose — two, in fact. Van Schreeven claims the maniac owner of this island is given to strange experiments. Loring, if that is so, is a guinea pig. He's being treated so he'll have the sanity, or the calm insanity, to seek revenge against Ralls. You remember Loring's face when the lawyer, Mr. Very, said that Ralls's whip had done the art on his back? Well, that expression might be sought for in Loring's face."

"Carter, that name — van Schreeven. Strange I can't place him. But what had Ruysdaal to do with the trial?"

"Perhaps nothing, perhaps a lot. You'll find out — soon."

2

Carter sat lost in thought. What, I wondered, wrapped his mind in a pensive cloak; his affliction, the creature of lovely curves, or hate for Ralls? Carter, too, was unpredictable, and I was not greatly surprised when he asked: —

"What's a word to rhyme with limited?"

"For what, Lord Byron? Piecing together some beautiful thread to amaze the world — posthumously?"

"Maybe," he said, "and maybe not. I could be fashioning a rhyme to knock the very props out from under you."

For a man so sick he possessed a remarkable snapback. Or was it that? But for the obdurate will to live until his purpose found the happy word *finis* ascribed in flowing letters, the beating he had taken should have broken him; but his magnificent callousness had the value of a symbol: he could endure the maltreatment of the man enemy and feed upon it; he had found a pabulum for his unyielding mind.

A presentiment met my thoughts there; it was an expected flavor to the feast of hate I saw all about me. What, I asked, would I pluck from the fricassee? I found myself in a lonely island that courted misanthropes. It was only natural that I viewed my condition without agitation or fear; the very character of the setting precluded alarm in a place where it seemed a necessity. Very wisely I faced it. I shared none of the repugnance of this place, except that which I held for Ralls; and that came through Carter.

"Limited, instead, behead, bled," he said aloud. I felt the wing beat of his fleeting impudence. It lifted my spirits.

"Death's-head, that's it!" Carter cried, snapping his fingers. "That looms like a hungry death's-head!"

"Drawing a portrait of Loring?" I queried.

"There are things worse, my chum," he said testily. "I think you'll agree when I tell you. I also think you'll agree with everything I've said about this home of rogues being a neat trap. Scoff if you like, but wait."

"Well, there's nothing like suspense," I declared. "I'll lean back and gaze at the moon." Sighing, I did just that.

Out of the mother of pearl moon Teleia stepped, her body a pink-bronze; mellow were my moments of transcendent pleasure, in which I sedulously courted the quasi-respectable. I sought a convoy of rapture denied me heretofore, and I was not immune to clearing dreamy highways toward its culmination. Revolting etchings, these, to chaste, unemotional folks, but nevertheless, in the past, the present, and always, a part of every man that lives at some time in his life.

The picture faded for want of fuel; no imaginative fire can burn inordinately without consuming the stores upon which it feeds. Past the tempo of my own ideology and its backlash, I peered again at the moon and started anew.

I traveled on, and back to the source of the beams, only to meet a heavenly face, one I had seen before: chaste and inspiring, Teleia's. In a state of bewilderment at my discovery I sought again, in challenge to the revelation, the moon-bathed body of Teleia, so great was my resentment to the truth that viciously proselyted me. But in vain. Her face, then, was the lasting force, the fire that burned with temperate zeal, never too hot, never too cold, never slaking the fuel with the insatiable tongue of a beast.

For long moments she met my gaze, she in the moon, I on the beach, and my first desires crept mildly forth to mingle with what I saw last. And as I lay there I felt the force of my inner words; I sat up, shocked, befuddled, and angry at the voice that kept saying: —

"Sam Rosen, you're in love!"

3

I scarcely heard Carter's mumbling though I trained my ear to his tongue in defense of self. Then I sought cover by telling the sane Sam Rosen that Carter's wounds must be properly dressed; but my unsaid words lacked all conviction.

"I've got it, Sam!" Carter exclaimed. "Ready for an earful?"

"Shoot," I said in abject manner. I stared at the palms in an effort to shake them out of their graven, mocking silence. It seemed they had heard my inner voice as it said: "Sam Rosen, you're in love."

"Very well, Sam. The poem I bring you is about Mijnheer van der Ruysdaal, and I'll thank you for your undivided attention. It is all revealing and it proves my powers of deduction." I turned an ear to him that seemed willing to listen. "Remember what I said about you and Ralls, about your conniving together, about his taking something from you? Answer me."

"I remember," I said. I was again normal, a mere man being whetted into a curious being.

"Well, when I finish this verse you'll see why my advice is manna from heaven. What I'm about to recite is the truth. You'll verify it when you visit the Dutchman's house for dinner — if you go."

The moon took a dimout in my befogged mind, and Teleia was completely forgotten when he raised his bottle and said: —

> Upon his wall hangs a plank
> That looms like a hungry death's-head
> To those who scuttled a ship so fine
> For lust of treasure of their kind;
> Returning, slinking to their find
> They meet the hollowed ivory head,
> A lettered plank to inspire dread:
> Reading — "Batjak, Limited."

Batjak. Ruysdaal. The *Red Witch!* They were one and the same in a concordat of revenge: Batjak had owned the *Red Witch*, of course; but —

"So Ruysdaal is Mayrant Sidneye!" I could not contain my surprise.

"Mayrant Ruysdaal Sidneye," said Carter, without voicing the triumph that was his.

I gave thought to the tangled threads of rumor, gossip of the pubs and quays. It seemed that Ralls and the powerful Sidneye of Soerabaja had much in common — a love for ships under sails, a propensity for intrigue and eternal feud. It was said that Sidneye had made Ralls rich, then poor; that Ralls had betrayed the tyrant's trust more than once. There were transient tales of all sorts running the seas. But all this was rumor, which Ralls never denied or affirmed.

And I had never so much as seen Sidneye, except as van der Ruysdaal. Nor would I have ever connected Ruysdaal with the newspaper picture of Sidneye. Therefore the revelation was nothing short of fuel for my anger at Ralls, who should have advised me of the fat man's identity. But Ralls had turned my question! And, of course, van Schreeven was no longer a puzzle; he fitted, instead, the pattern of Batjak.

Yes, Carter had succeeded. I was mad as hell — at both Ralls and stupid Sam Rosen.

CHAPTER VIII

I

MORNINGS go uneventful in the tropics; the low ebb of pleasure. One either sleeps off the night before or looks lazily ahead. In the cities an attempt is made to hold to the habits of the temperate zones. But the islands stretch slow muscles with a glorious awareness of that luxury known as languor. A cocoa-skinned maiden is slow in her stride with an armful of clothing to the water's edge. Her step is age old and timed to the voices she hears; at the fountain of fresh water she joins her neighbor, removes her coverings, and steps into the waters for a dousing of body. Amid indifference to shapes and curves, her sisters of a race do likewise, then beat their wet garments against the rocks until the coconut cleansing agent is driven out. The boys find a tree and mark it with the wet of their bodies and go their way in industry or indolence, but ever toward the seashore where a tramp steamer, ketch, or dinghy might wallow in close or tie up at a distance for the clamor from the outriggers.

A seafarer, however, finds the sun on the early rim and does not relinquish it until he bows to the tradition of his calling; only after the ship is tidy, and the word covers a multitude of chores, does he sweat in idleness. Tewelliger and Ripper were sailors first and human beings only after their salty incrustations were sweated from the shell. It was Tewelliger's hammer at work on the stern rail that brought the day around to me. The sun cast shadows that were short, and my appetite lent verity to their marking.

I was due a head that morning, I admitted, but its presence was joyfully missing. I stretched, and yawned into a noisy exhalation and threw a pair of fresh trunks about me, before setting my course for the rail. In a run I dove headfirst over the barrier and broke the water clean. In that moment I was awake. At the surface again I involuntarily ran an eye over the *Quean* and went under again, this time swimming under water to the other side of the ship. On the portside I came up, gasped for air, and swam toward the ladder. A rung was in my hand when a voice on the wharf caused me to stop short and turn about. I saw Ralls.

"You're wanted up at the Dutchman's house, Sam," he said slowly.

"Me?" I asked, surprised.

"Yeah. Old parrot face was here with this note." Without apology he read: "'Mijnheer Carter is seriously ill and asks for Mr. Rosen.' It is signed 'van R.'" I remained still, one arm on the ladder, the other resting in the water, and I must admit I was less concerned at the moment about Carter. My penetrating stare dwelled on the skipper, and the force behind it asked many questions: had the hurricane cooled, had it reached its pinnacle, or did it continue its sweep into a gale; was he steeping his mind for gold or pearls, or murder, or that baser scourge; what said the barometer of his face? For answer I met a sphinx. The glass of his eye shone through slits in that pliable, exquisitely tanned leather face, and his lips, a thin roll of cordovan, were set with purpose.

I covered my thoughts with a grin. I wanted then and there to voice my challenge, to promise him worse than he gave Carter, to swear eternal enmity. But I was not the fool to disclose my hand. I knew Sam Rosen, all right, and I was aware of how I came to be called a "cool un" from Bangkok to Suva.

"What's ailing Carter," I asked, hastily adding, "other than the usual?"

With placid evenness, he answered, "You should know, Sam. You pulled him from the water and drank out the night with him."

Instead of asking how he knew so much, I said easily, "Yeah, Skipper, I should." I lowered my eyes to the water; to have met his level eyes would have revealed my secret. "Ralls, I'm sorry you took it out on the kid," I said slowly. "You promised me to lay off of him."

"Yes, I did," he admitted, as if his memory had played him loose. "I'm sorry I broke my word to you, Sam. That's the first time I ever did it, isn't it?"

I eyed him quizzically before saying, "Yeah." Then I said, "You must be working yourself up to something bigger than the *Red Witch* — to forget things so easily."

"There's nothing bigger than that," he said.

"Well, we worked that in cahoots, that and several long shots since," I replied in inviting manner. A blue shark coasted slowly below me, sending a surreptitious glance my way, his appetite beckoning, his caution overruling. He was gone in another moment and I lifted my eyes to the greater evil. Coldly he eyed me, debating, I thought, on whether to guide this hurricane into the calm partnership of the past. Like the shark, appetite beckoned but caution had the final word. It was then I realized he was bent on more than pearls or gold.

"Well," I said, "I'll be getting on. I presume it's safe to walk into the tiger's lair. If I'm not in by sunrise tomorrow you can write me off or come after me." At the top of the ladder, I said, "If there's any message I can take from you just spill it."

"Take care of yourself," he said. "Until sunrise tomorrow, then." He turned about and walked off in the direction of the *Flores*.

How little it would have cost Ralls to take me into his confidence, I thought while shaving. To Ripper, I yelled, "Are my whites pressed yet?" Ralls, had he not flogged Carter and flung him to the denizens of the lagoon, might have kept the story from me. But he knew all about Sidneye and Batjak. The word brought a frown to my face; it seemed to ring evilly — Batjak — a definition for retribution. Ripper arrived with my spotless suit and a new cap, bestowing upon me a sidewise grin that chided me for primping. I gave him a piercing stare that drove the grin into his neck. He ambled away muttering, "Sa no good," over and over.

I thought of Carter's words: "It isn't a man's dress that appeals to a woman so much as his attention to dress. Reflect the bearing of boldness, of immaculateness, and the battle is half won." I tightened my lips before eyeing the mirror and spouting forth, "What the hell! I'm not interested in any battle except that of getting out of this place." The eyes in the mirror held mine and flung back at me all sorts of clamorous, silent accusations. "Sam Rosen, you're every kind of a liar." The hold Teleia had on me was a rope of horror in one moment, a heady garland in the next; as always, I sought refuge in anger.

On deck Tewelliger eyed me with raised brows, and I passed him by without a word, moving across deck with his "Well, well, Mr. Rosen the dude" look knifing me in the back. Over near the rise I saw the Moluccan and the parrot. As I drew near them I cast a glance at the *Quean*, and saw both Ripper and Tewelliger staring at me. I raised a hand and they both responded with lazy gestures. In another moment I disappeared from their view. I walked over the rise and into another world.

2

The heat was almost unbearable, it was always that way but more so that morning, and once over the hump of earth the air seemed packed in layers with nothing to stir it. Slowly, on the heels of the messenger, I curiously gave an eye to a new scene: on the lower side, to my right, were many creepers with hanging festoons of rare flowers, reminding me of the New Guinea swamps; ferns of every shape rose in tropical glory out of steaming surfaces, and twice I saw orchids growing in moss on the ground.

Suddenly the jungle growth was behind us, and I peered at the industry of a Netherlander. Tobacco grew in a wide field, and several coolies, Malays, slowly went about their work unmindful of our presence; farther on, at the edge of a clump of trees, several Malay boys rode slow and indifferent carabaos, going nowhere, it seemed, and in no hurry to get there. Some distance beyond a limp rag, the three stripes of the Netherlands, slept on a white pole with the British flag.

Approaching the residence I came upon a wall of sweet-scented shrubs that hid the tall steel fence with a single opening; a turbaned Malay came forward and asked me to relinquish my gun. Without a word I passed it to him, ignoring his grinning salaam. I was inside the province of van der Ruysdaal, or Sidneye, in a gorgeous garden of flowers and rock walls, gazing at a sunken arena of huge tulips that blossomed in patterned colors. Here, under the shade of an acre of cloth, was every imaginable flower, a botanist's paradise. Here the wild met the tame and found a breeding rich and indefatigable, a sexual fierceness of the nth degree. A barefoot Sumatran in riotous batik and brocade bowed low and relieved the Moluccan agent as we approached the house.

And the house: it was of three floors, having a long and rambling abruptness under the spreading inverted V roof. Twelve illusory doors, each crossed with an ornamental X from top to bottom, met my eye, though only two opened out for an entrance; above the rock columns, about eight feet in height, was a long veranda upon which giant striped umbrellas grew out of wooden tables; above this floor, a rustic balcony was topped by a thick tie beam. The walls were of timber, edged with a maze of seasoned bamboo that framed the endless run of windows as well as the array of doors below. The rafters extended beyond the walls some six feet on either side, and served as rain sheds for the rock walks around the house. The slate roof was of white and red, the wood of the half-timbered walls a live green of pale hue against white. All else was white — the surrounding houses, the shade arbors, even the sun dial. Only a bronze and polychrome statue of the goddess Devi traversed the outer color scheme: she, full-breasted and bent at the hips, wore a conical cap and rich sarong in her awkward pose in the central walk before the house.

Centered in the upper balcony was a huge shield, and in the dead middle a gilded quatrefoil stood out in a field of dull red. There had been a ship by that name, a tempestuous three-master that came to a bad end. But the quatrefoil, no mystery, was bundled up with minor mysteries and forgotten.

A sloe-eyed Malay met us at the door and my latest guide bowed out, leaving me in the company of the houseman. I was motioned to a long seat covered with a gorgeous shade of blue silk, dappled with large blue-white flowers. The rococo carving of the legs was too simple for a Chinese artisan, so I accepted the luxurious piece as made-to-order Dutch-English. No sooner had I taken a seat than two tawny men appeared with trays; on one were a decanter, a bowl of ice, and a syphon bottle; on the other hors d'oeuvres. Left alone with these delicacies, I soon had a drink concocted. Then I sat back to take in my new surroundings.

The pomp and ceremony accorded my arrival was silently augmented by a singular beauty. The room, forty feet square and walled in clear, lacquered eucalyptus, was paneled from the base some three feet above the floor; the latter was of red mahogany, fashioned into inlaid squares and matched in grain. The ceiling was, oddly enough, dead white, and trimmed in bleeding ultramarine some ten feet all around and circled in the center with the same fading design, which found its depth at the chandelier. On the floor a thick carpet seemed to throw its richer blue at the ceiling. A tressure, again quatrefoils in miniature and gilded against a vermilion back, hung on the wall; set apart from this piece was an oil of Queen Wilhelmina, in van Dyck style, by an artist who signed himself Huls; on another wall nearest the richly carved swinging doors was another oil, a three-masted queen of the seas — the colors were striking, and the sea swelled gently in shades of green and blue.

The odd size and shape of the room seemed cleverly, beautifully, overcome: against a wall, on a marble platform some three feet square, stood a statue of Krishna, with snakes at his feet, their coil meeting the marble — the flute, headpiece and all, in gilt and cloisonné; nor did the Hindu prevail throughout the room — I saw the white cast of Sophocles in another corner and the bearded head of Hermes in another; still another pedestal was topped with a sloop model, its balloon jib and spinnaker full to the wind. Under glass was a worm-eaten slab of old wood. The inscription read "Vogelkop," which was Dutch for bird head; and the plank joined the mystery of the surroundings.

There was only one window in the vast room; it was a huge affair some four yards wide and meeting the ceiling and floor without trim; only blue brocaded silk found flowing folds at either side, and a lighter blue bamboo shade shut out half the light.

At that moment two flashy houseboys opened the wide inner door and stood deferentially stiff to allow the entrance of one of importance. I held my breath, hoping to see Teleia van Schreeven. But I was disappointed. Slowly the wheel chair rolled through the opening.

He was the gracious host. "You'll pardon my tardiness," he said, smiling as he rolled to where I stood. "It was, of course, purposeful," he added. "The blue room softens one — usually." The implied hint was not lost upon me; I saw through his pleasant façade the strength of weakness, the monsoon behind pleasantries, the force of concentrated hate. Though indirectly it was meant for me, I steeled my trader's mind into a smile of acknowledgment.

"Won't you sit down, Mijnheer Rosen," he said.

There was the large black pearl on his finger; he was the same two hundred pounds of drugged flesh, with the varicose veins, with frambesia of face, a bald head, beady eyes, and thin, firm lips and bibulous nose.

"Thanks, Mijnheer," I said easily. "Would you join me in another drink? Your taste in beverages appeals to me more than your artistry." I grinned as I swept in the room with a motion of my hand. "For softening, or hardening, give me the liquid art."

"With pleasure," he said. The clap of his fat hands brought the Moluccan Methuselah — at that moment I catalogued the servant as Ruysdaal's personal attendant. Soon we drank, after words from the host, "To young Carter, may he recover shortly." Then he dealt me the first surprise: "I see a great future for the lad."

"You do?" I contained my surprise. "I had in mind a colony for him. There he could die peacefully."

"I don't think," he began slowly, and with emphasis, "Carter will be needing a grave for many years. You see, Mijnheer Rosen, there are vast fields of learning yet to be exposed, and explored."

And exploited, I thought, though I said, "That is indeed interesting. Mijnheer van Schreeven mentioned something of your experiments yesterday. I believe he said your interest lies in psychogenesis. An unusual avocation, I must say."

"It is more than that," he said. "Origination has its counter agent, generation its opposite. And, as we all know, development and evolution are mere stages of living clay. One molds objects in clay. From the same piece one can create an image of a cobra or that of a cherub. My greatest interest is in the antipode."

I replied in scholarly manner, "The universe is created of opposites, and the field is highly conducive to limitless imagery." His smile complimented me for my say, and under my straight face I said: You're welcome, you antipode to a cherub. I added, aloud, "Only one great obstacle attends the subject, that being the short span of years we're given in which to study the slow processes of evolution. Each flower in your garden, and I must extoll their beauty, requires an age to breed into a different flower." I was merely following a pattern; I was sparring.

"I, Mijnheer Rosen, see you are a student of nature. You will therefore understand me when I say I have been able to speed evolution."

"Then in Carter's case, I suggest the use of celerity, Mijnheer. He's on the road to the stiffness of a corpse. Before he's as cold as Devi and Krishna you'd do well to use your science."

"So. You recognize my Hindu images. Few do. Perhaps you wonder at their presence. For me? No. My servants love them. But — again to Carter. There seems to be a strong bond uniting you two." His hand was lifted in protest to any word from me at that point. "You see, Mijnheer, Carter draws a difference between you and — the senior partner of the *Quean of Melbourne*."

"Carter," I said, "is ever prone to stretch a point. I can't understand his loyalty. God knows I give him small reason for it."

"Let us then call it an inherent quality, Mijnheer, one that is in your favor." I translated his words without difficulty: they suggested that I prove myself not too hard to manage, that I lean over to the element opposing Ralls. His seven-veiled statement challenged my wits, called for an answer.

"Mijnheer van der Ruysdaal," I said slowly, evenly, meeting his eyes with assumed gravity, "little can be said in my favor — by Carter, or anyone. I reserve the significance of my leanings in any direction until my trader's intuition is fortified with complete facts."

"Well spoken," he said, smiling; he let his eyes travel to the tressure dotted with quatrefoils. "My brother advised of your powers as a trader. I regret we have nothing to trade, Mijnheer Rosen, for I should enjoy entering into heated debate with you over any worth-while, or worthless, article. Perhaps we can find such an item."

He grinned, clapped his hands four times, and bade the Moluccan bring cigarettes. I accepted without scrutinizing the long smoke, and after the gold lighter in the hands of the servant gave it flame I sat back and exhaled freely. It was indeed palatable, though a heavy flavor of perique lingered.

Patiently he talked on, awaiting my discovery. I was slow to grasp his opaque objective and I listened with interest to his fresh views on

93

horticulture. It seemed the soil of his native Java and that of his Little Soembawa had many points in common, as well as those expected differences. He had transported a shipload of Java earth to this island. That was all very interesting through the burning of the cigarette. It was not until I snuffed out the fire in a ruby bowl that I saw his purpose. I am sure that I started, though certainly not from surprise; as my eyes lifted to his I saw his steady, penetrating smile vanish. Again I lowered my gaze to the words in thin blue letters printed across the cylinder near the cork. They were: —

"Batjak, Ltd." Above them stood a gilded quatrefoil.

My host was ready with smoothing words. "You will, of course, remain for dinner. In the meantime visit your friend and enjoy all the comforts of Villa Quatrefoil."

"With pleasure, Mr. Sidneye," I said.

3

Carter lay in a trough of silk and down, framed by the handsomest four-poster and canopy I had ever seen. His room was cooled by circulating air. On a Chinese table near him great clusters of tropical jasmine gave off a heavy perfume. Underneath the bamboo blind, through a stretch of plate glass, the view of the side garden met my eye, revealing against a Chinese arbor the climbing purple bougain-villea; in the far background crimson hibiscus and flowering jasmine formed a shielding drop for the stage filled with riotous flowers.

Carter grinned feebly. "Swell layout, eh? Thought you'd like it here, Sam."

"I'm not sure I do," I said truthfully. "There's nothing to do here but go sweetly crazy. But how do you feel?"

"A little off key today. The doc, van Arken, says it's the Creeper. No new developments in the old stand-by."

"Why did you send for me?" I grunted.

"Put your leaden end in a chair, chum, while I call up refreshments. We have Scotch, gin, bourbon, rye, nectars, cordials, wines, brandies, and champagnes. Then we can offer iced juices, or tea from Tjisalak."

"Gin," I said.

"And ice, of course. You know this is a swell place to pass out from, Sam. I've already told Arken and Sidneye to fashion my last hours to a hold on a clear, perfumed afternoon. I can see all the beauty of the world from here — I can fade out slowly and without due pain, making my rhymes and giving them to posterity. Not bad, eh." He was serious. "Yeah, just passing out in a beautiful sleep with few regrets, with little

94

damage done to the world I lived to the hilt. Across these seas there's many a girl spared the knowledge of my going. I wonder which one will claim my last moments."

He pulled a cord which quickly brought a Malay. Soon a sterling silver tray was rolled in, laden with cold gin, mints, quinine water, huge glasses, ice, cigarettes, and dainty tidbits. "See, Sam, anything from a filet mignon to shark's fin. Not bad for the vanishing poet." The Malay bowed and turned about. Carter said, "Hey, Palebangji, bow once to Devi." The servant, giggling, obeyed.

I helped myself, stared at the pale face of my friend and wondered what sort of experiments he might be subjected to.

Carter said, reading my thoughts, "Who met you at the door?"

I gave him the story, as much as I cared to reveal, omitting nothing but my opinion of his host and the cigarette episode. I did not trust the walls; I was sure they had ears. Carter observed my darting eye and took it upon himself to advise that there were no hidden wires.

"That's swell," I returned. "For then no ear can be disappointed. I came here to see and hear, not to talk and be heard. I have no scrap with our lavish host."

"Perhaps your cigarette says otherwise."

"Perhaps," I said, staring calmly at the imprinted words. "Perhaps not. And if anyone wishes a tête-à-tête with me, I shall oblige him. So that's that."

"You bore hell out of me, Sam. I've given you plenty of opportunity to open up, I've given you reasons why, and I've extended an invitation to get on the right side. To set your mind at ease, I'll tell you there's no eavesdropper about, and I'll tell you more — I've been duly appointed to extend you an invitation."

"I imagined as much," I said. "But about the eavesdroppings, I'll lay you ten to one against your innocent opinion. However, it makes no difference." I raised my glass, sipped and said, "What time is dinner?"

"To hell with dinner!" he cried. "Why do you think I sent for you?"

"I'm sure it was a mere whim, Carter. Lonesomeness is a plague, I know. Or," I said, facing him squarely, "perhaps you thought my presence here would weaken the *Quean*. But, having kept us company for so long, you should know better. You see, violence is not expected in any form from the hospitable owner of this paradise. Even if it were, my being here would leave the situation unaltered."

"Just what do you mean, Sam?" Carter was genuinely puzzled; that's how I wanted him — and any eavesdropper.

"That I have nothing to lose," I said. No sooner were the words out of my mouth than he fell back to his pillows, laughing. To him I was the utter fool; to myself I was one who trod coals lightly. Before he could say more the door opened, without warning, to reveal a small man with coal-black hair, a pair of deep-set, intelligent eyes, and a Vandyke beard. The doctor, I thought.

He eyed me with sharp, unrelenting eyes that failed to upset me, acknowledged Carter's introduction with a stiff nod, and turned to his patient. He proceeded in the manner of one who knew his business.

"It is four hours until dinner, Mijnheer," he said in choppy English. "You should sleep until time to dress. Everyone attends this evening." Then he faced me. "You, Mijnheer, will be shown to your room."

"I'm in no hurry, Dokter," I said. "Tell the boy to wait outside." He eyed me with a look that said he was used to being obeyed instantly. I said, "Good-by, Dokter." Not for all the gold in Australia would I have moved until he departed; nor did I.

"Sam," Carter said, his voice almost pleading with me, "don't pull a runout on me. Promise?"

"On you?" I said, lifting my brow in surprise.

"Yeah, bo. I want to sit across the table from you tonight. Do that for me, Sam. I promise not to ask another favor of you, so long as I live. How about it?"

"Very well," I said, rising to go. "But if I should return to the boat, I'll be back. Sweet dreams of the poppy, chum."

From the windows of the stunning room assigned me I viewed the garden in all its glory. I yawned and eyed the bed, then glanced at the chilled glass in my hand, and again at the rock walkway below.

I awoke with a start, foggily glancing at my watch; I had slept nearly three hours. I, Sam Rosen, who had planned a visit to the *Quean* that afternoon. I got to my feet and saw, to my surprise, fresh clothing: a dinner jacket and trousers, a shirt and tie, as well as a dress handkerchief and all that makes up the outfit. There was a note pinned to it: "These will fit, Mijnheer Rosen. Dinner is at seven — van R."

After a second bath in one day, I donned the dandified clothes with the aid of a Malay lad, and made my way into the garden, smoking away at one of my own cigarettes while trying to convince myself that I did not enjoy the taste of luxury. Slow swinging steps took me past beds of colorful, and cruelly beautiful, flowers, the names of which I did not know. But I was less interested in them than in the beauty they brought into mind: Teleia.

The breeze held, and the surf outside the lagoon sent out its tide voice; the singing palms added a languid touch to even the perfume-drenched atmosphere; and I found myself eager for the presence of Teleia. As luck would have it I saw her just as the Oriental gong gave off its first resonant call to dinner.

Walking toward me, laden with cut flowers, she cast furtive glances toward the house. I stood awaiting her, unaware of anything in the big round world but her.

"It is good to see you again, Mijnheer Rosen," she smiled.

"You are kinder than I expected," I returned.

"We must all accept our disappointments," she laughed. "Are they not a part of every moment?" My eyes narrowed at this, and I wondered if her words were two-edged.

"You," she said, "find me kind, and Mijnheer Bullit, when he tells me of standing near the pool with a gun, is very disappointed when I slap him. So you see —"

"But why did you?"

"Because he should never spy on me." She said more with her eyes. "Thus, Mijnheer Rosen, disappointment reigns supreme in every moment."

"And what emotion, may I ask, did you experience as I left the pool?"

"A keen sense of sorrow, Mijnheer, that so good a man should find momentary weakness. Or, I could have despaired of your life, knowing you were followed. But of one thing I am happy, and that — Bullit's jaw is almost broken."

I grinned, an easy victim to the verbal uppercut she dealt. Pausing for a smile that could run only before pleasantries, she rocked me with: —

"Mr. Rosen, I know of no earthly reason why I should warn you — unless I possess an aversion to wolves outnumbering a lamb. Be alert, friend."

CHAPTER IX

1

As I entered the huge blue room I saw gathered there, and rattling off Dutch like a windmill on the Zuider Zee, a strange company, all traveling the same wind presumably, with sails set at various angles; the concordat found rule in the sovereign host — it better served the individual course that way. Dokter van Arken, standing stiffly with a colored drink in hand, and dressed like me, no doubt sought fame in the pursuit of Mayrant Ruysdaal Sidneye's psycho-isms; van Schreeven too had selfish reasons up his sleeve; else I was fooled. He eyed the corpulent invalid from a tanned face with smiling concern; Mr. Bullit, looking more like an overdressed frog in the white dress of evening, gulped huge quantities of liquor and disgustingly nodded out silent affirmation to every speaker's words; walking off alone and paying little attention to anyone was a young man I had not seen, a chap short in stature but otherwise measuring up nicely; my greatest surprise came when I saw the wizened Moluccan in dress attire and mingling as an equal; an island Mohandas Gandhi, a quick thought suggested, but nevertheless, a ripe surprise.

Toward the heterogeneous group I walked in nonchalant manner, pausing halfway to snuff out a cigarette. The host was first in extending a greeting, and with proper introductions under way I again shook the hand of van Schreeven, answered the Moluccan's bow with a bow, said to Mr. Bullit, "I'm pleased to meet you," not overlooking his dry twinkle and curious stare, returned Dokter van Arken's stiff bow with an enjoyable grin, and gave warmth to my clasp with the hand of the stranger, Jan Hooch, a junior partner of Batjak, Ltd.

Said Mijnheer Hooch, "Um-m. Rosen, did you say, Uncle?" I beat the Dutch uncle with a verifying statement: "Correct, Mijnheer. Of the *Quean of Melbourne* riding anchor in the lagoon." My tone was level enough to cause his youthful eye a second glance. I, of course, realized that I was the marked man of this strange dinner party, and I was ready to sort the insinuations, the sugar-coated narratives and concise utterances that were to be loosed for my benefit. A sense of pure enjoyment flooded me, and I set to work in an endeavor to keep it alive. I wanted, at that moment, to pull the strings of conversation, if merely to separate the dangling marionettes from their animating force.

Crudely, I said, "Mijnheer Sidneye, what kind of a host are you? I don't see my favorite — gin." Amid curious and surprised glances it was produced, and the host's profuse apologies were waved aside. I poured about four ounces into a glass and downed it straight. Crassness has its advantages: it subjects one to pinpoint comparisons, usually in disfavor, and sets one apart from those lipservers of decorum; therein the very force of the opposite is achieved, and opinions again take a tumble. Great fun, I've found, and, too, it's lucrative, after a fashion.

My manners were less crude, though I sawed against the grain, and purposely so, when I said: —

"Gentlemen, I propose a toast — Mijnheer Hooch, if you'll fill my glass for me." He did, not enjoying it. "Now, glasses up. To the health of our inimitable host, whose profundities amaze us, whose artistry is manifested by the beauty he gives his domain, whose inspiring presence is reminiscent of a dazzling lodestar. Truly, Mijnheers," I said, clicking my heels and bowing, "I am impressed." In that split-second exchange of curious and stunned glances, by all but host and the Moluccan, there was a painful softening of hard faces. I had broken the ice barrier to my objective, giving each man to know he was dealing with no mollycoddle.

Sidneye, shrewdly aware of my turning the faucet of initiative, merely smiled. He said, "You have scarcely seen anything yet." I accepted the easy end of his double-edged words and smiled my best.

"Come with me," he invited, "to the aquarium."

I followed the rolling chair through a wide hallway and into a long, narrow room; more than a score of long fish tanks met my eye, each framed in a stainless white metal and filled with the queerest creatures imaginable. My surprise was not feigned, and he smiled at my wide-eyed sweep of the room before saying: —

"Here is the South Pacific." I was ready to believe him. Soon the others entered and joined us in a slow walk between the tanks. "This little fellow," he said, pointing to a spotted puffer, "is known among natives as the Deadly Death. He is partitioned off due to his love of battle with his kind. This species, the *Balistapus aculeatus*, is from Fiji." A creature of marble black, white, yellow, and indigo, and lavishly striped, eyed us from coral stems. "And here," he said, "are squirrelfish and triggerfish. The lemon one is the yellow tang. Like to see a moray?" He pointed to the coppery black and white ringed eels, vicious guardians of reefs, resting under castles of coral.

"This," he said, "is *Pterois volitans*, sometimes called turkeyfish — though it is a lionfish. The long spines are poisonous — very." He said it in the manner of one who knows. I gazed at the hideous yet beautifully colored fish that had long pectoral fins like feathers. A tank of young gray sharks was next, and then — the horrible eyes of a squid met mine. How it was kept alive I don't know, unless by the constant flow of lagoon water through the tank. I'd heard they could never live in captivity, but there it was in a huge tank, barred inside triple-plate glass, waving its ten slimy arms at the tips.

99

"My pet," he said, and I could well imagine such to be the case. "Tjrid," he said, addressing a Malay, "feed His Majesty." Without further ado, the servant departed and soon returned with a young spotted hound, a reminder of my bird-hunting days in the States. He held the animal before the tank long enough for the huge eyes to find those of the canine: a low moan and a frantic spasm of fear on the outside; an awakening inside the tank. The monster shot forward, waving a thick arm before the glass and sending up a stream of bubbles.

Then the dog was carried up an iron ladder. And after the top bars were clicked, the sad animal was placed on a float inside the tank. The bars shot home menacingly and the Malay descended. What followed I shall never forget. The company remained for a while, but one by one they departed until only my bestial host, the Dokter, the Moluccan, and I remained. I felt the moment in all of its intensity, aware of the purpose behind the irrational show: it was for me, and for Ruysdaal's pleasure in rolling his eyes from the inhuman scene to my face. I, of course, accepted the challenge, the hardest task ever set before me; though neither squeamish nor afraid to watch death in an animal I did not enjoy such sights, and, too, I never saw a hound with more devoted brown eyes. They were round, kind, and loving; trusting eyes that wag a tail at one. At this juncture I felt the eyes of my host and his guests upon me, and I leaned against a center post in the room and placed my hands in pockets. Did I wish a cigarette? I did, though I suppressed the desire — indifference to their horrible whim must be my forte.

"A beautiful dog, Mijnheer," I said easily. "I should feed that damned squid a pig."

"Ordinarily, yes," he returned. "But His Majesty tires of a repeated diet. Don't we all?"

Once the dog straddled the wobbling wood raft, the baleful squid stared slowly, eternally, in anticipation of a flavorful gorging. An arm moved hideously out of the water, causing the dog to shrink in terror. A muffled whine and helpless bark were heard through the air holes in the lid. A second arm slowly appeared, transforming the torpid beast of long moments before into a devil of torment, anxious to evoke the last heartbeat from its victim through paralysis born of God-awful terror. The hound's eyes found mine pleadingly, and I was unable to withstand the glance. My eyes moved to the attacker as my fingers bunched into a hard fist inside my pocket. After that I was safe, though I almost dashed up that ladder to rescue the helpless dog. I thought of Ralls in that moment and swiftly compared his hurricanes to the degraded calm of my companions. Ralls would either enjoy the show or violently bring down a curtain.

Another tentacle rose, and the sucker discs, each surrounded with a ring of horny teeth, made ready to clasp the prey and bring it to the parrotlike beak under the huge, baglike body — there a vicious slashing will end any life. With two long tentacles on either side of the raft, the eyes, laterally placed behind the mouth, appeared above the water. An arm closed in, slowly winding about the shaking dog's ribs; he turned with an awful whine, eerie and ghastly, and bit at the rubbery thing. A howl followed and he frothed at the mouth. Then the second arm wound about his hind quarters and the raft tipped over.

Up came the shorter tentacles to reveal that grotesque and fearsome beak, open and ready to tear living chunks of flesh from the dog. The squid, a five-foot, slimy, cartilaginous devil of devils, evoked in one the fullest horror at a glance, but those unblinking mad eyes, those voracious jaws in action, brought forth the cold sweat of a greater dread than the word "horror" can give expression. The dog panted and struggled, and under water, except its head, felt the tear of the strong jaws that could snap leaders of steel. A terrible moan and spasmodic jerks preceded the blood that oozed into the water. I would have traded my interest in the *Quean of Melbourne*, in the treasure of the *Red Witch*, to have departed from the room and its occupants at that moment, but the bore of Sidneye's eyes and those pins of van Arken's fell against my face. I followed the whole scene without flinching, and when the floating hair barely moved with the stilled raft, with those darkened eddies of crimson-tinged water, I continued to stare — I was jailing my anger and loathsomeness behind bars of insouciance.

In the manner of a death knell the second gong sounded.

I turned to the quiet, unsmiling steadiness of three pairs of eyes and said blithely enough: "Mijnheer, my congratulations. I have never witnessed a more sensational show. One-sided, perhaps, but then, every man to his own whim. Now had I such an actor upon such a colossal stage, I'd give a different show — a Malay with a two-inch blade and His Majesty."

The trio stared at me; there was disappointment in the eyes of my host — and, too, there was a faint hint of admiration or wonder, or both. Even misanthropes sometimes show their secrets in their eyes.

It was small wonder then Teleia advised alertness.

2

Carter awaited us in the drawing room in formal attire; he seemed to lend clothes an added style. His smile beamed from flushed mouth and fevered eyes but none of his old-time sparkle was missing. Dokter van Arken was soon hovering over him. Why all this attention to a rank stranger, what had they in mind? The answer took me back to van Schreeven's words that had to do with opposites; and the ironical fact was more than ever emphasized.

Forgetting the queer lot, I listened to rollicking Carter. "Sam," he said, "you're not half so ugly when you dress up," to which I replied, "Thanks, Apollo."

Sidneye entered the conversation with: "Mijnheer Rosen typifies the Yankee." I cut my eyes his way for the explanation that followed. "He is loyal, stubborn, at times fearless — and gold mad."

"Well," I said, smiling, "you must remember that it was old Peter Stuyvesant who settled in New Amsterdam. Vanderbilt was three words in the old country, was it not?"

Van Schreeven chuckled, as did Hooch, at my sketchy rejoinder; the host grinned. "And," I said slowly, "the Dutch have never been at a loss to produce paragons."

"A philosophic cuss, isn't he?" Carter said. "His only burden is the company he keeps." At that moment I could have cuffed him with pleasure. He had jumped the gap all too soon, leaving only a poisoned atmosphere hanging over the room. That he purposely alluded to Ralls, I was sure.

"Another crack like that, chum, and I shall ask Dokter van Arken to send you to bed." I turned to face the slitted lids of Sidneye. "You'll pardon him, gentlemen, for such a *faux pas*. I shall mend the break in pleasantries with an old American saying — Said the governor of North Carolina to the governor of South Carolina, it's a long time between drinks."

Carter leaned back in his chair and roared with laughter. It was contagious. After some moments he said, "Sam, my apologies. I was just testing your fettle." To the company he said, "I warned you, he's the fox."

"A fox who," I added, "if these gentlemen aped you, would find himself in a den of wolves. But, of course, they don't know you like I do, Carter. Why not find your guitar and give them an island tune?"

"Do," suggested Jan Hooch. "All I can get on this infernal radio is Malay, Japanese, and Hindustani. The air is full of NIROM in Batavia. Manila fades out, and I'm hungry for music."

I grinned at Carter — sweet revenge. He said, "You make yours stick, don't you, Sam?" And I said, "Uh-huh." He ambled off after the instrument and we heard him tuning from the hall on his return. I advanced to meet him at the door, addressed him in low, menacing tone: "If you start playing that damn tune about the *Red Witch* I swear to slit your throat." He grinned in teasing manner, jerked his head to throw back a stubborn curl from his forehead, and softly began: —

"Oh the Amsterdam Dutch, the Rotterdam Dutch," and giving his words a ringing tone he named the other Dutch, ending with, "The Irish don't amount to much, but they're a damn sight better than the goddam Dutch." Jan Hooch laughed loud and long, and even the stilted face of Dokter van Arken unbent.

"Sam has a special request," he said, showing his teeth in a tormenting smile. I traced a finger about my throat, causing him a chuckle. Then his fingers slowly moved over the strings and he gave his voice to a romantic moon song, Polynesian inspired, and, after long months aboard the *Quean*, worked into a haunting, seductive melody with harmonizing words; it was my favorite. I relaxed, raised my glass, and drank to that Aphrodite at the pool.

The song continued, holding the attention of everyone, especially Jan Hooch, whom I had long since tabbed and filed: the not dangerous playboy. As I leaned against the blue seat I saw all eyes slowly turn and peer beyond me, then smile, and rise with their bodies under them. Carter continued to play as he stood, and I turned and got to my feet.

She stood in the doorway, smiling, her hands against the opening on either side. She seemed to sparkle, sapphire-like, into one's eye, to open like a perfumed flower in the morning sun to the music of the universe — and Carter created the slow stirring melody. Her hair rose at the forehead, curved back and fell in a luxuriant sweep; a frame for face and neck that met the light like a tropical halo. The rich translucent bronze of her face, neck, and hands was further enlivened by her costume, a scintillating white silk kabaja, or tunic, alive with small salmon-colored flowers against the merest hint of fading blue; the same design was wrapped tightly about her waist from upper hip to lower ribs, and tucked under in a receding point at dead center; there the kabaja met the most alluring of tropical garments, the sarong; also white, it burst into huge, wild, crimson blossoms — giant hibiscus against green leaves. A large pearl showed in each ear lobe and a tiny gold chain disappeared beneath her dress into the valley of her breast.

I struck a match to light a needed cigarette, but I stood staring instead of making use of it — until the Moluccan intruded with "So sorry," and raised my hand just as my fingers felt the bite of flame. Even then I failed to recover.

Carter's song faded out as she stepped into our company, and died into a murmur only to rise again with another strain: —

> With a ray of imprisoned passion,
> In the eyes of a golden typhoon
> And the sapphire of the tropics
> In her winy, whirling rune.

I saw the strange bright light in the eyes of Jan Hooch, once I was free to observe reactions, and I read of love in them; I snorted inwardly at such a union. Jealousy, yes, admittedly, for I was now sure of my love for her. I was the last to receive her warm hand, though by her look I was given to know I was not the least in her thoughts: the light of love was missing, I must confess, but there was interest — it stood out on the pin point of her twinkling eye in a wide background of challenge.

The third and last gong gave off vibratory notes and faded out. Hooch stepped forward and extended his elbow, causing her to eye him with a level and calculating gaze before turning the same expression my way. Instantly my arm bent to inviting angle, and she slowly placed her salmon-flowered sleeve through it; her other hand fell about my arm at the wrist as we led the march to the dining hall. She smiled up at me.

With little time for words I cast a wary eye about me, determined to deliver an important message before the opportunity departed. "I have something to tell you," I said in serious tone. "You must not leave the immediate grounds this evening. Do you hear?"

"You enjoy giving orders, don't you?"

"Quite the contrary," I said irritably. "But necessity demands. My partner is on the loose, wild drunk and — I may as well say it — in rutting mood." Her glance at me was quick, alert, and evanescent.

"Thank you," she said stiffly. "I can take care of myself." I noticed a cunning smile in play about her eyes and mouth as we entered the great dining hall. "I only hope you can," she added.

The same feeling of awe as that evoked by the blue room again enveloped me as I stared at the dining hall: done in red karri wood the walls glistened oppressively, and the anonymity of panels was affected only by an unbroken mural dropping down six feet from the ceiling.

In one corner stood a statue of Admiral de Ruyter, victorious over the British in the seventeenth century; the remaining corners were bare as were the walls, and only heavy silk curtains and an enormous chandelier gave further decorative touch to the room, excepting, of course, the huge table, and heavy brass-studded European chairs of an era past. The table was gorgeously set, and a cream-colored napkin with a red tressure bearing a gold quatrefoil framed each place card.

I was becoming used to my host's vagaries; the beautiful as well as the detestable found immoderate boundaries, reminding me again of his cruelty to the blacks that night, of the dog's eyes before the sea monster. The too heavy sterling tools, a too red surface of karri, joined, like the personalities of Sidneye, a too white ceiling.

Teleia dispelled my growing sense of malaise with: "Are you visiting the pool tonight?"

"I don't know," I answered, searching her eyes. "I'll no doubt have my hands full here."

She turned her face up to mine and said in all seriousness, "Yes, Mijnheer, I'm afraid you will. However —"

The others joined us before she could say more, so I buried my curiosity and took the seat of honor on the right of Mayrant Ruysdaal Sidneye. I could not understand why the table was set for ten when only nine were there. To my right sat Teleia, and next to her Bullit, then Jan; at the far end of the table was van Schreeven, and returning on the opposite side the Moluccan, Carter, and van Arken, in order named, leaving the seat directly opposite me, on the host's left, vacant. I had not long to wonder, however, for as the army of Malays — dressed in Paisley turbans, white high-collared jackets with braided shoulders, white trousers, and shoeless — took their places, Sidneye announced the tardy guest.

As he said the words I turned toward the door and saw him, the apparition of the Sydney courtroom, the chief mate of the *Red Witch* — Mr. Loring; and he was seated opposite me, with nothing to curtain the gleam of his eyes.

3

In my travels I had heard of it; I had once, when the *Quean of Melbourne* had been chased by a storm into the harbor of Batavia, been exposed to it, but never had I met squarely that famous epicurean delight of Java, *rystafel*, meaning rice table.

A score of servants were required to serve the traditional meal.

The first boy came with white rice, the next with a curry; number three boy trotted forth with a huge chicken loaf; number four arrived with boar en casserole, and number five with broiled jacks and pompano; another fowl dish followed in spicy sauce; then an interval of bamboo roots; and another dish, the roast of young *karbau* fresh from the spit; flounder done in a Chinese sauce, unlike anything I had ever tasted, was followed by rare nuts and condiments. Tiny shellfish, oysters en brochette, and even clam steaks, large and succulent in palatable sauces, joined small birds broiled in wine; the feast trailed off with *kroepoek*, dried fish. Many wines were placed before me during the long meal, each in harmony with the dish. *Rystafel* made a gourmand of a gourmet, and a glutton of the former.

But, as it was intended, other courses were served me, equally demanding of the senses, though not of taste and touch: Mr. Loring's presence had many facets. Conversations rippled and died out only to be followed by sharper topics under the superb control of our host. One by one the veils were lifted, and I, the guest of honor, was made to feel the keenness of every moment. With rice came Mr. Loring's penetrating stare from deep, deep caverns; augmenting the creepy travel of his eyes was the veiled amusement of host, Dokter, and Carter; with curried soup came the awkward words of Jan Hooch: "Mijnheer Loring, though fresh with Batjak by comparison to your service, I have followed your accomplishments." I was not surprised at the scowl his words evoked from Sidneye.

"We are very busy on this island, Mijnheer Rosen," said the host, retrieving discourse from its bungled state.

"Your plantation is very small," I said easily.

Sidneye, soup running down his double chin, chuckled. "You draw me on cleverly, Rosen. It is —" Teleia at that moment whispered, "Perhaps I had a purpose in warning you."

Sidneye frowned at this subdued conversation, at interlopers in general, and continued: "It is a nine-hour task to follow Dokter van Arken and his staff. You see he is my ever-obedient servant. I discovered him in floundering obscurity when he discovered in my dying body — life. That was long ago. Three years in Amsterdam, one in America, and many under my tutelage, have made of him a renowned scientist." He faced Loring with studious eyes.

"Mijnheer Loring is, as you can see, a new man." Loring's eyes glittered as they met mine, then dropped to his plate. "I brought him to Soerabaja directly after his wife began to exploit her body. Her objective was, at first, revenge, for on the night before Christmas of a year you must surely remember, Mijnheer Rosen, a Chinese messenger sought out the Mijnheer. He, thinking of reconciliation, accompanied the Oriental to a place on the waterfront of Sydney. There he was asked to wait in a small room for five minutes before removing a cloth blind from a door. It was very mysterious, but Loring obeyed the order implicitly. At exactly the moment the lights went out in his room, and —"

Loring raised his eyes to the speaker — pleading eyes, like those of the dog in the tank — and said, quavering, "Pray, Mijnheer, spare me that."

His plea was rewarded with a rigid face and cold, baleful eyes. "Calm yourself — at once!" Slowly Sidneye's face relaxed, and he turned again to face me. "Teleia, my dear, you will pay attention to another topic." She nodded and struck up a conversation with Jan, around the big frame of Mr. Bullit. Then the host continued in low tone.

"The blind was removed from the door, Mijnheer Rosen. What Loring saw held him suspended above a pit in hell. His wife, Etta Rose, had sent for him, that he might see with his own eyes what she saw when he admitted his perfidy — with a native woman. There on a couch was the woman he loved and a huge, gleaming New Guinea black."

He paused, eyed me triumphantly, a gleam of threat, hate, and joy traveling his eyes; then his heavy lids erased those lights and his next glance was that of a perfect host. "You'll enjoy this chicken loaf, Mijnheer Rosen," he said with all the charm in the world.

Loring's eyes were wet, and huge drops coursed his furrowed cheeks; his mouth was drawn tightly to corners, causing the upper lip to recede over lusterless gums and teeth that seemed to relish a gnashing of my throat. Sidneye was pleased; Dokter van Arken's eye dwelled speculatively on Loring.

"She, Mijnheer Rosen, flaunted her hips all over Sydney before she impaled herself. She jumped from a veranda onto a native spear implanted in the wild earth of New Guinea.

"Money," he said, jumping from tragedy to the first hint of the *Red Witch's* cargo, "is the root of all evil."

A helping of boar in delicious sauce, with yams and cane shoots, gave the conversation to Jan Hooch for the moment. "The boar was nowhere near me, I thought, when suddenly the native boy cried out, causing me to turn about. Not more than ten feet from me, his savage head lowered, his huge tusks gleaming, he charged with amazing speed. A shot rang out, but it missed, so I was left to defend myself. I stepped aside, more from fear than —"

Teleia sighed heavily. "It is always the same. He never deviates from, 'The boar was nowhere near me, I thought,' and he always steps aside at the fictional moment. Then —"

"A brave man, no doubt," I said, causing her to peer closely for the sarcasm I withheld. "He is your fiancé, I gather."

"Yes."

I eyed her with steely challenge.

"You have much to learn about all of us," she said. "My uncle is a strange friend and enemy — my father is merely the head of his empire. And I," she said, as though trying to deliver a message, "am a person with opinions of my own." She added: "You'll learn that."

I was learning much, I admitted: van Schreeven was a dominated being, like everyone else here; she was betrothed. But was she deeply in love with Jan, a favorite of the host? Teleia eyed her plate in silence, and I saw van Arken slip a white capsule into Loring's wineglass and beckon the man to down it; the eyes of Carter were glued to van Schreeven's face, and with the entry of number five boy with pompano, that end of the table snatched the conversation.

"Indeed," said Carter, "I enjoy sea diving. But in twenty fathoms, no." He laughed.

"Then you could not have enjoyed the trip. It was, incidentally, the seventh attempt to locate her," van Schreeven said, by way of entering a narrative. I lifted my ears, and I noticed that Loring did likewise. "My first, of course, and though I knew nothing of undersea methods, or equipment, I was in charge of the undertaking. More of a manager and purser, who followed one order — don't give up."

Carter said with a grin, "That's the type to stick like a leech. An education in diving is conducive to despair — like ample knowledge on any subject, for that matter."

"True," added van Schreeven, chuckling. "I earned the sobriquet of the Mad Skipper because of my Dutch stubbornness. Three American divers were in our employ, having failed to connect with the bank's or the Admiralty's units that preceded us. Batjak had sole claim to everything on that trip, and success would have enriched every shareholder with huge dividends.

"The *Klompen*, the wooden shoe, was heavy with tackle and provisions when we left Soerabaja on the morning of June fourth, and she steamed ahead with the sureness of all Batjak ships, on through to Manus Isle in record time. A Mandate patrol steamer escorted us through the islands and on down to the reef. We did not dare move at night once we were there, and for two days we encountered squalls and a choppy sea. Then came a fortnight of pleasant weather, half of it dead calm — excellent for our mission. For days our launch spluttered over the maze of water with an eye ever on the bottom. A hundred and a half miles around that reef, another one hundred and a half back again, and several hundred miles of exploring, netted us nothing. Only the American with the undersea camera was happy — we hauled his party along for a fee — Dutch thrift, you know."

The *Red Witch* was gradually taking over the conversation; slowly and gracefully done, I thought with an inward grin. It could not have been more skillfully handled had it resulted from painstaking rehearsal. It was, of course, prearranged. In casual tone I said: —

"You're speaking, Mijnheer, of the *Red Witch*, are you not?" And he eyed me at length before saying "Yes," in that tone that added an amused and deadly "of course."

"Back in Lorengau," continued van Schreeven, "I got the news to Soerabaja. It was impossible news, and not to the liking of the head of Batjak. I was ordered to refuel and cram the holds with provisions and do the job over again. The *Red Witch* must be there. Her treasure might be gone, but no person or group could remove the hulk. Weather charts were pored over for any disturbances of the ocean floor, and only the Rabaul eruption was given a passing frown. So again we haunted that position.

"At the edge of the ragged reef, after further weeks of fruitless search, we sent down our divers to explore the floor. One of them failed to return — only a stream of bubbles and cut lines told of his meeting a watery grave. But the *Red Witch* was not at Doppel Reef." He eyed me, as did Ruysdaal, Loring, Carter, and van Arken; their eyes asked: where is the *Red Witch?* Yes, where, Mijnheer Rosen?

"That *is* strange," I said. "Why didn't you try the spot given in the ship's log?"

"Rosen," said Sidneye, leaning forward with a leer, "let us not be facetious." Then, pulling himself back into the shell of host, he said, "Another death. Money is the root of all evil. That is the fourth death from the *Witch*."

"Only fools die for such," I said vehemently, drawing a quick rejoinder from my host. He said with a depth of meaning: "Yes. Only fools." I thought of the two men who died while the Japanese ketch towed the boats to Lorengau, of Loring's wife, of the diver.

"The fifth death came," said the host's brother, "when the sweetheart of the diver heard of the tragedy. In the French Quarter of New Orleans a young lady swallowed poison. She died on the steps of old St. Louis Cathedral."

"Gold," said Mayrant Ruysdaal Sidneye, "is the root of all evil." He hammered those words at me. "Then there was the banker who leaped from the suspension bridge in Sydney."

Before the last boy brought *kroepoek*, the list grew to nine; men and women whose epitaphs might well read: "Because of the *Red Witch* — may God damn her and hers."

And Loring, unable to contain himself, broke the awful hush that ended the meal with a peal of insane laughter. He leaned back in his chair, cackling and snorting with jerky, frothy utterances inspired by the devil himself. Dokter van Arken calmed him while our host eyed him serenely, while Teleia stared at a repulsive creature, and I — well, I viewed the whole scene calmly, for I had expected even worse. I was not in the least surprised when the crazed man at last wiped the dribble from his chin and pointed a quivering finger at me.

"You! You, Rosen! You know where the *Red Witch* went down! You're the son of the devil — like him — Ralls! I shall live to kill Ralls."

The dinner seemed, after all, a mild affair; it was that compared to the black diving to death in the lagoon. But in the days that followed its full significance reached up, like a bony hand out of the deep, to point a finger at me.

4

Teleia went to her rooms after dinner, and Loring was led back to his room by van Arken. Hooch and Carter strolled out to the veranda, with Bullit on their heels. That left me in the company of my host and van Schreeven, and of course the omnipresent Moluccan. We slowly moved toward the blue room where, I was sure, the proposition of our leaving this island would be verified or nullified. I was not kept in suspense very long; once inside the comfortable folds of a blue chair with van Schreeven and the Moluccan facing me from the divan, and Sidneye on my right, the core burst slowly out of its coverings.

"Mijnheer Rosen," said van Schreeven in conciliatory tone, "yesterday we had a talk. If you remember, I made you a proposition, the meat of which, for the benefit of my brother, had to do with your influencing your partner Ralls to quit this island at once. Right? Thank you. I believe we talked into the subject of price.

"Then my daughter walked in. Right?" I nodded.

"Mijnheer Rosen, just what is your price?" The question came rather unexpectedly and I, for once, showed surprise.

"You really surprise me, Mijnheer," I said. "Am I to understand that you are actually serious? Suppose we play our cards face up."

"You scarcely make yourself clear," he said.

"No? Well, just for the sake of conversation — but remember Sam Rosen is no fool — I'll play your game. I'll name a price — two pearls, one a perfect pear pearl, the other large, and black." My eye fell on the pearl on the puffy finger of my host, who smiled with the utmost ease, in a manner that said he was used to dispensing with trivialities by extending rare pearls as though they were gewgaws.

I sat back awaiting the hook. It came with his next words. "Only, Mijnheer, there is no reason for me to give you something for nothing. As a trader you'll understand that."

"Now we're talking sense," I returned, grinning.

"Yes," smiled Sidneye. "There's little reason for you to influence Ralls's departure — or stay.

"The afternoon your ship the *Quean of Melbourne* entered the lagoon, I was a very happy man, so pleased that I sat in my study and drank to the future — yes, while I gave an order that raised three iron bars to block the exit of the lagoon."

So Carter was right; we were prisoners on the lush island. Little Soembawa suddenly lost its beauty; its perfume turned into an odoriferous stench. And I, remembering the slabs of iron, felt myself the fool.

"Now about the pearls. Since you like pearls, friend Rosen — I'll gladly *give* you a few. You see I am most generous. But pearls have nothing to do with you and Ralls and the ship you helped scuttle. I was generous once before — that is why you and Ralls went free after the barratry charge. Why was I generous? Let us say I was biding my time. Yes, for your visit."

"Well, Mister," I said evenly, "you won't find Sam Rosen asking for any favor. And I imagine that goes for Ralls too."

"Of course," he said smiling. "But you have a choice. Ralls has none."

"And that?" I said, lowering a drink.

After some length, in which he eyed me with a merciless smile, he said, "Batjak might eventually find a place for a trader like Rosen — if he turned from Ralls to Batjak. What have you to say, Mijnheer Rosen?"

At last I said, "I don't know. There's something about your offer that is too free, that I can't quite understand. It is, of course," I said, as the idea burst into my mind, "one of your opposites. My greed is meant to rule me, is it not?"

There were indirectness and truth in his soft-spoken reply. "It seems that my agent in Rabaul, who sold Ralls a map of this pearl lagoon, found the answer to that question."

If Sidneye expected surprise to leap from my eyes at his revelation — and he did — he was due for disappointment. Carter had absorbed any shock on that score, thus saving my face as he had done before. But Sidneye hit hard and fast with his offer of leniency, and at a time when Ralls had provoked me. It would have been very easy to accept then and there, to say, "It's a deal, Mr. Sidneye." But there was more at stake, in fact everything, since only I had to live with Sam Rosen.

I frowned; I was left stranded on my own mental sands. "I'll need time to think this over," I said.

"Very well," came the answer. "We have ample time. So have you. Suppose you take a stroll in the garden — Teleia will be delighted to join you — and upon your return, if you have not reached a decision, I shall tell you a story."

I could not reach Teleia soon enough. But there she stood near the statue of Devi as if our meeting were prearranged. Perhaps it was, though she might have words designed for only my ears — so I thought with the true Rosen dubiousness fighting off any wishful thinking.

I opened the conversation with: "They deal strange cards. A deuce is an ace, and a king is a mystery." Teleia laughed lightly, knowingly, causing me to turn a sharp frown her way. "Suppose you enlighten me," I snapped, "since you know their brand of poker."

"There isn't really much to tell. I suppose you've gathered enough to know that Ralls and Rosen are long-awaited guests, particularly Ralls." We fell into step, moving down the luminous walkway, each gazing ahead in one moment, each turning in unison to stare at the other in the next. Silence claimed the period following that exchange. At last she spoke. "Of course your decision must come from your loyalty, or lack of it, to Mijnheer Ralls."

"How so?" I said, just before the answer struck me between the eyes. "Never mind, I see it now."

"Do you?" she laughed. "Aren't you forgetting your own skin?" I scoffed in an endeavor to work out of her conversational trap. "And," she added, "in saving yourself, won't you be sorry for it?"

"To put your words into the King's English, or the Queen's Dutch, you mean that your father and uncle are primarily after Ralls? That if I hold to him, woe be unto Rosen? That if I go against him, I'll always regret it?"

"Mijnheer Ralls is an interesting person," she said evasively.

"And one you'll do well to observe from a distance," I flung testily. Then I realized she said it purposely, admitting the truth while forcing the issue between Ralls and me. She remained a step ahead of me; she knew full well my feeling for her.

"I have every reason to leave Ralls on his own," I blurted.

"Have you?" She smiled. "Of course, you're in a tight spot, Mijnheer Rosen, one from which you might profitably escape."

"Which side are you on?" I said savagely.

"There are three sides, Mijnheer, the third being my own."

"Go ahead," I said, shrugging, "and talk in the stratosphere. Perhaps tomorrow I'll grasp your meaning."

"Yes. It will give you something to think about other than whimsical propositions from Batjak."

"You're not fond of Batjak, I gather. But your father —"

"I am also my mother's daughter. She was English and Balinese. She lived with me in America, where I was educated. She loved my father and — so do I; except for one fact: I cannot respect any man who is servile against his wishes." I frowned, asking myself if the moral of that statement was meant for me.

"But regardless, Mijnheer Rosen, Batjak is powerful. It is my uncle. Why don't you leave the island tonight?"

"Because, Miss van Schreeven, I never ran out on friend or foe, or a trade, in my life. Don't mock me with those eyes, for I'm not trying to impress you. No, I'm merely trying to face facts, trying to get used to the trap."

"If that is your decision — is it?" I nodded. "Then may I suggest that you seek out weaknesses in the men about you." She held out her hand to terminate our conversation. Reluctantly I took it and held it, reluctantly I allowed her disarming smile to draw it from my grasp, and at a moment when I desired recess from decisions. The night was made for us; too bad Sidneye claimed it.

"Dokter van Arken is a good subject, don't you think?" She added, "Then there's the Moluccan."

She departed, leaving me standing in the jungle of my own thoughts. Did she throw manna promiscuously, or was she a tool of Sidneye's? I thought of Carter's words: "She is, my chum Sam, the stronger lure." I sighed sadly and turned to the house. Through the window I saw the trio, host, brother, and Moluccan, sitting like statues, and I eyed

113

them for some time before moving on. I was tempted to follow Teleia, but I thought of my own words: "I never ran out on friend, or foe, or a trade."

Inside the room once more I walked to the one window, that gargantuan curtain-flanked square half shut by a bamboo blind. It loomed over me like a jinni of old, in quaint and modern dress, awaiting a signal from the corpulent Dutch conjurer to transport me to a distant decision.

"So you have not reached a decision?" said the Dutchman, breaking into my spell. "I have a very interesting story to tell," he added.

Out of the window, into my mind's eye, appeared the weak, ravenous face of Mr. Loring, the hard, cold eyes of Dokter van Arken, the penetrating calm of the Moluccan; and the mystery of my host and his strange satellites gathered in the opaque shadows beyond the painted lagoon. They faded into whimsical leniency, a proposition, and an answer. Suddenly I saw the window for what it was: a mysterious gap with a past — there was more to the scuttled ship out there in the sea than met my eye. The window in the Dutchman's house was then —

A window awaiting a house.

I turned to a drink, and my place in the blue chair. His words reached me and I fell into step with them. He began with: —

"It is the story of a quatrefoil — and a golden hind."

BOOK TWO

Quatrefoils, 1875-1925

INTRODUCTION

In THE long, lonesome wake of the Red Witch, I listened to Mayrant Ruysdaal Sidneye, ever hearing, as his strange tale unfolded, the churning foam from the stern of a dead ship whose gilded plate lay fathoms deep in the green mold of her grave. How lusterless was her echoic trail, and how like a welter of blood and foam. I followed his story. Aye, I peered beyond horizons, realizing that my image, like Ralls's, lay in the long trail of the Red Witch.

But Sidneye's, or Ruysdaal's, story follows; and it is told for its story value in story manner, with omission of that first-person narrative styling — I can give another's story a more coherent reflection by carrying it beyond the low pitch of its first blush, the spoken word.

He began with: "I was born in Amsterdam in July of eighteen hundred and seventy-five. But even at the beginning, Mijnheer Rosen, I get ahead of my story. It was thus . . ."

CHAPTER X

1

A HUGE man, evidently one of importance, slowly descended from a low-slung coach with the aid of two coachmen, and puffed considerably before scrutinizing the number on the wall a second time. He made his presence known and then preened himself while awaiting an answer. A man of proud bearing he was, and not unhandsome in a rugged sense.

A door opened as he cast an eye at the wall and then at a card he fished from a capacious pocket under an olive-green cape. Quickly he peered, lifting his eyes and jutting his head forward.

"Ah, *guten Morgen*," he grunted. "This is the address of Dokter Vrees-Teerink Sidneye? You are not Frau Sidneye's maid?"

"Oh no, Mijnheer —" The startled young lady of Oranje Street, forty-seven, recognized her error of address as she eyed the card. "Pardon, Herr von Streicher, Your Excellency — you see I'd forgotten. But I am her sister."

"It has been some time since I visited Herr Dokter, Fräulein, so I am not at fault for my error. He has married since I have visited. That is great. Indeed!"

He saw one to whom nature had given all the outward attributes of fecundity: plump cheeks, rosy and wholesome, framed by a sandy mass of hair, were centered by a piquant nose and blood-red lips; and the blue of her wide eyes told more than the slender neck, or the ripe bosom above a thin waist. She demanded an eye, thus freeing the observer from any guilt in viewing her.

"Frau Sidneye is to be congratulated on keeping such rare beauty in her family," said the German. "Hm-m. *Donnerwetter!*"

Blushing, she invited him inside. "The Dokter is expecting you. He awaits you in his office." Her eyes involuntarily moved to a portrait of Louis Napoleon, who had been dead some two years. The German's eyes followed; he frowned. The Dokter Sidneye had once attended the

Emperor, and a strange friendship had sprung up between the ill-assorted pair: Dokter Sidneye, by virtue of specializing, an oddity far ahead of the times, was in demand among those whose ailments were drawn to his lucrative hobby, be they prince or pauper residing in Barcelona, Bristol, Paris, or near the Zuider Zee.

"Herr Dokter, yes," he said. "And you also expected me, I see."

"Of course, Your Excellency, since my sister's illustrious husband advised me so. It is a great honor," she said, smiling feebly.

Von Streicher's second use of the word *Donnerwetter* was under his breath. Slowly he removed the cape from his barrel-like shoulders and placed a ham hand over the silk lining in the crook of his arm. He posed purposely, pardonably, for he was an impressive example of Prussia's military might, of the age of von Moltke and Bismarck. His eyes, however, were not boastful, although the timid Dutch in the young woman shuddered. His lips again lifted as his eyes fell to her breasts in a disrobing stare. Then his eyes seemed to ask her pardon.

"This way, Your Excellency," she said. The door closed behind him and she leaned heavily against it, her misty eyes staring at the wall of the far room. Then without a word she gathered her skirts and ran up the steps as fast as possible. Once in her room she flung herself across the bed and gave in to long, hard sobs.

There were many things that could have evoked such a mood in Zulinde Maria Schouten, the least of which might have been the man she had shown into the office. The last two days had taxed everyone in the Sidneye clan, for this time it was the wife of the Dokter, himself, and her own blood sister, who gave a belly swollen with child to the slow, obdurate pains of labor; at last, in the early evening before, the pains quickened and the unbearable dilating of the pelvis brought cries of anguish — and a son to the Sidneyes. The day was July the thirteenth, in the year of eighteen hundred and seventy-five. For hours fat Mama Sidneye and thin Mama Schouten had argued the name he should carry.

"Teerink, bah!" shouted the irate grandmother on the father's side to the recalcitrant equal on the mother's side. "Have I not used that twice — no, thrice? Vrees-Teerink, Pieter Teerink, and then Wilhelm-Teerink. Is it not worn by the handle until slick? Bah!"

"Then Hanszoon is such a pretty name for a he," suggested Mother Schouten.

"Hanszoon! Enough of the race carry the name. I had thought of naming him Kisar, but the name —"

"You," countered the other, "just you have a right to name my grandson? I hereby name him Roentjin Sidneye, after my great-uncle in Zuid-Holland! Attest me, Mevrouw Sidneye."

"That I shall not do! Did you furnish the he of the union, the he before it? No, I bore in great pain the thirteen-pound boy who now brings me grandchild. Humph, not so? Rather would I roll a cheese with my nose all the way to Zwolle!"

Frail Mama Schouten sighed, trained her eyes on the garment she mended, and hummed a tune out of pure spite, hoping to pique the other further. But buxom Mama to the great Dokter himself decided two could play such a game and she gave her voice a tune to drown out the other.

Or Zulinde Maria might have again let her thoughts roam to her sweetheart, one Hansel Stefan Meer, a Dutch sailor whom the family intensely disliked. Stefan had been at sea, plying between New Guinea and Rotterdam. Several months had elapsed since that meeting on the canal barge, and no letter had come from him. His departure had been a huff that volleyed into an explosion. Said he: "Then my weak Zulinde, have a choir boy for your man — the blue milk of his veins will match yours, and I, Hansel Stefan Meer, shall find a creamy lass, be she brown, yellow, or black. Either you marry me on my return, or my threat shall be fulfilled!"

Then, only yesterday morning, the barge boy had arrived with a tulip and a message: Stefan was in the city!

Under pretext of visiting the wharves for juicy fruits from the tropic islands to delight her laboring sister, she met the huge, bronzed, sandy-haired man she loved.

"Ah, my Zulinde, my pretty one!" he exclaimed. And his arms had roughly held her while she murmured, "Dear Stefan, it is so good to feel your strong arms," and he kissed her hungrily.

"Come, my cousin awaits. He has goods to run and we have the day with him."

"But I must hurry home, Stefan. Indeed. My sister is expecting any hour." Reasonable enough an excuse, he admitted in silence, but aloud he said: "Of all the times! I wait for months and this — this boy — he should wait until the day I return. May he have a worse luck when he reaches thirty and one. May he trip on a native girl and see twins, brown or black — aye, just fruits for keeping me in wait."

"Stefan! You don't mean that. Say you don't. When it is over I shall meet you here."

"Very well," he grunted. "Then I hope the unborn lad does not have twins when thirty and one — one will do him."

119

"Ah, Stefan, you're wonderful. I'd go to the end of the world with you, even if it isn't a boy my sister bears. My sweet," she said laughing, "if it isn't a boy, what then?"

"'Twill be a boy, mind you that. But Godspeed, and hurry back to me — or else I'll marry with seven harlots across the sea."

Secretly she called on Mama Sidneye for advice: she loved the sailor; he loved her; could she not change her heart, and thereby influence the others? The reply: "Well, child, as much as I'd enjoy going against your mother, I must say no. You cannot marry with so shiftless a man." Then: "So he is in Holland again! So! Then you do not leave this house. If you do, the milk of your sister's teats will curdle. Mark you, Zulinde Maria! Mark you well!"

Zulinde had contained her opposing forces until von Streicher arrived. All morning, and all the last night, the excitement of the new arrival held her emotions on a track that detoured sobs and thoughts of life without her beloved Stefan. But with the coming of the German the well of hot tears burst. As she lay in her room she was given to wonder: why should he upset her, what did he mean to her? Nothing, of course; he was the visible excuse for the tears when they were for dear Stefan who paced the streets awaiting her. Stefan had never disrobed her with his eyes, like the German. If he had — she suddenly sat up, startled — yes, from Stefan, she would not mind; suddenly she wondered why he had not.

2

"*Goeden dag*, Herr von Streicher, Your Excellency," said Dokter Sidneye, forcing a smile. "I have been expecting you."

His Excellency bowed in Prussian fashion, and adjusted his monocle before peering at the book-lined walls, the various apparatus of a professional man, and, at last, at the Dokter himself. A man of medium height, with dark skin, black hair, and Vandyke beard, met his eye; but a cold stare gave an unusual light to the calm, dreamy eyes, causing the observing von Streicher a faint smile. He advanced with heavy and choppy steps, aware that Sidneye's jaw, small-boned like the nose and chin, remained at a proud angle, matching, as it were, the defiance of dark, heavy-lashed eyes and erect shoulders.

"Must you bristle, Herr Dokter?" he put amicably.

"Have a chair, Your Excellency." The German obeyed, straddling the seat and folding his arms over the chair back, as he was wont to do in the long past. "I should apologize for my lack of courtesy, Streicher," he said, dropping all other address, "but I think we know each other. And, too, I am a bit weary — my wife delivered me a son last evening."

"Ah. Congratulations, Herr Dokter. Your first, I believe. Remember, Teerink, our pledge when in the university at Leipzig? Even then I was your greatest admirer."

"I remember," grunted the Dokter, "well." His heavy brow clouded and he turned in his screw chair to face a sheaf of papers on the desk top.

"You will, of course, keep your word, even though we are, shall we say, at odds." The words fell from the booted man in suppliant tone, causing the Dokter to face him with sharp challenge.

"Indeed, Your Excellency. A Sidneye never forgets the value of a promise." His shoulders sagged perceptibly. "Yes," said the Dokter, "he shall be named after you." Without further ado he pulled a cord and a muffled ringing of a bell sounded from another part of the house. Before long a fat woman opened the door and asked to be of service to the master.

"You will go to my mother and my wife with this message, Anna," said the bearded man with such force that the maid blinked. "Advise them that I have named the boy — Mayrant." For long moments she stared stupidly, departing only after frowning stares dispelled her trance.

"Now, Your Excellency, we shall finish the business at hand."

"Well done, Teerink. Well done. But you do not congratulate me upon my great office. You were in my thoughts, dear friend, when the great Chancellor von Bismarck-Schönhausen bestowed upon me high diplomatic honors in your country. Have you no word for my eager ears, no compliments other than the formality of address?"

"That is all, Mayrant. I abhor pretense, so I can only say I wish to God you'd died when in France. You can bring me nothing but trouble. You have come to collect, I take it. I regret that we have no set figures to deal with, for then I could borrow, or pawn, or else go to jail and be done with you. But, of course, your interest is less of money and more of the pound of flesh around my heart."

"Come, Teerink, where are your manners? Few Dutch folk would greet an old friend with such acid. I should enjoy a goblet of the choice vintage you once served."

Dokter Sidneye arose, pulled the cord for the second time, and gave himself to pacing, his fingers interlaced behind him. He stopped short and turned his head when the unwelcome visitor put into slow words a hint of his price: —

"A man in your position among his countrymen, Teerink, should possess the key to many of the intricacies of an inventive race. You are of high rank with financiers, as well as those at the University of Leiden. Is it not so, Teerink?"

"I listen, Your Excellency."

"In Zaandam, Utrecht, Groningen, besides Rotterdam and Amsterdam, there are various tidbits that interest my government. At Bergen-op-Zoom there is another. Of course, I am not at liberty to peer openly at the cores of *der Nederlanders'* fruits, Teerink."

"*Neen*," agreed the other, with noticeable satisfaction. "You are not."

"But, *mein* friend, you are."

The door opened and the same buxom woman appeared, wiping at her red eyes and beslobbered nose. Both men knew the name had not been received with joy, though neither remarked upon it. Wine was ordered and she hastily retreated. The host was first to speak.

"So you would have me betray my country."

"Your perception is magnified, Teerink, for, as you know, one can cloak perfidy in purple or sackcloth, depending on the desirability of the subject at hand. Consider your country in the light of a woman. Perhaps one doesn't want the whole woman, her aches, pains, and voluble organs. But only a part of her. Desire cloaks her in purple silk, though her tongue remains. You have desired in your time."

"Yes, how well you know."

The wine arrived and Teerink Sidneye poured. The German raised his glass with: —

"To our prosperity, Teerink. To a mending of our friendship."

"To the devil himself," replied the other.

"As I was saying there are things my country wants. Then, too, there are certain favors I, your close friend and confidant, would ask."

"It is still my privilege to refuse," said Sidneye, in a tone that seemed to find strength in the thought.

"But you won't. You must not forget, Dokter Sidneye, that in the year of eighteen hundred and sixty-seven a renowned specialist performed a very delicate operation in the rooms of Leiden; that he, protesting because of its illegality, was finally persuaded by the entourage of foreign notables to put science first — man-made laws second. That he failed, *we* know, and only failure creates crime. And crime, dear Dokter," he said sadly, "once uncovered, begets notoriety. Many are the heads that would fall in shame, many are the proud families that would flee like lowly gypsies should the sworn facts be loosed. The dossiers on the case are strong, authenticated, and they slept in peace until of late. Let us, dear Dokter Sidneye, work together to keep them that way. That is one of the reasons for my visit."

"Mayrant," said the Dokter with the superb calm of hatred ringing in his voice, "I placed my trust in you, a friend — and more — a friend among friends, I thought. How well you disguised your cunning and ruthless ambition. You, as my trusted secretary, connived with the war lords of Prussia on the one hand, and used my position and close friendship on the other as a steppingstone.

"That night, in the eating place in Kalverstraat, when you told me you were through with your apprenticeship, that you planned to use your knowledge for the furthering of your ambition, I was grieved. I offered my complete assistance. Did I not? But you said, 'I shall call upon you in due time.' You did. My influence was used in your country, my money, my labor, my very soul, in your behalf. I was building you into a colossal figure that sucked more of my blood as it increased in size."

"For which I ask your forgiveness," came the patient interruption.

"And," Sidneye's voice rose to a whine of anger, "now you return for all that is left. How can you? How can you, Mayrant Streicher!"

The unwanted guest sighed bitterly, frowning. "Teerink, I remember how you were duped by the Count. I regret that I turned your mind to that momentous decision of your career." His outward sincerity was lost on the Dokter.

"Stop it, Mayrant!"

"And remember the woman. How she lived for two days I don't know. I only remember her cries."

"Yes," came the weak reply. "Success would have brought science out of its darkened era. But —"

"Failure," Streicher said in resignation, "brought crime."

"What is it you want?" Helplessness and despair cloaked the words.

"And the perfidious Count," said the other, slowly, pensively, "refused my demands. Strangely, he was shot by one of our soldiers when he entered Paris. Justice." For moments he stared at the far window, then he got out of his chair and removed a packet of papers from an inner pocket.

"These," he said gruffly, as if the ordeal taxed him, "are the demands my country makes of me. I can only turn to you, Teerink." He walked to the window, turning his back on the Dokter.

With sagging head the Dokter slowly eyed the papers. Each sheet seemed to tug at his neck muscles, dragging lower the bearded face. Without a murmur or added frown, he slowly turned the sheets until the last was gleaned of its ignominious contents. Slowly he poured wine; then without a change of expression he added a powder. The mixture was swallowed in a single gulp. His face turned a chalky gray and he moved the papers aside and slowly lowered his head to folded arms.

"Well?" The rasping word came from Streicher. He turned about and walked to the desk, where he stood with arms akimbo and feet planted wide apart.

"Well!" The word rang impatiently. It sounded for the third time; only a spasmodic quiver met the eyes of Streicher — Dokter Vrees-Teerink Sidneye did not respond to words.

The German gently moved the head back and stared. Slowly he relaxed, and the form of the Dokter crumpled in the chair and fell to the floor. The bull neck of the benumbed visitor protruded and his beady eyes bulged in their sockets; a hand crumpled into a fist while thick lips curved slowly and savagely downward, as if seeking the flesh of his purple jowls. Then he retrieved his papers and searched out recent letters demanding money from Sidneye for secrecy.

He pulled the cord, as if to give his importune mission a climax. Then he stood, affrighted, trying to convince his turbulent mind of his own innocence.

It was only human that he should seek self-exoneration.

3

Stefan Meer was a godsend to the entire family during the period of anguish. Even Mama Sidneye eyed him without the ferocity of old, giving in its stead contemplative glances that harbored admiration for a man so able to take care of himself and others. Mama Schouten was no less convinced, though she, like her portly parallel, kept her opinions out of reach of her tongue.

The funeral, on a damp Sunday, was attended by the great, near great, and scores of devoted commoners; and not inconspicuous in the ill-assorted coterie was the man who wore the ribbon and cross of the Imperial German Government, a great man and a product of the deceased. He, in days gone by, had given his best face and humor to Mevrouw Sidneye. But he had changed, she observed with a frown, and he did not mourn in tone or word: perhaps his grief was of the deeper sort. She vividly remembered his face when, at the maid's scream, she ran the stairs to find her son dead; his words, "Mother Sidneye, my friend has departed from us," came from a face that was flushed and sorely confused. That, she termed, was the extent of outward grief in many folk.

Von Streicher's frequent visits to forty-seven Oranje Street were viewed with trepidation by Zulinde, for his eyes were ever the same as on that morning she had first felt them; and, too, he always managed to draw her off from the others that he might talk without the interference of curious eyes and ears.

It was on a warm afternoon two weeks and a day after the burial that he asked if he might enjoy Zulinde's company for a stroll: there were questions he must ask regarding certain callers who had done business with her sister's husband. His steady eye beat down all lame excuses she offered, and when he laughed and said to Mama Sidneye, "Is she afraid of me?" and the old lady replied, "Of course not, she merely awaits her lover Stefan," she blushed profusely and ran to her room.

"I tell you," Zulinde said to the matriarch after he departed, "he is a harbinger of evil. Watch him, Mama mine, he intends us harm."

"Nay, child," she answered, cackling, "he is but a man with an eye for a woman's charms."

"That and more!" came the retort. "When can Stefan and I wed?"

"Hush! Have you no respect for the dead? Shame on you, Zulinde Schouten! Thank heavens, you're not my child. Get you gone at once and see about your nephew's comfort."

"But — you don't understand, Mama mine. Listen to me — Stefan sails with the tide two days hence. He's going away."

"And you, Zulinde, you'd leave your sister with a child not three weeks in this world?"

"No — yes. Yes! I'd leave everyone and everything for Stefan Meer! And —" She got to her feet and walked to the window. "What's more, I shall!"

"*Neen,*" retorted the old lady, flinging her cap to the bed, and bending over her needles once more. At that moment Mama Schouten entered the room and, having heard only Mama Sidneye's negative rejoinder, she said with heat, "I say yes!"

"Yes to what, long nose?" said Mother Sidneye. "A guilder for you if you know of what we speak."

"I only know that you're wrong," snapped the Schouten side of the family. "Besides, Stefan is downstairs, and from the shape of his brow he's in a black mood!"

"Am I," cried the irate Stefan, when the form of his sweetheart showed at the landing, "to be tossed around for the bloody *Hansworst* who keeps visiting here? Am I to be put off forever? First it was the babe, and now the excuse of mourning." He stalked forward and planted his feet in fighting pose that complimented his handsome, ruddy face and sandy, short-cropped locks. "Am I to marry with you or not? Am I to sail with a wife or leave a purposeless coquette in my wake?" He said that and more, every word growing in volume.

She stood on the fifth step smiling at him, loving the sight of her man in temper. "Rave on, Stefan Meer," she returned lightly. "And when your steam is gone, I shall answer you."

"With what?" his bass voice roared. "More excuses?"

"No, Stefan, my love — with a promise to marry you on the morrow. Mijnheer Meer, my husband!"

Shocked, he could only gape awkwardly. The temper he had fanned so diligently was not to be wasted; it howled for outlet, and the *zeeman*, ever prone to obey the call of the deck, again flared forth.

"So! You, at last, decide. And why have you waited for days, months, and — why?" he thundered. "When you're my wife I'll make you over to suit me!"

She ran to his arms with, "Do, Stefan. I do so want to suit you." Her arms went about his strong shoulders, and the fire of his eyes retreated, leaving only the ashes of slow, smoldering coals. "And Stefan, with the whole world before us, our lives shall join our hearts in beating in double time for what we've missed. My Stefan, kiss me and say you love me." Her face was a glowing thing of beauty that radiated joy.

He frowned into his smile and said gruffly, "Kiss you, I shall. And when we're married I'll beat you every morning. Do you mind?"

"Never, my Stefan — begin now." Their laughter reached the ears of the two women at the head of the stairs and for once they exchanged smiles of agreement. Said the Schouten side, "Love is wonderful, isn't it?"

"Indeed," came the answer, followed by a gruff scowl and, "Who says so?"

CHAPTER XI

1

A FOPPISH man sounded the knocker at forty-seven Oranje Street at eight on the morning following Zulinde's declaration of independence. He gave an important sealed flap to the maid, with a request for an immediate reply. Soon he faced Mama Sidneye, who said in bewildered manner: —

"Tell Herr von Streicher we shall gladly oblige him with a conference at ten sharp. But why everyone should be there I do not know. Do you?"

"*Nein*, Frau Sidneye," came the blunt reply. "His Excellency scarcely confides in an underling."

"Then begone with you, my man," she said. "A sassy tongue is ever in a German head." She slammed the door and turned about, retraced her steps to Zulinde's room where preparations for a hasty wedding had reached an exciting stage.

"I'm afraid you'll have to be with us at ten, my dear child." She passed the note to the puzzled girl.

"Oh, he'll not need me," Zulinde cried. "For am I not of small consequence in matters of business? And, too, I'd rather not spoil my wedding day with the sight of him. Oh, Mama mine, does the rose go with this hood? Tell me —"

"Zulinde," said the elder woman with unusual seriousness, "you must be in the reception room at ten."

"And why should I come? I shall not!"

But at five minutes past ten she sat in a straight-back chair. Her mind was a whirl of valises, petticoats, capes, dresses, ribbons, and colors. Mama Sidneye frowned at her, causing her to placate the outward show of impatience. To her right sat her mother and sister, the baby in crib between them; thus the visitor sat facing her, and his eyes, while dwelling upon the others, swept her at every turn. And once he frowned at the foot she tapped impatiently against the floor; she placed her other foot atop it hurriedly, for her toes were recalcitrant things. Then, before she was aware of her error, she blurted forth: —

"Mama, my slippers! Will they — Oh!" The back of her hand swiftly covered her mouth.

"Fräulein Schouten," said the visitor, "you should pay close attention."

"Yes, Your Excellency," she replied meekly.

"Forgive her," said her mother, smiling, "but she is to be married this evening and her mind is naturally upset."

"Oh!" he said, surprised. "I had not heard. Perhaps —" He frowned, chopping short his words.

Zulinde's head cocked in bewildered fashion and her red lips parted slightly; the widow asked if the matter at hand might be serious, and von Streicher answered with a sober nod. Mama Sidneye screwed her face about and twitched her nose, and gave everyone there a look that

127

said she wanted no more interruptions. To Streicher she said: "Get down to facts, my boy."

"Very well. But I must remark upon the gravity of the situation — what I am about to relate caused the death of my friend Teerink." He paused for effect. "My sorrow for all of you in your hours of trial, and my aversion to the subject at hand, are only exceeded by attending duty. It was so when I came here to see Teerink.

"Now, I find it my sad obligation to bring out of the past a skeleton in Teerink's closet, a part of every man's life, I'm sure, no matter his claim to honorable achievement. I am truly grieved, Mother Sidneye, to acquaint you and yours with such facts, and only the pressing demands of those who would resort to chicanery could unseal my lips."

Zulinde's frowns were no less real than those of her kin; thus she shelved Stefan and the nuptials and lent an ear to the topic.

"It seems that in the year of 'sixty-seven certain intrigue flourished among wealthy and titled persons of a near-by country. It had to do with money, and passions — hate, greed, and wantonness. An heiress found herself married to a Count whose eroticism knew no bounds. He, she realized, sought her money, and was bent on seducing her younger sister. Such will suffice to explain the setting. The Count purposely brought about his wife's ill health, and then turned with feigned anxiety to the medical profession. Not a surgeon in France would do more than render diagnosis; there was constant fear of a loose tongue, scandal, and ruin.

"At that time — it was in April, I remember — I was, as you, Mother Sidneye, will verify, your son's closest friend and able secretary. The Count called for a conference and Teerink examined the written statements from surgeons of probity, many of them his fellow students at Leipzig and Leiden. I, in the capacity of business manager and adviser, listened, and then sought out cases, and, at last, the legality of that which the Count earnestly beseeched.

"The case interested Teerink, not from any sentiment or fee: science flung the challenge and he was sorely tempted to run the corridors of the unethical and illegal in an attempt to master that which baffled the medical world. I turned thumbs down on the case, advising that he risked, at even odds, professional suicide. I told him that failure would gnaw out his heart. Together we gave that decision to the Count who, amid tears of anguish, trebled the fee. At the moment I was tempted, by the monetary reward of course; and Teerink — well, the man's despair, plus the voice of the fickle goddess of science — reversed our decision." Streicher sighed, wiped at his misty eyes, and continued: —

128

"The case was falsified. Everyone was sworn to secrecy — and the great failure that cost a woman's life remained a secret until two months ago. Strife and impaired fortunes among the Count's friends resulted in conspiracy, and money could silence only one faction.

"Thus I, known to be a friend of Teerink, was sought out for the post of intermediator. A million francs was demanded by one group, high office by the other. Checking covertly, I found Teerink could not afford such a sum, even with the aid of his friends; that the Dokters in question were unsuited for any institution of learning. Their aspirations were, on the whole, ludicrous. But I must, I said, with the aid of Teerink, seek improvisations. Their gain would, of course, be nothing if the case found an airing, so I sought compromises of time and terms even before visiting here." He laboriously took his weight from the chair and paced the floor in silence. Then he said, "Thus the matter stands."

After long moments, in which the family stared straight ahead and not at each other, Mama Sidneye broke the silence. "Even with his death the matter stands? How can he seek office for men when he is dead?"

"That is why I have kept the matter a secret since the funeral," answered Streicher. "I have spared no effort to free the good name of Sidneye from ignominy since that day. Unfortunately the demand persists from both groups who now aim in accord — money. The sum jumps to two million francs."

"Mayrant Streicher," said Mama Sidneye pointedly, "how do we know all this to be true? My son grew cold toward you some years back, I remember. He said nothing, but then a woman sees things. I have always loved you, Mayrant, but in this matter I trust nothing but facts."

"Very well," said the man in resigned tone. "You may give these papers perusal. The names of the culprits are obliterated, for reasons of an agreement we made — for the safety of all — until the case is settled."

She read avidly, her face assuming mingled surprise and anger. "*Groote genade!* So it is true, Mijnheer."

"It is true," he said gravely.

"What do my husband's friends say to all this, Mayrant?"

"Frau Sidneye! Should I be so indiscreet as to consult them?"

"True. True," she said.

Herr von Streicher slowly walked to the window, his enormous hands at his back moving in agitated manner. There, with his back to them, he said with compassion: "There is no fame or disgrace in this world to compare with that which comes posthumously." He repeated his words more slowly. "Fortunately Teerink lives — now — the dead recipient of fame. Dishonor to a great man becomes even greater by contrast. And," he turned to face them one by one, "the son who bears his name finds a bitter legacy."

The widow turned her wet eyes upon the crib and sobbed bitterly. The matriarch scolded her severely, then said, "Two million francs, how many guilders is that?"

His Excellency answered with the truth. "Ten times as many as you can raise."

"Mayrant, what shall we do?" implored Mama Sidneye. "Can we compromise?"

"Read the last letter in the sheaf, Frau Sidneye," advised the man with a hopeless gesture.

She turned to the page and read: —

"'In answer to your request of the sixteenth of July, wherein you' — I'm not so good at French, Mayrant. Finish it." He took the paper and continued: —

Wherein you propose a settlement within the means of the family, namely two hundred thousand francs, we respectfully regret, Your Excellency, that we are less interested in means and more in our demands. The source of the payment is *à propos de rien* — irrelevant. Unless the money is delivered by the next month beginning we have decided to place the matter before the medical world. Surely the family of Monseigneur Sidneye can find certain men of science ready to clear the name of any impending dishonor.

With a flourish he affixed the paper to the sheaf, and said, "That is that."

2

The noon hour came, and with it a message from Stefan. It was handed Zulinde by the fat woman, who eyed everyone curiously and departed reluctantly with wide eyes. Widow Sidneye cried and the matriarch Sidneye scowled and beat a staccato on the arm of her chair with one hand while gnawing at a nail of the other; Mama Schouten sat in strained, worried silence, and Zulinde scarcely held the face of a bride-to-be — she sat mouth agape, staring into space. And her note: "It is from him, Miss," was accepted without any change

130

of expression. It was only when she read that her eyes softened and a faint trace of sunshine lighted her face. The note: —

My Zulinde, I can hardly await the hour. We shall stay the night in your new home — the *Quatrefoil*. She sails at dawn with the new bride, and may God bless her voyage and her bride.

Devotedly —

HANSEL STEFAN MEER

"Perhaps," she said apologetically, "I should go. I have much to do." She eyed her mother and Mama Sidneye, who offered no objection, and arose to go. "It is all right, sister dear?"

"Of course, Zulinde." A hand squeezed hers, and she started for the hallway.

"I apologize, Fräulein," said von Streicher, "But business is business and we must solve this problem."

"I understand, Your Excellency," said Zulinde.

Said Mama Schouten, "Mayrant is a friend in need."

"Have you any solution, any idea of how we can save ourselves?" queried Mama Sidneye.

"I am beginning, Mother of my friend, to generate an idea. Suppose you retire to your noonday duties and leave me in thought."

"Would you like sliced sausages, cheese, and a salt herring, Mijnheer?" said Mevrouw Schouten as they made ready to depart.

"*Nein*, only schnapps." He stood and bowed them out with, "*Guten Morgen*."

As the door closed behind them he stood facing it with arms folded, frowning in review of the short past. He moved away to await the maid's entry with schnapps. She was not long in coming and, once relieved of her burden, she seemed in no hurry to depart.

He said, grinning up at her, "What would you give to learn our secret — a kiss?" He seemed a jovial sort, and she, a merry, curious one, tittered and turned about coyly.

"How you tease. But all great men are given to their moments," she said, returning slowly to the center of the room. "And what a big man you are, Mijnheer. My Joris weighs, I venture, only a half as much."

"Which," he said, eyeing her intently, "makes you an unfortunate woman."

131

"How so?" she said flippantly, only to receive a laugh, and: "Why, a man, to properly mate a woman, should be able to lift her to a kiss Shall I show you?"

"*Neen, neen,*" she said. "I'll take your word. I'm afraid Joris can't do that, however. Once when I was yet single a *zeeman* lifted me and carried me fifty meters to a grassy *polder*. He was — ah how wonderful he was."

"And when he put you down, what then?" he said. She tittered and moved toward the door. "So you don't want to know what transpired here this morning? For a kiss, I'll tell you."

"What is one kiss, Mijnheer? I could spare it, but so great a man as yourself is easy to make breathe hard. The innkeeper in my home village did just that, and I would laugh at his reddened face."

"You're a vixen, my sweet one," he returned, laughing. "But I'm afraid you could not make me redden or breathe hard. Want to try?" He moved to the door and noiselessly shot the bolt.

She did not, she put to words, but her eyes danced with challenge. In another moment he had her hand in his, roughly kissing it, his lips traveling her arm. Soon he held her close, and she gradually loosened her hold on the tray and let it slide to the floor by the table. There it remained unnoticed for many long minutes.

At the door she said, "Mijnheer, I forgot to ask about the secret." Her face was flushed and she held the tray under one arm against her heaving bosom while she sought to arrange her disheveled hair.

"My dear woman," he said, the blood pounding at his temples, "haven't you been amply rewarded on this day?"

She unlocked the door, smiled at him appraisingly and answered, "Indeed. I made you breathe hard, did I not?"

Von Streicher threw back his head and laughed. With the heavy door between them, he said, "Peasant bitch, fool Joris is welcome to you."

3

Zulinde entered the room after her kin and found her chair of the morning. She loathed the sad interruption — there was so much yet undone, and, too, the meeting spread a pall over the house on a day when hearts should be merry. Stefan beckoned, and she smiled as she gazed at the long seat covered with worn silk and a crocheted piece; there Stefan's strong arms, the red and hairy limbs of a brave *zeeman*, had encircled her while he planned their future. She did not know what the German friend of the family had in mind — only that it would be, of course, a heroic attempt to save the baby, and all of them for that matter, from disgrace. Von Streicher was soon into the subject.

"Frauen and Fräulein," said His Excellency. "I had hopes of giving you a reasonable solution to the case. My mind has been racked in your absence for a way out of this. Of course I have influence, but using it is almost next to impossible." He stood and began pacing.

"I could," he continued, "bring to bear certain diplomatic pressure to quiet them. I could, I say, except for two reasons — one of which is that the dastards could squeal at my first move. However, there is a way to stop them." He debated aloud, more to himself than to his rapt audience.

"Yes, that would stop them!" he exclaimed. "My government boasts of the greatest secret network in the world. Such could close the matter without bloodshed."

He sent a hopeful smile in the direction of the aged Mevrouw Sidneye and said, stopping in his tracks, "Mother Sidneye, I have the solution! It is superb!"

"Yes?" she said.

"It is like this. I shall visit our capital. Our mighty Prince must bid me Godspeed. But — but wait. I have forgotten something." A cloud enveloped his brow and he sat down, a beaten man.

"What have you forgotten — Mayrant?" the mother of the Dokter said, her voice trembling. "I thought you could save us!" It was her first token of despair; skyrocketing hopes felt a jerking of the props from under them.

"I, Mother, have forgotten myself — my office." He eyed her fiercely, running agitated fingers through bristling hair. "I forget that even a man in my position cannot approach the rulers of Prussia with a motive that scarcely concerns him. They would laugh at me, and I should lose face. For what — they would say — a mere whim? They would say, 'We have a man in *der Nederlands* who is crotchety, who deals in vagaries.' Worse, though, their reply would be: '*Verboten!*'"

He was again on his feet. "'Herr Streicher,' they would say to me, 'are you representing us or your friends in the Low Country?' Then I would be asked: 'Are these people of your family?' I must say they are not, and receive for reply, 'It is too bad, Herr Streicher, for if they were we should take rapid steps to serve you — effectively.' Yes, yes, I should know. Too long have I known my masters."

133

Mama Sidneye leaned forward and asked, "You mean that if you were of us —"

He laughed hopelessly and shrugged, then walked to the window. "A thousand marks that such would prove true."

Heavy silence pervaded, and the builder of that helpless quiet let it hang. In sadness he walked to the table, and emitting a long sigh, reached for his gloves and stick. He was departing. The mother of the baby turned affrighted eyes upon him. Helplessly she faced her mother and her dead husband's mother.

"I regret, Frauen, and Fräulein," he said in conclusion, "there is nothing I can do."

"Wait, Mayrant — wait!" The weak plea came from a groping old lady who stared straight ahead.

"Yes, Mother," he said before turning to the crib. "Poor little Mayrant Sidneye. How I wish I could save his good name."

"Mayrant." The word came from deep within the old lady; it was commanding, strong, and challenging. "Mayrant, I shall adopt you."

"Nothing would please me more," he said. "But a stronger tie would be my government's demand."

"Then, then — Mayrant Streicher, do us a favor?"

"I stand ready with my very life," he said, with such sincerity that he was, himself, moved by its tone.

"Then, Mayrant, take Zulinde for your wife!"

"*Neen!*" It came in a shriek from Zulinde. "It cannot be!"

"*Nein,*" Streicher said after a moment.

Mama Sidneye was on her knees before the distraught girl. In another moment her son's widow, the blood sister of Zulinde, joined her; together they begged: "It would be for only a time — Stefan will understand — Mayrant would agree and thereby save us — would you not, Your Excellency?"

"Only as a means to an end," he replied without zeal.

"Please, Zulinde — please save my son — my dear baby and your nephew — the disgrace that must go with him through life! Oh, God, Zulinde!"

Only a tragic little cry was heard from the stunned girl, but it expressed the awful turn of her world. It could not be, she kept saying. Never could her own sister and mother sanction such a marriage. She screamed inwardly when she saw, heard, and felt their contradictory measures; they sought to toss her, youth and all, upon the altar of sacrifice! She was deserted. If only Stefan were here.

"Stefan!" she cried aloud. "Stefan, come to me!" Not until then did blessed darkness claim her.

4

Stefan, his lips pressed into a bloodless line, his jaw muscles contracting in unison with distending nostrils, his heavy brows frozen almost on a line with his slitted eyes, listened to the closing words of the tale Mevrouw Sidneye had for him. He stood with arms folded, the ends of which were working knots of bloodless fingers that sent nails into flesh; his feet were planted solidly on the strangest deck in the most curious storm he had ever encountered. For a half hour he had stood like that, never moving more than those muscles of the jaws, nostrils, and hands.

Mevrouw Schouten and her elder daughter eyed him from the chairs in which they had heard the drama of Teerink from the lips of His Excellency. The bride-to-be was missing at the hour of her wedding; and the church, and maids, and others necessary to the joyful event were by that time recovering from surprise. The word had gone out that the Schouten maid had at the last moment shunned the hand of Stefan Meer.

"Say something, Stefan," implored the old lady.

"I'll have the decision from the lips of Zulinde," he said. "Fetch her here!"

"She is in no mood or condition to see you."

"Get her here!" he thundered.

"Treat your tongue to manners, Mijnheer Meer!" scolded the Schouten dame.

"Unless you bring her here at once, by God, I shall go to her! I shall have it straight from her that she prefers an old pot of flesh to me. Now fetch her!"

When no one moved more than eyeballs for an exchange of glances, he strode to the hall door and slammed it hard behind him; the heavy tread of his shoes up the stairway met their ears in another moment, and then his angered voice as it reverberated through the house with: "Zulinde!"

Mama Sidneye shook her head sadly. "Poor boy," she said. Then her eyes joined those of her dead son's wife in a curious rest on the ceiling. The three listened with dire misgiving to the muffled sounds that came from the room above.

For long moments Zulinde clung to her man and gave herself to convulsive sobs that can only nest in a heart torn loose by its very roots. Her eyes lifted to Stefan and they saw through the wall of tears a vague image of a man who stared straight ahead. Two men held her, two Stefans, one whose arms held her close, another whose soul was partly stolen from her by luminous hatred.

135

In his arms — they were strong and tough — hope could not forever wallow in the ashes of tears, and her grief gradually subsided; jerky sobs lifted into a sigh; a smile, however weak, and a convulsive sob; a brighter smile and a red nose. With the consciousness of appearance, a tragic relation of actualities to unhappy thoughts, she knew herself stronger. Only a sniffle, and a further awareness of a cherry knob in the middle of her face, and Stefan claimed her.

"Oh, Stefan," she attempted, "I'm so glad you came. Something awful has happened."

"Yes," he said pensively, "I know. I had it from your *kind* folk." His use of the word sent her eyes into his.

"Oh — they mean well, Stefan. It isn't their fault. They only wish to save us, to save the baby, from disgrace."

"By trading your body, heart, and soul for his honor! By all that's good and bad, Zulinde, I'm beginning to hate the baby!"

"*Neen*, you can't do that. He is so young and innocent."

"Must you defend everyone and everything that's against us?" he flared forth. "Next you'll be saying the *verdomd* German means well!"

"He convinces me, against my will, that his sole interest is for the family. He was asked to marry me, Stefan, by the family. It was not his choice."

"So you think. How else would he go about it? A proposal on his part would have been unthinkable — so he is clever enough to twist it about."

"But, Stefan, why should he?"

He held her at arm's length, frowned down at her, and said, "My Zulinde, such a blessed innocent you are. Look in your mirror for the answer."

"I am convinced he means well for the family," she said. "But that and marriage to him —" she shuddered "— are widely different. Oh, Stefan, there must be some way out of it."

"Some way! Of course, there is a way. We shall walk out of this house and become man and wife. Woe be unto him who tries to —"

"*Neen!* Not until — Stefan, I cannot see the good Dokter's name tossed into slime, and my sister forever in tears, and little Mayrant a child other *kinderen* point at with sneers. *Neen!*"

"What is this mystery the German can solve?"

"They did not tell you?" she asked, surprised.

"Mama Sidneye said it could not be discussed."

"It is awful, Stefan. I'll tell you, but never let them know. Promise?"

Before long all she knew was also a secret belonging to Stefan.

"Fantastic!" he said. "What's more I don't believe a word of it. Sure — he would carry the proof, but doesn't everyone know that the Prussians are clever? Bah! I'll make him confess, the swine! But enough of this useless talk, Zulinde, and tell me if what they said was true — that you have agreed to marry him."

She was long in giving him an answer. "He promised it to be a temporary affair, one in which I would see no more of him than in the past. To prove to Bismarck he is of the family I must travel with him to Prussia, as a wife in name only."

"So you agreed!" he said in a fierce whisper. "You fool, don't you know he'd never keep his promise? Can't you realize he would stop at nothing?"

The next moment saw Stefan Meer take the matter in tow: Zulinde was lifted to his arms and carried down the stairs and into the presence of the startled women. "I am," he said, "taking her away before you three ruin our lives! You are cheap folk, and may this house be damned!" With Zulinde in his arms, he left the house on Oranje Street in long, rapid strides.

He was seized by the police — von Streicher's doing — just before the robed figure in a church many blocks away pronounced them man and wife; with Zulinde in tears he was thrown into a cart and taken to jail, where he remained until the owners of the good ship *Quatrefoil* secured his release just before the tide on the morning that followed. He strode on deck with the sad words of Mevrouw Sidneye still ringing in his ears: —

"They were married last evening, Stefan, my boy. By now they are well beyond the border."

CHAPTER XII

1

THE year was eighteen hundred and ninety-one. The harbors of Rotterdam and Amsterdam were alive with plying commerce. Great ships with tall masts rested at anchor in Rijnhaven, where the river emptied through the city of Rotterdam before moving on into the Waterweg and the North Sea; ships from Liverpool, New

York, Naples, and the Orient rested with the tides alongside Dutch ships that sailed in with cargoes of tea, copra, quinine, kapok, cinnamon, Java coffee, New Guinea mace, rattan for the furniture trade, and jute sacks filled with black pepper and clove from the Indies.

In the warm summer breeze of an afternoon in June the wharves stank sweetly of half-rancid copra and licorice, of heavy oils and hides. To the youngster, who seemed all eyes and ears as he turned his head to run the tall masts of a great ship — from foresail to fore-skysail, and back to the flying jib that met the winds of the mysterious sea at the bow — this was the birthplace of dreamy romance and fierce adventure. How he longed to climb the ratlines and rigging until the lapping sea, the squawking gulls, the raucous voices of the *zeemen*, joined in sweet salute to the great sailor fresh from school. Eagerly he scanned the deck.

Everyone was busy one moment, and in the next they laughed and walked to the wharves and away. He eyed again the solid masts and furled sail, and the desire to shin up the ladders of the sea was greater than the will to resist. He thought of his mother, of his step-father, and then of the woman who was his grandmother. He smiled.

"They would fly into fits if they knew I planned to climb the ratlines. But they needn't know."

With darting eyes, he again searched the deck and close wharf. The thrill of a deck under his feet was matched only by a look straight up into the towers. There spars and ropes raced in sweeping angles, some crossing, but mainly they sought convergence in romantic lofts.

The sailor with his back to the wharf did not look up from the paper in his hand, and, thought the boy, there were enough minor squeaks and other odd sounds on the ship to detract from any small noise he would make. So with the thought came action: he climbed and kept climbing, pausing only to test the steadiness of his head in altitudes that gave great and thrilling views of Rotterdam's waterfront; more of the magic of the sea claimed him. Wrapping his legs about the ropes, like the old salts, he slowly raised his arms and folded them.

And then something went amiss. His foot suddenly lost its coil about the rope and he felt himself falling backward. He clutched at air and completed a somersault downward, yelling as he fell, and only the oblique angle of the widening ropes furnished a net in which to catch and hold a foot. Some ten feet above the deck he swung, head down, hands frantically reaching for a hold.

Men came running from the wharf, and the sailor who pored over a paper minutes before was now staring up at him. One *zeeman* laughed and another said, "*Verdomd!* Did he fall from the sky?" Soon a huge man with reddened face and piercing eyes came slowly upon the scene.

"Just who be you, Mijnheer, and for what reason do you sail down on my ship? 'Tis a hell of a *zeeman* you be not to climb a ladder in no blow at all. Pieter, get him down."

Said the lad, "I can get down by myself. That's the way I got up — and what's more, I'll have you know I was sitting on top without holding."

"Well! Well!" said the captain of the ship. "So you couldn't ride out the calm? *Zeeman? Neen.*" He laughed and the men on the deck and wharf laughed. "And just who might you be — the ghost of Admiral de Ruyter, or did you come across the Noord Zee in an Englishman's balloon?"

"*Neen, Mijnheer,*" said the lad, after showing his skill at grabbing the ropes and dropping lightly to the deck. "Me, I am Mijnheer Mayrant Ruysdaal Sidneye. Sixteen years come July next on the thirteenth."

"Sidneye!" exclaimed the captain. His eyes bulged and his weather-beaten face and neck protruded like that of a goose, and his lips and eyes were fierce as he awaited another earful of those same words.

"That is my name, Mijnheer. Are you the captain of this ship?"

"Just where did you get the name Ruysdaal?" said the captain with a growl.

"Strange that you should know it wasn't given me," returned the lad. "I gave it to myself, and only for my dead father do I keep the name he gave me."

"So you are — and what, may I ask, brings you aboard the good ship *Quatrefoil?*" The exchange of glances among the men was not lost on the captain, and his anger swelled as he saw men nudge companions and slowly turn away to safer distances. The legend of the mad captain, known all along the waterways of Rotterdam and Amsterdam, was flavored with the name of Sidneye; the Schouten-Meer episode was hushed, of course, though never had it died. Nor would it as long as the truculent countenance of Stefan Meer frequented the grogshops and harbors of Netherland ports, as long as his name meant the toughest of tough skippers who sailed around the world and down under, as long as the word "Meer" stood among charterers as the name of an avenue to riches. It was said he had singlehanded routed a score of head-hunters in Borneo; that he, with a mighty pull at the helm, turned the huge *Quatrefoil* in a giant trough directly away from the teeth of a reef and into a towering wave. No greater *zeeman* was there alive, they said, than Hansel Stefan Meer. Rough but square, and as rich as Croesus, he was as sensitive as they came regarding certain happenings of the past. Men learned to bury their tongues while in his presence.

The lad answered fearlessly and without impertinent tone: "Nothing short of a desire to sail the seas brought me aboard this ship, Mijnheer."

"To sail, or climb about with the fancy of a New Guinea monkey?" returned Captain Meer, still staring at the boy. He was stocky like his father before him, only there was more beef on his bones; his nose and eyes were of the Sidneye family, though he had taken on much of the Schouten in lips and chin.

"I'm afraid I was only interested in the fancy part," answered the Sidneye lad. "My parents would not let me sail."

Stefan Meer knew more than the gaping crew or those idlers along the wharves: there was much they would never know, among such that he had cursed this lad for being born — for sixteen long years, never missing a day. His happiness lay fouled by this boy's birth, his and others', perhaps even that of the boy himself.

"Then you'd better stay off ships like this one — Mijnheer Sidneye. You're liable to sail without any consent."

"Could that be arranged?" asked the lad. The undertone of mirth from those not sailing under the captain reached the ears of Stefan Meer. The lad was either saucy or stark mad, perhaps both. At any rate he knew his own mind. "When do you sail?" he added.

"With the morning tide, but you'll not ride to sea on this ship, my tanglefoot *zeeman*." His tongue belied his burning desire. How he longed to ship the lad, to burn out his soul along with his flesh under a tropic sun — to see him rave with fever, with salt spray in open wounds when the sun split the delicate skin; it would be good to see this lad learn to curse with fervor, drink himself into fits of despair, and learn the hell of body from unclean women of the hot ports.

But Stefan Meer was not a violent man; once his anger was given time to cool, his surface reflected a calm. He was less furious and quick than he once was, and more given to the slow, patient workings of time. He therefore corrected his version of revenge and wished for fever not so hot, for inebriation less violent, and women who were minus searing contagion. There was nothing noble in his loosening of the screws, for he knew young manhood: given a taste of unknown ecstasies, youth would court mud like a grunting swine.

On the other hand, he was more noble than he knew. Honesty with others, a rough but frank show of that quality, was a part of him, and beyond his ability to correct. He was also clean in spirit, and free from the clutches of any woman who sought one of three things — money, husband, or manly vigor. He nursed his moments, to be sure, but he never allowed them complete freedom; thus they never gnawed at his conscience. He did not know that he was generous, compassionate, and ever ready to probe out the best in any man; Captain Meer's opinion of himself was thus: a savage driver, a hard man!

"So I'll not be on your ship then, Captain," said the lad. "And I'm sorry I came aboard your old tub." With that he squared his shoulders and adjusted his cap and walked proudly to the wharf.

The incident was almost at once forgotten by the crew and peering loiterers, but not by Stefan Meer. He retired to his cabin for a losing fight with past memories.

2

As the morning sun painted the easy sail in the loft, the cable rattled slowly up from the sea with a dripping anchor. The mooring lines were in when the baritone voice of the pilot called out, "Steady now!" Fore and main tops'ls and t'gallants snagged a high wind, and the ship quivered. Then a second command, "Easy into the wind!" The lookout yelled at the helmsman, "Easy! Easy!" And the chief mate cried: "Belay all!" Men up in the sails laughed and cursed intermittently, while a runt on the mizzen ratlines asked politely of a fat *zeeman* where the hell he thought he was; four heavy boxes, loosed from the derrick slings on deck just before the ropes were lifted from the land bollards, kept several huskies straining to get them aft; from the galley came the sounds of raucous laughter and profanity. The chief mate glanced at the bow and turned to the helmsman again with: —

"Into the Waterweg."

The *Quatrefoil* creaked and strained like a lazy woman awakening, easing slowly out into the basin. A spar rattled, blocks squeaked, and her black and red sides groaned. The foresail was freed, and it bellied sluggishly. Then they met a lull, staysail and jib hanging limp. The helmsman called for more sail. And the chief mate cried: "Royals, fore and main." The orders echoed from masts, and ropes danced about until upper canvas flapped and swung to, and bellied hard. The ship jerked easily and slid forward to thread its way among a hundred other seagoing sisters at anchor. A leadsman's perfunctory chant caused no comment. There was little need for him there, so he merely practiced.

Ahead the water sparkled and dirty gulls swooped down and through the maze of smaller sails. The sun made mirrors of new sails that hugged thin lines on the water farther on toward the bend leading to Hoek van Holland. Almost touching the sides were fishing boats trying for the sea in a wind high above their sails. The giant *Quatrefoil*, depending on her upper canvas, slid by them amid exchanges of laughter, cries of well-wishing, taunts, and requests for the loan of a breeze. "Where you bound, Mijnheers, Africa? No? The Indies! Ho! Ho! Tell my Vrouw in Borneo I don't love her no more. Take this guilder, Cap'n Stefan, and bring me a ton o' mace. Bring me a rattan bundle for to learn my old lady a thing or two."

A half hour later a fine breeze met them from the sea. The Waterweg was alive with incoming vessels, several as large as the *Quatrefoil*, among them several steamers. The *Jan Cocq*, a three-masted girl that plied the South American course, met them near the sea, her sails slattern and shredded, her foremast replaced with slipshod jury poles.

"Poor sailin' or a hell of a blow" met with "Blow, sure, for no amount of poor sailin' could take the whole fore," and "Brains would have saved the pole, boys. Don't pay attention to Telp." A good laugh joined with the discord of ribaldry.

"There's the *zee*, boys, I can tell by the callin' card — fog. Cheer up, Telp. Your face won't show blowzy in the fog. Ha! Ha! Ho! Ho!"

"Lay off, Reingold! I'd as soon crack your skull from the back as let you see a pin coming down. A fellow from Eindhoven kept at me like you're doing. That was two years back. Well, he's madder'n a loon, and living on Groot Banda — thinks he's a native chief."

"Yeah?" Reingold stuck his thick neck forward, narrowing his eyes in mirth. "I once knew a fat woman from Nijmegen who had such a glare no man could withstand her. But," he sighed, "she was not fat in the head like you."

"Ho! Ho! Ha!" The men bent double while squatty Telp frothed. "Reingold says Telp is fat in the head. Did you hear?"

"Quiet!" whispered a lean and whiskered *zeeman*. "Here comes the captain." All eyes sought the great figure, some warily out of yellow corners, others directly, and every man of them, including the imperturbable Reingold, resumed a slow mechanical speed. The shadow of Stefan reached among them, and every man knew his huge fists were quietly at rest on his beefy hips. Only one of the lot, a new addition to the crew, picked up in a grogshop because of his fierce eye and Herculean size, intruded upon the silence; and he, unaware of the captain's discerning eye, said: —

"I hope we make a landfall in the Society Isles. I tell you the women know how to welcome a *zeeman*. I tell you right, I tell you."

"Mijnheer Kuyter!" The voice of Captain Stefan possessed a minatory ring. "You will use your hands more and your loose tongue less."

Kuyter's blond head jerked upward and his washed-blue eyes narrowed. He had the temerity to address the skipper defensively. What a fool was this stranger Kuyter. "As long as I do my work, what's the harm in a little talk?" he said.

Reingold stared, and Telp blinked furiously, and forgot to fasten the rope that held a spar above the tar pot: the spar struck the pot and dipped a weak end into the black liquid before the counterweight flung it many feet in the direction of the mizzen and Kuyter. Hot tar struck Kuyter on the neck and shoulders, and his frantic clawing was punctuated, amid the laughter of all, with a volley of talented blasphemy.

Stefan Meer threw back his head and roared, and when his enjoyment tapered off, he said: "Mijnheer Kuyter, I saw a short-tailed monkey in Borneo once that did the act even better. Henceforth you shall be called Short Tail Borneo." With that he departed, and only the suppressed laughter of the crew nearest "Short Tail" joined with the noises of the rigging and creaking hull. Mijnheer Kuyter's tongue was shelved, though his roving eye remained glued to the moronic face of Telp.

3

The chief mate paused near the helmsman, glanced beyond the stern rail, and then turned his eye, like the man at the wheel, on the mizzenmast. In another moment both men plummeted weather glances and leveled their eyes each on the other.

"And why," said the chief mate banteringly, "do you gaze at a weather clew that's furled?"

Glotz chuckled. "My eye needs testing, Mijnheer Vossler. I was trying to pronounce the fly on the mast tip. I think it was a carrion fly."

"Very good, Mijnheer van der Glotz. I saw it myself, and it was a bloated carrion. Only I noticed it was minus a leg on the left side."

Both men chuckled. The two were close friends, having been brought up in Zuid-Holland within a stone's throw of one another. Glotz had remained single, no mystery, since Mate Vossler had himself taken the buxom Nand for a wife before Lidj could compose his tongue for proposal. It caused no ill between the two since the first mistress of one was that of the other — the rolling sea — and, too, each was his best over a cornucopia of dried sausages and schnapps, which, under any relaxed sky, be it over the Noord or Java Zee, gave them common felicity in word and taste. They gave guilders to the same priest, supported the same burgomaster in principle and voice, viewed the Prussian pomp with the same tongue-in-cheek disdain, hated the natives with equal intensity, and worshiped Captain Meer without surcease. Each kept his opinions and pet topics to himself, until those times when freedom from duties allowed a spread of food and drink: then, only from one to the other, were they shared.

Elongated Vee Vossler, bony, hard of muscle, harder of jaw, sent a monotonous blue eye filled with utter impartiality to every man on the *Quatrefoil*; for fifteen years he had ridden her decks under Stefan without inciting from any *zeeman* a word of slander. And so it was with chubby, amiable Lidj van der Glotz.

"I was not surprised to learn we were making Tandjoengselor on this trip," said Lidj despairingly. "Borneo has missed us for three years. And what a difference three hundred miles east can make. Ternate and the Moluksche Zee — like heaven to Borneo's hell. And too, it is closer to Soerabaja."

Said Vossler, "I have talked to Nand about moving to Soerabaja. We're at anchorage there more than Rotterdam. Only Nand would dry up."

"*Neen*, my friend Vee, as you well know, you're hunting other excuses and you lay them to the weather."

"You talk with wisdom, Lidj. It is hot there, but as you say, I dodge the main excuse. I want Raas and young Christiaan to attend Leiden."

"And miss the *zee! Neen! Neen!* Loving it as you do, you'd deprive your boys of such a life?"

But Chief Mate Vossler evaded the issue as he stared at the mighty ocean. After some length he said, "Borneo. You know, Lidj, we've never visited Borneo that trouble hasn't plagued this ship."

Lidj remained silent, though he too frowned pensively. Then, as was his habit, he smiled and said, "Nand will love Soerabaja."

4

The fresh vomit of the Neder Rijn had long since been left behind, and the salty spray of the Atlantic met them in a furious mood before the jutting north coast of France ended abruptly with Brest hidden behind the wall of advancing fog to the south; crew and officers saw Stefan Meer inhale huge gulps of winds that were land free, saw his expressions of joy, like a smacking of lips over tangy ale. Every man on ship, even those in the galley, heard his bellows blow his throat with: "Give her sail."

Helmsman Glotz grinned, wiped the salt from his left cheek with the point of his tongue, and eyed the weather clew. A great wave broke against the stern and sent a thin gray-blue sheet fringed with diamonds straight up and over the starboard side; the drops seemed to rattle on deck before the heavy wet tumble, and he grinned again as his face and shoulders caught their full share. His first love was upon him, that of guiding the mighty girl through the bouncing troughs, down into small valleys and through climbing waves. Sail meant a tearing through, and the gale, light but steady, was just enough to bite into the canvas and howl through the shrouds in the kind of conversation he liked — his first love, yes. Only two other loves· bowed before it, namely: good honest companionship with men like Vossler; and after all that went with the second — wine, pipes, food, and long discussions — was worship of God. Other loves he had, some light, others lighter, but none of these nested in the royals. He had urges, periodic hammerings from a too full spine, that caused his eye to give appraisal to a leg; but the opening of his sluice gates was more of a mechanical riddance. And after such relations — a swapping of guilders for flesh — he knelt on bended knee to give his soul lament.

But the sails, three sets to the fore, constituted his magic carpet to complete joy. He traveled with them as the guiding hand that kept the wind into them, and no matter how much they leaned or how proudly they stood they were a part of him. The *Quatrefoil* was good at scudding, though at times her stubborn soul tried to yaw. Laugh at her he did, saying: "My queen of the ocean, hold your temper — Lidj van der Glotz is at the helm. You'll keep a straight wake."

A towering wave sought to beat Stefan down as he stalked sternward. Wet to the skin, he did not miss a step, nor did he seem to know there had been a slapping wave. "How goes the weather, Glotz?" he bellowed. "Wheel heavy?"

"*Neen*, Captain," said Lidj, grinning. "Her cordage isn't creaking enough for that. I hear it way up the skysail first, Captain, and then set my arms and let her heel a fraction when it comes. She minds."

"You know her pretty well, don't you, Lidj? A ship's rheumatism does no harm. Well, her course is set, so hold fast."

"Aye, Cap'n."

Suddenly strange sounds of a commotion reached the ears of Lidj and the captain. Stefan Meer halted in his stride and hunched forward to peer at the apparition that struck him full in the eye. Forgotten were the noises of the shrouds, the sea hammering at the sides, and all things pertaining to weather and rudder. Chief Mate Vossler stretched his rubbery neck extra inches, and the furrow of his brow gave a downpour of spray right of way down his nose; the thick form of Telp, water dripping from his bulbous nose and dimpled chin, slowly turned about and froze into immobility; newcomer Kuyter, unaware of anything but the face value of what he saw, showed less surprise than the regular crew, while Reingold, on deck the afternoon before the *Quatrefoil* heaved anchor, stood bemused. Lidj stared at the square back of the captain. He knew the story from beginning to end, and, too, he was aware of a frown creasing his brow as he said to himself: "There'll be hell to pay now."

"Over here!" thundered Stefan, and two huskies labored with their burden, dragging the body and dodging the malodorous dribble retched from a hole in the chalky face of the victim. Groans were emitted with every retch, and words loud and strong regaled his assailants: "You goddamned beasts, loose me!" Then with a mad jerk he was free. The first move he made was to strike one sailor down, and the next was to stumble to the rail and bend over with an awful groan of vomiting.

Cries went up about the deck, informative ejaculations: "Stowaway!" Stefan Meer stared at his nemesis, Mayrant Ruysdaal Sidneye.

CHAPTER XIII

I

THREE days had elapsed since the maze of swamp and jungle on the dank coast of Borneo had last been seen over the stern rail. A heavy monsoon, standing down the east coast and crossing over the Strait of Macassar to one hundred and twenty east of Greenwich, before running its longitude in the west winds to the Flores Zee, left in its wake a calm unnatural and foreboding. It was deader than dead, no roll at all to the sea, and Borneo was no farther behind them than two days before. Not a block creaked, and every sail hung lifeless, dead and ghostly up there. The lookout on the fo'c'sle head was stilled, and the ship, mirrored with the slow, basting sun, was as motionless as if she'd been stilted in concrete just below the water line.

The stowaway, twelve pounds lighter, splotched brown, pink, and yellow from scalp to neck, and red-raw where weals on tender back, underarms, and shoulders caused him to wince with each move, leaned over the rail like the others and watched the fleet sharks stirring

146

up ripples on the glassy sea. He was without clothing above the waist since his body rebelled at every touch; the sweat in which he broiled added more to the misery of his sores. As he eyed a lean gray shark that rolled over and showed its belly and serrated mouth, a drop of hot tar struck the sorest spot on his neck. He jumped back and cursed the sea, the sails, and the world at large.

"What's wrong, Sidneye boy?" a sailor asked, grinning and nudging a companion.

"None of your business, *kass* head," returned the boy. For months he had flared at every word from the crew, since his entire voyage had seen him the victim of every indignity the inventive crew could heap upon him. It began on that day when he was dragged on deck like a culprit amid shouts of "Stowaway!" So he leaned again on the rail, after sour glances into the uppers, and screwed his face into a truculent expression that damned all he saw.

Sharks! Bubbling pitch! The god-awful heat of the sun! The *gewone menschen* that constituted the crew! The stink of the refuse from the boat that stubbornly clung to the spot on the water where it first landed! The hot water one had for drinking — and the awful running of his bowels! All these met a background in his mind: tulips, cool breezes, snow, clean, cool water for his innards, clean beds, and clean companions. Opposites all, and for even one portion of these good things of his homeland a year of his life, or more! But only water and dancing, stinking heat and sharks met his eye against a becalmed sea and ship that stared at a leaden sky.

What had he told Captain Meer that day? Oh yes: "Nothing short of a desire to sail the seas brought me aboard this ship." That's what he'd said. An ironic smile almost burst into play on his drawn face, but not quite — the hate in him rose to crush it.

"The goddamned land, sea, and air, and all the ships and people!" he said in a half-audible curse. "And that for Captain Meer, and — everybody except Mijnheers Glotz and Vossler. And goddam Kuyter and Reingold! And the galley crew, the dirty sons-of-bitches!"

"Sidneye boy," a voice behind him said, "the captain sends for you."

"To hell with the captain, Mijnheer!" returned Mayrant. "And to you, my gutless friend." But he ambled off, mumbling as he did so, pondering over what new surprise punishment the man he'd kill someday had concocted. Ahead he saw Kuyter.

"Well, if it isn't the beautiful boy! I know what the captain has in mind, Sidneye boy. Want to know?"

"Go to hell, you dirty —" Kuyter's laughter rang in his ears. Kuyter, too, would someday be paid in full and — how long was his list? Aye, how long? Suddenly his face brightened. He stopped dead still, turned about, and retraced his steps to where Kuyter had joined others of the crew.

"Mijnheer Short Tail," he said, and his face was pleasant for once. "I have a proposition for your ears."

"Proceed, Sidneye boy," said the big man in facetious manner.

"I shall. As you know, I do not like you, Short Tail Borneo. My dislike goes even further, I hate your goddamned soul, I do."

"Must I cry?" asked Kuyter, leaning against the rail and tossing a wink at a bearded *zeeman*.

"Not yet, Mijnheer Short Tail. I propose that the two of us, armed with a knife each, go overboard. One of us won't return. No. One of us will feed the hungry sharks out there."

Kuyter's sandy brow contracted and the lids narrowed over washed blue. Was the lad serious? Then he threw back his head and laughed long and hard. Reingold walked over from the starboard side and, after solicitous inquiry, bellowed mirthfully. Mayrant stood his ground, and gave the ribaldry a steady smile. Too quickly the laughter subsided, giving place to glances of concern over the shoulders of Mayrant. The lad realized Captain Meer was walking toward them, but he had found a new bliss, a reason for living, and the captain could do what he pleased and be damned afterward.

"Well, Short Tail Borneo?"

"Quiet, fool! The captain."

Mayrant raised his voice in answer. "Captain or no captain, Short Tail, do you have the guts?"

Captain Meer strode into the group, his eyes flashing fire. Every man save Mayrant exuded in some manner or another obsequiousness; Reingold's eyes darted about for a task needing a hand, and Telp bowed as if he had a tail curled between his legs, while Kuyter removed his elbows from the rail; others found their hands ungovernable and nervous tools of no use. They fawned before their master like dogs, thought Mayrant. How glorious it was to be free of that fear.

"Sidneye!" thundered the captain. "Did you receive word that I wanted you?"

"Aye, Baas Meer, I did."

"And what kept you?" His tone bespoke certain retribution; except for the captain's eyes, Mayrant would have missed no part of it.

"A proposition, Baas Meer. One I just made this man who has nothing but corruption for guts. Since I hate him more than any of

148

the rest of you — not much more, but enough to choose him first — I challenged him to leap overboard with knives. I'm waiting for his answer."

Stefan, unused to any show of disobedience, and slightly bemused at the sudden gravity of the lad's tone and expression, slowly placed a forefinger and thumb in pincer grasp upon his chin; his eyes traveled the boy appraisingly. In easier tone, he said: "Are you not aware of the laws of the sea, Sidneye?"

"That I am, Mijnheer Baas. But I've been goaded too far. Laws be damned when it's a matter of defense! I could knife him in the back, but I choose instead a fair fight. Look at him, Baas! A worthless hulk who slaves to let the other men carry his share."

"And you'd go overboard in the school of sharks with him — knowing that one drop of blood would be the death of both of you?"

"I would, Baas. And unless he agrees, don't be surprised if he's missing one of these days. I warn you, by the God in heaven, I warn you!" His tone was anything but trifling, rather it converged hate and lost patience into an ominous expression of fanatical determination, a trait none among them had even imagined a part of the boy. But his words hung mast high, and heavy as the leaden calm.

Kuyter gave evidence of the tension by a serious twist of his mouth and the lifting of one brow out of a fixed frown. The captain merely stood there, giving the silence lordly dignity, it seemed, while from the eyes of the lad concurrent flashes of hate and challenge flowed into the faces of each man with the slow turn of his head. The wave was broken when the long form of Vossler joined the gathering, and for a barest fraction of a second Mayrant hated him, too, for slowing the run of his thirsting wrath.

Stefan broke the silence, after it had been felt by all. "I'm sorry, lad, I cannot tolerate fighting aboard ship. Come with me."

2

The *Quatrefoil* was becoming foul on the water line; she was overdue in Soerabaja; and it was raining again, a slow dismal rain that would bring no wind; it was insufferably hot and, to top it all, dysentery raged on board; the men emptied their buckets but the putrescence rose out of the sea and only lured more oppressive visitors from the limpid depths; and still the dead calm rooted the ship.

Thus Captain Meer gave himself up to mental agitation on the afternoon of the fourth day of the calm. He stood with a hand on the mizzen fife rail, staring first out to where lusterless sky met opaque sea, and then at the halyards and brails and various gear coiled on the belaying pins. That his humor was bad needed no explanation, and the crew shunned him as much as possible. At such times not even Vossler or van der Glotz sought conversation with Stefan, the ogre of the good ship *Quatrefoil*.

His gaze lifted to the shrouds, to a clearing sky, and again fell to the sea where a shark rose violently above the mirrored surface and thwacked itself down, and repeated the performance several times before more of the monsters closed in and clashed in a violent flurry of blood and foam. His expression was fixed and he turned an indifferent eye to the foredeck. There with a gun in hand, shooting at every shark he saw, stood young Sidneye, enjoying more the cannibalistic show than the skill of planting lead in swift targets.

Captain Meer's eye changed expression. He reviewed his aversion to the lad, as he had every day since he first saw him. For long minutes he talked with Zulinde, for longer minutes he cursed Mama Sidneye, Mama Schouten; he turned a wicked eye on the sea, where out of the boiling glass rose the obese shape of Herr von Streicher. It was a glorious moment, and it received greater ecstasy when, at the exact spot of his transfixed gaze, a shark rose and met a charge from the gun in the hands of Mayrant Sidneye. A gaping hole showed in the tinsel-white belly and again the cannibals of the sea raced to the blood. So!

The thought struck Stefan squarely between his quickened eyes: a miracle had happened! Had not his eyes and the eyes of the Sidneye lad met at the same spot on the sea, out of all the millions of miles of it; and upon the vision of the man who had robbed one of sweetheart, and the other of father; and had not the lad's vengeance been taken in that split second; and had not the ghost of Streicher, who still lived, damn his soul, been brought down in blood to be fed upon by his own kind?

So strong was the apparition that it cascaded into every corner of his brain, a moment in the background, another moment in the fore; and then it found a nest, where it remained to undermine set opinions and fancies and the eye of his soul and brush them with unwanted compassion.

When next Mayrant Sidneye invaded his eyes, gone was the repelling stare; and in its place there was welcome — momentarily. But the old sore clung to that wrinkled scar of hate; Stefan Meer was not a man who reversed opinions on the spur of the moment, and thus obstinate dislike of the boy rose up in rebellion. As the battle raged inside him, Stefan turned his eye to a neutral corner, the sea, and prepared himself for the burial of one of the two — hate or compassion; there was not room in a Dutchman's soul for both.

The tropic night swallowed up ship and sea; and the warning lights threw long, still fingers into the desolate stretches of an empty dismal world, as if they were designed to mock ship, captain and crew. The *Quatrefoil*, the queen that had scudded before many a wind, that had leaned against waves with the grace of a water nymph, was now squatting petulantly, like the temperamental woman she was, in the cesspool of the seven seas. Below, in the heated depths, patches of luminescence moved to the waveless surface in bursting flashes as finned brother devoured some member of its family, or joined the packs that tore out living chunks of meat from another creature. Each forever stalked blood from minnow or whale. The sea, a horror by night, boiled with an unearthly glow that rivaled the motionless lights of the ship in prolonged ghostliness.

And Stefan Meer continued to stand by the mizzen fife rail, an obstinate old man in his moment, a refractory trader who looked at a world of cheaters, who childishly and fiercely combined all the good and bad of his lonely years in the debate: he was of no mind to give up hate of the boy and deprive himself of pabulum of the soul without tasting the merits of the alternative. It had centered on a set course — hating the boy or passionately joining with the boy's hate of Mayrant Streicher. The thought of teaming with the lad was inviting, but the imps of objection wailed forth: Stefan Meer, your hate would be overthrown by growing devotion to the lad himself. You have always wanted a son, said the kindly soul. But do not forget the hate you've enjoyed, countered the imps of objection.

3

While the captain wrestled with himself, the crew lined the rails, found their bunks and read by lamplight, grouped off in twos and threes to talk of things sweeter than a dead calm, eyed the mizzen fife rail, narrowed their eyes over greasy cards, or restlessly paced the deck. But not so with Lidj van der Glotz and Vee Vossler: grog and sausages met under binnacle in the latter's quarters on a table screwed to the floor between them.

Silence, except for the bottle meeting glass, spread its enigmatic cloak. It was Vossler, the mate, who spoke. "'Tis a sad duty. I must get the boy off ship at Soerabaja. Lidj, together we must send him back to Holland."

"Of course," agreed Lidj without surprise or question; if Vee thought so, then it was so. He grinned and said, "Drink, dear friend. Our sausages await us."

4

The boy trod the deck restlessly; why he peered into the night he did not know, unless it was for release from the tiger's cage in which he dwelled, its bars drawing ever tighter, its confines more oppressive and stifling with each passing moment. Anything to break the shackles of inactivity would have found welcome. At cards he was not taken seriously, in conversations he drew the spiked boot of ridicule, and his youthful soul could find no balm in reading words that assumed dull phrases. Where he sought adventure he found lugubrious burlesque: the world was an empty shell.

For want of something to unchain him from madness he slipped unseen into the captain's quarters and snitched a bottle of Dutch gin; before long he mourned with heightened splendor; his self-pity was steered into tears, his anger into a taut string of catgut that must snap with thrumming. And as he gave himself to these emotions the past rose up for closer communion, drove out the sorrow for self and lengthened the tremulant string over the vacuity.

He saw himself outside the balcony door of forty-seven Oranje Street, straining his ears for the soft words of his aunt, Zulinde Streicher, as she talked to another sister, from Boston, America. Harmenszoon van Schreeven, his half-brother, born seven years after the death of Dokter Sidneye, and only eight at the time, had fallen asleep on the couch in the big *dolen* room. Zulinde's past had been a hushed affair, a topic always stabbed with slow, hollow, but firm glances; and thus, when quite by accident he heard Zulinde mention Streicher's name, he sought the key to the mystery.

She had cried a bit, after telling Deena Stam about Stefan Meer, and Deena had replied in broken tone that Stefan might come for her — someday.

"No," said Zulinde. "For fifteen years I've waited, dear sister."

"Then time must heal your wounded heart, Zulinde."

He crouched low, moved an ear closer as the story unfolded; his eyes opened wide as she gave an account of her first wedding night: —

"Across the border from Nijmegen our coach came to a stop, and I heard His Excellency tell the drivers we would stay the night at Cleve.

And when he entered the coach, I noticed his eye was bold. He took a seat beside me instead of across from me, where he had sat in silence so far. I had learned to think him a noble man, one whose love of the dear Dokter exceeded mine. Then I would eye him, and imagine him as a husband.

"But when he sat beside me and took my hand in his I wanted to cry out. Instead I said, 'Herr Streicher, please remember our agreement — I am your wife in name only.' His reply — 'I shall not forget, my lovely Zulinde, but have you no kindness for a man's lonely mood?' I had none and straightway said so; and he, without a word, took his seat across from me. All the way to Cleve I was left alone with my love for poor Stefan, whom I had last seen being dragged away by the police.

"At the inn, I stood aside while he talked with the keeper, who turned his eyes my way with an expression that was quite strange. Soon I was shown to a beautiful room. Herr Streicher bade me *goeden nacht* and I, leaning against the closed door, sighed in most joyful relief.

"I turned all the bolts, and then undressed. I got to my knees and prayed — for Stefan, for our love to find itself, for my sister and kin, and for the baby Mayrant Sidneye. Then I went to sleep, and — it came near midnight." Her pause was long, and she sobbed once.

"My sleep did not last long — I was awake and sitting up in bed, wondering if I imagined a knock at my door. Then it came again. 'Who is it?' I said. 'An urgent message, Frau Streicher,' came the answer. I lighted the lamp and unbolted the door. Without a word the man strode in — my husband. He was drinking.

"I ordered him out of the room, but he merely stood before me. 'My *Frau* must drink with me on our wedding night,' he said. 'My beautiful *Fräulein* is now Frau Streicher.' I looked for my robe. And when I was seated on the bed, he caught my arms and drew me to him.

"I begged for his mercy, even promised to drink with him. I can hear my voice and laugh to this day, Deena. It was so weak and hollow.

"Calmly I reminded him of our bargain, and he spoke of a reward due him. I fell across the bed, sobbing hysterically. He merely eyed me, frowning, while he looked at my legs and body."

"My poor dear little sister," said Deena. And Mayrant lay quiet. He was beginning to understand; curiosity gave him no time for the hate that must be born later.

"He told me how he had tricked Mama Sidneye, my mother, and me. He told me he regretted that he had caused Mijnheer Dokter to commit suicide.

"I tell you, Deena, I fainted. I remember his arms pulling me to my feet, I remember his body pressed to mine; and then, I was pushed onto the bed."

"Poor child. Poor child." It came from the shaken sister.

"When I awoke, Deena, my hair was snow white, and —

"My soul will forever be crimson!"

5

Mayrant leaned against the bow and drank from the bottle. The hot schnapps evoked in him a sweet, sweet anger. He remembered all. He was again on the balcony of forty-seven Oranje Street, and his mind's eye failed to see the red arc of the leaping dolphin that rose out of the sea and splashed down again. Instead: —

While Deena sought to soothe Zulinde, he repeated, *"He told me he regretted that he had caused Mijnheer Dokter to commit suicide!* He was my father — my father!" Slowly he got to his feet and, giving his all to anger, he stalked into the room.

"I, Aunt Zulinde," he shouted, "shall never rest until Streicher comes to a painful and slow death!"

They had, of course, bundled him off to Rotterdam without delay. There his schooling was finished, almost. But a greater lesson he had learned: hate was less apt to cool if kept to one's self.

He gazed out into the sea, and ironically reviewed the present: the blessed calm, the joy of heat and sores, the beauty of the sharks and squid out there, the glory of the companionship of Kuyter and Reingold. Aloud he said, just as Stefan Meer was about to lay a kind hand on his shoulder: —

"May Streicher live until I am ready." The silence dropped its net into the sea and lifted a cool draught to his heated brow: the felicity of hate knew no peer. "Aye, may he live until then." He laughed.

"And may I learn to forgive the man she loves, Stefan Meer," he said before tilting the bottle to his lips. He stared at the bottle in his hands and flung it far into the sea, shouting to the top of his voice: —

"To you, Your Excellency, you son-of-a-bitch!" He leaned over the rail, peering intently, as if some answer must be forthcoming from the limpid depths below.

6

Captain Meer failed to approve of a stowaway's theft of gin, and Chief Mate Vossler saw no fair reason for excepting a stowaway.

But the two high officers of the *Quatrefoil* exchanged knowing winks — but no more of what was in the mind of each — and sent the culprit about his business. And that same night, when the clouds broke and gave the sails a mellowed silver and the decks a patchwork of shadow, both men frowned at the errors of clemency aboard ship.

The fight Baas Meer had denied the lad found its moment, and, as Meer himself admitted, it was a natural result of justified hate. But murder had been done, with Vee Vossler the sole witness to the deed. He saw the struggle quite by accident: as he moved aft he saw two men, pressed close to the port rail, locked in combat. Before he could cry out or reach them there was a sudden quickening of the bodies, and one of them leaned perilously over the rail — then only one stood on the deck of the ship.

The scream of Mijnheer Kuyter would forever ring aboard the *Quatrefoil* as he fell to the waiting sharks.

Both men agreed that a lad under age was worthy of leniency by the courts who must try his case. They pledged mutual aid on that score. But Vossler wondered why Baas Meer chose to adopt Mayrant Sidneye, while the protégé, in all ignorance of his good fortune, lay in the dark confines of his cell and cursed the rats that kept him company.

Toward morning the sweetest breeze that ever visited the Celebes Zee gave crush to the sails of the *Quatrefoil* and sent her, under the smiling eye of Lidj van der Glotz, creaking and rocking under her bellying sails toward Soerabaja and heaven.

CHAPTER XIV

1

THE year was nineteen hundred and two. Under full sail the *Quatrefoil* plowed before a northwest trade through the Badoeng Strait for anchorage at Benoa.

To Bali, where lived the ubiquitous gods, where the joy of living was personified. There artistry, naïve and enchanting, composed its own interpretation. From the southernmost tip of Tandjoeng Meboeloe, where the Indian Ocean hummed incessantly, to Tandjoeng Boengloelan, where the balanced rock meets the Flores Zee on the north, an accessible mythology, classical and Hindu in humor, reached out to claim visitor and native alike. It was generations old and piquantly styled to the magic of only Bali.

It was small wonder then that Stefan Meer chose such a setting in which to fulfill his version of retirement from the sea: a small plantation that clung to the open smell of the oceans, that was in a measure free from the grasping hand of Dutch, British, and American commerce, that failed to hold before his eyes a million visions of the same scene he longed to forget. Lush-green paddies, ornate temples, grotesque gods, translucent brown bodies, who knew the value of laughter and joy, could only alienate oppressive thoughts; here he would preserve the soul of a sailor in a heaven on earth. Perhaps, and who could foretell, the life near the circling sea might evoke in him a fountain of youth. Aye, who knew!

Baas Meer stood at the bow, his crates and sacks of burlap, his valises and hodgepodge, accumulated on the portside beam; he gazed across the violet mist that slowly unfolded stately shapes and green horizons. A flying fish rose from the pellucid water and dripped of sapphire as it glided toward the lazy harbor. The ceilings of palms were no longer gray-masked silhouettes against a wild field of blue; instead their swaying color moved to the syncopation of the island. Like the sun courting and flirting with the shadowed earth under the banyan tree, like a gorgeous flower nodding on its slender stem, the greatest and most pleasingly mystifying art exhibit of the Nederlands Indies beckoned. Even the natives saw no greener pastures — heaven was rebirth on the flowery island of Bali.

As Captain Meer stared, a pair of bronzed arms found elbow rest alongside him. Without a glance at their owner he said: —

"Aye, Ruysdaal, my son, it is all one could ask."

"It is that, Baas Stefan," answered the young man. "But another fact dims the beauty."

Stefan knew of what he spoke, and the words of the youngster, three years on the lean side of thirty, were music to his ears. A decade had passed since the day he had pleaded for clemency for his protégé — and he had said the word for all ears, even those of the crew — upon a promise to stake his reputation on the high seas, in every port of entry from Amsterdam to Melbourne, that young Sidneye's conduct could be guaranteed. Even the young culprit, who challenged the court of law with fierce unrelenting eyes, showed such surprise at the plea that his shell of armor cracked before an onslaught of tears. Kindness and affection tore asunder the incrustations of hate. A ludicrous sight, but the true colors of the son of Dokter Sidneye rose to stay the hand of justice. In truth he was adopted by the indomitable skipper of the great ship *Quatrefoil*, and the bond that was between the two, though much speculation reigned, was kept within the coffers of their minds and hearts. But something was there, said all, said the wharfmongers of Rotterdam, Batavia, Soerabaja, and a half-dozen other ports of call.

"My son," said Stefan, without glancing about, "you'll find your hands so amply filled that your heart will not have the time for lamentations."

"Then you know my heart better than I, Baas."

"*Verdomd!* You mean to tell me my confidence has been misplaced?" Stefan's voice imitated a gruff wind.

"*Neen*, Baas Meer. *Neen!* But because I feel as I do, the better skipper I'll be."

"More in line, Sidneye boy," said Stefan. He chuckled, "Sidneye boy. How long since anyone called you that?"

"Many years, Mijnheer. Many. But I lived it down with bloody fists."

"And learned to fight for respect from *zeemen* while you did it. 'Tis well. No milksop can drive a ship as you've done on these last two voyages. By all the blood in Borneo, I actually retired a year back and forced you to decide for yourself!" He chuckled once more. "Keep your shrewd eye, Ruysdaal, and counsel with the type of men you selected by your own self in the past. Vossler will be a good chief mate for many years, and Lidj — well, forever."

"But, Baas, that is what I have to tell you. Nand Vossler has decided to move to the Indies. It seems Vee wishes to be near her and the children — in Soerabaja — so he has tendered his papers."

"What!" thundered Stefan, forgetting the island, the palms and lavender mists.

"Aye. He's opening a trading house there."

"With what?"

"Well, Baas, I must tell you. I am financing it. I decided —"

"You? And with what, may I ask?"

"With, Baas Meer, the five thousand guilders you are going to lend me."

The captain's voice was heard by the men in the rigging, by those in the hold, and by the coolies with baskets of pigs and fighting cocks on the bamboo wharf, if they had ears cocked toward the Strait of Badoeng.

"Why you — you impudent *kass* brain! Me lend you five thousand guilders! Where's your senses, lad? Is it not enough that I bequeath

157

you a half interest in the *Quatrefoil*, after I cleared her in Rotterdam last June? Is it not enough that I go against my judgment, for which I have prided myself all these years, and entrust to a fool head the proudest, most profitable three-master ever to sail out of the Waterweg? Is it not enough that I turn you loose with stocked hold, stocked to her gullet, on a return voyage? And weren't you given a tidy nest above earnings last year? And you have the gall to ask me to finance another venture so you can divide your time and thoughts! Have you, Mayrant Ruysdaal Sidneye?"

A broad smile gave prelude to the answer. "Aye, Baas."

"What?" thundered the Baas, taken aback.

"Aye, Baas Meer, five thousand guilders."

Slowly the big frame of Stefan draped itself again over the rail; with eyes dancing and mouth working furiously, he said calmly: "You said five, did you not, lad? Will five be enough?"

"Aye! At current interest, beloved Baas."

Beloved Baas! The words were sweet to lonely Stefan Meer.

"'Tis a deal, Ruysdaal. And my apology for calling you Mayrant. I've a hunch you'll prosper if you work the *eilandens* more on your small capital and the big trade less. But what does Vee know about trading?"

"Enough, Baas. He knows that we should work the Moluksche Zee — Ternate, Amboina, Tanimbar, Banda, the Zuid Ooster and Zuid Wester. The *verdomde* Japanese can be beat there. Aye."

"Aye," he mused. "And when I get lonesome I'll hop over to look after things. Aye?"

"Good old Baas."

"Hm-m. Remember there's extra profit — if you buy from the first hands and miss the middlemen. You know, I might take a run with Vee to Moluksche. But what's he to use, a raft?"

"*Neen*," chuckled Sidneye. "In Soerabaja I bargained for a ketch. She'll do until we can outfit better. I named her — well, she's got a good name."

Stefan was quick to observe his hesitance. "Well, what did you name her?"

"The *Zulinde Meer*, Baas — the *Zulinde Meer*."

2

So Lidj van der Glotz became chief mate aboard the swift *Quatrefoil* in a ceremony that lasted well into the morning. Stefan's Dutch friend, Piet de Turffs, a huge man, and every bit as jolly as

158

he was large, drank level with his guests, and gave every man of the crew regardless of position the warm clasp of an equal on that occasion. He had sent his most trusted men to watch the *Quatrefoil*, after inviting the entire crew to his house in Denpasar, some miles inland. There he feasted them amid such brilliant entertainment as they would not soon forget.

A native orchestra moved into the yard, and under a bright moon lowered strange instruments and sat cross-legged on the ground. Intricately carved teakwood frames supported the bronze metallophones that squared off into center from the ten bronze bells, over which the performers held mallets — their sticks, hammers, and finger tips would later give variations of tone. Squatting in the center were the drummers. With gongs and cymbals ready, the *gamelan*, or orchestra, at a signal sent forth sweet, vibrant notes, the rhythm of which was gay and catchy.

Turffs, beckoning the native wine servers, leaned toward Stefan and Ruysdaal with a grin. "Just wait until the tinkling cymbal and the rattle of the *kendang*, the finger drum, pierces the night air. We'll have company aplenty."

The all-male orchestra wore nothing above the waist except brocade scarfs tied variously about their heads; colorful skirts completed their attire.

"See the young girl near the gate?" said Turffs. "She is the daughter of the mustached drummer. Watch her. She will surprise you with the *kebiyar*, the sitting dance."

Ruysdaal peered beyond the orchestra and saw the glint of moonbeams giving high lights to the snakelike floral design of her sarong, the golden sash that wound about her slim waist and held tight the firm flesh of her bosom. In one hand was a fan and in the other a headpiece, an elaborately gilded thing fashioned of buffalo hide. He could scarcely believe she was only eleven years of age.

The savage bar of his brow clouded as he studied his crew in holiday mood. Men like Ritter du Buys, Jan Zeen, and the Swede, Olaf Borjdst, and the German, Glaus Donner, had salacious longing written into their eyes and mouths. Their thirst for women had found renewal instead of appeasement in Soerabaja. Particularly he noticed Ritter, a swarthy, elongated *zeeman* whose fierce eyes lingered on the figure of the girl without restraint.

As the music died and slowly rose in a shifting of the metrical accent, the Balinese girl moved to the foreground, where she knelt behind the brass bells. On her knees she swayed slowly, undulantly, like a bone-

159

less beauty who, after successfully courting a rhythmic trance, followed the baton of an invisible maestro. Her arms, full, dimpled, and bronzed, moved with unbelievable motions, coaxing, it seemed, the nimble springs under the opalescent skin into her hands, one of which moved the fan with graceful motions of the fingers. The *kebiyar* dance continued.

The music was fading, it now hung in the air tremulously, making way for the single gong to emit a thin vibrant note. The *djanger* seemed to find new joy, in eye, lip, and muscle. The beauty of sweet surprise was in subsequent tinkling notes, an interpretation, said Turffs, of life and love. Then with passionate speed the fan fluttered. It was incredible; the moonbeams were churned by the fan as her body swayed in slow motion.

"Mijnheer," said Turffs, "there are muscles that are not meant to move, but watch her."

Said the *zeeman* Ritter du Buys to a companion, in a low tone that did not escape the ears of Ruysdaal, "I'd give ten guilders to see her teats shake without body aid."

Soon the gate was jammed with dance-loving Bali folk. They edged farther in, and soon lined the orchestra for an even more colorful background than the performers could give. One girl, bare of breast, darted mischievous glances toward the guests of Piet de Turffs and moved her sarong-clad hips in a most provocative manner.

Said du Buys audibly, *"God verdomd!"*

She came closer to reveal a white beauty dot between her eyes just above the exquisitely arched brow. About her ear was a lontar leaf. Her smile was magic and her lips evoked various impressions — strange and stirring ones — from the new skipper of the *Quatrefoil*.

He felt the clawing pains of manhood. How strange and sweetly lethargic flowed the rivers of his body; how swift and vicious in the same thought. The commencement of one beat ran into another, and continued in wild syncopation that matched the fluttering fan of the *kebiyar* dance.

The sultry green of her skirt, a background for the cyclamen petals of silken pink, reflected in broad moon streaks the flashing movements of her supple muscles — it was the synthesis. It was, too, the opposite of sanity. A longing for absolute kingship over her soul and body flooded his being. Too consuming is passion like that, though the aftermath is worse — for the fruit a man will kill, will turn his soul's lining to the parching sun. Ruysdaal's nails bit at the split-bamboo arms of the veranda chair with the force of steel incisors.

"She's a beauty, no doubt of it, Sidneye," said Turffs. In the instant Sidneye's face turned upon him, seeking to stay its greed, and yet asking if the girl might be obtained. Piet de Turffs turned the unvoiced question with the easy propriety of a great host: "But, alas, Sidneye, these people have quaint customs. The breasts of a maiden are always uncovered and are not intended to excite one. Should she show her calf, then — there is invitation."

"But who is she, Mijnheer?"

"Suppose, Captain, that you remember her as Lonyta," he said easily.

"Remember her!" cried Ruysdaal.

"Yes," answered Turffs, unperturbed. "Until your next visit. Perhaps she'll wait."

With an incredulous expression written into the violent mask of his face, Ruysdaal sank back in his chair. The suggestion made by his host seemed almost a promise. But the waiting: around the world in the troughs of waves, one setting sun lengthened into a hundred, a thousand orders voiced in half-dejected manner, with her atop each ripple calling him on and on, ever out of reach: a moment in the royals, again riding the bowsprit in answer to the *lelong* of the sea, to the brass-barred *gansa* of the storm, the drumming voice of the *kendang*.

Aloud he said: "God pity the crew!"

Smiling, Piet de Turffs ordered the wine server to fetch gin for his guest.

3

The magic shafts from the leaning moon joined the sweetened gin in giving libation to the night. Here was a garden of earth and sky, and who could withhold the complaisance due the universe? The murmur of the Balinese night seemed but the voice of the fierce moon. Savage as a tiger, imploring another physical effort by the wrinkled and effete, who harbor still the passions of yesterday, the moon rose higher, laughing, sighing, on over the tropics. Then, laughing like the tiger, it slinks out of the sky, pale and spent. The morrow returns the clear sights of sanity; and sorrow, if the tiger's tongue had licked a hand.

He who courts moon madness shall surely find it.

Captain Mayrant Ruysdaal Sidneye gave no thought to the morrow as he stole away from the show of gamecocks loosed to the kill. He saw the natives carrying the curious containers of plaited coconut leaves, looking much like a handbag, the colored tail feathers dangling from the opening, as they awaited the matches. He had no appetite for flowing blood and the squawking death cries from the cocks. *Neen!*

For his eye was on the slinking form of Ritter du Buys. Almost unnoticed the sailor had strolled into the shadows of the compound, in the same direction as that taken by Lonyta. As Sidneye was swallowed by the heavy patchwork of shadows from thick palms, the sounds of raucous laughter and spirited wagering reached his ears in slow retreat. A hush descended over the group and he was aware that the baskets had been cut to allow each cock the eye of an adversary. Then the shouting grew in fury. The cocks were fitted with gaffs. The battle was on. A flashing stroke, an eye was punctured, a coat of polychrome green and red was pierced and a white breast was stained with gushing blood.

He had no eye for such entertainment. The spoor of Lonyta was fresh, and his eye was heavily glossed with moon madness. He stalked on, dodging behind a tree when the wary eye of du Buys turned about. From tree to tree he followed the sailor; and ahead of him, by some few yards, he saw Lonyta. She seemed unaware of the man's nearness, and her song to the moon rose into the clear air.

The sailor halted and watched her. She sat on the ground, stretched her legs and leaned back on widespread arms, turning her face to the moon. Ruysdaal advanced with caution and it was not until he was directly behind the sailor that he stopped. For minutes he stood watching Lonyta before making his presence known. Then, tiring of inactivity, he nudged swarthy-faced du Buys.

Slowly du Buys turned and eyed his master. A cynical smile crept over his face as he stood erect with arms akimbo and said: "Does Baas Sidneye order me away, or does he wish to make a man-to-man stand?"

A moment of silence, and then, "*Neen*, Mijnheer du Buys. I left the captain of the *Quatrefoil* at the cockfight. Only the man stands before you."

"No grudges afterward, Mijnheer?" said the sailor.

"*Neen*," came the answer.

Du Buys smiled, hunched forward, slowly let his brown arms lift and hang grotesquely in air, and circled Ruysdaal with slow, guarded steps. Then his fist lashed out and Ruysdaal was sorely put to dodge the blow. It grazed his neck and carried the sailor forward. The taut strength of the master's hand buried itself in du Buys's belly just above the groin. A low moan from a writhing *zeeman* rose from the ground;

nothing more as he turned toward the girl who still poured out melody to the savage moon.

She faced him at an oblique angle, her legs separated madly, the sarong parting to show the wild curve of a knee and beyond. For an eternity of ten seconds he stared, and then, without a word, and only an animal snarl sounding in his throat, he advanced upon her. She saw him and, though her song was stilled, she eyed him with a smile of surprise.

In another moment he was beside her. He kissed her, his one arm tightening about her neck, the other roving at the bidding of a mad hand. Sweet dizziness and drugged eyes, complete surrender to passion and a careless disregard for the future — this was the whole eternity of yesterday, today, and tomorrow! Nothing else mattered but Lonyta, and her offering to his mood!

And for a time she seemed to respond: an arm rose slowly to his shoulder, and, quivering, it crept sinuously about his neck; after an age of languid fondling, he caught her skirt and tore it from her. Voicing fright, she tore loose from him with the agility of a jungle cat and rolled away, and to her feet. She ran toward the sound of the merrymakers. She was stark naked. He stared in hypnotic fashion after her.

From the ground, near a fibrous palm trunk, came the jeering laughter of Ritter du Buys.

4

The black cock with the white tail feathers and breast was a favorite of Piet de Turffs, and on its head he placed, laughingly, a hundred guilders, another ten, five, and three times, one. The challenging bit of color, a red and purple cock with a small comb, thin legs, and an eye for blood, danced about impatiently, drawing the eye of Stefan, and causing him to accept the hundred-guilder wager of his host.

The sailors drew closer, tense and expectant. Host and former captain fanned the spirit of the occasion with loud and challenging blandishments of favored cocks. The Balinese, lovers of games and fights, saw and heard, and babbled excitedly as they closed the circle.

Lidj van der Glotz, smitten with drink and dance, and excitement unequaled in many moons, approached his friend Vee Vossler with a wager of five guilders: —

"'Tis on Baas Meer's judgment I've faith," he said, laughing because he was in a mellow mood.

"Five guilders on the red, you say? Ha! Ho! Lidj, the red cock hasn't a chance. Baas Meer's eye has clouded. Aye, I'll take, and I'll raise it two."

"You're on. Seven it is, Vee, my friend. And the other three itches in my palm."

"So it itches!" responded Vee. "Well, so does my pocket itch for it. Here! 'Tis done."

The money was slapped on the veranda floor with much gusto, and Lidj, beaming, cried out to the wine servers. With two cups sparkling, one for himself, the other for Vee, he encountered Stefan, and rocked to a sudden halt.

"Ho! Baas," he laughed. "I follow you, with a ten-guilder wager you're right. Aye, Baas, and guess with whom I wager. Ho! Ho! Mijnheer Vossler, no other."

"Is that so, Lidj, my boy? Ho! Ho! Ho! A trader he is, and no eye for a cock? His sights must improve or he'll perish in poor trade."

"Aye, Baas!" He shook with mirth, and the brimming glass sent precious drops falling to the thirsty ground. "How's Captain Sidneye betting? With us, I'll wager three guilders!"

"Aye," said Stefan, rumpling the flesh between his eyes. "But where is Sidneye!"

"Hey, Kees," Lidj cried, "have you seen Captain Sidneye?"

"*Neen*, Mate Van der Glotz. Perhaps *hy is stomdronken*."

"Strange indeed," said Stefan. He sighed, lifted his glass and cried: "Attention, *zeemen!* Hey?" He roared and the sound smashed against ears taught to obey that voice. Had he shouted, "Reef the mainsails and t'gallant'sls and sky'sls," every man there would have reached for a rope. Thus all ears were cocked for Baas Meer's words.

"Boys," he said, "I have a surprise for you. Before the red cock cuts the liver from the black buzzard —" his boasting humor drew a long laugh and many merry jeers. "Aye, before, as I said, I have a great surprise. So, as a tribute to you who have served well Baas Meer, I bid each man among you step forward. Now, *zeemen*, while you form a line to the left, I shall tell you that Ruysdaal Sidneye is my choice of a ship's master to carry you through storm and calm and fair winds. He is a man among men, a man whom each of you can love and respect. Aye, and as you know, he's a weather eye second to none.

"Come forward, Sidneye." His pause was long and his eye was sharp.

"Well, *zeemen*, he ran out on his speech, I see. And if he can drive the *Quatrefoil* as he dodges a bit of oratory, we'll all be smothered in guilders. Eh, *zeemen?*" A loud laugh went the rounds. Baas Meer was a great fellow.

"Now, men, come forward. Here, Vossler, you're the purser. Who's here?" he boomed, as the first in line faced him. "Stan Volg, and how many years have you served under me? No, let me tell you. Twelve years, Volg, and a good man before the mast you've been. Purser — ten guilders for each year."

A rousing cheer went up.

The ceremony was short and to the point; the men gave their unexpected wealth to the warmth of wine, and sheer bravado in the choice of cocks was met with a let-money-talk answer, which, since everyone was richer than Croesus, staggered the sums bet on each of the impatient feathered warriors.

Said Stefan: "Now, every man is accounted for except the captain, and — du Buys. Hey! Send up du Buys." When he was not forthcoming, Stefan said to Vee, "We'll reward him later. The show must start at once. Aye, I've a thirst to see the black cock's blood!"

Genial Turffs widened the circle, and declared that all bets must be made then or never, that the fight was to a finish; and the first cock to throw up his legs in fright, or death, must be the accepted loser. Then at a signal, the natives loosed the cocks.

In another moment their antics — beautiful, graceful, and swift, and more dramatic because the weaker of the two must forfeit life — held the audience in gripping silence. The black awaited the attack, and when it came, his counterthrust, a flash of high lights in the moonlight, sent the furious red cock backward. Then, without awaiting a second charge, he gave his legs the speed of a mongoose in a stabbing advance. Blood was drawn. A light wound it was, and scarcely annoying to the frenzied red. A leap, a clashing of heads, a flutter of wings, and the gleaming gaff of the red gamecock pierced an eye of the black. It was a master stroke, a brilliant co-ordination of muscle and fury; the black uttered a squawk and shook its head.

"Ha! Vee," said Lidj, "the battle is half won! Look, he's bewildered!"

"*Neen!*" shouted a dozen voices. "He's the more stirred up. He'll kill now! He wants blood!"

As the black leaped into the air, his metal spurs churning moonbeams, the red tore in for the kill. A tense moment was at hand, for each failed to give ground. Blood spurted, and they were so close it was impossible to determine from which it came. Then, with a primeval lust for the other's blood the black gave his all to the attack: metal sunk into the head of the red, and the other gaff, in a flashing arc, tore out the feathers of his neck; and as his breast glowed of thick blood, a piteous though brave farewell to life sounded above the fray. The red spun in a crazed circle, leaped into the air, hoping in the utter darkness of oncoming death to find the black.

As the black gamecock stood in gorgeous triumph, the red lay still except for the spasms of reflex, dying in his own blood.

Such a moment evokes silence. Losers forget they have lost, and winners must await the end of a long split second before voicing victory.

Into that moment, strangely choosing it above all others of the merry Bali night, a figure ran through the circle, stumbled, and fell; she was naked as she fell atop the dying cock.

Lonyta!

5

Ritter du Buys groaned, and the blood he spat was accompanied by curses. The men, Turffs and Stefan in the lead, shouted at Ruysdaal Sidneye, but he, with the bloodstained sarong still clutched in his hand, continued to pound du Buys's head and stomach, glorying in each moment. When, at last, he was pulled from the wounded man, his eyes glowed like coals from hell.

Du Buys shuddered, gurgled his own blood, and lay still. Only a twitching, a reflex like that of the red cock, escaped him.

The men got more than they wagered for: the black cock; Mayrant Ruysdaal Sidneye who, hunched forward, his arms held tightly behind him by Vossler and Stefan Meer, sent wave after wave of blood-red triumph from his maniacal eyes.

Ritter du Buys was dead. First Kuyter. Then du Buys. The first was sacrificed to hate and independence; the latter to unrequited passion for a woman. Lonyta.

CHAPTER XV

1

ON each side of a red lacquered table in a warehouse in Soerabaja — the hot afternoon drawing out the sweet-rancid odor of copra and steeping it with the pungent cajuput oil from the Moluccas, mace, raw rubber, cinchona, tobacco, clove, and Dutch tea — sat an ill-assorted foursome poring intently over a document. The paper told of a year of operations. One of the four was a huge man with an eye of authority; he was clad in a planter's suit. The man on his right was tall and bony. Opposite the planter sat a brown man with white hair and beard, a Moluccan to those whose eyes could distinguish the races of down under, and a genius of trade among his own people; he had been adopted by the fourth man, a squatty, almost bald young man who smiled with the face of one who is proud of accomplishment. He, evincing leadership, raised an eye to each of them, then gazed at the tall masts beyond the window that hoisted a banner sprinkled with designs, each of which had four lobes.

Each of the three raised an eye to this man who had, only that morning, placed a sign above the door of the warehouse. An ordinary procedure, though this bit of plank was destined to conjure up hate for these words: SIDNEYE, VOSSLER, EN MEER. On each side it was adorned with gilded quatrefoils.

There was little said as the report bowed to a climax. Only the Moluccan cast devoted eyes at the owner of the first name on the gleaming placard, and Stefan Meer forwarded a glance of approval into the solicitous eyes of Vossler.

Sharp and thin, and pensively ambitious, were the eyes of Ruysdaal Sidneye: in them was the birth of an empire, a vast network of commerce from variform enterprises, which, with a score of fleet vessels scouring the seas from the Society Isles to Ceylon, could grin at Amsterdam, and all of Europe for that matter, in dictatorial manner. The great pool of trade in the tropics would rest in Soerabaja, in this very warehouse; a new era could be effected through price slashing, and the take should be on a great volume, at prices to crowd out the less foresighted; his ships would operate both ways, converging on Soerabaja with cargo, and plying the routes to Europe and America; further gain through F.O.B. Java prices could, as he knew, send many an otherwise half-loaded ship to his pool before turning its bow toward home, even though it should necessitate a run all the way from Sydney to his warehouses. And Sydney! Why not a branch office there! And America beckoned. Now that the Spanish were driven out of the rich Philippines, he must compete with thrifty shipowners from Frisco. A branch office in Manila, under an American name! Why not!

Aye; a dozen *Quatrefoils*. Thus he dreamed, and he was not one to gaze at wandering clouds without setting traps for them.

Said Stefan: "And without reservations, Ruysdaal, you have accomplished the miraculous."

"That I have, Baas Stefan. I am not yet done, however. The drafts for your shares lie before you. They represent profit on your investment beyond the interest rate on the five thousand guilders you loaned me a year ago. In short, Baas, you have in hand from this one transaction twelve thousand guilders.

"Friend Vossler, your ship's pay is indeed a paltry memory, is it not? You have earned a premium of three thousand guilders.

"Batjoek, my friend, have you fared well? Aye, with a thousand at premium!" He chuckled.

"Now, Baas, about the *Quatrefoil*. Here are her earnings. Look them over."

Stefan accepted the papers, his eyes dancing to the draft attached. Lifting his brows in a gesture of acute surprise, he leaned forward and ran the chart of cargoes, destinations, and, at last, the sum total. He saw in the lists more than met the eye: crowded holds, quick ports, incessant haggling, minimum voyage expenses, new ports for new cargoes, and wares never before put ashore in quantities to compare with the Sidneye sales; there were expenses the *Quatrefoil* was unused to, the hiring of advance clerks to chronicle her cargoes, but for every penny spent a thousand showed in the profit columns. And, too, Stefan saw: shortened rations from the galley; severe fines imposed on the crew, purely for the pinching of pennies; every man doing the work of one and a half men.

Ruysdaal had crowded an extra season into the year. He had dodged inclement weather. He had speeded up his crossings by cutting short, almost to unholy painfulness, his stay in ports of call — it was anchorage, quick bartering, and "Up wi' the cable and point 'er to sea."

"And, by God, here was a genius of trade! Here was brains!" thought Stefan. He'd do well to tag along and allow the lad his whimsies. The *Quatrefoil* had, by his blowing wind into her sails, by his vain swagger and merciless hand, found her earnings tripled. It was something to think about.

Ruysdaal cut his meditation short with: "And, Baas, here's a packet of mail from Rotterdam. Read at your disposal, after I make my next proposition."

Stefan, like Vossler, felt the authority of the former stowaway's mien; it was not intended, but inculcated — sharpened by quick thinking and crisp, blunt orders; he was unaware of his own disparity.

"Batjoek," Ruysdaal said, "you may check on the *Zulinde Meer*. See that she's under new canvas before she puts out for Fakfak. And — under no circumstances will we ship cajuput oil." The brown man bowed out.

"Why?" said Stefan, beating Vee to the question by a mere second.

"Because, Mijnheers, we are buying." His expression, a suppressed grin and a wink, further answered their question. It seemed to say: That which is scarce becomes more valuable with its scarcity.

"But, Ruysdaal," said Stefan in droll tone that sought more than an answer to a question, "the *Quatrefoil;* what about her commitments for the green oil?" Here was a test indeed, he thought behind a wrinkled grin, for the company must separate itself, in a measure, from the *Quatrefoil.* One could not suffer because of the other, or for the other's gain.

"I'm glad that arises," said Sidneye. "The letters have been mailed, Baas, and they say: we regret. But here's where each hand finds a bath of gold. Instead we ship cinchona belonging to Sidneye, Vossler, en Meer aboard the *Quatrefoil.* Trading profit for the firm, and cargo profit for the ship."

"Umm!" ejaculated Stefan, before glancing triumphantly at Vee.

Stefan eyed the young man not yet thirty, and he could not fail to see the whole of his makeup, the bone, the marrow, the flesh: of the bulk he was proud, of the offal he was ashamed; but there it was, interlaced with the better qualities, and flowing in the same streams. His mind went back to Turffs's gay night a year ago, to the sparkling revelry that inherited passion and murder, to the glamorous creature who unwittingly evoked the hell in Sidneye. Damn her for the trouble she'd caused!

2

The affair was not one that lent itself to a gentle hushing. Too many men had witnessed the killing of du Buys; and Turffs, a jolly fellow as a host, had turned into an outraged beast when he saw his house defiled. Nor could he be blamed for resenting such a reward for his elaborate pains. Nor could Stefan, who had bellowed forth his independence of any man: —

"We'll see the thing through!" he said, when the men volunteered — for reasons that were nauseatingly akin to fawning to their new master — to swear in a given direction. "*Neen!* No man shall ever live to cause me fear of his tongue. We'll see this mess through."

"Aye!" said the host with acid-fastness. "Dutch law prevails in Denpasar, and by God, it will not be cheated on my account!"

Vossler and Lidj sought to placate him, but their pleas fell upon ears that were numb to anything but the pumping of angered blood.

"The crime stinks to the high heavens," said Turffs, when he was again accosted by the sailors on the veranda. "For a man so to enslave himself to a swinging gut I have no sympathy. Fornication is one thing, but murder to achieve it shouts of insanity!"

Sidneye stood before them, listening, awaiting the order that would bring the minions of the law. He was aware of his madness, now that his deeds had cooled the fires of rage and lust, but in his soul he could find no compunction. He merely studied the men before him.

"Mijnheer Turffs," he said, "I don't like your words."

"Did I beg your advice or opinion of my words, murderer? But tell me, did you rape the girl?"

"*Neen.* But not because I possess any aversion toward rape, Mijnheer. She ran away."

"I am glad," said Turffs, in less violent voice. "Bali is a haven of peace and lovable souls, Mijnheer Sidneye, and you are out of place here."

Ruysdaal bowed low in mockery. "Then, why don't you send your dogs for the police? Your words bore me."

Stefan got to his feet and advanced to his protégé. "My boy," he said, half in anger, half in regret, "suppose you keep your counsel. That is all I ask." Then he turned away, beckoned Turffs to follow him, and left the men centered about Sidneye, and in the wake of a heavy quiet.

Strangely, the *Quatrefoil* turned her bow to the sea the following morning, and du Buys's body slipped into the waters of the Indian Ocean; all heads were bared except one. The matter died, and none, not even the new captain, knew how Stefan Meer paid for the silence of Piet de Turffs.

3

"Give us your plans, Sidneye lad," encouraged Stefan. "Then I'll open this letter, which I am sure both of us wish to read." The envelope was long and covered with many marks, the most interesting of which was the word "Hamburg."

"Umm!" said Sidneye. "There is no doubt of it." The eyes of the *baas* said more than words could outline: they told of one of his reasons for snatching the stowaway twice from the clutches of the law.

Vossler grunted in complete ignorance, though he placed the lid on a world of conjecture with the blankest of looks, as his mind's eye leaped to Zulinde Schouten.

"I propose," said Sidneye, "to expand our operations. We must either shrink or grow, and I see opportunities for the latter. I have, with the aid of Batjoek, conducted many strange experiments in the Moluccan trade, the result of which proves the wisdom of reaching out a hand and clasping monopolies. Aye! We find the world begging while we establish protocols. Let our wares mount with slow speed, and without the seeing eyes of our competitors, who must continue to look upon us as minnows in a sea of commerce."

"High sounding," commented Stefan, "though it is without props so far. But continue." He smiled his indulgence.

"We are centered, geographically, in a treasure, so I hereby take this compass and draw an arc. At two thousand miles we pierce Siam; we tip north of the American Philippines; at ten above the equator on the downward swing, Yap, and on the dot we strike at three below, Hollandia. Inside the arc are Borneo, the Celebes, the Moluccas, also Sumatra and the Malay States. From Oeleelhoue to Merauke, the Indies are ours. I suggest we work it."

His listeners gazed at the chart and built lesser images.

"Then from Sydney we draw a complete circle. New Zealand, Caledonia, the whole of worth-while Australia is ours to cruise systematically."

"With what?" asked Stefan.

"Yes, with what?" said the dreamer. "I'm glad you ask — while your dividends rest before your eyes. I have recently examined two seaworthy ships. Both are for sale, and one of them is priced far below her actual worth. The *Vrouw of Timor* is a steal. I've haggled for two days and, at last, when her owner was pickled in the juice brewed by Batjoek, he agreed to my price. The other, an inter-island ketch, goes on the block tomorrow unless she's sold. The lad who owns her doesn't want to watch such a ceremony and — well, he's now in an orgy of love with one whom I paid to lessen his obduracy. I understand she is a barbaric creature."

Stefan laughed. "You go to great lengths to achieve your ends."

"I do," said the trader in a voice of iron.

"And the name of the ketch?"

"We'll rename her. She's to work north of the Sulu Archipelago, and warehouse at Davao. The *Quatrefoil* will take on her stores."

"*Verdomd!* You've already got her on her course!" laughed Stefan. "But you haven't quoted prices."

"*Neen.* But a price is like a whore, merely a fancy. If it suits one, well and good. It is so simple, Baas. There are always others. But here." He placed a piece of paper before them, on which were listed the maker, age, capacity, and stores, together with the quoted price of each ship.

"Have you seen these vessels, Vee?" asked Stefan.

"I have, Baas, and I must agree with Sidneye. And, not to influence you in this matter, I am placing my full stipend here back into the deal."

Said Meer without glancing up, and without emphasis, "You were ever a practical man, Vee."

"Come, let me show you the ships," offered Vossler, "and you'll heartily agree."

"*Neen*," said Stefan. "I don't feel like the walk. You two are connivers after my money," he added, laughing, "so I hereby pass back my premium." To Sidneye he said: "Well, are you so poor a businessman that you pass up your part of the profits of the *Quatrefoil?*" His gruffness had the ring of a blessing.

"I do not," answered Sidneye. "That is your job, not mine. But first, beloved Baas, will you aid Vee in selecting crews for the ships?"

"No!" thundered the man. "I'm through with the sea!"

Sidneye nudged Vee openly, and together they laughed. Stefan's eyes narrowed as he stared from one to the other, but he soon joined them, giving his deep voice a rumble that came from his belly. They were thus engaged when the Moluccan entered the rough office and tapped Sidneye on the shoulder.

Sidneye's laughter died as he listened. Then he said, "What's that? Not the *Luzon Queen!*" Turning to his associates he said, his face growing red, "I must go. The Japanese are bidding for the *Alice Macdonald*, the ship I'd name *Luzon Queen!*"

4

Confronting the too polite saffron assembly aboard the *Osura Maru*, docked near the ketch, Sidneye, with an air of complete authority, ordered the young owner of the ketch, who should have been sleeping off an orgy, to stand aside. But the lad was openly defiant; and with a significant nod at Batjoek, Sidneye smiled, offered apologies to the sons of Nippon, and awaited the fulfillment of his unspoken order to the Moluccan.

It came soon: the owner of the ketch felt Moluccan sinews of spring steel; he was led from the cabin door, down the gangway, and ashore. Smiling broadly, Sidneye sought to placate the curious minds behind those slant eyes. To the Japanese translator he said: —

"A thousand pardons to our good friends of the north. Only my fond regard of your honorable and worthy talents, of your ancient customs, blessed by your ancestors and living in the great symbol, your emperor, gives me the freedom of such actions. Shall we go inside where we can talk without the ears of the wind?"

The four bowed and smiled profusely, darting shrewd and wary glances at one another as their bland smiles told of utter innocence.

"Enter," said the linguist in smooth Dutch. "We are proud to welcome so great a friend."

Inside the cabin Sidneye beamed as he produced a paper. The Japanese read in the swift tongue of his countrymen, raised his head and babbled a bit, evoking stabs at words from slow and quick heads that craned over the paper; and, at last, blank silence. Then he raised his eyes and asked: "Is this authentic, honorable one?"

"See for yourself," came the blunt answer.

Again the Japanese talked among themselves without pause for any answer; as suddenly as it began dead silence reigned. "And what connections have you, O honorable Sidneye, with the police?"

"Plenty. Enough to have the culprit jailed — even if he is my nephew."

"Nephew?"

"Aye, though I'm less proud of him than if he were a Fiji black, sons of Nippon."

"But he possessed the papers," said the translator.

"Aye, he's a thief! That's why I paid him a fabulous price for the tub — so he would steal less for his low women. But I know why he tried to sell you the ship. He hates the honorable Japanese and hopes to rob them."

"Then the vessel belongs to you?"

"Aye!"

Again the flowing jargon, and after much pantomimic clashing of opinions, the leader smiled and said, "We are greatly indebted to our great friend of the Netherlands kingdom. But could we purchase the vessel from you, honorable owner?"

"It is not for sale."

An oily smile preceded the velvety hiss of the linguist as he said, "But for a profit in yen equivalent to — to a thousand guilders' profit on your investment?"

Shrewdly the Dutchman eyed them. Here was profit for the taking, but why were the jackals so willing to pay more than the false figure, exceeding by far his actual offer to the lad, for that one boat? What did she carry that the owner could not see? He studied the faces alive with soothing smiles, and replied: —

"You fail to interest me. We are both aware of her actual worth as a ship, but we are also on common ground, honorable ones, when we view her worth to you." He grinned, heard his speech put into Japanese, and

173

sat back to await an end of their palaver. Fierce eyes met his and the volume of their speech rose and lingered. At last they faced him in a body, like toy soldiers who do everything in unison, while their spokesman said: —

"You are a great trader, O honorable Sidneye, and we are willing to increase our offer to the equivalent of ten thousand guilders' profit."

"Very well. I shall return here within two hours. Then, if I have decided to sell, I'll expect you to have the money in cash — guilders."

The terms were satisfactory and the four bowed him out, smiling. He was aware that with the contemplated Sidneye, Vossler, en Meer invasion of the northern trade routes he must return smile for smile. This he did.

5

He was soon aboard the slattern ketch, the *Alice Macdonald*. Pausing, he stared at the yellow sails with gaping holes, at the hazardous ratlines that soared into the forward mizzen. The two masts showed plainly of sea rot, and her ropes were frayed with age. The deck planks seemed to buckle and she was minus battens for her hatchway. A roaming eye dwelled for a moment on the cable, saw it was rusting in solid chunks. But for all her faults she could be made to order; he was already acquainted with her timber, and that, he said with a seaman's eye, was the pulse of any ship. With fresh canvas, and new planks, masts, and shrouds, she'd fly before a wind like a dragonfly on a pond.

But, God in heaven! She wasn't worth the sum he'd staggered! *Neen!* Even with paint on her hull and all the trappings of a yacht she wasn't worth the yen they bid.

With a cautious eye he went below, and soon Batjoek gave pretense of enjoying the fierce sun of the deck while his feet rested in the companionway. He had a strange and shrill whistle that pierced distances; it was like the wild birds of Halmahera, said some who had heard it, but by Mayrant Sidneye it was forbidden, unless it trilled in warning.

The owner lay in a corner of his cabin, outwardly subdued, but snarling. His adventure at sea had been financed by a fat parental purse, though he was now acquainted with poverty, with brusque refusals of more aid from his father in Melbourne. Thus he put his sole possession up for sale. A curly head and reddened cheeks gave his periwinkle-blue eyes, his mildly aquiline nose and strong, thin lips a certain masculine beauty that was appealing. His dress, as the ship's sails, shouted of last-penny erosion: he seemed lacking in all but spirit.

Sidneye stood smiling at him, before marching across the narrow cabin and helping him to his feet. The lad brushed him away, staring fiercely at this Dutchman who only yesterday was all smiles, and today the brute who gave his servant the nod for Oriental tricks that might subdue any man.

"You've got your nerve, goddam you!" growled the lad. "Now get off my ship or I'll set the law on you!"

"One moment, Mijnheer Younguer. One moment, please. What I did, my friend, was to your advantage. Sit down and let us talk. Just because you must sell this fine ship is no reason why you should be cheated. Or is it?" He smiled steadily and watched the boy who, almost convinced, but not quite, saw little to be lost by a few words; and, too, he was curious.

"Very well, *Mister* Sidneye. Have a seat."

"That is better," said the trader, reaching for a chair and straddling it without taking his eyes off his subject. "Now Mijnheer, let us hurdle any personal differences and get down to facts. You have here a very untidy boat and no means with which to repair her. You have offers from the Dutch and Japanese. Know what the yen is worth?"

"I'm no fool," retorted the lad. "I know the exchange rate as well as you."

"Do you?" said Sidneye, covering his sarcasm with a smile. "But do you know what they had planned for you? Do you? I thought not. You are bound for Sydney, are you not? They would offer you free passage, my foolish friend, and leave you penniless and without grounds for complaint, once you set foot on native soil. How do I know? I am a trader and traveler."

"I don't believe you."

"Very well. The door is open, Mijnheer, and you are free to trade with them. And — I shall withdraw my offer. Rather, I'd enjoy your plight." He saw the youth rise and start for the door, only to halt abruptly and cloud his face with indecision.

"Go ahead, Younguer."

The owner flopped into a chair and eyed his guest. "What is your offer?" he asked savagely.

"A little cash, a little stock, and a seaman's bunk aboard the grandest ship ever to sail the seas."

The boy laughed scornfully: it seemed to assuage his beaten pride. "There's only one ship in port I'd sign on. But you don't own her."

"And her name?"

"The *Quatrefoil*" — defiantly.

Sidneye voiced no answer as he fished his licenses from a pocket and flung them into the boy's lap. He was greatly pleased with himself when the belligerent eyes of a moment before slowly bulged with respect when they saw not only the *Quatrefoil's* skipper but her part owner.

"What do you mean by a little cash?"

"Enough for a nest egg — say one third of the price I set on the *Alice*. The remainder of the sum in stock shares."

"In what?"

"Sidneye, Vossler, en Meer."

"Never heard of them."

"*Neen*, my impulsive friend, but you shall. And should you learn the sea — and God knows you'll have the chance aboard the *Quatrefoil* — I'll make you a skipper of a Sidneye ship. Of course, you must study the sea, the people of every port, and learn to trade. I need men who are not merely content to run before a wind. Give me traders."

"It sounds all right, Mr. Sidneye, but — I don't know your firm. Your stock might be worthless."

"Aye," answered Sidneye. "That is for you to decide. Suppose you visit the British Consulate and inquire into the financial structure of the firm. Then check at the Javasche Bank."

The lad was torn with indecision.

"I'll hold the offer open two hours, Mijnheer Younguer, no longer."

6

He kept the Japanese waiting beyond the time limit. He was glad the Australian was sharp enough to look before he leaped — he wanted no future captain of a Sidneye vessel weighted with unpardonable gullibility; then, too, he was given a chance to turn the unkempt *Alice* inside out while Batjoek guarded the hatchway. This he did with the thoroughness of a Chinese designer of secret compartments.

The foul odor of bilge met him, but sweating and cursing he swore not to abandon his search. Again he moved to the lad's quarters and began sounding the planks one by one. He tore coverings loose, sought caches in furnishings, ever aware that Orientals seldom secreted objects or papers where one would ordinarily look. No doubt he was within an arm's length of that which gave preposterous value to the *Alice Macdonald*. Every inch of the cabin fell under his piercing scrutiny, and no sooner did his eye rest on wood or metal than his hand felt for springs and buttons. Tables and chairs were all but torn apart, and the lean galley was actually dismantled.

He stood, at last, in the companionway, disgusted and stubbornly clinging to self-control. Above him was the sunlight, against which Batjoek stood as a silhouetted watchdog; below were the planks that bridged the hold; and above the deck formed the immediate ceiling. It was indeed strange that no binnacle should hang there. In a storm the cabin door must be closed, particularly since the *Alice* was minus battens, and even on a placid sea at night there was need for a lamp.

Peering closer he saw the almost eradicated marks of screws. A lamp had once been there! Aye! And why should it have been removed? Soon he was atop the boxes piled against the starboard side and prying at the boards. There was a large square showing plainly its outline of cement. He pried and pushed to no avail, then sought a belaying pin to persuade the wood. At length it was opened.

He struck a light into the hole and saw nothing more than strings of pitch from the cracks in the deck. His hands felt about as far as they could reach into the dark and rested on plank and dumps of pliable pitch. With the pin he pried loose the smelly black heaps only to uncover timbered surfaces. Again he struck a light and slitted his eyes for a closer view.

Some yards away an unusual shape caught his eye. It was pitch-covered but sharper than the natural ooze of the suffocating stuff. As he sought a means to reach it, his elbow struck a fine string of black wire; he caught it, slowly tightened it until he saw the sharp outline move in the pitch bed. Soon the object was in his hands, and hurriedly, excitedly, he tore loose the covering of black glue.

In his hand lay a small pouch about five inches in length, its mouth sealed with leather drawstrings and fine ragged wire wrappings. Hastily he opened it, cutting his fingers until they bled.

Into the palm of his hand he emptied the contents: seven brilliant, rich green cuts of beryl — seven emeralds worthy of a diadem for a queen! Seven emeralds, and one giant black pearl! The sight of the last to fall from the pouch was enough to stay the breath of any mortal.

A mold that gave off the odor of death, that was green and mealy, fell into his hand with the gems. He brushed it aside without notice. But when it found the raw flesh of his hand where the serrated wire had dug channels, he winced. A drop of blood ran from his wounds, dripping of mold, down the sides of the gorgeous black pearl.

"God!" he exclaimed, forgetting the searing fire in his fingers. "It is worthy of — Lonyta!"

Later that same day, after the *Alice Macdonald* became the property of the Sidneye firm, after she was then sold to the Japanese aboard the *Osura Maru* at a fabulous profit, after the lad, Wilde Younguer, carried his sea bag aboard the queen of all ships and began an apprenticeship that would one day find its reward in Sidneye gold and power, Mayrant Ruysdaal Sidneye sat before his friends, Vossler and Meer, with the bland Moluccan, Batjoek, at his side. He gave an account of his doings.

To describe Stefan Meer as awe-struck is lacking in emphasis: his jaw dropped and held, and his experienced eyes literally bulged from their sockets; the profit on the *Luzon Queen* was enough to draw a shocked face into respect of hovering miracles; but the gems!

"The profits, and the emeralds, go to the firm," said Sidneye, suddenly wincing. "The pearl" — he raised the huge globule and gazed into it — "remains mine."

Then, without warning or apparent reason, the muscles of his face twitched in spasms that set in motion the encroaching fat of his jowls: the pain of his lacerated hand was excruciating.

The black pearl fell to the floor and rolled to within an inch of the wharf's edge, and there it slowly rocked back and forth in the hot winds from the Java Zee, as if undecided on its future course.

CHAPTER XVI

1

IN the ensuing weeks many doctors bent over an emaciated young man only to raise their heads, wipe away the sweat of despair, and stalk away. The peculiar malady took on a reputation, and even in Batavia men of science discussed the case back and forth. The definitions they gave were lacking in sureness, and each listener calmly swore to inject the missing resonance when his informal opinion was given voice. But with the words on his tongue he too was smitten with the curse of apocryphal speech. It was eventually dubbed "Sidneye's Smite." Veterans and apprentices beat a path to the house of Vee

Vossler in Soerabaja, where suffered the patient whose disease began with a cut hand.

Then one morning there came to the door a mere lad, one whom Nand Vossler eyed with subdued amusement. She led him to the waiting room, where three doctors sat awaiting the fourth to stamp out of the room in the agonies of a medical Waterloo. One of the doctors addressed the young man, and he grunted an answer; evidently taciturn to the point of snarling, thought the bearded three.

"Are you a Dokter?" the oldest dared a question.

"I am," said the youth, bristling.

The three men eyed him and sighed heavily: ah for the naïve blush of youth, the bloom of ambition. Then each felt a growing pity for the lad. He was so young, and no doubt so very susceptible to failure as to throw his life away once he tasted its dregs. Their run of thought was broken by the exit of the doctor from the patient's room.

"No?" said one of them, his single word carrying the full load of wonder.

"No."

After long hours in which the three departed in failure, one by one, the lad entered the room. He paused, drank in the setting at a single glance before directing dark eyes at the patient, who in turn eyed the one hundred and twenty-third physician and cursed him for belonging to so inefficient a body.

"*Neen!*" Ruysdaal exclaimed, trying to sit up in bed. "But you are too young." He ground his teeth and said: "What do you want?"

The young Dokter was Sidneye's equal in fierceness and his reply was gruffly sharp. "I want to help you. I can, Mijnheer, if, and only if, you believe me. Give me your answer quickly for I have no time to waste. A boat leaves for Amsterdam before noon. Have you more questions?"

Ruysdaal eyed him narrowly, menacingly, and at last, after sitting upright, said slowly: "*Neen.*"

"Very well, Mijnheer Sidneye. You have conquered your own doubt — I am a countryman of yours, and not an assassin. We are making progress. First, I shall introduce myself. I am Dokter van Arken, age twenty-three, of Zuid-Holland. My study of poisons, their marks and antidotes, their strange aftereffects, their numerous turns and almost unbelievable eccentricities, has borne a fruit I dare not proclaim."

"Why?" asked the inveterately practical Sidneye.

"That, Mijnheer, is none of your business. But since you've the gall to ask I'll answer. I pay less heed to accepted facts and more to my own theories. Such is not conducive to the praise of scientific bodies. Your

179

case, I hope, will give me the ears of the world. I intend to pronounce you well within a short time. Well or dead."

"Somehow, Dokter van Arken," said Sidneye, "you remind me of myself. And should you accomplish that I'll reward you. Only, however, if you agree to conduct your experiments with me as your patron."

For the first time the Dokter laughed. "Do I look like a fool?" he said. "I want only two things; the first is fame, the second independence. I had expected only the former in your case." Then he scowled at the patient.

For long moments the eyes of the men locked: in the savage exchange there was challenge that grew into respect; each was hungry for his own fame and fortune, each ruthless and determined.

"Very well," said the Dokter. "I shall begin at once. Get up!" The order came like the crack of a pistol. Ruysdaal stared at him. "Get up! Stand!"

"I — I can't. Why do you ask that?"

"No questions, Mijnheer Sidneye. I want nothing but implicit obedience from you. Nothing short of that will do. I work in a strange manner, Mijnheer, in the laws of the opposite. You cannot stand on your feet — so you think — but you can. Now!"

Mayrant Ruysdaal Sidneye could hardly believe his eyes: he was standing beside his bed gazing at the two purplish props that wobbled as they gave him support. Said Arken: "You should not be alive, but you are. Now walk to me." And Mayrant obeyed, his steps slow and uncertain, his eyes alive with fear, joy, and wonder, like those of a baby first risking a distance to a proud parent.

"Fetch me a glass of water," ordered the Dokter. A minute later he said, "Now stand before me." He moved back, and Sidneye, his mind forgetting his legs, moved forward more like an adult than a child. Van Arken laughed. "This act has little bearing on the case — except that it proves you can respond to force."

Van Arken stared at the nodules that had slowly worked up the arm and neck and on down and across Sidneye's body. "As I have said, you should already be dead. And within another month you will be — unless, of course, we experiment at once."

"Experiment!" exclaimed Mayrant. "I thought you knew the poison."

"Let us call it a fungus infection, the remedy for which I have not yet tried on a human being. Don't look so surprised, Mijnheer." Again their eyes locked. "Are you ready, Mijnheer Sidneye? The pill will be bitter. Do you relish the thought of my injecting the living bite of anopheles mosquitoes into your red corpuscles?" he almost shouted. "Which is malaria!" he added. "It is truly a departure is it not?" He smiled diabolically. "Are you ready?"

"I am ready."

"The agonies of failure are more merciful than those of success. But, the road is long and fierce. Your very guts will rise in your throat; a million hot needles, fever, and sweat, and who knows what else, since we experiment." He stared. "You're quite sure you're ready?"

"I'm ready!" thundered Mayrant.

2

Nand Vossler sighed with the sound of the knocker. Another medical man, she said under her breath, who must be turned away. Repetition was sufferable for a time, but she had reached the stage of nervous acuteness, wherein her body remained rigid and her mind's ear ever awaited another pounding on the wood.

For long weeks Vee had been at sea. The *Quatrefoil* must sail, he had said during the first week of Sidneye's sickness, and so with their older boy, Raas, he had hoisted sail and pointed the bow to the Moluccas; with them went Lidj van der Glotz, leaving only Stefan and, at regularly spaced intervals, the strange creature, Batjoek. But in these days Christiaan, the fifteen-year-old son, seemed to endear himself further to her. How kind and attentive he was; his eyes spoke as he gazed at her, saying: Mother dear, what else can I do to add to your happiness; have I failed in any way? And she had put into her eyes an answer that was the eloquence of a blessing. But beautiful Christiaan had been at the wharf weeks back when the young Dokter came.

She had, on that day, hurried to Sidneye's room; and, as she met the Malay couple assigned to him coming through the veranda door from the garden, she felt the end had come — simply because they had failed in their duty. Never leave him alone, she had ordered, and Stefan had also driven home the words. But there she met young van Arken, who bluntly made demands for the care of the patient, who said, "He suffers from sporotrichosis," adding without feeling, "I am injecting malaria. If that fails, and he lives, we'll resort to another experiment — iodine, given intravenously."

How lightly he spoke of experiments. Nand was shocked.

The night had been one of horror. No sounds came from the patient's room, but she lay awake even into the wee hours, listening, ever listening. With sleep the shock of the day took possession of her subconscious mind, and she saw again the mass of poisoned flesh. Only it pursued her, rolling, drooling, laughing, and assuming fantastic shapes. Then a jungle of living vines and moving tendrils coiled about her neck, arms, and body; and then, when the tentacles held her, the awful shape of a stem from a leaf, the body of Mayrant Sidneye, sought to pierce her.

Her screams brought her beloved Christiaan, and for long moments she held the soothing flesh of her flesh close to her. Sleep came while he stroked her forehead.

As the days wore into weeks, the dream repeated itself.

So Nand forced her body to the door that morning, paused to massage her temples before sighing despondently and raising her head in defiance to her mood. The door was thrown open; the shock was too sweet. She fainted in the arms of her greatly bemused spouse.

The Vossler house had indeed inherited a cycle of shocks, the greatest of which was to fall over the happy family reunion when the gong sounded the evening meal. It came about quite unexpectedly . . .

3

The volcanic range to the south seemed to brush away the mists for a farewell to the day; towering peaks and purple crevices were a blaze of color mellowed by tawny distances in one moment; and in the next, when the sun dangled in the moving western heavens, only the ridges drew a color that bowed toward Batavia; the rest was a parade of diminishing brilliance, made duller by the inflected rose and gold that hugged the western crags. Southward, on beyond the rugged horizon, lay the eastern arm of the mighty Indian Ocean.

The view from the Vossler house veranda was one enjoyed by Nand, Vee, Raas, and Christiaan alike; and on this evening by Stefan Meer and Lidj, as well as another man in their midst.

He was a young man with an unusual face, heavy in a way, though reminiscent of one's conception of masculine perfection. His eyes were bright and sharp, of a blue blue that was accented by a jungle of hair that ran over his brow. His nose was straight as a die, and thin. It was his mouth that attracted one in greater measure, for it seemed to strike a perfect co-ordination in breeding and character: it was a noble mouth. What it lent his face and coiling locks was, to men, strength of purpose; to women, a lively awareness of sex.

He was tall; not slim: balanced with the taper of a spinning top he exemplified a lively strength of body that seemed to lend power to his purpose. But he had a fault — though dressed as a layman, he told them he aspired to the robes of the Church. Fault? Indeed! No admiring young woman could look upon him as a future husband; therefore he was more desirable because of inaccessibility.

But how inexperienced was Harmenszoon van Schreeven whose bigoted mind was a field for portentous battles against heathenism. He fretted because he was not yet a priest. He said, as Nand compared him to her Raas, who sat beside her: —

"How utterly lazy is this world of yours. It beckons one to forget all tomorrows and find contentment in the present."

Nand laughed. "How I can agree with you, young man. When first we came here I dropped twenty years. But, like me, you must realize it will soon become a part of you."

"When I am a priest I shall rescue the souls who have become a part of it." He spoke in a mellow, inviting tone.

"The Indies are idyllic," returned Nand. "One's head becomes sweetly drugged. I pity the poor souls it turns forever — and there are many who never can be the same again."

Harmenszoon frowned. "I shall strive to remember your illustrations." He stood, moved to the edge of the veranda, and peered at the coppery hues against a spire of virgin rock many miles away.

Raas and Lidj had a game of cards going their way against Vee and Stefan Meer, and their laughter drowned out the copper and gold film in van Schreeven's eye. Nand made a laughing remark about her lovable children, its tone recognizing no disparity in the foursome.

Said the pious lad, "Someday I shall begin a great work of conversion. The sinner must relinquish his sin and fall at the Lord's feet."

Nand bit her lip, and Stefan, his eye and ear playing truant for the moment, frowned. Catching her eye, he winked slowly, and Nand, beautiful in her maturity of forty-and-six, was even more lovely as she gave her brow an arch that said: Poor boy, I wish you luck, but let's talk of other things. She enthusiastically put her question: —

"But your voyage, Mijnheer van Schreeven?"

"Ah, yes!" he laughed. "Never can I forget the conflicting emotions that assailed me from the Waterweg to your harbor, And I think Raas felt the same. I'm afraid he'll never become a *zeeman*."

"Raas?" she said, smiling. "*Neen*. His fancy runs to figures and books."

"It is just as well," said Harmenszoon wisely. "Just as well. The men of the sea are a hard lot. Were it not for my respect for your spouse, dear woman, I'd have beaten the profanity out of several of the crew."

"Eh! What's that?" asked Vee.

"No eavesdropping please," said his wife merrily.

"But I heard. And I must forever warn Mayrant's brother that a *zeeman* who does not swear is a landsman. Right, Stefan?"

"Right," said Stefan in booming laughter. "And by the Great Horn Spoon, Vee, we win a pot. Thanks to you, sweet Nand, for capturing his eye." His laugh died pleasantly.

"Does Mayrant swear like a sailor?" Harmenszoon asked frowning. Stefan, as well as Vee and Lidj, forgot their cards again.

"Harmenszoon," said Lidj, "you must not expect to see the brother you knew in Holland. You will see a man among men, my lad, one who is destined to become a power in this land. Indeed he swears, he does more. Aye! Because no man ever lived who could throw more wind in a sail, who could turn a guilder to a profit faster than he. *Neen!* So don't expect a man of your sort."

"I am amazed," said the lad.

"You needn't be," laughed Lidj, "and for the love of peace among us, don't betray your feelings."

"*Neen,*" said Vee. "Instead, act knowingly. And," he inserted a humorous lift to the topic, "do the opposite of your brother. If you do not you'll never wear the robe of the Church."

Harmenszoon laughed outwardly; he seemed for the moment an earthly human being. But with his half-brother's tormented soul at stake, he writhed inwardly and at last said that which a mind of experience would have shelved: "So my brother is not of the Lord's house. Then my first mission is to lead him there."

Silence cannot forever be soundless, and in that moment it took on voice: he felt the exchange of worried glances, of pregnant thoughts of pity from those older in years and reason; and he knew a flurry of anger at their refractory thinking, at their piteous glances that assailed him. In a flash he asked the Lord's mercy upon his countrymen who harbored the lethargic weakness of East Indian heathens. He saw the game come to an end before its rightful finish, thanks to Stefan, who pushed back his chair and raised a finger.

"Lend an ear, young man, to the voice of one who can save you many troubled thoughts. You do not know much about Mayrant. I do. Vee does. And Lidj. I can tell you now, and with fatherly advice, or with the roughness my years command, that you are not to approach your half-brother — should he live — with any thought of converting him."

The young zealot cocked his head in perplexed manner, then laughed. "But, Mijnheer Meer, surely you cannot expect me, his own brother, to leave him wallowing in sin."

"I can, and I do," said Stefan in the voice of the master of the *Quatre-foil*. "If you persist in such insanity I shall ship you out to Bali this very evening."

"But you cannot do that against my will."

"Can't I? Listen to me! Here in the tropics we take steps we feel are just. You are to report to your father's uncle in Denpasar, to Father Vandermeer? Your orders are to follow the bow of the *Quatrefoil* to Bali, aren't they?"

"Why, yes, Mijnheer," he answered curiously.

"And should I choose to sail tonight, could you remain?"

"I see. I see. Indeed you have me there."

"I really have you there, as you say," laughed the Baas. "And I'll do just that if you fail to give me your solemn vow."

"But why do you persist in keeping him from the word of God?"

"Because," said Stefan emphatically, "he hasn't got a soul to absorb it, if you must know. It's a long story, my boy, and one you'd scarcely understand. But, mark you, I'm telling you the truth. Lidj, do you bear me out?"

"I do, Baas."

"And Vee?"

"I'm afraid, Harmenszoon, that Baas Stefan is telling you the truth. But come," he added with a buoyant laugh designed to brighten all faces. "What kind of a host am I to allow our talk to run in gloomy channels? Nand, send out refreshments. Christiaan, tell me, did you long for your father?

"Aye, Harmenszoon, here's a lad for you," he laughed. His arms went about the quiet, effeminate lad and brought him to his lap. "He's inclined in your direction. Now Raas there — the rascal — he'll be a shipper's clerk, sure as you're born!"

"*Neen*, Father," said Raas. "I've decided to enter the firm. Baas Stefan has agreed that after an apprenticeship I can take over in Batavia."

"Wait," said Stefan. "I said if it suited Sidneye."

"Well," retorted Raas, with the smile of victory on his face.

"So," Vee cried, pretending annoyance at their secrecy, "you two connive behind my back! Well, everybody is joining the Sidneye boom. And what a boom 'twill be — if our genius of trade stays at the helm."

Van Schreeven frowned, made an empty gesture, and said: "It seems everything revolves about my half-brother! I don't understand. Is he the all-important man, and if so, why?"

Stefan seized the conversation. "He is the smartest trader I have ever

185

seen. He outthinks all of us, acts with the speed of a mongoose, and there — there's profit for all. Indeed, I'm afraid you underrate your brother's importance. He has made Vee rich, he has further enriched me, and Lidj cannot complain. He has broken all records for earnings of the *Quatrefoil*." Stefan eyed the perplexed youth before adding, "And you would change that?" He laughed.

"Indeed," voiced the lad. "Money is nothing compared to the Lord."

"And mark you these words," boomed Stefan, "the Lord is nothing to Mayrant Sidneye compared to his passion for gold!"

Harmenszoon, somewhat taken aback by the fierce outburst in company with the flashing eyes of the old sea dog, involuntarily fingered the lobe of his ear with distracted uncertainty. What was wrong with Mayrant, what was between him and the Lord that these people should decree his soul beyond repair; what crime was too great for the Lord to forgive? He hoped the tenets of his religion would in the years to follow equip him with the acumen to deal with such questions. He smiled as he thought of his future, a year under Father Vandermeer, then his study for priesthood.

Harmenszoon felt the winy air of the evening that, in some inexplicable manner, seemed to join with the words of Baas Meer, with the described soul of his half-brother. There was suddenly an explanation for everything; and then, equally unforeseen, the reason, the sane logic one could cling to, was snatched away. Even he, pious and strong, felt that which was utterly incongruous and sweet.

Christiaan was reciting a poem in Malay. Soon the thick notes of the gong announced dinner. The pitch, low and melodious, thinned as vibrations split the heavy tones. Harmenszoon frowned and gave thought to that which struck him: everything here was performed with magic. Exorcisms must, therefore, be labeled with the seal of Satan.

4

"Nand," said Vee, when they were seated around the table, "I forgot something that was written clearly into my mind for attention. The Australian lad was marked for this dinner."

"The Younguer fellow, Mother," said Raas. "It was his boat that Mijnheer Sidneye bought and sold to the Japanese. Part of the price was berth on the *Quatrefoil*."

"The boat in which the jewels were hidden?" said Nand.

"That's it," answered Lidj. "Never did I see such a collection of stones."

"It was the boy of whom I spoke," added Vee drolly. "I mention the moon and the company talks of the sky."

"A million apologies, Father," laughed Raas.

"I said nothing," Stefan added with feigned meekness. "But I'll add this, Vee. We bought back his ketch for a song. We named her —"

"I know," Nand said, leaning forward. "The *Luzon Queen*."

"Yes. She's quite seaworthy, now. Remasted, new planks, canvas, and paint. Batjoek has her now somewhere to the east. He's Timor bound."

"Timor," said Harmenszoon abjectly. "Timor. Perhaps I'll ask to go there when I am Father van Schreeven — after converting souls in Bali."

Stefan could not contain himself. "Young man, when you get through with Bali, you'll be bowing to Goenoeng Agoeng."

Harmenszoon smiled easily and replied, "Mijnheer Meer, you are accomplished in the art of underrating a man, it seems. That is, everyone but my brother." He eyed the cynical face of Stefan coldly before voicing an unexpected challenge: "In the nature of a wager, Mijnheer Meer, I'll stake my future on my ability to stand up against the devil. Suppose we meet here one year from now. If your judgment proves you wrong you will give the Church two thousand guilders. If I prove wrong, I shall forget any desire to wear the robes of the Church and salute the banner of Sidneye, Vossler, en Meer. What say you?"

Stefan grinned. "I'll do better than that — I'll make it five thousand guilders for your church."

Christiaan eyed Harmenszoon. "I hope the good Lord watches over you," he said. "I shall pray for you."

"He'll need it," said Stefan, laughing. "He's never seen a Balinese girl. Wait until his eyes pop in his head."

"Stefan Meer!" rebuked Nand.

The door at the end of the dining hall was suddenly opened. Nand, first to see it, said, "Oh, Dokter van Arken, come in. My husband has returned, and my son."

"I shall be pleased to meet them — later," said the Dokter, his voice striking harmony with his hard eyes. "But now I must intrude because of my patient — or I should say — what was my patient." He departed, leaving them staring after him, wondering. Slowly Stefan got to his feet, then Raas, and Vee. Nand, like them, read the message of death. In a moment the young physician was again facing them. He smiled with only his lips as he stepped aside and bowed.

Out of the darkness stepped a gaunt, emaciated figure, an apparition that grinned joyfully from bloodless lips and hollow eyes. His cheeks were made of colorless wax, taut, and thin; and only a few tufted strands stood out from the stretched dome of bleached ivory. To Harmenszoon — and his eyes bulged — here was the reincarnation of the devil.

"I am well," said Mayrant Ruysdaal Sidneye, advancing from the doorway.

CHAPTER XVII

1

CAPTAIN SIDNEYE, in greatcoat and woolens, stood near the wheel cursing the elements that were a part of the Noord Zee. A heavy gale sent every yard, spar, and shroud into its tune, and the whistling and creaking, and the slapping of canvas, had long since passed the stages of monotony. The brittle winds churned the sea and cracked with snow and sleet, washed up sheets of lusterless glass that froze into one's face and garments, that rolled over the deck and past the mizzenmast to form a solid layer of slippery crystal; the ratlines loomed like daggered ghosts, their points lengthened stalactites — a horror to the sailors who were ordered into the sails. Younguer was the last man up, and his progress had been made only with the hammering aid of a belaying pin against icy hemp. The *Quatrefoil* wallowed like a giant in chains, the tons of ice that could not be kept at bay her fetter.

A sailor passed the captain, his shoulders bent with balanced pails of steaming water for the deck. That he moved slower than necessity demanded was less from choice and more from fatigue: the safety of the deck called for shovel and spike to augment the steaming buckets from an overworked galley; and no man doubted that the ice would follow them on into Hamburg.

"More speed there, *zeeman!*" said Mayrant. "Do you want the steam to freeze? Here, Gaant, the fore-topsail's splitting. Send the men up! *Verdomd!*"

The weather gave the helmsman a chance to test the metal of his flesh under blue Singapore tattooing, and he voiced expletives that should have brought equatorial weather aboard the ship. The wind howled about him in one long eerie blast, shifting from northeast to north, and back again before the wheel could be hauled over. When the going got rougher the chief mate, Lidj van der Glotz, ordered less sail, and stood by the wheel.

"Land on the starboard bow!" The lookout's voice cut through the wind. Shouts of joy responded to the long-awaited sound; beyond lay the Elbe and smooth sailing on down to Hamburg. Men with axes paused to grin and stare, and seeing nothing but ponderous troughs and waves rushing toward the North German coast, they allowed their tools another bite into the white wastes. Grog! It spelled a warming of frosty gullets, a sensation of coziness. And soon, with sea bags in hand, they would court the waterfront inns and spend their money with careless abandon.

"Never again," muttered Mayrant, wishing for a kind monsoon from the Nederlandsch Indië to shut out the breath of the Arctic. "*Neen.* The Noord Zee can be a mountain of diamond-set guilders and I'll not be tempted."

The cargo awaiting the *Quatrefoil* was mock cargo; boxes would be taken on from which no material profit could be derived. It wasn't that kind of trip. Mayrant grinned. For the first time since he had assumed her command, the ship had pointed her bow north on leaving the Rotterdam Waterweg.

A second letter had been received by "Herr" Stefan Meer in Soerabaja from a quasi agent in Germany just as the *Quatrefoil* was nested for loading: —

Herr Stefan Meer,
SEHR GEHERTER HERR: —

I have the following to report: —
April fifteenth. Visited the town of Aurich and, after putting up at the Schwarzes Platz, I strolled in the direction of "19" *auf der strasse.* Passed the house twice, and seeing the place closed, I approached and knocked. Upon answer by an aged keeper (the same one reported in my last letter) I inquired of the master of the house. I was told he was in Berlin. When would he return? On the first May day. (My expense sheet is hereby attached for the period of waiting.)

May second. Not wishing to appear eager, I waited until the second of May. I had learned of his interest in objects belonging to famous people. Again the keeper came to the door and I was admitted.

"Well, Baron," I said, "don't you remember me?" And he said, "*Nein,* Herr Klingg, except that you returned my cane when I lost it at the races last summer." He is old, Herr Meer, but still arrogant. He is bald, and his big nose is red on the left side from rubbing. His face sags, and the teeth in his head are false. He sneers sort of one-sided like. But he's strong for a man of sixty-five. I tell you this because I haven't found a type cut of him yet. On his right ear lobe is a small scar which he rubs a good deal.

"What brings you here?" he said.

"I am on a secret mission, Baron, which wouldn't interest you, but I chanced upon an object that might cause you to open your eyes." He frowned at me and said, "Yes?" I leaned closer and whispered: "Of course, I am not the only one who knows about this, but I am the first to connive with the present owner." He asked questions after that, and when he learned that I could show him to the sword of Masséna he wasn't so high-and-mighty. "In fact," said I, "here is the paper giving me first right of purchase." I showed him my papers and he read them, and he seemed satisfied with the description of the property. I smiled slyly and told him to keep a closed mouth if he wanted to see the sword.

"I am interested in only a small profit," I said, using my hands like one of my race. "And what do you call small?" he said. Finally, I said, "About two thousand marks." He cursed, called me a *Ferkel*, and refused to have any business with me. I, of course, acted outraged. I stalked from the house, mumbling.

Before midnight he came to my room and bargained. For eighteen hundred marks I would sell him my paper, arrange a meeting — in the strictest secrecy — with the man who owned the sword, and see the deal through. "But," I said, "you must wait several months for his return from Australia." He agreed.

May twentieth. The Baron visited me today in Hamburg, where I am putting up at the address below. There I await your man. When he arrives have him ask for Herr Klingg. The advance money paid me was five hundred marks. This money is not deductible from the price we agreed on, Herr Meer, since I haggled it out of him. Also I convinced our man I had something to offer.

May thirtieth. At last I have found a type made of "19" in Emden in 'ninety-five. The job completed, so I await your next orders. But, as you can readily see, the price must be fixed by me, as I . . .

Then the letter dealt with money for two paragraphs.

2

Mayrant Sidneye stood before the keeper of a dingy place not far from the harbor of Hamburg. The strange glint in his eye was not a result of the flavorful schnapps his breath emitted, nor was it inspired by the touch of rouge he had forgotten to wipe from his face.

"*Goeden dag, Mijnheer*," said Mayrant. "I am told that my good friend, one Herr Klingg, lives here."

"Two flights up, first door to your left," came the answer in monotone.

Klingg met him, alert and curious, and at the mention of Herr Meer invited him inside. Mayrant's appraising eye dwelled on the agent for some length before he said more. The fellow's cupidity shone from small ratlike eyes in a pinched face. A small body, pale at the neck and hairline, was thin and stooped. Mayrant remembered the letter — "I smiled slyly" — and assured himself the act was not one to tax such a rogue beyond naturalness. Herr Klingg licked his lips eternally as if in cunning appraisal of his visitor, of his wealth and limitations.

"Let us get down to business, Mijnheer Klingg."

"Indeed. It has been very expensive to sit here waiting for a visit from Herr Meer's man," came the whiny answer. "First, my fee —"

Mayrant interrupted crisply. "I never discuss the price of an unknown value. You'll do well to sell me on what you have to offer."

The ferret face moved like a bobbing cork; a thin tongue again ran the inner lip and the eyes narrowed: Meer's man was no fool, much to his disappointment. "You have the letter, I see. Then, Herr Sidneye, you know he lives in Aurich, which means I'll have to send him a message and wait for him to come. Of course, we must work up some excuse for him to come here instead of us going to him."

"Then I shall be confined to my bed aboard ship. A bad case of grippe, Mijnheer."

"Hmm. Hm-m. Yes, that would do — that and your demand for secrecy. You are afraid to leave the ship. That would be good. You have many enemies in *der Vaterland*." He giggled, showed his yellow teeth and dead gums. "You refuse to leave your ship, and there the matter stands. In my letter I must give him a time limit."

"Two days — no more," said Mayrant. "And my cargo?"

"*Ja!* I have arranged for five thousand harmonicas, Herr Sidneye."

"Harmonicas! I had no such idea in mind. Empty crates or boxed earth will do."

"I'm afraid, Herr," said the man, wreathing his face in a most contemptuous grin, "you forget our port officials. Would you care to be questioned?"

"*Neen!*" Mayrant saw the disadvantages of doubt and explanations; he saw further: delay and suspicion would uncover his true identity, his false transaction, his basic purpose. Charges would then be made and, without any plausible excuse to cushion facts, they would hold fast. "*Neen!*" he said again with no lack of emphasis. "How much for the mouth organs?"

"Here's the bill of contract," said the schemer.

"*Verdomd!* And how much did you make on the deal?"

"Herr Sidneye!" There was the reprimand of innocence in his voice.

"Then you are a fool for trading without commission."

"Eh? What was that? I see, Herr, I see. But, of course, I could claim a fee. No money has changed hands. See?" He covered craftily, darting furtive glances.

"I thought you'd see my point. My name is to remain a secret, is it not?"

"Indeed. It is exactly as Herr Meer ordered. You shall be a sick man who is more grouchy and wary than ill. But now about the object of his visit."

"Yes, what about that, Klingg? Have you searched out a blade that will arouse his curiosity?"

"Have I! Just you wait until I lift a board here." He stood and eyed Mayrant before ambling across the room. There he stooped and ran his hands between two board ends. He was about to lift the shorter strip when he frowned, cocked his head and, with one eye closed, sent slow quizzical glances at Mayrant. He pursed his lips and then ran his tongue over them.

"Herr Sidneye, I believe on second thought we'd better discuss terms first. The sword, you see, is a ticket to prison for me."

"Why?" thundered Mayrant.

"Because, Herr, it is the actual blade itself."

"What! You lie, rat!"

"*Nein, Herr! Nein!* My brother smuggled it out of Norway. There is much excitement there. My brother demands a sum — or he threatens to —"

"So! I am to be mulcted by you. We shall see." Mayrant advanced upon the little man, saw his eyes widen with surprise and growing fear. As he cringed with one trembling hand thrust forward, Mayrant smiled. "I can get along from now on without your services, my greedy friend — and, too, without your blabbing tongue. I came here only to find a fool who thinks me gullible, who has no doubt made many mistakes."

Klingg attempted a smile and shrug; his hands turned palms upward with Jewish eloquence. "*Nein, Herr Sidneye! Nein!* I am out for a little money — can you blame me if I try? Just a little joke. Just a joke that

192

failed." He giggled again, watching each move of Mayrant's arms and body. "True, I have no brother, and it is also true that this sword is a fake. *Nein!* But am I glad you are a man one can respect! *Ja!*"

The sword was duly produced. It was ornate and well preserved; the engraving was given age by an artisan whose hobby was to lend antiqueness to metals — a profitable trade he had learned years before when a wealthy traveler sought Roman coins. The statement for the work seemed authentic, and Mayrant decided to accept it without quibbling.

Regardless of Klingg's money madness and petty duplicity, he was to be admired for his thoroughness. Sidneye eyed the culprit for future use. Commerce was without virtue and the time must surely arrive when such talents as the Jew possessed might come into play.

"One other thought. The Baron must not be seen approaching the ship, and his presence aboard her must not be known even by his servants. It would be better to lead him to another address and later to the ship. He must not be followed."

"As you wish, Herr Sidneye. I have a plan. Wait until you read the letter I shall write."

"Get busy then," ordered Mayrant.

"Indeed. Indeed." He paused to wet his lips before saying, as if to himself, "Of course, I haven't asked why you seek the Baron. It is none of my business. But for murder on my soul, I should rebel."

"Of course," said Mayrant facetiously. "But I assure you the Baron will not be murdered. Ah, no." His tone belied the words, causing Klingg to peer closely. An inner shudder ran the stooped frame and lodged in his tiny beady eyes. The nose twitched, and with it the face cracked with unwholesome wrinkles.

"Of course," said Klingg. Both men laughed. "My signal will be, in the evening of the second day hence, Herr Sidneye, a German drinking song. You will, of course, have your men posted, and be in bed?"

"Correct."

"And, pardon, but when shall we settle the matter of money between us?"

"In due course, Mijnheer Klingg. You see, you must be with the Baron — and the sick man."

3

The night, cold, clear, and silent but for the water lapping against the ship's sides, was ghostly; snow lay in never-ending nests on the wharf, roofs, atop posts, and aboard ship, reflecting mild phos-phorescence through the soft gray veil of evening. The waterfront emitted a twinkle of light here and there, from a warehouse closing for the day, from a half dozen ships anchored near by, and from a match that painted a face in orange somewhere along the plank way. Toward the sea a dim hulk loomed with riding lights aloft, and the sounds of a tug crew laughing and cursing intermittently was wafted by the spent north wind. The steam craft was guided to her wharf, some distance from the *Quatrefoil* amid short blasts of dismal horns, and there she came to rest; she seemed to sigh for a moment and then ask for sleep while her crew scampered off her to waiting bottles or women, or both, cursing the delay caused by the slow formalities of port entry. A cabin door opened on a three-masted Yankee clipper some fifty yards off the starboard bow and for a moment sent high lights to its furled sail; abruptly it was gone, and only the deserted night gave company to the two men on deck.

"It's colder than I thought, Younguer, or is it my thin blood driving out the virgin Dutch?"

"I was wondering the same thing, Mijnheer van der Glotz. But isn't the crew due to report about now?" He leaned over the rail, peering at the tiny street leading to the harbor, where a dim light caught the every movement of an important and ragged corner. He forgot his question as soon as it left his mouth and again turned his eye to the far-off tropics where the *Alice Macdonald*, now the *Luzon Queen*, wallowed in the lush beauty of her environment.

"I hear the crew," said Lidj. "And from the noise, a few will spend the night in the brig. I distinctly warned them not to drink heavily on this night."

Younguer laughed. "Being a youngster myself I can hear you telling the wind to calm."

"Aye," Lidj laughed full agreement. "But the ship must sail." He turned about, peered into her vast maze of shrouds and seemed to eye her top yards. "She'll be easy to handle since we picked a brace of wind that won't chop the sea."

"But why are we to play dead until the word comes? Shouldn't all hands be standing by for the cable to lift?"

Lidj continued to eye the lamplit corner. His reprimand would have done justice to any father: "Baas Sidneye, son, seldom asks or informs anyone of his reasons for things. After you take over a ship for him you'll learn plenty. Until then keep alive the industry you've shown."

"That I shall," answered the lad sincerely.

"And here they come," said Lidj calmly. "Gaant staggers, so does Dohle. And by the stars, so does Raas Vossler!"

"You'll log him?" asked Younguer.

"That I will," came the answer. "I see he's got a woman with him."

"Not bad for a German girl," commented Younguer. "I had one last evening and, except for her giggle, she wasn't to be scoffed at. Fleshy, all right, but I like them that way."

"How many marks?" asked Lidj in jocular tone.

"Marks! Hell, sir, I wasn't within a mile of the harbor. I splurged at an expensive inn. The girl worked at a bookshop." He sighed. "But she carried a flame in her belly."

Lidj walked to the gangway and stood eyeing the sailors. His words were calm and low, and for an instant Raas and Gaant stood rigid. Younguer strode in their direction as Lidj said: —

"You'll sober within a half hour or sleep in the brig. Stand by for orders. When the word comes this ship must move out in a hurry. Understand?" He watched them move off and then turned about.

Within the hour all hands were accounted for, even the giant cook who carried his liquor with phenomenal ease; one could always rely on him to laugh without pause when drunk; that was his only signal. Word had run the grapevine that the cargo was harmonicas — thousands of them, and the booming voice from the galley reached Lidj's ears, accompanied by eternal laughter: "Goddam, I play them all afore we reach Java!"

The grin on the face of jovial Lidj froze as he gazed again at the corner: under the lamplight were two men, one a stooped, emaciated fellow, the other a man of wide girth and, judging from his carriage, a man of importance. "It's him, all right. No doubt of it." The small man's voice broke into the song that was to serve as a signal.

"Mijnheer Younguer," said Lidj, "advise Baas Sidneye at once that we have two visitors." As the other scurried away, Lidj nonchalantly strolled to the plank to await the ill-assorted pair. Slowly they advanced, the wizened one casting a furtive eye over his shoulder. They were at the plank when Lidj challenged them: —

"Who goes there?"

"Herr Klingg," said the smaller, "to see the owner."

"What's your business, and are you alone?"

"We are alone," piped Klingg, "and our business is for the master's ears. Nineteen Masséna."

"Come aboard," grunted Lidj.

"What ship is this?" asked the large man.

"The *Alice Macdonald* out of Melbourne, Mijnheer," lied Lidj. "Come, wait here until I hear from the master. The Dokter is due any moment now, so you may be forced to wait."

Said Klingg: "And how is he today?"

"Improving, but one cannot predict the *verdomde* grippe."

"True. I had it last winter and my sister in Bavaria almost dug my grave. But," he added, laughing, and nudging his companion, "I was told by the Rabbi that I was entirely too mean to die."

Younguer arrived with a message — the master would see Herr Klingg immediately; give the Baron a taste of schnapps and bid him wait. Several minutes later Klingg arrived to escort the Baron into the presence of the owner of the sword of Masséna.

Lidj seemed the very quintessence of lethargy — until the pair disappeared from view. Then, with a lunge, he was at Younguer's side: "Younguer, get to the corner yonder and see if we're being spied on — Gaant, you sober? Good. Verryn, here! And Geyl, where's your trombone? Now, cornet, trombone, and violin. Play that German piece you rehearsed loud and long outside Baas Sidneye's cabin. It'll deaden the sounds on deck. Raamzen! Batten down the hatches! Mate ho! Easy with the cable! Mate ho! Haul in the ropes when I say —" Lidj was everywhere.

The three musical instruments soon belched forth discordance just outside Sidneye's quarters; the noise gave background to Lidj van der Glotz's orders. The echo of his voice was the easy, inculcated notion of trained sailors; ratlines were run, and sail ordered by the mate was on its way; the muffling of the cable, the hardest task before them, evoked a frown from Lidj, while his weather eye read the wind and sail before turning toward the lamplit corner where Younguer stood at ease. The pilot attended his duties in mechanical fashion, pausing at times to curse the makers of such foul music.

Little time had elapsed: the tugs noisily returned to the wharves, one of them waiting for the pilot, their crews lazily eyeing the big ship as she eased out close to the wind, her lights giving a dash of color to her sails; her wake was yet lazy and, picked up by the harbor lights, it flickered and died. The *Quatrefoil* moved slowly up to the North Sea.

4

As the door closed behind the pair, the Jew exercised the formalities of introduction: "Baron von Streicher, I present the owner of the sword." The Baron and the man abed eyed each other coldly, appraisingly, the Baron standing stiffly, one hand atop the other on the gold knob of his cane, his hat pulled close about the bony ridges, almost meeting the expensive coat turned up around his face. He nodded to the young man without smiling.

"Pull up chairs, and remove your wraps," said Mayrant. When this was done, without words to break the silence, each stared at the other's bald head; the seaman leaned on a pillow, the ex-diplomat sat at an angle with legs crossed and inventoried the cabin with a supercilious eye. The intermediary sat near the foot of the bed with legs crossed and sent his eyes in rapid travel from one to the other, all the while half smiling and tracing the pattern of his lip with an eternal tongue.

"Streicher," said Mayrant in a tone that searched his memory. "Streicher. I've heard the name somewhere. Were you ever in the diplomatic service in the Netherlands?"

"I was," came the cold answer, "some thirty years ago; long before your time."

"Yes, long before my time — perhaps. I have heard my friend speak of you. I remember now. You were married to his mother's sister. I believe her name was — he called her Aunt Zulinde."

"We shall get down to business," said the Baron. "I must catch the next train to Aurich."

"By all means, Baron. You came to discuss the sword, I believe." Klingg's tongue came to a halt in his right lip corner, his eyes narrowed; he was curious about the motive of his employer. "The object is behind the chest there." Streicher's eye slowly moved in that direction and he was about to arise when the sick man addressed him. "But before we view the sword, Baron von Streicher, I must make sure you are alone."

"I am very much alone."

"I see. Who knows you are aboard this ship?"

"No one. I gave my servants the address of the place I was to meet your agent."

"And you employed no one to follow you?"

The sounds of harsh notes almost split their ears; first cornet, then trombone and violin; Klingg started, and then settled back, while the Baron frowned and raised his voice in answer: "*Nein*, I am not followed. I say — *Nein!* Must such awful music be played right in our ears, Herr Captain?"

"It is a nuisance," boomed Mayrant. "But alas, I never bother to discipline the crew for a few drinks in port. Move closer, I say, and we'll get down to business."

The rumpled brow of the aged man moved closer. He seemed more than irritated as his lips thinned with his eyes. "Bring out the sword!" he bellowed, and Mayrant, grinning, bade the Jew fetch it. The wrapping of gray flannel was removed by Mayrant, who narrowly eyed the face of his guest; he was rewarded with a changing expression — sheer interest and greed driving out the flush of anger and the ice of aversion. The Baron was on his feet, leaning forward and adjusting a monocle to a perpetually swollen eye. Roughly he jerked the object from its owner and walked to the lamp, where he seated himself on the sea chest and produced a small metal-edged glass; for long minutes he examined the hilt, the outer metal of the blade, the ornate design, and at last, the depth of the plating.

Verryn and Geyl, both slightly drunk, continued to trumpet forth discordant notes, pausing only for breath; during the short interim Gaant sawed away at his violin monotonously. But suddenly all noise ceased abruptly. The trio laughed and talked about beer. Mayrant, waiting for them to continue, heard the bustle on deck: the ship moved a bit, telling him the mooring lines were in; and the grating of wood, the gangplank, barely preceded the vibrations from the anchor chains; he frowned when the clanking grew heavier and joined jarring thuds. The tugboat moved in noisily.

Streicher turned his head slowly, quizzically. "What noise is that — an anchor cable?"

"*Neen*," laughed Mayrant. "Some boxes — contraband — coming aboard. Such is no concern of yours, Mijnheer."

At that moment the ship jerked forward almost throwing the Jew and the Baron to the floor. Both were instantly on their feet, their faces glowing with bewilderment and suspicion. Then the violin sounded and in another moment the remaining instruments joined in to drown all sounds of the ship.

"What is the meaning of this?" thundered the Baron.

"Are we moving?" piped Klingg. "Yes — no! But we are moving!"

"Calm yourselves," said Mayrant easily. "We are only moving to another warehouse. The signal has come for us to load the boxes from Krupp of Essen. There are, my friends, certain islands in the South Seas where a native chieftain will trade a large pearl for every gun. I am a trader." His grin was iniquitous and thereby disarming. "Now about the sword, Baron, are you satisfied with its markings?"

For answer Streicher bestowed upon him a fierce stare, long and steady. His arms were folded and his feet were spread apart in the conquering manner of a Prussian facing a host of ragged prisoners. His gaze shifted to the Jewish mediator, its passion sending his startled eyes to the floor. Wincing, the Baron jerked a thumb and forefinger to an ear lobe and rubbed industriously.

The *Quatrefoil* creaked gently and harmonized her motions to those of the furious tugboats; the voice of Lidj was drowned in noise as he bellowed for sail. Only a fool, thought Mayrant, would accept for long the yarn of moving to another wharf, or a captain's patience with such poor musicians. But he was not lost to the situation that confronted him: something else sent accusation flashing from the Baron's eye.

"I am sure I asked a question of you, Baron," he yelled. "Why not speak instead of wasting the wrath of silence on me? I must warn you that I am not a man easily moved by a mere glance. About the trophy — is it what you seek?"

"The sword, Herr Captain, is a clever attempt at forgery. Remember this before you try to pawn off such upon another — Marshal André Masséna was Prince d'Essling, not Prince d'E-s-l-e-n-g. I regret that I cannot do business with you." He bowed stiffly and turned on the excited and worried Jew. "You, Herr Klingg, will return me the advance money — five hundred marks to be exact."

"But — Herr Baron, Your Highness, I — I haven't the money!" He whined and pleaded with the great one to give him time to produce the sum. "I am honest, Herr Baron, Your Worship, I am. I did not realize I was offering a fake. Never would I do such. Can't you understand I would never chance prison for so poor a reward?"

"My money, Herr Klingg — at once!" His one hand was extended, palm up, while the other menacingly brandished a cane.

Mayrant grinned. As the Jew cringed and Streicher bellowed and advanced, Mayrant laughed. The cane, in mid-air, came to a sudden halt, and the eyes that fiercely guided it turned slowly toward the man who was getting out of bed — the sick man was fully dressed. Streicher saw him walk to the door and open it, heard him dismiss the noisy trio and call for van der Glotz, then place his body in a chair and yield to fiendish laughter. Klingg, wide-eyed with terror and wonder, remained against the wall, his knees on the floor. He saw the door open and heard Sidneye say: —

"Lidj, remove the rat from the cabin. Put him to work in the hold, or let him scrub the decks. We need an extra hand to Soerabaja." He then turned to the perplexed Baron.

"Sit down, Baron, and make yourself comfortable. It is a long way to the Dutch Indies." He laughed. "Lidj, fetch us a bottle — the Baron and I have much to talk about that does not concern swords."

"Aye, Mijnheer Mayrant Sidneye," said Lidj.

The glorious moment had dawned; only one thing was missing: Stefan Meer. But he had dropped Stefan in Rotterdam.

199

CHAPTER XVIII

1

THE *Luzon Queen* belied her name. She had not sailed north of the equator, although her sails were a common sight in the Ceram Zee, the Banda Zee, the Gorong and Watoebela Eilandens, and the chain of islands running from Java to Tanimbar not ten degrees below. Only once had she crossed the Timor Zee to Darwin, and seldom had her riding lights been seen in the waters about the squid-shaped Celebes. The Moluccas kept the ketch busy, and besides, the genius of Batjoek was best exercised among his own people. There, from one hundred twenty-five to one hundred thirty east he was looked upon with awe akin to worship, with all a native can give a venerable brother.

And for Batjoek, one could scarcely know the life from Ternate to Amboina without tagging him with powers above those of most men, be they Moluccan or Dutch: the wisdom, patience, and ease of the aged met the vibrant and new of the young, causing the natives, for baffling reasons that were their own, to press him with gifts and favors. Stefan Meer, in giving credit to Sidneye for his uncanny powers in selecting men, also wondered, after viewing the workings of Batjoek, how his protégé had so conclusively captured the love and devotion of the native.

Only a few knew the story. The run of the narrative began in Vossler's hands when the Chinese seemed an unconquerable and costly force that threatened the young company, then in its first year, with certain defeat in the Moluccas. Cargo after cargo was sucked out of its hands, and for a reason: the fat Chinese bought monopolies in a most curious manner, using the more powerful of the islands' leaders to negotiate in their absence. In desperation Vee spent weeks in the archipelago in an effort to solve the trade mystery. The result, he was advised to consult a higher up, and this lofty native sent him higher. The wheel ceased its spin on Batjoek, a simple native who ruled by outward subservience, who bowed to the lowly and ordinary instead of the rich.

"A methodical old rascal," Vee commented, and thereupon set to work on him. But he returned to Soerabaja in defeat to await the *Quatre-*

foil and Mayrant. Together they returned and once more the paradox was approached. He had no powers, he said.

Then, somehow, the secret was out: Batjoek had endeared himself to the natives by his great knowledge of the black stone in the Kaaba, by his ready hand that aided all Moslems who sought to kiss the stone and drink the holy waters of Zamzam. He was honored, he was great among the *hadjis*, or pilgrims who had visited the Great Mosque. From mouth to mouth, from Ternate to Amboina, went the story of the simple man who used his wealth to send others to Mecca.

The Chinese paid him nothing — they supported his charities, ever adding to his fame, and — to their wealth.

Mayrant peered beneath surfaces: Batjoek possessed a primeval ruthlessness buried under his schooled humility. Thus the task before Sidneye was to combine fact and suspicion into a winning play for his man. It all came about one evening aboard the *Quatrefoil*. It was simple, too simple, but it is ever the smallest stone that tumbles the weight of a ponderous tower.

Batjoek was aboard to accept a gift of great value for his people in the north — a pouch of gold. Invited aboard for the festivities were many natives, and a dozen Chinese from the various ships that trafficked in the cream of the Moluccas. Hovering near this latter group was a giant Dutchman, named Handsmeer. He could draw coins from the ears and hair of any man, sometimes a deck of cards, and again a hare; so slow were his motions that the eye, it seemed, must surely be quicker — but not so.

The crux came when a prominent Chinese from a rich Java concern was approached by Handsmeer, who, with surprise and horror in his face, before the eyes of Batjoek, removed from the saffron neck a crucifix of gold.

"Look, Baas Sidneye! This man is a Christian!"

"So!" cried Mayrant. "Then he must be punished for his deceit. Lidj, fetch me the whip."

The protestations of the Oriental were in vain, and Mayrant brought the whip down across the shoulders of the victim. He then passed the whip to Batjoek, who handled it unmercifully. The remaining Chinese were, one by one, thrown into the water by the Moluccan and the captain of the *Quatrefoil*. The police were met by a surprised ship's crew as well as blank-faced natives, none of whom knew aught of such a crime.

Mayrant Sidneye was not satisfied with a mere trade agreement with the Moluccan. He desired rather a complete domination of his new friend. Combining persuasion and ruthless action he made his bid; his simple persuasiveness struck a chord of harmony in the brain of Batjoek: —

"There is only one way in which to wage a war with the defilers of the Mosque — you must sacrifice your simple life to their defeat in trade. You must bend your energies to the utmost in an effort to hold all profit from these dogs." There was more, and ever more.

"I shall guide you, Batjoek, so long as you obey me. I shall make you rich, so long as you serve me. I shall furnish ships and provisions for Mecca-bound pilgrims, so long as you bring me profit. But remember, my great friend, we must become brothers in blood instead of brothers in trade. No one will come between us, ever."

Batjoek replied: "No one, Baas." And the man of iron, Sidneye, was from that moment on second only to the black stone in the Kaaba. Thus many, many moons later, while the *Quatrefoil* slipped out of the harbor of Hamburg, the *Luzon Queen* was adding wealth to the growing empire of Mayrant Sidneye; that and more: —

She, under the hanging stars, was plying toward Macassar in the Celebes — to establish a prison for an infidel from far-off Europe.

2

Zulinde lived with her sister, the mother of Mayrant, and the wife of Pieter van Schreeven. Her mother had followed Mevrouw Sidneye to the grave years before, so far into the past, it seemed, that the house on Oranje Street had almost lost the echo of the perpetual feud between the two old women. But as the wintry winds howled and boards creaked in the attic, and the eaves emitted low whiny notes to these strange yet natural noises, she could piece them into some resemblance of the past and listen to her mother and rival in testy debate downstairs.

But every rap at the door was that of Stefan Meer, every canal barge was the property of his cousin, and every ship with masts was another *Quatrefoil*. He stood before her in the deep of night, rousing her from fitful slumber as he said over and over, "*Neen*, Zulinde." And all night long she would ask him why he said *Neen*, and never would he answer. It was a serious matter until the dawn broke, and then, when she made her way downstairs, the room swelled with the youth who had carried her bodily out that very door and into the street. Buoyancy claimed her for a moment — every morning of every day through every year it had been the same — and then the great truth advanced to dim and damn. How many times had she frowned and pinched herself, hoping to shake the dogged dream, and, failing, how many times had she given wonder to the weight of one infinitesimal moment? A rumble of thunder, a flash of lightning, and utter darkness.

Since that fateful evening she had never set eyes on Stefan. She knew, of course, that her nephew had sneaked aboard his ship. She was advised, by that nephew who swore vengeance, eternal and terrible, that Stefan was a great man who gave evidence of his fight with the clinging past. It was then she sobbed the nights through, asking of a forgetful God why the past must forever remain an ugly wedge between them. No answer came except a faint response, an echo above the thin air of the universe; it said he had heard, he knew! Perhaps his call had evoked in her the mood that cried her message.

Company was to arrive at six, and she sat before her mirror, wondering why she should care at all about her appearance. Only an old woman gazed back at her; perhaps fifty said the glass, perhaps forty-five, but no less. A silvery chignon topped a pale, thin face with kind eyes; a firm mouth had accepted the sadness of her years. The same curves were there, the identical cleft in the lower lip stared back at her. Where then was that life? Why preen for friends of Mijnheer van Schreeven?

Why?

Because it was expected of her, and because something was still alive inside her. The answer sent a faint quiver of hope into her eyes. She closed them in prayer, and when the plea was ended she arose without daring another glance at the woman in the mirror. Slowly she walked down the stairs, her face wrapped in a serenity that was only surface deep.

Van Schreeven sat smoking a meerschaum and reading a newspaper. He was a man good to look at; his wide, noble forehead still nestled its tufts, and void of wrinkles it reminded her of his handsome offspring who aspired to priesthood. He was a kindly man, ever prone to persiflage in her presence — she suspected why — and on more than one occasion, when the word Meer, or Streicher, fell from a careless lip, he hurriedly steered the conversation into another topic.

She had never regretted her sister's second marriage. To her there was something symbolical in the union; it was like a rainbow of hope to one whose soul keeps a body alive by bridging the chasm of the present; she gloried in the example set for her, and she lived only to imitate the pattern. But Stefan had been stubborn, and she did not dare make advances.

"How fine you look, Zulinde," said her sister's husband. "I vow every day that you are reversing nature."

"You will never cease to tease, will you?" she returned. "My next birthday sends my age soaring again, and it is not long off."

"Your next will find you another year younger," he said peremptorily. "Join me, Zulinde, in a toast to our close of kin in the Indies."

"A small sip of wine then," she agreed. "But where is sister?"

"Late, as usual," he laughed. "Her vanity exceeds yours, my dear. She glories in arriving last, the cynosure of all eyes." He rattled on while crossing the room to the cupboard where his wines and liquors caught shafts of light through ornate doors.

Her eyes fell to the newspaper at her feet, and, as habit prevailed, she turned to the list of ships. The *Adam's Nancy* of Liverpool, the *Bajon* of Java, the *Norfolk* of New York, and a dozen others made port. There was a list of ships sailing, and at the end of the column, a brief note among many others: the *Quatrefoil* of Soerabaja sailed on the fourth from Hamburg for the Dutch East Indies.

"The *Quatrefoil!*" she exclaimed. Van Schreeven turned his head and grunted. "Sailing from Hamburg! Then surely Mayrant was sailing her. And — at any rate we're usually paid a visit. I don't understand."

"Well, we can be thankful for the word of Mayrant's cure, although I must admit I'd have preferred his bringing the news in person." The decanter in his hand hung idle, and he made a gesture with the other before pursing his lips in silence and heaving a sigh. The red wine was duly poured and, with a smile, he extended the glass to the bemused Zulinde. "Here, my dear, warm the heart and mind and forget conundrums."

Her drawn face lifted and darted him a smile as she accepted the wine. Then her eyes again fell to the paper. She was drawn by some irresistible force to a small paragraph in a corner of the opposite page. The glass fell from her hand, spilling wine over the floor and rug.

"Look! Read this!" she said. A strange light entered her eyes as her stare fell on the far wall. Her hand was at her throat as she closed her eyes. Van Schreeven moved to her side. He read: —

HAMBURG — The disappearance of Baron von Streicher, retired, and formerly of the diplomatic service in which he served in the Netherlands, Denmark, and later in the home office, continues to remain a mystery. His manservant from Aurich has been in Hamburg for three days where meager clues are being followed by the Wilhelmstrasse. The Baron left his home for Hamburg on the morning of the fourth.

Van Schreeven sent his mind into the past; he saw his stepson rushed off to Rotterdam because of eavesdropping. "So," he said, a strange light playing about his eyes and smiling lips. "So!"

"Yes," returned Zulinde. "Brother dear, I shall not remain to greet your friends. Please offer my excuses — I am not feeling well."

He frowned. Should he give her the long awaited message from Stefan Meer? Stefan was coming!

3

Kintamani in the sunset. Almost forty miles north from the only harbor on the island, at Benoa, and high in the mountains where the headwaters of the Adjoeng send a stream due south to empty in the Badoeng Strait, the Sacred Mount of Bali, hoary Goenoeng Agoeng, brushed away the mists and caught the full shafts of the sun's inflected rays. A feeling of awe, of ineffable majesty, came with the evening's approach, and the chill air that rose up out of the stretching groves and feathery thickets of bamboo seemed to augment the magic that was everywhere. The peak that was the "center of the world" gave Brahmanism, in a passionate and grandiloquent metaphor, a sweeping righteousness that was too honeyed for active objection.

Harmenszoon van Schreeven went so far as to commit his thoughts to his tongue, with an awareness: that the voiced excuse for heathen life must evoke in him the reprimand of self; and he was again suddenly afraid. His kinsman, Father Vandermeer, to whom he had been assigned in Denpasar, had warned him, although the full weight of his words lingered as rigid, dispassionate tenets of religious science. Now he saw through the maze of words and silently rebuked the Father for extending mechanical disquisitions instead of pithy, full-blooded warning. After all, he was not a priest, he was only a man who found it a hard task to place the great Church first.

Again the changing colors assailed the white peak, and he was swept into that blissful state of lethargy and peace that loosed the shackles of complete religious responsibility.

The sun raced away from Goenoeng Agoeng and dipped into Java amid a ceremony of fierce color. The day died as the split ball glared in duller crimson at a triumphant march of evening shadows.

On just such an evening three months before he had landed in Bali; Father Vandermeer met him and together they had returned by cart to Denpasar and the monastery. The moon was full, he remembered, and his kinsman's words about the island fell slowly, a prelude to the mysteries and pitfalls he would later explain in full.

He had said, "So you wish to become a priest, Harmenszoon. I am glad. I can help you — perhaps. But our faith makes great demands, and he who serves it as a teacher must renounce sin; he must prove himself." In the days that followed he said more, but in scholarly and unclear manner.

Something like Nand's warning, only she, with the heightened innocence and concern of a mother, which she became to him on the eve of his departure for Bali, dipped once into the flesh of description, accompanied by a sudden rise of color to her cheeks: —

"Like a son of my own, I must warn you of the land of Bali. It is a strange, lazy land, unlike anything you saw in Europe, and only prayer and steadfastness can keep you as you are in such a setting.

"The native girls are beautiful and gay. Their morals are high, but look to your own."

How sweet was the wife of Vee Vossler, to whom he had given a laugh and a promise.

In Denpasar he spent many weeks in the company of men like himself, older men, of course, who had earned their robes, as well as the coveted title "Father." Each placed Church first, each seemed serene, each seemed blessed with the felicity that came with serving God and humanity. There were no shifty eyes among them; there was no penance, no furtive affair; there was not the stupid dishonor of any short exodus of the spirit. They lived in a world above him, though they, too, came face to face with the unholy and sweet, as painted by Nand. How he longed for their unclouded forbearance, even after his first surrender to the devil . . .

He was stretched in a hammock beneath the palms one afternoon, drawing lazy visions of sleep and sniffing the perfumed air, when into his life walked a girl he had searched out days back: a piquant face, a tawny skin, and two rose-tipped mountains rising out of a living valley. In response to the drug of beauty he forgot the pattern set for him. She smiled, startled. That she felt the avid shafts from his eyes he was certain, but she remained to stare at him, to loose that rhythmic language that shouted, by the very beauty of its cadence, the glory of Balinese women.

His eyes beckoned and she, unable to throw off a responding magic, ripened by slow flirtation, advanced slowly to where he sat. She paused before him and his hand reached out and drew her near. With both hands he grasped her shoulders and brought himself to his feet, where he stood gazing down at her; in the next moment his greedy lips joined with hers, and all distances, all environment, then disappeared into that blissful whirl of the new universe. The past was irrecoverable, and soon he lost all rhythm with the world.

There was no memory of the moments in which he led her to the hibiscus shelter, but how vivid was that moment in which he saw the shape of an avenging angel — a robe, a pair of feet, and the stern eye of Father Vandermeer.

The girl scurried away. Chagrined, Harmenszoon reddened and found his eyes anchored to the soil, and there they remained as the silent, understanding Father led him into the great edifice and into painful confession.

Kintamani was unendurable punishment without her. Chains of utter desolation were made worse by the hermit companion to whom he had been assigned: Father van Skike was a huge, reticent old man with rheumy eyes, a large nose that dipped into red, scowling lips that never lifted from a downward curve. His lower jaw protruded in bellicose manner and gave support to somber and penetrating eyes. Father van Skike never requested, he ordered, and Harmenszoon soon learned that punishment here was the very essence of the word; and he imagined the priest was stationed there for no other reason than to afford punishment to errant youth. He spent his time poring over books, seldom visiting the natives, and never seeking to christianize them. An erudite of the old school, he had, as Harmenszoon later learned, spent his productive years on the island of Flores.

And so it was night again; and Father van Skike awaited his return to the cage like a keeper of an unwanted animal. Slowly he turned about and faced the aged rock that stood, it seemed, to bless the temples of the heathens.

The priest eyed him with lingering disdain as he entered; he remained glued to the old rattan chair near the one table, upon which a flickering light sent ungracious beams to paint his worn eyes with crimson rims. In his robed lap a giant volume rested, the age of which went back into the early days of the century before; there one gnarled hand rested in the fold while another seemed ready to turn a page. The cantankerous stare held while he said: —

"You are late."

"I am sorry, kind Father, but the sunset gives one complete inventory of his soul."

"And among the chaff?" stormed the other in low, even tone. He gave the very silence a rumble of thunder.

"There is an awareness of wrongdoing, Father, that comes before sincere repentance."

"You are, at last, becoming wise." The thrust of his lower jaw seemed more pronounced when his mouth hung open, but it bespoke contemplation, the first the young man had read in the sour-visaged monk of Kintamani. "Or else you seek to deceive."

"*Neen*, Father," said Harmenszoon.

"Perhaps I am a foolish old man who seeks a cure for your wantonness because I would be rid of you. But to satisfy my conscience I can do no less than subject you to a test of faith."

"I would welcome such, Father. From the Holy Mother, I implore strength, and in the blessing I seek my life hangs in the balance. Without the benediction of the Church, Father, I am but a soul doomed to darkness."

Father van Skike grunted doubtfully. "I am but an eye of the all-powerful Church," he said. "My mission here is that of an observer, and not that of shepherd of pagan souls. From my study, and meticulous assimilation of what my eye meets, the Church hopes to destroy the temples of infidels. To my work I bend with a zeal your generation cannot envision. Many priests have sought the inactive mission facing the peak of Bali, but only those who have vanquished sin have been appointed. I am the third. I tell you this because it is my duty, not because I enjoy wasting words upon your childish ears. To acquaint you with my life of sacrifice is to strengthen the powers of self-denial in whatever soul you might possess, and to give you a foothold in a living example.

"By gazing upon a mortal who has not sinned in thought and deed for four decades your lustful soul should quicken with the agonies of repentance. And, in your case, is your soul heavier for the knowledge?"

Harmenszoon frowned out the run of silence. "*Neen*, Father. My soul is perhaps slow in grasping the facts you have suffered me to view in complete ignorance."

"You seek to rebuke me?"

"*Neen*, Father, I am but pledged to give you truth."

"Then allow me to voice a worthy opinion of your level head. Had you sought to leap the truth I would have kept you here another six-month." Harmenszoon shuddered and glanced at the slow fire in the hearth.

"On the morrow you return to Denpasar. Tonight you are free. I suggest you visit the pagan dance at the thatched shed beyond the storehouse — you will learn what the Church must conquer. Perhaps with the taint of your soul lessened you can work up zeal for the eternal task. Now get out of my sight."

The Balinese dance themselves into rhythmic moods, and then they seem to enter a weird trance, and then as the chanting or the orchestrations step to wilder, quicker tempos they become frenzied. About the conical brazier that evening the chanting chorus squatted and sought the gods without excessive gestures or apparent excitement. A boy sat on the ground draped like a girl with an elaborate headdress of gold and white. In his hands was a flower, an offering to the gods, and to it his eyes remained glued.

Harmenszoon found his roving eye seeing less of the dance and more of the translucent amber and bronze of the skins of countless girls: despite his fine words to Father van Skike, the roué in him came to the surface.

Toward midnight the moon invited him outside. Harmenszoon walked among the night revelers, hoping.

His eye lingered on a face not so appealing as that of his last amour; he lowered his glance of appraisal and warmed at the sight of her lovely body. He approached her and asked if she could lead him to a quiet spot where he could commune with the peak without molestation. Her laughing eyes agreed, and they sauntered off, apparently unnoticed. Past the many thatched roofs and storehouses, beyond the first grove of shadowed trees, and into the rocky stretches of a gentle incline they traveled, she chanting and casting furtive glances, he playing the part his habit demanded. They arrived at a tree-screened mossy shelf overlooking a cliff that gave view of the eastern landscape in a faint stretch of evanescent silver; beyond that the mists mingled with a vast and unbroken world of shadows. Goenoeng Agoeng lay behind that curtain.

The peak was not visible and his trip was for nothing, he advised, unless — would she sit near him and tell the story of the Sacred Mount? Not too close, of course, but near enough so he might touch her. He began to talk of love, and finding her eyes gleaming with interest he seemed more sure of himself. She listened avidly, and he grew bolder. He spoke of sensations, of ecstasy, and, at last, the ease of such discoveries.

She was stretched on the moss, her head supported by a tawny palm. He moved nearer, slowly taking her hand into his own, lifting it to his lips and kissing the palm, all the while holding his rushing blood in check. No objection was forthcoming, and he moved to her side. He continued to talk, priding himself on conquering the telltale quiver of his voice.

"May I kiss you?" he asked. "I can show you what I mean with a kiss." There was no answer. "Aren't you interested in what I have said? I can see you are. Come here." As if the coals of the brazier were between them, as if the echoic chanting conjured up a trance, she moved to obey. Her every muscle relaxed, except the arm that wound to his neck. Her deep brown hair trailed in the moss as she slowly reclined, pulling him after her.

He raised his head to find wind for another draught. "See, my pretty one, I am not a teller of wild tales. Now what do you wish?"

Eternally feminine is the woman. She had no word for it, but her eyes opened slowly in order that drugged lids might again emit flashes of invitation before her soft arms contracted and brought the mysterious pabulum of love again to her lips. He saw, heard, and felt the song of surrender, the magic trumpeting that the man beast must answer in triumph. Glorious triumph! He placed a kiss upon each eye, and cheek, and soon his lips touched her throat.

Only a murmur escaped her.

The only servant of Father van Skike was a squat fellow who clung more to the man than the new religion he did not understand; he was a sharp-faced one whom Father van Skike called Trost, a Ngada from the island of Flores. Ever reticent and all the more cunning, he had heard his master's guttural complaints at playing host to one whose visit was brought about by immorality. He said nothing but frowned in wonder. Unchastity among the Ngadas was a serious offense, and thus any man who sought the forbidden was guilty of a great crime.

Trost took his evenings as he found them, and on this night he, too, was a silent and meek spectator at the dance. He saw the seducer after the ceremonies, paused to wonder at his presence there, and, like the stealthy soul from a Flores kampong, he decided to serve his master by stalking the offender.

The study door opened without a rap and into the room raced the Ngada. Father van Skike, glancing fiercely from the sheet of vellum upon which he made the most correct observations, bade the prostrate one arise. There followed a question, a rapid flow of Dutch and Ngada jargon, and more questions. Minutes later Father van Skike stalked past a grove of trees, beyond a rocky slope, and, at Trost's motion, slowed as they approached the bushes that hugged the tree trunks. Carefully he edged into position and listened to the words of his charge as he asked for the lips of the girl.

"So!" he said *sotto voce*, his wrath widening its arch. "So!" And he sought control of his anger at the behest of his curiosity. He had not sinned in the manner of van Schreeven since he was twenty, and for two years he had suffered all the tortures that go with forbearance. Perhaps the youth would stop with the kiss; he prayed for God's intervention, though he was aware that such sin seldom cooled before reaching extravagant spasms. He watched patiently, holding his anger in tow as he waited. Turning about, he pointed a finger toward the village. Trost walked away.

He saw the kiss, he read the silent demand of the girl. He peered closer, his aged eyes dancing like rebellious lamps. In another moment he crawled to within scant yards of the stage. The grunt of a pig, the soft note of a nightingale, were the only sounds to pierce the silence of the night. Then the bodies were welded together by the moonlight over Bali.

Father van Skike shuddered; before him was the very essence of unholiness. Instinctively he recited in silence the musical chant of the Benedictus: —

"*Benedictus qui venit in nomine Domini* —" It seemed in the moment a monument to God's triumph over sin.

Then, in a rage, he cried, "Stop, in the name of the Lord!" In answer a snarling curse fell from the lips of the young man.

The walk to the house was without any word; but once inside the door the Father removed his robe and placed the table and lamp against the wall. Soon he was stripped of all clothing except the black cap. Only a cross adorned his neck. Following the pattern strangely set, Harmenszoon did likewise, as if in complete obedience.

"You, young rake, are incorrigible. Penance to you is something unknown. Advance and reap your reward!"

The old hermit priest of Kantamani had made enough observations of pagan life, of the white man's rule over the simple folk; in anger he made a resolve to tear out the pages upon which were annotated carefully expounded theories and utterly useless profundities; to ascribe gentleness to the inept and thoroughly wicked was to sanction the eternal menace. He would in the future engender faith by blood and flying sword.

Standing before Harmenszoon was a huge man, stooped and spent. But before long the same man, winded and glaring, stood over him, triumphantly shouting his faith. In comatose state Harmenszoon refused to believe what he had seen and felt. The penance was evinced by blood that flowed from a dozen places where the fists of Father van Skike had dauntlessly felled the devil.

"Now, beast and defiler of women," said the old man, "you may pack your things and come with me. We go to Denpasar. There you will be placed in the hands of your kin, or one Mijnheer Stefan Meer, who, I am told, lays claim to you on a wager of some four months' duration."

Thus the empire of Mayrant Ruysdaal Sidneye claimed another recruit.

BOOK THREE

The Golden Hind, 1925-1933

CHAPTER XIX

1

A VISITOR to Soerabaja in the year of our Lord nineteen hundred and twenty-five had not seen the city until the sight of a low-slung white building, sprawling over several acres not far from the waterfront, met his eyes; it housed the offices of the great firm that slowly, surely, spread its tentacles and sucked in a huge share of the commerce of the Far East. Lesser offices in Sydney, Melbourne, Singapore, Manila, Davao, Nouméa, Auckland, and as far north as Hong Kong, bowed to the island of Java with reports on twenty large ships, their cargoes and destinations, to-the-penny profits and losses on every traffickable product from forty-five degrees below the equator to twenty-five above. Untold wealth, flamboyant mystery and romance, awe and wonder, seemed to echo the name of BATJAK, LTD.

The history of the firm was, in a measure, distorted with legend: the white walls were the lengthened shadow of a famous ship reported lost in a storm off the western coast of the Celebes some twenty years before — the *Quatrefoil*. Many strange tales, some fabulous, a score only half-true, and some highly accurate, lifted the Croesus ship, as she was rightly dubbed, into a niche in the romantic history of ships that sailed the seven seas. There she remained, planting in the trades of the heavens the long wake behind her mizzen that foamed under the red, white, and blue colors of the flag of the Netherlands. Some said her skipper, Sidneye, had paid a dear price for every bit of driftwood he could identify as a part of the *Quatrefoil;* rumor also had it that fifty thousand harmonicas went to Davy Jones's locker with her, and that before a favorable monsoon on a clear, gentle night one could stand on the beach in Macassar, or ride into the harbor on a *soppe,* and hear the far-off notes of mouth organs played by mermaids — many swore that weird and tuneful music rose from the waves to their very ears.

But a visitor within the forbidding vine-clad walls was given a view of the model of the *Quatrefoil:* standing twenty feet high, and thirty or more feet in length, in mahogany and concrete, her sails furled, her every plank and rope in place. Only one brief inscription was at her hull; inscribed in gold was: —

THE GREAT SHIP *QUATREFOIL* 1874–1905

Some few remembered the high stink that surrounded the sea lady while she was yet fresh in her apocryphal grave. The newspapers of Berlin, Hamburg, Amsterdam, London, and Soerabaja listed accounts of startling accusations. Many clippings were locked behind steel doors in the sumptuous offices behind the façade of Batjak, Ltd. Excerpts ran as follows: —

AMSTERDAM, June 11, 1905 — Mayrant Ruysdaal Sidneye, Captain of the *Quatrefoil* and senior partner of Sidneye, Vossler, en Meer, a trading firm of Soerabaja, Java, was named today by agents of the Imperial German Government's Wilhelmstrasse as the man answering the description given by the innkeeper of Hamburg where Herr Klingg was last seen. Klingg was the last man to make contact with Baron von Streicher, whose disappearance the Wilhelmstrasse is investigating. Sidneye, a native of Amsterdam, is fighting extradition.

SOERABAJA, July 1, 1905 — The German extradition papers served today by the Governor of Java on Mayrant Sidneye of this city compel the accused to answer to an inquiry in Hamburg before December. The case has to do with the mystery surrounding a Baron von Streicher of Aurich, Germany, who strangely disappeared on the fourth of February of this year.

HAMBURG, Nov. 2, 1905 — In a resumption of the questioning of Herr Sidneye of Soerabaja, Java, the following came to light: he is an only son of the celebrated Dutch scientist, the late Dokter Sidneye of Amsterdam; he is related to the missing Baron by marriage, his aunt having been joined in marriage to von Streicher while he was in the diplomatic service in Holland in 1875. The hearing was attended by only Wilhelmstrasse agents and a few witnesses, all *Herrenvolk*.

BERLIN, Nov. 5, 1905 — Uncovered today in the files submitted by the Netherlands government, pertaining to the hearing in Hamburg (case of Mayrant Sidneye: The Baron von Streicher mystery), is the trial of young Sidneye for murder aboard ship in a calm off Borneo in 1892. In Soerabaja, he was championed by the captain of the *Quatrefoil*, one Stefan Meer of Amsterdam, who, it seems, was a suitor for the hand of the girl who married the Baron in 1875. Such complications must be unraveled before the Imperial German Government prefers formal charges or dismisses the hearing.

Soerabaja, Nov. 11, 1905 — Lidj van der Glotz, captain of the Sidneye ship *Denpasar*, was today questioned in the Philippine port of Davao regarding the strange cargo of the *Quatrefoil* last February when she sailed from Hamburg. He testified that the "harmonicas" were for Moluccan trade. His testimony was verified by a Moluccan, holding a high place in the Sidneye firm of Soerabaja.

Amsterdam, Dec. 15, 1905 — It is reported that the lingering inquiry into the disappearance of Baron von Streicher, in which a *Nederlander*, Mayrant Ruysdaal Sidneye, is involved, may force the return of the wealthy ex-resident, Mijnheer Stefan Meer, to testify in his own behalf. Meer's wife, it was disclosed, is the former wife of the Baron. Another item of surprising interest is: Mayrant Sidneye was named after Mayrant von Streicher.

Soerabaja, Dec. 21, 1905 — Harmenszoon van Schreeven, formerly of Denpasar, Bali, was today charged with the rape of a Javanese maiden. His denial of all charges was made by the firm of Cocq en Laas. Van Schreeven is a half-brother of Mayrant Sidneye, now in Hamburg as the central figure of the von Streicher mystery. Dokter van Arken, whose fame soared when he solved the mystery of Sidneye's strange sickness here, examined the girl and swore the charges were without reason, that the girl had no doubt had many previous affairs. The police are inclined to agree with the young Dokter. Van Schreeven is employed as a clerk by Sidneye, Vossler, en Meer.

Soerabaja, Dec. 27, 1905 — HAMBURG INNKEEPER CLEARS SIDNEYE!

Amsterdam, Dec. 29, 1905 — STREICHER INQUIRY CLOSED.

London, Jan. 7, 1906 — The Sydney, Australia, office reported that a man giving his name as Klingg was picked up in the Joseph Bonaparte Gulf which joins the Dutch Timor Sea. He died before giving any reason for his wounds. The only ship near by was the *Van Arken I*, mastered by a Captain Younguer, who knew nothing of the man. The name Klingg, as readers of the continent news will remember, is the same as that of a missing figure in the

Baron von Streicher mystery. Authorities express doubt as to whether the man who died aboard the patrol steamer was that Klingg. Berlin reports the Streicher case closed.

2

From nineteen hundred and five the newspapers gave only casual mention to the Sidneye, Vossler, en Meer firm, and even smaller lines to any of the vast group of individuals who answered to the roll call of the firm. There was little need for print while rumor was ripe, but several notices found space from time to time: —

SAN FRANCISCO, 1908 — Sidneye, Vossler, and Meer of Soerabaja were highest bidders for the steamship *Oregon Hound*.

SYDNEY, 1910 — The firm of Sidneye, Vossler, Meer, and Batjoek, Ltd. today opened offices at Circular Quay. Parent offices are in Soerabaja, Java.

SINGAPORE, 1912 — The Board of Trade is looking into the tin monopoly of Malacca. Van Schreeven, of the firm of Sidneye, Vossler, Meer, and Batjoek, Ltd., appeared before the board today. No details are forthcoming.

MANILA, 1916 — The riot in Davao last evening was quickly brought under control. Charged with the uprising is a Captain Younguer of the firm of Sidneye, Vossler, Meer, and Batjoek, Ltd. of this city, and Soerabaja, Java. Younguer refused to pay the market price for copra and threatened to sail the *Van Arken I* out of port. The firm is one of the largest buyers of copra in the islands, and the riot was a natural aftermath. Government trade officials called at the firm's offices here today, but were unable to locate the branch manager, Raas Vossler.

SYDNEY, 1919 — It is alleged the *Van Arken I* under the command of Captain Younguer refused to answer a call of distress from the Japanese *Oru Maru* in the German Mandate (seized by Japan in co-operation with the Allies). The *Van Arken I* is a ship of the firm of Sidneye, Vossler, Meer, van Schreeven, and Batjoek, Ltd., operating out of Soerabaja, Java.

TOKYO, 1920 — Right of purchase to vital metals from the Malay States by the Imperial Japanese Government has been refused by the Singapore firm of Batjak, Ltd. No reason was given for the blunt refusal. The firm of Batjak, Ltd. has enormous holdings from Hong Kong south.

3

The sudden tearing-down of signs above warehouses, the removal of gold leaf from the glass of office fronts, the scrapping of the huge metal sign atop the white building in Soerabaja, caused no end of comment; from Hong Kong to Tasmania ships put into port for long days of idleness, with no visible reason. The coat of paint over the firm name that had made history in the tropical seas was sensational. Banking houses in Manila, Singapore, and Sydney were no less concerned than the Dutch houses of Batavia and Soerabaja. Sidneye, Vossler, Meer, van Schreeven, and Batjoek, Ltd. was no more. The press and emissaries of financial powers were met, on that spring morning of nineteen hundred and twenty, by a trio of cynical, powerful men, dressed without pomp — except for the central figure, van Schreeven, who reflected the wealth of the firm — only to be advised there would be no change in the policies of the firm other than the name. Captain Meer and Mijnheer Vossler, dressed in sea togs, had nothing to say. The handsome spokesman then came forth with three words: "That is all."

And that was all, except that the new name, Batjak, Ltd., rode mercilessly over the seas after cargoes, gorged its many warehouses and factories, pulled its pools out of circulation in order to skyrocket prices on the one hand, while its relentless bush-beaters haggled on the other. Batjak, said wharf loungers — and bankers — meant barter, and the brief definition best expressed the name. Others said it meant blood; that if all ships operated in the manner of Younguer's *Van Arken I*, the latter definition took precedence over the first — skulls bleached in the out-of-the-way islands were echoes of Batjak trade. But every ship had its tales, its guarded secrets, its mystery; the *Van Arken I*, the *Denpasar*, the *Luzon Queen II*, the *Oregon Hound*, the *Zulinde Meer*, the *Lombok Djanger*, the *Keli Moetoe*, and even the sixty lesser craft, made up of schooner, ketch, proa, and sampan. Least known, and therefore the most mysterious of the Soerabaja line, was the big three-master, the *Golden Hind*, aboard which, it was rumored, rode the tyrant of Batjak, Ltd.

But everywhere the firm figured in the price of copra, copal, cajuput, cloves, cinnamon, cane, coffee, and cinchona, as well as the trends in hides, tea, nutmeg, rattan, ingots of tin, nickel, mother-of-pearl, wool, and wheat. Oil and rubber loomed like ponderous giants in the background. The largest buyers of phonographs, fountain pens, and other Western World gewgaws was Batjak. Merciless barter!

4

The layman from San Francisco to Rangoon heard and repeated many tales having to do with the change of name of the Sidneye Company. In the English Club of Hong Kong it was said for a fact that Batjoek, an old Moluccan, took over the firm during the hectic days of the war when submarines took their toll of the Sidneye ships flying the Union Jack. His financing was done, however, in Tokyo.

In Batavia a prominent Dutch planter told of the sinking of the first *Zulinde Meer*. Sidneye himself, he said, had thrown up his hands on the wharf in Soerabaja and cried: "This is the end." And English interests gradually claimed the ashes of the trade empire. In that same city another man of the Dutch Military said: "Meer himself saved the firm. He kicked Sidneye out, and handed the reins to van Schreeven and the Moluccan. The proof — do you ever hear of Sidneye?"

When van Schreeven married an English-Balinese girl in 'eighteen, and built her a huge palace between Denpasar and Bedoeloe, the papers named him "a head of Batjak, Ltd."

The most widely accepted story fell from the lips of a priest residing at the time — nineteen hundred and nineteen — in the largest of the Moluccan Islands, Halmahera. Father Duff was not a man to whom one might attach doubt: a man of faith and sincerity, the possessor of temperate mien coupled with positive sagaciousness, he seemed a symbol of honor, and he had no reason to deviate from the truth. His tale is briefly told: —

"It was in July of this year that I set out from Tidore in a tiny schooner for the town of Laboeha, on the island of Batjan. We encountered a heavy monsoon about halfway — right on the equator — and our boat was tossed about like a coconut shell, her masts ripped loose and heaved overboard, her hull drawing water like a suction engine. There was no steering a ship in such a sea and the native crew made ready to die. I must confess I prayed as I had taught others to pray.

"Clinging to a pitching deck, and gritting my teeth as tons of water sought to shake me from my hold, I opened my eyes and viewed an apparition: a great sailing vessel wallowing under storm sail was not more than a hundred yards away. She hailed us and, the wind with her voice, we heard. But hope died in me, for effecting a rescue in such a sea was insane.

"I shall not bore you with the details, but a miracle came to pass. The vessel, the *Luzon Queen II*, seemed to defy the waves; and she held her bow to the wind, while her beam gently drew nearer. Never was a ship handled with greater skill — I shall praise her builder and helmsman for the remainder of my days. We were taken aboard within two hours, all of us, including three goats.

"The Moluccan, the famed Batjoek, handled the ship. He met us and frowned without frowning — you know the native — at my robe. I was an enemy from that moment on, but as it happened, a friendly one.

"'We are bound for the Celebes,' he said. 'Your party must come with us.' We went, and before we passed Van Bone Gulf my Christian crew had again deserted the cross.

"We made port in a kind monsoon and I was told that Batjoek was traveling into the mountains — to Toradjaland. A shiver went up my spine. The Toradjas are head-hunters. They are the people who dwell in high-roofed kampongs and live for their funerals, their strange arts, and bullock horns. I could talk all night about the Toradjas, their queer ways and their weird *tao-taos*.

"My curiosity overcame my fear and I asked if I could go along. My request was granted. What he had in mind for me caused me little worry; and for some reason I trusted him. We left early one morning and followed the jungle road, twisting and winding into the hills toward the peak of Goenoeng Kalando. Then we turned south and followed the trails to the Mata Allo River and to the arresting Goenoeng Tindara. There we halted, and Batjoek was accorded a most unusual welcome.

"By the merest stroke of luck I saw the 'old man,' as he was called; he was a prisoner of importance, and without doubt German. Huge of bone, bald and wrinkled, and minus one eye, he was stark naked and in chains. A Dutchman led him about by a thong of hide knotted into his nose, and the 'old man' babbled and grinned at us. '*Guten Morgen, guten Morgen*,' he cackled, and then his mind asserted itself long enough for him to curse everyone in sight.

"I was seized when it was discovered I had seen the 'old man,' and only Batjoek saved me from death and a wooden *tao-tao* to honor my remains. Nor did he swear me to secrecy; instead he said it was time to move that which I *had not* seen.

"No, even if I were called to the stand to tell what I saw, I would deny having seen it.

"Then I was put to work. For five hours I helped haul gold ingots out of the caverns some fifty feet under the mountain. Enough for a king's ransom, and from what I heard Batjoek telling the Dutchman, it was exactly that.

"Said he: 'Baas Sidneye has his ships taken away, his jewels in pawn. For ten years I have sunk much of my gold here, mine and that from my friends in Ceram, and that which I have taken from the Chinese and Japanese. I could buy out my master and Meer — and Vossler. But no, I care little for gold or more than one ship. The war of religions can wait. I shall continue to serve Baas Sidneye.'"

That was Father Duff's story.

Plausible? Indeed! One could almost picture the rest of the story about a name: the many partners of Sidneye would have so weighted the firm name that no one could express enjoyment in its chant — Sidneye, Vossler, Meer, van Schreeven, Batjoek, van Arken, and Younguer, Ltd.! The compromise to a short resounding title was thus easy to imagine: the crisp, blunt euphony of Batjak, Ltd. honored its tawny savior, Batjoek; and one can well imagine that Sidneye thought of it at 12:01 and ordered the sweeping change at 12:02.

5

And the good ship *Quatrefoil:* She had not gone to her grave off the Celebes coast in nineteen hundred and five; instead, after weathering the storm, her masts splintered and her cargo of harmonicas dumped, she was coved and repainted secretly. Four years later she reached Dumbarton, Scotland, for a complete make-over — from wrought-iron hull, teak decks, and heavy brass, to the last rope. She retained something more — the proud heart of the *Quatrefoil.* It stood by, unseen and dead to the world, but very much alive inside the yellow hull that came out to run the seas.

About Mayrant Ruysdaal Sidneye: It was said, and without any to dispute the words, that he cared little for the onus of power, and more for the quintessence of the word; so, in order to free himself he hovered over Batjak, Ltd. as the power beyond the visible. At any rate little was known of him or his whereabouts after nineteen hundred and twenty-one, although great financiers and emissaries of governments never entered into business with the corporeal heads of the firm without the feeling that a hovering ghost must be consulted before any decision was made.

6

The year was nineteen hundred and twenty-five.

A Dutch secretary entered an ornate office inside the great white building in Soerabaja. Her eyes had long since become used to the arabesque walls, the gilded ceiling and mahogany floors; the verd-antique table some twenty feet in length and seven feet across, for the directorate of a far-flung empire, scarcely claimed her eye; nor did the white marble statue in the corner, an expensive piece from Rome, cause her any change of expression. Batjak, Ltd. was, as she knew full well, the symbol of wealth.

Stalking in behind her, and not pausing for any announcement, an old brown man with white hair and a mummy's skin flung himself into a chair. He wore little clothing, only a law-abiding covering for his emaciated body, and that was of cheapest white. But she, like other hundreds of well-dressed employees, bowed with respect.

The telephone was put aside and the big man behind the massive desk arose and extended his hand. The brown man did not rise; instead he said: —

"He died four days ago."

Without any expression the other sat back in his chair and said to the girl: "Has the *Golden Hind* reported?"

"I have it here," she answered, walking forward to hand him a coded message.

"Wait one moment, Janet. Here, Batjoek, I'll read it: '*Golden Hind* off Makin, Gilbert Isles, due south at 172 degrees from 3. Calm. Do not agree on wheat. Sell. Send agents to Curaçao, Americas. Buy aloin gum covertly. Hold. Batjoek to Fiji.'"

He frowned. "Ready, Janet. '*Golden Hind* message received. Will follow.'" He paused, whispered something to Batjoek, and continued. "'Nineteen dead four days. Wool low on Sydney market. Give order.'" He arose, hands in coat pockets. "Send in code four, and also in the same the following to Sydney: 'Sell.' To New Orleans: 'Harjaan to Curaçao, buy aloin gum.' To Denpasar: 'Stefan Meer, Nineteen dead four days. Love to my wife and Teleia.'

"Janet, you should see Teleia. She's seven now, and the image of her mother. I wish Raas would return so I could run down after her."

The secretary laughed. "Mijnheer van Schreeven, the last time she visited me she gave me a stick of candy. The rest of her sack was all over her face."

"Yes," returned the father, his face lifting above the chill of the glazed office, "to her Batjak means candy and dolls. To me," he added pensively, "Batjak means confinement. Batjoek, what does Batjak mean to you?"

Slowly the brown man answered, "It is the road to everywhere and everything." And for the moment the girl felt the stirring and mysterious breath of a vast empire's soul; then, its full portent beyond her, she again became a mere cog in a highly intricate machine.

The *Golden Hind* was almost a second *Quatrefoil*, and but for her master's whim (never again should any craft be blessed by that name) she would have been dubbed the second, and the four-lobed design might have continued to meet the spray of wide latitudes. Her sides were long, sleek, and gleaming of golden yellow, and her masts were high, and her varnished spars were new; her keel, like her every plank, was British, made to order by an old firm whose pride in worthy ships was a heritage of a deep past; and a pretty penny she had cost, since her owner had ideas that taxed the patience of blueprint makers in his desire for modernism, for luxuries not found aboard the *Quatrefoil*.

The *Hind* was the fastest thing under sails.

With her lacquered bow ricocheting the direct rays of the equatorial sun, and pointing like a tapering arrow to the heart of New Zealand some fourteen hundred miles south, she plowed the Gilbertese waters like a swan that had eyes only for the graceful purl of her own design. She aped a yacht, this cargo-mad ship, by the impeccable gloss that separated her deck timbers from the trim feet of her too neat crew, whose dress was the reflecting white of mast tips, forecastle, and bulwarks. A black streamer ran her sides from stern to bow, and her sails lifted the blue sea to white mirrors that towered and leaned with the winds. Ratlines, shrouds, and rigging, the maze of converging rope that ran dizzily aloft, still clung to the bleached complexion of a Manila hemp yard. Below decks she lost none of her trim, though the bowels of her shapely belly were fashioned less for beauty and more for the reaping of guilders; but her hold and compartments smelled of fresh paint and pitch blending with the sweet-rancid cargo of drying coconut meat. A picture of exquisite line and color was the *Golden Hind* — in every detail save one: —

The bald, meaty man in white that sat under the yellow and white striped canopy facing the north and the sapphire wake.

To Mayrant Sidneye the rhythmic glide over the gentle swells was lulling. The wide tropic sea, that began nowhere and ended without the chopped boundary of a palm shadow in the moonlight, cooed a lullaby that was matched by nothing else. The salty tang of the air, the soft wind ruffling the semi-disks of awning edges, were matched by creaking blocks, sighing cordage, and lapping waves. Into Sidneye's narrowed eye the white wake mingled with undisturbed blue and boasted of its adventure with a flying cloud as a highway of blue and green raced ever on and under the stanch ribs of Batjak's pride. That which he gave supremacy became law over the trackless sea. His self-contained ego was thus fed by the very foam off the stern.

The rattan chair, cushioned with heavy folds of yellow, was, like the white and yellow table and the copper container atop it, screwed into stationary position against the antics of the deck. A gin bottle rested in the copper circle in a silence matched only by the white-clad Dutch lad standing near the "king's tent."

"Why did you choose the sea, boy?"

Striking a rigid pose, the lad answered, "I scarcely know, Mijnheer Sidneye, unless I heard her calling my name."

"Did you ever long to steal aboard a craft like this while she lay in the harbor?"

"I did, Mijnheer, once while visiting Rotterdam."

"Then why didn't you? I did. Back in 'ninety-one. I was a stow-away."

"So I've heard, Master. And believe me, Master, I like to visit saloons and have men point to me and whisper — 'He's Sidneye's personal man — aboard the *Hind!*' Ah," he sighed, "I bit into good luck, all right." Mayrant chuckled and the boy continued. "Many a man approaches me with a small bribe for a kind word to your ears. I could earn a fat sum if —"

"If what?" Mayrant said, humoring his pause.

"If I didn't have to return to some of these ports." Mayrant's laugh and expression evoked a laugh from the boy. "And if I wasn't ordered not to admit you were aboard ship."

"Well, you're a fool if you don't take their money — and a greater fool if you don't bring to my ears the news of aggressive men I can use."

"You mean, Master, I've slept through a small fortune?" The lad's surprise was almost disbelief. "Great stars! I'll supply you with men you want, Master Sidneye."

"At how much — nothing? Fill my glass, Hekkin, and in the future consider every angle to make a guilder." The lad obeyed, his face wreathed in a newborn cunning. "And, Hekkin, if you have made half a thousand above pay guilders by Soerabaja, I shall elevate you. The alternative is discharge. Understand? And pour yourself a gin — I always seal a trade with cups."

His driving ambitions were interrupted by the wireless operator: "A message, Master." He advanced and stiffly bowed, extending the sheet in his dip. Mayrant accepted the paper and read.

The wireless man and Hekkin eyed each other. Mayrant Sidneye held a message that caused him a deep frown. The message was not

225

one designed to please — God, no! The squat figure was up and out of his chair, cursing the sea, the sails, the crew, and waving his arms like one gone utterly mad. The two stood rigid and calm, afraid to move, and the helmsman, near by, clamped his hands over the wheel spokes with such force that the blood was forced out of his palms. The mate on watch, the boatswain in the lower sail, the men in the rigging, knew naught of Mayrant Sidneye's dual reason for living; *neen!* Not a man among them knew of that second hold on life, of that long-nourished monster called revenge that lived sweetly as long as the "old man," or "nineteen," of the Celebes breathed air into his agonized lungs.

Mayrant von Streicher was dead!

The blow struck with the speed of cold paralysis and left a part of him dead: the passion of revenge that was half of Mayrant Sidneye. Emptiness in the wake of Streicher's death: no longer could the soul be tormented on earth; the opposite of glowing, living revenge was a boundless void.

He walked to the mizzenmast and glanced into its heights, a wifeless, childless man who had nothing upon which to lean but a ship and ships, but Batjak and a trade empire. Pitifully he reached for the wood of the mast, and ran his hand over its smooth surface in an effort to find in it some balm for his hollow soul.

Turning to the wireless operator, he said: "Batjak, Soerabaja — buy wool on Sydney market. Buy! Buy! Buy!"

CHAPTER XX

1

THE Gilbertese radiate a spontaneous charm, an ineffable smile that instantly blends into the Micronesian the legacies of the bronze Polynesian and the inky Melanesian: round, strong jaw, firm, chiseled mouth, broad nostrils, high aquiline forehead, and level brown eyes proclaim a proud race. Less voluptuous than her sisters from Hawaii to the Society Isles, the girl of the Gilberts is nevertheless a piquant sprite with a soul of melting romance. The graduations of definition are as one finds them: a lonely eye in the British Protectorate might gaze upon languor, while a colder eye could see only a hybrid with the mind of a child. Beauty, whether in London or Singapore, becomes more of a mood; but the world over, woman is eternal. And in the flaked coral that rises out of the equatorial flame of the Pacific, from Makin Meang at the north to Arorae, the same distance below the hemisphere divide, woman is the daughter of the sun by day, the ward of the stars by night, the lure and the fruit.

The island of Aranuku was no different from the other atolls of the Gilberts.

There — in the same hour Sidneye received the news of Streicher's death, when the *Golden Hind* was but a few hours north, and bearing down to flank the island on the west — a lone white man walked down the long street of palm-shaded houses. The thatched huts were without walls since the pandanus-frond screens were high into the eaves. Few clung to even the shaded open at siesta time, though the white man saw two old men in colorful waist mats and two younger men in loincloths moving slowly about their business. Under grass-skirted roofs children cried and women laughed. Before one house he paused, involuntarily raised a hand to set the worn sea cap to the back of his head, and peered closely: a native girl of marriageable age was undressing.

He lifted his eyes to the gray-green palm clusters bordering the lagoon, and then gave an ear to the muted surf beyond its coral fringes. Turning slowly he walked a few steps in the direction from whence he came and again retraced his steps, eyeing as he did so the girl who now exposed her body from shoulders to hips. The two old men kept their course to the lagoon; the younger pair moved on in the opposite direction.

The acrid odor of cooking shark assailed his nostrils and he turned slowly to survey the houses nearest the object of his attention. Across the coral-graveled street an old woman labored over an esteemed shark. For moments he eyed her. Quiet reigned, broken only by the surf, the whisper of the trees, and the echoes of tropical distances.

The native girl, unclothed, was plaiting her long hair, her back to him — a searing picture of firm buttocks and thighs and vigorous brown waist. Slowly he lighted a cigarette. Holding it between his teeth with lips drawn, he placed his brown knotted hands on hips and gave serious thought to the situation.

Frazier, the effeminate cruising deputy of the Resident Commissioner, whom he had visited when his small ship *Yucatán* beat herself to pieces on the reef, had warned him about the ancient ferocity of Gilbertese laws, some modified and others annulled by the British, but nevertheless given clandestine enforcement at times. There was little to gain in the punishment of a whole village for failure to observe His Majesty's decrees, he had said, and besides, it was too bloody hot for undue exertion.

"Y'know, old chap," he had said, "the day we put clothes on the women in these islands, we jolly well announced to the men that we covered prizes they'd appreciated only for the sake of custom and fertility. Nowadays let a virile youth peek at a leg and he's a victim of lust."

The skipper of the *Yucatán* thought of Frazier's words, of the quality of Gilbertese virulence. But to hell with the past! The old woman continued to hold ceremony over the smelly shark meat; the road to the lagoon was empty; the children no longer cried in the thatch up the street; the girl in the shade of the house finished one long plait, placed the stem of a lily into her hair and gathered the strands of the other side. She stood facing the lagoon now, giving a clear view of tapering breasts that were like full weighted pods. Without removing his hands from hips he spat out the cigarette, wet his lips, and lifted his brow in meditation: —

Frazier was by now snoring, the neck of a gin bottle clutched in one pink-white hand, a mosquito broom in the other. Within an hour he'd squirm, grunt, yawn, stretch, grunt some more, like a bull hippo, and raise his massive head for a bellowing noise that should bring his servant. Then he'd ask for ice, "All the goddam ice in Aranuku; and gin! And where the hell's my bloody shipwrecked friend? Get him, I say, and we'll drink till sunset. Tomorrow we'll move on to Abemama." Then he'd wallow himself down into the mat of his bed and blink the big eyes in his cherubic face, smile at tomorrow, and the yesterdays of Piccadilly Circus, and yawn ferociously. The first three slugs of gin merely lifted his lazy eyes to a normal brilliance; thereafter he slowly warmed, sweated in rivulets, and worked up loquacity. He ran the streets of London and Sydney with the glee of his stimulated memory, and wondered at the strange silence of his new friend and free boarder.

And the man from the *Yucatán* thought on: He'd best step into his decision now and get back for a fill of British gin. He walked slowly toward the house, up the walk of powdered and burned coral toward the pandanus corner posts and the naked Gilbertese girl.

2

The old woman stood over her pot of shark's flesh, moving her emaciated body in slow rhythmic motion; a tuneless chant evoked from the bestowers of magic a bountiful gift for her son's unborn child. The wife lay on a mat near by, sleeping, her belly almost ripe with the bulge of another generation.

> O see, by the flesh of the wild shark,
> The ferocious killer of the vast oceans,
> The courageous tiger of the mighty,
> That he is not nourished by the crawler;
> The slow fish that is turtle gives him not;
> The most flat and meek fish are not his food;
> Thus he is the soul of a sword;
> The soul of the Sun lies in his bowels;
> The earth and sea are his;
> His! His! His!
> He shall walk to the Sun and gaze fearlessly;
> He shall draw the eyes of all for his ferocity.

With her stick the old woman stirred, never removing her bright eyes from the pot. All sights of the world disappeared in her frenzy, and the ancestors of fierce creatures swam inside the pot and gave her great messages that had to do with the protection of the expectant mother from evil spirits: —

"Surround her mat with teeth of the shark and strings of hair from your son of the Sun, the dauntless seafarer who runs his craft far into the waters where dwell the bloodthirsty hags and whirlpools of the World's Edge. Sneer at the weak and stare not at the sapping soul of perfumed flowers —"

And on and on; the trance drained the old woman of strength and sanity. She spoke, she was answered; and the conversation was the same as that of yesterday, the day before. She hobbled over to the sleeping woman and drew a line around her with the dripping stick. Only then did she feel the drain of energy. As if to rest her body she gazed into the street — and then across the latticed shade of the cooling palms to the house from whence the sounds came.

In a land where there are no secrets, the hint of such provokes curiosity; the old woman shuffled into the open and across the street to the house that did not have its leaf screens raised to the eaves. She peered through the cracks. Taut, fascinated, she watched.

The white man whom she had seen with the British Protector stood before a girl stretched at his feet. A wild fierce light, the ecstasy of a strange magic, played in his eyes. A leather belt was wielded slowly but fiercely, singing and swishing through the air, to snap against the buttocks and thighs of the girl; and each stroke found quicker timing;

and the man's body grew more rigid and convulsive with every crack of leather against flesh.

The girl moaned, less from pain and more, it seemed, from hypnosis; she writhed, her body responding in spasmodic jerks as the belt cracked against her, but her mouth emitted only the low moans so desired by the white beast. The tempo increased to a climactic fierceness. Then, when the man fell prostrate across the maltreated body, the old woman scurried off to rouse the village.

Frazier, in his bed beneath the Union Jack, slept through it all. He yawned, rolled over twice, and thinking the noise from the lagoon a part of his dream continued his stertorous breathing, a dimpling smile on his face, a hand under his chin. Ah, the magic of distances, the echo of the voice-filled air in the palms.

3

All the while the *Golden Hind* raced obliquely with the wind and continued her uninterrupted course, her sail demanding a tight wheel in the helmsman's grasp. The flake of coral that was Aranuku was dead east of her when the sun reached far in the opposite direction and hung poised for the bloody dive into a vast concourse of tropical blue.

The helmsman echoed the order of one point to starboard and, eyeing the weather clew, moved his spokes and turned his ear again to the song that came from the ship's cuddy. His eye turned to the wisp far off the port beam without seeing the atoll or the wash of color. His watch would soon end and he could finish the letter to his half-caste Chinese mistress in Singapore, though God only knew when he could mail it. Ever a romancer, he gave thought to a wish: that he could exchange messages as easily as the great Sidneye. Surely he'd not rant and rave like the master, who'd given such a passionate performance only a few hours before. *Neen!* Not even if Lin Lee proved unfaithful. The sea was broad and there were more ports than that island eye of the Malay States.

Skimming toward the *Hind* was the triangular sail of an outrigger canoe; four brown men were aboard her, one lending his strength to the rudder, another gripping between his toes the mainsheet of the sail, while the other two stood on the outrigger like statues of a proud race meeting the sun and spray as they found them. Fleet were the native craft, fleet as the flying fish they sought in the sunset.

In bass Dutch a white-clad *zeeman* in the rigging bellowed: "Aranuku hard to port." An older man heaved the deep-sea lead and droned out the fathoms below. The song from the galley trailed off into nothing and gave way to a curse — hot grease against the singer's arms always evoked profanity; the helmsman grinned at the cook's wrath, then turned an eye to the racing canoe as her sleek hull sent sheets of spray in mid-air.

From his aerie in the uppers, a flaxen-haired youth thrilled at the sport of the Gilbertese fishermen, almost falling when the canoe seemed ready to dash her prow against the big ship. The canoe lifted her outrigger higher, causing the two balance-men to squat and hug their poles; shooting emerald spray against the ship, it turned in boiling foam just in time to forestall the inevitable crash. The natives emitted playful cries of "Ah-ee-ee-ah" as the outrigger splashed again into the water and the craft raced into the wake of the big ship and on across. Before long she leaned into the sunset, her sail a gold-lined silhouette against the western sky.

The captain of the ship walked beside the chief mate at the portside beam. Both puffed at cigarettes and eyed each other as if in mild debate. Van Cordtlaant, the captain, was tall, quiet, and amiable, but stern, a man little known in any port, and more of a mystery because of it; he sailed the "king's craft" without more background than that of walking aboard to take over — thus spoke rumor. Exceedingly handsome in a swarthy sort of way and calm as the dead of the Celebes Sea, he displayed a brand of aloofness that was rewarded with certain respect. He knew the sea, that much was evident, and that he knew her well was given emphasis by the very fact that he sailed the semi-yacht on which the empire ruler rode.

The chief mate was more like an open book: Teer Noord was a ruddy-faced hulk of a man who easily entered into a session of fisticuffs without provocation. He blustered and fumed when the sails had to be furled before a storm; he bellowed out his mirth when a young tanglefoot tripped on the ropes or clanked his cranium against the bulwarks. His nose was large and hooked, lending his sharp eyes a severity that reminded one of a hawk. The respect accorded Noord was founded upon background — from Port Said to San Francisco; but such an open book served to heighten the mystery of those closed chapters in the life of Captain Cordtlaant.

Both men proved what everyone knew: Sidneye was a master at picking his men.

The captain grinned at the serious squint of Noord's eye. "I say twenty guilders on my opinion, and I'll give the decision to Mijnheer Sidneye."

"You're on," boomed the chief mate. "His word is final, whether it's right or wrong."

"You'd do well not to doubt his opinion," reproved Cordtlaant with even emphasis.

"And you're right — except that I long since learned of the weaknesses of man, Captain. Of course, one must hew smooth edges at times, but am I an ape for every man's honesty? *Neen!* The eye of Baas Sidneye will dwell upon us both, and he'll be governed by the one of us that best meets the mood of his eye. If it was a storming I'd lay you odds he'd see in me the man that's right. But on an easy return trip he'll no doubt favor you."

Cordtlaant paused to eye his subordinate. "Your words have an unpleasant ring, Mate."

"No offense, Captain. I'll say the same to the man himself." A level gaze met that of his superior.

"Then we shall expect that of you." And Noord said *sotto voce*, "Damn his infernal aloofness!"

The island was lost over the horizon when the ship's officers strode toward Mayrant Sidneye. Both men eyed him as well as the newly emptied bottle in the copper nest, and each frowned at the chalky face of the attendant, Hekkin, who grinned sheepishly as he listened to the voiced resolves of a ruthless empire builder.

The two stood in silence behind the man, heard him ask for more ice, and heard his glass clink and rattle with it. Then they heard the *zeeman* in the rigging: —

"Man adrift dead ahead!"

Mayrant turned his head and cocked an ear to the sound. In another moment he arose and walked past his officers and toward the bow. Hekkin needed no word to spur him forward with his master's eyeglass.

"Easy to starboard," yelled Noord, "and make ready to lower a boat."

The red sun sent only a glare over the sea and into Mayrant's eye from the bow, and in a flash he moved to the forerigging and ran the ratlines. He cried: "Drop a charge into the water to drive off the sharks!"

Leaping toward Mayrant's eye through the glass was a picture that reminded him of a fact: to molest a girl of the Gilberts was to court slow death. Tied hand and foot with coconut fibers and lashed to a log was a white man. The log was in the water one moment and out of it the next, bobbing from the heavier outrigger. In this manner the log was minus a roll. The construction was so designed as to cause a rush of

232

sharks toward the dipping, helpless living flesh; only small chunks could be torn from the victim at one rush. Mayrant knew what had happened before: the quick sorcery and the lashing of the man to the log before swift canoes towed the defiler out to sea.

The sun alone was enough to finish a man facing the heavens after such baptism but the teeming sharks that split the surface added the last horror. Their baleful eyes and ragged jaws rising out of the water were made worse by their nearness. The fetid odor of their maws in one's face, then a rending of flesh from face, arm, intestine, or leg, and another rush and a searing stab of salt into the wound, would cause the most callous heathen to petition his gods for the mercy of a quick death.

But Mayrant saw no blood on the man. The sharks, huge and gray, charged, they whipped up a lather of foam about the log, and when almost upon the maddening flesh they craved, a sudden swerve and they were gone. Why? Mayrant squinted his eyes and peered at the man. Every shark, he saw, was greeted with a straining of the man's chest and a distortion about the mouth: he was saving his breath for the repeated noises that must soon drive him mad, or perhaps he was too spent to yell. The man's face seemed unduly calm for his predicament: he actually grinned at the devils with all the glory of contempt and hate. Or was it fear?

Within a quarter hour the victim was on deck; sitting in Mayrant's chair, his red face reddened by the sunset, he eyed the ship with interest, her master and crew with veiled contempt. The ship's surgeon whipped life into his body with a brisk hand and a smelly balm, while Hekkin, at Mayrant's order, refilled a glass with gin; and without the batting of an eye, the man who had cheated the Gilbertese of their revenge drank.

"He's had enough," said Mayrant; but the cool eyes that flashed level fire said otherwise, and Hekkin, torn between his master's words and the other's eyes, trembled at something unknown and obeyed the latter. Mayrant Sidneye was impressed as he eyed the tall, lean, heavy-biceped man whose age might be anywhere between twenty and thirty at one glance — between thirty and forty at the next; heavy black bars stretched above the black of his eyes and found certain harmony in the thin mouth and nose. A half-smile was warped before taking shape, and though by line it was a smile, it was, by co-ordination with his eyes, a Jolly Roger dripping blood.

Suave Captain Cordtlaant blinked as the level black eyes turned on him in hard appraisal. Teer Noord felt the stab of those eyes and winced, thinking as he did so that the brig should earn its place on the *Hind*.

The cynical face turned to the man who was ostensibly the owner.

233

There, in a flash of a second he discovered that which had forever evaded him: equality. Respect, mutual and eternal, was born out of the clash of two pairs of eyes.

"Who are you?" asked Mayrant.

"A man hard to kill," came the challenge.

"Quite plausible that, but your name."

"Ralls."

"Your full name?"

"Ralls."

CHAPTER XXI

I

SINCE Sidneye gave notice that all men, officers and crew, were to extend the guest, Mijnheer Ralls, every courtesy, Captain Cordtlaant went out of his way, without fawning over the man, to obey the order. While one could scarcely refrain from openly admiring the fellow, there were other qualities essential to the completion of a man — and in Ralls he saw more of what was lacking than did most men: Ralls was utterly devoid of compassion, of inward respect for any man.

It was on the day the *Golden Hind* stood between Fiji and the New Hebrides in her southward race that he decided to lengthen his feelers toward the guest. The sun bore down from its zenith on the cobalt blue, and the water heaved back its disdain of the sun. Passing through a sudden cloudburst the sails dripped of steam a bare five minutes and proceeded to hang limp and dry for the next half hour. Then a favorable trade filled the sails and the *Hind* was herself again, the queen of everything under canvas.

Ralls sat in Mayrant's chair under the awning while its owner lay asleep in his cabin. Cordtlaant approached, eyed a sailor at the stern rail, shot a glance at the helmsman, and turned a slow eye to the mizzen royal. He brought a cigarette to his parched lips and without a word proffered one to Ralls. Ralls, staring into the sea, accepted.

"Mind if I join you in a drink?" asked the captain.

"Help yourself," came the answer. "Can you tell me, Captain, where this ship is bound?"

234

"I cannot," he laughed, "for even I don't know. Only Mijnheer Sidneye knows."

"Hm-m. No cargo to speak of, and no port in mind. Rather odd, I'd say."

"On the contrary, the *Golden Hind* is not a ship to return profitless to her home port. Her cargo may crowd the holds or rest in the jewel box of Baas Sidneye, but she is the guilder mark of the line. Not even the *Van Arken I* tops her. I doubt," he added, lifting his glass to his lips, "if the *Quatrefoil* in her day ever matched her earnings. Did you ever hear of Batjak, Ltd.?"

"Who hasn't?"

"This is a Batjak ship," he returned with just pride.

"A ship of such a firm is usually routed, Captain. Why does Mr. Sidneye rule her? Just who is this Sidneye?"

Cordtlaant's eyebrows raised significantly: So! For all of his attention to this derelict, Baas Sidneye had sealed his identity. Smiling, he said, "The owners of Batjak are indebted to him and thus they humor his whims. You see, Mijnheer Ralls, he founded the firm more than twenty years ago."

"And just who heads Batjak now?"

"The Vossler, Meer, and Batjoek interests," he said in half-truth. "No one ever hears of Mayrant Sidneye."

"Yet, Captain, you say he alone knows the destination of this ship. Does any firm parcel out ships in that manner in this modern age? If so I'll take one and work the Tuamotus — up to the Marquesas." He eyed the captain with all the penetrating powers of his level eyes. "He tops the earnings of any other ship, you say. They humor him? Were I a laughing man, Captain, I'd laugh in your face."

Cordtlaant remained cool and lazily even. "A man fresh from a log in the sea, Mijnheer Ralls, should have more respect for his rescuers. That is, of course, until his position warrants the strength of his words."

"If my role is so insignificant, Captain, I am surprised at the route great men like yourself choose in seeking to cover facts."

"Suppose, Mijnheer Ralls, we smooth our feathers and drink together."

"Very well," returned Ralls absently. "So Mr. Sidneye is the head of Batjak. We shall drink to him, Captain."

"I don't remember saying that," Cordtlaant said crisply, "though I'll gladly drink to him."

"What an obliging fellow you are, Captain." Turning his head, he said with raised voice: "Come, Mr. Sidneye. We're drinking to you. The

235

'captain here just informed me that you were Batjak." Mayrant, hovering near, frowned and walked forward.

"On the contrary," said Cordtlaant, "I gave no such information."

"No," said Ralls, "he chose to try talking out of my head something that wasn't there, Mr. Sidneye."

Mayrant eyed the two with twinkling eyes: a duel of wits was a dessert he seldom tasted. "What have you to say for yourself, Captain?" he said jestingly, taking his chair as Ralls moved to a stool.

"To your guest, Mijnheer Sidneye?"

"Guest or not," said Sidneye, "your captaincy draws an equal to any man. Answer man or guest, as you choose."

"Thanks. But he draws his own conclusions about things, making you the head of Batjak in one moment, and choosing a ship to work the French Islands in the next."

Sidneye beamed and trained his eye upon Ralls, entertaining the picture of the rake mastering a Batjak ship. As if in answer to his doubts, Ralls raised his glass and said: —

"To Mayrant Sidneye and his loyal captain." After glasses were lowered he displayed all the shrewdness the situation demanded. "I rib too heavily at times, Captain, though I merely seek to draw the real man out of his shell. I must admit that the smooth tongue in your head merits the captaincy of even so fine a ship as this. But," he added in jocular fashion, "you're still a liar."

Cordtlaant's laugh eased the tension, though Mayrant seemed more pleased with Ralls's return. "For such words, Ralls," said the captain, "I'll speak to the Vossler en Meer interests about a ship for you. A ketch would suffice for a time, I presume."

"No," said Ralls seriously. "A ketch is not my idea of a ship."

"But we all began with a ketch," reproved the captain smoothly.

"So did I," returned Ralls. "But for the cargo I'm after a ketch is too small."

"And your cargo?" said Cordtlaant.

"You could put it in your pockets, Captain. I'm after pearls on a big-time scale."

"You choose to speculate rather than knuckle down to certainties," Cordtlaant grinned easily.

"Have it your way," said Ralls. "But do you call a handful of pearls speculation?"

"*Neen, Mijnheer,*" he voiced in silken challenge.

"Well, I know where they are. The only reason I don't own them now is because my machine gun jammed. We were almost upon the monolith where the pearls were, when I was captured by screeching native warriors. Ripper, my wop sailor, escaped. The devils even built a fire around me. I don't ask you to believe me — it makes no difference — but I wished for rain to put out the fire and got a deluge. By God, it was timely! The natives untied me, thinking I was a god who could put out their fires, and led me to my ship, making me a present of a pearl larger than yours, sir."

"Where is it?" asked Mayrant.

"In Honolulu. In hock. The *Yucatán* needed her timbers patched. But I made a landfall at Christmas Island without much more sail than the shirt on my back. There I boarded a tramp for Hawaii."

"On what island were the pearls?" asked Mayrant.

"Mr. Sidneye," said Ralls, "do I look like a fool?"

Before an answer could be put into words, the wireless operator was before Sidneye with a message. "Shall I wait for a reply? The hammer is hot today."

"*Neen*. You may go. Hekkin! Where the devil are you? Bring ice." He peered at the message with rising interest, then gave Cordtlaant a steady glance of quick appraisal. His eyes then jerked to Ralls; he laughed and said: —

"*Neen*, Mijnheer Ralls, you do not look the part of a fool. I take it you're willing to sail a Batjak ship? I thought so. Well, before any man can do that he must show his mettle." He grinned, his fat cheeks folding the flesh to his jowls.

"Cordtlaant — proceed at once to the Fijis under full sail. There's trouble in Suva. Younguer is charged with smuggling; he resisted arrest."

2

"No! I do not desert my captains, Mijnheer Ralls!" thundered Mayrant.

The *Golden Hind* stood in the harbor of Suva alongside the gaunt black timbers and aged sails of the *Van Arken;* beside her sister ship the yellow gleamed, her bulwarks glossy and blinding in the morning sun, her top hamper as neat as a bridegroom's tie. The deck of the black ship bore the marks of winches, derricks, of tracking stevedores, of bulky shapes denting her planks, of wood and metal sawed by dragging chain and rope; the acrid odors of mixed cargoes, and the frayed ropes, lusterless spars, and rusty sides, attested to her long run without fumigation and repair. But for a prize of Batjak's offering, any skipper would drive her to the full limit. Younguer worked for that top bonus: the *Van Arken* showed as much.

"I do not accuse, Mr. Sidneye, for it's none of my business," said Ralls. "You say that Noord is to sail out with the tub, and we are to take the *Hind* — without Captain Younguer. So, that being the case, I'll stick around this God-forsaken hole and see what turns up for me. Perhaps —"

"Younguer is unable to leave, Ralls. When he's out of the hospital, I'll have a dozen lawyers here to clear him of the charges."

"Just the same I'll stick around," returned Ralls. "There's only one thing that could change my mind."

"And that?"

"The *Golden Hind*." He arose from his chair, surveyed the ornate cabin: maple panels met mahogany and teakwood. He stretched his arms and yawned. "Well, sir, I'm obliged for the pick-up in the Gilberts. So long."

Mayrant eyed the ceiling. "Sit down, you fool, and pour drinks." Ralls dropped lazily into a chair.

"Very well, sir, but — shove the bottle here."

"Just what makes you think you are a better man than Cordtlaant?"

"If you want qualifications that a man is fool enough to declare, Mister, then you'd better stick to Cort. But between you and me, I'm the better man. Yes, sir, I'm the better man. Here's your drink, sir." He leaned against the table, face in hand, his sleeveless elbow against the layered veneer of the wood. "At your suggestion I'd dive overboard with him, both of us naked and with short knives. And I'll wager my Honolulu pawn ticket against the captaincy of the *Hind* that I'd come up without a scratch — alone." In the silence that followed, Mayrant's eyes slowly left the close ceiling and came to rest on the face across the table. "What's more, Cordtlaant is a great skipper — who knows only a ship, who is servile to you and her. Me, I know where there's treasure and I've got the guts to ride to it, whether you're along or not."

"And after that?" said Batjak's king.

"The seas are wide and deep, Mister."

"Yes, the seas are wide and deep," mused Mayrant. "But how do I know you can do what you say?"

"I've told you that I'm open for suggestions."

"So you did."

Ralls laughed. "I'll tell you what, sir. Suppose we lay our cards down flat, face up. We'll sail to the pearls. If I find them and get them aboard ship I get the captaincy of the *Hind* — you get a quarter share. How does that sound?"

238

"A half share, Mijnheer Ralls," corrected Mayrant.

"That amount would buy this ship, so why should I trade a ship for a mere captaincy?"

"Indeed, Mijnheer Ralls, and why should you offer a quarter share? I'm wondering just that."

"Because I'm broke," returned Ralls with lively challenge.

"That being the case we'll sign up papers to the trade — one half."

"And after that?"

Mayrant grinned, made a gesture with his hands, and replied: "The seas are wide and deep."

"Yeah, I said that, didn't I? But of your firm, what may I expect?"

"We route our ships according to cargo and demand. You're as permanent a fixture as you make of yourself. Our bonuses inspire initiative and on-the-side business, but Batjak takes the extra earnings of her ships — not her skippers. And unless a man respects Batjak laws and the name itself, he's out. If you, Mijnheer Ralls, brought in all the pearls of the seas and disobeyed the laws of the firm, we'd kick you out.

"There's Younguer. A rakehell if I ever saw one. He respects no man, or law, or convention in the gathering of his cargoes, but one law stands with him — the law of Batjak. Is he afraid of it? *Neen*. I do not court the fear of any man but my competitor, and I'll never tolerate fear from any skipper. A sense of loyalty and pride in the name 'Batjak' is the first step to our bonuses. Younguer's a rich man, Mijnheer.

"Why is he rich? I'll give you an example. In 'sixteen I sent his ship to the Sundras for copra our agents had booked at a price. He scanned the warehouses and sneered at the piles of first-grade meat, refused to haul it at the stipulated sum, and after a day of haggling took it on at a saving of several thousand guilders. The money was credited to the earnings of his ship, thereby giving him the most-coveted thing in a captain's life — time. Time for another profitable run, which means extra earnings. But another firm there ran up the price while he haggled, thereby creating personal strife. Ever full of ideas, Younguer caused the competitor's men to be jailed for certain reasons."

"Any law against murder, or staging a nice little tribal war at times?"

"Only — and remember this — only if you're so indiscreet as to involve the firm name. Then, after we claim full innocence of your crimes, we get the minimum punishment for you, if we can't free you. But Batjak can never use you again."

"Batjak's short on rules — and they're made to suit the occasion. Is that correct, sir?"

239

"The captain is law aboard his ship, if that's what you mean," returned Mayrant. "He's the soul of Batjak's cunning."

"Then I think I'll sign under her banner," said Ralls. "I plan to get rich and this seems the quickest route. So draw up the necessary papers, Mr. Sidneye, and then tell Noord to trail the *Golden Hind* with the *Van Arken*. We'll weigh anchor at sunrise tomorrow — out of Levu Passage and around Suva Point for the Koro Sea, and from there to fifteen degrees and due east."

The emperor of Batjak grinned. Here was his life, his passion, his joy; he forgot to mourn von Streicher's death; he gave no thought to the utter emptiness of a life without the comforting hand of a woman; men were his passion, their bearing upon his ego for discovery and development. He dedicated them to Batjak, which was nothing more than the intricate network of his soul.

3

The *Golden Hind* stood a furlong out from the bleached north shore of the atoll while the *Van Arken* lay a quarter mile to the south. Like vultures of the deep, the ships lay rocking in their shadows. Ominously quiet, strangely minus wind sail, too close together for any good, and too widely separated for freedom from suspicion, the pervading monotony was conducive to surface nerves even among the men on decks.

The water separating the ships from the steppingstone island was a searing sheet of blue-green that rose to a blinding emerald. The long fringe of the thin coast was one sight, one color, a shimmery dance of reflected heat against the anonymity of tufted palms. A lazy sail atop a moored outrigger clung like a fat leech to the serpentine shore that seemed to coil for miles about its treasure of pearls. Beyond lay a maze of small sails; beyond these, sad rugged peaks some three or four thousand feet into the sky.

Two pennants were run up on the *Van Arken;* the *Hind* ran up an answer. Teer Noord cursed and leaned against the rail. A motor launch was heard in the distance, and soon he saw a French craft point toward the *Hind*, her bow splitting the sea, her stern sending a long trailer of foamy white as she gave a display of her ready knots. Then the lookout said: "*Golden Hind* signals to move up"; and Noord, glaring at the sails of his ship, and then at the single pennant on the ropes of her sister ship, bellowed orders for sail: of all the foolish maneuvers of merchant ships, he was witnessing the prize show; who the hell did Ralls think he was playing for saps? Noord cursed passionately and then laughed: at least Cordtlaant's ego was taking a tumble before the intruder.

Aboard the *Golden Hind* Mayrant eyed his two captains, asking of himself which cut the neater figure. Both were lean, wiry, calm, and handsome. Stanch men, and dependable. Equals? He'd soon learn. Cordtlaant now had opportunity for uncovering his wares. He stood with glass in hand, lazily indifferent to the approach of the island launch. Ralls, on the other hand, kept his eyes glued to the craft.

At a motion from Ralls, a *zeeman* threw the ladder over. The white sides of the French craft drew close, and in due time her motors died alongside the *Hind's* starboard beam. Ralls grinned. The thin, heavy-nosed Frenchman, pale of eye, and laxly mustached, came aboard and eyed the trio. There was sharp, quick appraisal of the sails, the tidy deck, and then the stripes of Mayrant's awning, and, at last, the obese man sitting under it. The Frenchman had no apology for his stained clothing, brief shorts, and open shirt, white as a sheet against the black hair covering his deep bronze chest. Only his cap reminded one of elegance.

"Welcome to our island," he said in fluid Dutch, smiling broadly at Mayrant.

"Thank you," returned Mayrant. "Join us in drink, Mijnheer —"

"Jacques Desaix," said the man, bowing. "And I accept your hospitality." He added, laughing, "Our provisions are overdue from the island of Tahiti, and the absence of liquors is most annoying. Yes!" Hekkin placed a cold, sweating glass in his hand, and all the latent emotion of a true Frenchman rose in gesture and murmur as his lips touched gin. He turned the glass up and drained it of liquid and ice and stood smiling while he chewed the brittle lumps. Hekkin, ever attentive, walked forward and asked with his eyes if the guest cared for another.

"*S'il vous plaît!* Yes!" he answered. The second was as greedily consumed, and the downward curves of his smile, strikingly individual, like his mustache, held while he offered apology in word and shrug. Over the rim of the third glass he studied the men before him.

"Captain Cordtlaant, Mijnheer Desaix," spoke Mayrant, "and Captain Ralls. I am Mayrant Sidneye."

"An oddity, no doubt, having two captains aboard a ship," laughed Desaix. "But not for so worthy a beauty as the *Golden Hind*. I am pleased indeed to know you, Captain Cordtlaant." He stepped forward and shook the proffered hand vigorously.

"But as for Captain Ralls," he said, turning a flashing eye not quite covered by his smile, "we have met before. I dare say, Captain Ralls will remember me. No?"

Ralls seemed lost in a fog of perplexity. Stroking his chin and darting glances from the mizzen yards to Desaix and back again, he said, "You must have me confused with another, Mr. Desaix."

"Of course," came the facetious answer. "You were not aboard a craft called the — the *Yucatán* about eight months ago?" Then he turned suddenly to eye Mayrant, who cackled and spluttered over his drink.

"*Neen!*" laughed Mayrant. "Look closely, Mijnheer. The likeness almost fooled me. You're thinking of his twin, whose ship *Yucatán* ran afoul of the Gilbert reefs. Mijnheer Ralls put his rascally brother aboard a tramp for Frisco in Suva, not more than a week ago."

Ralls added with admirable sincerity, "That is correct, Mr. Desaix." Pausing, he said, "So my brother has visited this island. Did he cause trouble?"

"A thousand times yes, as you Yankees say! He plied me with so many drinks I was unable to chase after him. He was after the pearls of the monolith and —"

"Pearls!" Mayrant leaned forward.

"Yes, Monsieur. Around the monolith once a month a native ritual takes place. It is timed to the hump of the moon, between the half and full moon. Ralls remained here for a fortnight. Then — after the orgy of the pearls he overpowered the guards and, with a machine gun, wounded a dozen natives. I presume his plan would have succeeded but for the age of his weapon."

"I am sorry to hear that, Desaix," said Ralls with feigned regret. "I suppose he'll be picked up when he docks in San Francisco."

"No," said the Frenchman, smiling ironically, "I could hardly bring myself to file a report on the case — since I was abed and snoring off a drunk at the time. You can well understand my position." They could, and their laughter joined his to cement the cozy bond evoked by gin.

"But you spoke of pearls," said Cordtlaant casually. "Are they for sale or trade?"

"No, Captain. They are essentials of worship. Once every month, in the great feast I spoke of, one giant pearl is baked; its ashes are sprinkled into the waters on all sides of the island and into the lagoon. Then, after the ceremony, the pearls of the monolith are sent to the lagoon cavern of the pink octopus."

"Hekkin," said Mayrant, "the glass of our guest!"

"Thanks, Monsieur. The monster, I can see by your eyes, interests you. Well, it should. My niece, Angélique, a daughter of my brother in Martinique, went with me last week to view the monster. She fainted, but of course!

"See the bold run of emerald down the lagoon center, running into the west atoll?" He pointed and all eyes followed. "The depth there is not four fathoms. Southward, and down the center, is a deep trough. It is like a man-made excavation for a coral garden.

"As the flooring rises so does it recede; the most beautiful cavern God ever put before man's eye is almost on the north rocks. It is just this side of the row of leaning palms. I doubt if you can see it from here. No, Favu-Momo hides it. In the flat amphitheater, forty feet in diameter, are pearl oysters that no man can ever touch, except by ceremonious order."

"Why?" asked Mayrant.

"The religion of the tribes here makes them sacred. Whosoever brings up a pearl from the cavern shall die a leper's death. Then, too, few infidels would dare reach for them. Why? Inside the lowest cavern shelf there is a giant pink octopus."

Ralls leaned against the rail a few steps behind the Frenchman, and at Mayrant's glance he slowly nodded his head.

"And the pearls of the monolith," said Mayrant, "come from this cavern?"

"No, Monsieur. Only the one that is burned every month. A diver ventures below — a hero if he returns, an offering to the gods if he fails — to bring back the pearl. But since the visit of Monsieur Ralls's brother the pearls of the monolith are kept in a small iron chest — in the door of the monster's cavern."

Mayrant's grin was a challenge. He eyed Ralls.

"But, of course, you will put into port as my guests," said Desaix. "The day of the festival of the humpback moon is three days hence. We have fish aplenty, native fowl, coconuts, bananas, melons, mangoes, and other native delicacies. At Villa Desaix, Mademoiselle will treat your ears with excellent piano music."

Hekkin refilled all glasses. Mayrant smiled, caught Ralls's frown at a hurried acceptance, and said, "I'm afraid two merchant ships, with crews to feed and pay running like the clock, can't afford a vacation. Thanks for your invitation, Mijnheer, but —"

"Incidentally, Monsieur, I forgot to ask why your ship is anchored here. My report must be made, of course."

Mayrant was about to invent a fresh-water shortage when Ralls answered, "We're in need of repairs, Mr. Desaix. However, I'm afraid your tale is an invitation for us to look for anchorage elsewhere."

"But Monsieur! Help yourself to the cove. You'd perhaps enjoy a bit of idle pearling." He raised his eyes to the pennant atop the mainmast

243

and said, "Any and all ships under the quatrefoils are welcome to my domain."

Ralls, eyeing Sidneye covertly, raised his brows in acceptance, lazily, astutely. He was the head of the comet; mere men and the elements made up the nebulous train.

CHAPTER XXII

1

MADEMOISELLE DESAIX preferred the simple address of "Angélique," and the coterie from the two ships — Mayrant, Cordtlaant, Noord, Rostaars, chief mate of the *Van Arken*, and Ralls — eyed her in one accord, drawing complimentary comparisons of the person to the word. Said Mayrant, "A soothsayer must have named her"; he said as much to her. Her beauty could not be gainsaid, nor could her radiating charm. Supple and firm, and of medium height, she graced her share of curves, though another ten pounds, thought Ralls, would have given her rippling exquisiteness. She was a brunette with long undulant hair and deep, heavy-lashed eyes; while her skin seemed cream-white by the acute suddenness of contrast to the sheen of her coal-black hair. A narrow, delicate nose drew the eye to thin lips of hibiscus red as they parted in flashing smile.

A hothouse orchid, thought Mayrant, who, for all his fifty years, still dreamed of a rare flower, the living image of which stood before him. The raw tropics would claim her in a scalding blast before a baking wind; but for her a few years of vigorous and passionate blossom remained, and then like all orchids her season would end in the ghostliness of shriveled, colorless petals. But the future of her, of Mayrant Sidneye, was now. Thus he contemplated, laughing at his whimsical mind when her beauty and charm seemed a balm for his loneliness; he laughed less when the balm seemed more like a drug.

That she was deeper than her pretended shallowness was manifested by her dreamy eyes: they stared across the lagoon in pensive manner before again meeting the present with a serene challenge. All the while Mayrant grinned above his inward frown and eyed her physically and soulfully, stamping approval on her provocative lines while searching beyond them for the core of her — that reason in her own mind for her existence.

The men had accompanied Jacques from the cove, and soon they skimmed over the broad lagoon to the north, where the flat beach ran a few yards before being gobbled by advancing jungles that seemed to walk down the mountainside. Up a rocky path they trod, made easier by the bamboo rail running the full length of the trail; on each side ferns, palms, and creepers sought to cover the path with a growth so dense that only Tahitian machetes in constant use could hold it in check. A large hairy spider crossed the narrow clearing, pausing to eye them with poisonous disdain before moving slowly on; in contrast a giant orchid lifted its fierce beauty to their eyes. They crossed a bamboo bridge over a small valley and looked down some forty feet into a long clearing in which the fruit of the lemon and orange trees ripened on the same limbs with blossoms.

To the natives below them, Jacques cried, "*Kaoha*." The spontaneous charm of the Polynesian seemed to echo the full magic of the South Seas in answer. All but the aged responded, and they, ripe in wisdom, contented themselves with their memories.

Around a curve that skirted the valley, and up a winding path, they suddenly came upon a flower garden and a low stone wall; there, standing before them, was the Frenchman's residence. It was Parisian luxury in native basalt. Low columns of stone supported the thatched roof of the veranda overlooking the scene below. Mayrant saw the masts of his ships; tiny toys they seemed from the mountainside.

Desaix proved more than an equal to his promise of an excellent host: his house abounded with warm welcome — *à bras ouverts!* Trays of delicacies were set before them on the cool veranda; tall glasses of gin, and trays of orange rind, toasted pandanus kernels, tiny rolls of pickled octopus, and crisp fresh-water shrimp invited them to a gorging and lazy minutes of sleep. With the sunset they were greeted with the magic of evening, and the sincere words of Desaix and Angélique, "*Bon soir!* Come. The tropic night is made for living."

The evening meal had ended when a servant escorted into their midst a native guard and the wireless operator from the *Golden Hind*. Mayrant read the message and dismissed it with a laugh. Then, under a sudden frown, he gave orders to flood the markets with various products — to teach the natives of an area not to haggle too long with Batjak; to the Hong Kong office, a demand for more goods and less friction; to Sydney, orders to buy, buy; to Soerabaja's questions, no, no, and no. He felt the easy smile of dark-eyed Angélique; he caught and held her eye as she

245

said, "You are a man of big business, are you not, Monsieur?" Here was the strongest magic he had encountered in the vast Pacific since Lonyta.

His fierce eyes locked with her gaze of mild surprise. For a second they battled, but in the end her eyes fell before the onslaught, and she reddened perceptibly. Said the eyes of the emperor of commerce: Ever lonely is the throne, where jeweled pauper sits — alone!

She arose and walked slowly into the long drawing room, all eyes following her in silent tribute. For a moment she gazed out into the pearl-blue heavens, and then turned about and walked to a piano. There, out of sight, she seemed to stand before all eyes as the strains of a slow waltz broke the silence.

Mayrant Sidneye cursed the spell, fought the mood her fingers conjured up from the ivory keys, and sat back to enrich his coffers with French pearls — he found himself instead draping her with the silken quatrefoils of Batjak and placing a necklace of pearls about her neck.

Ralls was the only man in the smiling group who read in the layered streamers of cigar smoke the true passion of Mayrant Sidneye. His surface smile, thin as the final note from a gypsy guitar, was outwardly in tune with the evening's conviviality. He was first among them to applaud her offering. And quite easily he said: —

"What is your favorite, Mr. Sidneye; I'm sure Angélique would be pleased to do it."

"I have no favorites," returned Mayrant crisply.

Smiling, Ralls said in carrying voice, "*Ma chère Angélique*, Mr. Sidneye requests a stirring song of love and beauty. It is to be dedicated to you — from him."

Teer Noord cursed him silently, envying as he did so the granite polish of his bearing; Cordtlaant did not voice the thought of "Impudent dog"; Mayrant smiled beneath a flashing frown and hid the respect he was forced to extend.

And Desaix, aware of the tension of the moment, smiled and pretended mental numbness under a curtain of scrutiny.

2

There were pearls enough in the lagoon, and the natives did not need the sanction of Jacques to follow the bidding of Ralls, the son of the supreme god Taaro Tiki. For had he not, when Virgo first moved into the western heavens, called forth to his immortal father for rain to quench the fire blazing around him? Aye! But the revered one was interested only in pearls.

He sat on a crosspiece of the outrigger near the tiller, cyeing the shells that filled the dugout canoe. He watched the chief's son, Uti Mopo, as he knifed them and felt for pearls. Without show of interest he fingered the only fruit of the pearlers, peeling off the film and rubbing the warmth of his palms into the living gem — the color would forever glow without dimming. Since sunrise he had scarcely moved, had given no word to any ear except that one terse utterance as he stepped aboard the craft: —

"Pearls."

The sun was now cutting the blazing arc of heavens into a quarter slice, and the kin of Uti Mopo eyed the dugout for some sign of recess. None came, for Ralls intended to accept Jacques's offer — idle pearling — for its full worth; to be found lacking in white man's greed might cast suspicion on the lot of them who ran up no small expense with two idle ships. It was not strange that two pairs of binoculars up in the jungle hills watched his every move, counting every shell he touched: forewarned is forearmed; and he turned his eyes cynically toward the villa while the bronze men moved into deeper water.

A grinning youth with rippling muscles of back, arm, and chest stood poised for one fleeting second on the outrigger with a lead weight in each hand; amid a babble of words and laughter he leaned forward, cut the water like a tapered blade and, with quick stabs of his muscular legs, made his way to the coral floor. The handsome son of the chieftain leaned over the side, lifted a hand to his brow, and gazed after the diver. Ralls eyed Uti Mopo and observed his change of expression before taking a peep himself. Every native was on his belly, peering in silence. Then Uti Mopo uttered an exclamation—"*Haie!*"—and raised his face to Ralls. He beseeched the intrepid one, the son of Taaro Tiki, to save his worthy cousin — not even the chieftain's son dared break the tapu declared by the high priest: no mortal should draw blood in the sacred lagoon. Lazily Ralls studied his companions without seeing them; his thoughts were swift and calculating and without pangs of compassion for diver or crew — schemes ruled. Thus the diver must be saved.

Removing his shoes and cap, he grasped the largest leads. He placed the long knife used by Uti Mopo between his teeth and stepped into the lagoon. Once his head was under he seemed to somersault, to acquire unnatural diving speed from the swift maneuver; not once did his trailing legs fold under him and jackknife for propulsion — instead they were as one, rudder and tail fin of an underwater animal. Down into the sunlit green he sped, watching the youth below who fell back frantically from two huge heavy-barreled tiger sharks.

The tigers worked in deadly fashion, one moving nearer the victim while the other lashed out with a furious burst of speed; then back again, the other would whip the water to within an arm's length of the youth. Ralls knew these beasts, knew they must both move off for doubling — a long twenty-yard circle that would give the boy a break for the surface. Thus he rose toward the nearest shark with flying arms in an effort to frighten it: the beast, instead of racing away, drove toward him with a sudden upward lunge.

Ralls's knife ripped the gleaming belly for six feet, emptying entrails and blood. The youth seized his opportunity and rose to the surface, his lungs almost bursting, while Ralls moved toward the coral wall. The water was stained in red and pink layers: the blood spoor called for the pack of omnivorous creatures to rush in and slash their feast from the now berserk tiger. And out of nowhere they came.

The safety of the dugout above beckoned the sane man; the charging tribe held the demented Ralls, whose hatred, and thirst for further bloodshed, armed him with a hellish fearlessness — almost the synonym of invulnerability. The natives, flat of belly, had witnessed the timed slash, had rejoiced at the saving of their brother; and now, expecting the immortal's return, they saw his stance, the horrible mistake he purposely executed; their eyes grew wide as he leisurely swam through the stained water and back to the coral wall.

Cordtlaant and Noord had joined Angélique at the launch, and spying the sudden commotion of the natives a furlong away gave the launch petrol and steered straight for the outrigger. Noord sat at the wheel while Cordtlaant took a seat beside the girl under the trim red and white canopy.

"No, Monsieur," she said, laughing, "I have no ideas on the subject. You see I have been here only a short time. But," she allowed her smile a quick death, "something has them excited." Her thoughts turned to the sight her uncle pointed out days back: could one of the natives be battling the pink octopus? Shuddering, she turned her eyes away, just as the *Hind's* skipper lowered his glasses and said: —

"Mijnheer Ralls just went overboard."

Noord grinned and shouted back to his superior: "May his stay be a long one!"

"Why did he say that?" she asked.

"Oh!" Cordtlaant winced. "We jest heavily at sea, Mademoiselle."

She eyed him for some length. "I'm afraid I'm not so gullible, Monsieur." Then she smiled. There was no answer as Cordtlaant again hid his thoughts behind binoculars. "The undercurrent of feeling between you men and M'sieu Ralls finds the surface at times. Even Jacques remarked upon the fact — and to the man you serve."

So! Cordtlaant felt himself in for a reprimand. He frowned and made a grimace. There was many a slip between thought and tongue.

"I regret that you and Mijnheer Jacques have misunderstood. Ralls and I are the closest of friends." Her reply was a steady, accusing smile.

They were almost alongside the canoe when she said, "About Monsieur Sidneye — is he really the great man of the Dutch firm? I can't remember the name."

"Batjak," said Cordtlaant crisply. "Pardon, Mademoiselle, while we look into the trouble here." Without waiting for a word from her he stepped aboard the canoe and sprawled flat to peer beneath the surface. When at long last he raised his head, Angélique lay between him and Noord.

Ralls, spinning with knife in hand, broke the surface for a long breath before diving again in his peculiar fashion. As he reached a depth of two fathoms the shark flashed upward, belly and mouth rushing the surface at terrific speed, meeting the knife just below the serrated jaws. The sudden lurch of the shark caused Ralls a quick backward move that somehow dislodged the knife from the bleeding monster, and from his hand. It plummeted downward, heavy hilt first and blade trailing in its wobbly descent, and Ralls found himself face to face with not one but a half dozen of the blood-enraged killers. His quick mind was to be admired as he braved the sextet in a quick squirming dive for the priceless weapon.

Angélique murmured a terrified "Oh!"

There he stood, feet planted wide apart, in a maze of color, a field of madrepore rising about him in white, pink, and purple bushes from the gorgeous floor. He peered up at the sharks. The knife was again in his hand, and he leaned backward as a flashing shape hurled itself at him; the blade was driven home and again the emerald was stained with crimson. The slice was not nearly so long as the opportunity afforded — the wounded shark raced away in an effort to outdistance the pursuing pack.

Slowly, almost casually, Ralls rose to the surface. Uti Mopo and his consort rushed to his side and babbled long and loud; and then, with the trio from the launch looking on, the chieftain's son got to his knees and murmured eternal devotion before accepting the knife Ralls handed him. With it he severed the flesh of his wrist. Ralls did likewise; the fusing of crimson drops made them blood brothers.

Angélique did not know that her eyes ran him from tip to toe in slow appraisal, as fierce and primitive as the blood union she had witnessed. Her eyes had watched his drawing of shark's blood and his own, and each act seemed a wild call never before heard. It went, like a dagger's thrust, to the quick of her.

She whispered softly, "Monsieur Ralls, you are wonderful."

His eyes searched out the blend of that moment's emotions and, as ever, the mystery of woman rose up to baffle him: out of chastity is born a wanton moment, and a thin line must separate the two — so he reasoned — and never could a man be sure of a pair of eyes that were not augmented by embracing arms. Bluntly he flashed his questions. She was woman, if fact could give answer. Her eyes slowly fell before his stare.

Inwardly Ralls laughed at her. She sought the bridges of romance, the slow pathways of the moon for reserved acquaintance. His plans did not allow her to enter into his passions of body. She was more of a cog in reserve, a tool to be used at the right moment, if he expected to serve his one lord and master, Ralls. Thus he allowed his eyes a slow smile of friendliness, nothing more.

"Thank you, Angélique," he said. "What I did was nothing." The lie seemed to suffice; she stepped out of her trance.

Outwardly Ralls seemed pleased with the morning's catch of pearls. In his pouch were three pale blue-pinks, their collective value a matter of conjecture and therefore not likely to launch an experienced pearler into joyous outburst. Compared to what was at stake they constituted not a drop in the ocean. But for all concerned the catch was enough to match the blueprint of their visit. Mayrant would marvel at their shape and size. Jacques would take notice of the greed of his visitors. And greed had both men — a strongbox of selected pearls ready for market dwarfed the whole realm of mysterious riches awaiting them on the lagoon floor.

Two days remained until the feast of the humped moon.

3

Lowering his hand and placing the powerful lens on the table, Mayrant eyed Desaix thoughtfully before saying, "Captain Ralls has always intrigued me."

Desaix brought down his telescope without giving answer. Having witnessed the flurry of excitement among his charges, the blood bond of Ralls and Uti Mopo, the long moment of frozen stillness when Angélique and Ralls faced one another, he gave mental play to the hero's invulnerability.

"You are most fortunate in your selection of captains, Monsieur. Such versatility — adventurer, seaman, and businessman — is no doubt hard to find."

"Indeed. But a good captain is worth a dozen ships. In fact, every good skipper has bought me several of the best."

"Has Monsieur Ralls?" The ease of the Frenchman's address seemed to add to his bluntness.

Mayrant laughed. "I can see you still regard him with fingers crossed. You think he's the one who visited here, don't you?"

"Frankly, yes, Monsieur," he said, turning his level gaze upon Mayrant. "I do not intend a breach of etiquette, and I apologize as host to guest, but such a swashbuckling figure could hardly be a twin; and even if he were he's not the type to be carted back to America by a mere order, as you said. And too, I scarcely think the pervading atmosphere of law and order from Frisco east could contain such a man.

"Isn't it rather hard to imagine a one-man invasion of this island? True, it is a peaceful spot, friendly to all comers. It might seem easy to take single-handed, but no sane man in these times would challenge the flag of France. Yet Ralls did just that."

"There is little cause for alarm, my dear Jacques," laughed Mayrant. "No Batjak man is bigger than the quatrefoils."

"Just the same, I must say that I, begging your pardon, would recognize his greed as that of a lone wolf. He is, to my mind, loyal only to himself."

"Thanks for the warning," voiced Mayrant.

"You're welcome. I compare him to — Lucifer."

Mayrant grinned and said, "He would have made an excellent captain of a Batjak ship. I shall name a ship Lucifer."

A bit ruffled, the Frenchman poured a long drink and turned to Mayrant.

"Monsieur Sidneye, now that I think of it, you seem to be off your beaten paths; and with two very large ships." With the words out he raised his brow in eloquent fashion and eyed his guest.

Long moments of silence were broken by Sidneye's terse assertion, "Your statement has direction, of course."

"Yes. As your host I could never bend to such — er — boldness. You are, M'sieu, a legend in yourself, and a man whom all men must respect for many reasons. But on the other hand I am more than a mere host — I am the arm of the French Republic as well. I refer, of course, to the unannounced visit of your ships, one of which is captained by a man I suspect."

251

"Which, I presume," said Mayrant pleasantly, "points all too clearly to a second attempt at stealing the sacred pearls?"

"Precisely! That is, with your pardon, the gist of my thoughts. You, of course, can understand my position."

"Naturally. We shall sail with the tide."

"No! No! Nothing of the sort. I was merely leading up to a point. Perhaps I am the victim of fancies, but all I ask is your word that this dual personality, Ralls, will make no attempt to take the pearls."

Mayrant eyed him at length before opening slowly, fatherly, with, "Young man, I am not only older than you, I am far wiser. I am also richer, which fact can serve to atone for my blunt manner. If I say my opinions are infallible, it is because I have yet to meet a man who can turn a higher card. Call it luck or genius, or insanity, or whatever you will, but remember this — accomplishment drowns the voice of doubt.

"I have a half-brother who holds the highest office of Batjak. His name is Harmenszoon van Schreeven. He, as a lad, came to Java to conquer paganism; a knight who wanted to wear the robes of the Church. At that time, as now, I needed men I could trust, and I went to great lengths to get them. He was, as you'd expect, an obdurate creature. I paid a pretty price for the parade of temptations I set before his eyes. He lasted less than six months.

"I tell you this that you may view the rough avenues to the Batjak of today. I could tell you how I secured the services of the fiercest of my captains, a fellow named Younguer, or I could talk all day about my past; but the flavor, like baked clams, is ever the same. I was greedy, I am greedy, I shall be greedy."

Desaix seemed the essence of rapt attention. His mind labored to digest every word as it was spoken. That he filled the glasses absently only proved him an excellent host or a man whose nerves demanded a stroking of loose ends.

"But the men who serve me find me quite generous. My captains must become rich or I cannot use them. One might think their riches would make them lazy, but that is not so. My method is an injection of the drug of greed.

"But enough about facts. Let us pay call to the French *commissaire*, one Jacques Desaix. I shall introduce you to the man and let you form your opinion of him.

"To my mind he is a reserved fellow whose loneliness prompts him to invite into his domain those whom he actually distrusts. But he is calm, patient, and an excellent host; he's also glib and learned.

"At heart he is a sybarite who appeals to his guest for certain promises in order to bask as usual in the tropic clime."

Desaix grinned over his glass. "Monsieur, how accurately you build an effigy. I can only agree with your every word."

"Then it is a good beginning," said Mayrant forcefully. "Papeete, my dear Desaix, is the crossroads of Sydney-to-Panama commerce, the beeline route to Valparaiso, and as vital a link in the Batjak chain of suboffices as Suva or Auckland. I predict a vanilla boom when the great war of the Pacific strikes. But for the present enough traffic and produce flow through the Society Isles to warrant a Batjak office. I intend to move in for copra, and I must find a Frenchman who is utterly self-reliant, as well as wise, cautious, cunning, and captious — and trust-worthy. The man I select must be respected by the French and Polynesians alike; he must be willing to spend six months on a Bat-jak ship, another six months in her outposts. He begins at a good salary with a two-thousand-guilder bonus the moment he signs the papers —

"And three thousand on top of that if he is related to me — even by marriage."

Jacques started, sat up in his chair and choked on his drink. His apology was perfunctory and weak; he only stared at his guest through narrowed eyes before turning slowly toward the sweeping emerald of the lagoon. After long minutes he arose and paced the rock floor monotonously, ever pivoting at the same points. He paused, gave Mayrant a semblance of a smile, and said: —

"I shall be pleased to carry your message to Jacques Desaix. The double honor you extend should please him, Monsieur, and you may be sure I'll coax an answer from him by this hour tomorrow."

Again he paced like a lazy Malay tiger in a steel cage. "And in the meantime the French deputy is chained by a bribe — enabling Monsieur Ralls to mulct the natives of the sacred pearls."

Mayrant's eyes danced with enjoyment. "*Neen*, Mijnheer Jacques! Let us say that the deputy takes a well-earned vacation while the man, Desaix, matches his wits against his enemy, Ralls."

"So he is the same one who was here?"

"He is indeed," laughed Mayrant. "And he's after the pearls."

4

The sun was less than one hour above the horizon the following morning when Cordtlaant asked to see Mayrant privately. Soon the crafty builder of intrigue eyed his captain's swollen jaw and discolored eye with a grin of satisfaction.

"I seek your permission, Mijnheer Sidneye, to kill him."

"*Neen!*" said Mayrant. "I shall permit no murder."

"Then, begging your pardon, you'd better start telling the Lord and devil that — he almost killed Hekkin aboard ship last night. You see when I heard the danger gong I got up and went out to the *Hind*, and —

"Ralls was drinking heavily. After two bottles he came on deck; he slapped a *zeeman* hard for not moving out of his path, and then climbed atop the rail. He paced it until young Hekkin could stand it no longer. At his outburst, Ralls sprang to the deck and beat him severely. The crew surrounded him but he was too much for them; he seized a belaying pin and felled two of them and then tore into the remaining group with his bare hands.

"I found the ship in an uproar. When I faced Ralls with an order to leave the ship, he advanced belligerently. I must admit, Mijnheer, I was no match for him."

Mayrant pursed his lips, ran a hand over his bald skull, and said, "I shall talk to him, Cordtlaant. Does he show the marks of battle?"

The other grinned. "He does."

Mayrant grinned in response, then laughed lightly; and with the suddenness of a hurricane he threw back his head and laughed loud and long at the antics of his puppets.

CHAPTER XXIII

1

EVERY native knew the pose of the moon as the day dawned. A holiday spirit pervaded, and from the flat reaches of the pincer island to the highest slopes of the jungle mountain, joy and laughter met "*Kaoha*," and a thousand *Kaohas*, as the pilgrimage to the lagoon for the great feast began.

The slow trek down the hillsides continued all morning. A tattooed mother with a tiny babe and toddling child trailed behind a tattooed spouse, who carried a pole over his shoulder weighted at each end with loads of mountain fruit, goats, or boars for baking. Another could be seen from the villa with only a stalk of red mountain bananas that must be roasted before eating. Clad in bark cloth, French prints, and straight-cut dresses, ornamented with fish nets, the women and girls wore flowers in celebration of the gala occasion. A tawny face was enlivened by tiaras and necklaces of nuts, peppers, phosphorescent fungus for evening, by whale's-teeth earrings and pastes for olive faces, perfumed with saffron and native flowers. They were happy, gay, and their childish spontaneity was contagious. Every face, it seemed, sent out flashes of inexpressible, innate delight, individual, and tuned to the airy magic of the South Seas.

"*Kaoha. Kaoha!*"

To the spacious clearing, where one found latticed shade under slender palms, where the hut of Chief Ua Nuka Havu met the western convergence of the clawlike promontories that guarded the lagoon, there was heavy and excited traffic. There natives paved the earth's floor with palm leaves, dug pits for the baking of the flesh of land and sea, and met the hillfolk, the men in boats. A babble of voices at the water's edge drew a sizable crowd, and soon four grinning youths appeared carrying a long pole on which hung three octopuses. Soaked in lemon juice they were indeed a rare delicacy, and many mouths watered as the slimy creatures were paraded into the teeming enclosure. And while the youths launched into a jolly tale of their capture, the crowd turned to meet the steady influx of edibles: bundles of juicy sugar-cane sticks, sweet and chewy, and delicious with the juices of wild pineapple and orange; breadfruit, and coconut brandy — forbidden by French law; bushels of crabs and fresh-water shrimp, and sacks of yams and chestnuts. Ua Nuka Havu looked on, his face wreathed in one smile for his land and his people.

An old man of the village, wise of word and eye, looking for all like the bronzed and mustached English or French except for his tattooing, listened to the words of his brothers, said nothing, and then hoisted a bamboo flute to his nose and blew out a strange melody. He continued until the stalwart Uti Mopo, dripping from the lagoon, approached the group with a joyous "*Kaoha.*"

He sat among them, panting lightly. "The gods are good to us," he said. "There shall be a great feast with so much of everything for all."

Said the old man with the flute: "I remember when we had *puaa oa* at these feasts."

"Long pig! How tasted the flesh of a man?" asked Uti Mopo.

The old man stared into the clouds across the lagoon. "Tender like the banana, and sweet. I should enjoy another taste before I die."

A wrinkled man, equally old, piped, " 'Tis so. I remember how we

255

roasted the flesh on the sacred fire there in the center — only in those days, when your father's father was chief, the sacrificial fire was in the path of the sinking sun. Ah! After the sexual dance, we would eat the long pig! But the choice flesh was of the buttocks and the back, and all were allowed a morsel of the cheeks where the sacred pearl was roasted. Indeed," he sighed, "a long pig is like the meat of young pig boiled in the juice of cane. I, too, would welcome another taste."

"But," laughed Uti Mopo, "we are no longer savages. It is well that we refrain from the taste of our brother."

The old man said, before placing the flute to his nose, "I am not so sure."

A younger man said to the son of Ua Nuka Havu, "Who are the chosen ones for today?"

"I have not learned," answered the youth.

"There is some change due in the honor," returned the other. "For all mouths speak less of the dive for the virgin pearl. It seems that everyone speaks of the iron chest. It is true that the choice pearl must be torn from the cavern's floor, but the pink-monster guardian of the depths shall challenge the chest bearers. So the chest becomes the greatest honor in the eyes of our people."

"Tiki shall surely punish them for such thoughts," returned Uti Mopo. "Perhaps," he said, his face suddenly clouding, "I should speak to my father."

"Your father should summon his conjurers," piped the old man as he lowered his flute.

"'Tis true," agreed the lad. "I, too, have heard the talk. I gave it the same expression as my people — more like a sporting bout I viewed it, with all honor clinging to the sacred pearl."

"All the more reason, son of our chief, that the gods should advise us. You cannot challenge them without bringing us storm or famine. That is the wrath of Po. Go now and counsel with your father."

"Wait!" cried a little man, heretofore silent. "Is not the son of Taaro Tiki among us? Did he not run the flames into the ground by calling forth water?

"Indeed," said the small man. "How many sharks did he kill with his hands?"

"Three," said Uti Mopo. "I shall go to my father now. Perhaps he and the conjurers can talk with Taaro Tiki through his son. We shall see."

Said the small man after the departure of the youth who would someday become their chief, "He shall be a wise man when he becomes our ruler. He lends a listening ear to his people. His father's father was not so wise, and there came great winds that tore our coconut and breadfruit trees from the ground."

The old man, impervious to the silence about him, closed his right nostril with a thumb and blew into the flute. Life was a state of serenity, of beauty, of plenty; there was nothing he could wish for that was not within his reach save perhaps his youth, which was even more beautiful in echo. The young men in the group might have pitied his withered state, his time-dried fountains, but they envied his experience and sagacity.

2

Into such a world the *Golden Hind* had sailed — for captious plunder; and unlike the pirates of old who brandished a cutlass beneath the black Jolly Roger in a take-or-die journey to a speedy end, the moderns brought with them the wealth of background, the respect of a world of commerce, an unlimited supply of patience and cunning; and an arch-devil who was almost a god. Slow bribery served, even against the strong, as an agent to dull the wits toward any pressing problem; the element of time served to strengthen the props of the son of Taaro Tiki; a confusing lethargy that was too calm even for the clime claimed its moment, heaping bewilderment atop perplexity in the mind of the French host.

Jacques Desaix had often said, "Only one day of each month am I truly busy." And that day, the advent of the humpbacked moon was upon him. No set task for that day confronted him, nothing was required of him, and for all the duties well done that he could annotate for his superiors' perusal, he might as well have remained upon his perch. But on the other hand, the absence of the servant of the flag of France at the feast would be most conspicuous. Thus he was up with the sun after his second night of sleeplessness and indecision.

Three — no, four — problems ripped into shreds his state of complacency. He stalked slowly through the crowd, muttering in a perfunctory monotone, "*Kaoha.*" Each problem led directly into the other, tangled with it, moved on, and the procedure began all over again. Gritting his teeth, he said, "To the devil with it!" before realizing the devil himself was busily engaged in plying Ralls with advice. Perhaps, then, that was problem number one. No, for he must decide first upon Monsieur Sidneye's proposition, in order to determine his status as man, or *commissaire;* but before that Angélique's answer must be forthcoming — damn her reticence! — and even after that there remained his decision as to his own future; and that was ease and tropical pleasure against an almost lulled-to-death ambition. So! Should he forget the flag or rally to it when the culprit played his trump card? Should he arrest Ralls, and tell Sidneye to pull his anchors and be off, thereby throwing riches to the winds, and at the same time lose the golden opportunity of his niece? What niche was he carving in the diplomatic service? He shrugged mentally, thinking of a pin scratch on a diamond.

Before him stood a native girl with a shell of cool coconut milk. Of course he must accept and thank her. Soon a stalk of cane was in his hand. The smell of fish was heavy here and he turned to move in another direction. Directly ahead a pig squealed as if its fate were already known, and near by a small lad wallowed playfully in a basket of drying shrimp. Gas rose from the Frenchman's stomach and he asked of that organ one great favor, and that, to digest kindly the coconut milk that mixed with quantities of Dutch gin. The smell of ripened fruit saved him from nausea, and from the pile of assorted delicacies he selected a lemon and sucked its juice.

He stopped in his tracks when his gaze traveled the distance across the clearing and fell upon the chieftain's son; his eyes moved with the youth, who trotted in the direction of his father's house; he saw the rapt attention the natives gave the old hillman who fluted with unconcern. A stroll in his direction might be worth while.

"*Kaoha,*" said Jacques, "Keeper of the River and Sky. *Kaoha* to your friends."

"*Panhakanahau,* honored one," returned the fluter. "The gods are kind." He moved his arm in a wide sweep meant to include every offering to the feast. "The surf beats a song on the coral, the wise wind sings in the high branches, and there is shade for all."

"Your words are well spoken, Keeper. The cool waters flow down the mountainside because wise men counsel with Ua Nuka Havu. It has been so for many years." He squatted near the old man, and continued to suck at the shriveled lemon. The old man struck a shrill note, then laid his flute across his folded legs.

"Keeper, where does Uti Mopo go in such hurry?"

"There is need for a council. The sacred pearls of the monolith are receiving greater attention than the sacrificial pearl yet to be snatched from the sacred cavern." Jacques waited for him to continue. "Since the son of Taaro Tiki is among us, since he slew many sharks with his bare hands, since he provoked a deluge, he must say to his father, 'Oh, Taaro Tiki, father of the universe and spirit of my spirit, abide

258

with me; and send word to the sacred feast of the moon, to Chief Ua Nuka Havu, through me. Relate the importance of the pearls of the iron chest to your people.'"

Cautiously Jacques put his question. "Is this man truly the son of Taaro Tiki?"

"Have you doubt, Monsieur l'Administrateur, whose flag has long waved before our eyes?"

Evading the question, Jacques said, "Suppose there was doubt — how could he be tested?" Many long minutes of silence followed; the merest suspicion of Ralls's high role might lower his own prestige noticeably. At last the old man broke the long silence with: —

"Only one such test could clear him if doubt lingered in the mind of Ua Nuka Havu. He would then be forced to grapple with the monster."

Desaix got to his feet. A smile played about his eyes. "You are indeed wise, Keeper of the River and Sky." He turned his eyes toward the hut of the chief.

3

Indolently relaxing to the striped canvas hammock lay Mayrant Sidneye, a bare foot hanging over each side of his perch; he sipped from a frosty glass one moment, lowering it to a rattan table in the next, and placing his binoculars to his eye for a third movement. He grinned eternally. More like a Roman emperor he was, for his eyes were alive with anticipation of glorious entertainment to be furnished on this very day. His ruminating mind seemed immunized to the fatigue of weighing out his men. Just such pleasure had warmed the cockles of his heart when he drew Ralls and Cordtlaant into debate, but like a steam roller over a plant, Ralls, in one swift move, had surmounted any resistance from that quarter. Ralls, he reflected, should arrive for his reprimand at any moment now; he would see how "Mijnheer the rakehell" stood up under the fury of the Sidneye tongue.

"I wonder," he mused. "Even if he succeeds here he has yet to beat Younguer." He brought the powerful lens to his eyes and, after a sweeping search, saw Desaix moving indifferently toward the thatch of the native chief. His eye was drawn to the lagoon by the speedy white launch, and on its deck he saw the laughing beauty of Angélique. *Verdomd!*

Her eyes were not slanted toward Cordtlaant, they fell upon Ralls! So she had gone after him. His scowl gradually faded — there was no riding down his good humor of the day; it was greater fun to guess the moves of his marionettes. He laughed aloud, then downed the biting contents of his glass in a single gulp.

"Boys, it is your duel." He spoke as if Desaix and Ralls were standing near by. Desaix seemed a fool in many respects; but he knew his island, its people, and their tempo; he must surely know how to disrobe the false son of Taaro Tiki. Ah, well. He stretched his limbs lazily.

"Son of Tiki," he said, laughing. "How funny."

The sun reached into the lagoon in an effort to lift the very floor to his eye. Beyond, to the left, the vast Pacific sent its frothy breakers against the reefs where they broke into frenzied foam and joined the undertow; farther out a never-ending march of blue made avenues for relentless, endless whitecaps.

The old Sidneye retreated before the spell that descended upon him; forgotten was a ship, and a sea for its belly; drifting away was one captain after another; and before his heavy, drowsy lids closed his cradle rocked in the sweet contentment of peace, creaking ever so gently until its sounds faded away, creaking ever, "Angélique — Angélique."

The shadows moved slowly into their shortest lengths, remained stationed there for long easy moments before again seeking a slow stretch to the other horizon.

Ua Nuka Havu leaned against the wall half asleep. He was neither fat nor thin, except for his rotund belly, the folds of which were pronounced by the tight string of his *pareu* above the navel. He was naked above that marker. Heavy-jowled and meaty of cheek and neck, he was almost purple from tattoo markings; he could carry quantities of flesh on his big bones, it seemed, without creating a picture of corpulence. With graying hair, combed down to his right temple, he seemed possessed of an air of intelligence that was decorous with patience and compassion. Thus he was rightly interpreted, except that by inculcated indolence he was long on patience and longer in finding decision: he allowed most decisions to work themselves into favor; which fact, of course, added to his reputation for fairness and supernal wisdom.

At Jacques's insistence he tried to remain awake. At Jacques's last words his eyes were snapped into brief seconds of attention: "He has not claimed the honor you — you, Ua Nuka Havu, and your people heaped upon him. Only you are held accountable to your people. Suppose, and I say it for the hundredth time since I came to your house, he is not the true son, what then?"

Uti Mopo, wide-awake and minus his carefree smile, had heard all;

he was indeed shocked. Quietly, respectfully, he spoke his mind. Jacques listened patiently, and when the youth gave sign that he had finished, he said: —

"I do not challenge, nor do I intend dishonor to your gods, Uti Mopo, brother of brothers. I only say that he is known in far places as a white man who seeks to plunder. If he is the true son then he need have no fear; he will remain unscathed. But — should the monster conquer him, then we shall all know that he was not the true son."

Grunted the youth: "But alas, we cannot doubt. It is only to invite the wrath of Taaro Tiki for us to voice doubt."

Desaix sighed and made a gesture of utter hopelessness. Sadly his eyes alighted on the lean and bald creature who was Kuirinua, the one who proclaimed tapus. "You, Kuirinua, have never failed to convince Evututuki, the private god of the priests, who wrings water from the clouds unto the fields; you have talked with the gods so that there is always a supply of flying fish by torchlight. Your tapus have saved many of your people from the sharks. You are indeed a wise one, Kuirinua." He paused for effect.

"Would you advise your people wrongly? Would you defy Taaro Tiki by proclaiming for him a son who is not a son?" The old man was impressed, and Desaix felt the surge of fresh hope. "I can see the thunder and the black clouds piling into the heavens and sailing to our shores; I can see our palms snapped like twigs, our poipoi pits dry and empty, the waters of the mighty ocean pouring over us. Why? Because the man is an imposter, and because he was not given the supreme test first. Call him to you, wise Kuirinua, and say, 'The son of Taaro Tiki, and only his son, can remove the tapu of the cavern!' Do not express your doubt. Merely say those words and accept his answer for your decision."

The bald head nodded in palsied manner. "He is the son of Taaro Tiki. He, in the fire by the monolith yonder, defied the god Po; he called for water. Taaro Tiki sent water. He has been tested and he is the son of Taaro Tiki."

Uti Mopo smiled; Ua Nuka Havu opened his eyes and grunted confirmation; Desaix cursed in acid French, and said, "Then I, in keeping with the laws of the French Republic, shall arrest him and hold him for trial!" He got to his feet, brushed off his whites, and walked to the door.

"I am sorry," said the youth. "We have been friends and I do not cherish the ill will of a friend. *Faufau* — it is a bad thing."

The chief arose and smiled at Desaix. "Come, brother Chief, let

261

us forget we have seen disagreement. Let us say with joy, *Kaoha*, and again, *Kaoha*. A great feast lies ahead."

Thought Desaix: Of the four, I am the fool, the poorest student of diplomacy. The greatest of battles are won with smiles, and I am not yet beaten. Aloud he said, grinning, "*Kaoha*, Ua Nuka Havu! *Kaoha*, Uti Mopo! *Kaoha*, Kuirinua!"

4

To Angélique the proximity of Ralls was both pleasant and strangely forbidden, causing her deep, sultry eyes to dance in a dream of fancy that was childish, almost fairylike. Her long black lashes swept upward, revealing the clean whites of her eyes against spirited depths; and the iridescent cream-white of her skin reddened perceptibly; but it was her thin lips, parted in salute to the magic of clime, to the magic of man, that lent emphasis to her mood.

He stared dreamily at the far horizon. Only once had he given her a direct glance. She had wavered before it, as she had two days before, unable to find reason or excuse for the very fierceness of his message: it had given expression to nothing, and yet to everything foreign. An inner voice warned her of danger. That voice was not of the blood — it was sexless wisdom, opposed in its entirety to the lengthened stay of a chaste woman in those tropic seas.

Youth listens to youth, the only language it can speak. Angélique Desaix felt the drowsy run of her blood and accepted her moments of dreamy excitement as the setting dictated. The tropics ruled, and all else was imponderable. Forgotten were Cordtlaant and Noord, as she boldly ran her arm through his, and said: —

"Monsieur, do I fail to interest you?"

Ralls leaned on the rail, staring into the lagoon.

"Quite the contrary, Angélique. But I can show no sign of my feelings."

"Because of — Monsieur Sidneye?" He nodded. "Ralls, he has proposed to me through my uncle. You know? I can see you do. But how?"

"How do I know the blue shark yonder will dive for the wrasse? How do I know you're too innocent for me to ruin?"

"You don't!" she said with spirit. "Perhaps I'm not as innocent as I look." Ralls laughed at her, disengaged his arm, and moved to the stern rail. She followed, her eyes flashing, her lips quivering. "At least I'm not used to being snubbed."

"That," he said quietly, "is the least poisonous of my stingers. Perhaps you haven't heard of what I did last night?"

"I did," she replied, "and your face shows a bruise on the cheek. I also hear that M'sieu Sidneye is planning to — to give you hell — if you'll pardon my Americanism."

"I like your Americanisms," returned Ralls. "I've wondered why you call me 'Monsieur' when you're as familiar with the word 'Mister' as anyone on Canal Street. But have your whims, doll, and see if I care.

"About your uncle — he's after my scalp, I think. Can you add to that?"

"Only this," she said innocently. "Mr. Sidneye offered my uncle a bonus of five thousand Dutch dollars to take charge of an office in Papeete — if I was his wife — two thousand without me. So my uncle proposed to me for the Dutch tycoon." She laughed without any show of mirth. "Jacques also heard from his lips that you are the same Ralls who was here months ago, the man who hurt many natives and escaped by a miracle. He, sitting on his bags of gold, matches Jacques against you."

Ralls grinned. "But did you accept the great Sidneye?"

"I have given no answer as yet, Ralls."

The launch left a foamy wake trailing in sapphire and rainbow hues. Suddenly the motors were cut off, spitting noisily and erasing the bubbling white from the water. The engines churned again and the launch, coasting slowly forward, felt the pull astern and then strained herself backward. From the forward seat Cordtlaant's voice was heard.

"Here's the cavern, Mijnheer Ralls."

Her glance was quick and alive with surprise. "What are you up to, Ralls?" she asked. No answer was given her, unless the lazy smile he emitted said "Wait and see." His shoes and shirt joined his cap on the leather seats under the awning, and he stood with arms akimbo peering over the rail. He yelled out an order: "A bit to the starboard; good — hold her there." As Cordtlaant walked toward them he leaped overboard.

"Monsieur Cordtlaant, what is the meaning of this?"

"Calm yourself, Mademoiselle. Ralls just wants to look around a bit. Come, we'll watch from this side."

Despite her exclamations to the contrary she found her eyes glued to the crystal green of the lagoon into which Ralls had dived. The moments were slow pounding aeons that ran the gamut of seconds — sixty — one hundred and twenty — and another span; then he was up, his head in the air. Relieved, she spoke: —

"I don't understand you two. You're trying to kill one another one moment, and in the next you conspire like schoolboys."

With a smile and two words, Cordtlaant explained all: "Mijnheer Sidneye."

Ralls was under again. Down he went without more propulsion than a sweep of his arms after that quick surface act. At the halfway mark he swam around, peering below, and, as he seemed to sight his objective, he approached the far wall, eyeing an object which was no doubt the iron chest. Slowly he approached it, keeping a foot on the cavern floor — he might need just that added lift, Cordtlaant informed her, if he should meet with company down there. As Ralls moved nearer, cautiously, in slow stabbing jerks, it suddenly dawned on Angélique that she was witnessing — that she was a party to — the theft of the pearls.

"No!" she gasped. Her eyes locked with Cordtlaant's and then with those of Noord.

"An outrigger canoe to starboard," spoke Noord. In another moment he heaved a red stone into the water. She saw Ralls glance upward, straighten out that springlike foot, and rise to the surface; she saw more: he was no more than a fathom above the gorgeously colored floor when two long sinuous arms, thick and hideously pink, moved out of the serrated wall.

Ten minutes later the launch was moored to its post near the pathway leading into the hills. Ralls was again dressed and escorting Angélique up the first rise. Behind lay the outrigger and four puzzled natives. Not a word had Ralls spoken except to Cordtlaant — "That chest looks heavy — a hook and a rope are needed." Whether he meant to make another attempt before the feast, Angélique did not know or care; she was more concerned with her own wild surrender and rejection, with the shame that followed the thought of each.

Frigidly, she said: "Mr. Ralls, I beg of you to forget my insane actions of this afternoon. I assure you they will not be repeated."

He grinned easily, reached out and plucked the bloom of a hibiscus and placed it in her hair. "I'd not say that, Angélique. I had no time for you today. But perhaps someday —"

She stopped short. "And you'd have me marry another man when you — you could —" She did not dare conclude her thought with words. She so wanted to cry.

"I'm afraid, my dear, I have no choice but that — exactly that."

"Then, my dear Ralls, I can only say that I'll see you both in hell first!" The fire in her eyes had its appeal, the sudden evanescence of the flame was also provocative, but it was not until her expressions ran the gamut of emotions, and into ideas of calculated revenge, that he desired to pick her up and cart her off into the jungle. She was not aware of her victory — she had dented his armor.

"Yes," she said, startled by her own decision, "on second thought I shall accept Mr. Sidneye's proposal!"

"Then," said Ralls, eyeing her strangely, "I'd marry him before the mood vanished."

CHAPTER XXIV

1

THE last quarter of the day, to every native and visitor alike, was the beginning of the day; into it was packed the excitement and joy preceding the feast of the moon. Within two hours the swarm of outrigger canoes must groan under the weight of numbers in pilgrimage to the sacred cavern; everyone must see the pearl shells ripped from the breast of the undersea mother, must tremble with prayers to Taaro Tiki for the safe return of the hero divers. Anticipation, heightened and glowing, was further energized by sight, sound, and smell. Siesta was behind the refreshed tongues that babbled forth greeting and jest; flutes played and tattooed natives jumped about timidly, joyously.

And once the iron chest was drawn from the depths, after the sacred pearl was placed before the monolith to await the flames reserved for the gods, enormous quantities of food would be placed on the ground atop the freshest fronds while the moon hunched in the sky and proclaimed the feast. The gods were kind!

At the request of Ua Nuka Havu, Mayrant gave the ships' crews liberty, so there was further rejoicing aboard ships, not to mention the guilders awaiting impatient bets on divers. "*Neen*. I place two on the first being ate by the squid." "*Verdomd!* You're insane, Boolen. He'll bring the shell that'll hold the pearl!"

The man with a score of ships and an army of men under his thumb sat in a white iron chair before a table, talking in rapid Dutch. He emitted excited words, high-sounding, and for all like a whip. The ships must be ruled, and he alone would rule them; the crew had never before been maltreated, and standing above the laws of the stolid Dutch, and international maritime laws that forbade such, was Mayrant Sidneye, who would tolerate in no man, not even an upstart captain for a day, the abuse of man or men; for such crimes yardarms were made — to hold ropes — and for such nonsensical rashness, brigs were required — to rob a ship of cargo room. *Verdomd!*

Behind him stood Captains Cordtlaant and Noord, bubbling inwardly while their grave faces remained expressionless. How sad, said their faces; how glorious, said their minds. In the hand of each was a tall glass, and limping to fill them was the much-scarred youth of the *Golden Hind*, Hekkin, whose joy filled the full sails of his face; almost worth the beating was the privilege of listening in on the reprimand.

"I am almost ready to toss you back to the sharks. What assurance have I that the incident will not repeat itself? Could I trust such a man with a ship? *Neen!* By rights, and by God, I shall see that you perform your duty or be blackballed by every Batjak ship — you will extend an apology to Captain Cordtlaant, to young Hekkin, and to the crew! Now, what have you to say for yourself?"

Beyond the curtained doors stood Desaix and his niece, he with arm upon hers in detaining manner. He smiled full into his downward curve. The strange new emotion she had given birth that day, revenge, caused her eyes to narrow, her nostrils to quiver, and her lips to part with thirsty, cynical joy. She turned her eyes upon Jacques for the second time and shuddered in the moment she recognized the thin but eternal hate encountered there; almost as fierce as the eyes of the man she had courted. From the veranda there were more words from Sidneye and she listened closely.

"I call upon you, Ralls, to speak up for yourself. I can make or break you."

There was more, but she was content to cling to the words she had heard, to see her clean soul avenged. But her soul had been black when she warmed to him, or — perhaps she had merely given fascination a short run for the fun of it; never would she have done more. That was it, and he had looked upon her as wanton. How could he! Then she felt the utter rightness of Jacques's eye, and she justified it with all the savagery she could put into her lips and eyes.

But only for a moment. Angélique Desaix was unschooled in the art of hate. She was too true to herself to blame anyone for her conduct.

At that moment Ralls broke his long silence. From her point of vantage she had seen his steady grin, his cynical expression, his hoisting of the gin drinks as he slouched lazily in the bamboo chair with one foot hooked over the arm. She listened as he said: —

"Your whims, *Mister* Sidneye, are your personal property. So are mine. You, because you can afford them, and I, because I care little where the chips fall. I believe my debt to you, now and in the future, is frankness within reason." His eyes danced with black fire. "However, by the laws of the sea, I owe Mr. Cordtlaant and young Hekkin apology. I hereby tender them." He stood and gave each a bow that was baffling. Stubborn acquiescence, a means to an end, thought Angélique. But he performed with such ease and assurance that she could only admire him; and the spark of admiration flared again into the flame of desire. She smothered the emotion, and turned her eye to the great Sidneye.

He seemed surprised, infuriated, and pleased. Hunching forward, he stared at the only man who had ever dared voice impertinence after his reprimand; and it seemed the great Sidneye groped for decision. Angélique saw the smile on Ralls's face, saw him lower his glass, heard him beckon Hekkin for a refill, all so indifferently executed that he, instead of the bald Sidneye, might have been the man who owned Batjak. Then, out of the electric atmosphere, it was Ralls who snatched the calm that turned the situation.

"Now, Mr. Sidneye, if you're done with your day's lecture, we'll get down to matters of real importance." His glance fell upon Cordtlaant and Noord, in clear suggestion for their dismissal.

Mayrant obliged him; and when they had departed, he did a strange thing — Angélique, standing alone and peering through the cracks in the bamboo screen, saw it — he filled the glasses himself, and laid a hand on Ralls's shoulder in a gesture that could not be mistaken for anything short of affection.

Bewildered, she turned from the screen and sought her room.

2

It was only natural that earthly flesh begotten by the immortals should honor the festooned craft with Ua Nuka Havu, Uti Mopo, Kuirinua, the wives, and the old men of the wise council. The craft was minus sail, though its mast held aloft old and new shrouds that ran from bow to stern and to the outriggers flanking the cushioned dugout. The ropes were covered entirely by blossoms of every color and size, and the mast stood like a giant flower stem worthy of royalty and the guest from beyond the mists of the mountains.

Slowly the water exposition got under way: the towlines, running from the stern of the government launch to the bow of the canoe and forward log of its outriggers, tightened as the screw of the launch churned the placid green waters with foam. Desaix knew the ceremonious route and he pointed the thin white bow in the opposite direction from the cavern. As he circled to the right the boat nearest shot into line, and from the staggered row at the beach another and another followed until all joined the train. The placid water was broken intermittently by dotted canoes and the comb-tooth legs of outriggers. The forward line neared the pincers, beyond which the crosstrees and masts of the Dutch ships stood in silent salute.

At the mouth of the inlet Jacques swung into a wide portcircle, cut off the motor to allow the tail boats a catching-up. The towlines slacked a bit, then drew taut as the motor whirred, coughed, and the gears enmeshed with the shaft that turned the screw. When the waters purled from the white knife, in an opposite direction from the sea train, a great shout arose. A native song, strong, vibrant, and thrillingly savage, and yet magically Polynesian, was begun by Uti Mopo and picked up down the long line; the notes fell against the water only to be thrown back into the air and glide acoustically perfect across the wide expanse of water and beach. There is ever a strange magic in voices over the water, though only in the South Seas does music fall in séance so utterly pagan.

"It is — beautiful," breathed Angélique. She sat beside Mayrant under the canopy and let her eye roam at will. Behind them, forward to portside, sat Cordtlaant and Noord, with Hekkin, nursemaid to bottle and ice, in the close rear.

"Impressive," returned Mayrant, "to say the least." His eyes turned slowly from the chieftain's canoe and came to rest upon her. "But only you are beautiful, lovely Angélique. N'est-ce pas? Is that the proper French?"

"Perfect," she said, "except — it isn't so." She stared into his eye for a sweeping second before laughing lightly and turning again to the tail of the train. The slow, lilting chorus continued. "There's romance in their song, Monsieur Sidneye. I shall never forget this moment."

"Indeed," he agreed, feasting his eyes on her. "And what background could be better for your saying you'll marry me?"

"But — you have made a great mistake, M'sieu. You forget that you must first propose." For once his eyes snapped with incredulity. Then he laughed, and the sound was made more pitiful by his retreat into mirth at a moment when romance prayed for soft words. She frowned, thought of the stolid Dutch as a race of blockheads, and turned her eyes upon the son of Taaro Tiki.

Ralls wore his sea cap at a jaunty angle, a white flower at his left ear, an unmistakable sign among the natives of a man seeking a mate. Naked to the waist except for a large garland of flowers about his neck, he seemed unaware of the world about him; he almost symbolized the savage-flowered *pareu* Ua Nuka Havu lent him for the occasion. He leaned back against the colorful cloth, his legs crossed and giving view to blood-red swimming trunks underneath Polynesian attire. He could be the chief, she thought, if one judged with an eye to fierce beauty or imperious manner. With cigarette between his teeth he viewed the entire world with the true arrogance of the god he played. But the white flower?

"I thought your uncle gave you my message," said Mayrant.

"Yes, he did," she returned brusquely.

"Well?"

"I'm sorry, Monsieur Sidneye, but so much is lacking —" Coldly she spoke her true feelings, eyeing Ralls all the while. She saw Uti Mopo lean toward him, grinning, she saw Ralls raise a hand in gesture of agreement. The engine coughed and the launch jumped forward, almost snapping the hawsers. Mayrant's hand fell over hers.

"Angélique," he said huskily, "I shall tell you what I have never before told another woman. I love you."

The words, the slow emphasis of emotion, seemed to jerk her eyes to his. How deeply she peered she did not know, but in the fathomless depths she saw sincerity. Then he said it — would she marry him? And before her he laid his empire at a single glance. There was every reason to say yes, every reason to voice the opposite; and the native chorus sounded from the far-off boats, moving in the left circle, ever forward; and joyous natives waved flowers from crowded outriggers and canoes and raised their voices in glorious rhythm and tone; she listened, followed the line with enchanted eyes until they fell upon the towering pole of flowers and down into the canoe, upon Ralls.

His gaze was narrowed upon her, straight, penetrating, awakening, and ablaze with a message. As she stared the music rose into its most romantic notes while Ralls pinned her soul to its very background with his eyes. It was then he removed the white flower from his ear and tossed it into the lagoon. She felt a surge of hate in the moment.

To Sidneye's question, she replied, "Yes."

She was suddenly ashamed, and her face, she felt, was as red as the vermilion sarong she wore, as scarlet as the passionate blossom in her hair; she knew only pity for the man she'd promised to marry, only hate for the devil-god who swayed her soul. Biting her lip, she made a great resolve, and gave it nest in short prayer: Mayrant Sidneye must never regret this day — pray the Lord that she should learn to love him, but, regardless, that she should remain faithful to him — forever and ever.

Under her breath: "Amen."

She was aware of nothing else until the motor raced madly and the gears shifted, maneuvering Ua Nuka Havu's royal canoe into an excellent point of vantage at the western fringe of the undersea garden. Even then the kiss Sidneye planted upon her lips failed to draw smile or shudder. But with the awakening, her first act was to stab Ralls with an angry, triumphant glance. He merely gazed at her, but his eyes seemed sad.

The French boat then swung about and eased into a wide circle. It came to a halt against the starboard outrigger of the festooned canoe, stern to cavern, where Desaix, with the aid of a native uniformed policeman, lashed the sides to the outrigger. Other boats were coming up, and by the time the job was finished the wide circle was forming, every boatman careful to fling his red-stone anchor into the shallow shelf that encircled the sacred theater while his aides flung or snatched at ropes for tying one craft to another. As the circle neared completion many boats lingered outside; unable to find a place in the circle for canoe or outrigger, many natives began boarding the outriggers already lashed into an almost finished wheel above the cavern. The babble of voices, the rising of shrill, excited laughter, and the wail of scattered flutes playing against a wall of song and chatter were enough to cause the dead to rise and frown.

The sun hung hours above the horizon, though all glare was missing in the toned shadows of leaning palms just beyond the western circle of the canoes. Visibility was good and from the stern of the launch there was a detailed view of the world below; like a glimpse through a green-tinted sheet of plate glass arose a mighty pageant of coral and algae.

The deep, mysterious cavern was walled by many caverns, weirdly disappearing in the depths of a luminous blue, fringed by saw-edged coral in every shade. Down went the walls, almost precipitously. But it was the floor that reeked of mystery and beauty, that lent verity to the words of Desaix on the day of their arrival, "The most beautiful cavern God ever placed before man's eye." There lived beauty; there lurked greed and danger; and the fusion of colors became a living part of the deadly panorama. The scarlet spines of a sixteen-armed sea star, a brilliantly colored pincushion of the deep, were alive with a deadly poison; giant clams, a yard long and more, were man traps from which there was small chance of escape — three of them lay embedded in coral rock near the western wall.

A universe of colored fish, dazzling, unbelievable, swam in and out of the light beams that danced down from mysterious sources; living, lingering patterns were these show pieces of the South Seas; flitting on into ultramarine and cobalt caverns, where forests of living polyps dotted the lagoon floor.

All this in a few fleeting seconds was enough to set agape the mouth of a visitor — it did just that to many a Dutchman from the *Golden Hind* and *Van Arken* — and its rare treat was not lost on Angélique Desaix. She stared and lifted her eyes as if for breath, then lowered them again, trying in childish wonder to reconcile the scarlet beauty of the sea star with the very poison of its color. She turned her gaze, like everyone else, to the bottommost cavern under the intricate arch.

Ralls was no more than a dozen feet to their left. She sent him a glance that Desaix intercepted; he grinned as if to say: "Flirt on — while he lives." She ignored his meddlesome eye and whispered into Mayrant's ear.

"A capital idea!" exclaimed the tycoon. He cut a ludicrous figure, with a salmon hibiscus against his bald head, but for all that he offered her his world. "Jacques, you may announce that your niece and I shall be married by Captain Cordtlaant after the feast."

The Frenchman was unable to utter a sound. Struck dumb by surprise he opened his mouth to speak, closed it again and grabbed for the hand of the man who would pay him five thousand guilders — he almost reached for the money, thought Angélique, and for the moment she wanted to spur Ralls into beating him.

The gregarious Polynesians were unaware of the silent drama: their eyes sought a view of the iron chest and its horrible guardian; they awaited the words of Chief Ua Nuka Havu to commence the ceremony. But the chief was in conference with his son, the high priest, the wise ones, and the son of Taaro Tiki: should the people receive reprimand for elevating the iron chest above the search for the sacrificial pearl, or should they be given their moment of excitement with all reverent emphasis placed on, and only on, the one pearl? As Kuirinua rumbled his version, a long serpentine arm felt sluggishly of a coral finger, then another, and another, and, at last, the pink sack with great eyes moved into the light rays; for an instant it peered up at the strange company and, affrighted, moved quickly back into its mysterious home.

Ua Nuka Havu had his say, and the wise men were called upon for their opinions. Only Ralls remained without voice; and he seemed the essence of patience and ease. Desaix, quickly shelving the surprising news of his niece's good fortune, turned his ear to the powwow in the canoe, heard the various opinions, saw the devil incarnate in profile, and half closed his eyes in hushed expectancy. After endless moments of silence, he heard Ralls say slowly, dispassionately: —

"Did not the gods advise the all-wise Kuirinua to plant the sacred pearls in the custody of the pink monster?" Desaix scowled, silently cursing. He heard the wise men, Uti Mopo, and the chief voice agreement.

"Then," Ralls said, "is not the chest of sacred importance; does it not equal the event of the one pearl?" Only assent could follow. "Then your people, Ua Nuka Havu, have not blasphemed the gods." There was joy among the rulers and they babbled freely until Ralls, the son of Taaro Tiki, raised his hand for silence.

"I only hope, and I shall soon have an answer," said Ralls, "that the monster has not placed a curse on the pearls of the monolith. But the gods are all-wise and they shall speak to the great Kuirinua."

Of course, surprise and fear leaped into the faces of the royal party. Desaix glowered, while Ua Nuka Havu stood erect to open the long ceremony with a prelude of wordy supplication.

3

The pearl yield is scarce even in remote lagoons, as any pearler will confirm, which invites a pearling fleet to take on the thick shells, almost solid mother-of-pearl, and sail to port for the price per ton. But not so in the lagoon of the sacred cavern: countless generations had observed the rites of the cavern, long before the gods sent the pink monster into the waters. Pearls there were, and oyster shells covered perhaps one third of the floor.

After the rituals of speech, the wizened Kuirinua ordered five divers to make ready for the descent. Then, when the first diver split the water near the festooned outrigger, everyone felt the real excitement of the occasion. He was seen at the bottom, almost in the center of the theater, dislodging a cluster; he was up, grinning, with three large shells, his hopes high — the accepted pearl meant honor to the diver. Uti Mopo opened them. There were no pearls.

The second diver gripped the lead bars and cut a path to the bottom. His foot grazed the lip of a giant clam, and the snap of its irregular jaws was so sudden that those on the surface almost heard it. A murmur of approval. Soon he appeared on the surface and, amid shouts of praise, delivered his find to the son of the chief. One by one they were opened, and one by one discarded. Soon all five of the divers sat on the "bench of the fruitless," having brought up not a single pearl.

Kuirinua's voice rose to the heavens; then the first diver went below again. Emptiness repeated itself, once, twice, thrice, and the fourth lad was under. His foot, from stupidity or eagerness, or both, fell atop a sea star. Cries of dismay went up from the canoes, and as the clumsy diver hastened to the surface the remaining four went under with long sticks. On the bottom they turned the belly of the star to the surface and beckoned the injured one; down he went, and on the floor he placed his foot over the mouth of the star. Twice he came up for air and three times his foot was sucked; the spine and poison were no longer a part of him.

All the while the divers brought up pearls, four of them under the water at one time. It was the first diver who produced the shell with a pearl. Jacques leaned over the side to catch a better view of the find. Soon Ralls fingered it. With a word to the chief, Ralls placed the pearl in a pouch tied to the belt of his trunks. The show went on; only Ralls was the richer, it seemed.

At last, after three pearls nestled in the pouch, a huge black pearl was held aloft. Applause greeted the sight. Ralls stared greedily.

Ua Nuka Havu spoke. Kuirinua arose and poured coconut milk over two divers. Uti Mopo produced two long ropes of coconut fiber to which he attached a seasoned pole; completed, his handiwork had the appearance of a child's swing. The divers stood on the outriggers, one hand of each on the pole while the other gripped short spears. The weapons told a story; on this occasion the gods allowed them defense against their slimy servant, whose usefulness to the heavenly family must end when its coils were robbed of life by intrepid subjects of the earth.

A great shout went up, and without awaiting its echo the two gracefully split the surface, sending up sapphire drops as the lagoon closed over them. The hoist went with them. They were down one fathom, then another, and another, while the silence in the circle hung heavy over the water. Every belly on every outrigger faced the floor, and the canoes were strained at their sides by those who leaned over for a view of the last and final act.

On into the last fathom went the graceful divers, their feet at last touching the floor near the center. A group of spotted tangs swam near, then turned away. The amphibious Polynesians advanced slowly, warily, toward the great cave in a fantastic world of rocky blossoms and gauzelike inflorescence. Shelves of coral surrounded them, blending into fading, mysterious depths of purple and blue. Truly here walked the spirit of the tapu.

The vast cave with its perfect arch was no more than two yards away when they espied the rusty iron chest. A gift from a kind Frenchman long years before, the chest was fashioned into an oblong shape a foot wide and high, some twenty inches long; its top was hinged, and it was locked by a greased pole that ran through a series of ring-bolts, two of which awaited the pole of the hoist. It lay in a bed of red moss no more than two feet inside the castle door. Quickly they weighted the cross pole of the hoist with shells and advanced, spears poised. Into the vast, limitless cavern, into the indigo of absolute darkness, they peered, bending slowly and groping for the chest in which the treasure of the monolith was sealed. They touched its rings and bent lower to tug it to the haven of safety a few feet behind them.

Desaix, watching with such force that his eyes bulged and ached, felt his impotence, and cursed his luck; and then he stared again. He felt the hand of Angélique on his arm, squeezing hard; he heard her low moan as a long tapering tentacle was thrust forward, then another, and another.

The divers backed away as the bulb-shaped body shot into view, revealing baleful eyes against a sickly pink body and horrible sucker-adorned arms. The two forward inner arms wound in flashing coils about the iron chest, while the two long outer arms reached for the divers, one of whom stood in a trance gazing at the tentacle that found his leg. Suddenly he came to life and fell backward as his spear shot out of his hand. The other advanced, but as he did so a powerful arm moved up and wound slowly about his waist. Only one diver returned to the surface, and his leg, torn from the sucking arm, showed its marks.

Ua Nuka Havu stood and cried out to his people. "It is the power of Taaro Tiki!" Out of the silence that followed, Uti Mopo, rising from his belly, said: —

"It is too late to save him. Even now the monster moves into the cave."

"Who dares go after the pearls?" cried the chief. The Polynesians, dreading the tapu of Taaro Tiki, found solidarity in silence.

"Only Taaro Tiki can save the pearls," shrieked Kuirinua.

"Or perhaps the son of Taaro Tiki," said Desaix. Here was the beauty of brevity. The words, "If he is the son of Taaro Tiki," could only add superfluity to the tone in which he spoke, so he said no more as he leaned toward Ralls. But the words soared toward the Elysian heights of the Frenchman's hopes, exquisitely vague, blissfully real, and his smile coiled in rhapsodic hellishness to allow his venom outlet. And Ralls merely sat in the canoe, leveling his eyes upon his challenger, while the chief, high priest, and Uti Mopo stared inanely at the two.

Mayrant peered closer. The heightened drama had moved to the top of the lagoon. One native said to another, "The son of Taaro Tiki can save the pearls," and another passed the word on until the circle was completed. Cordtlaant heard; he grinned. So did Noord and young Hekkin. Only Angélique frowned as she gazed at Ralls, who seemed to define in that moment superb callousness. He was something strange, an imperturbable god — who spoke the rhythmic languages of force without termination, who raced on the winds of hoax in one moment only to descend to the earth and cause violent disruptions in the next.

Ralls turned his eyes from Jacques and lent his ear to Ua Nuka Havu. Inexplicably he said all without saying anything; he was both warlike and calm, he matched in spirit the velvety riot of color in the lagoon below, the peace of its deadliness. All eyes leaned toward him, all ears seemed to ask for his words, and in a silence so heavy a clap of thunder could scarcely penetrate he stood in the canoe and said in a voice of iron: —

"I shall go."

Only silence where applause seemed a necessity: but the stunning weight of his being, his brevity, his decision, hung over the group. Mayrant — like Uti Mopo, like the fleshy boatman across the circle, like Noord, like the scarlet-clad girl who would soon join him in marriage — stared hypnotically at the man who, despite every reason to the contrary, evoked in him the highest admiration he could give a mortal. No man was more worthy, he said, of the best Batjak had to offer.

Angélique, her voice quivering, cried, "No! You cannot do it, Ralls!"

He faced her, grinning, removed his *pareu* and cap, fished about the boat for goggles before stepping lightly into the water.

"A thousand francs, Monsieur Sidneye," said Jacques, "that he fails to return." He spoke with all the joy that accompanies a dream about to come true.

"I accept the wager," said Mayrant. His eyes said more — he had not placed the proper value on the cunning of Jacques Desaix, whose patience to his point was worthy of praise. He glanced into the eyes of the French Angel. Then he leaned near her and said: —

"May I call you Lonyta?"

She answered in abject manner; perhaps she felt the weight of his passion, or perhaps she did not care what he called her. Ralls was in danger — in many fathoms of man-killing water. Seldom, she thought, do men go down to the sea in search of basilisks. But seldom was there a Ralls.

4

On the coral floor Ralls peered about in every direction. He was in no hurry, a fact made known to everyone by his toying with a sea star before pinning it to the floor with the short spear of the unfortunate diver. He approached the chest without any show of caution, more in the manner of one measuring its position inside the cave. And there he stood eyeing the cavern, the shelf above it, the flat thin ledge to the right. He slowly turned around; in another moment he touched his foot to the floor in a light springy movement and shot to the surface. Nothing attempted, nothing gained.

For long moments he lay on the surface, breathing peacefully and stretching his long-limbed body. Then, executing a quick somersault that scarcely caused a splash, he dove headfirst and descended in a slow corkscrew circle, his feet the rudder, nothing more, as he conquered the pressure with prodigious ease. Soon his feet again trod on sand, and he strode to the arched cave, entered, and deliberately picked up the iron chest. It was only when he turned to the exit that he was aware that he was not alone.

From above the scream of Angélique broke the layered quiet of the ceremonious circle. Mayrant gripped the rail, and Jacques grinned. As Ralls walked into the inky den and bent over the chest, a long pink arm moved out from the shelf above; another thin coil followed, growing in size until it revealed a horrendous body oozing over the edge; and then, tentacles trailing, it shot water backward and moved entirely off the coral ledge to settle slowly, like a grotesque parachute, in the very mouth of the cave. The path of escape was severed — the son of Taaro Tiki must surely die a watery death. The waters would soon part to allow the spirit fitting return to the heavens. Kuirinua sat lost in profound thought: he should be ready to proclaim a tapu on the pearls; he should quote Taaro Tiki as saying to him: — "The guardian of the deep is now inviolate."

He was not the immortal son of Taaro Tiki — Ralls admitted as he gazed into the deadly, sorrowful eyes confronting him. The pink and tan dotted thing hung above the floor, slowly waving all but three of its mighty coils, and the three writhed on the coral as if to anchor the whole mass for a speedy stab forward. No Gilbertese log, this — no shark, child's play compared to this creature without sense of fear. He thought of a barrel of a Mexican's pistol pointing into his eye in a Yucatán forest, of a slithering cold snake he had mistaken for a vine in the jungles of northern Colombia, of advancing rats as he lay stunned and paralyzed on a beach in the Carolines — toys all. A half minute or more of his three minutes to breathe had elapsed. He wanted to kill this beast more than he wanted anything else in the world — not for the pearls, not for the *Golden Hind*, but for the sheer ecstasy of making the damned thing suffer.

Said Jacques, lighting a cigarette and toying with the match, "Only one shall emerge, Monsieur Sidneye."

Angélique shuddered. "You coward!" Weakly she sank into a chair, caught at Mayrant's arm and said faintly, "Isn't there something we can do? Tell them to send a dozen natives down with spears!"

At first Ralls desired a reversal of positions — the octopus should be in his domain, the defender, and not the cunning one who trapped the most cunning of men — and then he forgot to care. The chest was on his shoulder, and he was the one to lunge forward: the weight of the box plus his surprising advance threw the devil off guard and backward. He was out of the cave in that moment. A great shout arose from the web wheel of canoes and outriggers forty feet above him.

But the octopus seemed in no mood for battle; it moved to a shelf some yards away. There it settled down to eye Ralls sluggishly. In that moment Ralls was aware of the reason he was living: the thing was gorged on the flesh of the diver.

In a quick move he placed the pole on the hoist through the rings of the chest and saw it lifted; then he shot to the surface, sucked in precious air, and again felt for the bottom. Fool! Precious fool! He advanced upon the guardian of the pearls, and his flashing blade was matched only by the edge to his eyes. In self-defense a coiling arm went about his body, and in maniacal joy he dug deep the knife. With a hold on the inner shelf the octopus moved backward, pulling Ralls slowly into the narrow opening. Ralls slashed furiously in a fight for his very life; he was confronted by arms that sought to kill, that slowly, slowly but surely, dislodged him from striking position. He felt the second arm relax its hold as the awful ink-acid of the beast threw darkness before his goggles. The third arm coiled about his right shoulder and neck, while the fourth, fifth, and at last eight arms jerked hideously about him. Despair again gripped him, and to augment this his lungs grew hot, almost bursting from exertion. He tore at the arm that laid a huge flat undercover of suckers upon his shoulders, and he felt the monster's beak seeking to stab at his belly. The all-revealing greed of the thing; it sought to devour him as it fought to the death. Ralls lowered a taut arm before thrusting deep the blade of death. He felt the rending of tough flesh, the spasmodic jerks of the flattened bulb, the slow relaxing of the arm about his shoulder. Then he brought his knife into the sack, into the very brain and nerve core.

The blow was Ralls's last. In another moment he was freeing himself, pulling, tugging frantically at the outer walls. He floated out to the floor of the lagoon, just as complete darkness drew a tight curtain over mind and matter.

5

For an hour all she heard was Ralls's low moan, his babbling. "It took something out of me," he said over and over. Then, out of his coma, he slept. All the while the defeated, but not vanquished, Frenchman had remained outside the chief's hut with the chief and the horde of jubilant natives, the triumphant master of Batjak, his lieutenants and hirelings. And during that hour Angélique had labored over the son of Taaro Tiki, murmuring soothing words and applying strips of cloth, and potions of Kuirinua's balm. The sun had long since set; and the myriad stars, popping into view in the matchless dome of a tropical sky, were ordered into subordinate position by the splendor of a gibbous moon. Pale shafts of light were thrown down on Ralls, who had slept peacefully for almost an hour.

"No," she had said in peremptory manner, "I want no help, no company. I can best treat him if left alone."

He lay on his back on a fiber mat. Once his eyes opened, then their leaden curtains fell again. He was bruised about the shoulders, arms, and neck, ugly purplish-red weals against dotted blisters of blood; and his abdomen was slashed a half inch deep in a running wound below his navel. She dared not look further, though his hand ran to the joining of right leg and torso.

278

On hands and knees she surveyed her work, pronounced it good, then gazed at the face within a foot of her own. She murmured, "I have never seen a man like you." And then without pause she slowly lowered her body to hip and elbow, and pressed her face to his. Softly she caressed the fascinating stubble, moved nearer to feel of his mouth and forehead with her hands and warm loose lips. A thin moan escaped her as her breath steamed his cheeks; and pressing the side of her lips to his she fell flat to his side and dreamed sweetly of that which she held close. Her hand moved to his neck, to his chest, and there it lingered while she drank in the savage magic of wide-arched ribs.

To woman he belonged, and to that woman who found him the world must bow in envy and respect. How fierce were his kisses, how strong were his arms! Strangely she fathomed mysteries, viewing the eternal spring, the jungle lake from which supped the bird of paradise, the moon, the stars; her contentment could only begin in his arms — the soothing qualities of his mysterious being called in a voice stranger than the winds, than the pounding of the incessant surf, rhythmically, but louder and louder. She felt the surge of her blood, the very fusion of their spirits as her arm encircled him.

"Oh, Ralls — my Ralls!" she whispered.

Out of nowhere came his answer: "Angélique, I love you" — as if his words explained all!

"Then why," she said in pleading tone, "didn't you claim me?"

In the moment he was awake. He sat up, shaking his head; then, staring at her, he asked that she repeat the question. She did. After long moments he said: —

"Because you're the one thing in this world I've learned to love. And the barrier to our happiness must be conquered by me, not by you."

"I don't understand," she said, perplexed.

"You wouldn't. But it's there. Tell me, my dear, could you find joy in torturing me?"

"I don't understand," she repeated.

"Then I won't explain," he said gruffly, rising to his feet. He stood perplexed, his legs unsteady. Then he lay down once more. "But remember, Angélique, I love you. I'll win, remember that, and then I'll come for you. Now let me sleep."

Long minutes passed, in which he held her hand. Then he was up again, stretching his muscles and testing his legs. He grinned, saying he felt as good as new. Suddenly she was standing before him.

"Oh, Ralls," she said, smiling up at him, her hands clasping his.

279

"I'll wait for you — forever!" She stood awaiting his arms and lips. But he did not take her in his arms, he merely stared deep inside her, his expression ironical, accusing, and questioning.

At a moment when he should have answered her call, he said, "You might have to wait forever. No, Angélique, you'd do better with Sidneye."

A sharp frown erased her smile. "Ralls, why did you wear the white flower above your ear, why did you remove it? I don't understand." Her eyes begged for answer, received nothing but emptiness. "What have you to conquer that's stronger than love?"

"The devil himself," snapped Ralls.

"Then the devil is bigger than our love? If you feel that way, you don't love me." Out of unsolved mysteries, out of deeper humiliation, she grasped at the props of anger. But that, too, was evanescent. Lowering her eyes, she sighed heavily.

She said slowly, in resigned tone, "As another man's wife I'll have nothing to do with you."

How sincerely she spoke, how ludicrously positive; as if a woman could know her mind. But in his face she read of amusement, of love — bold, daring, and certain — of rescue.

He repeated: "I love you, Angélique."

In her upturned face, understanding and compassion vied with the enigmatic, dwarfing the pains of rejection and its aftermath, anger. It seemed her eyes made a gallant attempt at a smile while placing a value on her loss.

Ralls suddenly lifted her into his arms, and took several steps toward the opening. Then he halted abruptly. The startled expression in her eyes was short-lived; her face radiated dreamy contentment, and her arms instinctively circled his neck. In another moment their lips joined, and she no longer tried to solve mysteries. It was a long sweet moment that outdistanced eternities, in which his arms were strong pillars that defeated his words; his lips divine echoes of refutation.

Then he said, "My darling, my darling."

Her answer was a hungry whisper, "Ralls," and she held his face close to hers in eloquent invitation to a second embrace. And with no will to resist her, he obeyed; until he could no longer shut out visions of a beast — armed with a whip, an eternal Creeper — himself.

Out of the long moment, out of the long kiss, he lowered her gently to her feet, then stalked to the opening of the hut.

Almost savagely he said, "The feast awaits us."

CHAPTER XXV

1

BEFORE Ralls, on the intricately patterned frond combs that served for tablespread atop flat Mother Earth, a suckling pig basted in taro sauce joined a roasted red mountain banana, a quarter of wild pineapple, a dozen hot clam shells, in which the tasty flesh was fried, a whole flying fish baked in leaves, a pearl oyster shell of fermented breadfruit, a bowl of crabs in odoriferous, hot coconut milk, and a large coconut rind filled with its milk. With a quantity of Dutch gin under his belt and his irritably savage aches somewhat lessened, he fell to the spread with an appetite.

He was, of course, showered with choice gifts by the worshiping natives, Uti Mopo, Kuirinua, and Ua Nuka Havu. In his hair was a crown of tropical jasmine, while about his neck were strung flowers of every color. Sitting in the center of the royal group, he stared down the long line to the far end where sat the Frenchman, his niece, Sidneye, and his captains. Beyond, in the garish moonlight, the lagoon nestled like a jewel, her many facets sparkling as fish leaped into the air and flew about like live, wandering sapphires. The steady hum of insects met the joyous babble of voices intermittently punctuated with Polynesian laughter.

Ralls longed for the free soul of a native. In contrast was that ennobling sensation that entered his life with a sickening awareness: love for a woman. And were his soul free, unstained by a perversion that could only wear itself out, or go with him even unto death, he could remain in this languid setting forever, with her at his side. But it blinked at him in all its hideousness, like the riding light in the forerigging of a ghost ship. He shuddered, lifted a long second glance in Angélique's direction, and cursed himself for his softness.

Ambition ruled his many voices — to hell with a woman!

And for the artless natives he had little use. The fools planned to roast that huge black pearl. The cremation of a fortune scarcely appealed to him, not when there was a chance of getting his hands on the gem; and but for the infernal meddlesomeness of the Frenchman, he'd talk them out of that one. He could not cast his eye upon Angélique without viewing her uncle and Mayrant, and they spurred his two appetites — the *Golden Hind* went with Sidneye while the path to that gallant queen of the seas was blocked by Desaix.

But the food was good, and the time was not ripe for a claiming of wealth.

A native woman approached with a flat tray, the borders of which were lined with flowers and fruits. She placed it before Ralls, and the word went around the line of squatting natives and Dutchmen: a savage arm of the pink monster had been roasted for the son of Taaro Tiki! Adorning the smelly coil was one of its eyes, raw, and staring even in death. She bent to Ralls, and he kissed her forehead and invited her to partake of the meat she proffered. Jubilant, she accepted a coil tip and went her way.

The baleful eye continued to stare at him, and for want of some object upon which to settle his hate, he took the cold clammy thing in his hand with the idea of tossing it into the fire. Its very presence was an evil omen. Suddenly he grinned, eyed the sorrowful thing, and passed it to Kuirinua.

"Guard it well," he said. "Taaro Tiki now talks with me." The wizened one accepted it, placed it in a basket with other agents of sorcery, and stood. His words rang out: —

"Cease eating, every soul under the moon. Raise your eyes to the heavens — Taaro Tiki talks with his son."

Mayrant, a whole fowl at his mouth, grinned, tore off an enormous chunk of whitened breast with his teeth, and patiently awaited the expected shower of guilders. With mouth full and champing noisily, he leaned toward Angélique and voiced a thought. It was a gluttonous sound from thick, weighted tongue: —

"He has brains and power. I'm proud — of him." He grinned and swallowed hard.

Jacques glared. Such a display of hellish influence and nerve he had never seen. The awful battle with the octopus courted the admiration of even his hate-filled mind. The fact gnawed at him hatefully, like a cloud of midges buzzing about him, content in giving annoyance. And, as if to stay the tricolored power of the French Republic, Sidneye had, only a few minutes before, asked for his decision. "After the feast," he'd grunted sourly.

But the food, while not the cuisine of a Parisian restaurateur — which, he reflected with a scowl, his tongue's buds had almost forgotten — was good. He licked poipoi from his fingers, tore at succulent slabs of pig and goat, and gulped his fill of gin and juice. "And to the devil with Ralls! If everything else fails — " He smacked noisily, more over his thoughts than the flavorful meat.

Jacques was ever the sybarite. The gratification of his appetites had long since become his ode to life; the chores of the government were tolerated as a means to the purposeful pampering of his body. Nor were his luxuries, as one rightly guessed, confined to the senses of taste, smell, and sound. He courted the bottle, and when the slow rhythm of stimulated dullness found its stride, the man walked meekly behind, a servant to its moods; and the directions taken in these bacchant strolls were not in the least surprising.

So he drank to keep heightened callousness alive, and he ate to assuage his palate; but habit settled upon him as he imbibed of gin and a favored concoction of fish, and sent his thoughts to his favorite paramour, Haupua. With that comely amazon, whose thighs struck a Herculean rhythm, ecstatically prolonged, he had wallowed for long hours without respite. Ah! the tropics, aye the tropics! How easily he entered her drugged moods. He thought of his freedom for the taking, seriously considering his house and Haupua while his guests, and niece, followed the feast.

How perfect — except for Ralls. Once before he had locked with Haupua while Ralls set his stage for the rape of the monolith. To his niece he said: —

"Really going through with it?"

She turned a quizzical eye on him. "The marriage?" She added without emphasis, "That, I take it, pleases you."

He shrugged his shoulders, a gesture that said he cared little what she, or anyone, did. Her garrulous maid, Paunua, had spoken of his orgies, of his long hours over a bottle, of his equally long hours with a huge tattooed girl. Before her mouth could be closed, she had told of spying on the pair through a slitted blind.

So he was her uncle. She shuddered, thinking of her pious father, and for the moment she felt suddenly alone and unprotected.

"Oh Lord in Heaven," she murmured, "deliver me from temptation."

Mayrant's arm fell upon her shoulder. "What troubles you, my dear?"

"I was praying," she said. In that quick appraising second, he saw more of the woman he was to marry than mere flesh; and the weight of her goodness fell happily into his heart, causing him to think his first prayer since childhood: Oh Lord, give me strength to deserve her.

The moon rose higher into the low-hanging heavens, and floated through veils of luminous gauze ever westward — to dancing and singing, to fierce, unrestrained motions and tones. A song struck a stormy tempo, rose fiercely, whiplashed, lingered, and died — bodies swayed again to enchanting, slow rhythm, and the murmuring surf found its sweet monotony in the evening breeze.

The huge red stone, the focal point of god worship, came again into its own. Standing fifteen feet above the ground the grotesque shape was an attempt at a head with staring eyes and flat nose; a hulk of stone except for the chiseled gold-lined pocket that might indicate a hollow of a bent arm midway to the right. A fire roared at its feet on all sides, and the charred, shapeless skirt of the figure had known thousands of fires, while the hollow arm of the gods stood ready to receive the treasure of pearls. Below, in a stone bowl, the sacred pearl would be dropped for cremation.

The flames made Ralls shudder. He had once been tied to the belly of hot stone. He knew the heat, the utter hopelessness of staring beyond the fiery ring. He grinned, asking again, as he had in the short past, how the rain cloud happened to race out of the southeast to drench the whole scene. But that was of the past.

A semicircle of natives faced the dying flames. In another moment Kuirinua would tread the red embers without a murmur; he would feed the hungry image with a thousand pearls. He was even now on his feet, chanting. The time was almost ripe, thought Ralls.

Jacques, well up in the front row and facing the stare of the monolith, felt the tenseness of the moment. He stared at Ralls, saw nothing but a blank face and glinting shallows. He turned to study Mayrant. "What's holding your clown, Monsieur?"

"Mijnheer," Sidneye returned, in stride with the tone of the Frenchman, "we nurse the same question. But tell me, my dear fellow," he put with smiling sincerity, "are you the *commissaire* or the man?"

Desaix found great joy in his answer: "My wealthy friend, you now view a pair of them." His downward smile was anything but friendly. It sought to sever a jugular, or gouge out an eye, thought Mayrant. But Sidneye was immunized to threats and moods; he grinned.

Ua Nuka Havu arose; he stood before Kuirinua; and as the wise old diplomat pronounced the wisdom of the chief, his place in the sun, his all-high worthiness, the crowd remained hushed. The gods were pleased, he said in conclusion. Then the ovation was given, in cry, in word, in song. Only the praise of Taaro Tiki, his blessing upon them, and a word from his son, separated the rituals from the holy climax, the showers of pearls and a burning of the black jewel.

Soon Kuirinua stood before the coals; two natives held the iron chest. He took two steps forward before Ralls got to his feet and cried out: —

"At last, O wise Kuirinua, I have received the message. It is as I thought." Kuirinua, eyeing the crowd, his chief, and then Ralls, narrowed his eyes, and retraced his steps. Ralls continued: "Listen, wise one, and tell me that your ears also hear the mighty voice of Taaro Tiki. Do you not hear the thunder of Po, and lightning, and unkind winds — of parching throats, of fruitless trees, of dying fishes, and birds, and beasts? The winds are yonder, the fire of the sky is there," he pointed, "and the death of many people — it is there — in your basket."

Ralls approached the woven palm leaves, hovering over the tools of the high priest. "Only you, wise one, can hand me the token of evil, the eye of the demon. I command you." He pointed. Mystified, the old man obeyed, jumped about in the fashion of one bewitched — Ralls admired his astuteness — and proclaimed to all the voice of Taaro Tiki.

"Let there be silence," said Ralls. "For I must convey the words to your wise one. Only he can tell you what the winds bring." And into the ear of Kuirinua Ralls spoke, while the great audience, a solid, tense body, heard only the spitting of the embers, the distant rolling of the sea, and the wind in the palms.

2

Mayrant Sidneye grinned. He was well pleased with the message from the gods. Kuirinua had spoken; Taaro Tiki had spoken. The one long, uninterrupted message in monotone was a fierce, exciting revelation: —

"The walls of the heavens are bursting with anger — the new tapu Taaro Tiki has placed upon earthly things holds back the storm, the fire, the drought, the destruction, the dying hand that seeks to lay fingers on our people — no storm shall shake us, no fruit shall be dashed into the sea as long as we pay heed to the voice of the great one. The pearls of the monolith, of the iron chest, have remained in the sacred cavern for a moon, have been watched over by the infidel beast who failed to keep faith with the gods on this day.

"No — never again shall these gems reside in the sacred hollow of the arm of the image of Taaro Tiki — they are doomed to separate one by one from their brothers and fly over the face of the earth, eternally lost to the kind eye of Taaro Tiki —

"Not even the sacred pearl for the sacrifice can escape the tapu —

only the virgin pearls of the sacred cavern can appease his eye — and these shall be gathered one by one during the next moon, during the moons that follow — until at the last moon before the heavy rains, they too shall be cursed and held for the return of the son of Taaro Tiki — and only the son of Taaro Tiki can walk with them — with these in the iron chest — with the black pearl of the cavern. They are his to scatter over the world, to sow among the wriggling unbelievers, to take on the luster of the eye of Taaro Tiki who shall ever watch their destruction.

"Taaro Tiki speaks — he tells us to cremate the eye of the demon and scatter its ashes to the winds — that life shall remain —

"Taaro Tiki has spoken."

So Ralls owned all the pearls; even the big black! And every year more! The *Golden Hind* would stagger under her light load. Even then Jacques heard the muffled boom of the winch lifting the ship's anchor as she made ready for her run with the make of the tide; her rigging whistled in the wind, her sails flapped and bellied and pushed the hull forward — transport for the greatest fortune ever to rise from the sea. His mood was black.

He raised the gin bottle to his lips, drank it dry, then dashed it against the monolith.

His excitement was lost on none; even his mood did not dare interrupt the trailing ceremony. But before long the eye of the octopus was ashes, and the remains were reverently scooped up. Then — before the horde of natives found its feet — he did it.

With pistol in hand Desaix stood on his feet, rocking sidewise to plant his legs solidly, and cried out, "The son of Taaro Tiki is a hoax. He is a wandering scoundrel who has cheated you of your wealth. In the name of the French Republic I hereby place him under arrest. *Vive la France!*"

Ralls, with pouch and chest, turned to stare at the owner of that authoritative voice. Every native, the chief and his consort, Angélique, Mayrant, and every Dutchman there, stared, trying to believe shocked ears. Had not Taaro Tiki spoken? thought each native.

"Ralls," he said evenly, "do you submit to arrest?" He waited in stony silence for an answer. "Or do I have to show these people who bow to you that you can fall like any mortal?"

Mayrant was on his feet and at the Frenchman's side. "Mijnheer Jacques," he said, "I distinctly remember limiting the game to one of wits, not force. Unless you cease such play my offer shall be withdrawn." For answer Jacques pushed him aside.

No more than thirty feet separated the glaring pair.

"For the last time, Ralls." Jacques's gun hand grew taut and a stiffened arm moved into the line with his eye. "Very well, you bastard!" Only the sudden spring of a woman spoiled his aim: Angélique's hand was upon the gun as she hurled her body at her uncle. A shot rang out, reverberated in the sounding box of the enclosure, and died a vibrating death. The flesh of his niece's thumb gushed blood, as did the shoulder of Ralls. Jacques sprang out of the reach of lumbering Noord and raised his gun. But too late — Ralls had drawn the distance between them to nothing.

Before anyone could separate the two they staggered into the circle of coals and beyond the sacred ring. The next sound was the awful cracking of bone against the stone of the gods — bone was the weaker, and the sound was its macabre echo. The Frenchman, taut with hate and blood lust a second before, fell face forward into the glowing embers; a spit and sizzle, a twitching — *danse de la mort*, and —

Jacques Desaix was dead.

Angélique screamed inwardly though not a sound escaped her horrified lips. Only one voice rose in a dismal wail, telling of anguish at its highest.

Haupua would forever know loneliness.

3

Mayrant felt the ringing truth of Ralls's terse words, "I didn't plan that." The tempest had lifted from the son of Taaro Tiki, his show had ended with the pearls and there was no reason for any crude anticlimax. Thus by complete success he was exonerated, and the accident arising from his self-defense was merely the doing of the gods.

And Kuirinua pounced upon the popularity of that trailing coil of reason for all its worth; he built for the gods, and for Kuirinua, a new immortality and power that would remain unchallenged for generations to come; Taaro Tiki had spoken, defiler had met with destruction — who doubted the wrath of Taaro Tiki!

4

The wedding was, of course, postponed. The Dutch captains escorted Angélique to the Villa Desaix after attending her wound, while Ralls and Mayrant boarded the *Golden Hind*. The wireless sought the French seat of the archipelago with a message, and at last they received an answer: —

Regret death of Desaix. *Golden Hind* stand by.

Mayrant, tiring of his chessmen, it seemed, kept the air electrified for the remainder of the night. Soerabaja roused Harmenszoon van Schreeven from sweet slumber, and for hours the business of Batjak raced furiously across the vast sea lanes of the moon-drenched Pacific. Before dawn Suva was graced by the great one's attention; he would send Younguer his ship. Within the hour the *Van Arken* drew in her warps, heaved anchor, and creaked lazily, her helm alee, her close-hauled canvas tacking to starboard, and slid downhill into mighty fathoms. There was a certain beauty in her black smudge as she met the sunrise under full sail. In short minutes she dug into the wind and leaned gracefully, disappearing over the southern horizon with her many sails ever shrinking into one bright orange-yellow speck. She was bound for Fiji under Cordtlaant.

The tricolor was late in meeting the island breeze, though she gave vain ripples all the life of yesterday: the coming and going of her servants neither added to nor subtracted from her perpetuity. But the flag of France flew at half-mast. And the Dutch bars were dipped in similar respect.

While Ralls, the patient soul, seemed not at all concerned about coming into his own. When the time came he would assume his lead with a flourish; until then a fixed *sang-froid* attended his every move. He left the ship early, with no more fear of losing his share of the pearls in her safe than Mayrant had of losing his prize skipper. No word about them, no word of his captaincy, no word about anything, except the solid Dutch and native tale to explain away the death of the island's *chargé d'affaires*. The silence of separation was greeted by both men and each sought his own course without molest from the other, bearing out the fact, or supposition, that one twin personality is boring to the other.

Shortly after noon on the second day a French government schooner broke the southwestern horizon, felt her way inside the cove, and moored to the bamboo piling alongside the gleaming yellow hull of the *Golden Hind*. Ever observing, the lanky governor, clad in civilian white drill and wearing a wide panama, took notice of the flags' positions, as well as the quatrefoils on the mast tip of the *Hind*, and the dazzling brass and layered white of the ship's bulwarks. Trailing the official was a rolypoly caricature of a man in comical shorts and jacket.

Thought Ralls: Is the fat boy the new "Desaix"? But about the death of Desaix, it was deplorable.

"At the lunar month celebration," said Mayrant, "if you'll accept the truth without offense, Mijnheer, Desaix celebrated with abandon. There is no need for detail on that score." He paused, affirmed his own quizzical tone, and leaped the offensive hiatus with a knowing glance.

288

"In a spirited struggle, all in sporting manner, mind you, with my Captain Ralls here, he was thrown against the sacred monolith. His head was cracked." Ralls's bandaged shoulder, when questioned by the official's eye, was accorded three words: "A mere burn."

Debussie, the pudgy fellow, smiled in fatuous manner, voiced a regret he did not feel, and turned a slow eye upon his new domain. From the deck, through a stippled edge of palms, he saw the house on the hillside, and wet his thick lips before sighing. Ralls, more than Mayrant, evinced interest in the new ruler: to him the man meant an annual barrier or a free flow of the pearls of Taaro Tiki; he would court the latter.

And that he did, with Dutch gin, with formal introduction into the royal house of Ua Nuka Havu. The chief, his son, and the high priest were given instructions to pamper the new Frenchman, to extoll the son of Taaro Tiki at every opportunity, and — at the approach of the moon that should bring the son of Taaro Tiki into the cove in his gold water chariot, they must rob him of all alcoholic beverages: a thirsty soul would better appreciate the full larder of the gods.

The investigation fizzled out, the formality of a wake taking its place. The French schooner chased the sunset out of the cove, running away from her own shadow, taking with her the draped body of the ex-ruler of the emerald lagoon. Debussie, the puppet ruler, was last seen by the real czar of the island, the son of Taaro Tiki, lolling his indulged body in the triangular hammock overlooking the placid stretch of the Polynesian atoll.

And the *Golden Hind* lifted her anchor with the next tide and slipped laughingly into the slope of the sea. Captain Ralls, elbows on the stern rail, winked fond adieu — but not a last good-by — as the fringe of palms became a black mass, and then a tiny line that dropped into the bulky waste of the Pacific.

CHAPTER XXVI

1

THE lonesome archival vault in the long white building in Soerabaja held more than a score of huge leather-bound ledgers, into which was written the seasoned truth about Batjak's ships, crews, cargoes — and masters. To each ship a ledger, to each captain his just dues, the ever-steady hand of Vee Vossler ascribed in slow, painstaking neatness, his pen dipping into the well and scratching off words that smelled of spice and pitch, of steam and quatrefoils, of sails and blood.

To cover the travels of the *Golden Hind* under Ralls a million words could hardly suffice. The brevity of Vossler's entries — his pen a mammoth wine press, which he fed with details of events and corresponding facts to reap the juice of compressed data in blunt Dutch — best serves to chase down the story of Ralls. The man who sailed into the lagoon a fugitive from sharks, who sailed out of it a captain, has found proper introduction; he therefore pulls fancy from the factual pages of the ledger of the *Golden Hind*, throwing upon the screen of one's eye a between-the-lines story. But Vossler's annotations serve a purpose — they serve to bridge a yawning gap.

The entries began on page twenty-nine, the foregoing pages having to do with the ship herself, her speed, tonnage, clearance, size, cost, equipment, crew, signals, the names of her crew, her papers, her underwriters, and other factual data necessary to her history. Only one page bearing these words, "Sailing at Sidneye's orders," and dittoed down the page with the ship's position, marked the captaincy of Cordtlaant; the right column was filled with figures of her mounting expense from week to week, and under these figures at the bottom she surprisingly claimed the black ink of profit, with a brief mention of her strange cargo: "Rum to Oahu, T.H." It was no wonder she sailed light back across the international date line, standing down to five degrees before pointing westward and south to flank the Gilberts. Vossler said nothing about that but his packed entry said as much between the lines; it said more: Batjak played the game of tag in running rum.

Up to that mark on the page, the *Van Arken* under the tempestuous Captain Younguer claimed the ledger of highest profit, of unprecedented turbulence. But her star seemed dimmed as the colorful *Hind* grew to the feet of her new captain, who pressed her for more sail through squall and swelling sea, through patches of steamy sunshine, and into the remote islands of strange but on-the-line profits. The first entry, date prefixed: —

10–12–1925: Trouble procuring master's papers for Ralls. British, French, Americans revoked same in '23 and '24. P.O.B. set in motion, wins. Cargo, pearls. Position between 155 and 128 degrees west of Greenwich. Sidneye aboard. Crew impressed with Ralls's daring at source of pearls; further impressed by gift of pearl to every member of crew.

Golden Hind's prospects good. Angélique Desaix aboard.

1–11–1926: Wool Sydney via Soerabaja — cinchona, gin, tea via Davao to San Francisco. Ralls wins annual top prize over Younguer. Latter in bad mood. Ralls arrested in Honolulu for beating agent. Ship off course en route to San Francisco — reasonable — Vancouver anchorage. Six passengers to Papeete. Profitable report on voyage to date. Position Papeete. Sailing on 14th for Suva, Auckland. Sidneye no longer aboard *Golden Hind*.

2–19–1926: *Golden Hind* ordered to hold Suva. Trouble in Papeete.

3–10–1926: Position Suva. Trouble grows in French Islands. Ralls charged. Sidneye, angry, threatens Ralls with dismissal. Ralls wires challenge. Van Schreeven, Vossler, Batjoek, advise hasty discharge. Sidneye overrules, boards steamer *Van Dyke* under Capt. Cordtlaant for Suva.

3–18–1926: Ralls held in Papeete by French to face charges. Trial for beating Canadian girl (passenger from Vancouver) in Moorea under way. American writer and four Tahiti boatmen witnesses. Sadism belief grows.

4–1–1926: Sidneye procures native chief, son, and high priest from source of pearls to influence testimony of boatmen. Success. Charges beaten. Month lost to ship. Sidneye charges expense of ship to Ralls's account. Complete expenses not tabulated as yet — enormous. Ship sails from Suva to Soerabaja.

7–10–1926: *Golden Hind* all quiet. Position 19 degrees E. Long. 159.4 degrees S. Lat. Near Iles Chesterfield. No cargo. Free route to captain. Van Schreeven displeased.

7–29–1926: No word from ship. Last position of 7–10–1926.

8–11–1926: Somehow *Golden Hind* strikes fabulous windfall off Marion Reef 19.2 degrees E. Long. 152.7 degrees S. Lat. Gold. Australian Board of Trade intercepts. More hearings. Ralls follows trouble, but also luck. Sidneye, jubilant, rushes to Brisbane. Van Schreeven reprimands Ralls for unprecedented silence. Ralls retaliates, word for word. *Van Arken* in trouble on Great Barrier Reef — *Hind* sails to rescue; Younguer refuses aid from Ralls. Trouble between these skippers looms. Must route them widely apart.

10–20–1926: *Golden Hind* reports large harvest of pearls from "Feast of Moon." Position somewhere near Iles de la Société. Exactness precluded.

1–11–1927: *Golden Hind*, despite heavy expenses charged against Ralls — "Papeete Folly" — produced more than twice the profit of the *Van Arken*. Even van Schreeven pleased. Ralls wealthy man from share in Marion Reef find, half share in famous 1925 pearl find, and smaller 1926 harvest. Sidneye proposes a partnership in Batjak; van Schreeven, Batjoek, frown. Vossler hesitant. Perhaps he will go on his own — no reason for his doing otherwise, says Sidneye. Too stormy, claims van Schreeven, to last as lone wolf. Unanimous denial of Sidneye's proposal. No action by Sidneye.

1–20–1927: Matter dropped. Ship under repair at home port.

The years that followed were less turbulent; nothing sensational in profits, except for the pearls of the South Sea lagoon, and the mysterious disappearance of a sail reefer aboard the *Golden Hind*. Younguer, fifteen years older than Ralls, swore he lived to rid the firm, and perhaps the world, of the devil aboard the *Hind*. But such talk was given the smile, by Mayrant, and the firm forgot Younguer's complaints when long overdue news reached every ship of Batjak: —

Flags and banners at half-mast — Stefan Meer is dead.

2

Angélique welcomed the wrinkled old lady to the Sidneye palace high in the hills some twenty miles south of Soerabaja. And Zulinde Meer, smiling and sighing in her pensive gaze over the years, was quite happy to have had Stefan in even the long winter of their lives; in the quiet and peace of the strangest love, and often defined the sweetest, that holds through senility. She gazed over the foothills from the running veranda of arched stone columns and marble floor, smiling at the city of Soerabaja winking in the morning mists.

"Down there lies Stefan. I am content to remain here and watch over him." Every morning for six months she had said the same.

The sight of her tugged at a tear in Angélique's eye. How sweet was old age like hers; one thought, one mind, ever searching out the trivial million and one tiny threads woven into that major premise of undying love; one thought, one long season of accretion, like a tree of coral, its every pore a throbbing life until it meets with the drying sun to lose all color and pulse and retain only its bleached skeletons.

Even in the violet cast of her thin hair, in the slow blue of her kind eyes, in the welter of soft lines in a soft face, and the thin, yellow stretch of skin over long fingers, an echo of Zulinde's vibrant youth lingered in faint aureole. The white canvas, the towering masts of the *Quatrefoil*, were a part of her, and she a part of them — the good girl of the sea had supposedly gone in storm, while the lingering old lady, for whom she sailed first and last, for love and revenge, sailed on in the roadstead to peace; but of her was the ship, Stefan's ship, Mayrant's ship, the ship of retribution for Herr Streicher, the ship that pioneered an empire. Thus all that was Batjak was her child, and in reverence to its mother it dipped its quatrefoils in every tropic sea.

"Yes," she said, "I belong with Mayrant and his. With you, my dear, and your child."

"Yes," murmured Angélique. "Your Stefan would have it that way."

She turned her face to Angélique. Blossoming under a spontaneous smile she said, "Indeed. For I have my namesake to watch over. And where is she?"

"With her dolls in the nursery. When I left she was telling her Nina doll the story of the three bears."

Zulinde cackled. "My little Zulinde. What a child she is for a two-and-a-half year. If I didn't know Mayrant so well, I'd say he thought more of her than his *Golden Hinds* and *Van Arkens*."

"How silly, Auntie Zully! He loves his ships and his men, but he worships her." She laughed, more in welcome to Zulinde's lighter mood than at her own chance for playful scolding.

"*Ja*. And who wouldn't! Even the old shellface, van Arken, warms to her. That then is something." Again she laughed.

"That — indeed," laughed Angélique. "Until she was born he never smiled."

"And why should he?" snapped Zulinde. She had taken her chair and her sewing, and her words were addressed to her lap. "A man who has spent ten years over a stinking hobby like leprosy doesn't deserve to smile. It's like I tell him — 'Dokter,' I say, 'you and Mayrant are a couple of *Nederlander kameel* who talk about opposite this and that, about nodular and maculo-anesthetic, and chaulmoogra oil, and sodium, and the like.' And I say, 'What good is another bow from the world of science when you waste your life away without seeing or feeling the beauty of the universe?' And he — Angélique, sweet, ring the bell for my maid; I've no yellow thread — he says to me, stiff as a Prussian goose-step, 'We can save lives, I hope.' But I know his humor. Also, my dear, I know him. It isn't lives to save. *Neen!* It's fame for his own callous heart." She laughed, jocularity riding over mild contempt.

"Are you adding lace to the sleeves, or —"

"Now that is an idea!" exclaimed Zulinde. "You French run to frills, don't you? Well, if you do, so should your vain daughter. Lace it is."

"I am an American, Auntie Zully," corrected Angélique.

"So is the wild hellion of the *Golden Hind*," returned Zulinde. "But I guess the French and Americans are on a par when it comes to brains."

"Complimentary, of course," laughed the other.

"*Ja*," came the answer, persiflage-coated. "But yonder comes the mail. I hope Harmenszoon and Teleia are writing me. Since I left Bali I've been spoiled — a letter a day and a visit weekly. And Harmenszoon — as handsome as ever. Stefan loved the boy as much as he loathed him at first. And I was not the least surprised when he left Teleia a quarter of his fortune. Nor was I surprised when Christiaan Vossler, or should I say Father Vossler, got another quarter slice." She talked on at random, sewing slowly, enjoying every moment, and every word.

Angélique, quite content to listen, leaned back in a blue-flowered chaise longue, one arm hanging limply at her side, the other caressing the smooth silk of her kabaja.

"Childbirth," said the needleworker, "is an experience for a beauty like yourself, my dear. You were a smooth-petaled rose in bud before little Zulinde. And now the rose is opened. Indeed, you're more beautiful than the frail hothouse rose that spent a honeymoon in Denpasar; and having her plumped you into a glorious state. But I'm not a garrulous flatterer. *Neen.* I'm merely adding one and one for making two, my dear." She raised an eye filled with suggestion.

"You're suggesting I get plump again," Angélique accused. There was no answer from Zulinde, whose needle claimed the soft cunning of her eye. "I haven't forgotten the tightness of my breasts. And Zulinde kicked and squirmed for long days before she was born."

"Of course, she wasn't worth that," the old lady said facetiously. "There's no reason for Mayrant to want a boy."

"Of course not," said Angélique. "Except that I'll be gaining weight again — very soon."

Slowly the needle hand relaxed into the soft fabric in the other.

"Lord of Heaven," whispered Zulinde. "You sweet child! You love Mayrant, don't you? How wonderful that you know it, how much sweeter that he knows, and" — she gazed into the past — "how glorious is your union."

Angélique listened, repeated in silence those last words. Guiltily she said them over and over. The first child had just happened, almost as if she were self-conceived; she had given Mayrant's embrace the surface warmth of a luxury that was soulless. At first he was but an artless savage, but only because of her schooled aversion to intimacy with any man. But as she saw, felt, and heard the sincere outpouring of his lonely soul, she became tolerant, and kind, and loving. And then — when he discovered her growing tepidness, he was further energized, and his moods were long and clamorous — she surrendered herself upon his altar of passion, finding that distant, exquisitely vague splendor of a god's holiday. She embraced the freedom from Ralls and turned to the simple and peaceful façades of wifehood. Out of that beauty, that freedom from responsibility, life was sweet, and the blossom sprouted from the seed. Tiny Zulinde Sidneye was born of love.

The obstreperous past had not died; of late she sensed its return. Why, she did not know, but there it was, like a black horizon against a peaceful sea.

So she sought to build a wall around her future: she coaxed into her flesh another life.

"I hope it is a boy for him," she said, low and indistinct. "I do so want to make him a good wife, Auntie Zully."

It was then the tears of youth jumped the span to linger in a corner of an eye past its three score and ten; It was Zulinde Meer who peered through the northern mists at the sunny patches of youth; her gaze, too, was dimmed, for she had journeyed far beyond the limits of a true backward glance. Youth spoke its language, and she was content to wonder.

Blessed spring; blessed winter.

But neither knew that in that moment the hand of Vee Vossler was inking in a page of the ledger dedicated to the *Golden Hind*. Neither knew that he frowned as he wrote the following: —

6-11-1929: The area given the *Golden Hind* begins at the 150th meridian at 10 degrees S. Long., running north from that tip of Papua and west, where the route dips beyond the Ellice Islands to follow the international date line, standing down it beyond Tonga to 30 degrees S. Long. Thus the ship has free run of the Japanese, Australian, and French Mandated Islands over a great stretch of the Pacific. The *Hind*, according to Captain Ralls's wire, is forced to do business in Suva, Fiji, promising not to molest any business stirred into profit by Captain Younguer of the *Van Arken*. His last wire reads: "Sailing to Suva."

Nor did the two women know that Vee Vossler lowered his pen and moved to another table to open a similar ledger. His frown deepened as he eyed the dossiers at hand; he pursed his lips and heaved a sigh as he began to write into the records of the *Van Arken*.

6–11–1929: The wire from Captain Ralls relayed to Captain Younguer of *Van Arken*, requesting this violation of a rule be met with patience. Sidneye advises Younguer to stand by in Caledonia. Younguer advises he must sail on twelfth to Fiji or lose a cargo. His second message follows: —

"If it means my dismissal, I am moving to Suva. I have no objection to *Golden Hind* making port en route, or obeying orders for lifting rush cargoes or odd specialties. But Ralls's deal with the English firm of Manchester Ward, Ltd. is premeditated robbery. One of your ships is destined to lose a captain."

3

The *Van Arken*, well into Kandavu Passage, the roadstead to Suva, swung slowly round to portside, trembling and giving voice to every piece of tackle in her rigging, her stanchions leaning with her shift into the push of the wind, her sails cracking and doubling before her bow squared to leeward. The wind flattened a sailor against a ratline as the grinning helmsman shot the wheel and paused to eye him while lifting his serene gaze to the weather clew. Her cordage creaked and wailed, and her sleepy wake grew from a thin straight line to a wide lather of sea foam green full down the starboard side. In a moment, it seemed, her sail was set for the wind on her tail and she bolted forward, scudding like a true daughter of Neptune, her stern light and free.

Wilde Younguer, standing forward amidships, dipped his eyes from the converging masts and sheets and walked aft. Fiji lay dead ahead, Mbengga off the port bow, Kandavu to the port quarter, Suva Point meeting the thin eye of the bowsprit; the reefs on either side of Levu

Passage would soon meet the ship if the wind held; and the trade was deep, said his weather eye. Ralls would run down Nanuku Passage into the Koro Sea and, judging from his own bag of tricks, he should by now be skirting the southern Ringgold Islands. But it was of real importance to get there ahead of Ralls. He spread his thin lips into a tight grin and peered at the belly of the canvas.

He carried his years lightly. The owner of the *Alice Macdonald* at twenty, and a great admirer of Mayrant Ruysdaal Sidneye from the day when his slattern ketch became Japanese property, his life had been that of a stouthearted adventurer and trader. Under Mayrant and Lidj van der Glotz — poor Lidj had died off the New Guinea swamp coast with fever in nineteen hundred and ten — he learned seamanship, rising from a novice to a master who knew no peer at pressing canvas into greedy knots; from Mayrant and Batjoek he absorbed the patience, cunning, and diplomacy — and fire — that makes the down-under trader. He swore and raged, drank and sought women, all with moderation, though to his mood of a moment, of a day or week, he dedicated his every ounce of energy. He carried in his face a legible placard — *tread lightly on me* — and in every pub from Singapore to Suva men moved before its silent voice.

Blue, ringing blue, eyes flashed eternally from squint-wrinkled lids; he frowned easily, evenly, and, it seemed, constantly. He was neither forward nor diffident, and his face declared as much, just as his sensitive thin nose, with its close, nervous nostrils, and thinner lips shouted of his capriciousness. This trait — inconstancy — was however his stock in trade: he was mollified only by exercising a whim, be it running before the winds of a squall or cheating natives and traders. Cautious though bold, unruffled yet vitriolic, with no code but his own and that of the lazy, grasping tropics, he met the world with valiant shoulders and an easy step, carelessly challenging. He was roughly handsome to some, to others commonplace, and to a few notoriously trite. Wilde Younguer was Wilde Younguer, a well-known unknown quantity. He was, like most sons of Adam, inexorably bound to his own channel of life, expatiating upon his profits and pleasures, and ever minimizing his own frailties. But like his ship he would retain a proud bearing even in the suck and eddy of his last lonely moments.

And the proud ship plowed toward Levu Passage under full sail. No standing off and tacking in for the *Van Arken;* she pulled close, creaking and roaring in the wind before reefing sail. She went through with a bit in her teeth and leaned to starboard, her captain leaning all the while on the bow scanning the harbor as it came into view. He raised a hand to his chin in meditative fashion, rubbed at his sandy stubble and voiced a steaming oath.

The *Golden Hind* had won the race; she was moored, her sails furled, her yellow image dancing in the lapping brine like a jeering Chinese god. Wilde Younguer could afford his whimsies, he reflected, as he brushed past the swinging door of O'Bryan's pub. If he lost, no wife and kids would shower his grave with tears, and the few affected drops from the eyes of blond Nelly Duke or Copper-top Anne, or the Mexican doll, Inez Florencio Herrera, would keep the flowers alive for an hour perhaps. Then, as he put it, "Last curtain, last act. Play forgotten."

O'Bryan's came to life with the town: it yawned and emptied its fetid mouth at siesta, snoozed to the drone of its flies for a couple of lazy hours, awoke yapping and stretching, snapping its eyes at some object as if to determine where it left off, and slowly breathed up an appetite for swill and jazz, for an occasional round of fisticuffs, or knives. Then, mopping up its blood amid laughter and tears, and dousing the spot with a smelly disinfectant, it went about its life with iniquitous serenity, giving layers to its tempo until swift sunset met raucous evening. There arrogant Englishmen rubbed elbows with beachcombers, sailors, shipping clerks, shippers, the town's shopkeepers, and vaunted men of the sea.

To the latter class belonged the master of the *Van Arken*. His entry was like the boom of canvas meeting a spirited trade breeze. Straight to the bar he strode, the cynosure of all eyes. He was well known to Suva, since his narrow escape from death and imprisonment was written into the city's records when he resisted arrest on a smuggling charge.

"On the house, this one, Cap'n," said the plump, cherubic barkeep, O'Bryan himself.

"Thanks," returned Younguer morosely.

"And the next one is on me." The voice came from behind him. He turned about: Ralls. Their eyes locked for the duel of prodigious flashes; hate and appraisal flashed concurrently before dismal warnings; the contempt of one for the other, irreversible triumph seeking to drain the other of vigor, generated nothing more than a lengthened clashing of mettle.

"Sure," said Younguer, smooth as silk.

O'Bryan sauntered off, flashing surreptitious glances at the pair as they fell to their drinks. A distinguished Britisher of middle age, in immaculate whites and American panama, lifted his whisky and bitters and gazed at the pair because they reminded him of another pair he had seen somewhere; a slattern bleary-eyed moocher edged closer, seeking conversation with O'Bryan; an American tourist, pompous and giggle-tight, condescended to give the bum his bottle — it gratified his sense of importance and gave his ears something to take back home; a black boy no more than five, and well tanked, tapped the bar and wailed for another glass; the astonished tourist giggled and tossed the grimy child a cigar before voicing thickly, to the bum, his aversion to juvenile delinquency. The bum, of course, added garrulous support to such opinion, and fell into a story that ran the length of the bottle.

"I was sure your black tub would lumber in today," said Ralls. "She needs the kinks out of her hull, Captain."

"Yeah," said Younguer. "And how does the yellow *Hind* ride?"

"Proud and fast — like her skipper," returned Ralls. "Drink up, Captain, or am I supposed to slow down in honor of old age?"

"Like her skipper," mused the other. "You're right, Ralls. And I've heard the *Hind* called all sorts of names." His eyes stared dreamily into the shark's teeth decorating the back bar. "But we won't fall out over a little thing like opinion, eh, Ralls? We'll do it over bigger things."

"Of course. Any suggestions?"

"Well — now there could be. The case of the Manchester Ward cargo, for instance. That is more important than one sailor calling another names."

"To you, Captain Younguer, sir, a cargo is second only to a lady named Herrera. But, of course, how well she suits the word 'lady' is a matter of opinion."

"A matter of opinion, surely, for how else is a decent woman's name dragged in the dirt?" Younguer sipped, gleaning more intoxication from the sparring than from his cups.

"By association, I reckon," said Ralls, adding: "with skippers of black boats with sails."

Younguer replied casually, "You're good at dodging an issue."

After a moment of silence, Ralls said pensively, "Manchester Ward. Now that firm has a future — and I always look ahead."

"So do I. In this case I'm ten years ahead of you."

Ralls turned slowly, his eyes serious. "You *were* ahead of me, Captain. But seniority doesn't replace industry under Batjak — unless Sidneye has gone soft of late."

They slugged on, through one bottle which Ralls paid for, and on into the second, giving zealously, taking hard blows without flinching. Since their words were held to conversational tone the eyes of O'Bryan dimmed perceptibly, and his steady customers slumped back into their chairs, leaned against the tables to snooze, growl, or dream. The tourist vanished through the monotonous swinging exit, the bum on his heels. The five-year-old Fiji slipped into a corner and watered the floor, his young stomach clicking off timed hiccups.

Ralls, like Younguer, spoke into the mirror, eyeing the other there at infrequent intervals. "And I said to Sidneye," said Ralls, " 'He's not much of a seaman to try running the *Arken* through the Great Barrier Reef.' "

Younguer jerked his eyes from the mirror and faced Ralls squarely. "Yeah, Ralls, that seems to be your trouble. You're forever boasting about your standing with Sidneye."

"Boasting? I never boast, Captain."

Younguer replied, smiling scornfully, "Of course not. Why, I should apologize, Ralls. A man with your brand of arrogance doesn't know when he's boasting." Then his smile faded. "But your luck won't last forever. Then what will Sidneye think of his pet?"

"Pet?" Ralls lifted his brow. "So that's it. I might have known."

"Wait, Ralls!" said Younguer hurriedly. "Nobody gives a damn about your being Sidneye's little darling, or the woman beater that even Dokter van Arken couldn't cure, so it's rumored, after six months on the *Hind* — we're at odds concerning another matter, one that wouldn't exist if you'd kept out of my trade area."

"We'd be real chummy otherwise — is that what you mean, Captain?" Ralls chuckled. "That being the case, why the display of childish temper when I offered you aid at the Barrier Reef? Answer that — liar." But Younguer chose to glare in silence. "No, even then you dropped a few remarks about ridding the seas of me.

"Well, better men than you have tried."

"I'm not so sure about that, Ralls. But down to business. Do you think Sidneye actually approves of your lifting another captain's cargo?"

"You got Batjak's message, didn't you? He advised you to stand by in Caledonia, didn't he? It seems Sidneye approves, old man."

Younguer shook his head with pity and incredulity. "Ralls, Batjak sent me your wire. Here it is, and it says, 'I am forced to do business in Suva. I promise not to molest any business which Captain Younguer has stirred into profit.' " He raised his eyes to Ralls. "So Sidneye approves a damn lie, does he? Not that it makes any difference to me — since I sent the last wire. Too bad they failed to send you my answer."

"Well, Captain Younguer, even with all cards up, I continue to say Sidneye approves. And it's his approval that galls you, not the loss of a nice cargo — which is now being put aboard the better ship."

"We'll see, Ralls. Which ship is better depends, after all, on which of us is the better captain."

"Now I can't argue with you there," said Ralls. "Too bad you're not right oftener. If you had been you'd have been less jealous of my industry which won, and continues to win, the annual top prize. Nor would you have nursed envy of Sidneye's respect for the best captain on the seas."

"Damn, Ralls. The trouble you take to cover a lie. And a lie it is, except for a very important fact — you don't know when to stop. This trip of yours is only the beginning. And if Sidneye backs you, you'll think you own the Pacific."

"With his backing — which I've got — I can own plenty," Ralls said, smiling derisively.

"Sure. Sure. And that being the case, it's time somebody helped correct the bigwig's mistakes."

"Well, as I said, Captain, the cargo is now being put aboard the better ship. That should offer you a good beginning."

Younguer's eyes thinned. "Ralls, that's just what I was thinking. Suppose we get down to brass tacks."

"I've been waiting patiently, old man. I'm sorry your tale of woe hasn't aroused my sympathy."

"So I'm an old man asking for sympathy! Well, you'll find out — and goddam quick — you're off course there. You're good at abusing the weak. Now let's see how you hold up against the strong."

Ralls laughed at the other's rising anger; he said, in an effort to send it soaring, "Won't Sidneye chuckle when I tell him about this?"

With a mighty effort Younguer bridled his wrath and said in a voice low and calm: —

"At eighteen degrees south, Ralls, and one seventy-nine west, there's an island named Nayau — almost a hundred and fifty miles due east of here. Beyond the island, past Lakemba Passage, are tiny dots, the Lau Group." A cigarette was jammed between his lips and lighted, his eyes remaining in fixed position, full into Ralls's.

"Yeah, I know them," said Ralls.

"There's little traffic over there and what there is won't have too many eyes and ears."

"Continue, Captain."

"And there are dots that afford a perfect setting for what I have in mind." He grinned. "Just we two, Ralls, just we two. The ships can lie off and make bets."

"Bets — on what?" Ralls inquired, grinning.

"On which of us shall return," said Younguer soberly.

4

Late in July of 'twenty-nine, Vee Vossler pulled a leather-bound ledger into position and made the following entry: —

> A new captain has been named for the ship. The successor to the deceased was suggested by Batjoek and confirmed by unanimous vote. The affair has been hushed (each man aboard the ships received an extra bonus of one hundred guilders) and no repercussions, other than suspicion, have been heard to date: the *Golden Hind* and *Van Arken* cleared Suva on July 12 for a rendezvous in the Lau Group at 18 degrees S. Lat. and 178.2 degrees W. Long. Arriving with the sunrise after plowing a running squall the two captains, Ralls and Younguer, rowed from their ships toward a tiny islet, rising some twenty feet from the water — and disappeared. The time they landed, 7:00 A.M. The crews actually placed bets running into several hundred guilders. At 9:54 one boat was seen leaving the island, towing the other and rowing against a heavy sea. Upon his return the bruised and bleeding victor said the other had fallen into the sea in a school of sharks. Hoaglaand Rostaars's experience warrants his captaincy of the *Van Arken*.

Thus the *Golden Hind* ruled the vast Pacific from the Philippines to Easter Island, from Tasmania at forty below to San Francisco at almost forty above, a free lance of white sail above white bulwarks and yellow hull. Her priority in cargoes, her air of pomp — together with the very mention of her name — caused twenty Batjak captains, among them Cordtlaant and Noord, to slant their minds toward murder.

But that was in the year of 'twenty-nine, before the world-wide debacle of finance, before the *Golden Hind* met with the unexpected.

A hundred men prayed for the day when his power would be broken, when Sidneye's eyes would see the real Ralls. Even Vee Vossler ventured an opinion; to the tail of a page given to the ship's exploits, he added a personal note: —

> I think Ralls is the most hated man I have ever known.

5

Ralls left the *Golden Hind* moored to the pilings of her home nest in Soerabaja, and, in the company of his chief mate, a fawning fellow named Rodriguez, headed for the general offices of the firm. In due time he sat before Vossler, Batjoek, and van Schreeven, declaring his cargo and expense in detail. He gulped huge quantities of gin into his climax, got out of his chair when all routine lay in the wake, and sent Rodriguez away. No word was spoken as he again resumed his seat. Vossler's glance to van Schreeven merely emphasized the fact that the captain's will was his ceremony, typically, basically, eternally.

"Gentlemen," he said, "what are your orders?"

"They're quite incomplete, Captain Ralls," said van Schreeven, laughing pleasantly. "But, of course, the full cargo lists will be sent in by all agents tomorrow or the day after." He added a gentle reprimand, "As you should know." A free roamer hunting windfalls was not his idea of a stout business arrangement, and the very fact that Sidneye tolerated the adventuring had gone against the grain. True, the fellow had found more than his share of luck; he had pranced off with the coveted prize four times successively; he had earned more for the firm than any two ships, but — there was something unstable about the very structure of the arrangement. There was a quiet undercurrent of absolute distrust which van Schreeven dedicated to Ralls himself; and the future must one day overtake the past, like steam over sails.

"But I sail tomorrow," said Ralls peremptorily.

"There is no need for shortening your stay, Captain Ralls. Your ship no doubt needs repairs."

"I keep my ship in perfect shape," came the sharp answer. "And I sail with the evening tide tomorrow. Get life into your agents, sir."

Van Schreeven held to his veneered smile, saying, "Any other orders, Mijnheer?"

"Yes, Mijnheer van Schreeven. Get yourself another skipper for the *Hind* after this trip. I'm buying an Australian windjammer the day I complete this last run."

"My congratulations, Captain," the silky voice returned. "At last we shall meet worthy competition in the Fiji-Society group."

"Perhaps I'll not remain so far from my friends of Batjak."

"We should enjoy your company, Captain Ralls. My guess, however, was based on your success beyond one hundred and seventy Longitude. Of course, Captain —"

The door opened to admit Mayrant, Angélique, and their daughter, causing Harmenszoon's words to trail off unheard. Ralls, like the others, was on his feet, accepting the strong handclasp of Sidneye, his greeting of word and expression that was both sincere and warm. Angélique stood decorously aside holding onto Zulinde's hand, eyeing Ralls strangely underneath her surface smile.

"*Bon jour*, Monsieur Ralls," she said when his eyes traveled from Mayrant to her feet, then climbed to lock with hers.

"*Bon jour, ma chère. Oui! Enchanté!*"

She laughed, and Mayrant said, "Is there a tongue you can't butcher, Ralls?"

"Russian and Japanese floor me," he returned.

"And we're rolling out a Dutch carpet for you, Ralls," said Mayrant, beaming. "You're coming out to Weltevreden Villa for the night."

Van Schreeven, smiling, said, "But, Mayrant, perhaps you haven't heard. Captain Ralls is lifting anchor tomorrow evening. He's in quite a hurry — can't wait for cargo estimates."

"Humor him," laughed Mayrant. "Can't afford to lose our captain."

"But we are losing him," van Schreeven said, admirably cloaking a note of joy. "This, he says, is his last voyage for Batjak."

The bald dome slowly turned toward Ralls, the elated face losing its spontaneity before the rush of a bewildered frown. He asked why, and van Schreeven voiced terse words that had to do with an Australian windjammer. So the expected had risen to its moment — Ralls was to sail on his own. To a man of power possessiveness is a fault, particularly when a prize asserts independence; and thus Ralls's departure was almost desertion — it was treason. Sidneye's next words were typical of the man: —

"Then relieve him at once, Harmenszoon. Let's not detain Mijnheer Ralls."

"As you like," said Ralls. "I was only running out the year for the prize."

"Which," said van Schreeven evenly, "it seems you've already won."

Vossler, his face expressionless, said nothing.

"Then," said the sullen ruler, "if the prize is his, and he hasn't the gumption to hold the pearls for his own, let him complete the year. See that his trip is not hampered by our agents."

Angélique was glad. "But, of course, you'll spend the night with us," she said.

Batjoek, if he thought in terms of most men, viewed the scene with pagan indifference. The favorite's flag was already flying at half-mast; God speed the day when its lofty silk could be torn from the masts that were created for quatrefoils.

The door closed behind the visitors. Van Schreeven sat down and poured from a chilled container into three glasses — Batjoek's, Vossler's, and his own — and he eyed the liquid in brief silence, and said: "To the future, Mijnheers. May it be soon."

Ten minutes later young Hekkin entered; glancing nervously about for any signs of unburned bridges, he sat back and heaved a sigh of relief. Yes, he'd welcome a stiff finger of gin. The third was sloshing inside him before his tongue was primed for his tale. He smiled shrewdly, lifting one corner of his lips and screwing one eye tight with the fat of his cheek. Slowly he opened up.

"We made anchorage at Nouméa, standing off for the tide to make." For the better part of an hour he talked, drinking slowly, his lips reaching for sips long before a series of words linked into a single revelation. "And pulling sail into Java —"

He paused, leaned forward, and said: "Mijnheers, you know enough of Captain Ralls to feel the hush of a storm when he stands the rail." A nod of assent followed. "Well, he did it, last evening."

To remain vigilant under such warning could only give exercise to wisdom. But a ship, a port, a hellish adventurer, evoked questions without answers. Nor could the four have ever spotted the path of that hurricane born on the rail of the *Golden Hind* as she stood down to Soerabaja.

CHAPTER XXVII

1

OLD Semeroe peak, standing twelve thousand feet in the dying shafts of a Java sun, held their eyes with its splendor; a full moon rose above the horizon. Angélique, in the swift twilight, gave thought to his presence: Ralls shouldn't have accepted their invitation; Mayrant shouldn't have voiced it, and she should not be alone with him in the garden. The moonlight must find her nestled close to Mayrant. She thought of her daughter and her child in the making.

Ralls met the last fusing of color in the west with reverent eye, turning from the crimson ashes to stare at her in silence. Then the tropical night, hammering home its fierceness, fell with breathtaking speed. The hills rolled under lame shadows and the inflected rays of a heavy moon lent a pearl mist to the rooftops of kampongs down the slope.

Her haste called for plausible excuse: "I must see about my daughter, Ralls. Her bedtime."

"Then I'll await your return," he said.

"Ralls." She addressed him in a frantic and tremulous tone — there was little to be gained by prolonging the inevitable. "Ralls. I — I — shall not be back. Don't you understand?"

He merely stood there, quiet, contained, staring at her. The moon painted half his face. The jaunty set of his cap reminded her of a crown for the son of Taaro Tiki. The longer she stood there the swifter seemed her transport to the emerald lagoon, where he sat watching the divers, ruling the placid circle of canoes and outriggers in silence.

"Ralls," she murmured in self-defense, "say something."

"I love you, Angélique, I have come to take you away."

"No," she said evenly, "I cannot. I told you then — that evening in Ua Nuka Havu's hut."

"And I laughed, Angélique," he said, failing to smile. "I'd laugh now — only it's different."

"Quite," she returned.

"I wanted you then but I had myself to conquer. But now I'm almost free, and with you I can win. I have no choice, Angélique. I must take you with me."

She backed away from him in trepidation: it was not Ralls of whom she was afraid, rather it was Angélique, and the awful aftermath. He stalked her, and when she stumbled his arms went about her, drawing her soft, warm body ever closer. She stiffened in resistance, not to the son of Taaro Tiki, but to the loss of her child, the innocent, spontaneous Zulinde. Then came tears. They gushed from eyes that gazed upon a dispirited mother whose choice of death must come before relinquishing the precious fruit of her womb. Every whimper of her child was a part of her flesh. And strangely, but certainly, the child did not belong with a mother who went with Ralls.

"No, Ralls, I cannot go. Zulinde —"

"Your child? Then she will become our child."

"No! Let me loose, Ralls. Please —" A whimper escaped her lips. "And, Ralls, I'm to have another."

"Then we shall have two," he said. His face was close to hers and his grasp was strong.

"Are you merciless, Ralls? You'd take Mayrant's children away from him? No. I would never know a moment of peace."

"Then," he said, "I shall take you."

Out of the gloom a voice reached their ears. "Take her where, Ralls?" They turned sharply to see Mayrant Sidneye advancing in the moonlight. The eerie shafts fell atop the stretched skin in a grotesque dance and settled down into his sparkling, virulent eyes. Ralls relaxed his hold, and Angélique, sobbing, ran to Mayrant.

Not once did he look at her, so intense were the flowing shafts of fire he sent to Ralls. Then with a swift motion of his arms he caught her and flung her to the ground. There she lay at his feet, sobbing pitifully.

"So they were right," said Mayrant. "All of them." His lack of emphasis, like his easy smile, was deadly. "I should kill you, Ralls, but I won't. That is too good for you."

Ralls, for once, was minus that insurmountable wall of cynicism. He seemed to possess the humble soul of a mortal, compassionate, dutiful, and repentant. Mayrant felt his sincere condescension. But murder lacked that quality of self-appeasement; it left a gnawing hunger that was but a lengthened regret for failure to employ torture. He longed for the transcendental sweetness of his victim on the rack. He grinned. A Batjak blackball would serve as a beginning.

"Mr. Sidneye," said Ralls, "I love her. But can't you see she loves you? You are a fool, Mayrant Sidneye, if you let her lie there and lick your boots." Then his mood changed. His voice rose, like the thunder rolling over a vast expanse of trembling waves. "Pick her up!" he shouted.

Mayrant frowned, glanced at his wife, and slowly obeyed. Then Ralls turned on his heel and trudged through the gate to the road that ended in Soerabaja.

2

Even as the tide rolled in, the *Golden Hind*, under the dimmed eye of the weak western moon, cleared the port. Only three fourths of her crew were aboard, and these men, perplexed beyond words at their captain's rough disregard for their romancing, orgies, and slumber, heaved at sails and hawsers, pulled in her warps, brought the winch around with the dripping cable and anchor, and tore the pilings and hull from farewell embrace.

The *Hind* shuddered a moment and moved like a ghost into that misty union of night and day, her loft tapering off into shapelessness in the hovering gloom. The day was coming up rapidly out of Madoera Strait, over a sea that lapped up reluctantly in the morning tide. The *Hind's* canvas dripped of the cloud that moved swiftly in, that hung over the sides of the ship, and at arm's length from every weary eye aboard her, causing the port to resort to sounds of horns and whistles for safety. At anchor a ship could be rammed, and at three knots she'd do the ramming. But bantam tugs churned up all sorts of racket with unmuffled engines and screeching pipes.

A doltish mother had hold of the world that morning; the opening of her eyes and her bending to examine land and sea were performed with the witlessness of a drugged queen. And the mood of wind and sea was contagious on board ship. The boatswain cursed a maze of tangled cordage, and the ship's carpenter, replacing a ringbolt, shook like a man coming out of a dope jag; in the galley the giant cook tossed pans about in careless abandon, reaping a full share of discordance; Pieter Nisseen groaned at the helm, his head splitting from gross inebriety on the wane, and cursed the weather arm of the ship for not moving down to his defogged eye.

The captain stood at the bow peering into the impenetrable mist, not caring, it seemed, whether the ship walked or flew, letting Mr. Rodriguez do all the bellowing at the foggy ears above and below. And the mate howled out his mood, glad at having a crew of dullards to take the edge off his vitriolic tongue. His had been the glory of a dream come true when Mr. Ralls had barged in, eyed him and the *señorita* with disdain, and ordered him aboard ship.

"Heave, you blasted sleepwalkers!" cried Rodriguez. "And you, Thomasson, in the foresail there, are you thinking ye're a tern about to take off?" He drew his lips into an angered pucker and held his pose for further inspired imprecations. Turning to Ralls some minutes later, he said, "The course, sir?"

"East to one hundred fifteen," said Ralls. "All sail."

"That's to Sapudi Island, ain't it, sir?"

"Look at your charts and leave me be. And have the steward bring gin from my cabin."

"There ain't no steward, sir."

"Then make one!"

Rodriguez said "Yes, sir," meekly, much to the joy of the word-beaten Thomasson in the foresail, who, unable to clap a hand over his incautious mouth, laughed outright. A sudden all-together hush and relaxing at the ropes followed the laughter. As one eye they turned from Thomasson to the chief mate. Rodriguez stopped dead still, put his hands to hips, and gazed aloft.

"Mr. Thomasson, would you like a belayin' pin aimed at your head?" The decorous "No, sir" only infuriated the mate, and he cursed the sailor loud and long. Ralls continued to stare into the thick void, seeing nothing, hearing nothing that went on aboard the *Hind*.

The murky curtain lifted when they were well into the widening

308

strait, but only out of mast's reach; a sultry ceiling hovered above the peak, moving swiftly and without end northwest. Horizons stretched out no more than a furlong, beginning in a blur of dull gray and ending without relief. Then the wind came in gallantly across the starboard bow and with sail set to the elements the ship was lacking none of her smooth lift; her wake, streaming out beyond the edge of the dismal world, was but a lonely stretch of lusterless foam every bit as lonely as the sky it reflected. With Madoera flanking the portside, out of sight in the heavy pall of cloud, the ship roared on, bent for the open stretches that leaned circularly east by north toward the Kangean Eilanden, her captain still leaning to the sea in retrospective mood.

Before his eye rose the majesty of Point Venus in Tahiti. He moved on across the trackless expanse, past the encircling coral reefs of other islands, and into that lagoon where she had flown on the winds of her soul to his resisting heart. There lived the Angélique lost to him, a ghost in the gentle southeast trades, ever calling his name as the slow moan of the wind through the palms announced her presence. The sounds drew nearer, drowning out the lapping of the eternal sea, the volleying of canvas, an echoing moan — "Ralls," ever Ralls. Before his eye three wedge-tailed shearwaters, moaning, moaning, winged their way toward the island of Madoera. The birds, then, had invited delusion; he cursed them, the sound rolling with the wind across the deck and into the ears of the hoisters.

Slow, ripe drops of rain fell from the hanging pall, increasing as the ship charged into the wall of mist. They flew aslant at the captain, and he stood there, water streaming from his face — tears of the elements substituting for those he refused — until his body was sopping wet. The wind increased and the sky seemed intent on wringing out her grief over the ship, dumping to the deck a bubbling wash that rolled to port and slopped over the ropes, pins, and rail crates before cascading over the sides. Streamers sailed almost horizontally before the wind, pelleting the sails, riding lights, and forecastle with constant, roaring fury. The sea, choppy as the strait widened, choppier in the breath of the squall, rose up in turbulent troughs. Cries of "Batten down the hatches! Haul, you sleepwalkers!" rose above the pelter of rain and roaring sea on the wings of a gale, above the rattle and strain of yards, spars, and cordage.

Her captain continued to lean on the rail, his gaze running out the onslaught and dipping low over a Polynesian idyl.

Rodriguez approached. "The sail is pullin' hard, sir, and the lookout says he caught sight of big waves ahead, sir. She'll plow blind into them waves without risin' with 'em."

"Damn you and the lookout."

"Aye, sir," he said dejectedly. "And I've a steward for you, sir — Rameses Doom."

The cloud ahead grew notoriously black and, dipping low with the howling gale on its tail, it seemed a part of the black-green waves leaping furiously at the bowsprit. Down went the bow into a looming trough; the top-heavy *Hind* failed to pull out with the rise and plowed through like a dumb animal; the waves rolled over the forward deck head high, a swirling foam-crested mass, solid and thick. Rodriguez, hanging to a ringbolt, saw the captain's feet rise with the deluge and point straight out toward the foremast, and when the bow rose sluggishly to a heavy swell, he saw the master's arm locked to the rail.

"Mr. Rodriguez, shorten her and bring her more to windward."

The mate lost no time in obeying. Pieter Nisseen, forgetting his head as the spokes jerked at his hands like a wench gone mad, viewed the world as a lunatic paying visit for his sins, which he scarcely regretted, and turned his ear to the wind.

Thomasson hit the deck only to be ordered aloft, and his refractory whine was heard only by his own ears. The cook raised his voice and fists at the fools on deck who had no more sense than to give the hatch enough water to put out his fires. In the captain's quarters, Rameses Doom grinned at his freedom from a ratline, but not for long: Rodriguez turned the latch, letting in the howling wind, as unwelcome as any mate's angered face, and ordered him up into the loft.

"I can spit from here and it'll land in Soerabaja!" exclaimed a Dutch lad in the rigging. No one heard or cared what he said, for every precious glance from chore and foothold was directed at the captain.

The wind roared itself out with a long, howling reluctance to depart from the canvas, giving the sea an equal reign in which to jostle the ship about; but the thickest of the squall was striking hard down the strait and into Soerabaja, leaving in its wake a sullen, gnashing sea; and as it drove on there came heaving swells that accepted the loss of temper with, it seemed, a watery sigh of relief. The sky cleared in the southeast, presenting a bluest blue against a border of rolling white and closer gray. And, too, the position of the ship was revealed — precariously she sailed the edge of the deep — one could almost count the tufts in the palms along the Java coast. Nisseen did not wait long for the "Hard to port," and he swung her while the lads in the sail cursed. In another ten minutes she was well out from land. Clouds fell over her like a blanket of gloom, worse for the sight of the clear sky, and held onto the masts down below the sopping pennant of quatrefoils.

Said Nisseen, "This whole show is a poor piece of seamanship." He mumbled the remainder of his thoughts, eyeing the foredeck where the captain still lingered, quiet and unconcerned. "*Verdomd!*" he said, clearly expressing his every thought. Then the curtain came between him and the fore, lifted once, dived again, and held relentlessly for a full quarter hour.

The lookout yelled frantically. Every eye drew a bead through the curtain forward. "Ship dead ahead off port bow! Chinese junk!" A ghostly shape cut through the curtain of mist, revealing a huge three-master junk. Her excitement exceeded that aboard the Dutch ship; she veered madly to starboard, churning the sea with her antics. As a crash head-on was avoided by the Chinese, the *Golden Hind's* martingale slapped a howling Chinaman from the stern of the junk into the wash of both ships. Neither ship bothered to toss a line overboard. The junk righted herself after whipping the sea into a lather — luckily she came in a few feet off the port bow or the rending of ropes and masts would have dismantled both ships — and trekked on westward, hauling over and over as she disappeared into the hanging wet.

Nisseen said in dismayed tone, "*Verdomd!* A narrow squeeze. The chink was scudding, he was!" He turned his eyes to the bow, expecting to see the captain tuned to the present after that thrill. But he saw the same inane pose.

At noon the whole eastern horizon widened under the expanse of sunlit waters broken only by the disappearing coast of Madoera on the port quarter, the fringe of islands off the port beam, and one hundred fifteen riding into the bright patches over the horizon. The *Golden Hind* sensed her directionless course, and like a bird seeking to outdistance wintry blasts she flew eastward, paralleling the circle that must belch up Tanimbar.

Night came and the captain continued to stand by the port bow. The watch was relieved, and in the moonlight he stared into the sea that purled about the ship, that reached far into the east with a beckoning hand, always on the edge of the horizon, always motioning him onward. He gave no orders, snapped at those who offered him word or food, accepting only the inevitable bottle that must stand in place of the one tossed overboard. The watch changed again and again and there he stood, weight on elbows, meeting the phantom's eye with a fixed gaze.

The day rose up out of the sea, shot horizontal rays of the sun squarely into the bowsprit's eye, revealing the same man in the same stance, in the same mind.

In the lengthened days and nights that moved in from the horizon and disappeared with the ship's wake he stood there often; from Tanimbar, the edge of the world where the loneliness of the tropics reaches its highest pitch, where the sun grows sad in its own heat, where the water is glass that mirrors a circular, even horizon stabbed only by the ship's wake, a long tireless memory of what has been; into the gulf of Papua, alive with the crab-claw sails of the *lakatoi;* dipping below ten degrees and running into the trades straight around the Louisiades and making fast for the channels above the Indispensable Reefs; plowing ever eastward under the push of her canvas, rolling and bounding through troughs and black squalls, cutting the course above eight degrees, passing Fiji, deep off starboard; leaning upon a wind into Pago Pago; skirting Suvorov off the port beam; pointing her bow due east again, and calling upon the South Seas for a straight course into the archipelago — thus sailed the *Golden Hind*, paying no heed to the wireless that rattled in from Batjak, telling of a cargo here, of another there.

When the black-green peaks of a French island jumped out of the sea at sunset, Ralls sighed, and turned away from the rail. Directly to his quarters he strode, passing Rodriguez and a startled group of *zeemen* who eyed his beard and red eyes with growing fear. "Anchor off shore until the change of the watch," Ralls ordered. When next the mate saw him, around midnight, he was clean-shaven, dressed in fresh togs and climbing atop the rail. At his order the anchor rattled in and the ship, close-hauled, eased into the wind. Rameses Doom, stealthily coming on deck, whispered to the mate, the boatswain, and the ship's cook, who leaned against the mizzen fife rail in conversation.

"He drank two quarts, by the saints, he did! Marked each shot with a pencil and when the twelfth was behind 'im, so help me, his eyes was no longer red, but worse — they was black diamonds from the seventh hinge of hell!"

An hour later he stepped from the rail, after treading it like a lunatic conjuring up a one-act play to appease the devil himself. Then, as if the Prince of Hell were perched in the loft with a smile on his face and ready to applaud his theatricals, Ralls walked toward Pieter Nisseen and brought the whip into play. The ship staggered a bit, broached to, creaking and tossing as Pieter screamed. Rodriguez leaped into action, put the helm up, and cried for a lowering of mizzen staysails and a shivering of the after yards; the spanker was brailed in and she began to pay off. Then the devil said, it seemed, "Take the wheel, Ralls," and with the whip under his arm, its coils about his neck and shoulders, the puppet obeyed.

The low-hanging stars winked over the vast domain of smooth sea, throwing a pearl-mist transparency, matchless, tropical, and weird; an overgrown quarter-moon had already bedded down into the horizon of the central Pacific. Thus the sea accepted visibility for her horizons, for her universe of ripples, and, at last, for a ragged edge of black rising indescribably mute out of her bosom. "Island off the port bow," cried the lookout. Ralls stared, repeating over and over that one word: —

"Angélique. Angélique."

His tone was that of a returning lover. He peered over the water at the hump of the island's mountains, where the villa of Desaix still stood, now housing the pliable and fat new administrator; he listened, expecting the clear bell tones of her voice to rise and float over the magic emerald lagoon and spumy breakers in welcome. The cry should ring with all the glory of her; it should now be heard: "Ralls. Ralls."

He did hear the name, but from the chief mate. "Mr. Ralls." He turned slowly to the voice, his hand rising perfunctorily to the whip coiled about him. He stared, then let the hand drop to his side. Rodriguez placed a sheet of paper in his hand, held a light above it that the master might read.

GOLDEN HIND

CAPTAIN RALLS WILL RELINQUISH COMMAND AT NEXT PORT TO RODRIGUEZ. EVERY HARBOR ON SEA LANES NOTIFIED TO ENFORCE ORDER. NEW MASTER WILL STAND BY — BATJAK.

"I'm sorry, sir," said the mate meekly.

"Damn you and your sorrow!" said Ralls. "She's your ship, Mr. Rodriguez — after I make port."

"Aye, sir."

"Then give her sail," shouted the captain. "Full sail, Mr. Rodriguez."

"Aye — but — aye, sir."

Ralls's grip on the wheel tightened, while a gaunt, leveling serenity claimed his eyes and half-smiling lips. The island held his eye, and it was hard over wheel to leeward, shaking a man loose from the ratlines and sending him tumbling over the side: a splash, a line, a flurry of foam and a dismal cry; the line came in empty, and trailing its phosphorescent wake three fins cut the sea. In short minutes the *Hind* was scudding over the surface, gliding furiously ahead of her fevered trail toward an enlarged strip of land. On she tore until the milky breakers rolled ahead of one another in threes and fours, a sure sign of a coral shelf lazing under the surface. A dip to port, another, and the breakers flanked the starboard not a hundred yards away; and on, until the palm stems before the cove rose up to level their graceful heads with the ship. And then he shot the helm to starboard, amid a creaking and splashing, of ship bucking water and wind, of straining shrouds and beating sail, the golden ship leaped forward to ride the sea uphill, over the outer hump of the lagoon to a questionable anchorage.

Mr. Rodriguez knew the cove; so did the second, the ship's carpenter, the boatswain; on the forward deck they huddled, eyes bulging, mouths open, awaiting safe anchorage, said their hopeful minds — awaiting the inevitable crash, said their eyes. Incredulous. An insane man at the wheel of a ship that moved along like a racing cloud of white into a black squall. No power on earth could have checked her tremendous clip to give her safe anchorage. And no power offered aid to the proud lady. She tore on over the shoal, her keel scraping everything before it, and into the mouth of the lagoon. Between the ragged coral heads she ventured, straight for the narrows.

The *Golden Hind* struck with a jar that almost jumped her masts, throwing her all into the teeth of the lagoon. It was her last thrust, her final obedience to the southeast trades. She groaned at the mortal blow, her sides ripped open, her bilge meeting in metallic whorls the clear brine of the sacred lagoon. She stood there on even keel, her masts straight as a die, her stanchions like proud soldiers; there she would meet the tide running up into the lagoon, and there she would stand to meet the ebb, a monument to despair and thwarted love, an epitaph to the wild soul of a mortal man.

3

In due time Mr. Rodriguez gave his lengthy report to the attentive and silent faces around Batjak's massive table. Out of his necessary, though monotonous verbiage, an unnamed story, pathetic and weird, outdistanced all connecting details — the fall of a man. The nose of the mate, who had seemed so close to his dream of captaincy, was still in bandage; broken when the ship struck, it had been set in a wide sweep to the left by the ship's carpenter, the doctor having been injured beyond repair.

A dictating machine was set up to record the nasal voice, while on the left a bald head glared at the speaker; on the right a deep-eyed Moluccan sat without once moving a muscle; beyond him was the white-haired man whose eyes guarded the archives of the baffling firm; and across the table, alongside the hard knobby countenance that seemed as void as its dome, a handsome Dutch face winced when a word or phrase was led to slaughter — which was quite often; Mr. Rodriguez's lips were immunized to rhetoric. Beyond sat a newcomer, a barrister, and next to that stretched face was a youthful head on wide shoulders, arrogant and ambitious.

"— And he left the foredeck on that voyage only for a wink —"

"You may omit irrelevant details," said van Schreeven.

"Thanks, sir. Well, I ain't at a loss for facts, but they wasn't nice. He ate nothin' but a few sea biscuits, and there he stayed. Through squall, hot sun, and far into the black night."

He talked on, through the Papuan and Coral Seas, past Samoa, on to the French islands, beyond the wireless message, and directly beyond the white plumes of the dashing breakers and into the jarring crash.

"I was at the bow, me and the bosun and a few others, when her bottom cut a neat gash in the sand bar; and her point went as neat 'twixt the middle of them reef heads as a mortal could sail a craft. It was sooperb seamanship — I tell you — nothin' less than sooperb. Then the devil up in the 'gallants give up, hisself, cause she was doomed to shallows. Yeah, and closin' jaws.

"She hit, gents, like a sea plow, like a dame on pavement from ten floors up, and there weren't a beam of her, a yardarm of plank, or rope, that didn't moan and quiver. The reef slashed into her sides like a blade into a shark's belly. Lordy, the sounds was awful. My nose hit the rail in the sudden stop and cracked like a eggshell, blood spittin' out'n my mouth and ears. The lookout was thrown into the water and Thomasson hit the deck, breakin' both arms and a leg. The sleepin' men was tossed agin bunkers and a few cracked noggins showed up. The medico was done for when a spar struck him square on the nut."

"And Ralls?" said Mayrant.

"He was slung onto the wheel and slapped cold for a second. Head gashed up a bit. But as I run aft, stumblin' over everything that wasn't tied to, I seen him squirmin' slow like, and I says, 'Are you hurt, Captain?' And he gets up of a sudden and says to me, cold as the nose of a Bering Sea whaler, and smilin' through the blood runnin' down his face, 'She's your ship, Mr. Rodriguez.' Then, so help me, he turns a eye on the far hill and says, 'Angélique!' Some dame of the island, I guess."

"Of course," returned van Schreeven crisply.

"A swarm of natives in canoes and outriggers come about the wreck. They pointed to the water line that stood several foot out of the water.

The chief's son come aboard. Mr. Ralls walked toward him but the native backed away, scared out of his wits. Rameses Doom understood the jabber and said to me: —

"'Mr. Ralls ain't the son of the god Taaro Tiki any more. The high priest died two moons ago and on his deathbed he told the chief and the old boys that Tiki had removed his son's spirit from the man who came in big gold ship.'

"So there was the captain, half-starved, aboard the finest ship to ever track a sea — another derelict by his own doin' — and deserted by even them natives." Rodriguez sighed, felt of his nose lightly, and sat back in his chair. "Well, the remainin' crew was called to the for'ard deck by me and we held a session. By rights we should have locked him up, but we felt he was a sorry enough sight, so we let well enough alone.

"Well, the chubby little Frenchy arrived in about an hour, yappin' and stretchin' one minute, actin' excited as hell in the next, and then doin' it all over again. He peered at the holes in the ship's side, cussed in French, and said nobody but a fool would sail a ship into that coral head. He inquired me for a good half hour and then said he'd arrest the captain and hold him at his house in the hills. Then he ordered me to fling a few cases of gin aboard his new Diesel and make out a written report of the accident in detail. He was sort of wishy-washy.

"'Accident!' I says. 'Yes,' says he. But if he got my report, I thought to myself, or let me have my say to his higher up, there would be more than a accident to deal with. So I answers him, with these very words: 'Accident, hell, Monsieur Debussie! It took a damn good seaman to push this ship into the mouth of the reef.' To which he replies in a bluster: —

"'Well,' he says, 'you being the mate, I must arrest you too, and hold you incommunicado.' And whatever that was he done it, I reckon. But first he goes to the wireless room and fiddles around with the set awhile, and growlin' at Masterszoon, our ether hound, and at last movin' a few wires and takin' the platinum points off the key and the magnet off the sounder and droppin' 'em in his pocket — he done the incommunicado, all right. Next he appoints Doom to watch the ship and stay on board with the crew, and he takes me and Mr. Ralls to his craft.

"For five days I wasn't allowed to leave the house. Down at the mouth of the lagoon, I could see the old *Hind* standin' there blockin' the gate to the ocean. She stood proud, her sails reefed by that time, just like she'd her hook in friendly water, and was standin' by for orders. But on the sixth day the government schooner berthed in the cove outside and — I iterated and reiterated, and answered crazy questions.

"Captain Ralls was sick. He babbled about Angélique, and pearls, and such.

"Well, me and the crew, and the log, was taken to the official island where we was shipped to Papeete and held. Your man, Jennifaar, got us cleared of all charges, and —

"Here I am."

"Was Mr. Ralls sick when you saw him last?" It came from Mayrant Sidneye.

"Ravin' with fever," said the mate.

No word was spoken in the long minute that followed. Down one side of the table bounced the eye of the mate and back up the other, meeting the liaison that held the group together: blank eye met blank eye, evoking in the mate a sense of awe and respect for these bigwigs who dealt in ships, men, and money with a callous eye falling on all personal feelings and emotions. Thus they left the narrator hanging to the tail of his story with such realization that the truth, while acceptable, was long since a forgotten rumble, an agent easily fashioned to their whims.

Van Schreeven broke the brittle crust of silence with: "Mijnheer Rodriguez, you are, of course, aware of the value of your testimony in bringing this case to a just end." He turned a smiling, fierce eye on the mate, waited for no answer, and went on. "After due thought, we are not interested in tangling ourselves in the courts. There's nothing to be gained."

Rodriguez burst forth in nasally passionate tone, "You mean he's to get away with that crime!"

"To our way of thinking Mijnheer Ralls committed no crime. He —"

"But I tell you —"

"Silence!" roared the Moluccan.

"As I was saying, Mijnheer, though I see no need of shaping your opinion, Ralls's crime, as you persist in defining it, was paid for in full. The November crash of the New York financial world sucked him under to the tune of a quarter million dollars. Since he is penniless, sick, and friendless — and blacklisted — his suffering is the apotheosis of pain." He paused, eyed the mate. "Therefore we shall not prosecute. Neither shall we allow our underwriters a loss. You will, therefore, *Captain* Rodriguez, deny the truth in Papeete and in all your discourse in the future. We're placing you in command of an inter-island schooner, the *Galaxy*."

The surprised mate stared inanely for a moment before voicing his thanks for the promotion.

Said van Schreeven, with a faint trace of triumph, "The days of Batjak's free-lance ships are gone."

317

"To punish Ralls further," said Mayrant, grinning, "I have ordered the *Golden Hind* repaired. If it takes a half million guilders she will sail the seas again, and her launching will take place in the cove outside the emerald lagoon."

4

For two years Captain Cordtlaant sailed the *Golden Hind*, or the ghost of her. How tame, how meek she seemed, with her detailed course plotted by a Batjak pen, with her gallant sails minus the devil; she struck the Ceylon route, stood up through the Red Sea to Port Said and back again. For two years Cordtlaant sailed her, until he was stricken abed with Mediterranean fever in Rangoon.

And Ralls —

His fever cooled after long weeks, so the story went — rumor is sometimes lazy in making its rounds, and lazier with stale news of a man people like to forget — and how long he remained on the island few knew or cared. But there was one bit of information that found circulation in the pubs along the waterfronts; it concerned the *Golden Hind*.

The repair crews sailed in, the whole extravagant lot of them, with all sorts of tanks for air, with assorted tools and a giant derrick. They were not long in lifting her on stilts and draining the water out of her; carpenters and riveters sweated and toiled, sawed and fitted, while painters went aloft to varnish her every spar. New shrouds replaced the old, and her hull gleamed in the sunlight a pristine yellow. Within five weeks she was stocked, her crew ready to ship. For a week she moved inch by inch toward the cove and, at long last, amid the cheers of her crew and the joyous grin of Captain Cordtlaant, she kissed the water and upped her sails, and away.

Ralls, with a beautiful native girl hanging to his arm, watched the whole proceedings in unbroken silence. Not once did he say a word. The army of repairmen, the crew, it seemed, had strict orders to ignore him completely; he simply wasn't there. But with her leaning to the wind and clipping away to sea, he ordered the natives to pull out beyond the breakers in her wake. He stood, they said, and waved a slow farewell, a gesture every man described as pathetic and lonely.

A year later a Frenchman told an Englishman, whose brother captained a Batjak ketch, that Ralls lived with a native woman in a hut near the crab claw of the lagoon, that he beat another from the mountains at frequent intervals; that he favored the latter more and merely visited the former; this reversal seemed plausible.

Word reached Soerabaja that Ralls flew into a tempest in a Panama bar. Then from Vera Cruz came the rumor that he stood up the Eastern Seaboard from Cuba with rum.

Of such is rumor, sometimes more interesting than fact, but ever ambiguous, and designed to provoke a meditative brow. Fact, on the other hand, while sometimes less interesting — or more fictitious than imaginative fashioning — tends to hold in the sieve that which must otherwise slip through. And the fact that Ralls traveled down to Soerabaja was almost akin to the sensational.

He stood on a corner across from the building under the flying quatrefoils on a warm morning in March of 'thirty-two. A long black car moved past, came to a stop before the imposing façade. A man hobbled forth after kissing a black-haired woman and two children. The car then meshed into gear and moved swiftly away.

Ralls's voice carried across the street. "Mr. Sidneye." And the man addressed turned and stared hard at an apparition. He did not say a word, and his eyes remained fixed in doubt and complete perplexity. In the interim, Ralls walked the distance separating them and extended his hand. Reluctantly, still dazed, Mayrant accepted the hand and said: —

"Ralls!"

"*Ja*, Mijnheer, none other."

"Ralls, I can hardly believe my eyes. You don't look a day older than when I last saw you. Prosperous?" He crowded the distant tone of his voice with dismissal.

"*Neen*, as you say, Mister. But I've got a great idea. No. I'd rather talk privately." He threw a thumb at the entrance and lifted his brow.

"It must be very interesting, Ralls, if you've come to me with it. Very interesting." His tone was pensively frigid.

"It is that. But you're aware of my talents at picking long shots. My trouble arises only when I play my hunches singlehanded."

"Can't work for yourself, can you, Ralls? But you can make a million for others." He continued to eye the prodigal with a mixture of slow contempt and admiration, narrowing his eyes before turning that expression into a supercilious smile.

"We won't discuss that," said Ralls crisply. His smile was direct and cynical. Perhaps it was that old show of bravado, or gall, or whatever definition one cared to give his individualism, that won Mayrant's ear; it remains that Ralls invited the aging emperor of Batjak to dinner, that his invitation was accepted, that at the finish the bald man proffered a

319

check on the Javasche Bank of Soerabaja for a large sum, and raised his glass to the health of his companion.

Out of that dinner sprang a slow, eerie breeze, a sort of whirlwind, petty and inept, that brushed across several faces, leaving a taste of grit in a few mouths and sand in the eyes of others before moving on scarcely noticed; but from one to another it moved, gathering momentum, until it built a wall of howling wind, guilder-coated, and thus immune to the visibility of seeing eyes and hearing ears; but the two who stood in the vortex grinned and watched the spasmodic growth of their hurricane.

The death knell to Batjak's free-lance ships had sounded with Ralls's great mistake, thereby providing the more practical heads with a certain power that comes with proving the rightness of opinion. Their silent, I-told-you-so expressions had galled Mayrant somewhat, but there were two great reasons for his adherence to the dictum: one was Younguer, the other Ralls; the ships *Van Arken* and *Golden Hind.* And though he had the power to traverse the decision, he did not relish the idea of facing those under him with another failure to his credit. But the memory of the *Quatrefoil* under a younger Sidneye: a free ship with a swashbuckling eye to the lee; a spinner of adventure across the romantic seas; and of prizes; the *Golden Hind* of those years when the distant lagoon was a veritable gold mine, when the treasures of the deep rose up at the devil's behest to crowd her deck! Aye, memories. To a man battling old age, these memories had a voice.

The argosy of Batjak moved dully over the world's lanes, showing profit even in the lean years following nineteen hundred twenty-nine; a well-operated fleet, said the world. But lacking to the tempest of Mayrant's soul was the long gamble, the sensational windfall, the glory of the old line.

Thus he was unable to throw off the spell that came with Ralls. He had primed his mind with dreams, he had sucked long at his imaginative wells, and the return of the old favorite whose black soul was dotted with virgin gold, whose nerve was matched only by his luck, seemed to inject new blood into a decomposing body.

They talked of ships and contraband, of seas and helpless natives, of an unguarded treasure in the Australian Mandate; they talked more of ships, of a ship, and the weary Mayrant found transport to his youth. He, in the final courses of that dinner, built a ship, a great ship, and incarnadined her sides, and silvered her sails; at last glowing like a child as he sounded her name: —

"The *Red Witch!*"

5

In April of that year shipping circles were somewhat surprised when the following was announced: —

The firm of Batjak, Ltd. reports the sale of the *Golden Hind*, a three-master, that has upon occasion figured in suits and inquiries, to a Norwegian firm. The ship is to sail from Brisbane for Oslo on the twentieth of April.

Heaving a sigh of relief, Vee Vossler opened the leather-bound covers of the ledge marked *Golden Hind* and wrote therein: —

We are pleased at the decision of our worthy head, Mayrant Ruysdaal Sidneye, and are glad to write the end to the chapter of a notorious ship. Henceforth Batjak holds to steam. With the transfer of the ship completed on this day, Batjak marks the last entry in the ledger of the *Golden Hind*. Finis.

In May a London and Liverpool firm announced the purchase of a ship from a Norwegian firm. In June they told of its sale to a banking house in Singapore, agents for a wealthy Chinese.

It was on the afternoon of a day in January that a cocksure man left a huge Chinese junk in the Inner Roads of Collyer Quay, boarded a lighter for a run into the city of Singapore, and was soon eyeing the Bund, its teeming life, its buildings and sampans. He paid the Malay and stepped into a crowded pier. Standing at the appointed spot he was soon approached by a large and pompous Chinese who grinned and said: —

"Mr. Ralls?"

"Yes."

"Are you ready to visit the ship?"

The two men stepped into a wooden-shoe boat, a slattern sampan; and before long they hove in sight of a great tower of sail.

"Mr. Sidneye also controls our company," said the saffron giant, "but I think he bought into us simply for her." He pointed to the ship with a hidden past — how well she was covered was a source of wonder to Ralls himself. On her red stern in letters large and gold was written her new chapter: —

"RED WITCH, Singapore."

And for two years she sailed the seas a free ship under a free madcap; until her troubles uncovered her true ownership. Then, because a bald adventurer ruled his house, stormed at his underlings, and declared his dictatorship with huge hands filled with sixty-two per cent of Batjak's stock, she shook herself free of legal entanglements with the famed Power of Batjak and continued to sail the seas . . .

. . . A chartered ship until her perfidy was a forgotten vibration in the southeast trades. She met her end under Ralls, her lonely death unable to claim more than three ships' lives. But the words of her angel — the man who rebuilt her once from the ship *Quatrefoil* into the yellow and white sprite the *Golden Hind*, the man who made her into a stirring thing that carried the gilded lady in a field of red on her bowsprit, a crimson name that spelled out its integument of blood — lingered in the mind of the man who twice destroyed her: —

"Ralls, the value of a ship is nothing compared to the value I place in her master. Be kind to this ship, and remember — if ever the *Red Witch* meets abuse, I shall write off any loss except that of misplaced trust; and to that I shall swear eternal vengeance."

BOOK FOUR

Grave of the Red Witch, 1939

COMPENDIUM

THAT was the end of Sidneye's story, the odyssey of the Quatrefoil, of quatrefoils and Batjak — of the Golden Hind and Ralls.

With its finish, and there was much left unsaid, I experienced difficulty in severing myself from the past. I remembered I was Sam Rosen, a man whose past accepted, by association, the color of Ralls's feather. I remembered more: a squid gorging itself on a dog while my host probed me with scalpel eyes for telltale weaknesses; I remembered a dinner and its surprise — Mr. Loring of the Red Witch; and van Schreeven, who brought to mind the only pleasing reflection in this misanthropic setting — his daughter, Teleia. For an ephemeral moment I reviewed her. Trader Sam Rosen was in love! I checked that thought in a hurry, lest it catch me napping at a time when circumstances demanded alertness.

And circumstances. I came to Little Soembawa, completely unaware of its owner's identity. But Carter cushioned my surprise on that score; the same Carter upon whom Ralls had used the Creeper only a day before, thus splitting the team of Ralls and Rosen, joint owners of the schooner out there in the lagoon.

But what about this team of Sidneye and company who offered me clemency, with a hint that Batjak might eventually find a place for a trader like Rosen?

Yeah, I said to myself, what about this team?

One glance into the eyes of Mayrant Sidneye told me that he, too, was knitting the threads of the past with those of the present.

CHAPTER XXVIII

I

YES," said Mayrant pensively, "I told Ralls that — I shall swear eternal vengeance — eternal."

His long story out, he raised his eyes, blinked them furiously, and smiled. Need I say I viewed a different man from the host at that farcical dinner several hours before? I, Trader Sam Rosen, felt the weight of his story, his wealth of experience that sought to augment the pearls of my proposition, of his acceptance; he offered me clemency in trade for — for what? It suddenly dawned on me, like the rushing sensation of one's stomach in a fall, that I had nothing whatever to offer this strange man for his whim or his story. He was Sidneye of Batjak, of quatrefoils that soared above every trough of the seven seas. But how strange he seemed. Fatigue and hunger lay in the eyes that once ruled the ship with three souls. A bloated face surrounded eyes that lived in an abandoned world. A drugged and sickly skin — reminiscent of his sickness after the rape of Younguer's *Alice Macdonald;* a skin awash in the hues of sedatives and frambesia, that and a lusterless bald dome — against the man himself.

True, I sat out the complete silence that tossed furiously about in the echo of his tale. Across from me sat Harmenszoon van Schreeven, who had not been present when his weakness in Bali was painted into my eye. The Moluccan had long since departed, but need I say I failed to see the same wizened creature who kept company with a green parrot? So I gave answer to one of a dozen live questions: —

Neen, Trader Sam! Everything before you, everything behind you, has changed. You entered this house, not in nineteen hundred and thirty-nine, but in eighteen hundred and seventy-five.

The faces I saw before me were strange and familiar. They seemed justified; their moods, the expressions that stepped into their faces out of those moods, seemed less brittle and more rational. Though marked outwardly by the ravages of time, they depicted, despite one's

325

knowledge of their crushing power, new faces aureoled in the lights of tolerance and justice. In the face of Mayrant Sidneye I saw — almost — compassion. For a fleeting second it stood out from his lips and eyes like a ghost out of his courtship, or the scarcely mentioned love for his children. How clearly he had painted his weaker moments, his enduring weaknesses, his lovable traits, his harsh, to-the-death battles to appease his lust. In his more congruous love for Angélique, he had painted himself on the mellow wane, a man who owned all, yet who had substantially little until he found her. Of his passion for revenge, who could blame him? Streicher! Ralls! He gave revenge a magnificence — a superb rightness — did this man who found in his father's death a legacy to that end.

Mayrant Sidneye, the man of whims and passions, who could forgive again and again until he threw the helm down and scudded before the eternal winds of hate, had seen his favorite captain's arms about his wife, had picked her up at an order from that outsider only to forgive the deed and the word, and more. The weakness of his armor therefore could be narrowed down to a simple fact: he could not resist sensational boldness in any associate; such swept beyond the barriers of his better judgment to warm his adventuresome heart. His story attested to the fact. I should underscore that deduction, and hold it for future use, I reasoned. But I could not sit there in mute wonder for an endless age while the pair continued to sink the hooks of their eyes into me.

"You are quite gifted, Mijnheer Sidneye," I said. His quizzical brow sought release from ambiguity, and I, smiling, said: "In the art of spinning a tale." I added, "You build excellently. Such suspense calls for a climax."

"How so?"

"This layout," I said, with a wide sweep of my arm. "Is it only a spider-and-fly setting?"

"It is a beautiful place, is it not?"

"It is that," I said with meaning. The blue tones of the ceiling bled out before my eye, and the Hindu statue, queer art even after all excuses ran the gamut, glared at me silently, coldly; the gorgeous rug, the blue-in-blue color scheme, the rich, stiff walls, all claimed an admiring eye, though complete appreciation was impregnated with the grotesque; the whimsies of its artisan seemed to overcast the blue; I saw jaundiced tints. "Yes," I reflected aloud, "it is beautiful, but too perfect, and cold."

"Perhaps," said my host, his eyes frowning into mine, "the *Red*

Witch influences your opinion." Direct challenge that, seeking to draw out confessions of my guilt. But what mattered my part in this drama of hate and lust? I came upon the stage in minor role, in the last act; my lines were few and unrehearsed, my acting ability yet to be established. So I smiled easily, eyed him lazily.

"I am somewhat surprised, sir," I said, "that a man of your wisdom should draw such conclusions." The reprimand struck at his weak spot and drew a smile in that malleable face. The man was a direct target for well-aimed cool pertness. Too bad, I thought, that the hound hadn't bitten him en route to the squid's tank. He might now be gnawing at a bone.

Said my host: "My apologies, Mijnheer Rosen."

"Quite all right," I returned. "But back to your story. Your description of your wife was minus the fierceness you lend other topics. She is a woman to be admired, Mijnheer."

"Thank you, Rosen," he said. "She was a wonderful wife and mother. Perhaps if she had lived I should not have built this monument to revenge on this desolate island; or anywhere. But fate holds me in her palm, Rosen, giving me a fast pulse and driving soul that must turn to tempestuous doings. Otherwise the tempo is killing." Silence fell upon his pitiful confession, held for long moments, and evanesced only before his slow, painful speech.

"Angélique died while trying to give me a son, a third child." He sat there quietly, reliving the scene, said his eyes; burying her, said his soft, meek lips. His face lifted to the ceiling, to Angélique, it seemed. How eloquent was his love, how splendid was that recess; but for the stride of his spirit, he should have loved her memory like a fond, foolish, and lovable old man. He desired that above all, I could see, and the denial, no part of him, was heartrending.

Strange indeed is another's sorrow: sometimes so briefly displayed that a compassionate mind rushes forward to scan the dreary, tuneful interlineations; therein an ogre becomes a child one cannot but love; therein the part of man that is half-woman, kindly, commiserative, smiling, rises within the breast of her sons to give thanks for that unwanted emotion that softens the very world. I felt it, I was glad I could, and at the same time I felt the shame of my weakness.

I thought of Teleia, the face in the moon; I admitted my need for her. That, I said, with silent thanks to my Maker, was love, the opposite of wantonness. Aloud, I said, "And the children, there are three?"

"Two girls," he said. "They are dear to me, but the chord they strike is a rhythm all its own. They fill a spot, as Angélique filled another.

They are in a convent in the Indies — a better influence than their father."

I applauded inwardly. He knew the meaning of love. Ralls's avenging angel was showing a side that demagnetized my averse opinions. So, I warned Trader Rosen, careful — careful, Sam. Don't let that sort of cunning, if it is that, trip you. You saw the dog-and-squid episode, you heard its sequel. I should test his sincerity, I said, and I did with: —

"So Ralls had already met you, Mijnheer van Schreeven?" I shot a quick glance at Sidneye, saw his eyes freeze with his mouth at the mention of the name. Yes, he was sincere in his loves and sorrows. The former religious fanatic responded as I expected — one word, yes — and gave his half-brother the floor.

"Ralls," he said meditatively. "How dear to my heart is Ralls." I thought of Streicher, imagined more than I'd heard, and gave a mental shudder for my partner of the *Quean of Melbourne*, a man to be despaired of with the toppling weight of Batjak towering above him. "Brother," he said, turning to van Schreeven, "do you realize we have him in our midst?" He exuded the fatty deadliness of a spider in that moment.

In an effort to mask my desire for a straightforward digging into the bloody business at hand, I whipped back into his story with such curiosity as an idle mind might affect. "What became of Zulinde Meer, of Vossler, and the lad Christiaan; and, too, is the team of Cordtlaant and Noord still running the seas; what happened to young Hekkin?"

"Poor Zulinde. She died only a few months back. She outlived her world. Vee Vossler is alive, yes, but he is no longer able to move about. His elder son is filling his shoes in Soerabaja, while young Christiaan has risen high in his chosen field, the Church. Young Hekkin? Why, he's in charge of our fleet of seaplanes. A worthy lad." He smiled wickedly before giving answer to the remaining question.

"The team, as you call them, are on their way here. I'm sure Van Cordtlaant and Teer Noord will greet Ralls profusely."

"An accepted fact," I returned lightly.

"Yes, isn't it?" said my host. He eyed me narrowly before pointing his next words at my perplexed mind. In truth, I was never so torn between facts to an end and pressing decision; his question threw before my eyes the unsteady, uneasy position I had maneuvered myself into. "Well, Mijnheer Rosen, do you accept our offer?" His tone, brittle and icy, seemed to chop off cordiality that had hovered over us since my coming. He laid bare my indecision.

He was unaware of the last words between Ralls and me — our

covenant, "Until sunup, then." If I agreed with them, if I failed to return to the schooner, Ralls would come charging. If he walked into ambush, I could never forgive myself. And the sunrise wasn't far off. It all added up now, that reasoning of Carter's: Batjak, Ltd., the quatre-foils, the ownership of the *Red Witch*. Not only was my curiosity assuaged, my esteem for Ralls had risen and fallen perceptibly: because he had known all along the completeness of dovetailed ownerships, and passions, and plots; and he alone had heard the roaring winds of Sidneye's fury; and in the lagoon of fury he had chosen to remain, holding me a party to his escape or destruction. But I could not make any decision without first breaking with Ralls. I was chained to our partnership deep inside me; if and when I broke with Ralls, the severance must be clean and free of any tag ends of remorse.

"Mijnheer Sidneye, you are not dealing with a child. Why be lenient with me when I was as much involved as Ralls in the sinking of your ship? You think that, don't you?"

"Were you?" He mocked me, it seemed.

"That's for you to answer. I don't talk much, Mr. Sidneye." Rising to my feet, I grinned contemptuously, coolly. "I have a score to settle with Ralls myself. Do I make myself clear?"

"Yes — and no," said the confident head of Batjak. "You were willing to accept an offer to speed his quitting this island. Why?"

I smiled down at him. "Mijnheer Sidneye! I am a trader who never turns down a dollar when it suits my fancy. And getting him out of here suited my fancy." I expected him to ask if I was now in the same frame of mind.

He merely smiled. After a long monotonous stare, he said, "Sit down, Rosen." I obeyed because it suited my purpose. "Of course," he said, "you are aware that I have a reason behind my offer. I'll explain if you'll be so kind as to lend me an ear." His entreaty was backed with the welcome drink he extended.

"I am seldom hoodwinked, Rosen, and, as you have probably guessed, I take chances on minds more fickle than yours can ever be. If you worked for me I could expect the rigid loyalty I found in Younguer. The comparison, the mention of his name, Rosen, is a compliment. I seldom resort to such. You are scarcely enough of a scoundrel to deliberately sink a ship given to your care. I think I have catalogued you correctly — as far as I've gone. Stop me if I err, for believe me, this is no time for either of us to jest.

"You were the second in command of my ship when she was destroyed. You know more about the details than Batjak. Beyond that point I hold nothing against you. I have all I desire. I am not, as you might think, seeking to buy you in as a guide to the treasure of the *Red Witch*, though you alone, excepting Ralls and Arrezo, know the spot. How cleverly concealed," he said pensively, his fancy getting the better of his vein of thought for the moment. "More important things are at stake than gold. To me, the value of gold is but a symbol of power, and beyond that it is almost nothing. I should not be offering you anything of personal value, Rosen, if I offered you gold, a token I've learned to despise at times. So, when I offer clemency, I offer even less, by comparison. And in return for what?" He leaned forward to answer his own question: —

"For nothing," he said. "It is exactly as you said."

"Now we are getting down to facts," I said, chuckling appreciatively.

Van Schreeven yawned; I could use a little sleep myself, I silently admitted. Then I yawned, eyeing Sidneye, hoping he would do likewise. He refused. Thus I finished my drink, feeling spent, and numb even to the potency of alcohol. Morning was here; it was back of us and coming faster, its reddening blossom widening the rim of the east.

"Well, Rosen," said the host indefatigably, "again I say I must have had a reason for my offer."

"Yes," I said wearily. "You wanted to hold a stop watch on my desire for freedom, perhaps. Therefore, you feel I'll eventually come over to your side."

"Eventually, my friend, is closing in fast."

"And when do you think it will arrive?"

"Soon," he said. "Soon. Make up your mind. If I seem to rush you, Mijnheer Rosen, it is because I have a reason. I must know the color of your flag on an island where neutrality has no home. You are either with us or with Ralls; not that it matters much — to us."

"And the time limit?" I said.

He pondered a moment before replying. "Since Ralls stood the rail of his ship, time is short. Until sundown, then."

"Until sundown," I answered.

2

Clad in evening finery that was not mine, I walked out of the heavy atmosphere of the place unchallenged. Across his shrunken plantation I moved slowly, breathing the cool air of early morning and training my mind, as best I could, out of his possession and into the freedom of rest. At the edge of the swamp I paused for a deep

330

breath and turned my eyes toward the heavens, sending forth a sigh of envy as I viewed the battle of the dawn. How restful, peaceful, and sweet. Like nectar after quinine.

The day was stepping up rapidly from the sea, and the tide was running with abated fury against the coral barriers outside the lagoon. The finger of light in the east rose like a powerful, sweeping hand, so silent and mighty that it charged in noisily. A star directly overhead flashed once and went out, joining the half dome of advancing incandescence in becoming surrender. Swiftly others winked out and after a time the jib boom of the sun split the wet horizon — merely a glowing ship against the sky and flying quatrefoils, I said ironically. The mists lifted, and the day was again the winner over the tropical sky. Clouds, shaped like Arab dhows and rolling wheels, pulled hard with the lee of the sky. In their bosom a fast waterspout dipped into the brine far out to sea. A cool breeze eddied down from the clouds through the cavities of the palms and held in check, for a suspended moment, a flock of clacking goonies flying inland. I closed my eyes before its caress and actually found freedom from a Dutchman's hating mind.

Life is ever sweet in the roll of the dawn, in the inflected rays of a clement sun; and long shadows growing out of every rising object are coated with the promise of hope: they must grow shorter.

"I wonder," I said aloud, frowning before moving on into the dank mass of vines and layered rot. My eye was no sooner lowered than the crushing weight of discovery struck me squarely. I halted in my tracks, seeking an answer to the question I asked: —

"Has Ralls ever before been anything but a human hurricane on the night following his walk of the rail?" I sat down in the fog of retrospect right there in the middle of the swamp. I added my experiences to those of Sidneye and drew for an answer a cold, barren — No! Polynesian pearls, the attempted theft of Sidneye's wife, the sinking of the *Red Witch:* all following his hellish whim. Only the rush of the *Golden Hind* into the coral heads of the lagoon failed to strike a parallel, though a quick mood hastened his stride there. I argued hopefully — if he could shorten his punches he could also lengthen them. But somehow I felt the presence of useless and wishful thinking, admitting the awful truth: Ralls had walked the rail the night before last; thus he had thrown the whiplash of his hurricane while I listened to Sidneye's story. But where, and upon whom?

Teleia?

Then I surrendered to foolish fear, mentally and bodily. I was up and running as fast as my legs would carry me back over the path to

331

the Dutchman's house. The fear was rooted in me and I ran all the faster, panting, working up fury with every step. I conjured up awful scenes as I ran, slow deaths to the man who touched a hair of her head.

Then I paused, suddenly aware of my puerile actions in any other's eye — and after a time I walked slowly toward the entrance. The flat features of that symbol of Hindustani stood in the garden in the same monotonous pose of yesterday, and the tulip garden and adjacent beds of tropical flowers traveled the same carpet into my eye; and to even those innocents I addressed silent imprecations. It was as if the ghost of Ralls stood always ahead, romping before my eye in taunting glee. And then I was on the threshold, standing foolishly with my upraised hand knotted into a fist to announce my presence. Perplexed, I turned about, seeking an excuse to cover my true feelings. I was glad I'd humored the voice of caution, for it was then I saw her.

Between the endless rows of giant flowers she walked, in every way a living complement to their beauty and fragrance. She had not seen me, and I slowly walked in her direction, preening my face for composure while stroking the undesirable stubble of my chin. I was within thirty feet of her when she glanced up, and as her eyes fell upon me, faintly startled, then questioning, and at last smiling, I stopped in my tracks.

"Good morning," she said. I said nothing as I stood for a long count of ten before advancing with a frown of appraisal written into my countenance.

"Good morning — Teleia," I said, causing her eyes a curious thinning at the pause before her name, and at the tone I gave it. A woman is always a leap ahead of the dull male. I saw her gain, and I bowed to the handicap. Then I forgot all but the sure appeasement given my sorely tired eyes.

"You are out early, Mijnheer Rosen — after a full night of it."

"Yes," I said, "and for a reason. It has to do with you. Just where were you last evening? Wait," I said, when she smiled mischievously, "I'm serious. Perhaps it isn't any of my business — yet."

"Yet?" Her smile was taunting.

"Yet!" I returned vigorously.

"Mijnheer Rosen, I misjudged you. I thought you'd listen just so long to my uncle before visiting the pool. Don't look so surprised. Of course, there was nothing definite, but —" She smiled.

"And I would have rushed to the pool had I not been in the middle of a very important decision. My very health was — is — involved. You see, your uncle and father aren't very fond of my partner."

"You knew that, but did you learn enough to leave this island — and Ralls?"

"Not so fast. I came to ask you a question. Did you see Ralls last evening?"

"I did — around eleven."

"What! After my warning, after —" I was at her side in that moment, clamping tight her arms just above the wrists. "Well, what happened?" I said savagely.

"Mijnheer!" she said, smiling squarely into my eyes, her lips parting in provocative manner, her eyes staring lazily and raking the exclamation out of her last utterance. "Would it matter much — to you?"

"Matter?" I said, in exasperation. Then I saw that she teased. A romancer and torturer I defined her, but that, too, was as short-lived as my last breath. My hands relaxed and I saw the red marks at her wrists, and at the very moment she viewed them; no regrets there, and therefore no voicing of any lie — rather, at the moment I would have enjoyed putting red palm prints at other extremities of her anatomy. "You're stark mad!" I said.

"No," she said lightly. "He fascinates me."

"Hm — m," I growled. "He fascinates you, does he!" I thought of that fascination he held out to Angélique. I could see Teleia accepting the conduct of Angélique as exemplary, I could see her finding a certain rightness atop the shallow crust of infatuation.

"Impossible," I said.

"No, not impossible," she returned, lowering her gaze to a basket of blossoms before darting a mischievous eye my way. "He is the unconquerable type, and therefore interesting."

"I've got enough to worry about without adding you to my list. If you knew Ralls you'd remain on the grounds until there's an end to all this trouble. But on second thought I imagine you'll do as you please. Now tell me about your meeting."

After a time she began, "At the pool I stared into the water, since I was afraid to bathe without guards." I took the stinger without wincing, and she continued, "So I decided to go aboard the *Flores* for a while. I circled around the inner beach, passing your ship on my way. He stood on deck peering out into the palms, then at me, but never saying a word."

"Were you frightened?"

"No, only tense. I reached the *Flores* and told the Malay to stay on deck. I entered my cabin and was soon lost in a novel. I dozed off, and how long I slept, I scarcely know. But an unsteady vibration

333

aboard the ship caused me to open my eyes. I thought I heard a moan, but I laughed it off as the aftermath of the story I'd begun. Then, imagine my surprise —"

I was leaps and bounds ahead of her. "Ralls!"

"The door opened and there stood your gallant partner, the same cool character I've heard my father and uncle describe. I motioned him to a chair and mixed us a drink.

"He seemed puzzled that I should retain my composure, in fact he seemed momentarily disarmed. He helped himself to more gin and mixers and then took an enormous slug straight, not having said a word up to that moment. 'What happened to my Malay?' I asked. He merely shrugged and said, 'He'll come around after a time,' I realized I was quite alone with a man of unusual force, one whom I'd rather view from a distance; at least not alone. So I sparred for time, hoping you, or someone, might visit the *Flores;* after a tense interval, I said, 'Tell me about yourself, Mijnheer Ralls.'

"'I didn't come here to talk about myself,' he said gruffly. 'No?' I returned. 'Just what prompted your visit?' His answer, 'You, Miss van Schreeven,' was exactly what I'd expected.

"'I am sorry that I cannot encourage you,' I said. That was where I blundered. He informed me that he needed no encouragement. As if prompted by his own statement, he got to his feet and stared down at me. He was like a primitive man who lived long before laws and conventions were born."

"You need a guardian!" I snapped. Ignoring me, she continued: —

"In the next moment he seized me and drew me to him. He did not kiss me. He just glared into my eyes. I tried to smile but my mouth froze. I was scared." She paused, turned her eyes toward the lagoon, shuddering lightly.

She provoked hell out of me and made me like it.

"Then he ripped off my kabaja, and more. The next thing I knew he was flourishing a leather belt. There was nothing about him that resembled the man who entered my cabin. His face was long and hollow, all eyes and thin lips." Her hand fell instinctively over mine. "Somehow I forced a smile. It was weak, I know, since I was never more frightened in my life.

"He stood there with upraised arm, his eyes thinner than before. He seemed to have worked himself up to the highest pitch of fierceness. I tried to hold a smile on my face as I backed away. But with every step I made he advanced a step, all the while lowering and raising his whip arm, like a jungle cat flicking its tail before pouncing.

"I was growing frantic, and the realization of that fact helped some. I kept saying: Hold your head, Teleia. Think. There must be some way out of this.

"He was into his mad moment by that time, and I knew it was then or never. So I took a long chance. I said, smiling as best I could, 'I've heard the story of Ralls.' It was weak. So I added, 'I've also heard of his love for Angélique.'

"He paused, and frowned, and his arm moved slowly to his side. He seemed angry and uncertain. In that tense moment I said: —

"'Angélique said you were a great man, Ralls.'"

She sighed heavily, pausing to stare in the direction of the lagoon. I, anxious, snapped at her. "What happened?"

"That did it," she said. "He simply stared ahead, and after an age he said, 'I'm sorry, Angélique.' He said it again. Then he saw me and he seemed surprised. His next move was to turn his back on me and pour himself a long, straight drink.

"As I stepped to the closet for a robe he lifted his eyes to mine. They were the eyes of Ralls the man, a man who fought to rise above his weakness; they were clear, bright, and sane. Then without any word he stalked off, a pitiful, weak, though strong man."

"So he's interesting, is he?" I growled. "Well, all I can say is this — you're lucky! Damn lucky!"

"Ralls needs compassion and understanding, Sam. He's still in love with Angélique. And strangely enough, she did say he was a great man."

I could hardly view the scene or the man in that easy light; I was dubious, and puzzled, though I gleaned from Sidneye's story enough to imagine the power Angélique would hold over Ralls to his dying day. Then I felt the impact of another question: if he failed in one place would he strike in another?

"Yeah," I said. "It's lucky for you that you thought of Angélique."

I was fast giving myself up to a bitter rage, and its advance guard crept into my face. Instinctively she drew her hand from mine and eyed me seriously. After some time she laughed lightly, for my benefit; she hoped to draw me to her level. Then her simulated buoyancy died, and she said, almost in a whisper: —

"Sam — how I long for an end to all this slow hate. Yes, that's what it is. But it is my uncle, and Ralls is a part of it." Her dreamy, endless gaze pierced the western skies, seemed to join the morning breeze and the lazy lashes of the palms in an indulgent caress. She voiced my wishes. But it was no time for dreaming.

335

"Why not wish for the moon?" I said. "It would be easier to get."

I sought to encircle the maze of perplexing threads, to palm them into a compact ball and pluck at the edges for slow lucidity. I began with, "And you trust Ralls now?"

"I think so."

The opposite of Sam Rosen, I thought, who had answers aplenty for her, and about her, who was ready to toss the whole world over his shoulders with a horseshoe wish, not caring where it landed so long as she saw me in the light I viewed her. The breeze whipped at a lock of her hair, gave it dance upon a noble, tawny forehead; her eyes closed slowly, opened slower, and at last raised to mine as a hint of a smile and a quiver of her delicate nostrils voiced another mood.

"There is one question I wish you'd answer," I said, and her quickened eye told me she traveled with me. She waited for me to give it words, and I, a moment before tempted to ask her if she could ever learn to love Sam Rosen, suddenly, foolishly, said cowardly: —

"But I'm afraid if I don't put in at the *Quean*, all hell will pop loose." I turned on my heel and stalked toward the gate. There I saw her staring after me. Teleia, the magic image of Polynesia in drab Melanesia, almost pulled me back to her side.

"You gave me advice last evening — I could use more of it," I said, drawing from her an invitation.

"At the pool this evening — Sam."

3

The *Quean* sat lazily in the lagoon, her water line meeting the lap of water in lackadaisical manner, her warps tightening and giving slack with the push and pull of the breeze. A pair of our Malays swung brushes on the bowsprit in listless manner, while another pair worked up in the foresail; on deck Ripper and Tewelliger labored over a large sheet of canvas, our mainsheet; in our pearl boat at the stern another Malay team made ready to paint the portside. I paused on the beach, raising my brows and thinking: Going somewhere, Ralls? Industry again, for what?

Then I saw the skipper. Up the mainmast ratlines, a pith helmet on his head, his bare midriff meeting knee-jagged dungarees, he drew the sail needle where it was needed most. I almost yelled, "Where blows, Skipper?" but instead I frowned at a man I had never before seen. He, too, was a stranger with a familiar face, the son of Taaro Tiki, the master of the *Golden Hind*, the culprit tied to a Gilbertese log,

336

the mad captain who sailed out of Suva to put an end to Younguer of the *Van Arken*. He was a ghost, abandoned, weary, and yet alive; a spirit I had never before known. The new Ralls was every bit as surprising as Batjoek.

"Hello, Sam," he cried out. "I didn't let you down at sunrise. I saw you in the swamp running back for something." His steady glare asked what I'd returned for, and then answered its own question.

"Going somewhere?" I said coldly, craning my neck to hold his eyes.

"Yeah," came the answer. "And I think you know where."

I grunted. "But I'm afraid you don't." Grinning silence held him for some time, but he countered eventually with: —

"Converted, Sam?"

"No," slowly, "just prejudiced."

"There was a time when you weren't gullible, Sam old boy."

"Yeah. And there was also a time when we did things in partnership style."

"Meaning?"

"That the day is gone when your whims, that aren't a damn bit lucrative, are laying my neck on the chopping block."

Ripper slowly turned his fat, oily head my way, showing a grin of incredulity and curiosity. Tewelliger raised his head from the molded canvas and sent long, silent glances at me, then at the stern rail, and back again. Why he failed to stare overhead at Ralls, I do not know.

Ralls laughed — carelessly. Humor me, he would, and after a while we'd have a drink, and his friendly slap at my back would drive out the last sullen glint in my eye and loosen the gristle about my lips. I would smile reluctantly, and — another battle won for Ralls.

We would let the future decide that. I was in a bad mood, and anxious to clear the channels to a showdown, cautious enough, however, to build a stage on the steps of wisdom. A sail is ever as slow as the wind it courts and no sail enjoys a full rein in the teeth of a typhoon. Therefore, Sam, I said to myself, ride under storm jib. But I hoisted a sail high when I said: —

"Ripper, you and Tewelliger are wasting your time. This ship isn't going anywhere."

"Talk sense, Sam," Ralls said.

"To whom?" I answered, setting a foot aboard the ship and disappearing across the deck and below. Five minutes later I felt the lulling advance of sleep, and when I next opened my eyes the blistering sun threw the *Quean's* shadow straight to the bottom of the lagoon.

CHAPTER XXIX

1

A WEAK breeze greeted me when I appeared on deck. The lagoon was but a glassy mirror for the unadorned sky. Across the beam I peered at palms hanging limp in oppressive siesta while the beach danced crazily in the direct rays; no sound whatever, no lapping of water against the ship's sides, no creaking in the uppers, and not a bird or fish in sight. If the icy wastes of the polar zones throw a spell of loneliness that a man can hardly describe, then double the feeling in those wailing, mute solitudes of equatorial seas where, even in a lively trade that parts the hair in cool caress, a depression falls over the expanse of sky and sea that is nothing but sun and water, sun and water. The sea leaps up at one in dreary soliloquy with the red glint of sunrise; it murmurs crazed words until the sunset squall arrives to shed its grief atop the same long, trailing wake. Then a luminous night takes over, and a man will seek refuge in strange companions, in anything to drive out the hammer of repeated nothingness.

Suddenly I realized why I was lonely. I had tasted the luxury of civilization yesterday. The cool hand of Teleia beckoned. I shook the feeling as best I could with a word of advice that had a mock ring to it — get your business done, Sam, and then return to her.

"With what?" I said aloud. A tramp schooner, no worthy past, no lovely future, and no more wealth than her kin could expect of a small-time trader? Yes, that solved the conundrum, me — eloquently. Damn the heat, the loneliness of the day, and the self-reproof it evoked. I screwed my face into a scowl, and walked away, realizing I was courting low tide to a showdown.

I raised my voice then. "Ralls!" Again I did it, at last receiving a lazy grunt from Ripper: "He'sa no here. Gone ashore." I asked why, drew a worded shrug, and then ordered him up and fore. He came forward slowly, slattern as the word itself, his paunchy middle hanging bare, hairy, and greasy; his black oily hair fell forward against bushy brows, and his beard was days old. His sharp little eyes came to life when I said: —

"If you're not a hell of a sight." I moved my head sadly from side to side. "Now when I finish talking to you, I want you to bathe, shave, and get into clean clothes. Understand?"

"Aye, *Signor*, aye. But whata the sail?"

"Forget the sails, Ripper. Do as I tell you — if you value your worthless hide. I think I can save it for you if you obey me to the letter."

"She sounda bad, sor. The trouble she come?"

"Plenty. And you, as second mate of the *Red Witch*, are right in the middle of it. You had the helm that day, didn't you?" I saw a slow, dull frown creep over his face. The thrust hit home, all right, and I saw his brown bleach out, leaving him a tense, chalky statue of unproportioned meat. "Who threw her over on the reefs that evening?"

"But — but — I — I, sor, I no lika the job! I taka they orders — so wella you know!"

I scoffed. "That'll sound good to the man who owned the ship." He frowned again, then darted sharpened eyes at me. "Yeah, Ripper, I'm telling you the truth. The owner of the *Red Witch* is the man in the wheel chair." His hand drew instinctively toward his pistol. "No, none of that, you fool. If you value your life, obey me, even if you have to defy Ralls. Understand?"

"Aye, sor." He ambled off, staring at the mass of vegetation beyond the rise as if in its depths there lurked a patient hangman. As the stern of the *Flores* swung around I saw the skipper, hands in pockets, strolling casually toward his ship and my ship.

Queer tricks are played by one's powers of sight, and I felt the twist as I viewed Ralls, once again a familiar man; gone was the scourge of the seas, in its stead walked the cool soul who knew no hurricane. Here was Ralls; and six hours until sundown.

As he came close, I said: "Anything of major importance ahead, Skipper? If not the boys can row us out into the lagoon. There's something I'd enjoy showing you."

"Very well, Sam. I'm ready."

"That's fine. Now let's get going. I want to prepare you for a neat little surprise." I roused a couple of our stoics and ordered them to hoist a cover over the boat. While they labored I rounded up two pairs of sea goggles, and a full quart of gin. These I tossed over to the one we called Omar, and then went below for a deep-sea lead and a glimpse at our various stores for certain objects I had in mind. I grimaced as I scanned the paraphernalia, and then I grinned. There it was, and if my measurements paralleled the blueprint I had in mind, well — the Dutch had no monopoly on brains. I returned to deck and caught the tail end of Ralls's orders to Ripper: —

"— And get the foresail in shape. We'll be hoisting anchor if a breeze holds in the morning."

"Forget it," I said. "Ripper, leave the sails alone. They're good for any wind we'll get here." Ralls turned his slow eye on me as I said, "Do I make myself clear, Ripper?"

"Aye, sor," he said reluctantly.

Ralls turned to the wop with a freezing order, slow and without emphasis, but more deadly because of it: "Mr. Arrezo, we'll trim the foresail."

"Ralls," I said, "suppose you pipe down and let me give the orders for a while. Otherwise we'll have it out here and now." Our eyes locked and held for a time. "Well?" I said.

He shrugged, turned to the ship's ladder. In another moment I followed, and soon we sat facing each other in the boat, both smiling easily. I pointed, and Omar and Djengi bent slowly to the oars, carrying us away from the *Quean* and out into the coral patches in the blazing sun.

2

Relaxed, I tipped the quart and then offered it to Ralls. "So you're planning another trip to the wreck?" I said. "And just what'll you use for divers?"

"I'll do it myself," he said, lighting a cigarette.

"Think you can find her?"

"Uh-huh."

"Well, it's your go from now on, Ralls. I'm checking out." He merely eyed me without expression, slowly blowing out a long streamer of smoke. "I'm tired of chasing a will-o'-the-wisp," I said. "We've passed up our riches, you and I; we've searched for easy windfalls instead of cargoes. Personally I think the devil took the *Red Witch* and her bullion. Me? I'm out of it and, what's more, I'm sick of your playing me loose. You've thrown away my share of the *Quean* with your ungodly passions. You've taken chances beyond any sane man's wildest dream. For what — money? No. For your personal satisfaction.

"Two nights ago you walked the rail. I talked with you then, Ralls. I asked you to let Carter alone. You agreed. Yes, you let me think he was safe. Well, we both know what happened, we both know who pulled him out of a shark's mouth.

"Straight ahead, Omar, to the mouth.

340

"Well, Ralls, I met a group of people last evening. Like to hear about them? You knew van Schreeven was an officer of Batjak. You met him in their office in Soerabaja many times; you were aware of his dislike for you, as well as free routes of their ships; you knew Sidneye owned the *Witch*, in fact you inspired the ship, after Sidneye was finished with you for trying to steal his wife. You knew all about the warning he gave you — eternal revenge if you went against his trust — and yet you wanted to hang on here, making me a party to your loss. And loss it is!"

His expression remained unchanged.

"I met a Dokter van Arken whom you know well — and that unknown quantity, Batjoek. I also met a man we both knew years before. Crazed, loony Loring. He's there. And I learned more.

"Remember the fellows who mastered the *Golden Hind* when you floated out from the Gilberts on a log? Cordtlaant? And his second, Noord? They're your friends." I laughed ironically. "Well, Ralls, they are on their way to this island.

"What for?" He gave no answer. "Why all the sudden interest in this damned island by your enemies? Planned retribution is hot on your neck, Ralls. You thought as much when you saw Sidneye and Batjoek and van Schreeven; and yet you tied me hand and foot to your past."

"But," Ralls said slowly, "you can step out of the picture — as you've planned." I probed his eyes and tone for irony, but in vain.

"Yes, and I shall. But only after you and I figure things out." I gave him the details of the bickering of the night before; I cited the offer and then Sidneye's reversal of the terms. "Of course they're playing cat and mouse with me, simply offering me a chance to save my skin. I'm merely an accessory to a fact — you, Ralls."

The inner sand hump should come into view, its arrival scarcely timed to my finish. Thus I ordered the boatmen to rest on their oars until I gave further orders. I sucked at the bottle, giving Ralls the eye.

"All of which brings us face to face with certain facts, namely: they are after you to the death, and, judging from what I saw, heard, and felt, a slow death; the slower the better. And if I guess rightly, they'll plan their trap around your talents, letting you trip yourself; they expect action from you this evening because you stood the rail the other night — but that was a Dutch error — they forget that you always perform on the night after. Or do they?

"Which you did, even though you were unable to complete your beautiful work."

That brought his eye around fiercely. I found the emotion I was playing for.

I continued while his eye was glued into the backdrop of my mind. "Thus you are one jump ahead of the pack, since you'll no doubt meet the night sanely. That is one point in your favor, though it only serves to prolong the agony. Another step now. The *Quean* is half mine, but since I have to choose between you and freedom, the schooner is to be written off entirely, thus leaving me free to make an honorable decision. My half of the *Quean* is yours.

"Is it noble of Sam Rosen to let you down, Ralls? Let's consider. You always think of my interests — you'd not beat Carter after a promise, you'd never invite the vengeance of the Dutch by making hellish advances at a daughter of the vice-emperor. Of course not." I glared at him, smiling in the flood of my temper.

"But you did," I said slowly, in low icy tone. "And the fact that I don't like it is my affair and your affair, and no concern of the Dutch.

"I'll not let you down, Ralls. But you'll pull sail out of here alone." His eye again came around under a frown of complete bewilderment, the first I'd ever seen in his face. I wanted it that way.

He flung a second cigarette into the water, turned his head around to the lazy schooner mirrored in full length from trucks to water line. I followed his glance for a moment before peering slowly in the opposite direction. I measured the distance to the coral heads and felt the time ripe for getting on. At my order the Malays applied slow motion to the oars and I again turned to Ralls.

"That's why I stopped the sail repair — a dead giveaway. I also ordered Ripper to dress in his best.

"Pull, Omar. Now, more to starboard — this way, you dolt!" Ralls stared into the horizon until I spoke.

"Ralls, we've come to the parting of the ways. After tonight it's finis." He did not say a word, he merely stared at me, his expression solemn, blank, and lazy.

Omar jabbered in Malay, pointing ahead, and I sat up in the boat to stare at the cause of his excitement. Ralls turned a casual eye and then a fixed expression of interest on the spot where the inner hump of coral sand attested to the wash current of receding tides. I had expected more than I received; surprise that should have reached up into astonishment and shock failed to appear in his eye. Like a stagnant tide that refused to rise and churn white the surface, he clung to the unruffled bearing that was such a part of him. Exuberant calm. We were almost over the first of the staggered pop-up shafts

342

that blocked the exit to the wide, free Bismarck Sea, and my glance at what I knew would meet my eye evoked in me a sense of awe and dread. Batjak's shadow hung low.

Then I experienced a real surprise: the pillars weren't raised by compressed air — they were lifted by the maze of thick cable. Probably by a hidden donkey engine somewhere near the Dutchman's house. They simply sat there leaning toward us, half a fathom under, solid steel barriers to anything but a rowboat.

We followed the oblique run of the cable only to see the strands enter jagged prongs of a thick coral shelf. Thus it was impossible to trace the cable that closed the crude jail doors on a ship — and the lagoon was as ship-tight as if sealed by concrete. Slowly we crossed to the other head and drew for our trouble a similar picture. Outside freedom met us with a wide shelf of coral rock and sand and a blue-green, and the disappearing deep blue of a safe drop to mighty fathoms, holding out to us, not more than a hundred miles away, the gold of the *Red Witch*.

I laughed ironically.

Ralls calmly scanned the sea. I saw a strange light in his eyes when, after ordering Omar to hold the boat still, he looked at the overlapping shelves two fathoms under. There three caverns winked filtered rays in luminous blue shadows, and darting fish of lemon color played about the mouths, ran in for a game of tag and out again, a dozen black and orange striped creatures giving chase.

"Yeah, I thought of that, too, Ralls. In fact I checked the stores before we left the ship. But I didn't expect to find cable."

"It's possible," he soliloquized.

"With everything else being equal," I added peremptorily. "Meaning wind and sails, and a threading of the narrows before the hounds of Soerabaja can get under way."

"Yeah. But it's possible."

I turned to view the sheeted emerald glare. I picked out the blue depths of it for Ralls's roadstead to freedom. My eye had scarcely cut the lagoon halfway to the *Quean* when I saw a boat moving off from the beach. Two blacks and a white man. I gazed for some time through the parched surface of heat waves before asking Ralls for his glass. Without obliging, he said, after a penetrating squint, that the occupant was Carter. He said more: —

"Let's mark this spot and move away."

"You're really afraid of him, aren't you, Ralls?"

"I'm always wary of enemies," he said casually.

"And you've really got an enemy there, Ralls. Too bad you couldn't have controlled yourself. You might not have made one out of me." He said nothing as he gave me a look that said, "I'll get along," and marked the spot with his eye. "Well, Ralls, now that you know, let's get back to the *Quean*," I said harshly.

"No hurry," he replied. "We'll row over to the north lip of the exit. I want to think."

I could hardly refrain from a chuckle. I said, "I should think you would, Ralls."

Across the shelf of the horizon, that hid the large island of Rambutyo, a low-slung cloud bank extended across the whole northern rim; it moved in a long racing streak, dipping gracefully into the water just beyond the curvature of the earth. But even the empty sea, shooting white rollers incessantly at the land, failed to harmonize with the soul of Sam Rosen. I hauled my winds without gusts, pushing up vast and strange and waveless swells; my nerves were on edge.

The boat grated against sand and rock, and the Malays leaped into the knee-deep water and pulled us in. Ralls, half reclined, his chin in the palm of his hand and an elbow near an oarlock, gazed lazily at a tern flying north. Halfway across the lagoon I could now see that the face under the pith helmet belonged to Carter. Soon Ralls and I sat on the coral nearest the calm waters of the lagoon.

Ralls eyed me in the manner of a keeper who regrets giving an inmate recess. "Sam, you're a damn fool. Those Dutchmen and Carter, and the girl, have affected your mind."

"Your version, Ralls," I said. "They had something to do with it, all right. They added the two that makes me see four."

"Sam, you're in love with the girl."

"I am," I said flatly.

"So you'd end our partnership." He leaned back on elbows, staring ahead, apparently content to dwell on definitions and comparisons. Then he sent me an amused glance, and sat up slowly with bottle in hand and a fresh smoke in his mouth.

"Here's to you, Sam." He lifted the bottle, drank deep, and then held it out to me. I accepted and said: —

"And to you, Ralls. May you learn and profit." I then drank level with him.

Carter was out over the Dutchman's bars, staring into the water. Soon he lifted his eyes to Ralls and me. He rowed on to the rock where we sat, his eyes twinkling, his mouth a set smile. He got out and joined us.

"Greetings, Sam," he smiled, ignoring Ralls. "I see the Dutch have raised a gift for the admiral out there. Pretty, isn't it?"

"Whatever happens," I growled, "remember it's your funeral." He pursed his lips, ran a hand through his short curls, and walked to the boat for his guitar. Before long he was talking to Ralls, it seemed, through the guitar. Ralls pretended Carter wasn't there, until Carter spoke.

"I must write a poem about the blocking of the lagoon. Let me think. How's this? The admiral sat on a coral bank — staring at his tropic jail —"

"Enough," said Ralls, without turning his head.

"— In a sweet hangover mood was he — you see he'd stood the rail. Not bad, eh, Sam?"

"It's not good," I returned. "And not good for you."

Ralls raised his bottle before turning a calm face toward Carter. He said slowly, without anger or any emphasis whatever, "I wish you hadn't come out here, Carter."

"You're inviting it," I said to Carter. He knew what I meant, all right, though he merely grinned; his eyes were alive with that brand of sheer joy he always experienced when he tormented Ralls.

"Thanks, Sam. You're such a swell friend," he mocked. "But back to my poem. Since the admiral of Blup Blup can't escape by even a rowboat — that's fixed, too, just like the eloquent disdain of Miss van Schreeven, whose silken unmentionables he stole." He paused to laugh, striking a harsh finale on the guitar.

I was about to give him more advice — he inspired anger, even from me — when Ralls, with the noiseless agility of a cat, got to his feet and literally jerked Carter up. Before I could say a word, he threw a right that caught Carter's jaw and sent him, and guitar, six feet out into the water.

There was something in the punishment, or in me, that rose up in rebellion at Ralls's high-handed methods of settling things. Perhaps I was exceptionally tense, touchy. At any rate I heard my own voice in anger.

"Ralls, you're answering to me for that!" He turned, somewhat surprised.

His black eyes, dancing like the heat waves, gave me steady, almost desolate appraisal.

"Sam, you're a damn fool."

An accepted fact, I admitted in silence. But aren't we all? Only those placid folks who tread the clear paths of declared rightness, who neither breed nor cultivate emotions of greed, hate, and strife, are lesser fools. And why should I risk my life when I had a clear path to the opposite? The answer was simple: that something deep inside of a man that rises in defense of his freedom of soul as well as of body; there are times when the weak feel their blood rise, as though it were stout with color. It is then that a lamb's soul seeks the transport of a tiger's.

My feet were planted wide apart and I held relaxed fists on my hips; only my eyes were knotted. Ralls sighed heavily, almost in resignation, and tossed the bottle easily to the ground, his eye following its muffled landing and short roll. Then without further ado he stepped slowly toward me. The cigarette dangled from the dead center of his thin lips, as always, and as he stood before me his hand moved up to retrieve it for a flicking of ashes; that and no more, easily done, lazily implied, contemptuously inattentive. His whole attitude was merely a display of the strange qualities of Ralls, whose estimate of any man held to one word: inferior. Like a giant he eyed the dwarf and asked silently that the puny one strike first.

I eyed him in that split second, seeking to mask my fighting eye that sought a spot for a first blow. Without flexing a muscle, I decided upon a spot. Running parallel with my mind was the message of warning: I was not toying with dull native or inept fighter, but a man whose eye was deadlier than any single thrust. The eye had not fallen on me as yet, and — I must make the most of that. I had no fond hopes of victory over Ralls.

Carter was out of the water, rubbing his jaw, emitting that same taunting chuckle. One of the Malays rescued his guitar. It had all happened in a split second, it seemed.

The distance was short, the roll was perfect, and my hard knuckles thudded against Ralls's neck and jaw with such force that I was thrown backward. His body rose with the blow and he landed two paces away, his head burrowing into the sand.

He was sitting up in the next moment, a hand at his jaw working back and forth. His eyes blinked in bewilderment, and then they lifted to meet mine with that same cigarette-dangling expression predominating.

"Not bad, Sam," he said. "Though you should have thrown it nearer the ear."

"To hell with your advice!" I said, moving toward him.

Ralls was again on his feet, grinning, dusting his dungarees and helmet. As his step put him within my range I stepped forward with a right to his head and a left uppercut to the chin. He rolled out of both, having broken the force with a swift step backward. I charged, bowing my neck and swinging a long haymaker that whizzed by his nose; coming up short for another stab I saw his face lose its pleasantness, I saw the eye I dreaded gradually taking shape, and I knew that my opportunity for giving him his dues was behind me. I had failed miserably. But, like a boxer hanging wearily in a lonely arena hoping against hope for one last stab before the curtain that rings louder and longer than the bell, I met his step forward with a left uppercut. That blow had all of me wrapped up in it.

"This is a pleasure," I said, and I meant it.

It fell against his chin, the short crack of a pistol, and I saw him leave his feet, his head snapping back before his body followed slowly, limply. He lay in the sand while I counted: one, two, three — four — five — six — seven; and then got to his knees, shaking his head in groggy manner. Eight — nine, and he beat the imaginary bell by a downward drop of the hand.

"Thanks, Sam," he said. "I was about to lose my temper when you landed that one."

"That's what I've been hoping for," I said fiercely.

"Too late, Sam." He grinned at me. "Hell, I can't fight you."

Carter had not said a word. He glanced from me to Ralls and back again, his expression minus any joy, triumph, sorrow, or surprise; a lingering question stood out like the stump of a bowsprit on a wounded three-master. Ralls continued to rub his chin and jaw, all the while flashing me a quizzical stare that matched the silent lift of his mouth, seeming to say over and over again, "Nice work, Sam." Then he moved away, picked up the bottle and said: —

"Here's to the future, Sam."

I stared at Carter again. Upon his face was the wake of the excitement, a discernible impingement of poetic melancholy. In the moment I felt untold pity for him. I wanted to throw that left at Ralls again. But Ralls held out the bottle, and before his grin I broke loose from my spell of amazement, pity, and tenseness. My anger lifted, surprising even me. I grinned, took the neck in my hand, and said seriously: —

"To you, Ralls. You're a bigger man than I thought." Perhaps our partnership was deeper than the measure of my mind; perhaps Ralls had a hold on me I could never break. At any rate I found Sam Rosen asking himself why his anger cooled so quickly. There was no answer; to the puzzle that was Ralls I added the disturbing uncertainty of Rosen.

"Thanks," he said seriously; and then he shook me hard when he said, "That means a lot, coming from you."

347

3

All that was left in me was a sigh. I felt a certain soli-
tude creeping over me, and I gave Ralls, with every step of a measuring
mind, credit for a victory nobly won. Then I said that he would resort
to anything to win a battle. But I knew full well that Ralls had tri-
umphed over the twin minds of Carter and Rosen in the most wholesome exhibit of the real man we had ever seen. It had to be just that,
unless Ralls was weakening under the pressure of Batjak. I wondered.

We boarded our boat for a return to the *Quean*, Carter barely ahead
of us in his white boat bearing the tressure of quatrefoils. Ahead the
upper shrouds of the *Quean* snared a breeze, and the lazy coconut fronds
bent in and moved back into place; before we reached the schooner
the lagoon leaped up with a lively stir and we felt the breeze; the
Flores moved slowly back against her mooring lines; and the sun went
dim overhead, a point to the west, while behind us a light squall raced
on the tail of the dimming gray-white mist; a dozen large birds flapped
their wings and held their pace well ahead of the water sieve bearing
down from the southeast; a tern flew toward us from land, its white
breast mirroring the emerald of the lagoon as it coasted low and on
toward the Dutchman's bars. My eyes drifted shoreward, to a lovely
windfall — I blinked them to dispel or lend verity to what I saw: —
Teleia.

She stood near the *Flores*, staring out at the two boats, the breeze
caressing her hair; her flowing skirt whipped and held, etching the
limbs of a lovely statue. She drove out all dismal thoughts of the past
and present, and robbed me of that bitter study of the too close future.
If only the melody sounded, Carter's guitar striking into chord before
his mellow voice emitted the sweetest of his verse: —

> Like the gossamer threads of evening,
> Rolling in on a South Seas moon;
> And the perfumed essence of beauty,
> From a Balinese festoon . . .

Ralls broke the spell with: "Sam," seriously, "something's amiss."

I sat up, alert, sending my feelers ahead. Teleia waved us in, glancing first at the *Flores* and then the *Quean*. Ralls's intuitive sense seldom
jested; he nudged Omar and Djengi into greater speed, and as our
oars groaned in the whipped waters I saw Carter come out of his mood.
He stared at Teleia and then at the ships, at last turning his eye upon us.

The first heavy drops from the advancing cloud struck down at us, causing me to glance over my shoulder. A thick sheet was closing down over the coral shelf; and its roar increased, matching the sound made by the wind picking up the sea and throwing it against the outer barricade. The sun was lost in tons of winged mist.

"She's only beckoning us in out of the rain," I said.

Then the cloud was upon us, throwing an endless sea of large drops that seemed one continuous stream, heavy and cold, and so thick our every breath was a gasping fight against drowning; the lagoon seemed to rise into the belly of the cloud, thus building a wall of water, solid and high, from the coral floor below us to the fathomless cloud above. The burst lasted only a minute or so; it ran on into the palms and over the rise, roaring on beyond the glistening green that dripped its weight of freshness. With feet in water and sopping wet all over, I mopped the rivulets from my face and peered at the spot I had last seen her. She was gone, and I wondered if she had reached the *Flores* in time.

We made ship in another minute, and Ralls was up the ladder, almost searching out the picture on deck before his head reached the rail. He paused momentarily and his hand dropped over his pistol; but he thought better of it, so it seemed. He climbed on over. I was directly behind him, and when I felt the deck planks under me he had completely disappeared. I heard his voice through an open hatch: "Ripper. Tewelliger." There was no answer. With eyes narrowed I fell into role; I turned to scan the beach and the rise for signs of any enemy, forgetting I was taking the other side. Carter's head popped up, and he was soon aboard.

"What's wrong?" he said, and I, with arms akimbo, shrugged as best I could. Then I turned my eye on him, fiercely, before saying: —

"And just why should anything be wrong, Carter? Or were you sent out as a decoy while your friends boarded the *Quean?*"

"You're loony," he said in complete disgust. I grudgingly apologized. "Quite all right," he replied, "but here comes Ralls."

The expression Ralls had failed to achieve when my fists worked on him was no longer missing — and it was trained on me. Slowly he walked up to me, flashing his black mood until he stood no more than two feet away. There was no reason for his attitude until I heard his voice.

"Sam," he rumbled tentatively, "that was a lousy trick."

I gave him the expression Carter had given me. "Go on," I said. "Spill it."

"It's your time to spill," he said. "A neat trick that, getting me off on a wild-goose chase so the crew could go over to the Dutch."

"Are you insane?" I flared forth.

"No. Didn't you tell Ripper to lay off the sails; didn't you tell him to dress up?"

"I did."

"Why?"

"For the reasons I've already explained, Ralls."

"And you expect me to believe that?"

"I don't give a hoot what you believe. Everything I do carries my stamp." He eyed me seriously for a half minute before turning to Carter; he seemed to turn the lad inside out.

"We're both jumpy, Ralls," I said slowly. "Only a moment before you came up I pulled the same act on Carter."

The sun beat down on the wet deck, sending up steamy vapor. The breeze had arrived with the cool squall, had departed with it, leaving a heavy stillness in the air. How fitting, I thought, to the scene on deck, to the hollow emptiness of the *Quean of Melbourne*.

CHAPTER XXX

I

I SAT down and wrote the following: —

DEAR MIJNHEER SIDNEYE:

In my opinion you acted rather hastily, and, judging from our parting words this A.M. — "Until sundown" — I must charge you with undue meddling. I refer, of course, to your seizure of the ship's sorry crew.

Therefore, if you are the kind of trader you indicate — one who adheres to his own spoken bargain — you will send the wop, the American, and the Malays back to their ship.

It seems your token kidnaping should serve its purpose with their return, for nothing is so excruciating as the long, harsh shadow of a prolonged climax; that and the sight of a foolish crew on a ship going nowhere.

Respectfully yours,

SAM ROSEN

"Get it to the Rotterdam Napoleon at once," I said to Carter. "And tell him to stop his meddling until I get there. I'll arrive, tell him, with the up of the moon."

With Carter gone, I got out of Ralls's chair and walked to a port-hole. It was too quiet, almost funereal in the packed cabin, so I was soon on deck, down the gangway, and walking out to the rise. There I peered about for some time before strolling on down to the promon-tory where I had first seen Mr. Bullit. Then, letting my feet take me where they would, and knowing full well their direction, I soon looked up to see the *Flores* before me. Before long I was aboard the craft.

"Teleia," I called. A muffled sound inside, and soon a door opened.

"Sam! Come inside, won't you?" I would, and I was soon sipping at a gin drink, similar, I reflected with a frown, to that she had worked up for Ralls only last evening.

"What happened up there?" I leaned back, pointing toward the *Quean.*

She smiled, raised her brows wearily, and leaned deeper into the chaise longue. She exhibited something at our every meeting; this time it was the line of her jaw running away into a creamy, slender neck, and up into the wisps of hair at her ears. What would I see tonight, or tomorrow? I, who had seen her completely nude — but not half so beautiful as now — continued to gaze at her, stirring up warm, racy blood, and toning it with worship, holding the helm of my thoughts safely in tow to the mast of her eyes.

"I say, Teleia, what happened?"

"Sam Rosen, do you ever say the opposite of what you're thinking?" Her smile was accusing.

"Yes," I said slowly. "I guess so. Why are you so beautiful? Why do your chin and throat meet so nicely? And why do I get a more glorious thrill now than — than the view in the pool?"

"I asked for it," she said, coloring. "But it's for you to answer."

"Shall I?" I gripped my glass, and the same quickening must have found my eye, for her conversation listed heavily, and toward the *Quean.*

"I suppose I should tell you what took place."

"And," I thrust, "aren't you the girl who accused me of talking to port while shooting the wheel to starboard?" My laughter joined hers, and our eyes locked happily, failing to tear apart in that moment when mirth subsides before the onslaught of another emotion.

I growled aloud, got to my feet, and poured a stout finger of straight gin down my throat, pausing only to gaze at the rapt expression in her face. It lingered there despite my doltish actions; or did it, I asked. Then, more to recapture my bearing than to seize upon a lengthened moment, I took the three steps that separated us.

"Teleia, I love you."

I stood there, staring fiercely into her upturned face, as if my very expression must burn the words into her brain and heart. From a glare I traveled all the way for an answer.

Softly she said: "I know, Sam. I knew it at the pool."

"Well?" I said. It lay in her eye, deep and clear one moment and, like the squall cloud, a veil of mist in the next; but it came through, cool and sane, cleansed of everything but truth. The lashes fell slowly, hiding the hulk that was me, and giving her respite for much-needed thought. It was then I thought in the negative — she refuses to hurt me.

"Sam, I —"

From the door a voice: "Begging your pardon, Mijnheer —" I turned about furiously and saw the handsome man who was her father — "but your note reached us."

"And?" I glared at him, my hands resting on hips.

"Your request has been granted." He smiled blandly, ever poised, ever mocking, seeming to bow slightly as he spoke. "With reservations, of course."

"And that point, Mijnheer van Schreeven?"

"The man you gave the curiously correct appellation of wop — Mr. Arrezo. Mr. Arrezo has already gone to pieces. He told us the location of the *Red Witch*." He gazed level with my eye, his smile ever playing in a straight line.

"Otherwise, had his condition warranted his dismissal by Dokter van Arken, we should have complied with your request in full."

His bow followed, and I saw in it the thoroughness of manners, the glory of triumph: the man was almost as deadly as his half-brother.

"Now," he said, having given the pause of dismissal to one subject before leafing a page into another, "regarding your interest in my daughter. But first, accept my apologies for having heard your declaration, Mijnheer Rosen. I assure you I had no intention of eavesdropping. Can you forgive me?"

I answered with the word he disgustingly put into my mouth, "Yes."

"Thank you. Mijnheer Rosen, I do not forbid you to see my daughter. On the contrary, I imagine the island life is rather dull at times, and I'm quite sure Teleia is sometimes bored." He smiled and turned toward the door as if to leave his complete meaning suspended above me.

"Of course," he added with perfunctory sedateness, "when the storm subsides a wholesome peace will give us all time to devote to our hobbies. A more propitious day lies ahead." With that he was gone.

I stared after him. "What a sweet rebuke," I said. "I've never seen anyone more talented in the art of building a fire with ice water!" I spun about to see Teleia smiling in puckish manner.

"Mijnheer Rosen," she said in stilted tone, "a more propitious day lies ahead." Her laughter was sweet, and we drank to each other's eyes, and a sweeter meeting.

On deck I turned about and faced her. "Just what happened on board the *Quean?*" I asked guiltily.

"So that," she said, "really was the object of your visit." Her eyes smiled steadily, their candidness making a liar of me. I accepted the truth joyously, returned her smile, feeling free of all worry and care since rising buoyantly above the degraded mood of the island and its inhabitants.

"So you can relax long enough to smile. I like you that way, Sam." She almost said with her eyes: I love you.

2

Once ashore I drove her out of my mind. The task ahead was perilous and paved with ifs — if a breeze came; if it held; if the winding channel of the lagoon could be traversed in the dark of night, once its mouth were freed; if the latter succeeded. We needed perfect timing and inspired seamanship, plus more of a crew than the ship boasted, to free the *Quean*, and Ralls. With Ripper it could be done, without him the odds leaned heavily to failure. Thus I turned my mind to Mr. Arrezo of the *Red Witch*, wondering of his condition at the present. Then I weighed my chances of using him for a good hour; he knew the feel of the ship's helm, her weather groans, her every whim; and with his greasy hands on the spokes, with Ralls ahead in a boat, the under light burning, and Tewelliger shifting sail, the *Quean* might be half through the twisting course before bedlam broke loose. But we needed an ally.

The *Flores* sat light, but there was enough of her below the water line to thwart sane pursuit at night. I doubted if Mr. Bullit could get under way in time to catch the schooner, even if such a foolish attempt were made; and I'd gamble two to one on his backing down for the try. Anyhow, I'd keep Tewelliger's eye on the trim craft until the zero hour. I imagined her tanks were empty, and unless oil rolled across the open beach, she could scarcely churn the lagoon — unless — and what I needed to know was: had she secreted drums below?

On board the Dutch boat was a machine gun. If the *Quean* possessed that the odds might be lessened. But in trouble Ralls would use it with more zeal than was necessary to amend the unevenness of chance. But, if neither side had the gun — and therein a thought was born, one which turned me about-face with quickened step to the girl aboard the *Flores Tandjoeng*.

"Teleia, I need your help. You're aware of what's going on here, aren't you?"

"Yes." She sighed before saying, "It is Ralls, of course. Everything here begins with Ralls. It has been that way since my uncle bought this island."

"Correct," I said. "The trap is ready to close on him." She nodded. "You made some reference last evening to an ordeal ahead. You suggested I study certain men. Any other suggestions?"

She eyed me seriously before reaching into the core. "The *Red Witch* was in Ralls's trust — with you as chief mate." She frowned slightly, almost sadly. "I've learned to detest the men who wrecked her."

"Well," I replied vigorously, "I'm guilty as hell." And for the first time in all those years of her ghostly wake I felt my guilt in its fullest sense.

"Are you, Sam?" she asked with concern. "Weren't you in a measure helpless?"

To humor her I said, "In a measure, as you put it. But enough of the past. Ralls is going to make a break for the open sea. As you know the mouth of the lagoon is blocked. The cables run off to nowhere."

"No," she said. "Not quite that far." She smiled, and I stared. "So you are siding with Ralls?"

"No. I'm washed up with Ralls. I gave him my half of the *Quean of Melbourne;* I am remaining here to take my chances. I am also interested in what this island offers — you. But that's neither here nor there. The brush comes tonight after high tide. Too bad he can't pull with the current."

"So you're remaining to take your chances," she mused, smiling. "I wonder, Sam Rosen." Then she said, "If the lagoon bars were lowered — perhaps I'd find the answer."

"What?" I asked, surprised. I thought of a hidden engine, a windlass, a maze of cable — then Teleia. But somehow she didn't belong.

354

"Nothing, Sam," she said, leaning forward to place a hand over mine. "But which side are you actually on?"

"I told your uncle I'd notify him at sundown, then changed it — with this plan — to moonrise. By that time Ralls will be moving up toward Rambutyo, I hope. With the breeze and a clearing of the reefs inside, and a passage out into the free deep, he'll go free."

"But can he run the channel at night? It seems impossible."

"It's a long chance we'll have to take."

"We? And you think my father and my uncle would forgive you?"

"One thing at a time is my policy. After I help him out to sea then I'll face the ogres of Soerabaja, begging your pardon for the appellation, though God knows it fits."

Her gaze fell upon me like a pointed weapon, impaling me, it seemed, as she sought to turn me inside out for a better view. I felt her appraisal of my wits and brawn, my chances of success in my plan, as well as those in the mystery to follow.

But she spoke quite another thought. "Do you expect me to go against my people and help Ralls go free?"

Crisply I said, "I thought you'd perhaps hate bloodshed enough to deprive both sides of the machine gun." My eye fell hard into hers and she met it momentarily, but she gave ground at last.

"Is that all?" she asked, ostensibly pleased at my concern for others.

"That is all," I snapped, "unless you are willing to descend from your lofty perch and secure the release of one Ripper Arrezo."

She got to her feet. "I'm afraid you have made a serious mistake, Mijnheer Rosen. I am, after all, my father's daughter."

"Of course," I returned, smiling, "your dismissal proves that. Good day, Miss van Schreeven." In another moment I stalked across the polished deck and leaped the starboard bow onto the beach. What I didn't know about women!

With swift, angered steps I lessened the distance to the *Quean* to nothing, and soon walked the deck to the companionway. Ralls was below. Tewelliger stood at the rail with two guns slung under his belly. On the stern sat a Malay with a rifle, and up in the ratlines was his counterpart. I paused and peered up at the shrouds in the main gaff-topsail to perceive a gentle rocking. "By God, enough to carry her about — almost," I said aloud.

I ducked into the companionway and yelled out, "Ralls!"

"Here." The answer came from deep below, and I soon sniffed at the mixture of hemp mingling with the stench of bilge. "Anything new?" he asked before I was within easy range of his voice.

355

"Yeah, plenty — I think. But what happened to the crew up at the Dutchman's?"

Holding his tongue until I stood near, he said, not raising his eye from the assortment of explosives, "Ripper, according to Tewelliger, was taken first. It seems the fellow Bullit was on deck with two guns in hand and a dozen blacks hovering behind him. Sidneye directed the show. The crew was marched to the house and treated with rum and food. But not Ripper. Tewell' said they went to work on him at once, rushing him into a huge aquarium and giving him his choice of talking or being thrown to a big squid. Fantastic, I'd say."

"But I saw that squid," I said.

Ralls peered up at me. "Then I reckon Ripper talked."

I said, "Van Schreeven just informed me he gave up the location of the *Red Witch*."

A slow question at last escaped Ralls's lips: "Which one?" He shrugged; I grinned with him.

Pulling a cask close to him, I sat and began unraveling a length of wire, eyeing all the while the sticks of dynamite and caps, thinking of the toughness of Dutch cable as I did so. We sat there for ages, it seemed. I started to get up but Ralls detained me with a hand on my shoulder.

"Sam," he said, "I was just thinking." I lifted my brow attentively. "There's going to be a mad scramble here, and a run to the reefs. That's why the old boy sent for Cordtlaant and Noord. They'll follow up on Ripper's squawk, and soon." He stopped there, gave silence a ratifying pause before saying, "I've got an idea, Sam. Like to hear it?"

"Proceed," I said absently.

"It's too big for me to tackle alone, Sam. Now that I'm minus the best water eye that ever swung a tiller, I can't handle it." I felt his play for my aid. "But with your help, I think it could be done. Still want to hear it?"

"Let's have it," I said absently.

"I'll run this channel, Sam, if you'll set off the charge. Then we'll head for the treasure. Wait. I'm not finished. We can beat the Dutch to the *Witch* and I'll do the diving myself.

"Fifty-fifty, Sam. Enough to make us rich for life."

"Ralls, if Ripper gave a location, ten to one a ship is plowing toward that spot at this moment. If we got through, and the *if* is minus any odds in our favor, we'd meet an armed ship."

"Why let that stop us?"

"I don't know, Ralls," I said, nursing a frown. "My better judgment says no."

356

"It's worth a try," he said.

"Suppose, Skipper, you take the boat and Omar and plant the dynamite under the cable ends. Do a little diving on the way out and reach the ledge in a slow route. I'll handle this end, and do a bit of thinking on the side."

A half hour later I stood on deck watching the pair. I saw Ralls dive as if for pearls. I was thinking, and fast, hoping against hope my decision would be a good one. I walked down the deck, throwing an occasional glance at the boat as I did so; I saw Ralls pop up with a cluster of pearl oysters. Then I turned my eye to the beach, swept it clean from the hook on the north to the south beach, then pulled in my glance to the *Flores*.

I started when I saw Teleia. She leaned toward me, made a strange sign, and without further ado stooped and lifted something that went over and splashed, before shooting straight down into five fathoms. It was the machine gun.

3

The sun slipped into the last stretch of sky and hung there interminably, throwing splotches of palms across the *Quean's* deck, and a solid mass onto the beach and out into the water; only the upper ratlines and masts were minus any lengthening of the mad island that stretched its tentacled shadows about the ship. No sunset squall tailed the day, and no fanning wind swept across the desolate stretch of sea from the southeast. The breakers rolled in on their own power, and smashed against the rocks in a pounding noise of their own making.

Then I saw and felt the blanket of night, heavy, steamy, heady. It meant only one thing: action. I turned about and saw Ralls rise out of his lazy pose against the rail.

I trained my eye on the southern and eastern shoulder of the sky for any sign of a moving cloud against the low stars. I saw none. Then a crosswind dived low and moved across the deck, causing a rattle of loose tackle in the schooner's rigging. I turned about and saw nothing but the monotonous night, though I felt the breath from the northeast.

"How's that, Skipper?" I said, chuckling.

"Couldn't be better," he said. "Ready, Sam?"

"Ready. I'll handle the ropes here with the others."

"Djengi," he said, "get ashore and loosen the warps."

"Wait!" I whispered. "Someone is running toward the ship." I walked over to the rail, expecting any new trick or any resumption of the old; the feet on the beach beat a rapid thud to the water, and when there I heard a voice: —

"Sa me. No a shoot!"

"Ripper!" I exclaimed. "How did you do it?"

"The girl, she talka fast. I no say how, but *Signorina* have a way witha *Signori. Gesù Cristo!*" His voice quivered.

"Hurry aboard, Ripper," I said, "we're pulling sail."

"Sa good." He said it over and over.

"Ripper, can you run this lagoon in darkness?"

"Sa good. I try. You sinka the lamp and rida bow. I make it. Mother Maria, I make it!"

He was on deck shaking like a leaf. I sent Tewelliger after the bottle and held Ralls back until Ripper was fortified with gin. Then I stepped aside. "Where did you tell them the *Witch* went down?"

"One a forty-eight na four a tenth ata three na one a tenth."

"Doppel? And they believed you?" I said. "Come, Ripper, the truth."

"Why doubt him?" Ralls said.

"Because I heard van Schreeven tell how they searched out that position."

"Sa right?" he cried, backing off. "They tella me the same, but I saya she slida deep. I tella same and no change!"

"Well, we can settle that later," said Ralls. "Right now there's a breeze, and a big job ahead."

I said nothing. My mind went back to Teleia's last words: "Mijnheer Rosen, I am, after all, my father's daughter." From there I leaped the gap to a machine gun that now lay on the bottom, and up to the present and my second request — Ripper. And I was the man who had almost let Ralls talk her out of my life. I had a date with her at the pool. Would I keep it?

"Ralls," I said. "I've made up my mind."

He stopped short. "Yeah?"

"I'm staying," I said grimly. "But I wouldn't miss the trip to the mouth for all the gold in the ocean." There was no answer. I had expected none.

The ship was a ponderous hulk, a thing calling for motion, for just enough sail to ease her along, for all hands at stations. Djengi was aboard with the warps and the *Quean of Melbourne* gave a little to the wind, her bow lazily swinging out into the lagoon. Ralls took his position at the bow almost above me; I was in the boat below hooking

the under-lamp cord to the battery. Just when the point struck opposite the shore, dead east, I gave it the juice. The bow of my boat was
hooked to a chain running from the jib boom; I was more than half the
hull's length ahead of the *Quean*. But I could see ahead, and that was
what counted. Directly above, the boom pointed at the eastern sky.

"Easy to port," I said in low tone, aware that I must allow enough
time for our crew to supplement the action of the helm by a proper
trim of sails; and Ralls picked it up. "Easy to port," he passed to
Tewelliger, who stood forward of the foremast; and from Tewell' to
Ripper at the helm — "Easy to port"; and with little time separating
lamp from rudder, the *Quean* leaned to obey. Nicely and quietly done,
I said, grinning at the vision of Sidneye when he saw the lagoon minus
any schooner.

The wind back of us was a dream come true. Leaning over and
peering closely for the channel, I got an excellent view of the floor
many yards ahead, and by balling the lamp vision was good in any
direction. But I guessed on pulling for the opening twist out of the
nest, though the odds were with me since I'd traversed the course
only that afternoon in a rowboat. Then I saw it, looming like a huge
gap leading to the end of the world, my light digging just so far through
the crystal wet and then bouncing out against a thick wall of purple-
green.

"Hard-a-port," I said. The order echoed off Ralls's tongue, and I
heard Tewelliger's distant drone. No sooner did the *Quean* have the
wind full on her port quarter than I gave the next order, "Shift the
helm — hard over, and hold."

"Shift the helm — hard over, and hold," said Ralls.

Tewelliger's voice died out with "Shift the helm — hard over, and
hold," and the bow began its rake into a quarter circle, north to east.
Having Ripper at the wheel eased the tension. He seemed to lean all
the way from stern to bow, throwing a third eye ahead of a ship.

"A light on the *Flores*," Ralls said.

"Now, helm amidship. Forestaysail, Ralls — and sheet hauled flat
aft," I said for answer, adding, "What kind of a light?"

"Nothing unusual," he said, after the relay. I knew then that Teleia
was aboard; for only she would fail to blast a warning.

"Steady the wheel and hold the boys ready —" Something struck
my shoulder, and I peered back into the boat. I could see nothing
but I knew it was a flying fish. The light was beginning to call up all
sorts of curious life below. But the channel was dead ahead, and dark,
and sharp eyes were needed.

"Easy up there, Ralls. Steady! We're in the channel." Below, and always beyond my vision, horrible jagged fingers seemed ready to dive toward the ship, but the *Quean* slipped on into the safety of the light, her bow majestically leaning toward the Dutchman's bars.

"Excitement on the *Flores*," said Ralls.

We moved ahead in slow motion, though it seemed we were clipping along wing and wing. Danger stalked every inch of the black roadstead. "Steady helm, Ralls. Steady, and hold her ready to pay off quickly."

"We'll chance it with more sail," he returned. Soon the *Quean* seemed to leap forward.

It was his funeral and not mine. Then I forgot everything but what lay ahead. Directly toward the bow of my boat a pointed shelf of coral almost broke the surface. There was scarcely enough water over it to float the tiny craft I rode. To make matters worse I was unable to shout an order since I saw no visible path for the *Quean*. On it came, a chisel head tapering off to north and south, splitting the main road and preventing our swing in either direction. It was within twenty feet of me, then closer, when I saw it slope to starboard and sweetly under, leaving at least seven fathoms and a long play for the turn. But not enough considering our proximity, I said, pivoting the lamp back under to portside for a second glimpse of the hugging wall. No, scarcely enough to turn the *Quean*, but it was do or die.

"Ralls," I said, giving my tone a grim ring, "run down all headsails— fast!" Then I shouted, "Put her head to starboard! Hard over!" Measuring my distance from the fore point of the *Quean's* water line, I decided to hoist the lamp and chance a gutting of my boat so Ripper could maneuver her without tearing out the beam planks on the turn. I pulled the lamp and sat back tensely for the bite of coral.

And it came.

The reef tore a small hole in my boat but it lifted easily, swinging onto the cable and out of danger. The *Quean* swung around until she paralleled the beach; then the helm was shifted and she eased gradually forward, pulling slowly over onto the seven-fathom safety cushion, though widening the swing of the stern with every foot. The lamp was again under and exploring the southeast twist. It opened nicely, I saw, and I relaxed. But all too soon, for a scrape vibrated from the hull to the bowsprit and down the cable; I felt the ship falter, tugging as she lost pace in a wedge of coral.

Would she make it; could she? Excitement broke loose on deck, and I heard Ripper's voice shake as he pronounced the verdict: she was hung by her rudder. The swing, then, had been too much for her length; missing by inches the path I'd navigated. I unhooked the boat from the cable, grabbed an oar, and sent the waterlogged craft into a spin sternward. I made it quickly and verified Ripper's assertion: there she was, held fast by the coral.

"I told you we had too damn much sail! Get the boys down," I cried. "We can free her, maybe." We did, but not until flying jib, jib, forestaysail, and foresail were set to twist her off.

I was hooking the jib-boom cable to the boat when the whole sky seemed to light up. A flare burst and fell slowly from away up, painting the runaway *Quean* in vivid silver. A gun cracked from the beach, and its charge whined overhead. A second shot thudded against the mainmast, while a third, well put, brought a scream from Ripper.

The *Flores* was putting out, but I felt she wouldn't brave the channel at night. Then I understood her strategy; she could pull to the borders of the reef and find us an excellent target. That was exactly what she did.

Ralls returned their fire with pistol, while I yelled for him to spring sail and take the wheel. Soon the chains jerked my craft forward. The slow exchange of shots continued.

"I got somebody," Ralls said.

"Who's at the wheel?" I asked.

"Ripper. He only got a leg scratch."

"Then tell him that unless he steers like he never did before they'll finish him off. And hold all hands at stations."

I turned again to the circle of light before me, realizing for the first time the target I made. A bullet popped the water within a yard of me, sending a white plume of water into the air.

"Easy to port," I said, welcoming the turn that should put the schooner between me and the fire. "A couple of points more — another. Now steady your helm." On the turn a shot ended with a *ping* on the chain near my head; a whine, and a resounding spit as the bullet died somewhere in the water.

"Close," I said aloud. "Too damned close!"

The ship labored again under canvas too heavy for her track; it was plain crazy sailing all the way, with me sweating and staring hard into the beams ahead. With the sound of pistols and rifles cracking above and behind, with a shark's jaw moving to within a foot of me in the water, with ragged fingers of coral looming into the weakening rays of the lamp, I kept to my post. Gone was the thrill of the run that couldn't be made. It was a gigantic, thankless performance I'd taken upon myself to see through.

361

The firing subsided as we drove on out into the lagoon. The *Quean* pushed on, the water purling from her bow; insane, she seemed, twisting toward the exit in the black of night with a small bone in her teeth.

"Ralls," I said, "better slow her. We're getting close." With the slack I peered long and hard. "Let her coast," I ordered. "Breakers ahead — getting close."

For fifty feet she crept straight ahead. The first bar should be near. I peered, perplexed, then threw the light to the bottom. They were down, flat, like fallen tombstones in a lonely graveyard! Teleia! So I thought, before deciding that the Dutch might be playing us loose. But why? And so I thanked Teleia for the deed, though it was only a wild guess in the dark.

"Ralls! The bars are down! Give her sail."

"Yeah? It's cat and mouse then. We'll blast the cable just the same."

"You'll give her sail!" I thundered. "All sail, and fast!"

"Sure you don't want to come along?"

"Good luck, Ralls," I said. "See you someday, maybe." With that I shoved off, slowly pulling oar toward the dim outline of the barricade, wondering as I did so if the Dutch would raise the bars up under the schooner.

"The same to you, Sam," he said after long moments. "Here's to you, partner." I said nothing, but rowed on across the last of Sidneye's pop-up blocks, over the shelf where the sticks lay, and toward the coral rising slowly out of the sea. A bird flew down close to the water and upped just in time to miss my head, clacking loudly in surprise; a fish broke the surface, and the night, silent and close, gave itself up to the pounding surf outside.

The boat, almost filled by that time, was pulled up onto land some yards inside the lagoon, and I turned about for a last glimpse at the schooner. A dim outline held my gaze, a ghostly shape standing out quietly to the gap. Only the red glow of a cigarette told me that Ralls stood easily on deck, his eyes half closed, his composure at its peak. The *Flores* stood out from the beach far back, showing three lights in her ports. Then the *Quean* was over the bars. She was safe.

"And why," I said aloud, "don't they make some move?"

I raised my head for another picture of the schooner. The stars seemed to bend down from the sky to high-light her canvas, her bulwarks, the line of her bow. The silent *Flores* just stood there, her lights dancing in the water. I sighed heavily. No need for dynamite, though

I'd have welcomed the sound. All about me were silence, the roaring surf, and dull concentric ripples that moved on as if in perfect peace with the world.

4

I stood with arms akimbo on the very edge of the rock, the lagoon on my left, the ocean on my right; I saw the *Quean's* mainsail in the brisk wind, and above the song of the surf I heard a cracking as it bellied and strained forward.

"So long, Sam," cried Ralls. "See you in Singapore." As he said it, a second flare illuminated the whole world.

I turned away, why I don't know, but I was in the boat in another moment. Then, unable to hold back a farewell glance at the ship I loved more than I'd ever imagined, I turned about. Another flare went up before the second died, and as I stared at the stern pulling over the outer delta, it happened: —

The earth shook, enough to dislodge the oars from my hand, and the *Quean's* stern literally rose out of the water, splitting in half, it seemed; and the wall of water that reared its white head high caught and held the incandescence of the flare, shaped itself into a gargantuan plume, spotted here and there with timber and writhing ropes. The rudder held to one piece high in the air, and it leaned toward me with a strange companion, a long gray shark. Both landed off to my right, sending up another shower that drenched me before the white wall over the *Quean* had settled back to its home. A piece of flying metal tore an oarlock from the side of my boat before striking hard at my shoulder. Almost in the same moment something grazed my head.

A scream, then another, fitting echoes to the detonation of the sea; and then the fourth flare: in its silvery glow the *Quean of Melbourne* listed heavily, shot her stern into the sand floor at the ocean's lip, and slowly went under, all of her. She settled crazily, her bow at forty-five degrees one moment, and down she went, with only her foremast in sight. She seemed at peace in the coral sand. But not so. The outer hump, the summit of a marine hill, leaned to the suck of the ocean, tipped the scales, and sent her down. Slowly the mast glided seaward, and down, and the ship rolled into countless fathoms to find her grave.

I thought of the bell destined for Lorengau, almost hearing its sad solemn notes as it took its place in the carillon of Davy Jones.

Then everything went black.

CHAPTER XXXI

I

MORNING came with startling celerity. A portentous, muddy gap bridged the long hours up to my dismal awakening. I sat up in a strange bed in a strange room, my head pounding, my shoulder throbbing madly. Frowning at the repeated vision of a savage burst of water, of floating debris, a chorus of screams tuned to a departure from life, I glared at a bad dream. With a tighter frown of trepidation I slowly turned my eyes upon my shoulder. It was bandaged.

How foolish I felt. Giddy, and almost too weary to heed any remonstrance from my churning mind. Over and over I said, "Get a hold on yourself, Sam," but it was little use. I sank back and slept fitfully. When next I opened my eyes I stared up into the marble face of Dokter van Arken.

Without a word he bent to his task, the examination of my arm. I peered closely, wondering what I'd see, and if I could expect elucidation from that bigoted man with gimlet eyes. I decided against a try, and directed my full attention to the wound. Long and ragged it was, red raw and streaked under the skin; an unhealthy sight. He applied a strange ointment after burning several edges with liquid fire, and then gazed happily into my eye. I met his steady look with a smile of defiance and he turned to the knot on my head. He brought forth a nasty rag clotted with blood and hair.

"Remind me, Dokter, to inquire how the *Quean* met her doom. No hurry." I was rewarded with a silence that followed him to the door, and I felt no more alone after he departed.

I got up to survey the room, hoping I'd find a drink. I found fresh clothing in drawers and closets, a stack of books, a deck of cards, paper and pen, a bottle of citronella, and other hodgepodge equally uninteresting. But no drink other than a glass of quinine water. Frowning, I took stock. The furniture was matched mahogany, comparatively new and handsome; and paneled walls met maroon carpet and low ceiling; and a door led to a bath. That just about completed the picture. I stepped to the exit and tried the door.

It was locked.

"Well?" I said. "Well!" And the third time it gave off the thin hollow sound of a lead dollar.

The sun climbed high and then began its lean. A Javanese servant brought cold rice, mutton, and tea; an hour later he returned for the service, departed, and I did not see him again until just before sundown. Again cold rice, mutton, tea, taro, and, I'll never forget, a gin flask filled with quinine water. Excruciating? Find the superlative. All that day I did nothing but sleep, pace the floor, listen for the approach of visitors; I attempted a book, wondered about Ralls, Ripper, and Tewelliger, about Teleia; I asked who lowered the blocks, Sidneye or Teleia. No answer. I was another Loring. But Loring was merely a nervous wreck, and not an enemy. Another day of confinement and I'd express both eloquently. Late in the afternoon I settled down to an interesting session of solitaire, fancying myself in an air-conditioned gaming house, drawing five dollars for every card played up; I kept score and ended the day owing the house thirty-seven dollars. Sighing heavily I tossed the cards aside and greeted sweat, pain, and fever.

The second day rolled by like the first; there were no visitors other than van Arken and the servant; there were only a deck of cards and a wall of mystery. Surmounting all desire for freedom was my longing for Teleia. Her face appeared on the cards, and I saw it in the mirror while shaving. Toward midafternoon on that day, two days since our pleasant meeting, and two decades by the slow drag of my own company, I reviewed my declaration of love. I, a free man, had presumed upon my invincibility, upon our equality. Ludicrous indeed, I said, and I heard the ironical echo in my laugh. How had I ever been so blind; had I not been a penniless nobody running free merely because it fitted the whim of an avenging Dutchman?

"Yeah," I said wearily. "A fool is one who to his grave — pursues the clouds he cannot own — and leaves a wealth of things undone — his tomb a final steppingstone." I paused and said sourly, "Rot!"

I paced back across the room, saying between my teeth, "To hell with the dismal mood, Sam Rosen. Get your mind to working or you'll find this place your final steppingstone."

The sun was two hours under when I was honored with visitors. I would have welcomed the devil himself. And when the door moved slowly in I said I'd hit the jackpot — the devil in a wheel chair. He rolled in and came to a halt some three feet from the doorway. The Moluccan, Batjoek, and van Schreeven brought up the rear. Such procedure suggested a lengthy session, though I was at a loss. The three stared at me, level and blank, though Sidneye's face seemed alive with an expression of amusement.

Leaning against the pillow prop, I said, "Welcome, gentlemen, to Rosen Manor." I grinned, happy for their visit no matter its portent. "I regret I cannot return your hospitality of some evenings back, gentlemen, but you see my stores of liquors and such were unfortunately blown to hell a few nights back."

"Yes," Sidneye said slowly. "We understand." Turning to the door he cried out, "Bring in the refreshments." And lo and behold! Ice and gin, and hors d'oeuvres.

"A pretty sight," I said, smiling lazily, "though I'm scarcely tempted to indulge, Mijnheer Sidneye." I sought to leap ahead of the Dutch brand of torture, if such it proved to be, though I drooled inwardly, admitting I'd sell out, almost, for two tall ones. "A lovely place, this," I said, unbending an arm for a sweeping gesture. "Restful, quiet."

"Yes," he agreed slowly, mockingly. Then — "Mijnheer Rosen," seriously, "there are a number of questions I must ask, the first of which I hope will clear up the only remaining mystery." I said nothing as I frowned at his words, thinking Ralls and the entire crew dead. "Why, Mijnheer, did you engineer the *Quean's* sensational and foolish run for the sea and then fail to sail aboard her?"

"A fair question," I said, "though I'm afraid you flatter me. As you should know, Ralls is quite gifted with rashness."

"Was, or is?" he asked.

"That's your question. It so happens the world fell on me before the last plank descended into the water."

"Quite true," he said. "But you were seen sounding the channel with a light. Why, when we made known our discovery of the escape, did you not leave with your ship?"

"Because, Mijnheer, I intended beating the moon to you with my decision. Ralls and I had our parting."

"Yes. And so you thought you could help him escape and then return to us? Obviously you did, and I must say that your decision was that of an insane man."

"True," I said with all seriousness, "though I scarcely gave thought to what would follow. I was really fed up with Ralls, though I wanted him out of here, and free. I must admit that I went against you, Mr. Sidneye. Regrets? Not one, sir, not one."

"And you'd do it again?" he said.

"The circumstances will never be the same. I handled the situation according to my ideas of right and wrong. I washed my hands of

Ralls, helped him all I could, and if he is alive now I'll do nothing to help him — and neither will I rise against him. Nor is that all. In the first place I owed you nothing, sir, except an apology for one act. I refer to the *Red Witch.*

"Wait. Let me have my say, Mr. Sidneye.

"Ralls deserved, perhaps, what you had in mind for him, but I did not care to be a party to helping him into the shoes of Baron von Streicher. Therefore I aided him in his attempted escape, unaware you held the winning ace. I've played my hand and lost. That's my story. And — let me tell you this — I'm ready for your worst."

He broke the short silence with, "So you declare yourself our enemy?"

I laughed. "Quite the contrary, Mijnheer. These past two days suggest that you have taken that initiative."

His brows arched. "So they do, Rosen. But could you accept a drink?"

"I could," I gave off readily. "But only if you intend that I should drink it. I could also do with a cigarette, though I don't intend having one snatched from my lips."

"Your opinion of us!" he exclaimed.

"Is so foolish," I added sarcastically.

With a most delicious drink came a startling revelation: "We have come to seek your aid, Rosen." I leaned forward, genuinely surprised. "Yes, you heard rightly. Since you are a part owner of the ship we must call upon you to clear up a little matter with the authorities. It so happened that our flares attracted the attention of the Australian patrol boat on a regular run of the Admiralty Group. It was, unfortunately, within range of the sound, and upon its arrival the wreckage told a sad story."

"I see. But what can I do?"

"I have prepared a statement which I should enjoy having you write off in your own hand — after making sure you can answer any and all questions pertaining to the affair. Shall I read it?"

At my nod he read the following: —

The owner of a half interest in the *Quean of Melbourne,* a two-masted schooner of American registry, so forth, and so forth — I, together with my partner Ralls, and our crew named herewith — sailed into the lagoon of the island named for the express purpose of mending sails and repairing ship in general. En route to Lorengau with cargo listed as follows — we were detained for four days by the objective named. A most cordial reception from the owner of the island, Mijnheer Mayrant Sidneye, and his guests was extended us, and out of our conversations we agreed to accept for delivery in Soerabaja the following cargo: two tons of dynamite, the excess remaining on the island from that declared in Lorengau in December of nineteen hundred and thirty-six, so I am told. Its purpose: the widening and deepening of the lagoon for trading vessels.

With cargo cushioned properly we threaded the lagoon with the make of the evening tide on the eighth day of May, nineteen hundred and thirty-nine. We stood by for a breeze which came with darkness. After navigating the channel we hoisted sail just inside the lagoon and pointed through. Our friends were gracious enough to send up flares, and with the third we pulled for the open sea.

The explosion that followed was terrific, and there is no accounting for it — it simply happened, throwing the schooner's stern into the air, splitting her bottom and deck planks wide open. Something struck my head and arm, and I knew nothing more until I opened my eyes on the following morning in the home of Mijnheer Sidneye. Under the excellent care of Dokter van Arken, the noted scientist, I improved rapidly.

I mourn the loss of Mr. Tewelliger and the two Malays; I pray for Mr. Arrezo's recovery, though his condition is critical; but above all I grieve most for my partner, Ralls, missing, and presumably down on the bottom with the ship.

He eyed me narrowly. I remained silent and I slowly reviewed the casualty list. Then I said in abject manner, "An excellent statement, Mijnheer. Quite thorough," to which he replied: —

"Pointed, plausible, and passing. I take it for granted you're prepared to execute the document and lend it your signature." There was a world of invitation in his tone, and I, the trader, grinned into analogous mood, whetting my mind for a waiting tongue.

"Of course," I replied. "But first let us weigh the value of such a statement. I haven't the slightest hope of bargaining successfully with you, Mr. Sidneye, since all things are in your favor; but the law of this archipelago, I'm sure, would consider your actions a breach of trust."

"I don't follow you, Rosen."

"I think you do," I said slowly. "Mining a lagoon mouth is a dangerous and unappreciated act — for a foreigner. But you have the crater filled by now, I presume."

"Indeed. It was dragged before the Union Jack paid call."

"Which gives my statement the last sad note of a completed quest

— taps. I can almost hear the long notes bouncing across the waves, a farewell to a schooner and crew, to a wicked but brave skipper. To the individualist, Ralls." I paused for a heavy sigh, simulated, and dedicated to my outward gullibility. "So the climax comes, leaving only the American small-time trader, Sam Rosen, as the uninteresting anticlimax." I ran the four faces before me in silence for the slow count of one, two, and three, before closing in with the opposite of my mournful deductions.

"But, of course, with Ralls alive, and I am sure that he is, my statement to the authorities becomes more valuable to you. So, Mijnheer Sidneye, begin there with what you have to offer; a little above the par you had in mind."

"Nicely done, Rosen. There are errors, however, in your expression. Ralls, I'm afraid, has given his last order."

"Then, Mijnheer, why not open up with the truth?"

"Because, Rosen, the truth is ever irrelevant. Let us talk in terms we both understand — money."

"Your check for a million guilders would enrich me," I said. "There is so much I could spend it for in the confines of my room."

He grinned and said, "Now we are getting down to cases. Your first wish then is for freedom. However, Rosen, you are the only man outside of Batjak's top five who knows her authentic past. And you're aboard her present."

"I should enjoy becoming a member of that great firm," I said, grinning boldly. "But only after I learn who lowered your toy blocks in the lagoon."

"Any protégé of Captain Ralls," said the bald invalid, "has a touch of the *Golden Hind* in his blood." Thus he parried my jocular thrust. "You are free to come and go as you please on this island. You are my guest.

"As for money, suppose I pay you in full for the ship?"

"The *Quean?*" Bemused, I stared. "She was Ralls's. I gave him my half on the afternoon before she pulled out."

"Ralls," he said icily, "is no more. I am prepared, therefore, since your ship was not ensured, to pay you her market value, plus the estimate you place on the cargo listed."

"Wait," I said. "There's a catch to your proposition. Just what is it that inspires your paying out a heavy sum when I, as easily as Ralls, could have gone down with the *Quean?*"

He laughed aloud before replying: "Rosen, you have unwittingly done us a great favor."

369

I made no effort to fathom his meaning. Instead I asked a question — when could I leave the island? The answer was not lovely: —

"That," he said slowly, "will follow a cruise to the reefs. We shall then return here and remain for a few weeks. At that time we embark for Java.

"Teleia's wedding is set for July."

The brittle and cold glass was at my lips when he said it; to cover my feelings I downed its contents in long gulps, wishing in the moment that followed I'd saved half a finger. Full of surprises, he said: —

"She should be fully recovered by that time."

"Recovered!" I said, voicing all the surprise I felt.

"Yes, Rosen, from a bullet wound. The shot was fired from the *Quean's* foredeck."

2

If dullness hovered over me during the two days of confinement, its opposite reached out to claim me in the days that followed. With a mighty hiss and roar, like savage gusts from olive-green clouds, one event overlapped the other, with startling revelations ever standing down the coast of experience. Since I expected little if anything of importance to lie in the wake of the schooner's end, I sought enjoyment of my so-called freedom with a heart both heavy and numb. To Ralls I ascribed "Glorious finis"; to Teleia the same. But not once did I regret any direction I had taken.

Mystery is ever a balm to the sore heart, and I had in my possession an abundant store to spread over my sentimental wounds. First, Ralls; and was he dead? Then Ripper; and was he alive? No explanation was forthcoming from my host, and the statement, "Rosen, you have unwittingly done us a great favor," was inscrutable.

That night I moved about the house a guest. Longing to see Teleia and express my regrets, and sharing a strong desire to learn a few things from Carter, I found myself fighting patient wisdom. The latter won, however, and I retired early, after copying Sidneye's account of the *Quean's* end. With the sun I was awakened and asked to join a Britisher at breakfast on the east veranda.

He was a cynical sort, tall and bronzed, immaculately dressed in whites; he reeked with a superiority that is Oxford, impinged with British imperialism. But he was a man of experience, of thirty or thereabouts. Sheraton was his name. A twisted smile, emanating from a lean face, greeted my step onto the veranda; and I, appraising the new face, admitted the acquaintance of a strong character or a perfect fool. Over carabao tenderloins, tea, crumpets, and fruit, we stabbed out a shallow conversation, each feeling out the other's excuse for imposing upon the niceties of the present day and the world at large. He let drop in resonant, English-steeped tone a hint of his family tree; a twisted trunk with gilded bark, I thought. But Rosen, the lowly boatman, was more than impressed; he asked, listened, and was amazed; he all but fawned.

Before our meal was finished I saw his stare lengthen. He thought me a "deucedly vulgar bloke," whose questionable occupation, that of inter-island trader, was, by the loss of a vessel, reduced to the pitiful state of a beachcomber. But — since his duty was to investigate — he would extend tolerance where disdain seemed apropos.

He applied napkin in dainty stabs, and said: —

"Shall we stroll to the beach, Mr. Rosen?"

We were beyond the swampy land and almost over the hump that threw the lagoon at one's eye in a blaze when he made mention of the business at hand. "The *Quean of Melbourne* often docked at Lorengau, did she not?" I cast a sharp glance at him, nodded, and then stared at the empty space north of the *Flores*. "What was her business there?" he put mildly. I mentioned fuel and stores, trinkets from the Chinese boats, and other reasons. "Was not Mr. Ralls the master of the *Red Witch* when she went down?" At my answer, he said, "And you were chief mate?"

"Aye."

"Did the *Quean* go down with her diving equipment?"

"You jest, Mr. Sheraton."

"On the contrary, I'm serious. Strange, very strange, that you and Captain Ralls should pull in here. We've often said your host moved here in order to search out the *Red Witch*." At the water's edge he stopped short and sent his eyes deep into mine. "Mr. Rosen, suppose you give me the true account of the sinking of the *Quean of Melbourne*."

"Gladly," I said. "It's written here just as it happened." I handed him the paper I had executed the night before. Without haste he accepted it and read slowly. He then folded it nicely, eyeing me as he did so, and placed it in an oilskin pouch.

"Care to row out with me, Rosen?"

"If you do the rowing. My arm isn't up to it."

"Quite all right," he said, and we stepped into a slender boat I'd never seen before. He pulled oar slowly, tirelessly, and we were soon out over the glaring channel I'd last seen with the aid of a lamp. There ahead lay the coral jut almost breaking the surface, the same that hung the schooner's rudder.

"A nasty course," he said, peering into the water. I agreed heartily, and asked if he'd enjoy pulling a ship through in the black of night. "Couldn't be done," he said peremptorily, to which I also agreed.

"No?" he said, turning his face my way. "Yet in your written statement your schooner did just that." He frowned, and I, aware of an error that was as much my own as Sidneye's, smiled, and decided to shelve my tongue.

I grinned inwardly, wondering what his reaction might be, or might have been, to the shafts of iron rising from the inner sand hump. They would, of course, be removed, their long vigil completed. As we moved nearer I strained my eye for the long bars lying flat in the sand, and when we were into the last lap, I stared from sheer surprise.

There they rested on the floor!

"Something wrong, Mr. Rosen?"

"Yes," I said. "Here's where we stood when we upped sail. We crossed this delta and moved under full canvas out to sea. Then — hell broke loose."

"Mr. Rosen," he said menacingly, his eyes boring into mine. "Someone is dragging a dead herring before my nose."

"I — I don't understand," I said naïvely.

"You could, Mr. Rosen, after rotting behind bars a few weeks."

"Come, come, Mr. Sheraton," I said with mild defiance. "Suppose you explain what's on your mind."

"Of course," he said. "First, why does the *Flores Tandjoeng* show fresh bullet pocks? Second, why are Mr. Arrezo's wounds in the leg and arm bullet holes? Third, why was one of the Malays — washed up on the outer barricade where you and the Dutchmen failed to explore — shot through the head? Fourth, why didn't you write truth into your statement?"

"I'm afraid I haven't the answers."

"Mr. Rosen, you could be arrested for murder and other charges could follow," he meditated aloud.

"Thanks," I replied. "But tell me just how you arrived at Mr. Arrezo's condition? I haven't been able to see him."

"Easy enough. The Italian escaped last night. I found him on the beach this morning before dawn. He is dead, Mr. Rosen — dead!"

The Britisher was no fool.

3

The path back to the Dutchman's gave me respite. I used it freely for reviewing surprises before setting my quizzical mind free again. The quiet tropical day healed over, and the rhythm of land, sea, and air cushioned all shock. I turned the leaf that brought Teleia's glory into that settled rhythm; her face was in a cloud when I gazed aloft, in the long, sweeping coconut fronds as I lowered my eyes. My companion said nothing to frighten her away and I did not impinge upon his obstinate Sherlock Holmes mood. With the garden all around us, I lost the vision in my search for the corporeal. She was somewhere near, and her very presence evoked an impatience that soon turned into inconceivable loneliness. Then came the bitter thought of her marrying the young Dutchman of Batjak; and I felt it was incumbent upon me to do something about that.

Once inside the huge blue room Mr. Sheraton and I sat down to cool ourselves. Silence hovered over us like a dead calm over a windjammer. But not for long: in rolled the wheel chair, and trailing it was the expressionless, icy face of Dokter van Arken. I arose and greeted both men, while the Englishman shelved the threads of mystery for the moment.

"Good morning," smiled Sidneye in conciliatory manner. "Did you, Mijnheer, find everything to your liking?"

"Quite," returned Sheraton. "I do like to unravel a worthy crime."

Sidneye's brow lifted. "It would be a breach of etiquette to disappoint you, Mijnheer. But tell us more." His gaze roamed in my direction.

"Begging your pardon, Mr. Sidneye, but that is why I'm here now — I'd like you to tell me more. What brought about the fresh bullet holes on the *Flores?*"

"A direct question," said Sidneye. "One that calls for a direct answer. As a man, Mijnheer, I welcome your visit, but as the meddlesome official I do not. I'm afraid the answer to your question is simply this — none of your business."

"That," returned Sheraton calmly, "might suffice if I had not found a dying man on the beach this morning. He had two bullet holes in him. He was, by the way, once the second mate on one of your ill-fated ships. So, since circumstances warrant your arrest for murder, Mr. Sidneye, you might, quite by chance, wish to answer my questions. You may be sure that I'd not hesitate even slightly in taking you in to Lorengau. Think, Mr. Sidneye, what such an arrest would do for me. My future, sir, would be assured." He made his long speech with penetrating force, and I felt the Dutchman's error, and I saw respect rise above defiance in a Dutchman's eyes. But he had not warmed the throne of Batjak all those years for nothing. He rose to the occasion admirably.

"Quite right, Mijnheer," he said. "Your future would be assured. A man is easily broken when he aims too high. But back to your question about the *Flores*. Since I do not own the ship and cannot claim any moving craft a part of my humble domain, I suggest you see the owner, Mijnheer van Schreeven."

"That I shall. Now perhaps you can explain the death of Mr. Arrezo."

"I'm afraid that is beyond my powers. I'm neither psychic nor was I aboard the ship when she exploded."

I intruded with, "Perhaps our ammunition was in line of the blast."

"Likely," scoffed the officer. "Prove it."

"Mr. Sheraton," I returned, "suppose you disprove it."

"That is the court's duty."

"With all the evidence to the contrary, I'm afraid you'd present a poor case," I said. "Suppose, sir, if you really think you have a case against anyone here, that you arrest me here and now. I'll gladly stand before your court and, what's more, defy you to tie the *Red Witch* affair to this accident. Would Ralls and I have remained here a half hour had there been bad blood between Sidneye and ourselves? Would Sidneye have waited all these years for revenge? Would Mr. Arrezo, a mere hireling, be murdered, while I, the second in command, continued to enjoy the hospitality of the owners of the *Witch*?"

Said Dokter van Arken, "Mijnheer Rosen's logic is worthy of digestion." With that surprising remark he turned about and left the room.

"Perhaps you're right," said the visitor. I flashed him a dubious glance; I was aware of his strategy — he'd succumb outwardly and continue to stir the fricassee of surface facts and underlying suspicion. But he grinned and turned the conversation to lighter channels. Soon I made an excuse and departed.

In the lower hallway I met Carter. His mood was more on a plane with that of Tilden King Carter and minus the solemnity of our last meeting. And never was his style in better form, and never was I in finer fettle on the receiving end. I led him to my room, ordering a supply of ice and gin from a Javanese on the way. Once in the room I flung myself into an easy chair, and said: —

374

"Why so exuberant, Carter?"

"The doctor's verdict, Sam! But, of course, you haven't heard." He grinned. "You rested in the ward for the *non compos mentis*. And how does it feel to be nuts, and alone?"

"I'm nuts now if I'm not alone," I returned.

"I asked for it," he laughed. "But when are you to be arrested and hauled to Lorengau? For Ripper's murder, you know." He frowned slightly, heaved a sigh, and caught his grin once more. "Really, Sam, you amaze me. You can walk a tight wire longer, and with greater ease, than any man I ever saw. How in the name of all that's good and bad do you go free after pulling the *Quean* out for Ralls?"

"The Britisher," I replied. "But forget the present and past long enough to explain about yourself."

"Oh that. Well I was Arken's avid confidant several days back — in the early evening before the blow-off to be exact. I was told that my life could be prolonged, even better. Well — he's good. But to my case, which," he sighed, "seems more of an infection by fungi. Don't ask for more, Sam, but look at a guy with a future." In retort to my dubious eyes, he said, "You don't see my nose and ears enlarged, do you; you've never seen me suffer from mental depression, have you? Well."

Our drinks arrived and I set to work on one. "But how will he help you?" I asked bluntly.

"By proven agents — up to a point. Then, he said, by injections of such matter that my knowledge of facts would cause me to dread the ordeal. More opposites, he finally added."

"What about Loring?"

"I asked him about the old boy. He said Loring was actually crazy, incurable beyond a point, but — listen to this — by having a nurse read the whole account of the trial after the *Red Witch* once each week, the fellow holds his senses to earth by sheer force of will. He said: 'Mijnheer Carter, Loring should have died several years ago.' Imagine that."

"Hm-m," I said. "Carter, tell me, how is Teleia?"

"Doing fine. She got a shoulder wound."

"Where is she?"

"Across the hall, four doors down." He eyed me with amusement. "You love her, don't you, Sam? Oh, I don't blame you. But you might as well forget her. She's to marry the pretty boy of Batjak."

"Did she say that?" I queried.

"No, but you can readily imagine she'll do what her father says."

"Carter, between us, I'm not so sure about that."

"You're sticking out that neck again?"

"Wait and see." I poured another stiff drink and leaned back in my chair. I peered out the window at my left and saw the tall stately palms bending before the trade, their tufts standing straight out. Thin white clouds hugged the background of deep blue, coming in for a white drop against the brown-masked green of the playful fronds.

"Sam, a big dinner is planned two days hence," said Carter suddenly.

"A — what?"

"Forget her, Sam. Special guests for dinner two nights hence. Don't you repeat what I'm about to tell. But I promise you'll see the sight of all sights. So tune your ears to the future, my boy. The wave length is eerie."

"If anything more can happen here, I'd enjoy seeing it," I said wearily.

"And you will, never doubt that. You're still walking a tightrope, though you do it so nicely, so nonchalantly, that I'm afraid the Dutch are taking to you. Sam, you're a born trader, though I can't seem to remember anything extraordinary you've done other than save your hide."

"That's worth quite a lot in my eye," I said, laughing. "Here, Carter, drink up. It loosens your tongue."

"Yeah. I've been holding back until I feel the loquacious glow. It's about here, so I'll raise the curtain and dramatize the devil. Incidentally, has anyone told you what happened after the *Quean* lost her guts?"

"*Neen*, Mijnheer," I said.

"*Verdomd! Verdomd!* I was standing on the beach while Ralls and Ripper fired at the *Flores*. When the end came I was still on the beach, but I saw you slump in the boat. So did the party on the *Flores*. Teleia cried out: 'Look, Sam is hurt!' Yes, don't try to hide behind a smug countenance, Sam. She said just that in a tone there was no mistaking.

"I sprang into a boat and rowed like hell. They beat me out, of course, and were busy digging a splinter of the mast out of your head and arm when I got there. Teleia went along though she was bleeding profusely. I heard her ask for leniency in your behalf just before she fainted. Sidneye placed her in a boat with Bullit, van Arken, and you, chum, before he and his brother and Batjoek went on out to the barricade. I rowed on out and saw them pick up poor old Ripper; he was babbling and taking on like something that fell out of a coconut tree, bleeding like hell, and coming to only long enough to retch.

"Tewelliger was found with his head crushed in, poor fellow. I never did learn his secret."

"Nor did anyone else," I added. "But Tewell' was a good sort. Makes me choke up when I think of all the times we tortured him with tales of skeletons and such."

"Yeah — Omar was dead, too. That was a vicious blast, Sam. I saw the mainmast when it jumped clean of the deck. But back to what you don't know. Ripper came around the next morning, crying and pleading for his life. He was stark mad.

"Then Dokter van Arken asked if I'd enjoy staring at the prize patient of his career. Naturally I was interested, and we moved to the far wing on the third floor. I eyed the door narrowly and asked if he had the *oran utan* or the *Pongo pygmaeus*, wild man or ape.

"'Neither,' he replied, 'I have here the devil himself.'

"He casually unlocked the ornate door.

"The place was furnished exquisitely — mahogany, Oriental carpet, and toned walls. There were books aplenty, and gin. One picture caught my eye. It was an excellent oil of a red ship plowing through the dusk with a devil's head worked into the pattern of the cloud background. Only at a distance was the head visible; up close it simply wasn't there. The painting was lighted. Engraved into the brass plate were two words: —

"RED WITCH!"

My glass was almost at my lips when he said it. Then suddenly I forgot it, and it crashed against the floor. I was up on my feet and gripping Carter's shoulders.

"Ralls?" I said hoarsely.

"Ralls," he said, "and very much alive."

I thought of Mayrant Sidneye's words: "Rosen, you have unwittingly done us a great favor." And I had — for I had sprung the trap on Ralls. I thought of the Britisher down there, and more. And then I raised my bemused head and peered in the direction of the lagoon.

I had heard, unmistakably, the rattle of an anchor cable. A big ship was paying call.

CHAPTER XXXII

1

WHEN the *Quean* dived below the calm surface of the ever-beguiling sea, the romance of sails went with her. Gone was the glory of spray rising to kiss pale sails, the bellying, flapping rhythm of distending canvas, the soothing tunes played in the uppers. Spanker and jibs gave way to those dull appurtenances of steam and iron; and the day of fancy stalked the tail of the wind, leaning gloriously to the lee in a run for a final horizon. The trucks dipped lower and lower; then they were gone, leaving only the trackless sea, the roadstead to memories.

I gazed at the nondescript freighter anchored off the south entrance to the lagoon. She had a rusty look about her, sleepy, reminding me of a work mule. And somehow, as I gazed at the stubby bow, I felt, by comparison, the intuitive intelligence of a ship under sail; its very demeanor was spirited grace; an Arab stallion. The *Red Witch*, once the *Golden Hind*, the *Quatrefoil*, running to a landfall over the veiled horizons, meeting the sun on the hills of the sea, penetrating the heavy pall of cloud at a tremendous clip, and laughing past the roar of breakers piling over barrier reefs, seemed to race once more into the deep blue waters of the South Pacific. She mocked the screws of lumbering freighters, she easily gave them a close-depressed feeling of manifest failure.

The *Stefan Meer* belied her name. Why hadn't they called her, instead, *Sea Cow?* Did Sidneye warm to tubs? I didn't think so. Her motor launch was tied up at the bamboo wharf, and that legendary team, Cordtlaant and Noord, sipped with her owner.

"Their day of triumph," I soliloquized. "They churn in clumsily, fumbling for anchorage. They amble toward the Dutchman's house, drooling like cannibals over the living Ralls."

Carter's startling discovery had prompted my hand into a showdown, though the only cards to flatten face up were mine. I had walked straight to Sidneye and asked forthwith if Ralls had been rescued; I was asked if I chose to join the Dutch or champion a lost Ralls. So I said heatedly — "Mr. Sidneye, if you persist in hiding facts from me, my best bet is with the British." Thereupon he informed me I'd gone too far to reverse my stand, and I informed him that Sheraton was perhaps the better judge of that. The last laugh was his — Sheraton had boarded his boat at the mouth of the lagoon while Carter unraveled his tale.

To top it all, in walked the Dutch giants from the steamer. Cordtlaant, tall and rippling full, a handsome man, maintained the placid calm of Sidneye's description, while Teer,Noord, brawny, eagle-nosed, sharp of eye, and thin of lip, betrayed the fact that he gazed upon the chief mate of the *Witch*, a man on probation. My eye locked with Cordtlaant's after his own pattern; and with Noord it was the same, though Sidneye eased all tension with, "Mijnheer Rosen is my guest."

At their warming glances, given in respect to their master, I acknowledged their introductions in gentlemanly fashion, tossed off a drink with them, and departed, knowing I should see more of them later.

Invading Carter's room, I said, "I think it's time I talked with Ralls. The bids are high but I don't know if I choose to sell him out. I've damn near done so — with the Britisher. But unwittingly. So I'm the sap." Carter called me every kind of fool. Hadn't Ralls's folly cost me my only possession and means of earning a living; hadn't Ralls put my neck in a Dutchman's noose; why the hell didn't I wake up and accept the victor's proposition; and, was I minus all brains?

"So I haven't sold him down the river?" I said. Carter frowned, which meant I had not. "And is Ralls taking it lying down?"

"Why not forget him, Sam? You've walked the tightrope long enough. Instead, let us pay call on an opposite."

But Teleia wasn't allowed visitors, so said the Javanese maid. As I turned a sour glance upon Carter, I heard a voice, Teleia's: "Tell Sam I'll see him — tomorrow at ten." My face refused the mask to cover my joy at hearing her voice; I liked the music she gave the word "Sam." Carter grinned teasingly, then moved down the hall, laughing. On his heels I made a grimace and said: —

"One flower in a gilded dung heap."

"You're in Rome, Mr. Rosen, and you'll do well to sniff attar of roses." He chuckled, then eyed me seriously. "I imagine the big dinner tomorrow evening will convince you that such advice has merit. The guest star, I hear, is none other than the admiral of Blup Blup, his majesty Ralls."

"Perhaps," I added evenly, "they plan to talk him to death. Or — reform him. I can see Ralls's penitent face." It was my chuckle then, though it died on my face when Carter replied, quite casually: —

"I'll lay odds, five to one, that they break him." After long moments, he added: "Why not get on the right bandwagon, Sam — while you can?"

2

Slowly the day rolled into the next, and at the appointed hour I stood outside Teleia's room.

My rap had scarcely sounded when the door opened to show her fiancé in exit. I spoke and he nodded, the thinnest hint of formalities, and as he moved slowly away I walked upon the stage he had just quit. Somehow I disliked the fellow, not in that excusable sense of rivalry, but because his manner was too fulsomely agreeable. Perhaps it was the combination of round face, round eyes, soft lips and hands. Handsome, in a way, yes, though his fourteen-karat style was thinly effeminate, thickly contumelious. With a shrug I dismissed him from mind.

She was kind to my eye, too kind; I simply stood before her, staring in an effort to drink in all her beauty in one gulp. Her face was vibrant, alive, a frame for her talkative eyes. In one fleeting moment I caught the same expression I had seen in the moonlight at the pool. The pose of her lips was the same. And, as if by magic, the picture vanished and in its place I was blessed with a smile born of lengthened acquaintance; it soared above that stretch of her lips at the pool; it was a duplicate of her smile on the afternoon her father came upon us aboard the *Flores*.

Melodiously she said, "Good morning, Sam," and huskily I replied, "Good morning, Teleia." In the warm light of her eye I was rich again; to her beautiful cadences I'd ever step in becoming rhythm.

She steered out of the spell with, "You look none the worse for your experience."

"Thanks to you," I said.

"I did little," she said. "But, Sam, I'm so glad it's all over. Now you can resume your life on a better footing — on a higher plane."

I stared, amazed. I entered into joyous appraisal of her beauty — her hair up in a dainty chignon, her rich translucent skin scarcely paled by her accident, the living marble of her nose and chin moving decorously into her full lips. The visionary took over the practical.

"That higher plane, Teleia, stands before a man only when there's a reason for his eyes to lift. A man likes to stare up from the foot of a pedestal at the woman he loves. So it is with me — and the woman is you."

380

"You sound serious, Sam," she said blithely.

I met her eye squarely, almost fiercely. Her eyes quickened, smiled slowly into a serious drop. "One look at you is enough to send Sam Rosen overboard," I replied.

"Thank you, Sam."

"But I've been hearing things. First, from your uncle, then Carter. The news was a jolt, actually worse than the news of your stopping a bullet."

Sedulously she avoided my eyes, and I moved my chair closer. I was determined to have her or lose her, and on her decision that very day. If the case went beyond her, then I'd look in the direction necessary. But of her feelings, only she could act as spokesman. I peered closely while she stared at the running pattern of crimson in the rug. A smile fought for the corners of her mouth, quivered there for an eternity, and died.

"Sam, you'd better come back this afternoon."

I said bluntly, "Afraid to face the issue, or me?"

She had a way of leaning against the back of a chair with limbs outstretched that was all her own. The grace she displayed with the barest motion, or even in marblelike stillness, seemed to augment the beauty of the statue in the pool. I took her hand in mine, conjuring up a speech that fell short of expressing my true feelings.

"Teleia, I've been all over the U.S.A. and most of the Pacific. I must have been searching for you, though I wasn't aware of it until I found you. But now that I have I'm not about to bow out to Jan Hooch. Understand me? Looking ahead, there's everything with you, nothing without you. I have little to offer. I'm no junior partner of Batjak. I'm not a rich man.

"However, your uncle's check for the *Quean* is in my pocket, though it is rightfully the property of Ralls. If he survives, I'll give it to him, and start from scratch. If not, I intend buying a seagoing ketch. Jan Hooch might do better in worldly gifts, though I doubt his ability to match the feeling in my heart."

Her eyes lifted to mine in serious smile. For long moments she leveled her gaze in straightforward, appraising, and questioning manner. How deep she looked inside me I did not know, though I was sure she discovered the very essence of sincerity.

"A seagoing ketch," she said pensively.

"Yeah!" I spoke up with all the excitement her tone inspired. "We could pull east, down Samoa way, and over into the Society Islands. Just us. I'm a pretty good trader, Teleia, and I promise you wouldn't be bored." I was warming into my brand of enthusiasm.

"Somehow I can't see Jan on a tramp ketch," she said.

"Now you're seeing things with my eye!" I exclaimed. "Jan would put you on a stiff yacht."

"Sam," she said, with a frown and sigh, "are you free to leave this island; are you free of Ralls; is everything behind you in this strange episode of hate and vengeance?"

"No," I admitted. "But — soon, I hope."

"Of course. But for the present you are chained."

"I don't understand," I said, forgetting her hand in mine.

"Just this, Sam. At present I'm supposed to obey my parent. That is my chain. So until we are free, the ketch —"

Eternal interruption: Dokter van Arken's rap forced her hospitality; he entered at her word, gave her a nod and the parsimony of greeting of which only he was master. Beyond that the usual stern mien took over his face for a stiff nod in my direction, and he said more with a look than most men can put to words: he dismissed me eloquently, though I merely arose and walked to the window, where I stood until his examination was complete. With the door sounding his exit, I turned about quickly, unaware that I was due for another surprise. I saw her staring ahead, her lips and eyes blending into an alert and pleased smile. It was too fresh for any carry-over from our conversation; therefore it was van Arken's work.

"You were saying —" I stopped short as she pursed her lips and lifted her brow in what I thought was amusement. "Well," I added, "it seems van Arken for once left a smile in his wake."

"Yes, Sam, he did," she replied candidly.

"I've learned to expect interruptions here," I said impatiently. "We were talking about a ketch."

"A ketch? Oh yes, we were, Sam," she put teasingly. She seemed obsessed with another thought, and ostensibly determined to hold the conversation to lighter channels.

I frowned, leveling my gaze at her. What I didn't know about women, I said under my breath, would fill the seven seas and elevate universal low tide to the pinnacles of Dover's white cliffs.

"Sam." The sound, the tone, the very utterance surprised and pleased me. I saw her smile into the twinkling, joyous girl of Bali.

Her outstretched hand beckoned the uncertain male, and with a short step I moved to the soothing balm of her touch. "Sam, van Arken seems to like you." She smiled. "And — I like you too, Sam." Her eyes narrowed into an expression best described as a twin to her firm hold on my hand.

"You like me?" I said, crestfallen. "I had hoped for more, Teleia — for another word. You see I'm very much in love with you." She sighed and leaned back, her chin tilted upward. The answer was in her face, almost. Then it was gone.

"Sam." The word opened and closed a long sentence. It was then that I felt the inexpressible surge of understanding that no word can declare. There was no Jan Hooch between us, nor was there father or uncle standing imperiously in our world; only Teleia and Sam.

It was my moment, and I held the ready helm of the present; I threw it down and pointed to the sweetest windfall ever to draw my eye. I was leaning over her, then sitting beside her, my arms drawing her closer. Her eyes reached beyond the surface of mine, beckoning. Soon our lips touched, and long, sweet, and eternal was that kiss; the world had surrendered its sweetest to me.

"Sam," she whispered faintly, "I do love you."

And that was enough to give Sam Rosen every reason for claiming the world as his own. "My darling Teleia!" I whispered, adding, "Look me straight in the eye — and repeat it."

"I do love you, Sam." And I held her face close for sweet appraisal. Then she said, "You were talking about a ketch." Her smile was a lazy challenge, and her words an intrusion upon my mood as I tried to reconcile an unbelieving Sam Rosen to such a blessing.

"A ketch?" I teased as I held her close. "Oh yes." I smiled into her eyes, and drew her face to mine. "Yeah, the *Teleia*. Like that name?"

"I do," she murmured, her fingers touching my face. Our eyes locked and held, and they drew our lips together again. After a moment, she said, "Is a ketch roomy?" Her hand smoothed the hair at my temples.

"Cozy is the word," I replied. "If you're aboard; and you will be." She smiled happily, sighing, and I joined her — what romancers we were, tying our thousand and one unvoiced declarations to that imaginative fore-and-aft-rigged vessel. So a ketch was destined to become our romantic standard; that suited me, as long as she remained its heart. I said as much while searching out every detail of that lovely face so close to mine.

"Sweetheart," I said. "The luck of Sam Rosen!" I added, "You told me you knew at the pool, the second time I ever laid eyes upon you, that I loved you. Now when did you discover you loved me?"

"I don't know exactly. I think it was that same night — after you'd gone. Or it could have been after the dinner, when you came outside. But I was sure later that evening when you failed to visit the pool."

"And I had no idea!" I said, amazed.

383

"You were too busy, dear, nursing your transparent brand of belligerence." She smiled as she reached up to smooth my frown with her fingers. "Carter told me about you before I met you. I was interested even then."

"Still interested, sweetheart?"

"Now and always, Sam."

"Sweetheart. My sweetheart." Then, at a moment created for my proposal, I said, "When are you going to tell Jan Hooch?" It was a long leap back to the present, and I was the guilty skipper who moored to the dock of close-pressing events.

She laughed despairingly. "There you go sinking ships again." There was an interval of silence in which she, with head on my shoulder, studied the pattern of her dress.

"I don't know, Sam. There's so much ahead."

"You don't know!" I gasped. "Why? You don't love Hooch. That much I know."

"No, I don't love him. I love you, Sam."

"Then tell the — well, tell him that."

"We must wait, Sam. No, don't frown so. It won't be long, for everything is shaping into a final showdown. There's the dinner ahead, which I probably won't attend."

"Yeah, the dinner. But after that you'll tell him?"

"That, Sam," she said, smiling enigmatically, "depends more or less on what you do in the meantime."

3

Since a man in love unwittingly wanders into new and delightful transport — dreamy, aimless, tinged with rhyme and rhythm heretofore denied him — I was, during that sweet, evanescent day and the one that followed, almost rolled for the count. Naïvely I blundered into and out of conversations, lending my eye to an image that encompassed all but the sharp conversational exchanges of the close present. It was Carter who frowned hardest when I took my worst drubbing at breakfast.

On the veranda eight of us surrounded a table, and while I was not considered an enemy, neither was I revered as close friend and confidant. Thus the conversational topic soared above me like a mock cloud scudding before a loose helm. I heard only her words — "Sam, you were talking about a ketch."

And when Teer Noord — he was reminiscent of Mr. Bullit — said,

"'Twill be great sport to see Ralls's eyes widen," I continued to hear her rhythmic whisper: "Sam, I do love you."

"As well as to witness the surprise of his inscrutable partner," said Jan Hooch.

Carter replied, "Inscrutable?" Taking my reticence for cool reserve, he laughed, and added, "I think you'll see colors to your liking."

Sidneye, his eyes probing me like a ponderous lancet, said: "That remains to be seen. He fights hard to hold a neutral corner. But, of course, Mijnheer Rosen knows no more than we've told him about Ralls."

"Then he thinks Ralls dead?" bellowed Noord. He eyed me with sharp disdain before bursting into raucous laughter. I chuckled, and said: —

"Mijnheer Sidneye, there's a man of uncertain wit among us." Slowly I released his warlike eyes and turned upon my host. "Now will you be so kind as to tell me about Ralls?"

"There is little to tell, Rosen," he said in conciliatory manner, "except for his being alive and living in luxury."

"A most remarkable fellow," said van Arken, breaking his monotonous silence. "He puzzles me. I can find neither his opposite nor his parallel."

"You think he is superhuman?" I said. The question seemed to fill a captious abyss he had dug for my benefit.

"Mijnheer Rosen, you will join us at a most interesting dinner."

"Thanks," I said.

The conversation wore on, dull and uninteresting, and I turned my ear away. Abjectly I gazed into my plate, at the ashes of my cigarette, and at times I peered through the bodies and faces at the table as if they were silhouettes in crystal. I dreamed through the intricacies of their discourse, sitting among them like the center band of white, a fess in that escutcheon of Dutch red and white and blue. The talk wore on.

Hooch sighed out his impatience at long romantic engagements, then frowned at the mention of the long, probing vigil aboard the *Stefan Meer* for the treasures of the deep; and Cordtlaant, ever the gallant, emerged from his reserve with: "'Tis great fun, Mijnheer Hooch. But for you, why not be married aboard ship?"

"*Neen*," laughed Hooch. "I promised Teffin Borg he should be my best man. And then, Teleia has a voice, you know."

"Splendid," said Sidneye. "We can send for young Borg. All in favor of an early wedding say *ja*."

Carter and I remained silent in the chorus of approval, he staring at me in quizzical manner and thereby drawing all eyes to my face. Once more I lost the conversational thread, and feeling the weight of hammering questions, louder in that penetrating silence, I glanced up in startled manner.

"As one of us you must vote, Rosen," said Sidneye. "*Ja* or *neen?*"

Carter, reading my puzzled face, came to my aid with, "Sam, you'd just as soon see Mijnheer Hooch married aboard ship as in a Java church, eh? My vote is yes."

"And my vote," I said, "is a motion — that Teleia be allowed to plan her own wedding."

Carter groaned inwardly; and each man there, in the eloquence of his individual expression, accused me of being in love with her. I felt the weight of open pity and scorn. But out of the moment I gained one supporter: Mayrant Sidneye. In his eyes was admiration for sheer nerve.

Later Carter upbraided me for my witless answers and unpropitious timing. "You'll spoil our plans yet," he declared. Nor would he divulge what he had in mind.

4

Toward midafternoon I was about to rap on Teleia's door when I heard Sidneye's chuckle from within. I turned away but not until I heard him say: —

"So you have Rosen in tow?"

Frowning, I returned to the crack in the door and eavesdropped without compunction. Her voice broke the silence with, "Yes, Uncle, Sam loves me."

"Splendid," said Sidneye. "He was groggy at breakfast."

Was she, I asked, toying with me; what sort of game did she play, and upon whose stage? Then some inner voice calmed me; I couldn't believe her a fickle enchantress.

Another voice, her father's, joined the conversation. "Within two days the *Stefan Meer* moves to the reefs. We're all going, even you. You and Jan will be married by the captain."

"And if I refuse?"

"You'd dare to think of such?" said van Schreeven.

"I would!" she declared vehemently.

"Teleia," he said crisply, "if your mother were alive she'd be horrified at your choice of companions."

"Perhaps you're in error," she mused aloud. "While I'm sure you loved my mother, I'm beginning to believe you scarcely knew her. Batjak is a demanding master, it is —"

At that moment a hand fell upon my shoulder. I turned quickly and saw the level eyes of Dokter van Arken. How he got there, and whence he came, was of the past — the cold, relentless present was upon me. He removed his hand after ages, but not those deep, incisive eyes; folding his arms and raising one hand to the groomed Vandyke he seemed lost in study of me, or of what he should do with me. Then, without any expression, he made a motion with a finger: I should follow him. I gladly obeyed, choosing, I said to my trapped self, the frying pan to the fire.

He said, "To my office, Rosen," and that was all. Soon, battling out of a trance, I was seated in a huge chair in a beautifully furnished office of great size. I gazed in awe. He peered at me over a wide desk, his hands flat atop it, his motionless fingers pointing at me.

Then in walked the Moluccan; he seated himself without a word.

"Rosen, can you pierce Mijnheer Sidneye's armor at its weakest spot?" van Arken put slowly.

The question was every bit as surprising as his choice of it, and with it came a clear warning: there sits your enemy, Sam Rosen. My shrug failed to satisfy him; he insisted, and I, chancing the helm over the reefs of curiosity, said: "I think so, Dokter."

"And in your case, have you no imagination or genius? More than once I've seen you impress him — once while viewing the squid, again when you navigated the *Quean* out, and again this morning. That being true, Mijnheer Rosen, what would be his reaction to the sensational?"

I thought of Ralls, the South Sea lagoon, the brief fight with the Frenchman; then I studied the man before me, wondering at his sudden interest in men and plans, in me. An age of silence took over.

"It is said," he pronounced, "that a shoemaker's children go unshod. Quite true. The van Schreeven heir has no yacht of her own." His crafty eye sought to enliven my imagination; it was almost like skilled fingers massaging life into the dead cells of my brain.

"Yet, Mijnheer Rosen, the taking of a craft belonging to her father is not theft. A *zeeman* is all she needs, that and two Malay survivors of the *Quean*."

"I'm beginning to understand," I said. "But Dokter, your trap won't work."

"Stupid fool!" he flung caustically. "Batjoek and I do not deal in the dark. You speak of a trap, Rosen. You're already trapped, my friend. I offer you a key. Good day, Mijnheer. You'll find a thousand guilders in your pillow — after the dinner this evening."

The door closed; a stupid oaf — Sam Rosen — stood in the hall, wondering, asking: why the aid from those two; why the money, and what inspired their disloyalty to Sidneye — or was it that? Had Teleia a hand in it? Viciously I lit a cigarette and cursed. There seemed little else to do.

"Damn! The Moluccan didn't say a word," I growled.

"Well, did you expect a sphinx to talk?" I spun about. There stood omnipresent Carter, grinning.

5

Five minutes after the last gong eleven men sat down to the Dutch table; at one end, in his customary place, sat the inimitable host, and running the table clockwise were: Jan Hooch, Mr. Loring, Dokter van Arken, Carter, and Captain Cordtlaant; the chair on the end opposite Sidneye was vacant — I knew why — and the table followed the clock again, beginning with Batjoek; next came Mr. Bullit, van Schreeven, and Teer Noord; and I, as before, sat on my host's right. We were a clock, I mused, with van Arken the numeral nine, the empty chair twelve, van Schreeven three, and the invalid host on the dial at six.

And what a company: cannibals all, with the possible exception of Hooch, though he drifted with the tide because he knew nothing else; they sat there awaiting the feast of revenge on Ralls's soul. Sardonic eyes, cruel eyes, bestial eyes, all sharpened for the occasion — the awkward conversations that sprang up underscored the fact. Coolly I spoke to Sidneye, drawing a word picture of the panorama; he chuckled and praised my powers of perception.

"Beautiful, isn't it?" he said. "Only one is missing."

Every eye turned to the door; there, dressed in the becoming white of a yachtsman, stood the man of the hour; he smiled cynically, he stood with arms akimbo, his feet planted piratically apart; he studied every face there, and his swashbuckling gleam evoked in every man, I am quite sure, a measure of admiration. To me the sight was hypnotic, and I found myself standing, alone, in salute to his dauntless soul.

The moment was made to order for Ralls, and his arrogant stride through the thick silence to the empty chair was impressive.

"Beautiful, isn't it?" I said to Sidneye.

"It is that, Rosen," he replied. "He almost walks the deck of the *Golden Hind* again."

As I expected, it was rice table, *rystafel*, and the Malays, bare of feet and blank of eye, commenced the long service of forty courses. No word was spoken and the silence hung over us like a balloon ready to burst. Wine was poured, and I saw a gin bottle between Cordtlaant and Ralls. Hooch drummed the table with his fingers and Loring stared without respite at his nemesis. I glanced at Sidneye and saw his flashing smile, his steeped joy, and I thought the dinner would follow a pattern to the last curtain.

I peered into every face, and only in two did I see an unbroken run of purpose: Ralls's and Sidneye's. All others vacillatingly drooled or pivoted curiously. Van Arken and Batjoek hid behind impenetrable masks. For Hooch I felt a wave of pity, though it was suddenly evanescent; he said inanely, causing me to impute his words to a lambkin very much in a den of wolves: —

"Mijnheer Ralls, you're scarcely the type of man I expected to see."

Ralls smiled, eyeing the lad sharply before saying, "Rely on appearances, young fellow, and you'll not go far with Batjak." He spoke as though he owned the empire.

"Ralls should know," said Sidneye suavely. He added, "So should Batjak. You see, Jan, I erred twice in the case of Mijnheer Ralls — the *Golden Hind*, and the *Red Witch*." His eyes danced the table to Ralls. "My last mistake."

"The *Witch* a mistake?" scoffed Ralls. "She netted twenty times her price."

"And proved me a poor judge of men. Gold is the root of all evil." So he was beginning with monotonous proverbs; I groaned inwardly.

Then Ralls sent my thoughts back into the line of fire when he fanned a tiny spark with eye and word: "Your last mistake, Mr. Sidneye? Aren't you working on that one right now?"

"For your information, Ralls," smiled van Schreeven, "Batjak is of one mind, one soul — it is one solid vote." He sought affirmation in Sidneye's eye. "Batjak makes few mistakes — since the lesson of the *Red Witch*."

"No?" Ralls stabbed slowly, cynically. "No? Captain Cordtlaant passed up a fortune, did he not, in the Tuamotus last year? My friend Debussie wrote about some pearls in Matahiva. The captain, it seems, resents the practical advice of a sound seaman — Mr. Noord." To Sidneye, he said, "You'd do well to rid your line of high hats."

I saw Noord's face leap up with joy, before Cordtlaant answered frigidly: "Noord and I see eye to eye, Mijnheer Ralls."

Sidneye's eye beamed when Ralls completely ignored Cordtlaant
— he thought of his order to Cordtlaant and the repair crew he had
sent to the French lagoon: "Ignore Ralls." Noord, too, seemed pleased,
and I knew he'd salute Ralls's banner after that. The skipper — he
was that, and in fine fettle — addressed van Schreeven, his eyes and
voice thin and calm.

"So Batjak is one solid vote. Hmm, we'll see. At any rate Batjak is
minus the old guard's sparkle. It has lost its aptitude, the moving of a
cargo faster with minimum expense. The *Hind* and *Witch* used to pick
up loose wealth in remote places. But that's none of my business —
except that I hate complacency in an inept trader. Don't you — Mr.
van Schreeven?"

Sidneye sat entranced, living the duel of his puppets; his eyes asked
for more; his lips begged for that living word sauce to *rystafel*. While I
sat there tense, wondering if Ralls held anything in reserve. The company, and it was tough, had not dealt a card.

Smiled Sidneye: "Harmenszoon, you're the head of Batjak. Have you
no answer?"

Ralls interjected with a laugh, "Mr. Sidneye, I continue to believe
steam is slower than sails."

"*Ja!* I've always said it was true," answered Sidneye.

The livid face of van Schreeven was the cynosure of almost every eye.
Ralls studied the mural running the walls, while Sidneye applied a
studious eye to the coterie. Suddenly Ralls threw a glance. It impaled
Loring, it reached deep, evoking blunt, pensive words out of a face given
to slow contortions of hate. He seemed forced to speak. He said: —

"And here we sit, Mr. Sidneye, in the company of the murderer
who scuttled your ship."

"True," Sidneye averred, his face clouding.

"And," Ralls countercharged easily, "with a confessed bigamist,
a man who screwed up a compass by divine guidance." He added a
chuckle to his thrust. Loring was on his feet in an instant, his lips
quivering and nostrils distending violently, pointing, screaming at
Ralls.

"But you are a sadist, a hellhound! You beat women for sexual
satisfaction, and men for —"

"Enough," said van Arken placatingly. When Loring trembled all
over and sat down, he opened up slowly, softly. "Mijnheer Ralls is
not a sadist from choice. He —"

Ralls interposed with, "Leave it where it was, Dokter. You did
your best."

390

"I'm scarcely apologizing for myself," snapped van Arken. Sidneye cackled, while I sat back to enjoy the scientist's chagrin. But he was disappointingly calm when he said: —

"To give the devil his dues, let me say that I took a long voyage with Captain Ralls merely to study his case. I found exactly that which I expected, and I witnessed his antisocial manifestations upon two occasions."

Bullit's beefy head jutted forth curiously; Cordtlaant smiled his disdain, and Hooch stared at the man he had expected to see in the first place.

"But," Sidneye demanded, as if van Arken's failure improperly put must reflect upon the emperor of Batjak, "you did attain fair success in his case, did you not?"

"Or did he?" It came from van Schreeven.

"In a measure, yes," growled the Dokter. "I pored over his past and made suggestions; I followed the results carefully and, in a measure, sublimated the antisocial pattern. But such cases need constant attention, sane guidance, and — I think — ardent affection, a real love to lean upon."

He startled every ear when he said: "Ralls found that love."

I saw Sidneye and Ralls lock eyes, and the clamorous encounter almost sounded a name: Angélique. A Malay, serving Mayrant's plate, was brushed aside by the host when his arm broke that stare. Loring cackled, gazing at Ralls, and Cordtlaant merely sneered, but eloquently.

"And," van Arken added, "he refused it." He withheld reasons why, though Sidneye's eye almost made a bridge for the missing words.

Carabao roast followed fowl in Chinese sauce, and the dinner moved mechanically on; wineglasses were filled, lifted, and filled again. The impasse arrived with bamboo roots and shredded coconut; it lifted with roasted nuts and Sidneye's pensive outburst: —

"I've often wondered if the sadist or the man killed Wilde Younguer."

Loring chose the moment for: "The whip — the damned whip — like he used on me!"

"No," said Ralls, softly, slowly, "Younguer was a man."

"Yes — what happened to Younguer?" grinned Sidneye, red wine running down his chin. "What happened to the *Red Witch?* Mr. Rosen, as her mate, tell us about her end."

"Thanks," I said savagely, "I'll check it to Ralls."

"He," said Loring, pointing at me, his voice rising into a whine, "he helped Ralls! He helped ruin my life!"

"It seems you're involved, Rosen," said van Schreeven.

391

"Yeah," I returned, "since insanity has priority here."

Loring got to his feet. He leaned forward, hands on table, face to the ceiling. "The Lord shall take vengeance here and now."

He peered pitifully at the ceiling. Ralls laughed, breaking the spell, and before the ex-mate could sink into his chair, he copied the past: "I distinctly said two points to the north, Mr. Loring, and then due west. You will now go on deck and set the course."

Even Batjoek's eyes bulged when the fool straightened and said, "Aye, sir." But he rolled out of that punch, almost at the swift count of one-two, a rabid creature with eyes that followed a trembling finger. And Ralls smiled, calmly blew a smoke curtain in cold silence; his eyes seemed to court the joys of a descending Creeper.

Loring screamed: "You — you are the devil himself! You killed a dozen men!"

"I? Mr. Loring, Mr. Loring," Ralls reproved gently. "Calm yourself. You imagine things. Now, Mr. Loring, is it my fault that your godly mind could not conquer the sight of a native woman's body, that your lust made you the father of potbellied hybrids?" Loring stared, affrighted, it seemed. He quivered, his eyes losing one brand of madness in order to accept another. "Did I, sir, seduce your wife? No. But you violated divine laws, and the laws of man. Isn't the Lord answering your call for vengeance — upon you? You! You, Mr. Loring, and only you are held accountable for your sins."

Ralls wielded the Creeper — unmercifully. Truth, the sordid truth, was made manifest; the hateful truth, in which every man there felt for Loring, hating Ralls while he hellishly walked a conversational rail.

The ex-mate stumbled from his place. "May God have mercy on my soul. May God —"

"Mr. Loring," said Ralls, "who scuttled the *Witch?*"

"I — I," and he turned about at the door, "I did — didn't I?" That was the last I ever saw of Loring.

Van Arken stood. "Ralls, you've finished him."

"Yes," Ralls said. And I saw Sidneye's eyes — he idolized Ralls in that moment.

"But only Loring," said Sidneye, recovering. I was surprised when Batjoek repeated the words, and more so when Ralls turned a cool eye upon the Moluccan. I thought aloud: "Ralls evidently hit the twelve-mark last night"; and Sidneye agreed.

"You're a strange one, Batjoek," said Ralls. "I've always wanted to sail with you." I frowned, as did Sidneye, wondering what sort of game Ralls was playing. My interest reached new heights when he locked with that unknown quantity, Batjoek.

"Yes, I believe we'd make a team, Batjoek. I know of a windfall, a British payroll ship off the coast of Halmahera that has escaped even your sharp eye. I also think you'd have enjoyed my company when you held Streicher in the Celebes. Yes?" It was Sidneye who laughed and agreed.

A Malay tripped with a tray, though the incident attracted small attention as Ralls continued: "Of course, I merely dream aloud," he said in disarming manner, "but together, you and I might upset a lot of Jap and Chink shipping. We'd swear allegiance to the devil — and — speaking of promises —"

Sidneye murmured words of amazement, to which I, smiling in the face of extravagant anticipation, replied, "Nor have I seen such a man, Mijnheer."

But Ralls held the show: "Yes, Mr. Sidneye made you a promise, Batjoek. He said to you, as the world knows, 'No one will come between us.' But —" he lifted his eyes to Sidneye — "while he contributed to Mohammed and the black stone of the Kaaba, his half-brother remained a persecutor of your faith. Has he not been quoted publicly?" Ralls was captious, he turned the subject for a moment, then came back with: —

"Allah be praised. There is no god but Allah, and Mohammed is his prophet."

Batjoek, trapped into words, could only repeat; he was almost malleable after that, though van Schreeven said angrily, "We'll omit religion." But Ralls was moving up and down a rail.

"'No one will come between us.'"

"No one has," said Sidneye, leaning forward.

"There he sits," smiled Ralls, pointing at van Schreeven.

"Absurd!" said Teleia's father. In the moment a moving object caught my eye and for an age I forgot to listen. Teleia! Unobtrusively she slipped into the chair vacated by Loring. "We'll talk of other things," said her father. "Every man to his own religion."

Ralls leaned back in his chair, playing out words like a Chopin of discourse. "A brown man, a lowly Dutch subject, turns up with gold, enough to save a firm. The gold buys a crucifix for every neck in the Indies. Where are Sidneye's children? It's rumored they're in a Catholic influence." Thus Ralls lengthened his stride. "Do you hear denial? Aren't you merely a tool, a subordinate fool, Batjoek? Allah be praised," he laughed, "or Allah be damned?"

Sidneye laughed, enjoying the scene. But his eyes flashed amazement when Batjoek arose to extol the merits of Ralls's symphony. Condiments, wild boar off the spit, and wine; and the long voice of Ralls the sauce to unseen dishes. Van Arken's face was a sensitive scale, weighing, weighing the ponderous drama hanging in the balance of a fleeting moment.

Ralls said easily, "See, Batjoek, they serve pig to a son of Mohammed."

"That is purely an oversight," said Mayrant quickly.

"Mijnheer Ralls speaks the truth," said Batjoek. "For years I've pushed the truth behind me." There was no emotion in his voice, no trace of anger as he moved from his chair. Pausing to give van Schreeven a mild glance, and "Allah be praised," he strode majestically to the exit.

"Batjoek!" Sidneye spoke, and the brownstone statue in the doorway, quite used to obeying that voice, turned about. "Batjoek, return to your place. Batjak is first, and I am Batjak. Return!" The symbol of inexorableness stood there, an impregnable fortress, he seemed, withstanding terrific bombardment.

"Fool of fools!" cried Sidneye. "Obey me!"

Slowly the man yielded, and the empire ruler held to a throne of his own making; Batjoek returned, feathers ruffled, while Ralls eyed the emperor with amusement his uppermost expression. Silence mounted and fell until the pall beat against timid eardrums. The Malays seemed to juggle soft rubber plates, and I felt the fall of a curtain, the rise of another, Sidneye pulling the ropes.

"Mijnheer Ralls, you have enjoyed yourself, I'm sure," he said.

"Ralls, let us credit Mr. Arrezo and the American to your list of mounting murders. And your Malays. They joined the dead while you were gently lifted into the water. Ironical, isn't it? But how glad I am that you were spared. Why? Let us reminisce." He talked of a Sydney courtroom, of barristers, of testimony and words, at last asking: —

"Remember the banker-shipper, the charterer of the *Witch?* He leaped off the Rainbow Bridge! You know this, of course, but did you know that he was a stepbrother of Harmenszoon van Schreeven's wife? Yes, of Teleia's mother. That was the man you killed, Ralls."

I started, sending a quick glance at Ralls; he did not move a lash. Nor did Teleia, who leaned back in sober thought.

Then Ralls smiled and said, "So that's the reason the charterer was influenced into a contract that made him a party to any loss. If the usual charter contract had been drawn — and it would have, except that van Schreeven and the others caused you to fear a captain who chose his own routes — he'd have had no reason for suicide. So who killed him, Mr. Sidneye?"

"You, Ralls, when you deviated the *Witch* from her set course. The greed of one man," said Sidneye pensively. "Ralls, you hold aloft a feeble wax taper in the sepulcher of many families."

Kroepoek, dried fish, arrived, marking the end of the long service. I stared about me, asking: Who has scored, where is success? The answer came almost with Sidneye's next utterance, though not quite.

"But your day of reckoning is at hand. First we shall visit the grave of my ship. You will lead us to her, my dear Ralls. There's gold to be gathered — and then —"

Ralls needed little excuse for a run with any man; he proved it with, "Perhaps we can come to terms about the gold."

"Ever the pauper admiral," said Carter, voicing amazement. "Will you allow Batjak a guilder or two, Admiral?" Ralls showed anger, not at the shallow thrust, but because it came from Carter. I saw Sidneye's eager eye register the observation. I saw regret that he had not given Carter a star role.

"Terms," scoffed van Schreeven. "I'll see you in hell first."

Then Sidneye laughed loud and long. "Terms. The mouse bargains with the cat. Listen to me, Ralls. No man will ever again bargain with you. You're finished. Hear me? Finished!"

"Sure, Mister, I hear. And I said you were working into another mistake, did I not?"

"*Neen*, Mijnheer, *neen!*" Sidneye glowered and smiled, all in one expression. "Why, even Rosen has washed his hands of you." Turning greedy eyes upon me, he cried, "Didn't you declare Ralls dead in a statement to Mr. Sheraton?"

"I did," I replied. I glanced at Ralls, who did not move a muscle, who smiled on in the face of killing odds. "But," I said, rising, "I never sold any man down the river. Not even Ralls — who placed my head in this vise."

Then I walked to the far end of the table and placed the check for the *Quean* before him. "Yours," I said, glancing down past Cordtlaant, Carter, and van Arken. Teleia's eyes met mine with the kind of smile I liked, kissing good-by to that seagoing ketch.

"And I don't want a stuiver from anyone," I said, my jaw hardening.

"Sorry, Sam," he said, returning the check, while training a speculative eye and tongue-in-cheek smile upon me. "There are higher stakes."

As I stood there, bewildered, Sidneye chuckled, and said, "Higher stakes, yes — for you, Ralls, the Celebes. Yes, the Celebes." He turned to me with, "You, Rosen, since I sentence Ralls in your presence, think me either a fool or a man about to seal your tongue. But that is beside

395

the point." He produced a sheaf of papers. "Here is the legal touch — which I overlooked in Streicher's case — a contract for Ralls's signature, my dear Rosen."

I could not suppress a chuckle. "You simply hand it to him, he signs it — and presto! — he's your prisoner?" With that I returned to my place.

"Prisoner?" he said, smiling. "There is no such word in the contract. Rather he will be *employed* by Batjak for twenty years at a tidy salary." He paused for effect before saying, "To do what?

"Nothing." His eyes belied his gentle tone. "Twenty years of nothing! It is easy to imagine how Ralls will enjoy such employment. He'll receive his pay regularly, though he'll be unable to spend a stuiver of it — the same that Batjak once paid the captain of the *Red Witch*."

I shuddered inwardly: Sidneye had struck an inspired opposite in Ralls's case; the punishment rang like the highest note in a hideous sonata. Van Schreeven's smile underscored the fact. Here was the dessert to *rystafel*, the very reason for this dinner; faces came to life, leaped into expressions of greed, driveling over the long-anticipated treat.

"But I am a generous man," Sidneye said, causing every face there to turn apprehensive eyes on him. "Yes, I am a benevolent man who desires first of all to even one score.

"That, my dear Ralls, is a matter of pride — I should enjoy a profit, and the word has a double meaning, instead of a loss on your last run with our *Red Witch*."

"*Your Red Witch*, brother," interposed van Schreeven.

Ralls spoke up with, "I've already said we can come to terms about the gold."

As van Schreeven leaned forward menacingly, Sidneye said, "Suppose we face facts, Ralls: I am a judge imposing a sentence. The jury — every man here — says you're guilty. However, if you perform to our satisfaction — by leading us to *our Red Witch* — I shall shorten your time in the Celebes by ten years."

"No!" cried van Schreeven. Sidneye merely smiled; and Ralls eyed both with sharp, smiling eyes that seemed to harbor cunning.

"Let me see the contract," said Ralls. He was soon scanning it, his smile widening as he turned a page. "So I'm to pose as an ornithologist," he mused aloud. "Quite an avocation for a mild man." He glanced up, adding with a smile, "I think I'll begin by studying birds of prey, particularly buzzards." There was a long pause before Ralls said, "Mr. Sidneye, my compliments. The whole thing seems in order — so I'll sign it." He did.

Slow surprise was manifest in every face, including Batjoek's and van Arken's — and my own, I'm sure — as eyes pivoted under deep frowns from Ralls to Sidneye. And Sidneye! He seemed a man engaged in taking his own brain apart in search of a flaw in his strategy. Ralls's easy acquiescence proved a flaw existed; it did more: it robbed Sidneye of the flavor of a triumph that had been his. He seemed nonplused, and for a good reason: he had hoped that Ralls would at last squirm.

And out of the shocked silence Ralls said, "Now that we've settled that, let's turn to more important matters." He smiled at Sidneye, whose lips thinned bloodlessly in a fast reddening face. "Now that I work for Batjak again, gentlemen," and he aimed the thrust at van Schreeven, "I must refresh your memories on one point. My voyages always pay off better when I'm given a free route to a prize. Now that's the way I want it in this case. Well, do I get my wish?"

"Technically, yes," Sidneye answered in the manner of a man seeking to retrieve a loss. He added, chuckling, "If a doomed man cares to look at it in that light he should be humored."

"Thanks," returned Ralls. Then, to my amazement, he said, "Now, Mr. van Schreeven, you never liked a freehanded skipper, did you? It wasn't your idea of a stout business arrangement. Nor did such ever appeal to Batjoek or Vossler, or van Arken. But here it is, the way Mr. Sidneye likes it." I thought he was a fool who talked against himself, who divided the lesser lights only to bind them solidly together with the mention of a buried fact that had in the past singled him out for Batjak's disfavor, for Sidneye's admiration. And even as Ralls said it Sidneye beamed.

I saw van Schreeven's hand on the table as it drew into a fist. But he merely laughed scornfully, saying, "Ralls, you'll never roam the seas in a Batjak ship again."

"Harmenszoon," said Mayrant, "we'll humor him."

Van Schreeven got to his feet, his face empurpled. "Humor him! You said those words for years, Mayrant! You humored him with free routes and a closed eye against the objections of all of us. You got for your pains a ship jammed in a lagoon entrance — and a *Red Witch!* I'll be damned if we humor him again with an inch to crowd into a mile.

"And, you're doing exactly as he said — you're working into another mistake! And every man here will agree." His angered eyes peered into every face for support.

Hooch stood up in a hurry. "I agree," he said. Then Cordtlaant rose with, "And I." Sidneye frowned, his sharp eyes dancing around the table and pausing on van Arken before leaping toward Batjoek.

397

Slowly van Arken stood and said, "Twenty years, after he finds the *Witch*." Then Carter got up, and just before Batjoek said, "I agree with Dokter," cried out, "Make it a hundred years!" Soon Bullit and Noord joined in.

Ralls chuckled. "Well, it's like you said, Mr. van Schreeven, Batjak *is* one solid vote — against Mayrant Sidneye."

Sidneye sat there glaring at Ralls, then at his rebellious puppets. "Fools!" he flung, enraged. "Sit down, all of you!"

Then Ralls grinned, and stood as if to make his exit. "Too bad, Mr. Sidneye. Too bad we are outnumbered. When do we move to the Celebes?"

"Celebes!" exclaimed Mayrant.

"Yes, I wouldn't think of moving out to the *Witch* until Batjak is one solid vote." With that he strode arrogantly to the door, where he turned about and said, "Yes, one solid vote on how much it will pay in money to look down at the *Red Witch*."

CHAPTER XXXIII

I

I AWOKE early next morning, my mind churning every word uttered at the dinner; over and over. I tried to forget, though I continued to wonder at the skipper's game, asking just what stakes were higher than the fancy price Sidneye paid for the *Quean*. Ralls did not have a chance at the *Red Witch's* gold. Or had he?

At the moment an idea leaped out of the mirror. "Yeah," I said aloud. "If the *Flores* is good for my getaway, why not take Ralls along?" We could split the money if he continued to refuse all — perhaps in Lorengau. Then we'd part forever.

But could I reach Ralls? It was worth a try, and I placed the attempt second on my list; the first being Teleia, of course.

I quickly took stock of my possessions, which included the money Dokter van Arken contributed. I examined my wounds, feeling surprise and pleasure as I did so — ordinarily the tropics retard the healing of cuts and sores — so thanks again to the scientist whose knowledge and skill were made manifest in my healthy cut. Teleia's wound was less

398

dangerous, I said in support of an exciting plan, and there was little question about the attention she received.

I had slipped the money in an oilskin, having ended a search for seaworthy clothing, when I thought of Carter. I could not just pick up and vanish without a word to him. At his door I hurdled the formality of a rap and barged in. He opened a frowning eye, then another, and soon he sat up in bed eyeing me sourly.

"What do you make of it, Sam?" He meant the dinner, of course. I shrugged. "Is the admiral mad?" he asked, leaning forward.

"In a measure," I said with a slow dubious ring. I studied him for telltale reaction, expecting to see a grin of triumph; instead I saw a sad, wan little smile. "But," I said, "he came back on springs of steel, the old Ralls.

"But here, Carter, I'm losing time." Thereupon I rattled off the whole plan, including the aid of van Arken, and I drew from him an exclamation of, "Well, I'll be damned!" And nothing I could say seemed to stop his getting dressed — he would round up the Malays and hide them in the grove near the *Flores*. Well and good, since he was hell-bent on throwing in his half-stuiver's worth.

"We'll pull a couple of hours before sundown," I said. "So there's no hurry."

2

The shadows were long grasping claws seeking to retain their hold on a dying day when I tapped against her door. Soon she stood before me in a gay flowered *pareu*, and the coral tints, rising from the silken background to vivid blossoms, seemed to reach out and lift the tawny cream of her skin to pellucid heights. Thrilled, I closed the distance between us and gave myself up to her warm lips. We both staggered out of that blissful meeting, smiling, and viewing the other with appraising eyes, eyes that saw nothing short of perfection.

"I'm so glad you came," she said. "I've expected you all day." Her dark eyes burned into my heart.

"And I," I returned, "have been rather busy."

"So Dokter van Arken said." I frowned, then grinned, asking if someone had spilled the news of my plan. She masked her eyes and voice, saying, "I know nothing." But the smile belied her words. "Who would reveal secrets to me?" Her eyes twinkled.

"Who wouldn't?" I laughed. "You're not exactly a Dutch definition of just an ordinary person."

"Then what am I?"

"You? Why — you're towering sails of pure white silk on gilded arms and masts. Yes, and your cordage is of purple and gold and silver, meeting a sapphire-studded bowsprit, and diamond-set bulwarks of solid sterling."

"I'm a ship that would sink," she laughed.

"Yes, right into my arms." Then I turned serious. "You're that and more, sweetheart. And you and I have a job ahead."

"You include me, Sam? Why, and just what is the job?"

"Sit here by me, sweetheart. First, tell me you love me. You do? Well, so far, so good. Now tell me something — just who let the bars down in the lagoon? This is an important question, since it has a bearing on an even more important one I'm planning to ask."

After a long moment she answered. "I did, Sam. I didn't know about the mine."

"I knew it!" I said joyously.

"Now just what did you mean when you put off breaking the news to Hooch with — 'That depends more or less on what you do in the meantime'?"

"Just what I said, my darling," she smiled. "And you came through with flying colors — you did put honor above our ketch."

"So that's what your eyes said when I held out the check to Ralls?" She nodded, her eyes alive with admiration, and more. "So that was it. Well, we'll have our ketch, all right, if it never sails any sea but the sea of our dreams."

"I understand," she replied seriously, and for ages we sat there gazing dreamily at the future and the present that nestled in our faces. Then I said it, I gave voice to that all-important question.

"Will you marry me, Teleia?"

Seriously, fondly, she reviewed, it seemed, our every word and glance before giving answer.

"Sam," she said, suppressing almost a twinkle in her eye, "you are not obligated to propose — just because I lowered the bars in the lagoon."

I winced. "None of that," I said seriously. "The reason I asked who lowered the bars was — well —"

"Well — what?" she asked, smiling.

"Just call it a bridge to my last question — as it happened your answer bolstered my nerve. But enough of that. Will you marry me?"

"Yes, Sam."

I had never heard sweeter words. Huskily I said, "I'll love you always, my darling. I'll live to make you happy — always." I don't know how long I held her before sighing and holding her at arm's length.

"Sweetheart, will you leave this island with me today?" She allowed her eyes a moment of surprise and incredulity before speaking one word: "Sam!"

"Yeah," I grinned, "we're stealing the *Flores!* We're eloping, Teleia."

She drew back instinctively. "Sam, are you mad?" she exclaimed in low tone, smiling into my mood, almost.

I said stoutly, "I'm serious. Together we'll board the *Flores* and thread the lagoon. But we must do it before the light is gone." Her answer meant everything.

"But, Sam, you're impetuous," she deliberated aloud.

"Perhaps I am. But Dokter van Arken suggested the idea and laid a thousand guilders on its success." Thus I laid my plans before a partner whose love of adventure flashed in her eyes. But there was more than evanescent thrill to meet my direct gaze: there was that trust a woman in love places in her choice of man.

She murmured, "Sam, we're both mad." And Sam Rosen sighed from sheer relief.

"But aren't we sailing the same wind?"

"Yes."

"Then you'll dare it?" I said.

"I'd go anywhere with you, darling," she said, placing her hand in mine; and the maleficent atmosphere of that Dutchman's Little Soembawa seemed clean and free under the long shadows that now reached for the night.

"Then we'd better move into our future," I said. "And remember, my dear, fate isn't always kind to lovers. We may fail. But remember this — we are one, and never shall anyone come between us. Say it after me."

"We are one — and never shall anyone come between us."

"That's a vow, sweetheart. That's the soul of our ketch."

She joined me in forgetting the past. Her next words, "Sam, dear," were but preludes to a dream that called for a voice. She seemed unhurried, now that we were launched upon a plan to make us one. She forgot Ralls, Batjak, and Hooch; she forgot, as I did, that she had ever lived a moment before our meeting. She continued with, "We'll be busy just being happy, won't we?"

We decided to move out to the veranda, as though we were busy killing time on a lonely island. So, with simulated expressions wrapping

401

up the secret of our betrothal, we walked slowly down the long, wide hallway, her step and mine, her heart and mine, in perfect rhythm.

We moved on toward the pool, and once behind the screen of trees and bushes, we broke into a run. Circling the beach was but a matter of minutes, and we arrived on the open beach before the *Flores* while the sun hung suspended three lengths above the onrushing night. The lagoon was never so beautiful.

The gantlet wasn't quite run — Mr. Bullit showed his face from behind a stanchion and hastily changed his frown into a grin. Teleia eyed me, as much as to say she would handle him; and she did, by telling him to report to her father. With his departure, I scanned the tropical hedges for Carter. He emerged from the south bend with two Malays as soon as Bullit hit the jungle. We were soon on the *Flores*.

Teleia stood there, watching me. I was suddenly conscious of standing in swashbuckling pose, hands on hips, and ordering Carter to take a look at the screw; somewhat taken aback, I said in jocular tone: —

"Mrs. Rosen-to-be, am I captain of this craft?"

"Aye, sir," she said, her dimpling face eager.

"Then you'll be roustabout as well as chief mate. Get below and check the provisions. But give me the fuel supply at once."

From Carter, running up the gangway, "The screw has been repaired, Sam. And what's more, so have those toy steadying sails."

From below came Teleia's voice: "Captain Rosen. Fuel — quarter of a drum."

That was bad, and I said so. "But," I added in resigned tone, "I've a foggy idea in mind. Maybe it'll work. Carter, like to ride out to the mouth with us? Perhaps the *Stefan Meer* can send you back in a dory." He seemed tickled at the idea.

And five minutes later I heard the spit of the engine. Easing the screw into gear I heard a sweet purring, and a churning of the water. With Teleia by my side I set the ship in motion, dead astern, and cut her into a half circle before shooting the white stem out into the dangerous roadstead to freedom.

3

Ralls cropped into my mind once more as I watched the lagoon, expecting all hell to break loose on the beach at any moment.

I had come upon Ralls early that morning — just after leaving Carter. He sat reading in the garden, causing me to stare at an apparition;

I expected him to be safely stowed away. It was then I realized that he was figuratively behind double rows of bars. Advancing, I made no mention of his quasi liberty. Instead I voiced my proposition, cold and pointed: I was planning to depart from Little Soembawa before sunset — aboard the *Flores;* would he care to shake the island? Expecting an easy answer in the affirmative, my surprise turned into amazement when he said: —

"Thanks." He sighed heavily. "I've got other plans."

4

The tide was coming in fast, and above the subdued grind of the engines I heard the breakers crashing against the coral shelves of the barricade; one continuous pounding, plumes reaching high and falling back for the undertow, and another snow-crested roll at the inexorable wall. Meeting the *Flores* was the current, strong through the lip of the lagoon, and boiling through the pathway I sought to follow.

Pulling a ninety-five-foot craft through was not child's play. But compared to the *Quean* she was easy; she should be safely at sea within the half hour.

I grinned ironically, evoking from Teleia a question easily answered. "Quite the opposite of the *Quean's* run," I said tersely.

Teleia's hand rested upon my shoulder as we crossed the bars and maze of cable. I could feel her warm, pulsating breast against me as the two ugly fingers of coral parted for our exit; and we were through, meeting the wide-open sea, the limitless freedom of sky and clime; then we were beyond the spot where the sea rose up for the *Quean* on that night aeons and aeons back.

Carter turned about, sighed, and forced a smile. In rueful tone he said, "Congratulations, Sam. You're out, and free. And as for you, Teleia," he said, "you're getting a rakehell, a trader, and a level head. Keep him well ginned, but otherwise hold a tight rein on him." And we rolled forth a bottle and banter, all the time lessening the distance to the iron ship standing out to the south.

Anchored some distance out owing to the uneasy sea, the *Stefan Meer* sat there after slugging it out with the sun. She lost her glowing red as we pulled closer, assuming in its place the anonymity of any cargo ship one might have in mind; she was long, with waistless cargo decks, derricks flanking her jumped center, and gray lifeboats staring out like useless eyes. Her prow reached high in opaque scarred black, broken only by the great holes for her anchor cables. She squatted there, a fatuous sulphur-bottom whale with sleepy eyes, the Dutch *zeemen* moving about her topside like swishing suckers. The dingy forecastle showed the laundry of many a sailor, and as we hove-to several of the Dutchmen, looking funny in their sea garb, moved to the rail. One fellow stood stripped to loincloth. As we drew near he scurried aft amid the jeers of his companions.

"Ahoy, *Stefan Meer!*" I cried. "Mijnheer Steen, please." He was, said Teleia, a law of the sea in his own right. Soon a tall man appeared, sharp of eye, nose, and chin. At his appearance I gave Teleia the job of spokesman.

"Hello, Mijnheer Steen," she said, displaying her best smile. "We haven't met since Soerabaja last year." He wound up his face, threw it into a pleased expression by spreading his heavy lips into a wide grin, and returned her greeting. "We're sneaking out to fish, Mijnheer. Could you, would you, be a party to our mischief by setting out a drum of fuel and some deep-sea tackle?"

If there had been a *neen*, it was melted down into fawning acquiescence. All he said was "*Ja, ja, ja,*" bowing as he did so. Soon we had the fuel and tackle, and he said in guttural Dutch, "Careful, Juffrouw, you don't get caught in a storm. The sea acts like an old woman working up to a fit."

Smiling, she scoffed, "We'll also bring you our prize catch, dear friend. And, by the way, Mijnheer Steen, will you send our friend here back to the house? Splendid." She blew him a kiss.

Carter surprised us. "I think I'll go along. Every fisherman needs a best man. After the ceremony I'll work my way back. Perhaps with Mr. Sheraton." I glared at him, then joined Teleia's light laughter.

It was then Carter said, "Maybe before the ceremony, Sam. Look who's coming."

I spun about, my eyes alert: there, moving in lazily from the north, was the Australian patrol schooner, Mr. Sheraton standing on the port quarter eyeing us. I could almost feel his mocking eyes, and his triumphant chuckle seemed audible to my mind's ear. I glanced at Teleia, and she at me, disappointment ruling our faces.

Covering a curse I groaned, "Well. Well. This calls for quick thinking, or —"

"Don't kid yourself, Sam," said Carter. "Sheraton isn't about to let you out of his sight." As I sent him a glance that said, "You don't know Sam Rosen," he added, "Wait and see, simple Sam."

Carter was right. The patrol craft moved past the lagoon entrance, reefing her slattern sail as she closed the distance between us. Soon she swung in to parallel the *Flores*. Mr. Sheraton leaned on elbows, his face minus any of the triumph I'd expected, as he said: —

"Going somewhere, Mr. Rosen?"

"I was," I returned. "To Lorengau — to get married."

He shrugged. "Sorry," he said almost as if he meant it, "but I'm sure that can wait until we investigate further. There is a little matter in which you seem to be involved — murder — or murders, let us say."

"Well," mourned Carter, addressing Teleia, "our runaway scheme didn't pan out."

"Yours!" I almost shouted. "This idea was mine."

"Sam," said Teleia, her hand on my arm, "Carter and I planned this several days back. Please, Sam, don't look so fierce. You see it was my idea even on that night when my uncle told you his long story. I'd have gone with you then. Remember I said, 'Dokter van Arken is a good subject, don't you think? And then there's the Moluccan.' Remember?" I did.

"Well, Sam, I went to work on van Arken that same evening. Carter was a good ally — and so was Batjoek, though his sole reason was me — my wish. And you — you came through with flying colors when the Dokter suggested the plan."

"But van Arken?" I said. "Why did he and Batjoek go against Sidneye?"

Her answer was a smile and shrug. Perplexed, I lifted my eye again to the deck of the patrol schooner. And there I saw trouble standing in to a showdown.

5

Mr. Sheraton ordered me to put the *Flores* inside the lagoon; reluctantly I obeyed. His craft followed, and her anchor splashed just as she crept over the Dutchman's bars. My brows lifted and I said speculatively: —

"So he plans to block the lagoon this time." I asked Carter to take the wheel, and I moved aft where I stood studying Sheraton's seamanship in preoccupied manner: he allowed her to swing head to the wind, the anchor holding her by the head, and hove short, while she was made fast aft by the kedge anchor to port and a hawser to the starboard shore. She could scarcely sheer in a light wind. But I was thinking less about the craft and more about the threat she seemed to voice in her odd anchorage.

"Sam." It was Teleia. "The welcoming committee! Look."

"Yeah," I replied, crestfallen, "I expected that."

After the age in which I stood at the bow directing Carter at the wheel, we moved into the anchorage from which we had departed. There in the pale light I saw steady faces, mocking, silent, and grinning faces: Mayrant Sidneye; the contained father, Harmenszoon van Schreeven; the stoic, Batjoek; the divided team, Cordtlaant and Noord. The most fatuous grin emanated from the revengeful face of Jan Hooch, while the silence of a funeral showed in the eyes of Dokter van Arken.

Sheraton was not long in arriving. He did not pause for any greeting, he simply said, bluntly, "Gentlemen, no one will leave this island until I've searched it thoroughly. Is that clear?"

"Naturally," Sidneye replied. "We are more than anxious to please any guest — even an uninvited one."

It was about nine that evening when I was called to the blue room, at Sheraton's order. I was forced to reiterate my every statement bearing upon the *Quean of Melbourne's* mysterious end. Soon I was told to stand by for further questioning — that new light had been shed on the case.

"The new light on the case, sir?" I said.

"Oh, just a trifling clew," he returned. "Mr. Ralls has been found — alive."

How genuinely I feigned surprise I shall never know.

"Frankly, Mr. Rosen, we have no case against you. However, through you we hope to solve the mystery of the Dutchman's place." His eyes dwelled upon me, and I leaped into a bit of fast thinking. "Of course, you may refute your statement and speed up the matter, though we're in no hurry." Why wasn't he in a hurry, and how was Ralls discovered; was I a sucker because I believed that polished voice?

"Sir," I said, prompted by my realization that here was my one and only opportunity to help Ralls, "if he is on this island, why not arrest him? Your case might end there."

"No hurry," he said in the manner of one addressing a child. And I, sitting there with a universe of knowledge, found my tongue chained by circumstances.

"Why?" I said. "Who knows, you might be doing Ralls a favor."

"So I thought, Mr. Rosen. However, I talked to Mr. Ralls. I offered him the haven of handcuffs. Like to know what the bloke said?

"He said, 'Thanks, Tommy. If I move out now, both you and I will lose what we're after. Suppose you casually move down on the *Stefan Meer* tomorrow — she'll be five miles north by west from the southern tip of Doppel Reef.' He offered a proposition — for the information he could give about the wreck of the *Quean*, I must see that the *Red Witch* case was not reopened."

My amazement was genuine.

"Unfortunately we cannot agree to such. The *Witch* looms over the sinking of the schooner like Gibraltar over a pebble. Of course, the case is closed, but — there's the gold."

Sheraton shrugged. "So you see I'm aware there's something big brewing."

"I still say you should arrest him," I piped.

"No," said the power out of Rabaul. "We might then lose the thread forever."

"Then why tell me all this? Don't you know I'll blurt it out to Ralls and Sidneye at the first chance?"

"Yes," he said, smiling slowly.

But why had Ralls given Sheraton a false position? I continued to ask the question until, through the window of my room an hour later, I heard the patrol schooner's anchor cable rattle in as Sheraton made ready to quit the island again. He, emulating the cat, would allow the mice, Ralls and Sidneye, room for a run. I admitted he seemed less foolish and more clever, a man who recognized an even chance at startling success on the morrow.

But tomorrow was another day, I thought, sighing heavily; the night continued its rule. And no sooner had I completed the thought than a Malay servant brought a message: —

Would I join the others downstairs?

6

As I stood in the doorway of the huge room all eyes turned my way. Cadavers all they seemed, silent, and strange under the yellow light thrown against the blue of the room; they soaked up a hellish glare: the bald pate of Sidneye glowed like a moon on the wane and the Moluccan's face absorbed the color like a blotter of deep umber; van Schreeven's ruddy complexion was tinged with an ashen film, while the pink face of Jan Hooch seemed drained of color; Cordtlaant, standing between Carter and Noord, was less ghostly; but Ralls — there was the apparition. I moved into their midst to accept the tint in store for me, saying under my breath, "Why doesn't Sidneye bring in the squid and make it unanimous?"

"Sit down, Rosen," said Sidneye. "We've been expecting you." Van Arken entered and everyone sat down. The chairs formed a large circle. Drinks were served, though I declined a bracer of gin as I thought of Teleia, whom I had last seen when I kissed her, just before Mr. Bullit took over the yacht.

Sidneye broke the silence with, "Mr. Sheraton has departed." He laughed contemptuously. "He was very disappointed at the lack of evidence here."

I was about to say Mr. Sheraton was a wily creature who would bear watching, when Ralls said, as though he spoke to a group of hirelings, "You may rest at ease, gentlemen. Thanks to Mr. Rosen, he finds nothing in the sinking of the *Quean* that hints at crime. Sam, you deserve a medal."

I eyed him coldly. "My chest is covered with such conversational gewgaws. What else have we to talk about?"

"A reef, perhaps," smiled Sidneye. "A reef you remember, Mr. Rosen."

"Well — out with it," I blurted.

"Sure," Ralls said. He sat opposite Sidneye in the circle. "I told them I had promised you half of the treasure, Sam." I winced, glowered at Ralls, and replied in low acid tone: —

"Why not lay the cards down? In the first place you can't locate the *Witch*, nor can I, nor anyone. In the second place I've renounced claim to any part of the treasure. I wouldn't touch it with a ten-foot pole!"

Van Schreeven surprised me with, "I'm beginning to agree with you, Mr. Rosen."

I was in no mood to agree with anyone. I said, meeting the steady gaze of van Schreeven, "And I might tell anyone who's interested that I could now be on the patrol schooner and free of this horseplay in wits. And the reason I'm not is Teleia." I laid my fiercest eye on Hooch, who sat next to Carter. "My dear lad, you've lost. Are you man enough to stand on your own hind legs and wish her well, or do you propose to chase after an illusion?"

He blinked his eyes and lowered his gaze. I'd been a bit rough perhaps.

"Romance knows no barrier," Sidneye mused, before saying crisply: "But back to Ralls and the treasure. Rosen, I disagree with you on one point. Ralls is a *zeeman* who can smell out any track in the sea."

"Very well," I smiled ironically, "suppose you are right — what then?"

"Just this," he said quickly, menacingly. "You, too, have a part — since you were a willing witness to the scuttling of our *Witch* you will more or less guarantee Ralls's performance."

I chuckled. "Damn, Mr. Sidneye, it seems the Celebes ticket should do that!"

"Unfortunately it doesn't," he replied.

"Nor will Sam Rosen," I returned quickly. "I suggest you enlist the aid of the devil."

"We've considered that," he said scathingly. "But since you are involved, and since your stay in the Celebes is also considered, I think you'll see it our way."

I stood, angry as the word itself. "Mr. Sidneye, I've said I'll have nothing to do with the gold of the *Red Witch*. I mean it. And your threat doesn't scare me a damn bit. Why? Because you don't intend for Ralls — or Sam Rosen — to spend a single day in the Celebes!"

His lips thinned and his face reddened perceptibly, though his eyes regarded me with wondering esteem.

Van Schreeven, delighted, raised a hand and faced the circle of faces. "What did I tell you? Even Rosen knows the Celebes was a hoax cleverly prepared for our benefit."

Ralls frowned, and van Arken stroked his beard thoughtfully, while Batjoek remained a sitting statue. But all eyes seemed to acknowledge the truth of Harmenszoon's words.

"You'll see!" flared Sidneye, gripping his wheel chair and almost rising up out of it. Then with a mighty effort he managed a smile and turned upon me. "Very well, Rosen. You've spoken your piece. Now I'll say mine. Your childish outburst has done nothing to improve your already precarious position. I think —"

Ralls interposed with a laugh and, "Forget it — Sam's in love." I chose to ignore the thrust.

"Yes," smiled Sidneye, "and all the more reason why he should prove himself manageable. But the Celebes. I think my past should prove a point there. Never would I think of denying Ralls the pleasures I extended Streicher. As for Rosen," he shrugged, "who knows?

"But — since we all realize the utter uselessness of threats, which Mijnheer Ralls chooses to accept with a smile — let us turn to the sole remaining influencing agent: money. We have a job ahead and money will expedite matters. Do you agree?" The coterie wasn't sure; Sidneye's turn from punishment to reward seemed to bewilder them.

"If Ralls can lay the shadow of the *Stefan Meer* on the *Red Witch* tomorrow, I'll present him with fifty thousand American dollars. I'll do more," he added, studying Ralls closely. "I'll set Rosen free."

I started; so that was Sidneye's reason for mentioning the Celebes for me — and, I admitted with further surprise, the threat was a brilliant play, the means by which I, or rather my safety, should guarantee

Ralls's performance. But how did Sidneye know of that weak spot in the skipper's armor?

"*Neen!*" cried van Arken and Batjoek in union. "Rosen is guilty." Hooch and Cordtlaant supported them, while van Schreeven objected to paying Ralls a stuiver.

"I say yes — to both!" Sidneye thundered, his face coloring vividly and holding past the first flush. An ashen purple then took over, reminding me of thunder over the horizon.

Batjoek spoke: "I propose we pay Mijnheer Ralls the money. Then, until Sheraton cools off, we stand on the island, or check on the treasure in Halmahera. We can decide on suitable punishment after that — for Ralls and Rosen."

"A good idea," said Sidneye.

"Preposterous!" cried van Schreeven. "They'd steal the gold in the meantime."

"And I," said Ralls, "accept the offer of Batjak. I'd expected more money, but — well, Sam's freedom means a lot."

I was surprised at his quick acceptance: Ralls thought in terms of hundreds of thousands, which he had claimed as his own ten years before. Thus he was staking all on the success of some fabulous, undeclared scheme, while putting his weakness concerning my safety up as a pawn for his gambit. And, of course, his words tickled Sidneye's vanity — they proved the success of his strategy in threatening my freedom.

"I say again I am heartily averse to any agreement between ourselves and Ralls," said van Schreeven in the smooth voice I'd learned to respect. "We have sworn to rid the Eastern World of him, and unless we do we'll have all this to do over in a year or two. I suggest we forget the reefs and proceed at once to the shadows of Peak Latimodjong. Don't you agree, Batjoek?"

"I have spoken," said Batjoek.

"Yes, you've spoken," countered van Schreeven. "And do you believe a man like Ralls could be sincere when he puts Rosen up as his reason for accepting Mayrant's offer?"

"I've spoken," said the Moluccan crisply. I saw the twinkle in Ralls's eye, in Sidneye's.

"Gentlemen," said Ralls. "You continue to underestimate me." I saw Sidneye's eyes widen. Ralls added, "The cards are stacked, and I'm the dealer."

Everyone felt the weight of Ralls's words; right or wrong, he packed conviction into them. Sidneye seemed impressed.

"Suppose then, Mr. Ralls," van Schreeven spoke with mild contempt, "you tell us just why, if you pull the strings, you can be placated with the paltry sum of fifty thousand dollars."

"A timely question, and one worthy of an answer. I cannot salvage the bullion without capital. Batjak possesses that. You remember the pearls of Polynesia, of course; alone I could not touch them, but with the *Hind* and mighty quatrefoils behind me I struck a fortune — for me, for you. Regarding fifty thousand dollars, I am quite sure I can up the ante — but it will do for a starter."

Van Arken came to life. "I think Mijnheer Ralls's last statement emphasizes beyond any doubt the eternal problem confronting us. We'd do well to divorce him, as well as Rosen. Therefore I say that you have yet to come forward with any intelligent suggestion."

"We should welcome one, Dokter," said van Schreeven, smiling acidly.

"I'm beginning to wonder," snapped the Dokter. "The Celebes could give birth to repercussions, just now, or had you thought of that, Harmenszoon? Freedom invites future visits from Ralls, Mayrant. Batjoek has the right idea about the Mandate officials, and on one other point he and I are in perfect accord."

"And that?" said Mayrant.

"Need not be divulged," answered van Arken, "at this moment."

"No?" Van Schreeven was on his feet. "I think I have the answer to that, Mayrant." He staked his all, I could plainly see, for victory here, for a firm hand on the helm of that Batjak empire the inner man so despised. "Van Arken and Batjoek conspire against you; I'm beginning to see it all. They fear, Mayrant, that you are under the spell of Ralls. His temerity, like Rosen's, they think, finds your weak spot."

Sidneye gripped his chair tensely, his color rising. He stared at three faces, van Arken's, Batjoek's, his half-brother's.

"Yes," flung Harmenszoon caustically, "I'll wager they had a hand in Rosen's theft of my yacht, and daughter — for the same reason — they feared his surface boldness; van Arken stands in fear of losing his place in your eye, Mayrant. Hooch saw Rosen and Batjoek enter van Arken's quarters on the day of the dinner."

"Fool!" said van Arken. "Fool of fools!"

And I — Sam Rosen — was beginning to see the light. That, then, had been the true reason behind their gift to me of a thousand guilders, their mapped plan before a word had been spoken. Teleia was a party to the plot, as Carter, though she was ruled by variform and sweeter purpose. But van Arken's jealousy, his weakness, lay bared for all eyes to view.

"Damn!" I said, as Sidneye brought up the present.

"So!" He repeated it over and over, running his eyes from van Arken to the brown man, and then to his brother. "Who speaks the truth?" He seemed to read denial in the silence of the accused.

"I," said van Schreeven. "Do you hear from the traitors?"

A few short steps separated van Arken from the accuser, and he took them; then his open hand flashed up and to a most startling destination — van Schreeven's face. Cordtlaant moved forward, and I saw Teer Noord's eagle nose and eyes move ahead of his body; hands on hips, his smile dedicated to sweet combat, Noord stepped directly into Cordtlaant's path. The latter's arm rose in a swift arc, and it was Teer Noord who fell, his nose spouting gore.

Sidneye stared anxiously, torn between love of battle and a greater love — success in uniting his lieutenants at this crucial stage of the game into a solid Batjak. And out of his ephemeral indecision Cordtlaant advanced, van Arken his goal. Perhaps the greatest surprise came when the *Stefan Meer's* captain was halted, actually downed by a blow I didn't think was a part of the lad — Carter.

Ralls laughed. "I should regret the trouble I caused you, Mr. Sidneye."

"Thank you, my dear Ralls. Some day in the near future, I'm sure, I shall say the same to you."

But no throne is empty until the ruler is unseated; and the son of Taaro Tiki joined me in witnessing a performance I never expect to view again. It began when Mayrant Sidneye threw one word with clipped, incisive voice: "Quiet." In its wake was frozen attention, which he viewed with sardonic amusement. He was authority in that moment.

"Your antics," he said, "are disgusting — amusing, childish. Look at you! Harmenszoon, look at yourself — a madcap spouting untimely accusations. Van Arken, stare at a childish hand that slapped your partner. Cordtlaant, at last you bow to anger — and before Ralls. Noord, you are less of a man, more of an ape." Slowly he eyed them, slowly he upbraided them, following the pattern around in another vicious circle.

"Brother, you will apologize to the Dokter and Batjoek for calling them traitors."

"I'll do nothing of the kind."

"But you will," smiled Mayrant. "Yes, Harmenszoon of Bali, your conscience must engender forgiveness — as it did when you seduced the maiden of the cloister, the maid of Kintamani."

"Enough!" van Schreeven snapped. He stood, his face red and minus inculcated composure. "You dare humiliate me?"

"And old Father van Skike beat you at fists for your weakness. And

412

the rape of a girl later, in which van Arken lied to save you." He then turned his gaze upon Cordtlaant, as if in respite. But no, he sought a quick rung in a second ladder.

"Cordtlaant, you'll shake Noord's hand!" he thundered. Success was behind him in another moment. "And you, van Arken, will extend your hand to my brother." There followed moments of tense silence. "Then the man I built into an international figure is a traitor. *Verdomd!*"

"*Neen*, Mayrant. Neither is Batjoek," said van Arken, extending his hand.

"Harmenszoon, you will obey me now — you have the word of Batjak, the word of Mayrant Sidneye, that I will allow you one minute to obey me. Otherwise, I swear to break you."

Batjoek's word carried weight when he said: "The Baas never jests." His statement seemed to rise out of the long, relentless past, packing conviction, and more — it said the strongest of Batjak's lieutenants bowed before its ruler.

"All of Batjak is one mind," said Sidneye slowly, without any emphasis whatever; the lack of force seemed to echo deadly earnestness. The seconds ticked off into the past, and Sidneye, eyeing the watch in his hand, said, "Harmenszoon, you're finished — through! You aren't worth the trouble I took when I placed a parade of temptations before you in Bali." When van Schreeven's face slowly paled — as if emptying itself of all expression in order to accept the flood of surprise that ran fast into a strange and ill-omened amazement, before leaping into the throes of utter stupefaction — Mayrant continued scornfully, mercilessly: —

"I saved the Church trouble, though I've wished often that you had attained priesthood instead of Batjak's figurehead."

"Mayrant," van Schreeven managed weakly, "you jest — surely. You — you could not have done that to your brother."

The implacable voice of Sidneye reached his ears quickly. "But I did — everyone knows it but you."

"No!" he cried. "No, Mayrant!" He quivered all over, reminding me of Loring at the dinner; he could reconcile himself neither to the fact, nor the deed, that had changed his life from the course the inner man continued, after long years, to favor. Then, as if the shock of the awful revelation joined with the unbelievable duplicity of his brother to drain him of physical stamina, he clutched spasmodically at his heart and sank slowly to the floor.

Dokter van Arken bent over him and, after a lapse of long moments, he peered up at Sidneye.

"His heart. You almost finished him, Mayrant."

"I! You dare say I did it? *Neen!* He brought it upon himself."

"Yes," Batjoek said, "Baas is right. He did not do it. There sits the man — Ralls!"

"*Ja!*" cried Hooch, then Cordtlaant.

Van Arken slowly got to his feet, turning his glare from Ralls to Sidneye. "Yes, Ralls is responsible, Mayrant. Ralls, the man to whom you persist in offering clemency. I say we should proceed to the Celebes at once."

"*Neen!*" shouted Sidneye.

"*Ja!*" sounded the defying chorus led by Batjoek; the trailing voice of van Schreeven rose up from the floor.

Ralls laughed — and I could not help bowing inwardly in respect to the genius of hard and nimble wit, the lone wolf who scored again over the pack of the Western Pacific; Ralls had divided that house of Batjak from its master at *rystafel* with the power of his tongue that matched, it seemed, the hand that brushed off Desaix and Younguer. And he had done more on this evening: he, with the aid of outcropping jealousies, which he evoked to the surface, had almost dissolved the firm.

At that moment I was sure Ralls nursed a mighty scheme; his reason for splitting the firm soared above that of mere shallow enjoyment — if I knew Ralls: he would pursue his course unmolested while they continued to snarl at each other.

"Well, Mr. Sidneye," he said, "do we visit the *Witch* tomorrow?"

"*Ja! Ja!*" And Sidneye grinned out his fierceness, his large teeth bared, even as everyone filed out of the room in protest, van Schreeven supported by van Arken and Batjoek.

The show could not go on forever, I said. The timetable called for one more destination — finis.

CHAPTER XXXIV

I

WITH the sun I was aboard the *Stefan Meer*. I heard the buzz of the winches on deck, and the strokes of the crank shafts in the engine room; the derrick strained and cargo chains groaned before the thuds of slings meeting deck, as diving equipment was hoisted aboard; the smell of hot oil and mists of steam, the rattle of the anchor chain, the hoarse shouts on deck, together with a dozen and one other familiar odors and noises, said the *Stefan Meer* was making ready to leave Little Soembawa. Soon I moved to the forecastle for another hour of sleep.

When I came on deck we were under way; the island lay behind the northern horizon. I found that which I sought, the white yacht up ahead. Under its stern shelter I saw Teleia. She leaned against the rail, her red and white kabaja sweeping with the wind to starboard; at her side stood the junior partner of the firm, her suitor. I moved toward the port bow, lifting my feet over calking kettles, oakum, coils of rope, and links of anchor chain, and soon I stared at her across a hundred yards of limpid water. Wishing for an enormous boat hook to reach out to the yacht and hang an equally fanciful ringbolt, I threw her a hand that first touched my lips. Sweetly it came back to me.

We veered slightly westward. The *Flores* held her distance ahead of us. I remained at my position near the cathead for some time, peering at Teleia, then the roil of the water behind the yacht, all the while matching the present against the future. I was lost to the present when I heard a voice back of me.

"Hello, Sam." I turned about to see Ralls. "Got a dry match?" I had one.

"Where have you been hiding, Skipper?" I said easily.

"Making charts."

"Just what is your game, Ralls? You had a chance to go scot-free with Sheraton. These boys are after you with money now. Then they'll take you to the Celebes for a slow death. Twenty years of it, Ralls!"

He grinned. "You'll see, Sam."

"And what's more, why did you give Sheraton that cock-and-bull yarn about locations — five miles north by west from the southern tip of Doppel? The law here is your salvation."

"Sam, you amaze me. Don't you realize I knew the blokes wouldn't agree to a wink and a closed eye about the *Red Witch*? If the treasure is lifted east of the Purdy Isles, I'm a liar to the court. Thus it must be taken in a hurry, and the world must think it's still in the tight fingers of Davy Jones."

"Hm-m," I chuckled. "I seem to remember the court proved you a liar years back. Why again, Ralls? Perhaps you're playing up to Sheraton to avoid questioning about the *Quean's* end. Is that it?"

"Could be. But when he doesn't meet us there, since we'll be miles to the south, he won't wait long before turning this sea inside out.

Then I shall see to it that I'm placed under temporary arrest for sinking the *Quean*."

"With a sack of gold bars?" I said, chuckling. "Not you, Ralls. And you spoke of upping the ante — how?"

"Wait and see, Sam. But you know I missed you last night when I made twelve marks on a couple of bottles."

"That's the usual number, Ralls."

Shrugging, he said, "Too bad you fell in love. We could have turned a neat trick here. Love is all right, though it puts a man on the defensive. Take yourself, for example. Your initiative is gone, and you spend your time worrying about my neck." He grinned, flashed his vigorous eyes, and said, "Don't deny it, Sam. It's true. But she's a beautiful girl, almost as beautiful as —"

"Angélique," I said for him, ripping his armor to shreds. He sought solace in the hot desolate horizon, where nothing but the monotonous sun beat against the edge of the world.

"Too bad you didn't take her for your wife in the thatch of Ua Nuka Havu. You'd be a different man today. But the pearls and a Batjak ship were worth more at the time. Weren't they, Ralls?" There was no answer. His eyes, like the eye of his soul, sought the far eastern Pacific; and he, once again in the outrigger, faced the stern of the French craft and the radiant brunette who loved him more than Sidneye or his gold.

"Yeah, Ralls, you'd better hit the marks past twelve once more. You'd better drink every last drop to your memories. Something tells me you're to lose even them." With that I turned about to leave him.

"Wait, Sam," he said persuasively, pitifully. "Let's team up for this once. It's a great gamble, and I hold a pat hand."

"Ralls," I said slowly, "I'm more interested in getting you free of this crowd. I'll team with you for that and no more."

"Sam," he began slowly, forcing his words, I thought, "I was sincere last night — about your freedom." I could see he meant it, though I wasn't about to admit it. "I am now. Perhaps it's best that you don't join me."

"Sure," I said, smiling sourly. "You weaved in your concern of me nicely last evening — for your future use."

After some length, he replied, "Yeah." Then he sighed and said, "It seems strange that no divers are aboard this tub."

"Perhaps they're on the *Flores*."

"No. I checked there," he said, peering up at a seaplane moving toward us.

416

"Just why are you interested in divers?" I eyed him narrowly, suddenly interested. The amphibious bird, in the meantime, had circled. She was now purring down to the water, her pontoons popping, her twin motors sounding behind the flash of silvered propellers. She taxied alongside the *Stefan Meer*, and I saw, in gold and red on her silver sides, the quatrefoils of Batjak. And soon I saw more.

Three men alighted; they were soon on the *Meer's* deck. I overheard a Dutchman as he said: —

"Two divers and their boss."

Frowning, I stole a glance at Ralls. He smiled, almost, as his narrowed eyes fell upon the trio in lazy appraisal. But I knew Ralls's every expression — indeed — enough to realize a fact: his mind's eye was never more alert than in those moments.

"Well, Sam," he said moving toward them, "wish me luck."

"I do, Ralls." I did.

2

The *Flores* allowed the *Meer* a catching-up, and the smallest man of the diving trio, who was the expert, I thought, went over to the yacht for a talk with Sidneye. I was tempted to go along; Teleia beckoned. But for some reason I remained on the freighter. I strolled about for a time, at last moving toward the captain's cabin. There I came upon Ralls.

He sat drinking with the two divers. I took a chair, refused a bracer, and listened. He spoke of the *Red Witch*, and the pair sat entranced. At last one of them asked if he might peer at a diagram of her hold — he would like to study the route to the gold.

Ralls replied in disarming tone, "That will keep, fellows, until we find her — and that's the big job now."

"But," the man protested, "our *Baas* said you'd acquaint us with her innards."

"No. There's little use in worrying you with that now." He seemed unaware of their exchange of bewildered glances as he said, laughing, "So — let's talk of things more pleasant — women, for instance."

3

I boarded the *Flores* when the undersea expert moved back to the *Meer*. The noses of the two ships pointed down to the sea for a slow pivot around the coral jaws of lazy Doppel Reef. Under an escort

417

of noisy birds beneath the solid expanse of a cloudless dome, the *Flores Tandjoeng* lifted her steadying sails and churned into a long pull ahead of the colorless freighter. A long trailing wake ran parallel with the frothy track of the larger ship, and as the sky lifted high its inferno, the highways emanating from the ships' bellies assumed the sparkle of sapphire and bleached emerald. School sharks picked up our trail at three degrees under and their fins cut the water tirelessly for the remainder of the voyage.

As the morning advanced I sat with Teleia, her father, who remained out of bed against van Arken's order, Sidneye, Hooch, and Carter under the stern shelter of the *Flores*. We talked even as the powers of Batjak argued — Teleia's eye spoke of romance, and I, unmindful of her father or Hooch, returned, with Carter's songs in soft background, as good as she gave. The seaplane hovered in the distance.

My mind was frequently drawn from Teleia to the skipper. The more I wondered at Ralls's game, the more my mind went back to his interest in the divers. I sensed danger, realizing Ralls would scarcely hesitate in sacrificing the pair for his gain. The thought grew until I eyed the *Meer* with soaring apprehension.

But the morning wore off on the dull side, and except for her presence — a brush of her hand, the flash of her smile, and the depth of her eye — the freight ship offered better company. We had skirted the upper extremities of Doppel Reef, had moved on down past the southern and larger portion, our port bow knifing off a slow curve into four points. Across the now choppy sea the waves were broken by tiny coral dots where the reef rose almost to dry itself in the sun. At noon we were moving directly into the east, with Doppel on our port and Albert Reef breaking far out on the starboard horizon. And we kept on our easterly course until Sidneye said our position was four degrees south and one forty-eight and five-tenths east of Greenwich.

"With the top of Albert Reef miles behind us," he added.

He arose, gave a signal, the raising of an arm, and soon a motorboat was put over the side of the freighter. A quarter hour later Ralls pulled alongside the yacht, and without a word to anyone he walked straight to the wheelhouse and took over the helm.

The *Flores* leaned forward noticeably. Then under all power we shot into the west, bearing off the merest fraction of a point southward. I was standing near the stern rail when we straightened out, and it was then that I felt the heavy, heavy past pressing against every cell in my brain.

Teleia saw me pale; she witnessed the unnatural quiver of my hand

as I sought to lift a cigarette to my mouth; but she could never know —
there aren't words to describe it — of that communion, eerie and
cadaverous, I held with the ghost of the ship we sought. Her towering
sails talked with the winds in my ear, and her tackle rattled with tormenting laughter; Mr. Loring's cabin door opened somewhere behind
me, and the store of gold bars reposed innocently under their seal down
below; the leadsman grunted from sheer surprise, calling off no bottom,
then nine — and the sun dipped straight into the horizon, a bloody
hand reaching from Albert Reef to meet the gallant lady.

Aye! We followed in the last wake of the *Red Witch!*

"Sam?" she said, her hand falling on my arm. "Darling, what's
wrong? You seem upset."

I gripped the rail and frowned at the sea, then I turned the same face
slowly in her direction. "Yeah, I am. We're in the *Witch's* wake,
sweetheart."

Her reply was soft, and serious: "This, darling, will be our forgotten
sea."

Holding her hand tighter I said pensively, "The forgotten sea." It
seemed just that.

I stared across the waves, green and blue, rolling in white froth, graying with the sky and inking with the night. They seemed to laugh up at
me, daring me to deaden their passion for another wreck on the stretching coral tombs of the sea. Aye, for Ralls ruled the helm, and he
traveled the wake of a dead ship with his mind's eye glued to that lonely
stretch from her stern; and he felt again the scraping of her sides; once,
twice, mere warnings of that which was to come. And he traveled the
path again, guiding the shallow draft of the *Flores* over a sea that would
enjoy reaching up to claim the heavy iron ship lumbering behind.

Ralls had downed a prodigious quantity of gin. He, like the hurricane he nursed into a wild, wild wind, roared on to perfidious horizons,
his destiny unknown to any but himself and the devil.

A *rystafel* boy served sandwiches and beer in the shade of the stern
awning. Conversation was rife with continued discord, though we sat
apart from it. Whether I should speak to Ralls or Sidneye, or both, or
neither, I argued with a sense of values that engulfed the lives of the
divers as well as the blood and bone of Ralls. Then I dived into the
respite one needs before reaching out again to claim a decision, a retrospective view. How odd, how uncanny — Ralls and I on the trail of
the ship we'd stabbed to death — Ralls at the helm, the Dutch unsus-
pectingly behind.

A word from Teleia, and I accepted a beer and raised it to my lips

419

before flinging it overboard and stalking forward to the wheelhouse. There I opened the door, glanced at the indicator — FULL AHEAD — before staring at Ralls. He turned his head my way and grinned.

"Right in the wake of the *Witch*, aren't you, Ralls?" No answer; I had expected none. "And she scraped long before she went down. Remember?" Again silence. "The tub behind us hasn't the shallow draft of this boat. Shall I tell Sidneye that?"

He laughed lightly, which proved I was in error, a fact I had known from the beginning. But I was merely drawing him out. Then I plucked at the core, watching him closely for any change of expression.

"And you seemed very interested in the divers, Ralls." He turned quickly, his eyes thinning. "Of course you wouldn't be planning to lead the lambs to slaughter, or would you? Now that would really cause Sidneye's eyes to pop."

Slowly he turned, ordered Mr. Bullit to the wheel, and for a moment his eyes burned into mine. Then his arm raised in a flash, and I saw a universe of hanging stars before the black of night wiped them out. I fought my way out of a whirling world and opened my eyes. Blood ran down my face; and my head, against a bulkhead of the wheelhouse, throbbed painfully. But there was Ralls standing straight and serene, gazing ahead.

What followed was simply the belated joy I sought on that afternoon when I showed Ralls the power of my fists: we slugged our way out of the tiny room and past Teleia's cabin door; I backed away and he stalked me, this time in deadly manner; on past the starboard alleyway, the *Flores* lurching madly under us, and out to the open space near the lifeboats, and it was there I found room for an offensive. I charged and drew blood, though I gave up as much and more — from my nose. Carter led the surprised group, Sidneye bringing up the rear, and at Teleia's cry I landed a punch that threw Ralls's head back against the rail.

But the devil and a hurricane seldom succumb to the puny blows of mortal man, and before I knew another second I was overboard, with Ralls's sharp eyes drawing closer. I slashed at the tepid water for my life; I went under. When I opened my mouth again to breathe the sweet, fresh air, his fist shot out like a brass piston, but not before he said: —

"Fool! Why should I want to harm the divers?"

When next I opened my eyes, I gazed past the soft smile and caressing hand of Teleia, and saw the *Stefan Meer* stood well out to starboard a good mile away. I wondered, my hammering head seeking a normal focus, why Ralls evinced interest in the divers. The skipper looked ahead in this, the biggest game of his career. And though dazed, I knew in the moment that this game, and not pearls or women, had been working in his mind long before we entered Little Soembawa's lagoon; that had the *Quean* made the run out that night, the Dutch would have followed. Albert Reef was inevitable — with the Dutch furnishing a ship and equipment.

No, Ralls had not been duped by the Dutchman who sold us that map in Rabaul — he had known of Sidneye's presence on the island!

4

I awoke with a start. The sun drove harsh rays into my face, and I found to my surprise I lay sprawled on the stern divan very much alone. Thirst claimed priority over everything but loneliness. As I felt of my jaw with misgiving she came into view with tall frosted glasses.

"Up already, Sam? I've only been gone a moment. Father was put to bed." At my side she gently adjusted a bandage, and I squinted to bring the *Stefan Meer* into line of vision.

I picked up the binoculars and peered. She came on, but slowly, carefully, and I could see the leadsman sweating as he drew in the line. Again it went over and the freighter inched along, her bow scarcely purling the water. She threw a midafternoon shadow as lazy as her stride, and the smoke left her funnel in a thin streamer that traveled straight out and with the lee.

"We're not moving," I said, frowning.

She laughed. "Sam, you're slow this afternoon." I gazed at her steadily, smiling despite the pain it brought to every muscle of my face. Lifting her glass, she said: —

"To us, Sam." It was then I took her in my arms and kissed her.

Someone behind us cleared a throat. "I beg your pardon," he said. Startled, we both turned to see young Hooch. "Sorry to intrude," he said, "but there's a little gesture due — I feel I should apologize for having waited so long."

Teleia and I exchanged puzzled glances, while he stepped to the stern center and gazed for a moment at the Dutch flag standing straight out with the southeast trade. He moved ceremoniously to the ropes and, to our surprise, sent the lively bars of red, white, and blue to half-mast. Then he turned about and stood facing us with a wan smile and a forlorn eye. He bowed.

Exit the Dutch! He walked up to me and held out his hand. I took it, my emotion soaring with his; and there we stood, the three of us. It was all over and he walked forward of the ship, his head low, his heart sad.

A shout rolled across the water. It was Ralls, standing in the launch a half furlong off.

"She's here!" he cried. I stood there shaking like a leaf, glued to my tracks. The words rang out, slowly vibrating against my eardrums; I seemed to hear a bell's hollow notes from an ocean grave.

"She's here!" And out over the glaring sea the *Stefan Meer* clanked ahead, the noise of her deck reaching our ears as the leadsman carried the ship forward step by step. And the *Flores* obeyed the indicator in the hands of Mr. Bullit, shuddering as she moved into Slow, turning her graceful nose toward Ralls. The seaplane dipped and slid to the water.

"She's here!" I squeezed Teleia's hand until she uttered a little cry. Before me a ghost of the sea seemed to rise up — a misty wraith, a long red hull and graceful bow; a figurehead reaching beyond countless horizons, her breasts of gold provoking wharfmongers into wagers as to the size of her nipples; a proud tower of canvas, another, and still another, and a spanker waving at the luminous ribbon she laid on the sea; the crush of her sail as she met the capricious winds from the emerald lagoon of the distant South Seas; the sighing of her shrouds as the spray spoke the tongue of the lady of the bow.

I gazed, my eyes bulging, at the vaporous outline she threw against the western sky, her every rope and arm moving toward me like a sylph under a gibbous moon — the *Golden Hind* and her sweet cargo, Angélique; and then the *Red Witch*, the devil's own ship forever. She faded in tears, it seemed, a squall of her own making; and down into the somber sea she slid, her splendor unbroken as her intimate, sad moan rose with the suck of the sea.

"She's here!" cried Sidneye. "*Ja!*"

The *Red Witch* struck, and the boats were lowered. Mr. Loring was placed in position and Ralls stood against the luminous sky — never again would she glisten in the sun, her pennant high, her ears attuned to the shouts in her foretops. A banker in Sydney leaped from the Rainbow Bridge, and a seaman met a shark with his name indelibly stamped in the creature's belly; another went over; and Mrs. Loring turned a whore before impaling herself. Death and violence followed her.

The trail of blood, emanating from the spot upon which my eyes remained glued, incarnadined the blue sea. I saw it, felt the weight of my part in the crime.

The *Flores* coasted a few yards, then churned the water astern, converging with the iron hull of the freighter at a point where only fifty feet of water, and Ralls in a boat, separated us. The seaplane rose up in a whir and her pontoons dripped of sapphires as she glided into the sun. Mr. Bullit's dome was encircled by a radio headset and I heard him talking to the plane — "The Australian boat — give her location." The plane, soon a tiny speck in the sky, evidently responded. A quarter hour later Mr. Bullit said, "Sheraton's schooner is moving west by north into anchor off Doppel — fifty-five miles off."

"No time to waste," said Sidneye. He sparkled like a schoolboy in his first long pants. "Cordtlaant, Noord!" he cried. "Fetch up the divers. You, Steen, get the derrick winches warm! *Verdomd!* The diving bell — get it to the beam." A clatter of wood and a clanking of metal followed, and the men sweated; a hiss of steam and a donkey engine's raucous sounds; a smell of oil and iron, of sea and — the perfume of Teleia. Only the tone of her murmur steadied me.

Ralls, standing in the sea-eye boat, arms akimbo, gave a contemptuous eye to the furor of excitement. He seemed wiser than the lot of them, he seemed aware of a power greater than steel and pumps. He, too, felt the ghost of the gallant lady as he stood over her.

"Like to peer at her, Sam?" he cried.

"No," I said. "How deep is she?"

"Some fifteen fathoms," he returned evenly, "and balanced on the edge of the world."

I heard Carter's voice down the rail as he gave off the cheerless words: —

> And Neptune's hand upon her breast
> Drew fathoms deep the red *Red Witch*.

"Cut it!" I cried, and Ralls, unmindful of Teleia, cursed him. And Sidneye once more sent a puzzled gaze at the only man who seemed to hold a power over Ralls. He seemed to view the Carter I knew.

"Sam," she said, "you're upset. Come, let's move back to the shelter."

"No," I said. "No, sweetheart, I couldn't be moved from this spot with a derrick. Bring us a good stiff drink." As she moved off, I added, "But wait! On second thought all I want is you near me."

5

On the deck of the freighter a close-cropped head was swallowed by a grotesque undersea helmet. All the apparatus was moving up in good order, having been checked and rechecked by another man I'd never seen before. The pumps were given the all's-well signal, and the busy fellow who directed the first act of the subaqueous show was lowered into the boat beside Ralls. On his belly he peered at the ocean floor, arose, and raked a finger across his sweaty forehead, saying so all could hear: —

"Fifteen fathoms or less, I'd say."

The leadsman pulled in the deep-sea lead, emitting in guttural Dutch, "Sixteen three and a half."

Mr. Bullit cried out: "Sheraton's off Doppel Reef, anchor up. He points to the west." Thus Sidneye remonstrated with the crew for delay, for useless testing of all apparatus, almost bungling the job at the beginning. But the director, in the boat with Ralls, advised Sidneye brusquely that all gear would be tested or there would be no diving. As he said it one diver fell when the derrick moved wildly across deck, and it was Teer Noord who struck the lever man down.

Ralls was the only man save me who knew where the bullion lay. For fifty thousand dollars he'd not give up that secret. Whatever his game might be I could only hold my breath and watch it unfold. And it did.

The divers' boss called for a conference. Ralls joined Sidneye, Batjoek, and van Arken on the deck of the *Flores;* the divers came aboard with Cordtlaant.

"Now," said the little director, sweating and wincing, "the location of the bullion."

"Yes," smiled Sidneye, excited. "Give it to him, Ralls."

Ralls's eyes stabbed me with one of his "Schooner alert" glances as he searched his pockets. "I must have lost it in the wheelhouse when Sam and I threw our fists. Sam, you'll help me find it." I followed, my mind racing into and beyond a maze of questions and answers as to the meaning of this play.

Once we were out of earshot, Ralls turned upon me, his voice low and fierce. "Sam, has anyone asked you about the location of the gold?"

"No," I admitted. "They've been too busy squabbling about your future to think of that."

"Good," he chuckled. "Now, Sam, you were very interested in the continued good health of those divers a little while ago. Are you still?" I nodded slowly, perplexed. "Then," he said, "stick to what you implied last evening — you don't want any part in this affair." With that he turned about and joined the others. I followed, still wondering.

"I must have lost the diagram in the water," he said to Sidneye. "But here, give me a pencil and I'll sketch it." This he did, causing

424

the director to curse steadily in low monotone. Ralls turned to the two divers with: —

"Well, it's up to you, lads. It's probably no worse than any other job you've done. However," he added apprehensively, "every damn hulk is treacherous." Slowly, evenly, and almost sadly he eyed the undersea men.

"Do you care to chance it?" he asked at last. They weren't sure, and they asked to peer at the *Witch* while discussing the matter among themselves. Ralls was in the boat with them when Sidneye said: —

"Ralls, I once sailed the *Witch*. I know her every nook and cranny, her every mood. I should think you'd have raised the weight — say, to 'tween decks, at the ship's middle. The bow and stern would have risen more easily to the force of the sea, and she would have been less liable to ship seas — and, she'd have answered the helm quicker."

Ralls stood in the boat, grinning. "Correct you are, *Zeeman* Sidneye, except that you forget details. We carried wheat — scarcely enough for ballast; so — with a few bars of gold we were still light."

Sidneye eyed him speculatively, and said, "Ralls, Mr. Loring, as mate, kept a record of the position of all freight in the cargo book. From what he said your sketch here is contrary to his entry."

Ralls took his time in replying. Every eye there stared at him — he reminded me of a giant magnet drawing shreds of steel. I noticed the baffled faces of the divers, their penetrating eyes alive with growing trepidation.

"Very well, Mr. Sidneye," Ralls shrugged, his tone both resigned and accusing, "I've completed my part of the bargain — there's the *Meer's* shadow over the *Witch*. So go ahead and send these fellows down on a damn foolish errand." He then got out of the boat and took a chair on deck.

Sidneye's eyes, I noticed, had not moved from Ralls's face. They continued to study him as he said, "Batjoek, what do you think?"

"The cargo book would have been accepted as evidence at the trial," said Batjoek. "Though it went down with the *Witch*, I'd take Loring's word."

"Don't listen to Ralls," said a voice back of us. I turned to see van Schreeven's wan face. "Why not ask Rosen?" he added.

"I wasn't mate long enough to even see the cargo book," I said truthfully.

"We're wasting time!" cried Sidneye, when Mr. Bullit announced Sheraton's location. "I'm inclined to listen to Ralls," he added. "If he's wrong then we can search elsewhere."

"You'll regret it! Wait and see!" said van Schreeven. Batjoek and van Arken agreed, and Sidneye cursed them.

Then Ralls stood, smiled at van Schreeven, and joined the divers, who now seemed minus all zeal. The boat moved out a few yards and Ralls pointed to the *Witch*, talking in low tone as the men peered below. Twice I saw the men glance sharply at Ralls; and soon they were staring into each other's eyes, making grimaces and shaking their heads gloomily.

"Are you ready?" asked the director.

One of the men spoke up. "That ship hangs over the edge of the world, sir. I ain't going down." He turned to the other for support. It came.

"Hell no, sir! This job wasn't meant for me," said his companion. "I've got a wife and two kids."

And no amount of coaxing, or offers of a rich prize, could induce them to don a helmet.

Again every eye turned slowly to Ralls. In that moment I admired him as never before; not for his fiendishness, but for the power that rose up out of the mere man; his was not backed by great fortunes, nor did it rise from kingship — it was the apotheosis of the preternatural. And I saw his plan: he had planted a seed of fear in the divers' minds that morning; and I realized that the position of the *Witch*, plus Ralls's gloomy lie about the location of the gold, had terrified the divers; with the patrol steamer moving nearer, he remained the sole hope. Out of the heavy silence his voice rang like a silver bell: —

"Mijnheer Sidneye, your mission has failed."

But Sidneye remembered the pearls of the cavern. "Ralls, you win," he said. "What is your price?"

"Half the gold," came the sharp reply.

"*Neen!*" voiced van Schreeven. Ralls shrugged.

"Half?" said Sidneye in contemplating tone. "I'll make it a quarter."

"Half," said Ralls. "Mijnheer Sidneye, the Australian patrol moves toward us."

"A third," said Sidneye, raising a hand. "No more."

"A half, nothing less."

A breathless silence, then, "Very well."

But Ralls wanted the deal annotated; he said that I should hold the paper; that Teleia and I, if he failed to return, should collect the bonus of fifty thousand dollars. In due time he moved up the ladder of the *Stefan Meer* for a suit of undersea togs. The devil and a hurricane moved into the sea, as I cried out, "Good luck, Skipper." The waters parted for him, then closed over him.

Down, slowly to the depths of the lonely sea, went Ralls, his speed measured by the snakelike tubes and strands of cable moving slowly under. After long years, it seemed, during which Teleia gripped my arm convulsively, there came an abrupt halt; the little man in the boat said Ralls was on the leaning deck searching for a hatchway.

"He's in!" he cried. "And he wants more line. Slow there." Then, "Hello, below," and he conversed with Ralls.

Sidneye, eager — aye, greedy — asked that the hoist follow him. He saw the fabulous wealth from Kalgoorlie's once famous "Golden Mile," reputedly a hundred and ten bricks, each worth more than eight thousand dollars, and he wanted to see, to feel of that gold. The spectators, and they were many, stood tensely quiet about the rails of both ships, and all eyes seemed glued to the air tube.

Mr. Bullit sang out: "The patrol schooner is driving southwest in our direction." Within a minute the seaplane droned into view, circling us slowly as it drove on into the north and out of sight.

The line jerked and the little man aboard the freighter lifted his voice to Sidneye. "He's through the hatch, calling for the receptacle." A quick drop of the lines — they slipped another ten feet within a second — was followed by slow, quivering motions that sucked them under a foot at a time. There followed an interminable quiet, an interim that brought the steel-meshed basket into play at the bottom of the sea. Seconds, long and burdened with suspense, multiplied into minutes; and the sun slipped closer to the oblique swampy coast of far-off New Guinea.

Said van Schreeven: "And Ralls wins, damn him — thanks to Mayrant!"

"Father," said Teleia, "you must not get excited."

"I'm sorry," he said weakly, "but I've hoped for years we'd never find this hell ship." He sweated laboriously, and his face twitched painfully.

"Father!" She moved to his side. A moment later she asked me to go with her, and together we helped him to his cabin. Hooch arrived a moment later.

"Send for — van Arken," gasped her father. Hooch went after him. Soon he arrived and, after an interval, ordered all but Teleia out of the cabin. I moved to the rail.

No sooner had I propped my elbows against the brass than the basket broke the surface; water poured from its sieve as the derrick juggled it into a swing for the deck.

"Give it to me!" screamed Sidneye. "Here, I want it!" His eyes gleamed like mad balls seeking to leave their sockets, and his lips quivered. Soon the contents were brought to the *Flores* and he bent over the two slimy, colorless bricks, rubbing his hands with glee. He reached for one of them and — just as his hand closed over it, a foot, seeming to move out of nowhere, was planted atop it. That foot belonged to Carter.

"No, Mijnheer. You're in no shape for this." Carter was right; and Sidneye stared. Carter was fast coming into his own. "Remember the *Alice Macdonald*, Mijnheer," he said. He was a sparkling Carter. Their eyes locked in challenge, pristine, uplifting challenge to Sidneye: it bespoke a spontaneity that was the opposite of hate. Therein lay the power over Ralls. Therein Carter shone in his true light — he was worth more than gold.

Van Arken arrived. "Your brother, Mayrant, is seriously ill. Come."

"In a moment. In a moment," said Sidneye. He sent his feverish eyes again to the basket, just as the kettle hooks disappeared under the water. Nor could he take his eyes from the spot; he remained there, a man turned from his senses by sheer lust for revenge more than any desire for the gold of the sea.

Before the basket reached a depth of ten fathoms the connecting link between Ralls and us moved about as if shaken by a monster of the deep. A jerk on the line evoked an astonished yell from the little supervisor: "Trouble!" It seemed that he left the rest to those among us who knew Ralls. "Easy there!" he cried. "He's in the hold — in trouble." He spoke into the tube, at last saying: "He says he didn't go down there to talk. Damn!"

"*Neen!*" shrieked Sidneye. "*Neen!* He must not be in trouble!"

The winch, however, thought otherwise; it buzzed, and the lever was thrown. The cable rose swiftly, a foot every second, jerking, evoking from the little director disparaging words for the fools who handled the lines. A welter of bubbles broke the surface. Someone cried for the diving bell, and I saw it moving over the side. I looked down at my hands and saw them gripping the rail like bloodless claws. With a mighty effort I tore them loose.

Then in a quick dive I was over the rail into the tepid water, coming up under the bell before it popped water. I found myself seated across from the astonished little fellow who directed the show; and I heard his fitting epithet, "Insane fool!" though I paid him no heed. Instead I stared down into the water that closed over us, seeing for the first time the dim leaning hulk, far down on the bottom of the sea.

Rigged under full sail, the strings of rotted canvas and ropes lay in rough tangle on her foremast. She sat perched lengthwise between sloping walls, her deck at an angle of about twenty degrees, her fore half drawing a sharp outline against the vast bottomless blue over which she seemed precariously balanced. The main and mizzenmasts had snapped in her settling. But I wondered at her balance, how she hung there, fore over the ledge, stern on coral. One glance of surprise, one glance of remorse, and I painfully sent my eyes to the threads leading to Ralls. They slowed, and held normal. I breathed a sigh of relief. Our narrow chamber seemed to move at a snail's pace, but the wreck moved closer, and the pressure increased.

Then I saw more than lines at the hatchway: I saw Ralls moving out slowly, surely, tugging at a heavy bar. It was placed in the basket and again he disappeared through the hatch. In the interim I peered at the bowsprit, viewing dim lines of the figurehead underneath; she gazed down into those shadowy depths, into the eternal mystery of a deep watery void. The splintered mizzen stump caught my eye; it was ragged and almost healed over by the sea. Up the deck I walked again, Chief Mate Rosen; and I lingered at the spot where Camille and Sharnwort had fought to exhaustion. The *Red Witch* was a lonesome thing down there, depressed, desolate.

"My God," I said, as I almost heard her roll my name.

"He's safe," said my companion. Then I noticed our bell was no longer moving down.

"He's up with another bar," spoke the man. "A damn good diver."

"But what could have caused the flurry down there?"

"Any number of things," grunted the fellow. "But he moves a lot of line — almost as if he moved aft. Just where is the gold?"

"Aft," I said witlessly.

"Aft!" he cried. "Aft? And he said it was forward." Then he cursed Ralls, as well as the divers and himself.

Soon I saw the robot-like figure emerge from below decks. Another bar, another four thousand dollars for Ralls. I felt his slow, patient grin as I stared at the grotesque shape of him dumping that bar into the hoist.

For an instant he stood straight and threw his eye about him, impervious to the undersea. He peered up, as though he made ready to shout, "All sail!" And then the long run to the stern claimed his eye: "Mr. Arrezo, a point into the lee!" He stood near the starboard beam, almost amidships, a small figure as my eye traveled the forty-four feet between her snaggle-tooth rails. Below him to stern, coral; below him to fore, the fathoms of Davy Jones's domain. And he seemed to straddle the brink! He peered down at his find, the ruling passion that had claimed years of his life — and mine — gold. Two bars in the basket, the crimson lady's virginity, two bars added to those above, two more crimes against her. Then he moved on to the opening and below, into the womb of the girl he had murdered.

The rape continued.

I have said a ship has a soul, I have ever compared a sprite under sails to a glorious woman of variform moods — a sensitive creature, given to laughter and tears, to moments of pensiveness. Horizons her ambition, she'll pull for them with the constancy of her melody, as the woman corporeal answers to the touch of a good skipper's hand on the helm. It's then a long run into the cobalt, the everlasting waltz of the sea playing in her rigging, a capricious lean to a note, thin and raptured. A caress as the wind hand lovingly steals about her. A brassy sky — no horizon but shimmering heat over a glassy expanse — that is but a moment of evanescent pain, which she accepts with the same faithful smile she gives to those inclement moods of the sea. If a woman is made to endure pain, a ship is her pattern. And the heart of a ship — where is it, at her bowsprit, in the mizzen, or in her royals? I do not know, though I'll swear she has a heart.

And hearts can be broken.

My eyes saw more than a slattern hulk down there, they conjured up a soul. And I'll never regret the unmanly tears I shed as I sat there listening to her long wail. Perhaps they were manly; they simply rolled down my face, causing the director of the show a frown and a word: —

"A seaman don't like to see them dead."

The third bar moved up, and into the basket, and the silent retriever again moved toward the hollow hell of a derelict's insides. The cable clanged against the iron bell, and a flurry of bubbles pulled for the surface. I watched them soar, like tiny balloons they were, racing to the surface, unafraid of the bends or other perils of a diver's life; the laws of land and sea said they would return safely. I was in unlovely mood, wishing for a cigarette, for Teleia's hand, for Carter's ebullient chatter; I was in turbulent mood, wondering about the final accretion from this end-of-the-trail run. Ralls? Sidneye? Over and over, one question atop another unanswerable question. A hell of a mood for a bloke who has just won fair lady. And so it was I upped the foreroyals of my spirits.

The moment was, however, ephemeral.

Ralls moved in slow motion toward the basket. The colorless bar rolled out of his hand, and he paused for another gaze about him. What was his mood, I said; was he speaking to the lady in endearing manner, renewing his acquaintance with the twin souls he knew, speaking softly, ever softly; or was he that Ralls with Creeper in hand? What he said to her I shall never know; but I do know a broken heart can wail on into overlapping eternities, or it can choose an opposite; it can enact a Zulinde Schouten or a Loring's wife — it can sip from its fountain of sorrow or turn bared teeth.

The lady of the *Red Witch* chose her moment for one or the other — at any rate she shuddered, settled to starboard slowly in a move that almost drew level her sloping deck. Her sails, one mast, and tangled heaps of stumps and rail, seemed loath to follow, so slowly did she come to life. Ralls moved aft as fast as his cumbersome weight would allow, and there he stood, placating the scarlet lady or wielding the Creeper. Evidently he won, for instead of yanking for a lift, he took a step to the fore.

Again the hulk leaned more to starboard, and Ralls moved on unafraid. I said, "Tell the fool to come up. The *Witch* is mad!" The man stared at me, and then below, slowly lifting the tube to his mouth, while I sat there a slave to agony and suspense never before equaled.

So he had used the Creeper! Whether then or on the day he stabbed her, he had used it — for before my very eyes the powers of heaven or hell lent an unearthly hand to the scene. Choosing that moment, of all the long, hollow years in which the broken heart of the ship heaved lonely sighs in the ragged depths off Albert Reef, the *Witch* was fighting back. It was nothing short of a battle between Ralls and the red lady. Ralls, even then, when the stern lifted a good fathom, was slow in signaling for a lift.

In the hollow of an iron cage, I writhed. And the man spoke into the tube: "Trouble. Up with diver!"

The cable jerked, banged clamorously, and lost its slack. Ralls felt the deck leave his feet.

But the ship was adamant. Why she had been content to hold aloft her dazzling bait of wealth, why she had shelved there, awaiting the greedy eyes of man all those years, evoked in me vague, unanswerable questions; nor was I seeking in vain to bridge a gap of plausibility when she upped her stern once more and leaned her bowsprit down below the shelf on which she rested.

Perhaps she had waited there for her master. It is said — a ship rests better with her captain at the helm. It was then I recognized her heart. It was not of sail or bowsprit, nor yet of figurehead. Once perhaps, but her revenge had long since planted her heart in the gold.

And only the few bars of gold, those on the deck of the *Flores*, and those in the meshed hoist, had held her balanced against the suck of the sea. Her heavy heart held the balance, and with the shifting of its weight, the fore was then the heavier.

She slid forward in a slow, quivering motion, her bow reaching out for a moment of buoyancy, a glorious second of gracefulness; and she seemed to hang there in balance on her beam before lifting up her stern and moving off the ledge into the last launching of three gallant ships of the sea: the *Quatrefoil*, the *Golden Hind*, and the *Red Witch*.

But in the lift of her stern there was retribution: as the stern rose high, the cable that strained with the weight of Ralls dug into the stump of the splintered mizzenmast. Then down moved the ragged stump, following the cable like an engine of death on a greased track. It raced down upon the helmet where the shape of man writhed in combat; it trembled for an instant, then bore straight down, taking Ralls, cable and all. And on down she surged, nestling like a leaf in a gentle wind, carrying Ralls to a cadaver's reunion at the bottom of the sea.

A mighty rush of air to the surface — and ship and gold, and Ralls, ended the long, long wake of Batjak's *Red Witch*.

6

The Australian patrol ship came with the sunset squall; Mr. Sheraton had arrived too late, though in his eyes I saw the curtain had not fallen on the enigma of the *Quean of Melbourne*. He was a tenacious sort, his persistence accepting more than its share of temerity. I say this because he foolishly underestimated the Power of Batjak — which eventually broke him.

But the long mystery of the *Red Witch* — a higher court had rendered a final decision: death to Ralls. Perhaps that court would reincarnate his spirit: with Ralls the skipper of the winds of the sea, hurricanes could only howl the louder.

7

To the victor go the spoils, though victory is sometimes robbed of its sweetness. Mayrant Sidneye, his feet planted upon bars of gold, saw the cable writhe in its madness, heard its gnashing at the derrick, and then its last snap; he heard the verdict and, with the crew of the *Stefan Meer* staring across at him, he cried like a baby.

"Ralls! Ralls! What have I left?" His pitiful wail was but a copy of his grief aboard the *Golden Hind* on that day when the wireless informed him of the death of Streicher. Gone was a subject for those strange impulses of his soul. And while he bemoaned his plight, Dokter van Arken brought him the news of his half-brother's death. He stared in disbelief for a moment, then again sent his wail after that intrepid enemy swallowed up by the sea.

As I drew near him, I saw his round, bewildered eyes peering through their wet lashes. They searched for something, or someone, in a manner that rolled back horizons; they stared at my feet and slowly moved up to my face; the king had found another favorite, those pitiable eyes seemed to say.

"Rosen!" he said. "Sit here by me."

"Sorry, Mijnheer," I said, "but I think Teleia needs me more than you." It was a good beginning. At least, he should forever understand that she was my all, my beginning and end; that perhaps we, together, might smile down upon him and bathe his grasping soul with the over-abounding warmth of our happiness.

Sadly he peered at the sea, suddenly turning his hungry gaze upon Carter, whom he asked to sit. And Carter moved toward him saying: "Sure, sure, Mr. Sidneye, of the Amsterdam Dutch. The Irish don't amount to much —" he grinned — "but you've been a bad boy long enough."

Thus the curtain dropped on the Bismarck Sea. When next it lifted a lovelier scene emanated from a lovelier stage — and the part seemed made to order for me.

And Trader Sam Rosen obeyed his heart on that peaceful sea of love in the two and a half years that followed, finding in his wake a ketch, as well as an unearned success; he became the strongest voice of the three commanding Batjak. And Mijnheer Tilden King Carter struck his own tempo; he — and Batjoek admitted it to be true — was the greatest bush-beater the firm had ever known; with grin, guitar, and guts he conquered. While he poured out his songs and verse to Teleia and me, and later to our young lady in an ornate Dutch cradle — Angélique Rosen — he stepped as ever into his own rhythmic, innate lightness: "Imagine Mrs. Carter's lad a big shot! Feature me, will you, a Dutch vice-pres!"

And Mayrant Sidneye found a spot in his life to match that in his heart for his lovely daughters. Ever pensive, he gazed out over the hills and kampongs to the towering peak of Semeroe in the south before turning his eye, in a vast sweep of the seas of the eternal Pacific, to Soerabaja, and fluttering quatrefoils in the southeast trades. But beyond, out of the north, his third great passion was in the making. It came in the year of 'forty-two, roaring down over wide horizons, sweeping across the islands one by one. But of Mayrant Sidneye and the northern typhoon — therein lies another tale that has nothing to do with the treasure I pulled out of the long wake of the *Red Witch* — Teleia.

And so my story ends; and those windows that awaited a house yet to be built drew a final prop with this last plank: —

I, Sam Rosen, once free of the spell of Ralls, found peace and success where he had failed.

ABIGAIL E. WEEKS MEMORIAL LIBRARY
UNION COLLEGE
BARBOURVILLE, KENTUCKY